THE THEFT OF MAGIC

Camber drew back and watched Dom Queron blink and tense for just an instant in sheer, naked panic, then twist around and stare at Rhys in undisguised horror. Emrys looked equally stunned, the only time Camber had ever seen the abbot's composure shaken.

"Sweet Jesu, what have you done to me?" Queron cried, beginning to tremble as he realized just what Rhys *had* done.

He clapped both hands to his temples and shook his head several times, unable to assimilate what he was missing. Then he subsided weakly, as if he had no physical strength to cope with his helplessness. Instinctively, Emrys gathered him into the circle of his arms, staring at Rhys in shocked disbelief.

"You took away his Deryni powers!" Emrys whispered, his tone both accusatory and awed. "One of the most powerful Healers I have ever trained, and you made him—human! Blind!"

Also by Katherine Kurtz
Available from Ballantine Books:

The Legends of Camber of Culdi

The Chronicles of the Deryni

CAMBER THE HERETIC

*Volume III in The Legends of
Camber of Culdi*

Katherine Kurtz

A Del Rey Book

BALLANTINE BOOKS • NEW YORK

A Del Rey Book
Published by Ballantine Books

Library of Congress Catalog Card Number 81-66657

ISBN 0-345-27784-8

Manufactured in the United States of America

First Ballantine Books Edition: November 1981

Cover art by Darrell K. Sweet

For Sven Lugar and John Innis

Contents

PROLOGUE

But ye are a chosen generation, a royal priesthood,
an holy nation, a peculiar people.

—I Peter 2:9

The document was written in the tight, crabbed court
hand of one of the castle scribes, and covered an entire
large sheet of creamy vellum. The man reading it had
thought it innocent enough at first glance—dull, routine
procedures for the running of yet another royal commission—but now, as he scanned it a second time and began
to catch the more subtle nuances of phrase and intent, he
looked up at his companions in amazement.

"Murdoch, I don't know what to say. This is brilliant—
everything we could have hoped for. He'll never sign it,
though."

"He already has," Murdoch said in his thin, nasal
voice, taking the document and handing it to a third man.
"I slipped it in among a stack of other routine documents
yesterday. This is only a copy."

The third man, who was also the youngest of them,
glanced over the text with hungry eyes that did not miss
a thing, an oddly academic quirk in a man so obviously a
soldier in every other way. Big-boned, well-muscled, solid
but not fat, Baron Rhun of Horthness was a rising star in
the army of Gwynedd at only thirty-two. The sparse,
wolfish grin now spreading slowly across his face was a
feature which had made friends and enemies alike refer
to him as Rhun the Ruthless.

"I assume that Cullen hasn't seen this," Rhun said, his
tone clearly confirming a fact rather than asking a question.

Murdoch nodded, steepling spiderlike fingers in a gesture mixed of confidence and arrogance. "He hasn't, and
he won't," he said. "As far as our dear chancellor is concerned, the king's will remains exactly as we all witnessed
it last fall. And because this is not a change of the will,

1

but only an alteration of the guidelines for a potential regency council, there is no reason that he *should* see it until after the king is dead and it cannot be changed. God grant that the king's death may be painless, and soon," he added piously.

Rhun chuckled at that, a low, dangerous rumble, but the first man did not even smile. As he glanced at Murdoch again, his expression was thoughtful.

"Tell me, does anyone know when Bishop Cullen will be returning?" he asked.

"Too soon to suit me," Murdoch said. "The king sent Jebediah to fetch him yesterday. Knowing the way our illustrious earl marshal rides, he should reach Grecotha by tomorrow at the latest, even allowing for bad weather. That puts Cullen back in Valoret well before the first of February. I had hoped he would winter at Grecotha, but—" He shrugged, a surly twitch of the narrow shoulders. "At least this will probably be the last time. The king can't last much longer."

"He's that ill, then?" asked the third man.

"I wasn't certain he would survive past Twelfth Night," Murdoch replied coolly, "though the Healer Rhys seems to have kept body and soul together rather better than I hoped. Curse the miserable Deryni, anyway!"

The exclamation elicited a short, taut silence, as each of the men considered what the king's death might mean to him personally. Finally Murdoch rolled up the document and bound it with a length of vermillion cord. As he glanced at his companions again, he tapped it several times against the heel of his hand.

"Well, I'm off, then. I want to show this to Hubert before I put it away for safe-keeping. Either of you care to come along?"

"I will," said Rhun.

After they had gone, Earl Tammaron Fitz-Arthur, Third Lord of the High Council of Gwynedd, sat quietly for several minutes, thinking. If things went according to plan, he could very shortly be the next Chancellor of Gwynedd.

A few days later, on a snow-clogged road leading south toward Valoret, the Deryni Camber MacRorie and his escort trotted at a steady pace, the sound of their passage muffled by the snow and carried away by the wind.

Camber, whom the world knew as Bishop Alister Cullen, one-time Vicar General of the powerful Order of Saint Michael and now Lord Chancellor of Gwynedd, had received the king's message before dawn, grouchy at being rousted from his warm bed until he realized that the king's messenger was his old friend Jebediah of Alcara, Grand Master of the Michaelines as well as Earl Marshal of Gwynedd. He and Jebediah read the words of the royal missive together in the bishop's study—terse and typical of King Cinhil. Jebediah then gave Camber the true gist of the message.

Yes, the king was sick. Alister must come. Yes, his condition was serious; and yes, he had seen the royal Healer. No, he was not about to die until his good friend and chancellor, Alister, got back to the capital—and maybe not even then, if he could help it.

But Cinhil had also made it abundantly clear that he would brook no delay in Alister's coming. And though he had not made it precisely *clear,* he had certainly implied that there were other reasons for calling the chancellor-bishop back from Grecotha so soon after Twelfth Night—reasons which might not be consigned to the written word, even in the hands of his earl marshal.

At that, Camber had begun to hope—both that the king's condition was not so grave as he had first been led to expect, and that Cinhil might have reached the decision which Camber, as Alister, had been urging for more than a decade.

And so the Bishop of Grecotha had summoned his household guard and set out for the capital just after first light, riding hard through the snowdrifts of late January and pausing only to change horses and occasionally take a hot meal. At this pace, they would be in Valoret before nightfall. As they rode, Camber had time for reflection, for wondering, for playing the tempting game of *if only.*

If only Cinhil were not dying. *If only* his final illness might have been delayed, even for a few more years. For that matter, *if only* Cinhil had been younger when they put him on the throne. A man in his mid-forties was hardly of an age to be starting a royal family, especially if he hoped to see that family grow to maturity.

His eldest son had been poisoned as an infant, before Cinhil even came to the throne. The twins, next in age, were not quite twelve, a full two years and more from their legal majority. The youngest was just ten, and their mother dead these nine years of bearing a final son who

3

outlived her by only a few months. Even when the twins came of age, it would be several years before the first of these, young Alroy, could be expected to rule competently on his own. Until that time, Gwynedd would continue to be effectively governed by a council of regents.

Camber had feared that this day would come; had known, when he and his children had placed the reluctant Cinhil on the throne, nearly thirteen years ago, that it would likely come far, far too soon—but he had never given up hope that the inevitable might be delayed for yet a little longer. Even now, a potential regency council not entirely of Camber's liking had been named by Cinhil; and many of them watched and plotted and waited for Cinhil to die, solidifying their influence over the three young princes, prodding and undermining the spirit of human-Deryni coexistence which wise men of both races had tried for years to inculcate both in the future heirs and in the people of Gwynedd—and Cinhil would not see the danger.

Now the anti-Deryni factions were about to get their wish. Cinhil would die within the year, probably within the month, if Rhys' estimates were correct, and young King Alroy would be ruled by his regents. The last of the Deryni loyal to the Crown would be ousted from their offices, their positions of influence, no matter that many of them had served Gwynedd and its present king well and with distinction. And then the ostracism would begin, and the persecutions, and finally the bloodshed. It had happened before, in other lands, in other times. Perhaps it was happening already.

And so Camber hurried along the Valoret road to the summons of his king, himself still young for his seventy years, in the guise of a man ten years younger still, and by appearance and action no more than fifty or so, to meet his children and his king and try to accomplish the goal they had set when they began this road, now fourteen years before. Then they had made a former priest a king and given him powers equal to any Deryni—though the king had always been reluctant to use those powers. Now that king must pass on his power, or at least its potential, to his young sons, in hopes that they would learn to use it more wisely and with less fear than he had shown.

Camber did not know whether or not they could succeed, for time was running out; but he knew they had to try.

CHAPTER ONE

*For of the Most High cometh healing, and he shall
receive honour of the king.*

—Ecclesiasticus 38:2

Rhys Thuryn, perhaps the most highly respected
Healer in all the Eleven Kingdoms, paced back and forth
in the Earl of Ebor's sleeping chamber and tried to decide
what to do next. On the bed beside him, the earl tossed
and writhed in unrelieved agony, perspiration drenching
his high forehead and dampening the reddish-blond hair
and beard, even though the room was chill on this last
day of January, in the year 917.

Cinhil himself had sent Rhys to Ebor. When word of
the earl's accident reached the king, he had nearly
worked himself into a coughing fit in his anxiety, barely
able to gasp out the words when Rhys appeared in answer to his summons. Nothing would appease him but
that Rhys go to Ebor at once. No other Healer would do.
What if the earl were dying?

Despite Cinhil's agitation—and perhaps a little because
of it, though another part of him was chilled at the news
—Rhys had demurred at first. Even though the king was
somewhat improved now that Camber had returned from
Grecotha, Rhys still did not like the idea of being several
hours away when Cinhil might need him. The king was
not going to get well this time. At best, Rhys might be
able to ease his discomfort in these last days or weeks.
The sickness in Cinhil's lungs was beyond the ability of
Rhys or any other Healer to cure. Neither he nor Cinhil
harbored any illusions about the eventual outcome of his
illness.

But neither did the king harbor any hesitation about
the urgency of assistance for his injured earl. Gregory of

Ebor, though a full Deryni adept of remarkable ability, had nonetheless won Cinhil's great respect and friendship in this past decade on the throne; he had been appointed Warden of the Western Marches only two years before. Rhys *would* go—and go, he did.

But now that Rhys was here with Gregory, he had to admit that he was uncertain how to proceed. He knew Gregory very well, as Gregory knew him. For the past five years, Gregory had been a member of the powerful and very secret alliance of Deryni known as the Camberian Council, so-called at the insistence of Archbishop Jaffray, also a member, who had felt the name appropriate as a reminder of the ideals the group strove to uphold. Rhys and Evaine were members, as were Joram and Jebediah and Camber himself—though Jaffray and Gregory, of course, did not know that last.

Over the eight years of their existence, the Camberian Council had done much to police the ranks of less responsible Deryni and to keep the peace between the races, Deryni and human; and Evaine's continued research, now supposedly in conjunction with Bishop Alister instead of her father, had unearthed a wealth of hitherto lost knowledge of their ancient Deryni forbears. Grecotha, where Camber now made his home, had been and continued to be a mine of magical information. And Gregory, Earl of Ebor, had been a part of much of it.

Now Gregory lay in a delirium from which he seemed unable or unwilling to escape, neither royal patronage nor Camberian affiliation able to help him quell the unbridled energies which ran amok in his body and sometimes in the room. Even his eldest son and heir, a studious young man not unskilled himself in the channeling of Deryni might, had not been able to break the cycle. The floor before the fireplace was still littered with shards of smashed crockery and glass which none of the servants were bold enough to clean up—mute testimony to the potential danger of a High Deryni lord apparently gone mad.

Pensive, Rhys paused before one of the earl's expensive colored windows which had thus far escaped destruction and laid both palms flat against the sun-warmed glass, wondering idly how the earl had missed them. He and Evaine, his wife and working companion of nearly thirteen years, had tried on arrival to ease Gregory's pain and ascertain the extent of his injuries. The two of them were strong enough psychically that the earl could not breach their shields and do them serious threat in his incoherent condition.

But their patient had thrashed about so violently when touched that they dared not maintain the contact for a proper reading, lest he blindly begin flinging objects once more in his delirium. Nor was his thrashing doing his physical injuries any good.

The injuries to his body were easy enough to assess. A dislocated shoulder he surely had, by the angle of the arm inside the loose blue tunic; and most likely a fractured collarbone, as well, though Rhys could not be certain of that until his patient permitted a more thorough examination.

That left some other explanation to account for Gregory's irrational behavior—perhaps a severe head injury, though neither his son nor his steward could remember him hitting his head at the time of the accident. Still, a Deryni of Gregory's proven ability simply did not lose control for no good reason.

Rhys's amber eyes narrowed as he let them focus through the red and blue glass. With a resigned sigh, he ran one hand through unruly red hair and moved back toward the fireplace and his wife. Evaine sat huddled in her fur-lined travelling cloak, quietly watching her husband and the man they had come to heal.

"What are we going to do?" she asked, as he crouched beside his medical satchel and began rummaging inside.

Rhys shook his head and sighed again. "We're going to have to sedate him, first of all. We may even have to knock down his shields. I don't really want to do either one. He could have been a big help. We can't have him destroying the place while I try to work on him, though."

He extracted a green-sealed packet of folded parchment and read the fine script on the back, then closed the satchel and stood.

"We'll try this first," he said, carefully breaking the wax seal. "I wonder if that horse could have kicked him in the head? Pour me a small cup of wine to mix this with, please. The sooner we get it in him, the better."

With a nod, Evaine MacRorie Thuryn, only daughter of the sainted Camber of Culdi, rose gracefully and went to a low table nearer the fire, laying aside her cloak as she knelt. Though she was now thirty-five and the mother of three, her face and form were still those of a very young woman. The wool and leather of her riding dress clung to every gentle curve, the dove-grey setting off the fine blue eyes as no other color could. Her hair, shining like burnished gold in the firelight, had been twisted into a neat coil at the nape of her neck to keep it tidy for riding, but a strand near her face kept escaping from behind one delicate ear and added to her youthful image.

Carefully she poured half a cup of wine from a flagon on the table, holding it out thoughtfully to receive Rhys's powder. As always, when they were together, they were in a light rapport.

"You're right, I suppose," she said, swirling the contents of the cup and watching the drug dissolve. "He's certainly making things worse by his thrashing. And if he starts throwing things around again—well, I don't know how much more this room can take."

Rhys sniffed the cup delicately, then gave her a wry smile.

"Have you no confidence in my potions, my love?" he chuckled. "I guarantee this will take the edge off."

"You have to get it into him first," Evaine countered. "Just how do you propose to do that?"

"Ah, there lies the Healer's secret!" He stripped off his Healer's mantle and tossed it in a heap on top of hers, then crossed to the door and flung it wide.

"Jesse, would you come in here, please, and bring a couple of your servants with you? I'm going to have to give him a sleeping draught before he'll let me touch him. Don't worry, I won't let him do anything dangerous."

Cautiously, a husky, olive-skinned youth peered around the doorjamb and then eased his way into the room, followed by three blue-and-white-liveried servants. Jesse, who had sent to Valoret for Rhys, was a quiet but intense young man whose concern—and healthy respect—for his sire's abilities was evident in every line of his bearing. Neither he nor his men made any effort to move closer to the great bed where the earl tossed and fretted, though they did glance surreptitiously in that direction.

Rhys took Jesse's arm and urged him and his men toward the bed with reassuring words.

"Now, this isn't going to be as difficult as it may seem," he said easily. "He's going to be all right, and so are you.

8

Nobody is going to get hurt. Now, you men—I want you to pin his legs and his uninjured arm when I give the word. Sit on them, if you have to, but keep him still. My potion isn't going to do him any good if it isn't in him. Jesse, I need you to help me hold his head. If you can keep him from thrashing around, I'll worry about getting his mouth open so that Evaine can pour the stuff down. Do you all think you can manage that?"

Jesse looked dubious and a little scared. "You're sure he won't start throwing things around again? I mean, I don't suppose he would hurt me, but what about the servants?"

"You let me and Evaine worry about that," Rhys said, gesturing for the men to move closer. "Is everyone ready now?"

Reluctant but obedient, the men eased in gingerly around the bed and made assignments among themselves, watching as Rhys and Evaine took positions near the head and Evaine readied the cup. A moment they paused, one man surreptitiously crossing himself before the expected struggle. Then, at Rhys's signal, all of them pounced.

Pandemonium ensued. Gregory arched his body upward in reflex, almost throwing off even that array of physical force, and the bed began trembling from more than his movement. Rhys heard something smash against the floor behind him as he forced the earl's jaws apart, but he ignored that as he tried, at the same time, to apply pressure for temporary unconsciousness. Gregory let out a terrified animal gurgle as Evaine began pouring the drugged wine down his throat, but Rhys's skillful touch evoked a swallowing reflex once, twice, a third time, and then it was done.

Releasing Gregory's head, Rhys signalled the servants to withdraw to the safety of the doorway, then stood back with Evaine and Jesse and tried to dampen the effects of the earl's temporary wrath. A bowl and pitcher of water across the room toppled to the floor with a crash that made them all jump. Then a pair of swords over the mantel came careening through the air to clatter against the opposite wall, narrowly missing young Jesse's head.

Finally, the earl's pale eyes began to glaze, his head to cease its fitful tossing from side to side, as the drug at last took effect. He moaned several times, obviously still fighting, but it was evident that he was losing the battle. As

9

the earl at last grew quiet, Jesse gave a great sigh of relief and shuddered, hugging his arms across his chest against more than physical chill.

"I *told* him not to ride that stallion," he whispered fiercely, almost to himself. "The animal is a killer. Valuable stud or not, he should be destroyed!"

"What, exactly, happened, Jesse? Were you there?" Rhys asked, beginning to relax a little. "Do you know whether he was thrown against something, or did he just hit the ground?"

The young man shivered again, closing his eyes as if that might keep him from remembering. "I was there. I wish I hadn't been. The stallion threw him into a fence, hard, and then I think he kicked him, though I can't be sure of that. It all happened so fast."

"But he was unconscious for a time?" Rhys urged.

"Either that or just stunned. The master of the horse said he thought it was just a dislocation and the wind knocked out of him, at first. But by the time they got him up here, he was moving the way you saw and raving with the pain. That was last night. Things started flying around the room shortly after that. Our household Healer is away for a few days, so that's why I sent for you."

"I see," Rhys said. "Well, I'm pretty sure he has a fracture and a dislocation. And given his psychic activities, there's probably more at work than that. Anyway, we'll see what we can do, now that he's manageable. You can wait outside, if you'd rather."

With a nod, Jesse swallowed and slowly backed toward the door, finally turning to flee with the servants. Rhys suppressed a smile with some effort until the door had closed behind them, then laid an arm across Evaine's shoulders.

"Well, love, shall we try it again?" he asked lightly.

Evaine took her place at their patient's head and laid her hands on his temples, Rhys moving in opposite, at the man's left. This time Gregory calmed immediately under her touch, slipping swiftly into an easy, profound sleep which was intensified by the sedative they had given him. A peaceful stillness descended on the room, dispelling the previous agitation of the man beneath her hands, as she centered and held their patient's consciousness for her husband's touch.

Rhys could feel the change of atmosphere, Evaine's readiness. With a sigh of relief, he unlaced Gregory's tunic and eased it back from the injured left shoulder, gently slipping his hands inside to curve around the broken angle of joint and clavicle. Extending his senses to probe and explore the extent of the injury, he traced the damaged muscles and nerve-ways and mentally felt out the dislocation of the joint, the clean break in the collarbone, physically eased the dislocation back into place before lining up the ends of the snapped bone and beginning the processes which would regenerate it.

Profoundly centered now, as his Healing talents took over from mere intellectual sensing of the injuries, he closed his eyes and let himself drift into his Healing mode, let the power flow, feeling life-force channel through him as it had so many times before, a part of him marvelling yet at the miracle of Healing which had been given into his use.

He could feel the bones knitting beneath his fingertips, the swollen and torn muscles shrinking back into place and mending, the bruises fading and healing. He could sense the warmth of increased blood flow through the injured area, carrying away damaged tissue and speeding the growth of new.

Finally, he opened his eyes and let more usual senses confirm what his soul already knew, pressed sensitive fingers along the line of previous break and dislocation, and knew that this part of his work was essentially done. His patient might be a little stiff for a few days, but that was small price, indeed, to pay for the outrage which had been done to his body. He did not think that Earl Gregory would begrudge that small discomfort. Now he must try to discover the reason for the rest of Gregory's symptoms.

As he raised his head and let his eyes refocus on the visual world, Evaine caught his attention.

"I think I've found why he was so uncontrolled," she said, running the fingers of one hand lightly along Gregory's skull just behind the left ear. "He's got a knot here, hidden in his hair. I think he did get kicked. There's a slight abrasion. You'd better take a look."

Frowning, Rhys moved his hands to the man's head and probed, his eyes glazing lightly in his concentration. After a moment, he nodded.

"There's swelling inside the skull, as well as outside. That could well account for his behavior. I'll see what I can do."

11

Again he sank into trance, his eyes closing, and this time the questing was much more draining, the Healing more demanding. He had far more difficulty visualizing what should be inside the skull, and he kept getting tangled in Gregory's sedated thoughts.

But there was relief in his eyes as he emerged from this second Healing, and he allowed himself a soft but satisfied sigh as he straightened and stretched.

"Hmmm, I wouldn't want to do that every day, but I think he's going to be all right now. You can let him come to. The drug should be just about out of his system. After a good night's normal sleep, he ought to be fine."

"With a bit of a headache, I should imagine," Evaine replied, easing out of the controls she had been maintaining. "Can he have some wine?"

"Certainly. He's going to want something to eat, too. He needs energy, after what he's been through."

With a final glance at her charge, Evaine went to the door and ordered food and drink to be brought, for the previous wine had been a victim of Gregory's crockery-smashing. By the time Gregory's pale eyes were flickering open, she had managed to get a servant to clean up the mess and was ready at his head with a cup of warm milk laced with spirits stronger than wine. Raising him with an arm under his shoulders and head, Evaine put the cup to his lips and let him drink; she and Rhys watched with approval as his look of bewilderment diminished and he appeared to reorient to his surroundings.

"Rhys," the earl murmured, focusing first on the Healer's red hair, then on his face. He blinked several times, trying to put things into perspective. "What are you—how did I get here? I was riding that—oh. . . ."

"That's right." Rhys nodded. "You're starting to remember. You got thrown and kicked, and you're lucky to be alive. Your son sent to the king for a Healer, and the king sent me to put you back together." He smiled reassuringly. "I must say, you didn't seem very eager to have me work on you, though. You were throwing things around the room and making a terrible scene."

"You mean, I fought you?" Shock and embarrassment flashed across the earl's narrow face. "I used my powers? Rhys, I *am* sorry. I—"

He froze for just an instant, a look of increasing consternation growing in his eyes as he turned his mind inward—a look which quickly changed to one of incredulity and fear.

"Rhys? I can't sense you, Rhys!" Like a drowning man, he reached out blindly and grasped the Healer's arm. "What's happened? What have you done to me?" His other hand went to his temple in alarm.

"Rhys, I can't See you with my mind!"

"What!"

In an instant reflex, Rhys sent his mind out in quest, almost recoiling in horror and surprise as he realized that the other's mind was totally open to him. Gone were the customary Deryni shields which should have been reestablished with Gregory's return to consciousness, gone all evidences of power which were the trademark of a skilled and powerful Deryni like the Earl of Ebor. Suddenly, he was *in* Gregory's mind, able to find no vestige of the tremendous strength and ability against which he had been struggling not a quarter hour earlier!

He could feel Evaine's concern mingling with his own shocked disbelief as she slipped into rapport with him, sounding out the emptiness, the lack of resistance, as if Gregory of Ebor were a human of the most unsophisticated background. What could have happened?

Shaking his head a little to clear it, he slipped his hands to either side of Gregory's head and pressed him back gently onto the pillow, splayed fingers cradling the back of Gregory's skull as the thumbs rested on the damp temples, mind deepening the link. The earl did not resist, staring up at him with frightened, accusing eyes which held no awareness of the Healer's mental touch. He was helpless, vulnerable.

Closing his eyes against the sight, Rhys reached out his mind and exerted gentle but firm pressure, easing his patient back into merciful unconsciousness while he continued to probe and explore. He had never heard of such a thing! Deryni did not lose their powers. Had *he* truly done this?

What happened, do you know? came Evaine's clear thought, cutting through his bewilderment and dismay.

It must have been something I did in Healing his head injury, while I was very, very deep, he responded, only part of him paying attention to her query. *Stay with me, love. I have to find it again. It has to be about—there!*

As he ended the communication, he forced himself to slip deep, deeper, exploring all the possible avenues he might have touched in some unaccustomed way. For a long time his trance was so profound that even Evaine could not follow, so deep that all she dared do was watch and monitor, making sure that his body remembered to breathe, his heart to keep up its slow, controlled, regular beat.

He was so deep that even he was not consciously aware when he had found the right spot—knew only that he had found it and set things right. One last scan to make certain that everything was, indeed, restored, and then he was taking a deep breath and coming to the surface again, looking tired and still a little puzzled, but satisfied. His hands shook a little as they slipped from Gregory's head to his own, and he allowed himself the utter luxury of sinking bonelessly to the floor beside the bed, leaning his head against the edge of the mattress as he took another deep breath and then yet another.

Evaine darted around from the other side to take one of his hands in hers and search his eyes anxiously, her other hand caressing his cheek.

"Rhys, are you all right?" she demanded, relaxing a little as her senses confirmed what his nod declared. "Where were you? I've never seen you go so deep."

Wearily Rhys shrugged and smiled, drawing his wife into the circle of his arm. "Me neither. That's probably one of the oddest things I've ever experienced. I still don't know how I did it, either. It's going to take some digging to bring it to the surface." He paused, then continued thoughtfully. "You know, this is something your father should see. I wonder if he'd come here, if we sent a message."

"Can't it wait until the next council meeting?" Evaine asked. "He isn't going to want to leave Cinhil alone, even for the few hours it will take."

"Cinhil will be all right for a few hours," Rhys replied. "Tavis is always there, if another Healer should be needed, and there are other Healers in town. But I really think that this should be checked out before Gregory has a chance to reorganize and possibly mask what happened. Maybe he can even help me figure out how I did it."

"Hmmm, you're right. And there's certainly no one better qualified for that. How are we going to persuade him to come, though? You can hardly tell him what's happened in a written message. Suppose Cinhil saw it?— not to mention the messenger."

"That's true. On the other hand—"

Reaching inside his Healer's tunic, he caught and pulled on a narrow green silk cord until a dull silvery medallion appeared, the size of an early walnut. This he fingered thoughtfully, absently rasping his thumbnail across the heavy carving while he considered his next move. Then he gave Evaine a hug and got to his feet, letting the medallion dangle as he gave Evaine a hand and helped her rise.

"See if you can find some writing materials, will you, love? We'll ask the good bishop to come to his injured friend, the Earl of Ebor. We'll appeal to his duty as a priest and bishop, as well as a friend, but I'll add another short message in the seal that only he can read. The outward words will be enough to make him come, and for Cinhil to let him go, and the seal will tell him why we really want him. I'll have a messenger saddle up and prepare to ride, while you get started."

CHAPTER TWO

And in his estate shall stand up a vile person, to whom they shall not give the honour of the kingdom: but he shall come in peaceably, and obtain the kingdom by flatteries.

—Daniel 11:21

Cinhil Haldane coughed fitfully into a napkin, then moved an archer on the inlaid gameboard, his glance darting quickly to his opponent's face as he settled back in his chair. Across the board, the man the king knew as Alister Cullen smiled and moved a mounted scout in reply.

Cinhil frowned.

"Now, why the devil did you do that, Alister? The caradot's lair is over there, you know that. Sometimes I really don't understand you."

Camber shrugged and raised a shaggy Alister eyebrow, masking a smile with one casually raised hand.

15

"I am aware of the caradot's location, Sire. I am also aware of the strength of my archers and cavalry."

"Your archers? But, I—oh."

Cinhil's voice trailed off as he studied the formation of the pieces in question, but then he seized another of his own archers and moved it in counter-attack.

Slowly, almost languidly, Camber reached out and pushed his war-duke to the next square. At Cinhil's gasp of surprise, he held up a forefinger.

"You have one chance, Sire, and one only, to extricate yourself from your present situation. If you can find it, you can also win. If not, you must resign the board."

"What?" Cinhil blustered. "You haven't got the strength to—oh. I see." He sighed. "Damn you, Alister, do you have to be so bloody good at everything you do?"

At Camber's repeated shrug, Cinhil furrowed his brow and leaned his chin on his hands to stare at the board more intently, chewing at the edge of his grey-streaked mustache in concentration. He stifled another cough, but he could not entirely mask the pain the effort cost him.

Camber pretended not to notice, leaning back in his chair with half-lidded eyes and twisting the amethyst ring on his right hand with his thumb, but he knew the king had not fooled Joram, who sat reading quietly in a window seat across the room, out of earshot but not sight of the man who was actual as well as spiritual father to him.

Joram was nearly forty now, though he still looked the fit young Michaeline knight he had been almost a score of years before. He still wore the blue of a Michaeline priest and the white sash of his knighthood, but now he served as private secretary to the Bishop of Grecotha, his former superior in the Michaeline Order. The position was an excellent cover, for it enabled him to continue working with the man whom most folk thought dead these thirteen years now, and a saint, at that. So far as anyone outside Camber's immediate family knew—and not even all of them knew the true story—Camber *was* dead, slain in the battle of Iomaire in 905, while trying to defend his friend and battle-comrade, Alister Cullen, from the Princess Ariella. Only Joram, Rhys and Evaine, and the steadfast Jebediah of Alcara knew that it had been Alister and not Camber who had died that day, and that Camber had magically taken his dead friend's shape and memories, the better to carry on his work of guiding the new-crowned king. The secret had been kept now for nearly

16

thirteen years, and the gamble had paid off. By and large, Cinhil had been a good king. The success of the next reign depended at least partly on Camber's secret being kept yet a while longer.

Joram had raised his head in inquiry at Cinhil's cough, freezing in a listening attitude which had become all too common at court of late, but Camber gave him the slightest shake of his head and returned his attention to Cinhil. The king coughed lightly again, then moved his priest-king to threaten Camber's archbishop.

"All right, try that one, Alister."

As Camber's hand glided out to counter the attack, there was an insistent knock at the door. With a sign of exasperation, Cinhil rolled his eyes heavenward and shook his head.

"Not now, please!" he muttered under his breath. "Joram, will you answer it? I don't want to stop now, just when I've got him on the run!"

"On the run, indeed!" Camber scoffed good-naturedly, as Joram got to his feet with a nod and moved toward the door. As it opened inward at the priest's hands, Camber could glimpse a tall, lanky form wearing the unmistakable colors of Carthane. It was Earl Murdoch himself, one of the human governors of the young princes and a staunch opponent of anyone or anything Deryni. He was also, Cinhil had informed him somewhat apologetically a few months before, to be one of the regents for young Alroy, if Cinhil died before the boy turned fourteen. When Camber had asked him why, Cinhil had simply said that Murdoch seemed to him a pious and temperate man, well-suited to such authority. Besides, Murdoch had sons only a little older than the twins.

Earl Murdoch's gaunt face mirrored intense annoyance as he encountered Joram at the door instead of one of the royal squires.

"Excellency," Joram murmured dutifully, standing aside and making a precise and correct bow.

Murdoch tried unsuccessfully to cover his displeasure with a brusque nod of his head in return, but the movement was hardly gracious. He was well aware that Joram's father had been an earl of even greater seniority than himself, and that Joram, if not for his priestly station, would have been Earl of Culdi after him—and Murdoch's senior in rank. The fact that Joram was *not* the

17

earl made no difference to Murdoch. He still resented a Deryni in any position of authority, real or potential.

"Father MacRorie," Murdoch replied, each syllable clipped by his dislike. "I would have audience with the King's Grace. Be so good as to announce me."

Secretly enjoying Murdoch's aggravation, Joram made the man another bow of strictest formality, then turned slightly toward the two men seated in the sunshine.

"Sire, His Excellency, the Earl of Carthane."

Cinhil, his back safely to the door, was able to indulge in a tiny sigh of resignation before turning his profile to the waiting lord. "Ah, Murdoch, can't it wait? I'm just trouncing Bishop Cullen at Cardounet."

"My most profound apologies, my liege," Murdoch answered, giving Joram a glance of purest disdain as he pressed past the priest and bent to kiss the king's hand almost reverently. "I thought to acquaint you with the progress of the royal princes' studies, as you did request, but if the time is inconvenient, I can come back another time. My Lord Chancellor."

As he straightened from Cinhil's hand, he gave Camber the curtest of nods, and Camber inclined his head graciously in return, knowing that his politeness would gall Murdoch far more than any incivility on his part. Murdoch's mouth took on the appearance of a man who had been eating lemons, but he hid that from Cinhil as he turned away briefly to draw up a stool, having been bidden by Cinhil's gesture to take a seat.

"Nay, you need not come back later, my lord," Cinhil said. "I did ask after my sons, and you have done right to come and tell me. Are you and their other governors satisfied with their progress?"

Murdoch settled on his stool with a flourish, watching Cinhil toy with one of the captured pieces. He masked his annoyance well, but Camber could tell that he was less than pleased to have only Cinhil's divided attention. His voice was nasal and irritating. Camber wondered, not for the first time, what Cinhil saw in him besides his ancient human lineage. He had met Murdoch's sons, and counted them no particular enhancement to any family line.

"Prince Alroy progresses well, Sire. His Highness has a flair for languages, and Bishop Hubert is very pleased with his studies of the scriptures. He is also growing stronger daily. He will make a worthy king to succeed

18

Your Grace—though of course we all pray that will be far in the future."

"Yes, yes, go on."

"Of course, Sire. Prince Rhys Michael is yet young, of course, but both Earl Ewan and Lord Rhun agree that he shows great promise as a strategist and tactician, as well as skill with weapons. If he should one day become king, you need not fear for the welfare of this land."

"Oh, come now, the boy's only ten! What about Javan?" Cinhil asked impatiently.

Camber tried to keep his face impassive as Cinhil turned his full attention on Murdoch. Beyond the king, he could see Joram perched gingerly on the edge of his seat in the window embrasure, felt Joram extending his senses so that he might overhear all through Camber's mind. At one time or another, Joram had been tutor to all three of Cinhil's children, and Camber knew that the crippled middle prince held a special place in his son's heart.

He turned his attention back to Cinhil, feeling for the king as well as Joram as the royal lips drew back in a tight-lipped grimace.

"Why do you hesitate about Javan?" Cinhil asked quietly. "Is he a problem for you?"

With an embarrassed shrug, Murdoch began a minute inspection of a gold thumb ring on his left hand. "Well, his swordsmanship is the best he can manage, under the circumstances, I suppose," he said depreciatingly. "And Earl Tammaron says he rides rather better than anyone ever expected he could—better than the other two boys, if the truth be known," he admitted grudgingly. "But— the devil take it, Sire, he's not fit to wear the Crown after his brother, and you know it! The people won't tolerate a cripple on the throne. Not only that, I don't like the ideas that young Lord Tavis is putting into his head. Bishop Hubert and I did warn you about a Deryni tutor, Your Grace!"

"Yes, you did warn me," Cinhil replied neutrally, glancing aside uncomfortably at the most decidedly Deryni Bishop of Grecotha and at Joram. "However, Tavis O'Neill is a highly qualified teacher, and a fine Healer, as well. With Javan's—handicap—it seemed an ideal pairing."

"What ails Prince Javan cannot be helped by a Healer, Your Grace," Murdoch retorted coldly. "Forgive my bluntness, but you know that is true. And meanwhile, that

Deryni poisons the boy's mind against those who are entrusted with his care and education. He *hates* Rhun. He undermines the authority of—"

"Have you proof of this, my lord?" Camber interjected, quietly, but with such intensity that Murdoch was cut off in midsentence. "It appears to me that you are accusing Lord Tavis of sedition, a serious allegation. Unless you have proof—"

"Sire! Must I be contradicted in the performance of my duty?" Murdoch retorted, drawing himself up like an angry spider. "If the King's Grace insists upon surrounding his royal person with Deryni, *such as slew Your Grace's noble family many years ago,* that is certainly the royal prerogative! But Your Grace has given me the responsibility of raising up the future heirs of this realm, and if I am to fulfill that responsibility, I must have *some* authority. The royal nursery is not the place for Deryni, Healers or no!"

Camber opened his mouth, then closed it, glancing at Cinhil for some guidance as to how and whether he should proceed. Cinhil had gone white at Murdoch's words of accusation, his grey eyes darting to Camber almost as if the bishop personally had drawn the bow which sent feathered shafts of death into his great-grandfather's body, plunging the kingdom into those dark years called the Interregnum.

All at once, Camber was poignantly reminded of the delicate balance he constantly walked with Cinhil, despite nearly a decade and a half of close association, both as Camber and as Alister. And in all that time, the core of royal doubt about Deryni had not really diminished—not in that private heart-of-hearts to which Cinhil still retreated under stress.

Camber did not move, only his ice-pale Alister eyes pleading with Cinhil for a return to sanity, a denial of the insinuations which Murdoch had just flung out like a gauntlet. The Interregnum times were past. Cinhil knew that in his head. The Deryni who served the present Haldane line were of a different breed than those who had put the Festils into power nearly a century before.

But Cinhil must say that, not Camber or Alister Cullen.

For a seemingly interminable moment, Cinhil did not stir, his grey gaze darting from Camber's face to Murdoch's and then back again, until Camber thought he must burst from the tension.

Then Cinhil took a deep breath, as if about to make a major pronouncement—and started coughing instead.

As Murdoch watched, Camber grabbed a goblet from the table next to their gameboard and filled it with wine from a silver ewer, upsetting half the pieces on the board in his haste to get to Cinhil's side and ease the wine past his lips.

Cinhil drank in grateful gulps between coughing spasms, gaining some ease after he had gotten a few swallows down, and Joram hurried to his other side to offer the king a napkin to wipe his mouth, picking up fallen gamepieces awkwardly as the red-faced Cinhil fought to control the coughing.

Camber laid hands on the king's head, willing the coughing to subside and perhaps even succeeding a little. In any case, Cinhil managed to stifle one more coughing bout, then stopped, cleared his throat, and spat into his napkin. His face was composed if ashen as he eased back onto his chair, and he would not let them see the crumpled cloth in his hand.

"I apologize if I have caused you distress, gentlemen," he said, in a weak but steady voice. "I seem to have a touch of a winter cold." He cleared his throat again, then swallowed noisily.

"Murdoch, would you mind if we delayed the rest of your report until later? I have been aware of your concern about Javan and Tavis for some months. I think the matter can wait a few more days. However, I hasten to point out that when Tavis was sent away for a time last year, the boy sickened and refused to eat. Under Tavis's tutelage, he has thrived—at least as much as he is able. The fact that Tavis is Deryni does not concern me nearly as much as Javan's unhappiness and ill health when Tavis is not about."

"You coddle the boy, Sire. It is not good."

"I do not coddle him. I face the realities of his—deficiency. You are aware of my feelings on that subject."

"I'm sorry, Sire. I meant no disrespect."

"I know you did not."

Awkwardly the king reached out to press Murdoch's shoulder in reassurance, and bowed his head as the younger man seized the royal hand and pressed it to his lips again.

Camber almost could not bear to watch, amazed that Cinhil could let himself be so deceived. Cinhil could even Truth-See Murdoch if he wanted to; but Cinhil rarely used the abilities which Camber and his children had given him so many years ago. Please God, Cinhil's children would not be so blind!

"Please forgive me, Sire, but it's only that I care so much," Murdoch was whispering.

"I know. Fear not. You yet are in my grace," the king replied.

He stifled another cough, and his face went a little paler against his scarlet robe.

"Please go now, Murdoch. I think I must rest now. Alister, stay with me awhile, old friend. Though you are not a Healer, your company does much to ease my discomfort."

"As you wish, Sire," Camber replied softly, moving closer to stand with his hand on the king's shoulder. "Earl Murdoch, my secretary will see you to the door. His Grace will surely send for you again later."

With that, he turned his attention to Cinhil, bending closer to the royal ear. "Try to relax, Sire. Take a slow, steady breath—not too deep, or you'll start yourself coughing again. That's right. Now exhale. Let the pain detach. . . ."

Murdoch rose in annoyance, ignoring Joram's polite and precise bow as he made his own way out. Joram, when he had closed the door after Murdoch, returned to stand attentively beside the stool Murdoch had just vacated. After a few minutes, Camber straightened up and glanced at Joram, signalling him to sit as Cinhil slowly opened his eyes.

"Is that better, Sire?"

"Yes, thank you," Cinhil whispered. "It helps. It really does. I should know better than to let myself get so agitated. I don't dare breathe too deeply any more, or it starts me coughing all over again."

With a raise of one eyebrow, Camber leaned down to retrieve the napkin which had fallen from Cinhil's hand after he stopped coughing, noting the browning-red stain on the fabric. Calmly Cinhil reached out and took it gently from the bishop's hand, folding the napkin so that the stain could not be seen. When Joram started to open his mouth to speak of it, Cinhil shook his head and carefully laid the napkin aside.

"I know, Joram, I need no lectures," he whispered, very matter-of-fact in the stillness which his acknowledgment had created. "I am very ill. Only Rhys and I know precisely how ill. And this matter of Javan—I need to speak of it to both of you. Believe me, I trust Tavis. He is a fine young Healer. But—"

A short, staccato rap on the door stopped him in mid-phrase, and Camber flicked a glance in the direction of the door. He recognized the mental presence on the other side, but it was obvious from Cinhil's sigh that the king did not.

"It seems this discussion is not to be," Cinhil said resignedly. "No matter. See who it is, Joram."

As Camber had known it would be, Lord Jebediah of Alcara eased past the door which Joram opened.

"Your pardon, Sire," he said as he approached, making a slight bow in Cinhil's direction. "Alister, one of the Earl of Ebor's men just delivered this. He said something about Gregory having been injured in a riding accident."

The greying earl marshal was dressed in worn blue riding leathers—from his rosy cheeks and the amount of mud liberally spattering his body, it was apparent that he had been jumping his new hunter in the castleyard—but he was carrying a clean packet of parchment in one gloved hand, the green of a Healer's seal bright against the creamy white.

Cinhil perked up immediately. "Is he all right? What's happened? I sent Rhys and Evaine to him this morning."

As Jebediah shrugged and handed over the packet—this was obviously the first time he'd heard of the accident—Camber broke the seal and unfolded the stiff parchment. He read the few terse lines of script, penned in Evaine's precise hand but in Rhys's unmistakable style, then refolded it and thrust it into his wide sash with a sparse little Alister smile.

"It seems our friend will be all right, Sire."

"Thank God!"

"Rhys says his memory is a little hazy, but his injuries have been completely healed. Apparently Gregory isn't convinced, however, and insists I come at once to give him the Last Rites."

"Last Rites?" Cinhil sputtered, almost bringing on another coughing attack.

"Now, Sire," Camber soothed, "under the circumstances, I think simple Communion will probably be sufficient. I suspect Gregory is merely being dramatic, to make excuses for falling off his horse. Still, he has asked for me, and you're doing well enough. May I go to him? I should be back by dark, and Jebediah can fetch Tavis, if you should need a Healer before then."

"Last Rites, indeed!" Cinhil repeated, shaking his head in outraged disbelief, but chuckling just the same. "I'm supposed to be the one who's dying, and *he* wants the Last Rites. Oh, go ahead and see him, Alister. But you tell him that I'll expect to see him here at Court for a full explanation, as soon as he's able to ride again!"

"That I shall certainly do, Sire," Camber replied, returning Cinhil's chuckle. "Good day, Sire, Jebediah. Joram, we'd best ride, if we're to get back by dark."

When Camber and Joram had left the room, Cinhil sat quietly for several seconds, his grey eyes focused through and beyond the disrupted gameboard, then beckoned Jebediah to come closer.

"Jeb, I need you to do something for me."

"Of course, Sire. What is it?"

"I want you to visit the royal nursery and observe my sons. Talk to their tutors, if you can. Especially, talk to Lord Tavis. You're Deryni. Perhaps he'll listen to you. Try to make him see why it's important to get along with Murdoch and the other governors. Murdoch seems to have some concern about his influence over Javan."

"So far as I know, Javan is doing well, Sire," Jebediah replied, a little guardedly. "His weapons mastery is improving markedly. He hasn't the agility on foot that his brothers have, of course, but he makes up for it in other ways. And frankly, his wit is much quicker than Alroy's. It's too bad that the good points of both boys couldn't have been put into one."

"Aye, there should never have been two," Cinhil sighed wistfully. "I wonder why that happens? Their mother was overanxious to give me another heir, God rest her sweet soul. But do check on that for me, will you, Jeb? My time grows short, and I would not leave my sons totally unprepared."

And in the corridor outside, Camber drew his son into an alcove and looked furtively up and down the passageway, silencing Joram's incipient inquiry with a glance and a shake of his head. Taking Rhys' letter from his sash, he opened it and scanned the lines again, running his fingertip thoughtfully over the seal at the bottom of the page.

"There's more to this than meets the eye, Joram. This is no mere whim of Gregory's. Even injured, he would not summon me without good reason. He knows Cinhil is ill. Nor would Rhys send such a message for him."

"I didn't think it sounded like either of them," Joram replied. "Is there something more in the seal, perhaps?"

"I think so," Camber murmured, holding it closer and scrutinizing it more carefully. "Keep watch, will you?"

And as Joram turned to the business of scanning the corridor, Camber held his sensitive fingertips on the seal and closed his eyes, letting his breathing deepen and then slow as he triggered the light trance which would enable any other message to come through. For several seconds he reached out with his mind until he caught and held the thought beyond the words penned on the parchment. Then he opened his eyes and exhaled softly. Joram returned his attention to his father.

"Bad?"

"I don't know," Camber said puzzledly. "I'm still not sure what he's talking about, but the implications are staggering. It's Rhys's message. He thinks he's taken away Gregory's Deryni abilities!"

CHAPTER THREE

He that loveth his son causeth him oft to feel the rod, that he may have joy of him in the end.
—Ecclesiasticus 30:1

By midafternoon, Jebediah was finally able to make his way to what was still called the royal nursery, though its young charges had long ago outgrown the term, at least in their own minds. He had meant to get there earlier, while the boys ate their noon meal, so he would disrupt their routine as little as possible, but half a dozen urgent matters had suddenly presented themselves for solution almost the instant he left the royal apartments, and he was several hours finding answers. All of the problems *seemed* as urgent as his officers said they were, but he could not

25

help noticing the timing. He hoped that it was only his imagination that Murdoch, Rhun, and Udaut all seemed to have such convenient crises which only he could resolve.

In any case, the royal nursery was very quiet when he arrived, and he could tell by his reception that his visit was neither expected nor welcome. In the large dayroom, huddled by one of the two great fireplaces, he found Crown Prince Alroy still at his books with his tutor, though it was usual for formal studies to be finished by this time of day. Brother Valerian, the boys' Latin master, was standing over Alroy with a very stern mien, emphatically pointing out the correct translation of the military commentary which Alroy apparently was supposed to have prepared for the day's lesson and had not.

Alroy smiled tentatively when he saw Jebediah come in, for the earl marshal was something of a hero to the sickly lad, but Brother Valerian immediately whacked the scroll beside Alroy's hands with a willow switch and pointed to the text. Jebediah had the distinct impression that it would have been Alroy's fingers and not the scroll which would have gotten whacked, had the marshal not been present. He supposed such discipline was necessary but he felt sorry for young Alroy, all the same.

By contrast, Rhys Michael, youngest of the three princes, had been allowed to set up his toy knights and archers in the previous day's ashes at the edge of the other hearth, and was confidently explaining deployments and troop movements to another boy whom Jebediah did not recognize. Rhys seemed sunny-dispositioned and content; and a quick perusal of the strategy he was explaining to his classmate caused Jebediah to raise an eyebrow in surprised approval. It was the classic battle of Rhorau, and the boy's words and gestures showed that he even understood it! The lad definitely had a head for military tactics.

A somewhat more involved procedure was required for locating the third prince. Jebediah did not see him at first, and was loath to ask for fear of bringing on reprisals after he was gone. Judging from what he had seen of Alroy's treatment, that appeared to be within the realm of possibility.

He had traversed nearly the length of the chamber, inspecting several other clusters of young boys and their school masters, before he spied Javan sitting on a bench

26

in the window alcove across the room, next to a grisaille window which looked out onto the winter-dead garden. A large tree just outside the window cast an eerie network of shadows upon the prince and the young man who knelt motionless at his feet. The man's back was to Jebediah, but his dark red hair and Healer's green robe proclaimed him to be Tavis O'Neill, the very person with whom Jebediah had hoped to speak.

The pair did not appear to notice his approach. It was not until Jebediah reached the window alcove and mounted the two steep steps that Javan looked up and frowned. Now Jebediah could see the reason for Tavis's stance; the boy's deformed right foot was cradled in his cupped hands, its specially constructed boot stripped off and laid aside so that the Healer might work. Tavis was massaging the foot very gently, his eyes half-closed in trancing, obviously in his Healing mode, but it was evident from Javan's occasional grimaces that something was amiss.

Cautiously Jebediah moved closer, not wishing to disturb the Healer's concentration, but he was unable to see precisely what Tavis was doing.

"Is anything wrong, Your Highness?" he asked in a quiet voice.

Javan's face flushed red, and Tavis started and then recovered, covering the deformed foot beneath his hands with a casual gesture which was not lost on Jebediah. He did not turn toward the earl marshal.

"My Lord Marshal," Tavis said softly. "What brings you to the royal schoolroom?"

"Concern for Their Highnesses," Jebediah replied. "It appears that my concern is well founded. What are you doing?"

"His Highness's tutors are not always gentle in their training, my lord," Tavis murmured, still not turning toward the grand master. "This morning's training was particularly brutal."

"Brutal?"

Tavis pivoted on his haunches, his face almost white with fury. "Yes, brutal! They made him walk a five-mile march this morning in the snow, wearing full mail and carrying an adult-weight sword and shield. He finished," he said, fiercely proud, "and not far behind his brothers, either—but this is the price he had to pay. And I have already eased much of the hurt!"

As he spoke, he raised the foot he had been cradling and glared at Jebediah in challenge. The marshal, finally gaining a clear look, had to exert great control not to flinch openly.

The boy's right foot was raw and angry-looking, where it was not purpling with bruises, the pale skin chafed badly all around the thick, misshapen ankle. The other foot was also chafed and red, though not as severely. Beside Tavis on the wide windowsill, Jebediah could see a basin of water and several damp towels, a glass vial containing what looked like soothing oil.

"Who is responsible for this?" Jebediah asked, his voice deadly calm and even.

"It was—"

"It doesn't matter," Javan interjected, cutting Tavis off before he could say a name. "If I'm going to be a warrior, I have to be tough. I have to be able to keep up with the others. I have to be able to lead them. I'm going to show them that I can."

"Sheer physical ability is not the only requisite for leadership, my prince," Jebediah said, biting off a harsher comment he had been going to make about whoever had been responsible. "Who has told you that it was?"

Javan stiffened, his lower lip quivering a little in his indignation. "If I am possibly to rule after my brother Alroy, I must be strong. Do you think they will allow another weakling to sit on the throne? Gwynedd needs a warrior king."

"Gwynedd needs a king who is wise," Jebediah countered. "If he also happens to be a warrior, that is fine. But it is not required. Your father is no warrior, and he has done well enough."

"My father." The boy snorted with a dejected derision. "Aye, he is no warrior. Would that he were, and had been, from the beginning. But, no, he must abandon his vows and be neither prince nor priest, and accursed by God. If he had not, I would not be thus, with the sign of God's displeasure for all to see!"

With that, he jerked his deformed foot from Tavis's grasp and tried to hide it behind the other one, turning his face away and knuckling angry tears. Jebediah, aghast at what he had just heard, looked at Tavis for some explanation.

"My lord, have you been filling his head with these mad tales?"

"It is not I who teach him history or religion, my Lord Deryni Marshal," Tavis said bitterly. "Please leave us. Haven't you upset His Highness enough for one afternoon?"

Jebediah could find nothing to say to that. As Tavis stood and gathered the crippled prince in his arms, to carry him away from the eyes which now stared from every part of the room, Jebediah felt like a monster. He watched them go, wondering how he was going to explain this to Cinhil and, even more, to Camber.

But at that moment, Camber's thoughts were far from the princes and from Valoret. As he and Joram followed Jesse up the outside stairs from the castleyard, into Ebor's great hall, he reviewed in his mind the little he had gleaned thus far about the situation for which Rhys had called him.

It was unusual for Rhys to ask directly for his help, for Camber had never really been able to learn any of the Healer's Art which Rhys had mastered so well and so many years before. Camber had been considered a great non-healing adept, and Alister was not unaccomplished himself; but neither aspect of the man who now nodded greeting to Gregory's various servants and retainers could compare with the specialized abilities of a gifted Healer like Rhys.

And yet, if Rhys *had* somehow managed to take away Gregory's Deryni powers, then that was, indeed, a subject of great interest, both to Camber and to the part of him which was Alister. It was a thing which could touch all Deryni. Camber had never heard of such a thing happening, except in occasional head injuries which were so severe that other functions were also impaired; and in those cases, function could almost never be restored, and the patient surely died. Nor had he ever read of such a thing, though over the years he and Evaine had worked with some very ancient documents, indeed—records which sometimes spoke of many wondrous things not normally thought of as falling within even a Deryni's abilities. The ancient texts said nothing about taking away a person's powers deliberately.

Jesse led them up a winding turnpike stair for nearly two floors, then doubled back through a narrow gallery walkway which skirted along the length of the hall and overlooked it. At the end of the passage, a heavy, metal-studded door stood ajar.

The earl's great, tapestry-hung bed could be seen through another arched doorway across the entry-room, the green-clad figure of Rhys sitting wearily on a chair beside the sleeping Gregory while Evaine stood behind him and massaged his temples. Rhys looked up as Camber and Joram entered, his face creasing in a relieved smile as he rose to greet them.

"Am I glad you're here, both of you!" he said, laying his hands on their shoulders in a dual embrace. "Jesse, thank you for bringing them up. We'll call you if there's any need."

Linked minds exchanged in an instant what lips would have taken long minutes to recount, even as Jesse backed out deferentially and closed the door. Evaine, too, joined in the rapport, the mind-brush of her affection reaching out to caress both father and brother. Even as their link receded to more usual levels, Rhys drew them all physically into Gregory's bedroom, to stand along the near side of the bed.

"You're sure he's all right now?" Camber asked in a low voice.

"Perfectly normal. I only have him in forced sleep because I wanted to be able to talk freely with you. I know that I can duplicate the effect, though. We won't even have to wake him. I don't think he'll remember anything out of the ordinary, either. He was only conscious for a few seconds, and he was still in a bit of shock. Do you want me to show you what I did?"

"Not just yet. Are his shields malleable?"

"To the four of us, yes. Do you want to read him?"

"I think so."

Moving closer to the bed, Camber unclasped the heavy riding cloak he had been wearing against the outside cold and shrugged it into Joram's waiting hands, then blew on his fingertips and rubbed them together briskly to warm them before touching Gregory's temples. As he let his fingers slip easily back into the thin reddish hair and took control, Gregory gave a little sigh and seemed to relax even more.

Deeply Camber delved, exploring the traditional pathways through which the Deryni potential was usually carried, appreciating the discipline of this particular Deryni mind and marvelling that anything could have neutralized it, even briefly. Then he withdrew both mental and physical contact and turned to Rhys.

"He seems fine to me. Perfectly normal, other than being open to the controls you've placed upon him for Healing. Now, what did you do to him before?"

With an indrawn breath of apprehension and resolve, Rhys moved in closer and laid his hands on Gregory's head. "You'd best not come with me while I do it, at least the first time. Just stand by for a moment."

"Very well."

As Rhys closed his eyes and went into his deep Deryni trancing, Camber watched neutrally, aching to follow what the Healer was doing, but respecting his opinion that it were better not to do so. After a moment, Rhys opened his eyes and drew back a little.

"Take a look now," he said, a twisted little smile on his lips. "Even knowing something of what to expect, I think you're going to be surprised."

"Indeed?"

With the arching of one bushy Alister eyebrow in skepticism, Camber laid his hands on Gregory's head once again and extended his senses—and encountered no shields, no resistance, nothing—nothing at all which gave hint that the being beneath his hands was Deryni! Despite himself, he looked up quickly at Rhys, at Evaine, noted both their hesitant, slightly troubled little smiles. Without taking his attention from Gregory further, he motioned for Joram to move in and read with him, felt the increased potential as Joram's familiar presence bolstered his own awareness of the mind they read.

Backed by Joram's steady touch of mind and hand, he let himself sink into his own deep trancing, reaching out at successively lower levels for the telltale signs of Deryni potential which were no longer there in Gregory. He could feel Joram's incredulity in tandem with his own, felt a slight twinge of dread as the thought simultaneously crossed his and Joram's minds that use of this particular technique could be a threat to any Deryni; thanked God that the Healers were bound by so rigid a code of ethics. What a weapon for Deryni to use against Deryni!

But he dared not dwell on that further. Surfacing enough to function on a physical plane as well as a mental one again, he signed for Rhys to join them in the deep rapport, to work his Healing magic and restore what he had taken away, while he and Joram observed. He felt

31

Rhys join the linkage and withdrew enough for Rhys to take control, felt the Healer slip deep into union and reach out.

A twist, a psychic wrenching, gentle but persistent—and suddenly Gregory's mind was as it had been, sleeping and controlled still, but completely restored to the fullness of his Deryni potentials. Camber was shaking his head even as the three of them withdrew, too stunned by what he had witnessed to do more than stare at his son-in-law in amazement. He could not seem to find his voice. Rhys finally broke the silence.

"You didn't really believe me, did you?" the Healer said, as he reinforced Gregory's Healing sleep and then broke off all contact. "Let's go into the other room. He needs to rest."

Without a word, Camber followed, his mind still examining the implications of what he had just seen and felt. When they had settled down on stools and in chairs beside the fire in the outer room, it was Joram who spoke.

"All right, how did you do it?"

Rhys laced his fingers together on his knees and shook his head slightly. "I think it's a Healer's function, Joram. I did it inadvertently the first time, while working at a very deep level, and I couldn't reverse it until I'd gone down deep again. The process seems to require the same kind of energy expenditure as an actual Healing."

"Is it more difficult?" Camber asked.

"No, it's—different. I suspect that one could become quite adept at this, after a while, but I don't really see that it's worth the effort. I mean, what good is it to take away someone's powers? Now, *giving* powers this easily—that's another story."

Joram snorted as he shifted closer to the fire. "Humph. I can't say that it's done Cinhil that much good to have such powers. Nor would I have been unhappy to see Imre or Ariella lose theirs. It could have saved a lot of needless deaths."

"True," Rhys agreed. "However, gaining Imre's and Ariella's cooperation might have been another matter. Gregory was easy. He was drugged to a fare-thee-well the first time, already in Healing sleep, totally trusting me to do what needed to be done. One could hardly ask that of an enemy. At this point, I don't know whether I could have done it to a conscious subject or not."

"You mean, if Gregory hadn't already been unconscious, you don't think you could have done it?" Camber asked.

"He probably wouldn't even have discovered it," Evaine said.

"She's right," Rhys agreed. "And remember, we know one another's mental touch, from working together in council. If we hadn't had that advantage, he wouldn't have been so open." He shrugged. "But this isn't the place for further speculation right now. I don't even want to tell Gregory what's happened until I've had a chance to think about it some more."

Camber nodded. "A wise decision. Given all the pertinent factors, though, how soon do you think he'll be able to ride? Cinhil thought Gregory was being melodramatic." He chuckled as he remembered the king's outburst. "He seemed to think Gregory was trying to steal his thunder, with all this talk about dying, so he wants to see him."

"I can imagine," Rhys chuckled. "On the other hand," he continued on a more serious note, "I didn't want Cinhil thinking he had to get on a horse and come charging out here, in his condition."

"Oh, I don't think he would have——" Camber began.

"He would have, and you know it!" Rhys disagreed with a grin. "He's the second most stubborn man I know."

"Myself being the first, I suppose." Camber smiled. "Well, you're probably right." He sobered as his thoughts returned to Cinhil. "The trip certainly wouldn't have done him any good, though. I don't like the sound of his cough."

He looked to Rhys for reassurance, his hope fading as the Healer did not deny the fear he had so lightly posed. "How much time *does* he have, Rhys?" he asked, almost inaudibly.

"A matter of weeks," Rhys managed to reply. "A month, at the outside. I don't think he'll see Eastertide."

A chill slithered down Camber's spine. *Weeks! A month at the outside!*

And Cinhil *knew,* he realized, as he thought back on their last conversation. Cinhil was aware that he was dying, and had started to tell Camber and Joram about his concern for his sons when Rhys's message had called them both away.

Now Cinhil was alone at Valoret—or, not alone, for

Jebediah was with him; and Tavis was available for the basic work of Healing. But Jebediah was not trained to cope with what must occur before Cinhil died—and Tavis must never know!

"We must get back to him," Camber breathed, unclasping cramped fingers and reaching for his cloak. "How soon can the two of you leave?"

He stood as Joram laid the heavy cloak on his shoulders and fastened the clasp. Rhys and Evaine also stood, almost frightened at the intensity of Camber's reaction.

"We need to be certain Gregory is free of any aftereffects," the Healer said. "Under the circumstances, with he being who he is, we really should spend the night here and plan to leave in the morning."

"So long?" Camber murmured. "God, I wish I hadn't left Cinhil! What if he—"

"*Father,* he isn't going to die tonight!" Evaine insisted gently, sensing Camber's increasing anxiety and knowing it to be unwarranted, as yet. "Unless he was much worse at noon than he was this morning, he has time."

With a weary sigh, Camber clasped both their hands to his breast and shook his head.

"I'm sorry. I know. You're right. Nonetheless, I must go back to him. We've come so far. . . . Return as soon as you can. God keep you both safe."

Chapter Four

Judge none blessed before his death: for a man shall be known in his children.

—Ecclesiasticus 11:28

They delayed at Ebor longer than Camber would have liked. The horses had been fed and watered, the men of their escort provided for, while Camber and Joram were in the earl's chambers; but when the two emerged, nothing would do but that they take a light meal with Lord

34

Jesse and the steward—for Jesse was hungry for news of the capital and the king, and knew that the bishop had just left the court that morning.

So half an hour was lost appeasing Jesse. When at last Camber and his men rode out again, the hazy shadows were lengthening beside the muddy road, the sky dulling to a close, leaden grey which bespoke ill weather to come. With luck, a full moon would light their last miles almost as bright as day, reflected off the pale and silent snow-drifts. And if the promised new snow held off for even a few hours, they would be back at the king's side before Compline. As for a storm—Camber preferred not to think about that.

But so far, the weather seemed to be holding. They had been riding at a steady, ground-covering canter for some time, Camber and Joram leading, the four guards following in pairs, when Camber finally reined back to a brisk walk to let the horses blow. As he caught his breath, he overheard one of the younger guards wondering softly to his colleague how such an old man could set such a pace. It was all Camber could do to keep from smiling as Guthrie, the guard sergeant, shushed the man and urged his mount alongside Camber's, on the opposite side from Joram.

"Your Grace, do you intend that we should take this road all the way back to Valoret?"

"Now, Guthrie, that's an odd question," Camber answered, cocking his head curiously at the man. "This is the shortest route. You know I want to rejoin the king as soon as possible."

"Of course, Your Grace." The man bowed respectfully in the saddle. "The men merely wondered whether you were aware that there is another road just ahead, scarcely half an hour's ride longer, which would take us past Dolban. If you would consent to a brief stop, they would like to visit the shrine there and pray for the king."

Dolban.

The name of the place touched unwelcome associations in his mind, and he had to suppress the urge to shudder. Nor could he ignore Joram's mental shiver of apprehension. Neither of them had any wish to go to Dolban.

Dolban had been the first of the shrines constructed by Queron Kinevan and his Servants of Saint Camber. It was at Dolban that the formal canonization ceremonies had taken place eleven years before, when the supposedly-dead Camber of Culdi had been declared a saint, worthy of veneration for what he had done for his people, his king, and his God; an example of what Deryni *could* be, even in the estimation of humans.

After Dolban had come a succession of other shrines —Hanfell and Warringham and Haut Vermelior and a dozen other places whose names Camber had no wish to remember. Defender of Humankind Saint Camber had become, and Kingmaker, and Patron of Deryni Magic, as well, though the latter was not so widely touted lately, as anti-Deryni sentiment became more widely espoused by the humans surrounding Cinhil's dying court. Camber knew it all to be based upon a lie.

"Your Grace?" the sergeant asked, breaking into his reverie. "Your Grace, is anything wrong?"

"No, no, nothing is wrong. I was just thinking about Camber. I really—"

He broke off as the drum of hoofbeats and whoops of raucous laughter suddenly intruded in the dusky silence. By the commotion, at least a dozen horsemen were approaching from beyond the next curve, and fast. Simultaneously, he was aware of Joram already taking stock of the situation and estimating the odds—though it was obvious that they would be greatly outnumbered, if it came to a physical confrontation.

Frowning, Camber reined his grey to the left and signalled Joram and the guards to do the same, though all of them kept riding slowly in the direction they had been going. In the face of such a situation, they must proceed as if nothing were amiss, as if they had as much right to be on this road as did those approaching. He fervently hoped that there would be no trouble, for they *must* get back to Cinhil!

All at once the approaching riders burst into view from around the curve and thundered into the long, straight stretch, riding at a reckless gallop. They were no soldiers —their bright, multicolored clothing proclaimed that at a glance, as did their lack of discipline as they rode. Bright caps, some of them with plumes and jewels, shone on most of their heads, a few of them banded with fillets that looked almost like coronets, and might have been. Velvets and furs on cloak and sleeve and saddle trappings glowed in the waning light, swords and daggers flashing at every hip. A few of the riders brandished swords in gloved fists.

They laughed raucously as they approached, their guffaws and shouted comments becoming more ribald as they noticed the somber little band proceeding toward them. In a flurry of movement, they nearly surrounded Camber and his party, their fine horses jostling the more ordinary mounts of the four guards and making Camber and Joram's greys lay back their ears in protest.

"Give way, my lords!" Joram shouted, flinging his mantle back from his sword arm and laying a gloved hand on the pommel of his weapon. "We would not dispute the road with you. Observe the King's Peace!"

"Why, 'tis a lone Michaeline knight!" one of the young toughs sang, to hoots of derisive laughter from a handful of his colleagues.

"One Michaeline and an old man and a few paltry guards to stand against all of *us?*" shouted another. "Let's dump them off their horses and let them walk like the last ones!"

As one man, Joram and the four guards drew steel, though they did no more than hold their weapons at the ready. Camber still had not reached toward the sword at his knee—calmly sat his horse and surveyed the surrounding riders with grim expression, but without apparent alarm, forearms resting casually on the high pommel, the reins held easily in one gloved hand.

His sobriety apparently touched some chord of response, for one of the riders jostled the elbow of another of his comrades and gestured urgently toward the black-cloaked figure sitting so calmly in their midst. The man so jostled took a hard look at Camber and then held up the riding crop in his hand. The sniggering and the catcalls died away immediately.

"Hold, lads. The old man thinks to outstare Deryni. What say you, old man? Why should we not have our way with you?"

For answer, Camber let his shields flare to visibility, though he did not permit himself to move, even then. Apprehensive murmurs rustled among the men as the silvery mantle of his Deryniness glowed unmistakably in the twilight. Several riders lowered their weapons sheepishly and tried to melt into the shadows at the edge of the road, though most held their ground with undiminished belligerence. A few flashed their own shields to light momentarily, but they did not persist when their leader disdained to follow suit. That one stared across at Camber with stony defiance.

"I see," he murmured.

"Do you? I don't think you do," Camber replied, barely trusting himself to speak. "The fact that I am Deryni like yourselves alters nothing. The shame upon you all is that so many should set upon so few of *any* race, who have done them nary a harm. Has the King's Grace endeavored to protect the land and guard its roads only to have his nobles flout his laws for their own sport?"

"The King's Law? Human law!" One of the men spat, a contemptuous, bitter gesture which was repeated by several of his colleagues as the man continued. "Our forbears ruled this land and helped to guard its borders. We were held in honor and esteem, as well we should have been. Now this human king gives over all our honors to his *human* toadies!"

"And you play directly into their hands!" Camber retorted. "Don't you see how you give our enemies precisely what they want?"

The hand of the band's leader tightened on his crop, and his dark eyes took on a cold, steely gleam.

"How dare you speak to us that way? Just who are you?"

"Why should that matter?" Camber countered, halting Joram's indignant beginnings of protest with a sharp gesture. "You do our race as much harm as the very toadies you claim so to despise! What better excuse does a man like Murdoch of Carthane need than the irresponsible actions of the likes of you, giving the proof to his lies?"

That accusation brought angry mutterings to more lips, and one brash soul spurred his horse hard into Camber's to grab a handful of black cloak and attempt to pull its wearer from the saddle. A deft evasive movement on the part of Camber forestalled the intended result, almost transferring it to the perpetrator, but the move was also sufficient to throw the cloak back from that shoulder and expose the collar of golden H's and jewelled pectoral cross lying on and across Camber's chest. As their significance registered, several gasps of recognition rippled through the band.

"Good God, it's the chancellor!"

Beside Camber, Joram allowed himself a tiny sigh of relief and lowered his sword, though he did not sheath it just yet. The four guards remained at the ready, sensing that their chances of survival had just shifted back in their favor, yet not precisely certain how that had been accomplished. Tension was sustained for several heartbeats, but then the leader of the band brought his crop up to his cap in salute and bobbed his head in slightly mocking deference.

"Sorry, Your Grace, we appear to have made a mistake."

"I'll say you have!" Joram muttered under his breath, starting to sidestep his horse between Camber's and the leader's.

But Camber's tongue-lashing, plus the discovery of his identity, had apparently quelled any further desire of the young lords to bully the six they had met. At their leader's signal, the band crowded past Camber and his escort with astonishing precision and galloped away on the road back toward Ebor, quickly disappearing in the growing twilight. Joram and Camber's men made as though to follow, their outrage written plainly on their faces, but Camber held up a hand and murmured, "No!"

His men returned obediently and fell in around him, but it was obvious that they were resentful at being held back. Joram allowed himself a final, murderous glare in the direction the marauders had disappeared before sheathing his sword with a vexed snick of steel seating in steel-bound leather.

"Young ruffians!" the priest grumbled, under his breath.

Guthrie, the guard sergeant, was less circumspect.

"How dare they? Just who do they think they are?" he blurted. "Your Grace, you should have let us go after them!"

"To serve what purpose?" Camber replied. "You are all fine soldiers, but you were also greatly outnumbered, in strange territory, and at dusk, when all three factors would have worked against you. Furthermore, they were all Deryni; and except for Joram, you are not."

"His Grace is right, Guthrie," Joram reluctantly agreed, "though I, too, would love to have thrashed them all soundly." He turned to Camber, Michaeline composure restored as was fitting in the chancellor-bishop's secretary. "Under the circumstances, Your Grace, do you think it wise to divert to Dolban? The king should be told of this incident as soon as possible."

Joram's words gave perfect excuse to omit the visit if

they chose—an option which both Camber and Joram would have preferred, rather than subject themselves to the emotional strain of a visit to the principal Camberian shrine; and Queron Kinevan was the last man that either of them wanted to see, after their few encounters at the time of Camber's canonization—but unfortunately, a similar argument dictated precisely the delay they otherwise might have avoided. Queron Kinevan, as Abbot of Saint Camber's-at-Dolban, had primary responsibility for keeping of the King's Peace on the roads surrounding the abbey lands, and it was he who should be informed of the band of young Deryni bullies first, even before the king.

Camber reminded them of that, before leading them into a bone-jarring gallop on along the increasingly dim and icy road. They had not travelled a mile further toward the Dolban cutoff before they came upon the first signs of their marauders' earlier exploits.

They slackened pace as the muddy footing of the road changed from fetlock depth to nearly knee-deep, noting without comment how even the snow-banked verge beside had been churned to slush by the recent passage of many horses. As they continued cautiously into the next curve, they checked before a ragtag assemblage of perhaps a dozen liveried men on foot, though the men's high boots and mud-fouled spurs gave mute indication that they had not begun their journey thus.

The men drew their swords and stood their ground, darker shadows against the indistinct grey blur of the hoof-churned mud beyond. At the side of the road, in the shelter of a winter-bare tree, a youngish man in once-fine riding garb was attempting to comfort a weeping young woman. The woman's fair hair was uncovered and coming unbound, and she clutched two muddy handfuls of clothing and cloak to her breast as she wept in her comforter's arms. An older man in tonsure and clerical attire, also muddy, looked on helplessly and wrung his hands.

"Hold where you are!" one of the retainers shouted, brandishing his sword and pushing his way to the front of his men. "If you've come back to molest her ladyship again, you'll have to kill us this time!"

Immediately, Camber backed his horse a few steps and raised his empty right hand to show he was not armed, at the same time parting his cloak so his collar and cross could be seen.

"We mean you no harm," he called, trying to make out the men's badges of service in the dim light. "I am Alister Cullen, Bishop of Grecotha. Were you set upon by the men who just rode off yonder?" He gestured back the way they had come.

"Cullen?" their lord exclaimed, thrusting his lady roughly into the protection of the cleric before heading toward them, hand on sword hilt. "Hell and damnation, it's another Deryni! Haven't you hooligans done enough? Just wait until I tell my brother what has happened!"

As the men shuffled aside to let their lord stalk through their midst, Camber glanced back at Joram, caught the slight shake of his head.

"I'm sorry, my lord, I don't believe I know you. You are—?"

"Manfred, Baron of Marlor. My brother is Bishop Hubert MacInnis—and when he finds out what has happened here, there'll be hell to pay, believe me!"

"I quite agree, my lord," Camber replied, cutting off Manfred's tirade smoothly, though he hardly raised his voice. "I am no more pleased by what has happened than you are, and was on my way even now to report the incident to the abbot at Dolban. We, too, were set upon by—"

"D'you think I care a whit for your problems?" Manfred interrupted. "As for your precious abbot—I hardly expect justice from the Deryni leader of a cult which venerates a Deryni saint!"

"The abbot, besides his religious and Healing vows, is the king's sworn man in temporal matters," Camber replied a trifle haughtily, despite his intention to forbear and not further offend the brother of Hubert MacInnis. "I am certain that Abbot Queron will render you and yours the same justice which is due any loyal subject of the Crown of Gwynedd. That your attackers should have been Deryni only makes me doubly anxious to see them brought to justice. My lady Baroness?" He turned his attention deliberately from the baron and guided his horse forward slowly, its feet making sucking noises as it picked its way through the mud.

"My lady, I am most sorry for what has happened. I would not remind you of what must have been a terrible ordeal, but may I inquire more specifically what was done against you?"

The lady, who had frozen at Camber's direct address,

only resumed her nearly hysterical weeping. The cleric held her close and stroked her disheveled hair as if she were a distraught child, finally raising his eyes uneasily to Camber's.

"They—were not gentle with her, Your Grace," the man said haltingly, "but neither did they—use her. They —tore her garments and—threw her to the ground. But then they let her go," he added, almost puzzled. "It was a taunting sort of play, as if they meant no real harm, but only sport—"

"Sport!" The very thought set off Baron Manfred again, as he slogged his way back toward the pair and Camber. "Nay, priest, do not side with them and call it sport! They have offered grave insult to me and to my wife. For that, they shall pay!"

"And so they shall, my lord," Camber soothed, "and I shall inform the appropriate authorities immediately. I take it that your horses were run off?"

"Do you see any horses besides your own, you fool?" Manfred raged, his hand clenching white-knuckled on the hilt of his sword. "We are stranded here afoot, and it's getting dark, and likely to storm, and you prattle on of—"

"I shall have horses sent from the abbey as soon as possible, and an escort to see you safely to your destination," Camber said smoothly, gesturing for his men to come closer. "In the meantime, I shall leave you two of my men and four of the horses. Guthrie, you and Caleb stay with his lordship until the abbot's men arrive, then join us. Torin and Llew, leave your horses for now and ride double with Joram and me. It's only a short way to Dolban."

The moon was just rising above the frosty trees when they came within sight of the abbey gates. Torchlight illuminated several cowled figures walking guard duty above the gatehouse, and the brands flickered and spat in the light mist which had begun to descend.

Externally, the complex had changed little in the years since Queron Kinevan and the zealous Guaire of Arliss had bought the then rundown fortified manor and begun its restoration—though, according to reports, the inside no longer bore any resemblance to the modest manor house originally built there.

Neither Camber nor Joram had ever set foot inside the

walls, nor had ever wished to, but it was obvious from Llew's hoot of recognition behind Joram, and a monk's answering wave from the gatehouse, that he, at least, had been here numerous times and was well known. Even though it was nearly full dark, the gates were opened promptly at the sight of the two double-mounted horses. By the time they had drawn rein in the courtyard and dismounted, it was clear that Camber and Joram had been recognized, too. Grey-clad men and women were gathering on the steps of the chapel which fronted the yard, even as several of their brethren took the horses away toward the stables.

Camber fidgeted a little as he drew his cloak more closely around him, wondering whether he had made a mistake in coming here. He had not realized his own household was so rife with the cult of Camber, and he knew himself to be on unfamiliar ground. He dismissed his men to go on to the shrine, then stiffened as a small, wiry man in grey robes eased his way through the waiting brothers and sisters and approached them. His face was guarded, a little anxious to one who knew how to read it, but his manner was brisk and efficient. It was plain that he still was not intimidated by either the Bishop of Grecotha or the son of Saint Camber.

"Bishop Cullen, Father MacRorie, we are honored by your visit." He bent one knee to kiss the episcopal ring on Camber's hand, then nodded formally to Joram. "Brother Micah said you rode in mounted double. Is anything wrong? Is it the king?"

The familiar Gabrilite braid was longer by a handspan than it had been eleven years before, and streaked with grey, where once it had been a rich, reddish brown; but aside from that, Queron Kinevan did not seem to have aged appreciably. The bright eyes still looked out with as much intensity as they had that week in Valoret when Queron and his Order had first brought their petition before the Synod of Bishops.

"Nay, the king was fine when last we saw him late this morning, Dom Queron," he replied, trying to keep his tone as neutral and matter-of-fact as Queron's. "There was some trouble on the road, however, both to ourselves and to another party which we encountered later. We left two of my men plus the extra horses with them until you can send assistance. You *are* responsible for patrol of the royal road in this area, are you not?"

43

"By day, yes, Your Grace. But no one has charge of the roads by night, especially in winter. What trouble did you encounter?"

With a hitch at his sword belt, Joram gestured back toward the closed gate.

"A band of young Deryni nobles—younger sons, by the feel of the situation, sir. Perhaps ten or fifteen of them, all looking for trouble. They took us for human at first, and thought to harass us, until they recognized His Grace."

Queron clucked his tongue and slowly shook his head. "A sorry business. I do apologize, Father. And to you, especially, Your Grace. What of the other party you mentioned?"

"Baron Manfred, the brother of Bishop MacInnis, his wife and chaplain, and about ten or twelve retainers," Camber replied. "All angry but unharmed, and horseless now. I told them you'd bring fresh mounts and escort them to their destination." He sighed. "I hardly think I need warn you how MacInnis is going to react, when he learns of this."

"Indeed, not. Excuse me a moment, please."

At Camber's nod, Queron turned away from them and conferred briefly with a number of his monks, several of whom disappeared immediately in the direction of the stables. After some further discussion with more of them, Queron returned to Camber and bowed again. The second group of monks went to meet the first, who had returned with horses and weapons from the stables.

"The baron and his party will be rescued immediately, and some of our brothers will drive off the marauders, if they are still in the vicinity, Your Grace. I am told that this kind of incident is becoming far too frequent on the roads around the capital. I regret that our kind are being driven to such acts."

"I regret it, too, Dom Queron."

"As you say." Queron sighed. "But, no matter. It will be taken care of, you may rest assured. In the meantime, you *will* stay long enough to see our shrine, will you not?" He glanced back and forth searchingly between Camber and Joram. "Father MacRorie, I especially understand your reluctance to come here before now, but ours is a shrine of the Blessed Sacrament, as well as of your sainted father, you know. Besides, the rest of your escort will not return for some little while. Surely you will not leave without paying your respects."

Though Camber had, for a moment, considered doing that very thing, he heard Joram's minute sigh of resignation and knew that he, too, realized they dared not. This time they must play out the charade or else risk offending Queron and the many Camberian brothers and sisters waiting expectantly in the background. As Bishop of Grecotha, Camber could not refuse to visit any shrine unless there were very pressing reasons. Alister Cullen would never have considered such neglect of duty.

"Very well, then, Dom Queron," Camber said quietly. "We may not stay long, for we have pressing business with the king, but we shall pay our respects. One favor I would ask, for Joram's sake. May we have some privacy inside the shrine?"

"Of course, Your Grace," Queron replied with a bow, turning to make a hand signal to one of his monks. Then he looked long and compassionately at the younger priest.

"Poor Joram," he murmured. "After all these years, you still cannot accept his sanctity, can you?"

With difficulty, Joram swallowed, would not meet Queron's Healer's gaze, and Camber knew he was remembering how he had been forced to face Queron's questioning in another time and place, when the legend of Saint Camber had yet to be proven.

"It is very difficult to be the son of a saint, Dom Queron. If only you knew how difficult."

"But—"

"Please, Dom Queron," Camber interjected, sensing a long, involved disputation if he did not get Queron and Joram separated. He laid a comforting arm around Joram's shoulders and urged him toward the doors. "I'll— see your people when we come out, and give them my blessing then." That was the Alister part of him talking.

"For now, though, let's go inside, son," he said, drawing Joram toward the plain, metal-studded doors.

Very soon they were alone, standing quietly at the rear of the nave with their backs against the doors and their nostrils filled with warm air and the familiar scent of incense. Camber heard a door close at the far end of the church and surmised that it marked the exit of his guards.

For an instant, it was all deceptively familiar. Camber did not know what he had been expecting. He cer-

45

tainly was not prepared for the sight which met his eyes. He supposed he had anticipated the usual overdone treatment which was so often afforded a saint's principal shrine, gaudy and grandiose in taste, cluttered with candles and statues and other over-pious accoutrements. This place was not.

For beginnings, the chapel had a somewhat nonstandard layout, perhaps because of its manorial origins. The nave was the usual long and narrow basilica plan, with a double colonnade running its length and dividing off a clerestory aisle to either side, like any proper church; but there was no southern transept. The southern wall, set against the former outside wall of the manor's living quarters, was windowless and mostly blank, except for a mosaic design of red and gold surrounding each of the fourteen Stations of the Cross.

The northern wall was quite another story. Several side altars and chapels had been built into that wall, and there was a transept. As Camber and Joram began walking slowly down the left clerestory aisle, they passed a circular baptistry done in mosaic of reeds and doves and flames, a delicate Lady Chapel of gold and lapis and, in the transept, an altar dedicated to the four great Archangels, colored lamps burning at the quarters to signify the angelic protection.

At the end of the nave, in the sanctuary, was the altar guarded by Saint Camber, the vaguely lit statue of the saint standing to the left of a simple but spacious altar and retable of rose-marble. The statue of the chapel's patron saint loomed larger than life, carved in a pale grey stone which gleamed almost silver in the light of a thick candle at its feet, arms upstretched to support a jewelled replica of Gwynedd's crown of intertwined crosses and leaves. The pale tones contrasted subtly with the delicate rose of the altar itself, and paler pink marble veined in smoky grey faced the walls of the sanctuary and formed the altar rail, the color heightened by the glow of the red-shielded Presence Lamp which burned at the right of the altar. The Monstrance on the altar below the Rood Cross glowed like a ruddy sun in the wash of rose light.

Camber let out a low sigh as he and Joram came up to the gates of the altar rail, doggedly fixing his attention on the Monstrance and its sacred Host as he sank to his knees and signed himself with an automatic gesture.

46

Keeping his mind to his customary set of prayers before the Sacred Presence, he closed his eyes and shut out the sight of the statue, willed a little of the serenity he derived therefrom to flow into his son, kneeling at his left elbow.

But when the prayers were finished, he had no choice but to open his eyes and look up at the figure which the world now knew as Saint Camber. His annoyance at the idealization they had made of him was overshadowed, as it had been before, by the enormity of the lie he had been living.

What colossal conceit to have allowed it to continue! True, he had not yet been struck down by lightning or otherwise shown the measure of Heaven's wrath; but he could not, in conscience, believe that there would not be a price to pay for what he had done.

His intentions, of course, had always been as pure as he could conceive. So far, though the fight was far from over, he and his children had managed fairly well to keep alive the ideals they had hoped to preserve from the beginning, by placing Cinhil on the throne of Gwynedd.

There had been setbacks, to be sure, not the least of which had been Alister's untimely death in battle with Ariella. And the human lords who had flocked to Court in the wake of Cinhil's restoration had gained far more influence than Camber and his kin had hoped they would.

But to balance that was the closeness of Cinhil and Camber, which had endured for nearly fifteen years now, though of course Cinhil did not know that it was Camber and not Alister with whom he had dealt so intimately and on so regular a basis for the past twelve. That, alone, had been worth the price Camber had had to pay, if all the factors be totaled.

That price, of course, was another story altogether. Though the world had accepted him as Alister Cullen, Bishop of Grecotha and Chancellor of Gwynedd, Camber knew that this part of his life was a sham. True, he had legitimated his raising to the episcopate, by being properly ordained a priest before allowing the late Archbishop Anscom to consecrate him bishop. And he had never offended the letter of canon law—though he had bent it —and the spirit of that law had doubtless been broken times too numerous to count.

What distressed him most, on those rare occasions when he permitted himself to think about it, was that he had been forced to stand by and witness the travesty of his own canonization, powerless to object any more strongly than he had, lest he lose all for which he and his had fought.

And what of those who believed in Saint Camber? In some ways, that bothered Camber even more than the obvious accounting he would have to make concerning the Alister-Camber impersonation. For the people, both human and Deryni, believed in Saint Camber, ascribed miracles to his intercession, venerated his image and his memory in scores of shrines and chapels across the land, that he might act in their behalf.

For the thousandth time, he asked himself whether faith alone was sufficient to account for the miracles— for, as Deryni, he was well aware how important mere belief could be in effecting cures, in helping cause things to happen. For many, belief in Saint Camber seemed to bring comfort and assistance. Who was Camber to say that such belief was not valid, if it produced results?

Suppressing a sigh, he glanced aside at Joram and was surprised to see his son gazing up raptly at the statue. Joram had been against the impersonation from the start, though he had reluctantly agreed to help, when there seemed no other choice. Through all these long years, he had stood by his father, regardless of the shape he wore, and defended both Alister and his father's name against all attack.

Camber wondered how the shrine was affecting Joram —the statue, the chamber, and what they all evoked now, for so many people. And in that moment, Joram turned his head and looked him full in the face, reaching out with his mind and willingly opening to his father's probe. As minds leaped the boundaries of usual sensation, they knew one another's most secret thoughts of Camber and of sainthood, and they plunged into even more profound communication.

But there was none of the old bitterness in Joram's mind now, that combination of fear and outrage which had for so long ruled his inner balance. Something had finally enabled Joram to accept the inevitability of the situation, to forgive the dogged determination which had moved the man who knelt now beside him.

That decided, it was as if a great burden had been lifted from Camber's mind, as well; he realized that he, too, could let go of the guilt, the uncertainty, the shadow of apprehension. Together, the two of them were doing all they could to hold back the Darkness, to preserve the Light. What more could any mortal ask?

With a smile, Camber reached out and patted his son's hand, then let the younger man help him to his feet. Together, arm in arm, they walked back up the center aisle to speak with Queron and his Camberians, before heading back to the capital and Cinhil.

Statues would never haunt either of them again.

CHAPTER FIVE

For the vision is yet for an appointed time, but at the end it shall speak, and not lie; though it may tarry, wait for it; because it will surely come.
—Habakkuk 2:3

When they entered the torchlit yard again, Queron Kinevan was far easier to face. He had gathered the entire complement of the abbey while the two of them were inside the shrine, and all knelt respectfully as the bishop appeared at the portico.

But Camber was no longer anxious at having to be among them. After chatting amiably with several of the brothers and sisters, he pronounced a general blessing on the house and the work. Then, with apparent reluctance, he requested that his party's horses be brought around, Guthrie and Caleb having returned. Queron thanked the bishop for his visit, then himself held the stirrup so that Camber might mount.

Soon Camber and his son were on their way to Valoret once more, their road lit by torches and the ever-brightening moonlight and their number swelled by half a dozen monks whom Queron had insisted upon sending with them for their further safety. They reached Valoret shortly after Compline.

The king was not yet abed. His eldest page met them as soon as they had stepped into the great hall, before they could even divest themselves of their heavy travelling cloaks. Cinhil was waiting for them in the private chapel adjoining his apartments, kneeling at a *prie-dieu* in heavy scarlet nightrobe and a fur-lined cap with lappets that covered his ears. He raised his head and half-turned toward them as the page went out and closed the outer door.

"Alister! It's about time! Is Gregory—"

"He's well, Sire," Camber reassured him. "He should be able to ride in a few days. I gave him your message. He had nothing to do with our delay."

"No?"

Camber let Joram take the damp cloak from his shoulders while he began peeling clammy gloves from fingers stiff with cold.

"Unfortunately, not. We met Bishop Hubert's brother and sister-in-law on the way back, near Dolban. Manfred, I believe, is his name. I expect you'll be hearing from him far sooner than you would like."

"Why?"

"He and his lady wife apparently were harassed by a band of—ah—young Deryni nobles," Camber said tersely. "Joram and I had encountered them ourselves, a short time earlier, but they cried off when they found out who we were."

Cinhil brought a fist down softly on the armrest of the *prie-dieu* and swore a mild oath.

"The blind fools! How can I hold off reprisals against Deryni when Deryni themselves keep agitating the countryside? God knows, we don't need another incident like Nyford. Would you like to see one of your Michaeline houses burn next? How about Grecotha? Or Jaffray's Saint Neot's? Or perhaps Valoret itself?"

Camber sighed and took a seat on a stool which Cinhil had indicated. The king did not need to say more about Nyford. The previous summer, rioting peasants led by a handful of disgruntled human lordlings had utterly destroyed Nyford town and slaughtered most of its inhabitants. The spark which began it had been a senseless incident of irresponsibility not unlike that which had just occurred on the Dolban road.

Nyford lay on the point at the confluence of the Eirian and Lendour rivers, where Imre of Festil had begun the construction of his ill-starred new capital nearly twenty years before. Though the palace and surrounding administrative structures had barely been begun in Imre's time, other folk had occupied the abandoned building site after Imre's fall, humans and Deryni, and a thriving community had sprung up. A Healer's *schola* and several other Deryni groups had also moved in, including a religious community which founded a church and primary school dedicated to Saint Camber.

Water trade also became firmly established, as was almost inevitable, given Nyford's fine, well-sheltered harbor—the last in the mouth of the vast Eirian estuary. A group of Forcinn Michaelines organized a sea-service out of Nyford, hiring on as pilots for the river ships which plied the waters north to Rhemuth, and west, well into Llannedd lands, and east into the Mooryn, as well as on their native sea.

Deryni business acumen had built a thriving river town on the ruins of a far less successful Deryni venture; but human neighbors of lesser resourcefulness gradually felt mere resentment and jealousy shift to blind hatred—an attitude fueled by the increasingly rigid anti-Deryni stance of many churchmen and high-ranking nobles. It was symptomatic of the attitude in much of Gwynedd, though never so blatant or so strong elsewhere as in Nyford. As the taunt of mere existence grew, pricked from time to time by the spurs of occasional Deryni arrogance, not to mention Deryni dominance of most of the area's economy, human sensitivities were increasingly irritated. It had been a grave error of judgment to concentrate so many Deryni in so localized a place. When, in the heat of a particularly severe summer, tempers had seethed with the rising temperature and humidity of the Nyford delta, little was needed to spark the fire of violence.

Nyford had burned for a day and a night, but not before rampaging humans had put to death all the Deryni and Deryni sympathizers who could be found. Deryni-owned or piloted ships were burned to the waterline where they lay at the quays, after being robbed of their cargoes. Deryni shops were vandalized and looted, their proprietors usually dying in the process.

The *schola* was brought down stone by stone, after all its pupils and masters were put to the sword or clubbed to death. Many of the dead were no more than children. Saint Camber's-at-Nyford, church and school, was desecrated and torched, after the sacrilegious murder of the brothers and sisters of the order which had founded it, most of them not even Deryni. The piles of bodies lining the streets fueled fires whose smoke besmirched the clean skies above the delta for most of a week.

Shaking his head, Camber dropped his gaze for just an instant, knowing he had tried every plea and argument possible on this particular point, both with the king and with the myriad Deryni and human lords with whom he daily came into contact. Cinhil understood the problem of balance and order between the races, though he had been only marginally successful at maintaining it; his human ministers were not so understanding. Camber's sigh, as he raised his face to the king's once more, was one of a man momentarily weary even beyond his years.

"Sire, I certainly cannot dispute history," he said softly. "These young firebrands are playing right into the hands of their worst enemies, but they don't see that. They see only that they seem to have no function in a non-Deryni regime."

"That isn't true."

"I know it isn't. But that's what they think. They equate the King's Law with human law. They see no place in it for Deryni."

"Well, damnit, they'd *better* see, or soon there really *won't* be a place—and maybe precious few Deryni! I can't hold back my other nobles forever, you know. And my sons—"

As his voice broke off, he turned his face away from both men. After a second's pause, Joram caught Camber's eye to ask whether he should withdraw and, at Camber's nod of permission, gave a brief bow over the cloak he held across his arm.

"I'll leave you now, Sire, if you have no other need for me. I really should see to the comfort of the monks who came back with us from Dolban."

"No, stay—please. What I have to say concerns you more than Alister, in all truth. Except that I know that you will do as I ask. I do not know whether Alister will."

Surprised, Joram glanced at Camber and got a quick mental image of total mystification. Cinhil had buried his face in his hands, rubbing his eyes wearily, and as Camber shifted uneasily on his stool, trying to imagine what Cinhil might ask that he would not do, Joram shrugged out of his own wet cloak and laid it and his father's in a damp heap to one side. Cinhil lifted his head and stared for so long at the crucifix on the wall behind the altar that Camber and Joram both began to get a little anxious.

"Sire, is anything wrong?" Camber finally whispered.

Cinhil, with a light shake of his head, reached out to touch Camber's arm lightly in reassurance.

"Nay, do not 'Sire' me, old friend. That of which we must speak has nought to do with kings and bishops and such." He turned his attention to Joram. "Joram, it has been near fourteen years since last we spoke of this, but the time has come when I must break my silence. I have thought long on it, and confess I have harbored many bitter thoughts toward you—and toward your father."

He faltered a little at that, his eyes flicking momentarily into some unseeable realm where the ache of memory and disappointment still aged and festered, then returned his gaze to Joram.

"But, that is past. And though I fathom the reasons that he did what he did, and hate those reasons to this day, still, I cannot deny that the end was—desirable—for Gwynedd."

Camber, sitting quietly on his stool, could sense his son's tension as the younger man slowly moved closer to stand behind him. He felt Joram's hand brush his shoulder where Cinhil could not see it, as Joram gazed down guardedly at the king.

"Sire, you know that it was ever our intention to guard and protect this land—and its king. And I hope I need not tell you that we never meant you any enmity."

"I know that, Joram. If I believed otherwise, neither you nor any other who had aught to do with what happened would be alive today. I—fear that I have learned, over the years, how to be a ruthless king as well as a compassionate one. None can say that my enemies have prospered in these years of change."

Camber glanced at his feet, knowing it was useless to bring up the hidden, more insidious enemies which Cinhil had *not* subdued—the men who even now plotted at the heart of the future power of Gwynedd, who had the charge of Cinhil's heirs and would be their regents until the eldest came of age.

He could feel Cinhil's gaze upon him, and knew by the other's sigh that Cinhil had guessed what he was thinking, though the king did not try to reach out with his powers to confirm it; he never did.

Shakily, Cinhil lumbered to his feet with an assist from Joram, annoyance clearly nibbling at the edge of his control. Camber, too, rose, to gaze across at Cinhil with compassion and expectation. He knew they would not quarrel again over *that* issue. On that, the king's mind was made up.

"Thank you for not arguing with me on that," Cinhil said softly. "I have not much time, and the time I have must be allocated for what is now the most important thing yet remaining to me." He shifted his attention to Joram.

"Joram, I need not remind you of what happened to me fourteen years ago, in that hidden chapel of your Michaeline Order." He swallowed painfully and glanced away for just an instant, then resumed. "I—hated you for it then—I hated all of you. And there are powers which you awakened in me then, the use of which terrifies me to this day." He clasped his hands and took another steadying breath.

"But, there are—other aspects of those powers which I believe it might be desirable for a king to have, perhaps the most important of which is the ability to read the truth in another man's heart, even if he wishes to lie. This—and the ability to defend one's self against magical attack, when one is threatened. I have made little use of these abilities, but I—wish for my sons to have the choice when I am gone."

Joram's expression had not changed as he listened to Cinhil's words, but Camber could feel the rising tension in his body, and felt his own anticipation welling in response. In a single, wordless communication, he and Joram exchanged their plans for how to handle the situation—a situation they had long prayed would come to pass.

Joram drew breath slowly, carefully, weighing the words he must speak to the king.

"Do you know what you are asking, Sire?" he asked softly. "What you ask can be done, but the energy required to do it is considerable. It would also require your full participation, under the circumstances."

"I am aware of that," Cinhil whispered. "I would wish it, in any case. I would not have my sons endure such an ordeal without their father nearby to keep watch over them."

"Sire, there is another aspect which must be mentioned," Joram continued haltingly. "When we performed this office for you, my father was alive and we were four

—Rhys, Evaine, myself, and he. Since you speak thus before His Grace, do I correctly infer that you wish Father Alister to take my father's place?"

Cinhil turned his gaze on Camber, almost reluctant to meet the other's eyes. "Will you do it, my old friend? I know how you feel about direct participation in such things, but you are aware of what went on that night. You were the guardian outside the door. I remember you standing there as I passed by, stern and grim in your harness, naked steel in your hands as you passed us into the chapel. Will you wield a sword again for me, this time within the confines of a holy circle?"

"Sire, I—"

"Nay, not 'Sire.' Speak to me as Cinhil, your friend, who needs your aid—not that poor, beleaguered man who wears the Crown at Valoret. Say that Alister will help his friend Cinhil to do what must be done, so that his sons may survive whatever may come in the future when Cinhil, both the man and the king, is dead and gone. We must not talk in circles, Alister. I will die soon. You, who are several years my senior, must surely have thought of death. It comes to all of us, and we must all make preparations in our own time. A king must think of it more carefully even than an ordinary man."

With a sigh, Camber bowed his head, his token Alister reluctance now satisfied.

"As friend, I cannot refuse you, Cinhil," he said softly. "What you ask, I shall perform to the best of my ability, no matter what the cost." He held out his hands to Cinhil, the palms up, and Cinhil laid his own on Camber's.

"Thank you."

With a nod, tears welling in his eyes, Camber brought Cinhil's hands together in a gesture of reassurance, bobbed to touch his forehead to the royal hands in a gesture of humility, then turned away and sank to his knees before the altar, face buried in his hands. Cinhil watched him, stunned a little at the apparent depth of his friend's emotion, then returned his attention to Joram. The younger man had not moved.

"I believe there are—arrangements to be made, Joram," the king said softly. "Will you see to them?"

"I will, Sire. Did you have any particular time and place in mind? Rhys and Evaine have stayed the night at Ebor with Gregory, but they should be back well before noon tomorrow."

Cinhil nodded distractedly, his attention fixed once again on the kneeling Camber. "That will be fine."

"Then, do you wish to plan for tomorrow night?" Joram asked.

Cinhil nodded, still not looking away from Camber.

"And where shall we plan to do it?" Joram insisted. "I do not advise using the chapel where your ritual took place. It is still an active Michaeline establishment. There is danger of interruption."

"Here, in my private chapel," Cinhil murmured. "It will suffice, will it not?" At last he turned his gaze back on Joram, sincere question in his grey eyes.

"It will suit quite well, Sire," Joram replied, making a bow and beginning to withdraw. "I shall make the necessary arrangements with Rhys and my sister. May I also include Jebediah? We will need another guardian."

"Do so."

And as Joram withdrew, closing the door behind him, Cinhil eased himself to his knees beside Camber and joined with him in prayer, never realizing that the part of his friend with which he was interacting was only the surface of another man whom he had thought long-dead —a man who, far from being apprehensive at what his king had just commanded, was already planning how this long-wished-for event might come to pass, and how best the awesome powers of the Haldane line might be instilled in the Haldane heirs.

Camber remained with the king for nearly an hour more; and while they prayed together, Joram set in motion the plan which he and his father had long ago formulated to deal with what now appeared to be an impending certainty. After dispatching a messenger to Rhys and Evaine, he summoned a bleary-eyed Jebediah to his father's chambers to tell him of the king's decision; for in addition to Jebediah's part in what would now ensue, the earl marshal must be prepared to be dismissed by the ambitious and mostly human regency council which would assume rule in the name of the underage Alroy, if Cinhil did not survive the next night's work. The very thought of placing command of Gwynedd's military forces in the hands of non- and anti-Deryni lords gave the Michaeline grand master nightmares, even though he had a sizable cadre of Michaeline-trained men already placed in key positions of authority, who could hopefully keep more reactionary overlords from too drastic action.

And so Joram and Jebediah discussed the military implications of Cinhil's possibly imminent demise, and tried not to show their anxiety when Camber at last joined them, several hours before dawn. The king had finally succumbed to troubled sleep, Camber told them, but his health was even more precarious than they had feared. There would be miracle, indeed, if he survived what must be done.

The cathedral bells tolled Lauds in the leaden, predawn silence before their plans were complete and the three retired for a few hours' much-needed sleep.

The dawn did not bring relief from the bitter cold which passed over the land. The bells of Prime and Terce never rang that morning from the high cathedral tower, for a savage ice storm raged across the Valoret plain soon after sunrise, immobilizing outdoor movement and leaving in its wake a world of white and silver silence.

Rhys and Evaine, stranded at Ebor for nearly four hours with Joram's messenger and their escort, could only fret and listen to the wind and wait, until at last, near noon, their guard commander judged that it was reasonably safe to go on. Even then, the road was slickly treacherous, every frozen tree and bush and tuft of ice-laden grass a cruel, razor-edged obstacle for man and beast. When they reached the city at last, hours later than anticipated, all were nearly frozen, their cloaks stiff with ice.

The spent horses shivered as they trudged the final weary mile through the city gates and up the steep cobblestone street to the castleyard, even though they bore thick bardings to ward off the cold. Their legs were red almost to the knees from breaking through the icy crust on the road and sometimes falling, and their steps left bloody hoofprints to show the way that they had come. As they drew up in the yard, heads lowered and blowing, Rhys slid from his mount gratefully and staggered on numbed feet to help his wife from the saddle.

Joram was waiting for them at the top of the stair, bundled in his Michaeline greatcloak and looking anxious and worn. For the benefit of their escort, he informed them that Bishop Cullen was awaiting their arrival. When they had hurried to the bishop's chambers, they found a tired but hale Camber waiting for them by a roaring fire, with bowls of steaming stew and mulled wine and warmed fur-lined robes to wrap around themselves while they thawed out from their ride.

He would not let them speak until they had gotten some of the hot food into their stomachs and stopped their shivering, preferring instead to outline the previous night's events to give them background. He finished his synopsis at about the same time that Rhys set aside his empty bowl and accepted another cup of mulled wine from Joram. The Healer drank deeply, then absently held out the cup for another refill, his attention fully on Camber. Beside him, Evaine was finishing a piece of bread spread thick with butter and honey, licking the sweet stickiness from fingers no longer red and stiff with cold.

"How is Cinhil taking it all?" Rhys asked.

Camber sighed and laced his fingers together in a gesture which was at once his own and Alister's.

"He is resigned, I would say. You will be better able to judge his physical state, of course, but though he is weak and knows it, he seems resigned to what must be done and to the possible price he may have to pay. I don't think that even he expects to survive this night, but somehow that does not seem to alarm him now. He is past fear."

"Past fear," Evaine whispered. "Would that we all could be. When he is gone—"

She shuddered, not with the cold, and Rhys reached blindly to his left and took her hand, gave it a reassuring squeeze.

"Well," she said briskly, "we'd all best see about reaching that state, oughtn't we? We knew this day would come eventually. It's just a shame it has come so soon. Father, has he given you any idea what kind of ritual he would like, or is he planning it himself?"

"He wishes it to take place in his private chapel," Camber replied, "and he has given us leave to make the physical preparations. I reviewed the essential elements of an effective ritual with him this morning, but the rite is to be of his guiding. He made that quite clear."

"Can he be trusted to do it?" Joram asked. "He has deliberately given himself as little experience as possible, in using his powers. Suppose he breaks under the strain?"

"In that case, we must be prepared to step in," Camber replied. "But he is not to know that. For as long as we can, we must let him believe that he is truly in charge. And he may even surprise us."

Evaine nodded, then glanced at her brother. "Joram, how much has actually been done in preparation? Is the chapel ready yet?"

"Not entirely. I had the servants give it a thorough cleaning after Mass this morning. I was waiting for you to arrive before tackling any more specific preparation, though. If you've rested enough, we can get started whenever you're ready."

"Fine. It will keep us from thinking too much."

She got to her feet and cast off the extra robe she had wrapped around her white she ate, touching Rhys's hand a final time. "Rhys, will you need any help with the children, or can Joram and I get started with our part?"

Rhys shook his head. "I can manage. I'll see Cinhil first, to make certain he's resting. Joram, can you meet me at the nursery-end of the passage when you've finished helping Evaine? Shortly after Vespers will be fine. I'll let you in."

"Good enough. By the way, what about Tavis O'Neill? He's been spending a lot of time with Prince Javan. He's never far from his side."

With a sigh, Rhys laid his hand on his pouch. "I'll ask Cinhil on that one, but if worse comes to worst, the drugs I have will put him out of commission, just like the other servants. But before I go drugging other Deryni and royal princes, I intend to see His Grace—just to make certain that this is what he wants."

A few minutes later, Rhys found himself being admitted to the king's apartments by a solemn-faced squire who bowed him in and immediately withdrew. Cinhil was ensconced in a pile of cushions and sleeping furs before the fireplace in his sleeping chamber, half-reclining while he perused a well-worn scroll of devotional readings. A bank of rushlights on the floor at his elbow cast a warm glow on his face.

At Rhys's tentative knock on the doorframe, he looked up as though brought back abruptly from some other, more serene world, the grey eyes blinking in the light of rushlights and fire as he saw and recognized the Healer.

"Rhys! How glad I am to see you!"

He started to struggle to a more upright position, stifling a cough, but Rhys, with a protesting shake of his head, crossed quickly to his side and knelt, there to take one thin, cold hand in his and kiss it gently.

"Please, Sire, do not bestir yourself for me. You should be resting."

Cinhil shook his head, his tight smile revealing a genuine affection for the Healer which he rarely permitted to show.

"There will be ample time for resting when all of this is done, young friend—an eternity of resting. For now, though, these holy words are my best comfort. These, and your presence. Alister would also be a comfort, but he is busy making preparations, as you no doubt know. He sent you to me, did he not?"

"Aye," Rhys whispered, lowering his eyes. "And I am sorry that it could not be he instead of me. I know what comfort he affords you—and you, him." He allowed himself to meet the grey eyes again, a touch of his customary banter returning to his voice. "But for now, will you allow me to see for myself that all is well with you? For all your wisdom, and his, you have not a Healer's touch, you know."

"Well do I know," Cinhil sighed, glancing away at the fire. "And all is not well."

He let the scroll under his hand curl back on itself with a crackle of brittle parchment. Rhys laid it on the furs beside the king before resting his hand gently on the king's arm again. Even with Camber's warning, he had not expected Cinhil to be so weak. Just the mental commitment to the night's work must already have cost Cinhil a great deal.

"Let me help, Cinhil," he whispered, slipping his hand to Cinhil's shoulder when the king did not protest. "Relax and let me see what can be done."

When Cinhil still made no move of protest, Rhys shifted to the right, toward Cinhil's head, and let both hands slip to Cinhil's shoulders from behind, supporting the king's head on his lap. He felt the tense muscles relaxing as he extended his Healing senses, and he let himself begin to sink into his Healing state, to monitor the body which lay beneath his touch.

At first, he thought Cinhil was going to resist him; for though the body yielded to his touch almost immediately, the churning mind inside did not. Several seconds passed before he felt Cinhil's thoughts slacken and go still as well, sensed the surrender of conscious control to his Healer's touch.

A moment's deep but gentle probing confirmed what Cinhil had said, what Rhys had feared increasingly for many months. The king's lungs were very weak, his general condition frail. And there was nothing Rhys could do save to ease his discomfort, to try to pour more energy into Cinhil's meager reserves and give him strength for these final days or hours—for even a Healer could not reverse aging.

Drawing from deep within his own reserves, Rhys channeled all the excess energy he could spare into the king's tired old body, at the same time setting a strong but overcomable inclination to rest until the last possible minute. Then he withdrew.

But as he shifted back beside Cinhil, and the king opened his eyes again, Rhys knew that he had lost that particular battle. Cinhil's eyes were bright and a little defiant, aware of Rhys' suggestion and already overriding it.

"You do not intend to rest, do you?" Rhys muttered accusingly, shaking his head in resignation.

Gently Cinhil echoed his headshake. "I told you, there will be time enough for that." He picked up his scroll again. "Be content, Rhys. You have done what you felt you should. Be free to go now. I believe you have business with my sons before this night's work begins."

Jaws tightening with emotion, Rhys gazed across at the king for several seconds, then sketched a stiff nod of agreement and reached into his belt pouch to withdraw a folded packet of parchment sealed with green wax.

"If you refer to this—yes. I wished to be certain that this is what you want."

"A sleeping potion?"

"Among other things. Working with children, it is more certain than the—techniques we used before your own assumption of power."

"What other things are in it?" Cinhil whispered, not meeting Rhys' eyes. "Tell me. They are my sons. I have a right to know."

"Would the names mean anything—?"

"Yes!" Cinhil insisted, turning his grey gaze on Rhys with an intensity the Healer had not expected. "I have read. I wish to know!"

With a slight shrug and a nod of his head, Rhys held the packet in his palm and returned Cinhil's gaze.

61

"Cinquefoil and poppy extract, for sleep. Wolfbane, a very minute amount, for Vision. And another drug known only to those of Healer's training. I may not name it for you, but I promise it will not harm them. It will place them in a receptive state of mind for what must be done. You were given the same substance the night of your power assumption, though you may not remember it."

Cinhil's eyes glazed slightly, and Rhys knew that he was casting back in memory, reliving that night so long ago when a younger Cinhil had stood entranced in a magical circle and watched them prepare a cup; knew he was finally making the connection with the rain of white powder which had fallen from Camber's fingers onto the surface of the magically charged wine, the wine which Cinhil had then been compelled to drink.

Cinhil blinked and shook his head slightly, and the spell of memory was broken. With a little shudder, the king glanced quickly at the fire.

"It is a Deryni drug, then?" he whispered.

"Yes."

"But, it works on humans and Deryni, alike?"

"Not precisely alike. But unless activated by the kind of activity we plan tonight, it acts primarily as a sedative, gentle but insistent. I had thought to give it under the guise of a physick against colds. I am told that Alroy has been abed with coughing for much of the week, so we can surmise that the other boys are similarly inclined toward such ailments, and a physick will not be suspected. Also, it is safe enough that even if others should taste of it, it will only make them sleep."

"Tell them you act on my authority, that I am concerned for their health," Cinhil said softly. "And if the squires sleep in the boys' chamber, they are to partake, as well."

"I understand," Rhys said. "What of Tavis O'Neill? I am told by Jebediah that he and Javan are inseparable these days."

"You are a Healer and his senior," Cinhil said shortly. "Can you not govern him?"

"I can try. But he *is* a Healer. If he inspects the 'physick,' he will know something is amiss. This is no remedy for colds, as he will well know."

Stonily Cinhil turned his face back toward the fireplace.

"Then he must drink, too. And you must erase all

memory that aught is amiss. You are a Healer. I leave it in your hands, Rhys."

"Very well. There is nothing further I can say to persuade you to rest?" he asked.

"There is nothing."

With a deep sigh, Rhys started to turn and go, but then he saw Cinhil begin getting to his feet.

Grimly, Rhys helped him to stand, led him to a seat in the window embrasure where he might watch the fading western sky, and tucked a sleeping fur around the frail body to insulate against the cold radiating through the leaded glass.

"It will be my last sunset," Cinhil explained wistfully, as Rhys adjusted the draperies to give him an unobstructed view. "One might have hoped for a less grey one, but any is better than none."

Rhys could not trust himself to answer that. Swallowing a lump which had been building in his throat for the past few minutes, he bowed profoundly, touching the king's hand in understanding, then turned and fled the chamber.

He found a scene of unexpected tranquillity when he entered the nursery suite, and the contrast was soothing to emotions as keenly edged as his had been in the last hour. Rushlights had been lit to dispel the gloom of the gathering dusk, and the princes were just finishing their baths, in preparation for supper and an early bed.

The boys had outgrown their childhood nurses the summer before, those stalwart and loyal ladies having been replaced by a corps of eager young squires of suitably noble birth and a brace of royal governors appointed by the king. The former, most of them hardly older than their young charges, saw to the business of dressing, serving meals, and otherwise assisting their masters in learning the manners and mannerisms befitting young gentlemen and princes. The latter were gone now, the day's lessons done. And though the close proximity of so many boys and very young men at times became more than a little raucous, tonight that was not the case.

Huddled sleepily beside the fireplace in the main dayroom, a yawning Prince Alroy was nursing a cup of warm milk laced with wine. His squire combed the raven hair as it dried by the fire's heat. The eldest prince was already dressed for bed, long white woolen nightshirt covered by a fur-lined dressing gown of crimson wool. Matching slippers embroidered with the Haldane lions showed beneath the hem of the gown. The boy's thin shoulders were hunched down in the fur against the cold.

From behind a lattice screen at the far side of the fireplace, Rhys could hear the childish exclamations of the youngest, Rhys Michael, apparently disputing the entrapment of his head and arms inside his nightshirt while his squire tried to free him. Said squire, a lanky, goodnatured youth of only a few more summers than his young master, could be seen towering head and shoulders above the top of the screen, his adolescent face creased in a grin as he labored to extract the royal hands and head from their fabric prison, roughhousing to an extent he would not have dared with the more delicate Alroy or the serious Javan.

As for Javan, Rhys had to look for him at first, but then spotted the crippled prince seated quietly in a nearby window embrasure with Tavis O'Neill, a glowing charcoal pot at their feet. Javan seemed oblivious to what went on in the rest of the room, eyes closed, his hands resting open-palmed on his knees and covered lightly by Tavis'. Even from where he stood, Rhys could discern the high energy level surrounding both of them, and surmised that Tavis was working some kind of healing with his young charge.

Just then, Alroy noticed Rhys' arrival and put aside his cup of milk, smiling tentatively, the grey eyes bright and a little feverish-looking.

"Lord Rhys!" he called, his words eliciting a cough which sounded of nerves as much as any physical ailment.

His greeting resulted in a squeal of delight from behind the screen and then the launching of a small, shirt-clad body into Rhys' arms, staggering the Healer with the force of his arrival.

"Lord Rhys! Did you come to have supper with us?"

Rhys hugged his namesake and tousled the dark hair gently. "Thank you, I've already eaten. Now, get back to your squire and get dressed before you catch cold like your brother."

As Rhys Michael scurried to obey, Rhys moved closer to Alroy, who had hung his head at Rhys's words. Lightly he touched the boy's forehead to check for fever.

"And how are you this evening, Your Highness?" he asked easily. "Your father tells me that you've not been well this week."

Alroy flashed a wan, tentative smile and cleared his throat, trying to muffle another cough. "I am well enough, Lord Rhys. Sometimes I cough a lot, but I'm better than I was last winter."

"You feel a little feverish."

"It's the fire," Alroy insisted, moving a little back from the flames. "I'm better. Really, I am."

With a smile, Rhys took one of the prince's hands lightly in his own, extending his senses, then shook his head lightly and dropped it.

"You're better than last winter," he agreed, "but you're not well enough. I think it's early to bed for all of you tonight, and a physick against colds to boot."

"Oh, Rhys—"

"Now, none of that," Rhys countered, gently but insistently. "I assure you, it's tasteless. I'll tell you what, though. We'll make it in the nature of a special treat." He glanced at Alroy's squire. "Gavin, while Their Highnesses are at supper, would you go down to the wine cellar and bring up a flask of that sweet Fianna wine, please? You've all been wanting to taste it, and His Grace said it would be all right just this once."

Young Gavin's grin was like sunlight in the gloomy room.

"I'll go right now, m'lord. *I'd* even take a physick for the chance to sample that wine!"

"Then, you shall have that chance," Rhys grinned, slapping the boy on the shoulder and sending him off toward the door. "Go and bring it, and a brace of cups, and we shall all sample."

"You're sure it won't taste nasty?" Rhys Michael asked dubiously.

Rhys gave a good-natured chuckle. "I promise. Now, tell me how your studies are progressing, child-of-my-name. Here, you can sit on my knee and make a full report."

Smiling broadly, Rhys Michael took the seat offered and began rattling off a list of the things he had been learning since he and the royal Healer had last visited. In the next room, Rhys could hear the sounds of the supper being laid, the voices of the servants setting the table and laying out the food. After a few minutes, a servant finally announced that supper was ready. The two boys immediately scampered into the other room, followed shortly by an annoyed-looking Javan, who eyed the elder Healer suspiciously as he passed. When the boys had said grace and begun eating, Rhys drew back into the common room and turned toward Tavis. The younger Healer had not moved from his seat in the window.

"Is Javan ill?" Rhys murmured.

Tavis shook his head cautiously. "No, not ill. He is not strong, though. I try to give him energy each day."

"That is admirable," Rhys replied, "but is it in the boy's best interests? He will not always have you there to help him."

"I know that." Tavis looked away, trying to hide the pain in his pale eyes.

"Tavis," Rhys asked softly, "are you aware of what must be the destiny of these boys? Cinhil is dying, and Alroy will succeed him, almost certainly as a minor."

"Alroy is the eldest. That is his right."

"He is also the weakest," Rhys continued. "I hesitate to say it, but we Healers must face realities, even if others will not. Alroy may not live long enough to get an heir. And if he does not, then the crown falls to Javan. If you make him dependent upon you, how will he bear that weight when you are gone?"

Tavis' head shot up in challenge.

"I shall never leave him!" he whispered fiercely. "No one else cares for him. They think that because his body is flawed, his mind is likewise unfit. But he will show them, some day. I want that for him, Rhys."

"If God wills that he someday may be king, then I want it for him, too," Rhys replied. "But you must not shelter him so much that you stifle his growth."

"It will not be I who stifle him," Tavis retorted, a little defiantly, though he did not raise his voice.

With that, the younger Healer picked up a scroll from the seat beside him and began reading intently, not looking at Rhys any more. Rhys stood there for several seconds, then went back into the room to glance through some of the boys' lessons lying on a table near the fireplace. He and Tavis had never been able to communicate very well.

Young Gavin returned with the wine just as the boys had finished their supper and were beginning to drift back into the room with the other two squires. All six boys watched with varied interest as Rhys pulled the folded

66

packet of parchment from his belt pouch and tossed it onto the table.

"So, we have the grand physick against colds, to be taken in some of the finest Fianna wine ever to grace your father's cellar." With an exaggerated flourish, he unstoppered the green glass flagon and sniffed the contents, rolling his eyes appreciatively as the bouquet reached his nostrils. "Ah, marvelous! And let me tell you, I had a devil of a time convincing the King's Grace that this would not be wasted on the untried palates of a gaggle of schoolboys. You'd better not make a liar of me, now."

As they laughed, except for Javan, who merely grimaced, he took up the packet and broke its seal, then poured its contents carefully into the wine.

"Here are cups, m'lord," Gavin announced, setting them out expectantly as Rhys swirled the flagon.

"Good. You've brought extras. Well, there's enough for all of you," Rhys said, half-filling six cups with the doctored wine. "This is a sweet wine, but light—one of the Fianna varietals. Go ahead and try it."

The squires did not need to be invited a second time, though they did manage to restrain themselves from grabbing until their young masters had taken up their cups. Rhys Michael held his to his nose, sniffed it in imitation of Rhys with the flagon, then tasted and gulped it down. Alroy sampled his somewhat more conservatively, but he, too, clearly approved of the treat their father had allowed and quickly drank it to the dregs.

Only Javan seemed somewhat reluctant, casting a questioning glance at Tavis for reassurance before cautiously sampling it and then draining the cup resignedly.

So much for developing that *one's palate,* Rhys thought ruefully, almost wishing he had left some of the wine unadulterated, for his own consumption. But of course, neither he nor any of the others who would be involved in tonight's ritual had eaten or drunk anything since midafternoon, or would tonight.

He never saw the squires drink—only their empty cups and pleased smiles bearing mute witness to the fact that they, too, had partaken. When all the cups had been replaced on their tray, Rhys smiled and clapped his hands for them to be off to bed, following them affably into the sleeping chamber. He was aware of Tavis gliding down from the window seat toward the half-flagon of wine still remaining, and he made short work of his good-nights.

The squires were nodding off, too, finding their sleeping pallets, as Rhys slipped back into the common room. He was not surprised to find Tavis waiting for him, accusation in his eyes.

"You lied," Tavis whispered.

"I did?"

"That was no physick against colds," Tavis continued, gesturing toward the flagon, eyes flashing like pale aquamarines in his anger. "You drugged them. You gave them enough cinquefoil to put them asleep until tomorrow. I could smell it! What are you up to?"

Mentally and physically steeling himself for what would probably have to be done, Rhys feigned a look of innocence and inserted himself casually between Tavis and the door.

"Up to?" Rhys replied. "Why, I'm simply following His Grace's instructions, seeing that the children get a good night's rest."

"Rest in peace, more likely," Tavis muttered, touching a fingertip to the dregs of one of the cups and tasting it analytically. "You won't mind if I check with His Grace, will—what's this? Wolfbane and *mer*—Rhys, you didn't!"

His shields were up, his mind shuttered behind the impenetrable controls of a highly trained Healer, and Rhys knew he could not breach those defenses except against great resistance.

So before the younger man could react, Rhys stepped forward and slammed his fist into Tavis's solar plexus, caught him as he collapsed to the floor with a startled whoof of expelled air.

"I'm afraid I did, my young friend," Rhys whispered, snatching up the flagon of wine and holding it to Tavis' lips as the man gasped for breath and tried to struggle back to control.

He forced Tavis to swallow the equivalent of a full cup of the drugged wine, amid choking and sputters of combined pain, indignation, and fear, then eased the younger Healer to a half-sitting position against one knee as he set the flagon back on the table. He watched sympathetically as Tavis regained his breath and the drugs began taking effect.

"I'm sorry I had to hit you, Tavis," he murmured, laying a monitoring hand on Tavis's forehead. "But it was necessary for you to drink, since you had the ill-fortune to be here tonight, and I doubted you would do so of your own accord."

"But, *why?*" Tavis croaked out. "My God, Rhys, you've given them *m-m-merasha!*" Tavis managed to mumble, around a tongue which was fast growing too big for his mouth and losing its coherence. "And—and *an-halon, Merasha* and *a-a-anhalon,* and they're not even Deryni!"

"It has been done at His Grace's command, and with his full knowledge," Rhys said softly. "Beyond that, I may tell you nothing more. And even if I might, you wouldn't remember . . . would you?"

Tavis's gaze became a little more distant, his eyes less focused, and Rhys could easily follow the increasingly confused and slurred surface thoughts as Tavis tried to analyze his reactions and identify their causes.

But his shields were also melting away. Gradually, Rhys began to extend his control into the other's mind, gently but surely, nudging the increasingly sluggish mind toward sleep and forgetfulness. Tavis gave token resistance, and a part of him raged that he should be so invaded against his will, but after the weakest of struggles, he succumbed to unconsciousness, totally at Rhys's command.

Rhys, after carefully erasing what had just occurred, and inserting new memories to account for Tavis's sleep, gently picked up the sleeping Healer and carried him to a pile of furs before the fireplace. Arranging him there amid a pile of pillows and covering him lightly with a sleeping fur, he laid Tavis's scroll near his relaxed hand and checked the depth of his sleep a final time.

Then, after emptying the last of the drugged wine down the garde-robe shaft, and rinsing it and the cups with water from a ewer, he poured a little of the leftover table wine from dinner into the flagon and added yet another powder—this one truly a sleep-encouraging physick. A little of this he splashed into each of the cups, then emptied all into the garde-robe again. Now, even inspection of the dregs would not reveal what had been done.

Finally, he went to a tall wooden closet in the corner of the boys' sleeping chamber and pressed a series of whorls and depressions in the heavy carving. A panel slid aside in the rear of the closet to reveal a bored-looking Joram sitting on the stone floor beyond, bundled closely in his

Michaeline greatcloak. A narrow passageway stretched into darkness beyond him.

"It certainly took you long enough," Joram whispered, getting to his feet and brushing dust from his posterior. "I thought you were going to find me a stiff, frozen statue. Everyone asleep?"

Rhys nodded. "Sorry for the delay. As I feared, Tavis was determined to stay about, so I had to drug him as well as the squires. He won't remember anything in the morning, though. Come on. We'll take the twins through first."

CHAPTER SIX

Neglect not the gift that is in thee, which was given thee by prophecy, with the laying on of the hands of the presbytery.

—I Timothy 4:14

Trying to remain unobtrusive, Cinhil Haldane peered through the doorway of his private chapel and watched the preparations which were taking place. That long-familiar refuge for so many years of his life had taken on a strangeness under the ministrations of Joram and, especially, Evaine—a strangeness he had sensed building for hours, even as he napped and read and prayed in the adjoining royal suite.

They had all come to see him privately at some time during the day. Alister had come first, just past Terce, later than was his usual wont but the more rested for having slept a few extra hours. Cinhil knew that the bishop had not had much chance for sleep last night, for the two of them had prayed together nearly until Matins.

After Alister had come Joram; and then Rhys, Evaine, and finally Jebediah—whose visit had been perhaps the saddest of all, for the Michaeline knight would not be able to share in this last task—had already said his final goodbyes. Even now he was arming himself to stand guard outside the royal suite, that the work inside might not be disturbed.

Now, there was another Deryni who did not fit the traditional mold which humans would ascribe to all of that race—a gentle and a compassionate man, for all that he was warrior, born and bred. The king wondered why Jebediah thought the regents would not keep him on as earl marshal, once Cinhil was gone. Cinhil had assured him that his fears were groundless on all counts, but he was not certain that the earl marshal was convinced.

One fear which was not groundless, however, was the likelihood of Cinhil's impending death—not that Cinhil himself was particularly frightened by the prospect any more. Even the means of death did not dismay him, or hold for him the stark, soul-withering terror it once would have. This magic was of his choosing and his direction.

Dispassionately he accepted that his life would likely end within these walls tonight—and that he was content that this be so, if only he could accomplish his last intentions. And such an end, in the service of his sons, was infinitely better than dragging on and on, ever weaker, eventually bedridden and coughing out his life in a final fit of blood and pain.

He had told Alister so. He had made his final confession this morning and received absolution. After, he had secretly celebrated his last Mass, with Alister to assist him, reverently donning the beloved vestments technically forbidden him since a long-ago Christmas Eve when a long-dead archbishop had pronounced him prince instead of priest. That Cinhil had resumed his priestly office and continued to exercise it faithfully over the years was a secret which only he and Alister shared, a secret of the confessional which both men would carry to their graves. His reception of the Sacrament as priest, one final time, had lent him strength to face the rest of the day's demands. Later, Alister would give one final sacrament, in its time; and after that, there would be peace. He would welcome peace, after the life he had been forced to lead.

With a sigh, he glanced into the chapel. It seemed almost stark compared to its usual appearance, dark but for the Presence Lamp and a single taper on a small table in the center of the room. After the servants had finished the general cleaning, Evaine and Rhys had removed everything except the heavy altar against the eastern wall and the thick Kheldish carpet which covered the tile at

71

the foot of the altar steps. This last they had moved to the center of the chamber, and brought in a smaller one which they spread in the northeast corner. Then Joram had disappeared through an opening to the left of the altar which was there and not-there, almost in the blinking of an eye. Evaine and Alister and Jebediah had continued the preparations.

New, fresh altar cloths and hangings had been laid in place next, the altar candles replaced with new ones, the sanctuary lamp replenished with oil, woman and bishop and Michaeline knight performing all these tasks with reverence and a serenity which seemed to extend even to the doorway where Cinhil watched. Four candlesticks with colored glass shields in gold and red and blue and green now stood at the cardinal points of the room, very like those which had stood guard at his own rite so many years before, though his had all been white.

He was momentarily startled then by a fully-armed Jebediah brushing past him, well-burnished mail clinking softly as he moved, the white belt of his knighthood gleaming against the dark Michaeline blue of surcoat and greatcloak. He bore Cinhil's sword of state in his gloved hands, the jeweled belt wrapped loosely around the carved and gem-studded scabbard.

Jebediah nodded respect to the king as he passed, but he did not pause. Crossing the chapel to where Alister looked up expectantly, he bowed to the altar's Presence and then knelt to lay the sheathed weapon across Alister's outstretched palms. Alister bowed over the sword, then laid it on the altar and began lighting the altar candles with a taper kindled from the Presence Light itself. After that, he knelt on the altar steps and bowed his grizzled head in prayer, gnarled hands folded loosely on his knee.

Jebediah, when he had seen the candles lit, bobbed his head in obeisance once more, then rose and left the chapel as quickly as he had come. Cinhil felt a pang of loss as the knight disappeared through the outer door. He knew he would not see Jebediah again.

Small sounds: the chink of metal against glass. In the center of the room, Evaine was arranging objects on the table—a thurible; a small, footed cup of white-glazed clay, filled with water; a slender silver dagger which Cinhil thought he remembered having seen at Evaine's belt on several occasions. Its metal gleamed in the light of the taper, potent but somehow not sinister. Underneath the

72

table, though he could not see them for the white cloth brushing the carpet all around, where Rhys's medical kit, a pair of mismatched earrings made of twisted gold wire, and three small pieces of parchment already appropriately inscribed.

These last he had copied out himself this afternoon, his final legacy to those who must wear the crown after him. The words were not much, but they would have to suffice. He had nothing else to leave them except life itself, having given them little more than that. Still, they were his sons, bone of his bone and flesh of his flesh.

Movement caught his eye in the shadows to his left, and he was startled to discover an opening which had not been there an eyeblink before. Rhys and Joram emerged by the glow of a pale sphere of greenish light which floated near Rhys's head, and Joram gently deposited a small, fur-bundled form on the carpet in the corner. A twisted foot protruding from under the furs proclaimed it to be Javan.

Rhys laid the sleeping Alroy beside the small table, tossing the child's furs to Joram, who then disappeared through the opening again, though this time it did not close after him. When Cinhil looked back, Rhys was already laying his hands on Alroy's forehead, eyes closed, while Evaine quietly brought out the medical kit from under the table.

Cinhil must move now. As he crossed slowly to kneel by Rhys's side, unfastening the wire which held the great cabochon ruby in his right earlobe, he watched the Healer swab the right earlobe of his eldest son with something whose pungent aroma almost made him sneeze—stared with fascination as Rhys's bright needle jabbed through the boy's fair skin. No flicker of awareness crossed his son's face as the Healer withdrew his needle and wiped away the little welling of blood, then held out his hand for the stone.

The Eye of Rom, they had called it, when Rhys and Camber had given it to him so many years before—cut from a stone which fell from heaven the night of the Savior's birth, the legend said, and brought to the Child by the Magi, wise men of the East who had known that this was a stone for kings. Cinhil felt a twinge of loss as he gave it up, for he had not been without it for all these years now. The stone was one of the keys to the powers they had given him on that long-ago night. And as he watched

Rhys insert it in his son's earlobe, he knew that it would protect that child as it had protected him.

He blinked—and realized that Rhys had moved, that the Healer was now kneeling beside the sleeping Javan, his needle once more flashing in the candlelight which Evaine had brought. He heaved himself to his feet, but by the time he had made his way to where the two worked, Rhys had already inserted the wire of twisted gold which would hold the place for the Eye of Rom to lodge, should Alroy die without heirs.

Joram returned with the sleeping Rhys Michael then, the mysterious opening shushing shut with hardly a whisper of sound. As the priest laid the youngest prince beside his brother Javan, Rhys shifted his attention to that one, and Joram gestured for the king to join him in the center of the chamber. With a sigh, Cinhil crossed slowly back to the table with the Michaeline priest.

"I believe we're almost ready, Sire," Joram said in a low voice, kneeling down beside the sleeping Alroy. "Have you any questions, before we begin?"

Cinhil glanced past Joram at Alister, still kneeling before the altar. "No, I have none for myself. But, what of Alister? Will he be all right?"

Joram's handsome face creased for just an instant in a gentle smile. "You need not fear for Father Alister," he said softly. "He is a man of conscience, but he has worked with us before, very satisfactorily. He knows what he must do, and is far more reconciled to this kind of work than his outward demeanor would have one think. Do not underestimate him."

"Nay, I have never done that," Cinhil murmured, laying a hand on Joram's shoulder briefly. "Alister," he called, raising his voice only slightly, "will you attend us?"

He watched the grizzled head rise, watched the gnarled hands brace against cassocked thighs as the bishop got to his feet and turned toward them, his seamed face calm and without apprehension.

"I am ready, my friend," the bishop said softly, turning to take up the sword from the altar before joining them beside the table. "Are you content, Cinhil?"

"Content?" He watched his friend lay the sword on the floor partly beneath the table and again felt a flutter of apprehension which he quickly damped.

"Aye, I am content," he breathed.

As he spoke, Evaine and Rhys returned to the center of

74

the circle and knelt by Alroy. Cinhil watched Rhys close his eyes and take a deep breath, slipping into his meditative state, then watched as he laid his hand on Alroy's forehead and seemed to wait for something. Immediately, Joram, too, took a deep breath and let himself sink into trance—and Cinhil knew that they were forming the rapport which would keep Alroy controlled through what must be done. Beyond them, Evaine had set the charcoal to smouldering in the thurible and now moved with her taper toward the candle standing at the foot of the altar steps, invoking, as flame flared to life behind the amber glass, the Archangel Raphael to guard the eastern quarter.

He noted Alister watching intently as she moved on to the south, toward Saint Michael's candle with its ruby glass shield, apparently totally at ease now that things were beginning. The fire blazed up crimson, then moved, golden and pure on its white taper, to cross behind them all, where the glass shielding Saint Gabriel's candle would turn the fire to azure.

Rhys had withdrawn his hand from Alroy's forehead now, and Joram as well, and the boy slowly opened his eyes upon a scene which he would not remember in the morning—indeed, would not remember at all until it should become time to pass his gifting to his son. The boy's eyes were wide and slightly glazed, registering his surroundings at some deep level but beyond his ability to react with the fear or anxiety which he might otherwise have shown. Cinhil knew that he was aware of his father's presence as Joram and Rhys helped him to sit, but he knew also that he was far from the forefront of Alroy's thoughts as the boy was made to stand easily beside the table.

Evaine had lit the last candle now, the green-shielded ward guarded by Uriel, the Dark Archangel, but she paused just past the northern ward until Rhys had confirmed Joram's control over his charge and then withdrawn toward the other two sleeping boys. When he had passed through the gate she had left, pausing to brush her lips lightly with his own, she continued on to the east and closed the circle.

Joram was waiting for her at the eastern quarter, the thurible smoking in his hands as he censed her with its sweet smoke. To the ancient Psalm of the Shepherd, he began retracing the circle she had defined, the smoke and the echo of his words hanging tangibly in the wake of his passage and somehow contained by the boundaries of the circle being cast. As before, the only other time Cinhil had watched them at work, he was almost certain that the limits of the circle now glowed.

As Joram passed between Cinhil and the watching Rhys, outside the circle and in the northeast quarter, Cinhil was sure that there was *something* between them. He continued to be sure, even when Joram had completed his circuit and moved into the center of the circle to cense the rest of them standing there: Cinhil himself in the east, though he was no Healer; Evaine, again standing in the west, as she had so many years before; and the implacable Alister in the north, where Camber once had stood. Alroy, too, was censed; and Cinhil wondered whether the boy was experiencing any of the same emotions which Cinhil had felt on the night of his own magical initiation.

Then Joram was returning to Alister and giving the thurible into his priestly hands, that the bishop might cense him, in turn. Joram bowed his head as Alister swung the thurible with his customary dexterity, taking it back and setting it on the table with another bow when Alister had finished.

That done, Joram knelt and brought forth Cinhil's sword, drawing it partway from its gemmed scabbard and extending the hilt toward Cinhil with bowed head.

Cinhil knew what he must do now. He steeled himself as his hand closed on the familiar hilt, but he drew the weapon with a smooth, sure motion. He and Alister had jointly blessed the sword the night before, adding their own consecration to the one already placed on the blade the day of his coronation. The very air around it seemed to vibrate as he raised the quillons before his eyes and walked slowly to the eastern ward. There was no doubt in his mind that the weapon was now, even if it had not been before, an implement of magic.

The candlelight was golden from the eastern quarter candle, and he let that light stream into his mind as well as his eyes as he raised the sword in salute to the Presence signified by the Light above the altar beyond. With a short, scarce-breathed prayer for courage, he let the tip of the sword sink to the floor beside the gold-lit candle and turned slightly toward his right as he began to retrace their circle a third and final time.

He did not know the formal words for what he did; he did not want to know. Instead, he spoke extemporaneously from the heart, trusting that Those who listened would recognize his good intent. He was surprised to find his grip firm and sure on the weapon beneath his hand, his voice steady and confident.

"Saint Raphael, Healer, Guardian of Wind and Tempest, may we be guarded and healed in mind and soul and body this night."

He had reached the red-lit southern ward, and he inclined his head a little in acknowledgment as the tip of his blade passed by.

"Saint Michael, Defender, Guardian of Eden, protect us in our hour of need."

He walked on, feeling the inexorable building of energy and knowing—and somehow taking comfort from it—that he was a part of its source. He was in the west now, and the color of the west was blue, the color of the Lady's mantle. Again he inclined his head in passing, his lips now in invocation of the Western Guardian as his sword continued to inscribe the sacred circle.

"Saint Gabriel, Heavenly Herald, carry our supplications to Our Lady."

And on to the north, where green-filtered fire reflected eerily off his blade.

"Saint Uriel, Dark Angel, come gently, if you must, and let all fear die here within this place."

Another half-dozen steps, and it was done. Returning to the east, where he had begun, he drew the final stroke which bound the circle, then raised his blade in salute a second time. As the sword sank from that salute, suddenly much heavier in his hands, he turned to look at all of them, paused, then moved a few steps to the left to lay the sword along the northeast arc of the circle. Blindly, then, he returned to his place before his son, facing the altar and settling his thoughts into calmness once more.

He had done it! It was begun.

After a moment, he heard Evaine draw breath behind him, listened transfixed as she wove the same spell she had made so many years before.

"We stand outside time, in a place not of earth. As our ancestors before us bade, we join together and are One. By Thy blessed Apostles, Matthew, Mark, Luke, and John; by all Powers of Light and Shadow, we call Thee to guard and defend us from all perils, O Most High. Thus it is and has always been, thus it will be for all times to come. *Per omnia saecula saeculorum.*"

"Amen," Cinhil whispered, truly in union with all of them now, as he had not been for many, many years.

He crossed himself and closed his eyes in silent prayer; was aware, through his meditation, of the soft rustle of his companions' robes as they went about their next tasks. He caught a whiff of incense as Evaine brought the thurible to his right, was abruptly conscious of Alister and Joram moving into place at his left.

He turned toward them and candlelight flashed in his eyes as he looked up, glinting from the blade of the dagger which Alister carried across the rim of the white-glazed earthen cup. Nervously, Cinhil took his son's shoulders and turned him slightly away from the knife, knowing the boy would remember none of this, yet sensitive to the fear of the present. A little self-consciously, he pulled from his left hand a heavy gold ring set with garnets, the central cabochon surrounded by smaller, brilliant-cut stones which caught and fractured the candlelight into hundreds of fiery flecks which danced on his dark robe. He could sense his son's dazed attention on the ring as he handed it to Joram.

"This, properly charged, will be the trigger. When I am gone and he puts on the ring, his powers will be complete. But he will not know of them unless he needs them, and even then, he will believe those powers his by Divine Right, because he is king."

"A reasonable rationale, under the circumstances," Joram nodded. He gestured toward Alister's cup with the piece of parchment he also held. "For our part, we have chosen water rather than wine for this rite. Wine had a particular significance for you, but we felt that water was sufficient for the children. It will hold the charge as well —unless, of course, you prefer wine."

Cinhil shook his head and contained a shiver, remembering that wine, dark and bitter, throbbing with power. With a deep, sobering breath, he took his son's slack hands in his and met the glazed grey eyes with his own.

"Son, forgive me for what I am about to do to you," he said in a low voice. "What I must do, I do for your good and the good of all your people. I know you cannot understand that now, or what is happening to you, but I want you to know, at least at some level, that despite what may sometimes appear, I—care for you greatly, and would never willingly permit you to come to ill."

Gently his thumbs chafed the two small hands resting

so still within his own, then brought the right one to his lips and kissed it. His eyes misted as he glanced away at the parchment which Joram now held within his vision, but he did not need to read the words penned there.

"I will declare the decree," he said, never faltering as he recited the words of the Psalmist. *"The Lord hath said unto me, Thou art my Son: this day have I begotten thee. Ask of me, and I shall give thee the heathen for thine inheritance, and the uttermost parts of the earth for thy possession."*

He glanced into the boy's eyes again, fancying he could see some comprehension written there, then released the boy's left hand, took the dagger from Alister and tested its sharpness against his thumb.

"Alroy Bearand Brion Haldane, Crown Prince of Gwynedd, be consecrated to the service of thy people," he said, the while squeezing Alroy's right thumb close in the grip of his free hand.

In two quick motions, he jabbed the boy's thumb with the point, then turned the blade on his own. The boy did not flinch—only watched dreamily as his bleeding thumb and then his father's were pressed briefly to the parchment, to the ring. As Joram cast the parchment on Evaine's brazier, Alister wiped both wounds with a strip of linen which he then laid across his left arm, maniplewise.

Cinhil watched the fresh smoke of the burning parchment spiral upward, to curl lazily against the confines of the protective circle. Only when the parchment was but a crisp of brittle ash on the charcoal did he move again, this time to take a pinch of ash between thumb and forefinger and sprinkle it on the surface of the water in Alister's cup.

"Give the king Thy judgments, O God, and Thy righteousness unto the king's son," he said.

He took the blood-stained ring from Joram and slipped it into the cup as well, sensing their surprise that he had now literally made this a blood-rite, but he could not let that deter him. Somehow he knew that it was necessary, and what further he must do.

As they took their places once more, Joram to his left and Alister to his right, he drew strength from his own resolve. Impassively he took the cup from Alister and turned to face the altar, raised the cup slightly with both hands in salutation to the Divine Presence.

"O Lord, Thou art holy, indeed: the fountain of all holiness. In trembling and humility we come before Thee with our supplications, asking Thy blessing and protection on what we must do this night."

He turned to face his son, lowering the cup to extend his right palm flat above the rim.

"Send now Thy holy Archangel Raphael, O Lord, to breathe upon this water and make it holy, that they who shall drink of it may justly command the element of Air. Amen."

A moment more he held his hand motionless there and forged his will, his heart pounding in the unbreathing silence of the warded circle. Trembling, he let his right hand slip down to support the cup with its mate, felt the ring beneath the water vibrating against the snow-white glaze.

A breeze stirred his robe, a lock of hair, wafted a curl of incense smoke past his nostrils, began to circulate with increasing force within the confines of the circle. He saw the wild look in his son's eyes as the breeze became a wind, a vortex which snapped robes tight to bodies and whipped hair against faces which did not flinch or turn aside.

Evaine's hood was swept from her head, her hair coming down in a cascade of tinkling golden pins which showered the carpet at their feet. Yellow and iron-grey hair stood out like living, writhing haloes on Joram and Alister, but they did not move—only stood with hands crossed still on blue and purple-clad breasts, serene, implacable, though the bishop did close his eyes briefly, Cinhil noted.

Then, suddenly, the storm was past. Almost before anyone could react, the wind had captured more of the incense smoke and coalesced in a tight spiral centering over the cup which Cinhil still held. He was aware of all their eyes upon him, of an eddy of surprise that he had called up this imagery for the work they did. But there was an undercurrent of acceptance, too—of acquiescence to this approach—and he knew that they would follow his lead.

He watched as the breeze subsided to a tiny, controlled whirlwind hovering above the cup, did not dare to breathe as the funnel sank and touched the surface of the water, stirring it slightly and then dying away.

When all movement on the surface of the water had

ceased, when all that stirred was the renewed shaking of his hand, Cinhil closed his eyes briefly and passed the cup to Joram. Joram, apparently unmoved by what he had just seen, bowed solemnly, grey eyes hooded and unfathomable. Holding out the cup beside the entranced Alroy, he extended his right hand over the rim as Cinhil had done.

"O Lord, Thou art holy, indeed: the fountain of all holiness. We pray Thee now send Thy holy Archangel of Fire, the Blessed Michael, to instill this water with the fire of Thy love and make it holy. So may all who drink of it command the element of Fire. Amen."

A moment, with his hand held over the cup, and then the hand was drawn a little to one side, though still it hovered close. Fire glowed within the hollow of his palm, growing to an egg-sized spheroid of golden flame which hung suspended but a handspan from the cup. The flame roared like the fire of a forge, filling the warded circle with its might.

After a few heartbeats, Joram turned his hand slightly downward and seemed to press the fiery sphere into the surface of the water. Steam hissed and spat for just an instant, then ceased as the flame subsided to a cold blue which brooded, barely visible, on the surface and around the rim.

Carefully, reverently, Joram turned toward his sister and extended the cup to her. She tossed her wind-tumbled hair back from her face with a quick, graceful gesture and took the cup, held it close against her breast for just a moment while she gazed into the water.

Then she raised it high in supplication, her eyes focused on and through the glow of flame.

"O Lord, Thou art holy, indeed: the fountain of all holiness. Let now Thine Archangel Gabriel, who rules the stormy waters, instill this cup with the rain of Thy wisdom, that they who shall drink hereof may justly command the element of Water. Amen."

For an instant there was silence, a growing electric tension in the air. Then lightning crackled in the space above their heads, and thunder rumbled, and a small, dark cloud took form above the cup.

Cinhil gasped, his resolve shaken at what Evaine had called, but the others did not move so neither did he. Evaine's face was suffused with radiance, her blue eyes focused entirely on this thing she had called.

Thunder rumbled again, lower and less menacing this time, and then a gentle rain began to fall from the little cloud, most of it falling into the cup but a few drops splashing on those who watched. Cinhil flinched as the first drop hit his face, restraining the almost irresistible urge to cross himself, but the rainfall ended almost as soon as it had begun. Abruptly, the cup in Evaine's hands was only what it had been before, though fuller by perhaps a fingerspan than it had been. The outside of the cup ran with water beaded on the glaze, dripping a little on the precious Kheldish carpet as Evaine handed it to Alister with a bow.

Cinhil drew another deep breath as Alister glanced into the cup and raised it to eye level with both hands, focusing his attention on the point above their heads where the cloud had manifested itself seconds earlier.

"O Lord, Thou art holy, indeed: the fountain of all holiness. Let Uriel, Thy messenger of darkness and of death, instill this cup with all the strength and secrets of the earth, that they who shall drink hereof may justly command the element of Earth. Amen."

Instantly, the cup began to tremble in Alister's hands, the ring inside to tinkle against the cup, the water to dance so that it threatened to spill over the rim. At first Cinhil thought it was Alister's hands which shook, as his own had done; but then they all became aware that other things were rattling and trembling, that the very floor was vibrating beneath their feet.

The tremor increased, until Cinhil feared the very altar candles must be toppled from their places. But then the shaking subsided, as quickly as it had begun. Alister raised the cup higher and inclined his head in acknowledgment of the Power which had been manifested through his hands, then lowered the cup and turned his gaze on Cinhil, extending the cup to him.

"The cup is ready, Sire," he said in a low voice. "What remains is in your hands."

Slowly, soberly, without a trace of fear anymore, Cinhil took the cup and held it close against his chest as he bowed his head and spoke a final, humble prayer in his own mind. In front of him, the trembling Alroy had not let out a whimper, had not moved, but Cinhil could see the fear and dread in the grey eyes as he looked up and searched his son's face. His hands were steady as he lifted the cup between them.

"Alroy, you are my son and heir," he said. "Drink. By this mystery shall you come to the power which is your divine right, as future king of this realm; and even so shall you instruct your own sons, if that should someday come to pass."

Slowly the boy's hands rose to meet his father's, tipped the cup to his lips so that he might sip once, twice, again. He shuddered as the cup was taken away and handed to Joram, closed his eyes, and began trembling more violently as the *geas* came upon him. Coolly and dispassionately, Cinhil laid his hands on the boy's head and sent forth his mind, finding no resistance now that the cup had done its work.

Forcing ever deeper rapport, he plunged Alroy into the full awakening of all his Haldane potential, imprinting irresistible compulsions which would hold and guide him in the use of that potential for so long as he should live.

The boy cried out, a quickly stifled sob of pain and fear, but Cinhil dared not relent. Though the boy staggered under the outpouring of his father's will, moaning anew as the final compulsions were set, Cinhil did not ease the flow of energy until his task was completed. Then he drew the boy to his breast and cradled the raven head against his bosom, embracing and supporting him as the lad slipped into unconsciousness. He did not heed the tears which now streamed openly down his own fatigue-drawn cheeks.

"Sire?" Alister whispered.

"Not yet."

For a little while longer, Cinhil held the boy, withdrawing slowly, erasing all conscious memory of what had happened, easing the last vestiges of pain. Finally, he slipped his arms more closely around the limp little body and picked the boy up, holding him in his arms with some effort.

"He will sleep now," he murmured, making a half-hearted attempt to dry his tears against his sleeve. "He will remember nothing unless there is need. Even then, he will not remember this night unless it falls that he must perform a like office for his son someday."

He drew another deep breath and buried his face in the boy's black hair, which muffled his voice as he added: "Alister, would you please open a gate so that I may take him to Rhys? I fear I may have drawn too deeply on my own strength. Help me."

He was aware of the bishop striding quickly to the northeast quarter of the circle and stooping for the blade. But by the time he had made his slow, shuffling way to his friend's side, Joram and Evaine supporting him at his elbows, the gate was open, Alister standing aside with the sword at rest beside him while Rhys reached out for the unconscious Alroy.

Cinhil gave the boy tenderly into the Healer's keeping, then sank to his knees outside the circle's gate, forcing himself to breathe slowly but not too deeply, for the last thing he needed was to trigger a coughing bout. He waited while Rhys laid his son on a sleeping fur, checked his condition, signed for Joram to come and take Javan into the circle. When Joram had passed inside with the boy, Rhys scrambled on his knees to Cinhil's side. His Healer's hand touched Cinhil's in deep concern.

"Cinhil, are you all right?"

"With your help, I shall endure what I must. I need your strength, though, Rhys."

"What would you have me do?"

Cinhil closed his eyes briefly. "There is—a Deryni spell for banishing fatigue. I—know it, but have never used it." He paused. "Will you help me work it now?"

"There is a danger. You know that. In your weakened state—"

"In my weakened state, I shall surely die if I attempt what further must be done and do not have this help," Cinhil chided gently. "Come, Rhys. You know that I am dying. At least let me accomplish what I must, before I go. If I do not leave this circle alive, once my task is finished, it does not matter. But it does matter that I finish my work. I cannot, without your help."

A flicker of compassion stirred behind Rhys's amber eyes, and then he pressed the royal hand in acquiescence.

"Very well, my liege. You shall have your help. Open to me and let me enter. I promise, you shall have the strength to finish your work—and you shall feel no pain."

CHAPTER SEVEN

*Or ever the silver cord be loosed . . . then shall the
dust return to the earth as it was: and the spirit
shall return unto God who gave it.*
— Ecclesiastes 12:6–7

At Cinhil's nod, Rhys took a deep breath and let himself begin to sink into trance, though he did not close his eyes just yet. Slipping his left hand along the side of Cinhil's neck, his thumb resting lightly behind the right ear, he brought his other hand up to touch the front of Cinhil's head, his hand's weight urging the weary eyes to close. A moment more to collect himself, and then he was sending forth his mind across the bond now being formed, urging Cinhil to let go, to surrender control to the Healer's touch, feeling the king's slow, pained response.

Beyond Cinhil, he was aware of Camber and Joram watching from the gateway, of his wife kneeling beside the sleeping Javan and collecting the golden pins which had fallen from her hair. He sensed Camber's wordless query as to Cinhil's condition, but he could only catch the Master's eye and shake his head minutely, his glance and lightning thought telling Camber all there was to know of Cinhil's chance of lasting out the night if this went on.

There was no appeal from Cinhil's self-imposed sentence, however. Both Rhys and Camber knew it. What Rhys had been asked to do would sustain Cinhil through the other two imprintings, which was what Cinhil wanted, but it would deplete the king's resources past possible renewal. And Rhys, whose vocation it was to prolong life, was now being asked to take action not for length but for quality of life. Still, Rhys thought he understood.

Resignedly, then, he let himself slip deep into trance with Cinhil, blocking Cinhil's pain and cancelling out fatigue and doing what Healing he could. Some repairs he was able to effect for the present, but he knew they would not hold for long under the stress to which Cinhil would soon subject himself again. Rhys would be able to do more Healing after Cinhil had finished with Javan, and that would give him yet a little more time, but that would be the limit, both for Cinhil and for him. He could not answer for Cinhil's life, once the third imprinting was complete.

Quietly, gently, he did what must be done, then withdrew mind and hands and opened his eyes. Cinhil did not move for a few seconds, but when he did look up at Rhys again, he appeared to be greatly renewed. A faint smile split the grey-flecked beard, becoming wider as he explored the new limits and comfort of his renewed body.

"Healers do, indeed, work miracles," he said softly, gratitude lighting the grey eyes. "What a fool was I, ever to doubt it. Thank you, my friend. You have done me and Gwynedd great service this night."

As he got to his feet and headed back into the warded circle, Joram and Camber stood to either side of the gateway and bowed him through. Another glance passed between Rhys and Camber as the Deryni Master laid the tip of the sword at one side of the gate and drew it across, sealing the circle once more.

Rhys checked on his two charges briefly—the one still unconscious, though recovering and approaching normal, if drugged, sleep; the other sleeping still in blissful ignorance of what lay ahead—then returned his attention to the circle. Through the veiling mist of the circle's power, he could not see them clearly, but he could follow their progress from the shadow-shapes.

He watched the shadow that was Camber bring the knife again, watched Cinhil take that knife and prick the thumb of the unresisting Javan standing in their midst. Joram held the parchment, the charged water in its cup, and Cinhil let a drop of the boy's blood fall on each.

Smoke rose from the censer as the parchment burned, but Rhys could not smell it. Sound was muffled and almost other-worldly, somehow apart from the real world where Rhys knelt outside the circle.

We stand outside time, in a place not of earth . . . , he recalled.

He had expected it would be thus. He had been inside a warded circle many times before; he certainly was not new to the practice of ritual magic, especially since his association with the MacRorie family, so many years now.

But never before tonight had he been on the outside, trying to look in. The experience was a little unnerving.

Outside the chapel, he was aware of all the normal sounds of a royal castle at night; but inside, all of that seemed suspended. It was as if the warded circle soaked up sound and light like a giant sponge, deadening normal perceptions so that the perceptions of *other* might be more readily discerned.

Fully caught up now in the magic of the moment, he rose slowly to his feet, for the crux of Javan's imprinting was about to be met. He knew that those within the circle did not need to repeat the four-fold invocation they had made before. This rite was an additive one, bringing Javan into the spell by the adding of his blood to the already charged cup, binding him into the succession in ways which mere lineage could never, ever challenge. When Javan drank from the charged cup, he would be assuming all the compulsions which Rhys and Camber and Evaine and Joram had imposed on Cinhil twelve years before, as well as the will of Cinhil himself, who controlled this rite and was its author.

And if the time came when the elder Alroy should die without male heir, then Javan, too, would assume the royal Haldane heritage by the expedient of putting on his father's ring. That ring still lay in the bottom of the cup which Cinhil now extended to his son, bathed in the water which was charged not only with ash and the blood of three Haldanes now.

Thrice Javan sipped; then Cinhil was handing Joram the cup and laying his hands on his son's head. The boy's body went rigid as the royal will was imposed.

For a long time, nothing moved within the circle save the slight, slender form of Javan, struggling feebly to escape the power being thrust upon him. Cinhil drew him close against his breast as he continued his relentless patterning, finally raising his head to let Joram take the collapsing boy. Wearily he sank to his hands and knees.

At once Camber was moving to the edge of the circle and catching up the sword, cutting another gateway in the circle's dome. As soon as the gateway was open, Rhys dashed inside, pausing only an instant to touch the unconscious Javan's forehead and confirm his safety before throwing himself to his knees beside the exhausted Cinhil. Slipping a supporting arm around the king's shoulders, Rhys touched his fingertips to the royal wrist, fearful of what he would find. Cinhil's eyelids fluttered weakly and then gazed up at Rhys.

"I just about did it that time, didn't I?" he rasped, fighting back a cough. "You must get me through the last one, though, Rhys. I've never asked anything so important of you."

In Rhys's arms, Cinhil's body seemed to have grown lighter, more frail, and Rhys knew that he was burning himself out with the massive energy consumption—and that nothing could persuade him to stop now and save himself. Rhys moved his hands to monitor the pulse in Cinhil's neck—quick and thin and thready—then slipped his touch back to the side of Cinhil's head to read the growing fever, the life-fire brighter, more intense than the old man could sustain for much longer.

"I know, my friend," Rhys murmured, embracing the king close in the circle of his arms and drawing them both into soothing, Healing rapport. "Let go now, and let me do my work. You *will* get through what you have deemed you must. I promise. Relax now and let me bear the pain for you a little while."

And Cinhil did relax, his shields falling away even faster this time. With firm, steady strength, Rhys carried them both ever deeper, ever more centered, letting his healing touch spread out and through the two of them, easing away Cinhil's fatigue and pain once more, numbing the resistance of flesh pushed too often past the danger point, knowing that even now the damage was done, the final processes irreversible.

He floated with Cinhil for several minutes, letting his healing forces mesh with Cinhil's mind and body and cushion him from the pain, not letting himself think about what would come after, not letting himself think anything at all. There would be time enough, after Cinhil was gone, for thinking. . . .

And outside the world of Rhys's mind, Camber stood quietly beside the open portal, his hands on the quillons of Cinhil's sword, and followed the surface of Rhys's thoughts and sensations, feeling for the Healer, feeling for Cinhil, both of whom knew full well the cost of what they did.

No sound disturbed the tranquillity of the warded circle. He could not even hear Cinhil's breathing, now that Rhys was in control; and the others were outside with the three children, Joram and Evaine keeping watch until

Rhys could return to his guardian duties. From time to time, Evaine glanced back through the gateway at her husband, but neither she nor Joram moved until those within the circle began to stir, Rhys raising his head groggily and then helping an oddly peaceful Cinhil to his feet.

Evaine and Joram, too, stood at that, Joram bending to scoop up the sleeping Rhys Michael. No words were exchanged as Rhys left the circle and Evaine and Joram went in, though Rhys did pause to touch his namesake's head in passing, ensuring the boy's response to Joram when the time was right.

When Rhys had once more taken his place between the two remaining boys, Camber bowed slightly to him and then drew the sword across the gateway's threshold and sealed the circle again. He took his time as he bent to lay the weapon back in its place along the edge, straightened, and moved slowly back to his place at Cinhil's right, palming the silver dagger as he passed the table.

Joram was rousing the groggy Rhys Michael to semi-wakefulness, speaking to him in a low voice as the boy got his feet under him and managed to stand under his own power, still supported by Joram's hand under one elbow. Cinhil watched all with greater serenity than he had yet displayed this night, and Camber was more certain than ever that the end was near.

The king would find the strength to do what must be done. Camber knew that Rhys had removed the last of warning pain signals from his body, so that he might complete his work without distraction, even to the end—and that Cinhil was content with that. With a gentle smile of unity, of total acceptance of what the king had chosen, Camber laid his hand on the royal shoulder for just an instant, felt Cinhil's answering surge of appreciation, of affection.

Then Evaine was moving into her place behind Rhys Michael, the thurible spewing incense smoke, and Joram was bringing the cup and a third small piece of parchment.

For the third time, the now-familiar ritual moved through its sequence until Cinhil had delivered the final invocation, standing before the altar with the cup raised in both his hands. A moment he paused, head thrown back and eyes closed in supplication. Then the cup was sinking back to eye level, to chest level, and he was turning to face Rhys Michael.

Camber, watching as Cinhil gazed across at his son, saw the boy's instant response of trust and resolution, in contrast to the others' apprehension. Suddenly he knew that here was Gwynedd's future, for better or for worse, in this youngest child of Cinhil. In a flash of prescience, the likes of which he had seldom experienced in all his long life, Camber saw an older Rhys Michael mounting the throne of Gwynedd, at his side a tawny-haired girl who wore the crown of Gwynedd's queen. There was something familiar about the girl, but Camber could not quite place it. Besides, his attention was for the youthful king, who could not have been more than fifteen or sixteen—but old enough to rule outside the strictures of the royal regents who would have plagued his older brothers.

And, what of his older brothers? If Camber's glimpses of the future were correct, then both Alroy and Javan were destined to die young—would produce no male heirs, if, indeed, they married at all in the short time allotted to them. And if these two died young, what kind of turmoil must lie ahead for Gwynedd, to lose three kings in twice the years?

As quickly as it had come, the image was past, and Camber was watching Cinhil extend the cup to Rhys Michael, wondering whether his flash of insight had been that or only fantasizing, as the boy slowly raised his hands and laid them on his father's. Though the child moved somewhat jerkily, his movements slowed both by the drugs in his system and the controls placed on him, it was as if the actions were as much of his own volition as they were of any other's ordering. He leaned forward to meet the cup as it was brought toward his lips and drank without hesitation. Camber could see the muscles of his throat working as the cup was tipped back and he swallowed once, twice, a third great gulp which drained the cup and set the ring to rolling with a brittle tinkle against the glaze inside.

The boy dropped his hands then, swaying a little on his feet as his father handed off the cup and took a step nearer. Camber could feel the tension building in the very air between father and son, a static energy which arced with an almost visible spark just before Cinhil's hands touched his son's head. The very air seemed to blur around the two of them. Camber blinked and passed a hand in front of his eyes in an attempt to clear his vision. It did no good.

He was aware of Joram's and Evaine's expressions of surprise, their involuntary steps backward, away from what was happening between Cinhil and his son, and Camber, too, felt almost compelled to back off. He could not decide whether the exchange was just sloppy because of Cinhil's fatigue or actually more intense, but whichever was the case, it was not comfortable to be as close as Camber was. He yielded to the pressure and let his feet carry him back a step, two steps, not because he must but because he chose to, until he could endure without discomfort the slippage of energy which was spilling over the link which Cinhil was forging with his son.

It was soon over. Finally he saw Rhys Michael stagger, as the contact was withdrawn and Cinhil's hands left his head. Instantly Joram moved in to catch the boy as he started to crumple, endurance spent for the moment. And as the boy was swept up in the strong arms of the Michaeline priest, Cinhil, too, faltered, reaching out a blind hand toward Camber.

"Alister, I need you!"

The voice was weak but penetrating in the silence of the warded circle, and Camber was at his side before he could take another breath. The royal legs buckled at the knees as Cinhil turned his head to look at Camber in surprise, not comprehending why his body should suddenly cease to obey him. Gently Camber eased him to the floor, motioning for Evaine to cradle the failing king's head against her knees as he scrambled to his feet again and dashed to the northeast quadrant where the sword lay. Rhys was waiting outside the circle, Joram approaching from behind with the spent Rhys Michael, as Camber kissed the sacred blade, touched it to the floor, and swept it up and down to cut the doorway once again.

Then Rhys was inside and racing to tend Cinhil, Joram stepping outside to deposit his unconscious charge gently beside the two older boys. Camber remained at the threshold, the sword motionless under his hands.

"Joram, we'll need the holy oils and the ciborium. The oils are in the aumbry, there to the left of the altar." He turned to the inside of the circle. "Evaine, come tend the boys. Rhys will manage what little can be done for him."

Without demur, Evaine came out of the circle, settling down among the sleeping children. Joram opened the cupboard Camber had indicated and removed a black leather-bound box which he brought to his father, along with a sleeping-fur to pillow Cinhil's head. Then he returned to the altar and made a deep genuflection before opening the door of the tabernacle. Camber knelt as the ciborium was removed from its sanctuary, bowing his head as Joram passed back into the circle with it and placed it on the little table. He stood as the priest came back to his side.

"Shall I leave?" Joram murmured, glancing from his father to the supine Cinhil stretched by Rhys's knees.

Camber shook his head. "No, I think he would want your assistance in these Last Rites." He passed the sword to Joram and picked up the holy oils. "Wait here and close the gate when I tell you it's time."

Briskly he moved to Rhys's side and knelt, laying the leather-bound box aside. The Healer gave a deep sigh and raised his head slowly, removing his hands from Cinhil's forehead. The king seemed to be resting easily, his eyes closed, though his face was pale against the dark fur of his pillow.

"I've done what I can," Rhys murmured. "It's up to you now."

"Thank you. You'd best go outside with Evaine. This is best suited to priestly hands." He raised his voice as Rhys moved toward the threshold. "Joram, close the gate and then join us."

Cinhil's breathing had eased with his reception of the Sacraments, and now he gave a small, contented sigh and raised his eyes to Camber's. Joram had withdrawn to the closed gateway to give them privacy, and stood now with his back to them and his head bowed over the quillons of the broadsword. Cinhil glanced in his direction, then returned his gaze to Camber. The bishop still wore the narrow purple stole he had donned in his priestly office, and Cinhil raised a feeble hand to finger the strip of fabric fondly.

"It is nearly finished, old friend," the king whispered. His hand moved on, to search for Camber's, and Camber took it between his own.

"You have been good to stay beside me," the king continued. "I could not have completed this night's work without you."

"I think your thanks should be to Rhys, not to me,"

Camber replied gently. "And to yourself, for realizing in time what needed to be done."

"Was it in time?" Cinhil asked, searching Camber's face. "Will my sons be able to follow me as they ought, Alister? They are still children. And what if you are right about Murdoch and the others? I have trusted them, but perhaps I shouldn't have. Alister, what—"

"Rest easy, my liege," Camber murmured, with a little shake of his head. "You have done what you could, what you thought best. Now it is for the future to decide what will come of them."

Cinhil coughed, then shuddered a little, his hand tightening on Camber's.

"It's cold, Alister." He closed his eyes briefly. "I feel as if my body were no longer my own. Is—is this what it is to die?"

"Sometimes," Camber whispered, remembering the only other death he had come close to experiencing, when Alister Cullen's dying at Iomaire had had to be relived, that awful night so many years ago. "They say, though, that when one comes easily to death, and at peace, it is a moment of great joy—that the passing is gentle and most welcome."

Carefully Cinhil took a deep breath and let it out, a look of delighted surprise slowly coming across his face. Incredulously he raised his eyes to Camber once more, but already he was seeing otherness which was not caught within the confines of the magical circle or the world it held back.

"Oh, 'tis true!" he breathed in awe, searching his friend's eyes. "Oh, Alister, come with me for just a little while and see! 'Tis a most fair realm that I would enter!"

"Cinhil, it is not yet my time. I dare not—"

"Nay, be not afraid. I shall not compel you past what place is safe for you to go. I would not take you untimely from my sons. But, oh, the wonder! Have we not shared other marvels in our lives, my dearest friend? Let me share this with you, *please!*"

With a weary nod, Camber closed his eyes and let his thoughts cease, let himself open along the old, familiar link which the Alister part of him had formed with the king so long ago. He felt Cinhil's presence, somehow refined and *different* from what it had been before. And then, gradually, his mind began to fill with what he could only describe as sound, though he knew it was not that—

a light, hollowly resounding tinkle as if of tiny bells mingled with the hush of many voices chanting a single Word on tones which blended in indescribable harmony.

The music of the spheres, a part of him thought sluggishly—*or perhaps the voices of the heavenly hosts—or both—or neither.*

For a moment, there was a swirl of foggy, opalescent color, a feeling of disjointure—and then he seemed to be looking down at Cinhil through eyes somehow more perceptive, though objectively he knew that his physical eyes were still closed.

With his Sight which was not sight, he Saw the years melt away from Cinhil's face, knew Cinhil's awe as the king gazed up at the form which was no longer quite the Alister Cullen whom he had seen and known for the past twelve years. Whatever was happening had stripped away the facade, leaving his psychic form naked, for Cinhil to see in all its many facets.

Camber? came the king's tentative query, somehow past shock or anger or fear.

And Alister, in part, came Camber's meekly tendered answer.

And with that, he offered up the rest of the story to Cinhil's clearing consciousness, leaving out no detail—for he could conceal nothing in this dreamlike, awesome realm in which they both hovered now. In an immeasurable stretch of time, the deed was done, the tale told; and Cinhil's awed expression had changed to one of beatific acceptance.

Through double vision now, as Camber and Alister, he watched Cinhil sit up, seemed to feel the feather-brush of Cinhil's hands on his shoulders as the king embraced him like a brother. Then Cinhil was on his feet and stretching out his hand to Camber, and Camber was taking that hand and rising.

A part of him knew he still knelt by the dying king, the royal hand clasped in his; but the more important part now rose and walked with Cinhil toward a brilliant light which seemed to come from outside the circle, just beyond where Joram stood. He could see Joram's shadow-shape silhouetted against that light, head bowed over the quillons of a sword which glowed with ruby clarity against the golden light of what lay just beyond.

But between Joram and the light lay the circle, a cold silver boundary which Camber suddenly knew Cinhil could not pass. Cinhil saw it, too, and came to a halt an armspan from Joram, his hand still clasped in Camber's.

You must help me to pass, Camber-Alister, he said. *Beyond here you may not go, but I must. It is time. They are waiting for me.*

With a chill of knowing, Camber felt his image nod; and it was with a sense of profound loss that he let the king's hand slip from his and backed a few steps toward the center of the circle. There he could see his body kneeling by Cinhil's as he had left them. Wearily he let himself settle back into his own.

He started as he opened his eyes. Cinhil lay silent beside him, a look of peace on his face, his breathing stilled. Across the circle Joram still stood unmoving over his sword, apparently oblivious to what was taking place behind him. He could not see Cinhil's image with his eyes, but when he again shut them momentarily, he could See Cinhil standing there expectantly, one hand raised slightly toward Joram and the gateway he guarded.

"Joram, open a gate," Camber said softly, opening his eyes again and once more seeing only Joram.

Joram started and turned slightly toward him in surprise, but Camber only shook his head to stave off any questions from his son.

"Open a gate," Camber repeated. "And then kneel down in homage to the one who passes."

With a strange look on his face, and a quick, stricken glance at the unmoving form of Cinhil, Joram gave a slight, confused bow, then turned back toward the circle. He raised the sword in salute, let the point fall to the edge of the circle at his left, then arched it up and back down in one smooth, graceful motion. Where the blade passed, the circle was breached, finally showing a high, arched doorway taller than a man. Outside and to the left, Camber could dimly see Evaine and Rhys kneeling and watching the gateway attentively, could sense their question as they watched Joram kneel with the sword still in his hands.

Then Camber was closing his eyes a final time, turning his magical Sight toward the image of Cinhil once more. Once more he Saw Cinhil standing behind Joram, watched the king raise a hand in final farewell.

Then Cinhil was moving through the gateway, his face transformed by a shining light which grew around him. Dimly, past the slowly receding Cinhil, Camber thought he could see others standing and reaching out to Cinhil —a beautiful young woman with hair the color of ripe wheat, two young boys who were Cinhil's image, others whom Camber could not identify.

In a rush of wind and the illogical impression of wings, four Presences seemed to converge around Cinhil then— *Beings* with vague shadow-forms and sweeping pinions of raw power which somehow sheltered rather than threatened.

One loomed massive and overpowering, vibrant with the hues of forest tracts, feathered green-black wings shadowing the entire northern angle of the room as it passed over an apparently oblivious Evaine and Rhys. Another seemed to explode silently into existence right before the altar, bursting either from the gold-glass gleaming of the eastern ward candle or from the altar's open tabernacle, shining like the rainbow fire of sunbeams caught in prisms, so bright Camber could hardly bear to look, even with his mind.

The third was winged with fire and sighed with the roar of infernoes, the heart of the earth, though its great sword of flame was raised protectively over Cinhil's head as he stepped outside the circle without a trace of fear. And from the fourth Presence—a shifting, liquid form of blue and silver shadow—a shimmering horn of quicksilver seemed to take form.

A soundless, mind-deafening blast of titan resonance assailed Camber's senses, reverberating in every particle of his being; and suddenly he could feel the circle beginning to fragment around him, as if the horn sounded some note which the fabric of the circle's dome could not withstand. He *heard* the energies which rent the dome asunder—knew that all that saved him from eternal, mindless madness was the ciborium with its consecrated Hosts, resting on the table close beside him.

Then, even as the shards of shattered circle were still falling to the tile, there to disperse and melt away like flakes of snow, Cinhil and his ghostly Escort began to recede—slowly at first, but then faster and faster until nothing remained but a shrinking point of rainbow light suspended between Camber and the altar candles.

Then, even that was gone.

CHAPTER EIGHT

Now I say, that the heir, so long as he is a child,
differeth nothing from a servant, though he be lord
of all; but is under tutors and governors until the
time appointed by his father.

—Galatians 4:1–2

Abruptly the spell was broken. Camber, his body reminding him at last that it was time to breathe, gave a gasp and shuddered, opening his eyes with a start. Through stunned and disbelieving vision, he saw Joram twisting around to stare at him in awed question, Evaine searching the air over their heads in vain for some vestige of their magical circle. Rhys was ministering to his three young charges, but it was clear that he, too, was aware that something extraordinary had just occurred, even by Deryni standards. The majority of his attention was on Camber and the king.

"Father?" Evaine whispered.

"What happened? Are you all right?" Rhys demanded.

"Is he dead?" Joram questioned, laying down the sword and scrambling to his father's side.

"Rhetorical questions, all, I hope, in light of what I have just witnessed," Camber murmured softly, disengaging his hand from Cinhil's to touch Joram in reassurance before crossing the king's arms on his breast. "But I think we may not all have seen the same thing. Evaine?"

Evaine, getting slowly to her feet, took a few steps toward where the circle's boundary had been and put out a tentative hand, as if to test what her other senses told her.

"It was incredible. I never saw anything like that before," she said, her voice edged with amazement. "It was as if the circle were made of glass and something struck it simultaneously from all directions at once—except that it didn't fall straight to the floor; it slid down the curve of the dome, from the top. What did you *do?*"

"That's all you saw?"

"There was more?"

"I see. And you, Rhys?"

Rhys shook his head from among the sleeping children. "Only what Evaine described. Did *you* break the circle?"

With a sigh, Camber echoed Rhys's headshake. "No. And if I told you what I *thought* I saw, I don't know whether you'd believe me. You'd probably think I drank from the same cup as the children, and was seeing visions. No, don't interrupt." He held up a hand at their beginning protests. "We haven't time to discuss it now. There's work to do. The king is dead, and the new king must be told. And we have to put things back the way they were, before anyone else finds out what really happened."

"Understood," Rhys said, slipping his hands under the sleeping Alroy and gathering him up with an armful of sleeping furs. "If the three of us take the boys back to their room, can you and Jebediah manage the rest?"

Camber nodded, patting his daughter's hand lightly in reassurance. "I'll manage. Evaine, after you've helped Rhys with the boys, you'd best go back to your quarters —make certain you're not seen—and stay there until there's sufficient commotion in the hall to have awakened you. I know you would rather be here, but it might appear suspicious. Joram, you and Rhys can come back here, since you had reason to be with Cinhil at the end."

After what had just occurred, they would not have thought of questioning him further. As Rhys carried the sleeping Alroy into the opening which reappeared in the chapel wall, Evaine leaned over to brush a kiss against her father's cheek, then picked up Rhys Michael and followed her husband.

Joram did not move until the others had gone, head bowed and eyes hooded in unreadable contemplation as he knelt by the dead king. Finally he lurched to his feet and went to pick up the remaining prince, muffling him in the last of the sleeping furs they had brought.

"I have just one question," he murmured, only half-facing Camber as he paused, just outside the opening of the secret passage.

"Very well. One question."

"Did he know, before the end, the truth of you and Alister?"

Slowly Camber let his gaze shift back to the face of the dead king, tears stinging his eyes.

"Aye, he knew."

"And, did he accept that knowledge?" Joram insisted.

"You said one question," Camber replied with a slight smile. "But, yes, son, he accepted it. I will swear that he did not know before tonight, but we made our peace, he and Alister and I. I wish you could have shared it."

"That you and he shared it is sufficient," Joram whispered, blinking back his own tears. "Somehow, it makes the lie vindicated, after all these years." He swallowed, then shook his head. "I'd better go."

Camber remained kneeling there for several seconds, staring after Joram. Then he recalled himself to the tasks at hand. With a sigh, he took up the ciborium and rose, starting to make a perfunctory bow of respect before putting it away. But then he winced and almost gasped aloud as the image of the shattered dome of energy flashed into his memory.

God! How had he endured? As he recalled again the massive energies which had been loosed at random as the circle crumbled, he marvelled at the miracle of his own survival.

A shudder of far more than cold shook his body then, and the cold, hammered metal of the ciborium seemed to sear his flesh for just an instant. Shocked, he stared at the small, jewelled cross projecting from the cover and took his hand away, at the same time realizing that his left hand, which held the sacred vessel, had felt no more than cold.

He sank back to his knees at that, carefully lifting the golden cover and setting it aside. In the glittering bowl of the chalice lay perhaps half a dozen of the precious, consecrated Hosts, exactly like the one he had given to Cinhil so short a time ago. Respectfully, he reached in with thumb and forefinger and extracted one at random, gazing at it attentively.

Unleavened bread, the uninitiated would call it. Flour and water. And yet, in this morsel of the plainest of foods resided the greatest Mystery of his faith, something which he could not begin to explain or understand with his mind, but which was nonetheless true for heart and soul.

And had that Mystery protected him tonight? Perhaps it had. Cinhil had shown him a half-forbidden thing, not realizing, even in his heightened awareness and grace, how broad was the sweep of the wings of the Angel of Death.

Or, was it simply not yet Camber's time? Did the Lord

—that same Lord present, or so he believed, in the consecrated Host between his fingers—did the Lord have other
plans for him, other work for him to do?

He doubted he would get any further answer tonight.
With a short but fervent prayer for continued mercy, and
a little shiver as if physically to shake off this line of speculation, Camber deposited the Host with its brothers and
replaced the cover, took the ciborium and the box of holy
oils back where they belonged.

After that, he collected the now-cold thurible and
Evaine's silver dagger and locked them away in a cupboard in the north wall of the chapel, adding to them the
earthen cup, which he elevated a little toward the altar
before fishing Cinhil's ring from the dregs of ash at the
bottom. He dried the ring carefully on the hem of his
cassock before replacing it on Cinhil's hand, then
sheathed Cinhil's sword and took it and Rhys's medical
pouch into Cinhil's sleeping chamber, where he hung the
sword on the bedpost at the head of the bed and laid the
pouch on the carpet beside. Finally, he went to bring back
Cinhil.

He was amazed at how light the body seemed, as he
carried the dead king back into the room—like cobwebs
or down or wildflowers, though none of these images truly
satisfied him. With infinite tenderness, he laid Cinhil on
the bed and arranged the bedclothes so that they covered
him to the waist, then refolded the hands on the still
breast. When he had finished, he moved wearily to the
outer door and laid his hands on the latch, leaning his
forehead against the cool, sleek oak for just a moment before opening the door.

Jebediah had sensed his presence, and stared at Camber in apprehension as he slipped through the opening
which Camber allowed.

"It is finished, then," the grand master murmured,
reading confirmation on Camber's drawn, weary face.

"Aye, his work is done and he has found his rest,"
Camber said in a low voice.

Jebediah crossed himself with a heavy hand. "May
God have mercy on his soul," he breathed. "I had hoped
that you and Rhys were wrong, that he would have more
time."

"So had we all," Camber whispered. "God grant that
the time he did have will bear good fruit. I do not envy
any of us the next few years."

100

"No." Jebediah gave a heavy sigh, grey-winged head bowing momentarily in sorrow. "I suppose that I should inform the other regents," he finally said, looking up. "Are the princes to be brought here right away, or do we wait until morning?"

"Bring them right away. And if Murdoch or any of the others try to delay, remember that you're still the earl marshal, at least until the first meeting of the regency council." He shrugged resignedly. "After that, I suspect many of our folk will be out of jobs."

"Don't worry," Jebediah whispered, laying his hands on Camber's shoulders, while his mind echoed, *Don't worry, Camber.* "I'll keep your fellow regents in line, at least temporarily. Meanwhile, is there anything I can do to help you, before I go?"

Camber had no need to respond in words. He sensed Jebediah's presence, surrounding and permeating him, and he let a weary smile flicker across his face as he closed his eyes and basked in Jebediah's strength, pulling in the energy and comfort which the other man offered.

Finally, he took a deep breath and reached up to lay hands on Jebediah's.

"Enough, Jeb. You, too, have tasks to perform. We must delay no longer."

With only a nod for answer, Jebediah withdrew mind and hands and went out, disappearing into the turnpike stair. When he had gone, Camber closed the door and returned to the chapel. Yet a few more tasks remained before he might abandon himself, at least temporarily, to further contemplation of what he had witnessed tonight.

And in another part of the castle, three equally weary Deryni, each carrying one of the hopes of the Haldane line, paused at the end of a chill and narrow passageway while the first of their number scanned through a peephole into the royal nursery. No one stirred. Even Deryni senses could detect no sign of waking consciousness.

As Rhys fingered the mechanism which would give them access to the closet, he glanced back over his shoulder at his wife and her brother.

"It's clear, but let's move quickly and quietly. There are three squires and Tavis who must be taken care of, before we leave."

Rhys quenched the pale, verdant handfire which had lit their way thus far and eased open the outer door of the closet which disguised the entrance to the passageway. He could hear one of the squires snoring softly as he stepped into the room and headed toward the empty beds.

"Sleep yet a while longer, little king," Rhys whispered softly, as he laid Alroy in his bed and smoothed the raven hair across the pale forehead.

The boy whimpered once in his sleep and curled up on his side; Rhys tucked the sleeping furs close around him. Quickly, then, he moved from one squire to the next, touching each one briefly and securing his memories while Evaine and Joram put their princes to bed and similarly ensured harmless recollections of this night's events.

A while longer Rhys lingered at the side of Tavis O'Neill, extending and then withdrawing his controls far more carefully than had been necessary for the three human children or the squires. A final survey of the room, to ensure that nothing was out of place; then Rhys was moving quietly to the outer door and listening, casting about with his senses for any sign of danger or watchfulness.

The way was clear, so with a quick gesture and a kiss, he sent Evaine out to make her way back to their quarters, but a scant few doors down and around the corner. Joram was waiting in the passageway when Rhys returned to the sleeping chamber, and conjured silver hand-fire as Rhys stepped through the closet and pulled the outer door carefully closed. A moment more to set the passage door itself in place, a final scan of the princes, and then they were on their way back to Cinhil's apartments.

The chapel had been restored to its customary arrangement when they came back through the last doorway and closed it, and they found Camber kneeling motionless beside Cinhil's body, which lay on the great state bed. Candles had been lit around the room, the fire built up in the fireplace, and Camber had laid a lavishly embroidered cloak of wine-dark velvet over the body to the waist.

"All's well," Rhys announced in a low voice, moving to the opposite side of the bed to gaze across at Camber. "They'll not remember a thing of tonight, and any residual grogginess can be ascribed to shock, grief, and the lateness of the hour. You've sent Jeb?"

Silently Camber nodded. "He will return soon, with all of them. But God help us, Rhys, for now our test begins, in truth. I hope we've done the right thing, letting him give magical potential to children."

"I hope so, too," Joram breathed.

Nearly a quarter of an hour passed before anyone else came, and it seemed like twice that. As the three men knelt in silence, each alone with his own thoughts, the sounds of the night's quiet were gradually disturbed by increasing activity in the great hall below, men and horses moving in the snow-muffled fastness of the castleyard, and then by the tolling of the great cathedral bells outside the castle walls.

First to arrive was Cinhil's former squire, Sorle, newly knighted at Twelfth Night, followed shortly by Father Alfred, Cinhil's human confessor of many years, who cast Camber a wounded look for not calling him sooner, as he sank to his knees at the foot of the bed and began reciting prayers for his dead master's soul.

Many more of the royal household gathered outside the door and at the foot of the narrow turnpike stair, there to huddle together apprehensively and await the arrival of their new young king. The approach of the royal party was evident to those inside the royal bedchamber by the hush of the waiting household, even before the chamberlain's staff rapped the requisite three times on the closed door.

"The Lords Regent of Gwynedd, with His Royal Highness the Crown Prince Alroy and Their Highnesses the Princes Javan and Rhys Michael, request admittance to the royal presence," the chamberlain's voice rasped, hoarse in the damp, late night cold.

Murdoch, looking sly and almost predatory in the candlelight, led the delegation, his hand resting possessively on the stooped shoulder of a haggard and sleepy Alroy. The boy seemed bewildered, and kept knuckling his eyes and yawning.

On the prince's other side, the usually unruffled and impassive Rhun of Horthness was somehow managing to look thoroughly dissipated in a long dressing gown of black wool and fur, and Earl Tammaron, oldest of the regents after Camber, was a stolid and expressionless shadow just behind Rhun, overtowered by a head by the younger man.

Bishop Hubert, the fourth regent, loomed behind Alroy with enough bulk to make up for several men, blue eyes and blond-fringed cherubic face belying the hypocrisy which Camber knew lurked beneath the wine-cassocked breast. By careful attention to the children's whims and pleasures, Hubert had managed to endear himself to all three of the young princes, and they liked him perhaps best of all five regents—which was unfortunate, because Hubert MacInnis was not a nice man.

Jebediah brought up the rear of the little party, one hand resting comfortably on the shoulder of each of the two younger princes. Rhys Michael appeared bright-eyed and curious, none the worse for his ordeal of an hour before, but Javan's face was tear-streaked, and he clung doggedly to the hand of a pale and stunned-looking Tavis O'Neill.

As Camber moved forward to greet the new king, Rhys sent him a lightning synopsis of what he had been forced to do to Tavis. That information filed away, Camber could turn his full attention to the matter at hand—the cementing of the new young king's status. He would not allow his fellow regents to usurp Alroy's position at this early date.

As the last of the party entered the room and the household pressed into the doorway, Camber moved a few steps closer to Alroy and sank deliberately to one knee.

"The king is dead. Long live King Alroy!" he said in a resounding voice, regretting the necessity for the boys' sake, but knowing it had to be established for the benefit of the other regents.

"Long live King Alroy!" Rhys and Joram and Jebediah and the others of the royal household echoed, also kneeling as the regents belatedly did the same.

Alroy stopped dead and looked all around him, his lower lip trembling as he forced his gaze to slip past the still form that was his father's body. As his eyes met Camber's, the bishop rose and bowed again, taking the boy's small, cold hand and warming it between his own as he drew him slowly toward the high state bed.

"Your Grace, I am sorry to have to tell you that your beloved father died peacefully a little while ago. He received the final sacraments, as you would have wished. But then, before he died, he asked that you accept a gift from him—a gift in addition to the crown and throne which now become yours by right of birth."

As the boy's mouth gaped, Camber urged him across

the final few steps to the bed and leaned across the body, deftly removing the Ring of Fire from Cinhil's hand. Before Alroy could question or protest, Camber caught his left hand and slipped the band into place. The ring was huge on him, of course, but even as it slid home on his finger, Camber sensed the trigger being activated, felt a slight psychic shudder go through the boy's young mind as the potentials were released, though he knew there was no conscious awareness on Alroy's part that anything had happened.

"This is my father's gift?" Alroy asked shyly, staring into the fire of the stones and pursing his lips in wonder. He could not know that his own blood had added to the stones' luster.

"It is your father's gift, my prince," Camber said. "Ah, I know it is too large," he continued, removing the ring and putting it into Alroy's hand, now that its work, at least on this Haldane, was done. "But you shall grow into it—or it can be made smaller, if you like. I believe it was your father's intention that this become part of the regalia of Gwynedd. Perhaps one day your son shall wear it at his coronation."

Alroy smiled tentatively and closed the ring in his hand. "I should like that," he murmured. His face took on a more serious mien. "But, do you think I shall ever have a son, Bishop Cullen?"

"Of course you shall," Camber began. But then he was cut off by Murdoch moving in and taking the boy's arm, almost jerking the prince away from the bed and from Camber.

"There will be time enough for idle chit-chat later on, Bishop Cullen. For now, it is late, and the princes need their rest."

"Certainly, my lord," Camber returned smoothly, making a slight bow. "I simply thought His Highness should have his father's gift to comfort him. It is not an easy thing for young boys to lose their father."

"Their *father* felt that a council of regents was best suited to determine what is best for the princes, Bishop Cullen—not a single man," Murdoch said softly. "You would do well to remember that." He thrust the confused Alroy back into the hands of Rhun, who towered over the boy with his hands resting firmly on the young shoulders.

"Furthermore," Murdoch continued, "you are advised

that the regency council will convene its first meeting to-morrow. You will be informed of the exact time and place. I would advise you to consider carefully the role which you wish to play in the new administration. I know that you will abide by law and custom in all things, as you have hitherto."

"My sole aim is the service of the Crown," Camber replied neutrally, though he wondered to himself why Murdoch had chosen those particular words.

The earl's gaunt face showed a semblance of a tight, artificial smile. "Excellent. Then we shall all get along splendidly. Goodnight, Bishop."

And, turning on his heel, he spread his arms and herded all his party out of the chamber. Those who remained exchanged resigned glances and began moving toward the door also, Jebediah beginning to shepherd the household back to their duties while Rhys and Joram paused just outside. Sorle disappeared into the adjoining bathing chamber, preparing to do final squire's service for his dead master, and even Father Alfred withdrew a little from his recitation of the Litany for the Dead, to give the bishop a last moment alone with the dead king.

Sadly, Camber moved closer to the head of the bed and gazed down at the familiar form, laid his hand lightly on the cold ones crossed on the still, silent breast.

"Good night, my prince," he whispered under his breath. "I shall do my best for your sons, as I have always done for you."

But he could not go on after that, and had to content himself with a final bow of his head as the tears welled in the icy Alister eyes. He did not remember leaving the room. It was Joram who put him to bed for what remained of the night.

Camber's fellow regents wasted no time in making certain their hold on the new king. By noon, while cathedral and church bells tolled the old king's passing, Cinhil's body had already lain in state for three hours in the main chapel of the castle, not far from the chamber adjoining the great hall where Cinhil's council had customarily met. After a noon Mass, which Archbishop Jaffray celebrated in that same chapel, young pages delivered the summons to convene the regency council. Camber spent a few more minutes in meditation, praying

106

Divine guidance for the young king, then made his way into the council chamber, Joram at his heels.

The other regents were already there—Murdoch, Tammaron, Rhun, and Bishop Hubert—standing in a little cluster to the right of the king's chair and talking with Earl Ewan, son of the ailing Duke Sighere. Others of the regular council were also there: Udaut, the constable, and Archbishop Oriss, and Baron Torcuill de la Marche, the latter sitting in the chair directly to the left of Camber's accustomed place at the foot of the table. None of these three men were strangers to the political arena, both Udaut and Oriss having been among Cinhil's original council lords, and Torcuill going back even to Imre's council. But Udaut and Oriss would probably survive the reorganization which was surely about to take place, where Torcuill would not, for Udaut and Oriss were not Deryni. The regents themselves were entitled to seats on the regency council by statute, as was the person holding the office of Primate of Gwynedd—currently Jaffray of Carbury, a former Gabrilite and most certainly Deryni. All others served at the pleasure of those six men. With only two of the six Deryni, Camber and Jaffray, the odds were not overwhelmingly reassuring.

Alroy sat at the head of the table, looking uncomfortable and abandoned in his father's carved, high-backed chair. Though they had set a cushion under him, the illusion of greater height did not really disguise the fact that the new king was still a frightened boy of not-quite-twelve. The grey Haldane eyes were dark-smudged shadows in the pale face, the tunic of unrelieved black only emphazing the boy's fatigue and recent illness, as well as his usual pallor. His only royal ornaments were a silver circlet bound across his brow and his father's Ring of Fire, which he wore suspended from a fine chain around his neck. The Eye of Rom was obscured by his collar-length hair, but Camber knew it was there; and should anyone notice and inquire, Alroy would "remember" that his father had given each of the boys an earring a few days before, when he knew he was dying. On the table before Alroy lay his father's sheathed sword, the weapon appearing rather more innocent by daylight than it had by magic's light the night before.

Camber suppressed a smile at that, wondering whether even the other Deryni in the room, other than Joram, could sense the aura of power around the sword—though even they would doubtless sense it only as the proper hallowing of a king's sword, not a magical blade. With all the dignity of his three offices—regent, chancellor, and bishop—he strode quietly into the chamber and paused beside his chair at the opposite end of the table from Alroy. The thought of his fellow regents swearing their oaths of office on a magical sword was some consolation for the calculating looks they gave him as he made his bow to Alroy.

"My liege. My lords."

The boy nodded nervously, and Murdoch turned to give him a curt, haughty nod, only just concealing his outright loathing for his adversary.

"Please just be seated until the others arrive, my lord chancellor," he said.

With that, he turned back to Tammaron and murmured something in a low voice. Camber could not hear what passed between them, but it was fairly apparent from Tammaron's expression and the amused chuckle of Rhun of Horthness that the remark had not been complimentary.

As Camber took his seat, exchanging a troubled glance with Torcuill and Joram to his left, Jebediah came in with Bishop Kai, the third of the Deryni bishops in Gwynedd. After a crisp, military bow to young Alroy and a nod to the other regents, Jebediah slipped into his seat at Camber's right and laid his marshal's baton on the table before him. Bishop Kai sat to his right. After a slight pause, Jebediah leaned slightly toward Camber and whispered from behind a casually raised hand.

"I don't like the feel of this. Murdoch looks entirely too pleased with himself. And what's Ewan doing here? I thought he was tending his father."

Camber intertwined his fingers and rested his elbows on the table, likewise speaking from behind the barrier of his hands. "I rather expect he's to be your replacement, Jeb, since he's here today."

"My replacement?"

"Why else would he be here? I would have guessed Duke Sighere, but no one knows whether he will ever be well again. In Sighere's absence, what more logical choice than his eldest son and heir?"

"Ewan, eh?" Jebediah sighed resignedly. "Well, we could certainly do worse, I suppose. It could have been Rhun."

Camber shook his head. "Too young. Even Rhun knows that."

"But not too young to be a regent," Jebediah reminded him.

"I never said I understood Cinhil's criteria for selecting regents," Camber replied. "Ah, here comes Jaffray. I have a feeling that's all they've asked for this first meeting. I suspected that they'd want to keep it small, at least in the beginning."

They half-rose as the archbishop reached his chair and bowed to Alroy, but even his arrival did not bring a hint of a smile to the boy's face, though Jaffray had been a frequent visitor to his father's table and chambers.

Have they poisoned him against even Jaffray? Camber wondered, nodding to Jaffray as the archbishop sat down. He and Jaffray might well be the only Deryni left on the council, if the other regents did as thorough a housecleaning as Camber anticipated. He did not envy the archbishop.

"My Lords, if we could please come to order," Murdoch said, rapping with his knuckles on the table for their attention. "My Lord Marshal, would you please convene the council?"

Everyone stood except Alroy, who obviously had been coached. Jebediah picked up his baton and saluted the king, then drew himself to attention.

"My Lords, this, the first council of King Alroy Bearand Brion Haldane, is called to order. Let Justice, tempered by Mercy, prevail in all our judgments."

"So be it," Murdoch replied, in an almost flippant tone.

As seats were taken again, Murdoch gathered a sheaf of parchment documents on the table in front of him and jogged them on the edges, a self-important gesture carefully calculated to draw their attention to him.

"First order of business will be the recognition of the Lords Regent," Murdoch said, no longer able to control a slight smirk. "As was previously made public at a court of our late beloved King Cinhil, the following persons have been named to act as regents during the minority of King Alroy: Earl Tammaron Fitz-Arthur, Bishop Alister Cullen, Bishop Hubert MacInnis, Baron Rhun of Horthness, and myself, Murdoch of Carthane, earl."

He consulted the top sheet in the stack of documents in his hands, then surveyed the table again. Camber had a quick, almost indistinguishable flash of foreboding, and wondered what Murdoch had in mind. Everyone knew who the regents were to be. Everyone also knew that the next item on the agenda should be the swearing in of those regents. What game was Murdoch trying to play?

"Ordinarily," Murdoch continued smoothly, "said regents would be duly sworn to office at this time. However, under the terms of a recent edict signed by our late beloved King Cinhil, which sets forth detailed procedures for the operation of a regency council—" Camber sat forward, suddenly alarmed. *He* had seen no such procedures. "—I find that it is the prerogative of any four regents to expel and replace a fifth of their number if they unanimously adjudge him to be incompatible."

His gaze was directly at Camber, a clear challenge.

"I am sorry to have to inform you all that Earl Tammaron, Bishop Hubert, Baron Rhun, and myself do adjudge Bishop Alister Cullen to be incompatible with the aims and operations of the regency council of our beloved King Alroy, and we do, therefore, expel him from our number."

A low muttering of astonishment, both approving and disapproving, rippled through the assembled men, but Murdoch held up one hand for silence and continued speaking.

"We do also, according to the wishes of our late beloved King Cinhil, and with the consent of our Lord King Alroy, choose Duke Sighere of Claibourne to be the fifth of our company, and do appoint his son and heir, Earl Ewan, to serve in the capacity of acting regent until such time as Duke Sighere's health may permit him to assume the office in his own right. Bishop Cullen, am I to gather, by your stern expression, that you do not approve?"

Camber did not give Murdoch the satisfaction of seeing him stand—only leveled his icy Alister gaze down the length of the table to look the human lord in the eyes. Around him, he could feel the consternation of a great many other people, Deryni and human alike, but he feared that it would make little difference. Murdoch would not have dared to take such a preposterous course of action unless he had the document to back him up. But Camber could not imagine how Cinhil might have signed such a document, knowing what it was.

"The Earl of Carthane is an astute observer, as usual,"

Camber said evenly. "How clever of him to deduce that I would disapprove of such a document and its use against me. He can, of course, produce the alleged document, and unimpeachable witnesses to its signature?"

"He can, of course," Murdoch said disdainfully. "And should anyone take it in his mind to destroy said document, it should be known that this is but one of three originals, all signed by the king and witnessed by Lord Udaut and Archbishop Oriss—both of whom, the chancellor will note, are not themselves regents."

With a condescending little smirk which could no longer be controlled, he passed the top document on his stack along the table to Oriss and Udaut, who glanced at it and then nodded apologetically to Camber as they passed it on; to Jebediah, who could only sigh; and then to Camber. Camber scanned the text closely, seeing how the division of lines in the tightly penned script might have been misread or skipped over, even if Cinhil *had* been reading carefully—though, if it had been buried in the midst of a great deal of routine correspondence, Cinhill might *not* have been reading carefully, in these last weeks of increasing illness—then confirmed the date and witness seals.

Even when he had finished reading it, he did not know what he was going to do next. Though he was now certain that the king had, indeed, signed it, he was equally certain that Cinhil had not realized what he was signing—not that one could prove royal intent now that the king was dead. Murdoch simply had won this round. It now remained to be seen how well he could follow up on his advantage.

With a resigned sigh, Camber passed the document on to Torcuill, who glanced at it and almost shook his head; then to a stony-faced Jaffray and on past Rhun and Tammaron back to Murdoch. The man who had now emerged as a spokesman for the regents replaced the parchment on the stack in front of him and folded spidery fingers neatly before him.

"I trust that the document meets with your approval, Chancellor?" he asked softly.

"Not my approval, but my acceptance," Camber replied coolly. "It bears the signature of our late beloved king. As a loyal subject and servant of his Crown, I am bound to accept it."

"Well spoken," Murdoch said smoothly. "There being

no further reason for delay, then, the Regents of Gwynedd will now swear their oath of allegiance to King Alroy. Archbishop Jaffray, are you prepared to administer the oath?"

There was nothing else Jaffray could do. With a resigned, apologetic glance at Camber, Jaffray stood and bowed to Alroy, waited as the five regents stood and laid their hands on the sword lying on the table before Alroy. Camber did not even listen as Jaffray administered the oath. As the regents and the archbishop took their seats, the swearing done, he knew that the next item of business was going to be even worse than they had thought, earlier.

"Our next item of business is the customary resignation of the old council," Murdoch said matter-of-factly. "Dispensing with formality, under the circumstances, let us simply say that the Lords Regent have advised His Royal Highness to accept the resignations of the following: the Lord Chancellor, Baron Torcuill de la Marche, the Earl Marshal, and Bishop Kai Descantor. It is His Highness's pleasure to retain the rest of the former council."

Magnanimous, isn't he? Joram's thought whispered in his father's mind, though the priest's expression did not change. *That's all the Deryni except Jaffray, and he can't fire Jaffray. What are you going to do?*

Do? What can I do? Camber returned. *The best I can do is to strike a last note of caution before beating a prudent retreat. We'll figure out finer strategy later.*

As Camber met Murdoch's stare, the other three dismissed Deryni glanced to their senior for guidance, none of them moving from their places. For a time that seemed to stretch forever, Camber only returned Murdoch's gaze, not blinking, showing no emotion, deliberately fostering the impression that he just might attempt to defy the regents.

Only when every eye was upon him and the tension had grown so thick as to be almost palpable, even to a human, did Camber slowly reach to the chain of office on his shoulders and lift it off over his head.

As he laid the collar of golden Haldane H's gently on the table, his fingertips resting fleetingly on the pendant seal, there was an almost imperceptible sigh of relief— which was quickly cut off as he stood at his place.

"My Lord King, your sainted mother, Queen Megan, presented me with this chain of office only a few months after you were born," he said gently. "I return it now into your keeping, as your regents have requested and as is customary. It was my honor and my privilege to serve your later father, and I would gladly have served you, in turn."

The boy lowered his eyes in embarrassment, and Murdoch and the other regents, saving Ewan, glared down the table at Camber; but none of them yet appeared over-anxious to keep him from speaking further. They had known he must make some statement to save face.

"But Your Highness's Lords Regent—"

"Careful, Bishop!" Tammaron warned.

"Your Highness's Lords Regent have decided otherwise," Camber continued smoothly, "and perhaps feel that the usefulness of an old man like myself is at an end, that this is a time for fresh beginnings. That may be. I should only like to say that I think your father was well served, and that I hope that those who serve Your Grace will have your interests as much at heart as we have, who have served faithfully and without asking aught in return."

His gesture included the other three Deryni being dismissed as he continued.

"My Lords Regent." Here he turned the pale Alister eyes on all the council. "I shall leave you with but this one thought. You have been entrusted with a precious charge. Our late Lord King judged that you would be wise and responsible counselors to his tender, minor sons. I charge you likewise to keep faith with—"

"Bishop Cullen, do you threaten us?" Hubert interrupted, the fanatical light in his eyes belying his cherubic appearance.

"Threaten? No, my lord. But I do warn. All of us are aware what issues will be brought to the fore in days to come. I ask only that you put the good of the kingdom and the king above your own concerns. There are many, many good and honest folk, both human and Deryni, who have given much to put the Haldane line where it is today, and they have an abiding interest in the continued health of that line. We will be watching you, my lords."

"And we will be watching *you!*" Rhun retorted, staring hard-eyed down the table. "Take care that you do not overstep your place, *Bishop!*"

Camber did not reply to that. With deliberate dignity, he turned his head to gaze at Alroy, who was almost

113

cowering in his chair at the intensity of what had just transpired. Camber smiled at the boy, desperate to put him more at ease, then laid his right hand on his breast and bowed profoundly, turned and walked slowly from the chamber. Behind him, as Joram rose to follow, Jebediah picked up his marshal's baton and strode quickly to the head of the table, knelt between Alroy and Bishop Hubert, and offered up the symbol of his office with bowed head.

"It has likewise been my honor and privilege to serve Gwynedd, my liege," he said in a low voice. "I pray you to give this into the hands of no one who will not guard Gwynedd's peace as diligently as I have done. If ever you have need of my services again, you know you have but to call."

Alroy said nothing; but when Jebediah felt the boy's hands on the ivory baton, he raised his eyes to Alroy's and caught and held his gaze, shifted his hand to take Alroy's and press it to his lips in homage.

He did not stay to see the shocked incomprehension on the young king's face. He was only vaguely aware of Bishop Kai and Baron Torcuill making their bows of leavetaking as he fled from the chamber. Outside, he found Camber in close conversation with Joram.

"We must meet tonight," Camber whispered, as he caught Jebediah's sleeve and drew him into their counsel. "Will you and Joram see to the summoning? What has just happened puts an even greater urgency on our plans."

Jebediah nodded agreement and Joram glanced around casually as Bishop Kai and Torcuill emerged from the council chamber. Camber turned his attention to them and shook his head.

"It is as we feared, gentlemen. Jaffray now remains the only Deryni to guard us from the likes of Murdoch and Rhun."

"And Hubert MacInnis!" Kai sputtered. "That so-called man of God is—"

"No more, Kai," Camber warned, laying a hand on the younger bishop's arm and glancing around meaningfully. "There may be other listeners. His brother is at court now, too, and has no reason to love Deryni."

"Aye, I've heard the castle gossip." Kai seemed to deflate. "Well, there's nothing more for me to do here, in any case. I think I can accomplish the most good by getting out of Valoret and lying low. I was not made an itinerant bishop for nothing. My flocks have always been in the countryside. Where will you go, Alister? Back to Grecotha?"

Camber nodded. "That seems the best plan. Do stay in touch, though," he murmured. "There may yet be work for men of faith and conscience."

"Perhaps. But they will have to stay alive, and I do not believe Valoret is the place to do that well. Tell Jaffray to be careful."

"Jaffray?" Joram asked. "You have some inkling that he is in danger, Your Grace?"

"Danger? You might call it that. If you were Murdoch, and hated Deryni, and Jaffray were the only Deryni left to mar the purity of your regency council, what would *you* do?" Kai muttered.

"We will try to warn him to be careful," Camber agreed. "And Torcuill, what of you? What are your plans?"

The baron shrugged. "Return to my marcher lands, I suppose. It will seem strange, after so many years' service here at Court, but Kai is right. This is no place for a Deryni to be."

I wonder if there is any place for a Deryni to be, Camber thought, as they went their separate ways. *What will happen to us, now that we cannot stem the tide in the council? Can we survive?*

CHAPTER NINE

Woe unto thee, O land, when thy king is a child.
—Ecclesiastes 10:16

Camber slept the rest of the afternoon and into the evening. He had slept not at all the night before, though he had not told Joram or Rhys that. When he drifted back to consciousness, the Compline bells had just finished

115

ringing in the cathedral nearby. It would have been dark for nearly five hours.

He allowed himself the luxury of a giant stretch and yawn, trying to remember the last time he had indulged in such simple pleasure. Memories of the night before began to surface, but he nudged them gently aside while he settled into a series of meditations, gradually tuning his energies to their customary fine balance and then trying to resolve in some rational way the knowledge which finally he allowed himself to acknowledge. He succeeded in the first of his endeavors, but not the second, even when he engaged the more objective part of him which was Alister to try to find reasoned explanation for the night's events. Cinhil and the phenomena of his death refused to be compartmentalized.

Oddly, he felt no particular anxiety over that discovery, and no real grief over Cinhil's passing, as such. Not that he would not miss the king, even in his exasperating stubbornness—not at all. But it had been so clear—if anything of that night had been clear—that existence continued, and that Cinhil had gone a willing traveller into whatever realm came next. Other than those few ecstatic times when Cinhil had soared free in the ritual of the Mass, Camber had never seen him truly happy for more than a fleeting instant. The nearly fifteen years of their association had been fraught with conflict and frustration —for both of them, if the truth be known.

Even so, Camber regretted once again that he could not have been more open with Cinhil all along, that it was only the Alister part of him which had been able to interact with Cinhil on those deepest, most spiritual planes —though the notion that he and Alister were really still completely separate, after all these years, was, perhaps, a little naive. Perhaps the blending had been happening all along, from his interaction both with Cinhil and Jebediah, the former who thought him only Alister and the latter who knew him to be both Camber and Alister. If the two aspects had been drawing closer over the years, that would certainly help to explain Cinhil's easy acceptance of Camber's revelation, there at the end. Perhaps it had not been revelation at all, especially in light of what else had been revealed.

He sighed and sat up in bed, yawned once more, then swung his legs to the floor and stood. By the time he washed and dressed and located something to eat, mid-

116

night would be fast upon him. By then, he must be in the chambers of the Camberian Council.

The Camberian Council, so-named by Archbishop Jaffray when the group was formalized seven years before, had grown out of an idea which Camber and his children had discussed increasingly over the years since Cinhil's restoration. Eight years had passed since the five of them—Camber, Joram, Evaine, Rhys, and Jebediah—had begun working out the structure and exploring such of the old Deryni lore as they thought might be useful in inaugurating a larger body.

Mahael's *History of Kheldour;* the Pargan Howiccan sagas of the previous century; Sulien's *Annals,* from far R'Kassi; the whole of the Protocols of Orin; and numerous other lesser works—all were consulted in order to expand their knowledge.

By the end of their first year, at the time of the Winter Solstice, they were ready to expand the Council to eight, adding Dom Turstane, a very skilled Healer-priest and philosopher recommended by the venerable Dom Emrys, who had declined the position on the grounds of age; Archbishop Jaffray, also Gabrilite-trained, whose credentials as Deryni and priest were impeccable; and Gregory of Ebor, one of the most talented and skilled Deryni laymen Camber had ever met, with neither Gabrilite or Michaeline training, though his abilities certainly did not suffer for that. Gregory had been the recommendation of the Alister part of Camber, and at times, Camber almost wondered whether his alter-ego sometimes occupied a ninth seat at their council table.

These latter three members were never to know the secret of Alister Cullen's true identity, which the others shared; but in all other things, they were peers, and presented a formidable array of talent and power. In the seven years since their formal coming together, they had accomplished even more, in some respects, than Camber had dared to hope. In addition to rediscovering several magical operations thought lost over the generations, and forging a powerful group mind with which to wield them, they had codified many of the ancient Deryni dueling standards, secretly assisted in the establishment of several additional Deryni training *scholae,* diverted a goodly number of Deryni of unrealized potential to be educated, and disciplined numerous of their race whose actions might otherwise have brought about serious repercussions on all Deryni from those not tolerably inclined toward magic. If the feared persecutions came, they were determined that there should be recourse for at least a few, that the race and its knowledge should not die.

Their number had decreased the previous spring, when the beloved Dom Turstane died in a fall—but while they began evaluating several potential candidates to replace him, they found that somehow the balance of seven plus the vacant seat worked, even better than when they had been eight.

Whatever the cause, they gradually stopped even talking about filling the empty place. Sometime during that period, Jebediah made a joking remark about the seat being reserved for Saint Camber, perhaps sensing unconsciously what Camber had been feeling all along, and the name was seized upon by Gregory and Jaffray, who both were ardent supporters of the Camberian movement. They called it Saint Camber's Siege. The Camberian Council remained at seven.

Now one of those seven hurried toward his appointed meeting with his fellows, clasping cloak to throat and slipping along a shadow-girt corridor toward Jaffray's apartment and the Portal it contained. The archbishop would not be there by now, but its Portal would. With its use, Camber would be at the council chambers in the blink of an eye.

He passed no one in the corridors at this hour, and for that he was grateful. When he reached Jaffray's door, he scanned beyond it briefly, cast up and down the corridor in either direction, then bent to the door latch and reached out with his mind, found the pins, nudged them gently with that particular Deryni skill which not all of his race could wield with this degree of accuracy.

He kept a little tension on the latch while he worked, finally feeling the handle drop beneath his hand. With a smile—he had not lost his touch—he eased the door open and entered, closing and locking it behind him. But a few muffled steps, felt-soled indoor boots quiet on carpet, and he was slipping into Jaffray's sleeping chamber and across to the far wall, drawing aside the curtain to step into Jaffray's oratory.

He stilled his mind and visualized his destination, let his awareness of the place's power flow through him. A moment he took to center in, to set his destination firmly in mind. Then he reached out with his mind and bent the energies, and was no longer in the oratory at Valoret.

As his eyes came into focus, he saw Jaffray himself standing just outside the Portal with a candle in his hand. The archbishop was muffled from chin to toes in the same deep violet of cassock and mantle as Camber, his dark, grey-streaked Gabrilite braid and jewelled pectoral cross gleaming in the candlelight. He nodded nervously as Camber's eyes met his.

"I'm sorry about the regency, Alister. I wish there were something I could have done."

Camber shrugged, stepping out of the Portal with a resigned expression on his face.

"We underestimated Murdoch. What can I say?"

"It wasn't your fault," Jaffray murmured, shaking his head. "None of us thought he would be that brazen. By the way, did you hear they'd named Tammaron chancellor?"

"I rather suspected that they would," Camber said dryly, glancing toward the entrance to the council chamber.

Jebediah was waiting there with Jesse, Gregory's eldest son, and Camber's grandsons, Davin and Ansel, now-teenaged sons of the martyred Cathan MacRorie. The three were regular visitors to meetings of the Council, for they had all spent many months over the past several years riding the roads of their respective lands with their retainers in an effort to keep down the activities of bands such as that which had accosted Camber and Joram a few days before. More than a few young Deryni firebrands had found themselves hauled before the local courts in Culdi and Ebor and fined or temporarily incarcerated for the deeds of themselves and their men. Based on such experience, the opinions of men like Jesse and Davin and Ansel were often invited. On the shoulders of such as these would rest the eventual future of all Deryni in Gwynedd.

As the three made respectful bows to the two bishops, Camber smiled his greeting and wondered why they were waiting outside with Jebediah—then reasoned that Joram and Evaine were probably awaiting his decision on whether the matter of Rhys' newfound talent should be discussed before those not of the Council. There was no question in *his* mind about that, however. He nodded to Jebediah and pressed his shoulder in reassurance and affection, as he and Jaffray passed.

Torches blazed in golden cressets to either side of the great hammered doors, reddening the already ruddy bronze and throwing the carved scenes into bold relief, making the figures seem to come alive as the doors opened and the shadows flitted across the incised panels. Evaine and Joram were already there, standing restlessly by their places at west and south, respectively, of the eight-sided table. Gregory, the only other member yet present, was strolling back and forth before a panel of wood-limned ivory set into the northeastern wall, pretending avid interest. Three more of the eight walls under the faceted amethyst dome held similar panels, depicting scenes from Deryni legend. The north wall was taken up by the huge, ceiling-high doors, and the other three were still blank stone—for the chamber was still not finished inside, after seven years of work.

Gregory glanced up eagerly as he heard them come in, striding eagerly to embrace the older of the two men.

"Alister!" He stood back to look at Camber from arm's length. "I'm told you came to visit me when I was injured, and I don't remember a thing. You must think me a terrible host!"

"As I recall, you were in no condition to host anyone —except, perhaps, the Angel of Death, if Rhys hadn't intervened," Camber replied dryly. "Did Evaine tell you anything else about that day?"

"I haven't yet, Father Alister," she replied, making a casual curtsey as he came closer to the table, "though I think it's something he should find out about tonight. Rhys was on his way to check on the princes when I left him, but as soon as he returns, I think all the Council should hear the whole story. I also invited Jesse and Davin and Ansel to join us. Do you mind? Their evaluations may give us some fresh insights, under the circumstances."

"I have no objection," Camber replied. "Jaffray?"

"None here," came the archbishop's response.

"Then, it's settled," Camber said, taking his seat between Evaine and Saint Camber's Siege, in the north, as Jaffray seated himself on the other side of the empty chair. "Gregory, would you ask them to come in, please?"

As Jebediah and the three young men entered, Joram waved his two nephews to stools on either side of him, and Jesse nervously took another stool between his father's chair and Evaine's. Camber gave Jesse a warm smile to put him at his ease, then glanced across to his right at his grandsons as Jebediah took his place directly opposite.

"Welcome, gentlemen," he said, including them all in his greeting. "Jesse, I know what you've been up to lately. How about our younger MacRories? What news from your part of the kingdom, while we wait for Rhys?"

Davin, seated to Joram's right, flashed his famous grin, all shiny, even teeth in the fair, nearly beardless face. Though he did not know Camber as anyone other than Alister Cullen, both he and his brother had been close to the bishop for many years now.

"We were hoping you might be able to give *us* news, sir," Davin replied. "There have been a lot of rumors, but precious few facts."

"There are always many rumors in times such as these," Camber said enigmatically. "I assume that you've heard about the king?"

Solemnly Ansel nodded, almost an identical image of his elder brother. "I received a private letter from Dafydd Leslie around noon today, sir. Dafydd said that Cinhil died sometime last night, and that the regency council would be meeting for the first time today. Did it?"

"Such as it is," Jaffray said in disgust, as all eyes turned toward him. "Murdoch found a way to oust Alister from the regency."

"No!"

That was clearly news to the three newcomers, and to Gregory, as well, who stopped pacing and then groped his way numbly to his seat.

"Aye. They chose Duke Sighere to succeed him, with his son Ewan sitting in for him, and then they dismissed all the Deryni from the council that they could. I'm the only one left."

Joram snorted. "And they would have gotten rid of him, too, if they could have found a way."

After a short, shocked silence, Davin found his tongue.

"How—how did they oust Bishop Alister?"

"A mysterious document, allegedly signed by the king," Jaffray said, almost singing the words in his sarcasm. "Oh, it was Cinhil's signature," he added, seeing the indignation growing on Davin's face, "and duly witnessed.

121

Unfortunately, there's no doubt about that. We could have fought a forgery."

"Who witnessed it?" Jesse broke in.

"Oriss and Udaut, neither of whom probably knew what was being signed, any more than the king did," Jaffray replied promptly. "Oh, it's a bloody mess, all right. Alister is out and Sighere is in, for regent; Alister is out and Tammaron is in, for chancellor; and Jebediah is out and Ewan is in, for earl marshal. They also fired Torcuill and Bishop Kai. The only reason I'm still in is that they can't get rid of me. The Archbishop of Valoret stays, whether he's Deryni or no—at least for the moment." He sighed. "And all of that is fact, not rumor. I was there."

His ascerbic assessment of the situation brought a silence to the chamber which was not broken until the doors opened about a minute later to admit Rhys.

Jaffray's briefing had saved time, though, and they were immediately able to launch into a discussion of the situation at hand. They talked about young Alroy, now king, and his ill health, and the fact that he was thus far bearing up poorly under the stress; Rhys had had to put him to bed with a sedative before coming to join the others tonight. They talked about the regents, each adding his or her observations about each man so that a unified assessment of the potential dangers from each began to take shape.

That led them to a discussion of the roving bands of Deryni: the reason, in addition to the shakeup in the regency, that the meeting had been called. And Camber's recitation on their encounter with the band which had harassed Manfred MacInnis's party led to the reasons for his travel on that road in the first place, and what had happened at Ebor.

Ebor brought discussion to a crashing halt. It took two tellings, one from Rhys and one from Camber, and a demonstration on the disbelieving and almost hostile Gregory himself, before even Gregory would accept that it had happened.

"I just don't see how it's possible to take away a person's powers," Gregory finally muttered, still unable to articulate his sense of violation. "And not to remember that you were even in my mind, Rhys—and you and Joram, too, Alister—nothing like that has happened since I was a very small child."

"If it hadn't been a life and death situation, I would never—" Rhys began.

"Oh, I know that," Gregory said impatiently, cutting him off. "I'm not angry that you intervened, God knows. Otherwise, I might not be here. It's just that—damn it all, Rhys! I've not had the benefit of your fancy Gabrilite training, or Joram's and Alister's Michaeline discipline, but I've studied with some good men—and women," he added, with a nod toward Evaine. "I would have sworn by all I hold holy that I could have detected a memory lapse like that. It's—unnerving!"

"I'm sure it is," Rhys returned quietly. "If it's any comfort, I think your head injury is responsible for at least part of the amnesia. Memory loss of an accident and the time surrounding it is quite common. Sometimes one eventually remembers—sometimes not. And when you add in the fact that you were sedated—" He shrugged. "What still amazes me, though, is the ease with which I was able to take away and restore your abilities, once I knew what was happening. Oh, it took energy, I grant you—no magical working is free—but no more than any other advanced Healing function. It's a shame Dom Turstane is no longer with us. I'd like another Healer to see this, so we could compare perceptions."

Jaffray cocked his head thoughtfully as he ran a smooth finger along the gold set into the tabletop. "Fortunately, Turstane was not the only outside Healer to whom we have access," the archbishop said. "Frankly, though, I doubt that even Turstane at his best could duplicate what you've apparently done."

"No *apparently* about it," Joram commented under his breath. "Ask Gregory whether he only *apparently* lost his powers."

"All right. *Concedo.* I must confess to being more than a little mystified, though—and a bit frightened," Jaffray admitted. "I thought I'd had access to every bit of esoterica that the Gabrilites had to offer—and their records are probably among the most detailed in existence in one place. Over the past seven years, Alister and Evaine have shared with me the additional wisdom of the Ancient Ones whose records Alister and Joram continue to uncover at Grecotha. None of that has prepared me for this. Being able to take away a Deryni's powers goes against everything we believe or were ever taught."

"You say that with a note of almost ecclesiastical disapproval, my Lord Archbishop," Rhys said with a tiny, wry smile. "How so? We've *given* Deryni powers, at least under carefully controlled circumstances. Why, then, should it seem so illogical that they could be taken away?"

"That's entirely different, and you know it," Jaffray said reproachfully. "Giving power to a human and taking power away from a Deryni are two different things."

"I tend to agree," Evaine said, not noticing the effect their words were having on Davin and Ansel and Jesse. "Giving power to Cinhil was a magical operation, based partially on Cinhil's own unique potential. What Rhys did to Gregory was something else entirely."

"Was it?" Joram pursued the point. "Rhys was involved in both operations. Maybe he was responsible for our success in giving Cinhil his powers. You have to admit, he *is* a common factor."

Davin, who had been exchanging silent looks of amazement with his brother and Jesse, could not longer keep silent.

"Just a moment, please! You mean that the three of you *gave* magical abilities to Cinhil?"

"You could say that," Evaine replied, "though that knowledge must never leave this room. Actually, it would probably be more accurate to say that we—discovered a potential for the assumption of power in Cinhil, and then we devised a setting whereby we could activate that potential in him." She glanced at Rhys. "We never thought in terms of a Healer being a necessary component of the working, though. And I honestly don't think it was a factor for Cinhil. A Healer does seem to be necessary for what Rhys did to Gregory. *I* wasn't able to do it."

"It should be easy enough to test, then," Jebediah said. "Let Rhys see whether he can give Deryni powers to just any human. Have you ever tried that, Rhys?"

Rhys shook his head. "No, but I don't think it would work."

"Why not?"

"Because I think Cinhil and his line are a special case, where that's concerned. There *may* be others, but I've never met one. As for a Healing connection, quite frankly, it never occurred to me until Joram mentioned it, but I don't think that's valid, either. I can feel the power go out of me when I Heal, and I didn't feel that with

Cinhil. Besides, a similar working was done on Cinhil's sons last night, and I wasn't even an active part of that. I was outside the circle almost the entire time."

Jaffray rapped with his knuckles for their attention. "All right, I think that's a moot point, then—the giving of power. Rhys, you might run some tests on a few selected humans, but I have to agree that I don't think anything will happen. Let's go back to Gregory, though. Do you have any idea how long his condition would have lasted, if you hadn't restored him?"

Rhys shook his head wistfully. "I would have to assume, based on our admittedly limited knowledge to date, that it would have remained in effect until the process was reversed. Oh, it's possible that one's powers might eventually return spontaneously, but who's to say? It's equally possible that the results might be permanent, if no one intervened. And with a memory block, one wouldn't even know to try to regain one's powers."

"What a chilling thought!" Evaine breathed, unable to prevent a small shudder of dread. "Pushing that concept to its horrifying but logical conclusion, imagine what could happen if—well, I don't suppose humans could learn to do what Rhys does, but if they could subvert enough of our own people who could be taught to do it, why—within less than a generation, there might be no Deryni at all!"

"Wait a moment. Wait just a moment!" Camber murmured. "Rhys, did I just hear you say it was possible that Gregory's powers might have returned spontaneously?"

"I said it was possible," Rhys said cautiously. "At this point, anything is possible."

"Then, we could be talking about a—a *blockage*, rather than a removal of powers," Camber murmured, shaggy Alister eyebrows nearly meeting in his concentration. "If they were *removed*, they'd be gone. One would only be able to get them back by—by going through something similar to what we did with Cinhil's sons. But we didn't have to do that with you, Gregory. What Rhys did worked like a simple Healing function. No magic."

Gregory's narrow face contorted in a grimace of speculation. "But, if my powers were only blocked, why weren't they detectable? It seems to me that a Deryni of Rhys's training—"

"No, wait," Camber interrupted. "Maybe that's the

beauty of it—if we can use that term in this context. It's a blockage, but it's such a deep one that even another Deryni can't discover it, unless he knows exactly where to look. Now, that could well be useful."

"To be Deryni and not know it and not have it detectable?" Joram asked. "You call that useful?"

"It's useful if a human can't prove whether you're Deryni or not," Camber retorted. "If the persecutions come, that could be very useful."

"I don't know," Gregory said doubtfully. "If the persecutions do come, I think I would want all my powers intact, so I could defend my family."

"And if you and your family did need defending," Camber replied, "do you really think that there aren't enough soldiers in the service of the crown to hunt you down and take you? If enough people are against you with swords, where are you going to find the time to use your powers for defense? That's the point that most humans don't understand, either. They seem to think that these great armies of Deryni, bristling with arcane armament, are going to come swooping down and enslave all humans with their evil, magical powers."

"Didn't the Festils do just that?" Evaine commented archly.

"That was a coup mostly from within, and you know it," Camber replied, "as was the ouster of Imre. The point is that in anything dealing with sheer numbers, with mere physical overpowering, the humans are going to win almost every time. And the more we use our powers against humans, even in justified defense, the more excuse they have to hold that against us and claim that we're allied with—oh, demons, evil spirits, the forces of darkness—you name it!"

Jaffray shifted uneasily. "All right, all right, I can see where you're leading, Alister. And I agree that it's obviously an advantage if a Deryni can't be detected by humans. But I'm not sure we've proved that Rhys's talent does render a Deryni totally undetectable. You know, as well as I, that there are numerous drugs which will act only on Deryni, or only on humans, and some which act differently on Deryni and humans. Are we postulating that such drugs might cause a different reaction in a Deryni who'd had his powers blocked?"

Rhys shrugged and shook his head. "Unknown. What I gave Gregory is hardly a fair test. There were too many other factors at work. It raises another important point, however. While it's true that the drugs you're referring to have legitimate medical uses, it is equally true that such substances have been abused in the past, and employed to detect and temporarily neutralize Deryni. I'm told that royal warders use a derivative of *merasha* to control Deryni prisoners; they learned it from Deryni who were Imre's jailers. Which brings us to the possibility that occasional Deryni will, for whatever reason, aid in the detection and destruction of their own kind. It's another danger we must especially guard against—that this knowledge, if it can be passed on, does not fall into the wrong hands."

"Aye, we have always had our Judas goats among us, haven't we?" Jebediah said softly. And Camber knew he was remembering such a Michaeline, and a dead prince who slept in a tiny tomb beneath a Michaeline stronghold.

"But what about the effect of the drugs on those with blocked powers?" Jebediah continued. "Will they react as humans or as Deryni? Rhys, you're the Healer among us. What will happen?"

"I suppose we're going to have to find out," Rhys replied. "And if the drugs do work in the usual ways, I foresee many headaches and other unpleasant side effects to be suffered in the cause of discovery. Jeb, you seem to be volunteering."

Jebediah gave a rueful chuckle. "I wasn't, but I will. I'll do whatever's necessary."

"Thank you. Evaine, light-of-my-life, how do you feel about a *merasha* hangover in a good cause? And Joram?"

As Joram nodded resigned agreement, Evaine blew a kiss across the table to her husband and smiled.

"I am yours to command in all things, my lord and my love—even *merasha* hangovers," she added, "which, fortunately, you can ease. However, I do think we ought not to lose sight in the meantime of what it is you're actually doing. It's all very well to study the effects, but we also need to know about the cause. Right now, we don't even know for certain whether this is a real Healing talent, hitherto undiscovered, or just a special quirk of yours. We don't even know whether you can do it to anyone besides Gregory. For that matter, maybe it's something odd in Gregory.'

"Now, see here!" Gregory started to sputter.

"No, she's absolutely right," Camber said, leaning back

and surveying them all. "It *could* be something in you, Gregory—though I don't think it is, judging by what I saw. But until we have some answers, and even once we do, I suggest that we all consider how this rogue talent of Rhys's might be put to some constructive use—in a desperate situation, of course, since taking away any Deryni's abilities—or blocking them so that they can't be used or remembered or discovered—is going to have to be a desperation measure. Jaffray, your assessment is liable to be especially valuable, since you have Healer training."

"I'll do what I can. I know some excellent Healers who could—"

"Ah, not yet," Evaine interjected, shaking her head and holding up a restraining hand. "For now, I have a very strong feeling that we should keep this matter strictly within these walls, almost as if it were under the seal of the confessional. If word of this were to get out, if humans got it in their heads that there was no way they could detect Deryni—never mind whether or not it was true—the reaction could trigger a bloodbath that would make the Nyford massacre look like a summer children's festival."

The horror evoked by her words produced a stunned silence which hung heavy and oppressive in the room for several seconds. Finally, Jebediah coughed and shifted in his chair, releasing then to move uneasily as he plucked at a clasp on his tunic. His sigh, just before he spoke, told volumes of all their weariness.

"Evaine is right, but perhaps she is a little too close to the situation," the grand master said. "Rhys's new talent is not the real issue. Oh, there's no doubt that a danger exists in this regard," he added, to cut off several would-be challengers who had taken exception to his words. "I have a cousin whose demesne lies not a day's ride from Nyford. I've heard what it was like."

"Then, what is your objection?" Evaine asked.

Jebediah shook his head. "My objection is that I think every one of us has missed the real point of this meeting, running off in all directions about this new talent which Rhys has discovered. Think about it. Which is more important from a *practical* view: a new, wild talent which *could* be dangerous *if* anyone else can learn to use it and *if* it fell into the wrong hands? Or very real young hooligans who are even now riding our roads and gen-

erating ill will toward our people by harassing humans?—
some of whom make very serious enemies."

"He's right," Camber had to admit. "Which definitely
brings us back to the original reason for our meeting.
Gregory, you and Jesse have been patrolling the roads
the longest of any of us. Any suggestions?"

As Gregory glanced at his son, Jesse gave a shrug.
Though he was the youngest present, and had said little
thus far, it was he who had led most of the patrolling
action in Ebor, since his father was frequently too busy
with other duties to do so. The experience had given him
a maturity far beyond his sixteen years.

"It's hard to be specific, Your Grace. Usually those
who are attacked don't recognize their attackers. I don't
suppose you'd seen any of yours before?"

"No, but I would know them if I saw them again. For
that matter, I could link with you and let you have a look,
and Joram could do the same with Davin and Ansel.
Would that help?"

"I'll say it would," Ansel chimed in. "The main part
of our problem has always been one of identification. But
Deryni evidence against Deryni culprits carries rather
better weight than human word against Deryni, don't you
agree, Jesse?"

Jesse nodded eagerly. "Absolutely. I don't know much
about all those other things you were discussing earlier,
Your Grace, except to be scared, but I do know many
of the local lords who ride the Dolban and Ebor roads. If
you and Joram can identify particular offenders, the
MacRories and I can find some pretense to round them
up. At least it would get them out of circulation for a
while."

"That sounds like a reasonable plan to me," Camber
agreed. "Unless anyone else has something to add, why
don't we adjourn, and Joram and I will brief our young
associates here. Jeb, will that satisfy your objections for
now? I see nothing further to be gained tonight, and it's
been a very long day for all of us."

There were nods and murmurs of agreement to that,
followed by a general exodus of all but the five in
question, though Camber knew that Gregory, at least,
would be waiting outside, and probably Jebediah. As soon
as the room had cleared, Joram settled down with his
nephews to either side and quickly went into rapport with
both of them at once, for they were well accustomed to

such interaction. Camber turned his attention to Jesse.

"Well, Jesse, do you have any particular approach you prefer to use for establishing rapport with someone new? I don't believe we've worked together before, have we?"

"No, sir, to both questions," Jesse murmured, looking across at Camber trustingly. "My father trained me, though, if that's any help. I know you've worked with him."

Camber smiled and stood slowly, signing for the boy to remain seated. "Well, this should be easy, then," he said, resting one hand on Jesse's near shoulder and moving quietly around to stand behind him. "It's been a long day, and I'm tired, so let's just make this a nice, easy, passive link, and I'll feed you the information as soon as you're ready." He slid his hands to rest on both the boy's shoulders, kneading the tight neck muscles briefly with his thumbs.

"Center down and relax," he breathed, feeling the boy draw breath deeply and let it out in response, already accommodating to his instruction and first tenuous contact. "Excellent. This is going to be a pleasure, I can tell. Breathe again now, and let it out. . . ."

With that, he dropped down two levels at once and found the boy's consciousness sinking in perfect unison with his, approaching a linkage and touching and merging as smoothly as he could have wished for. He closed his eyes in response to the growing rapport, knowing that Jesse no longer saw through sight either, then simply let his hands rest easily on the boy's shoulders, the need for physical contact no longer necessary except that it would have been more bother to move than simply to remain standing where he was.

Jesse's shields receded with a practiced ease which Camber should have expected, knowing Gregory, and the link was forged and the memory of the encounter near Dolban exchanged with no more effort than the wink of an eye. A moment he lingered in quiet balance and communion, then withdrew easily before the returning shields and opened his eyes to see Jesse turning his head to look at him. The boy wore a pleased and fascinated smile, as if he, too, had been surprised at the ease with which they had adjusted to one another.

"Well done, lad," Camber murmured, giving the boy's shoulder an encouraging squeeze before he sat down again. "There's no doubt whose son you are. Do you recognize any of our young toughs?"

"I surely do, Your Grace. I'll get our men started rounding them up the first thing in the morning, and check with Earl Davin and Lord Ansel, as well. And thank you, sir."

"Thank *you*, Jesse."

He watched appreciatively as the boy went out to join his father, then turned to see Joram watching him. Davin and Ansel were already gone, and Joram was smiling slightly.

"Just offhand, I'd say young Jesse gave you a pleasant surprise," Joram said.

"Just offhand, I'd say you were correct." Camber indulged in an enormous stretch and yawn, then stood. "Either I'm getting better in my old age, or else the younger generation is better trained. That Jesse is as smooth as silk, even better than Gregory. I shiver to think what he might be like with some Michaeline or Gabrilite training."

"My, how we *have* spoiled you," Joram replied. "I don't remember your saying that sort of thing before you turned Michaeline."

Camber grinned and threw his arm around his son's shoulders as they moved toward the double doors, quickly casting out with his mind to be certain the other side was clear of all but Jebediah before he replied.

"You're absolutely right. I was an insensitive, unappreciative sod. Now, let's get back to Valoret and get some sleep. Lord knows what those bloody regents will have in store for us tomorrow!"

CHAPTER TEN

*But at present it is expedient for thee, and for thy
house, to be grieved.*

—III Hermas 7:12

Camber invited Rhys and Evaine and Jebediah to join
him and Joram in his quarters the following evening, ostensibly to dine, though Rhys had brought his medical kit.
The Court was in deep mourning until after Cinhil's funeral, now less than a week away, so no formal meals
were being served in the great hall. Most of the staff were
taking simple fare in their own quarters.

Cinhil's body continued to lie in state in the castle's
chapel, guarded by selected members of the Company of
Royal Foot and a succession of mostly human nobles
chosen by the regents as honorary sentinels. The princes
were brought daily to pray beside their father's bier,
and were even permitted to stand short watches with the
regular honor guards, so long as at least one regent was
present, but other than that, and Alroy's brief appearance
with the heralds and regents at his acclamation as king,
the boys remained in seclusion. Suspension of regular
court activities for the week lent an extra air of heaviness
and gloom to the already bleak winter days.

That air was scarcely alleviated by the tone of the
meeting which Camber now convened with his children
and Jebediah, for after a meager supper, the five must
settle in to further explore the limits of Rhys's rogue talent. They decided that Jebediah should be Rhys's first subject of the evening, since he had not been involved in the
incident with Gregory. The Michaeline grand master
seemed resigned but curious as he settled into the chair
provided for him before the fireplace and Rhys perched
on the arm beside him. Evaine took a place slightly behind and on Rhys's side, while Camber and Joram

drew up stools opposite to observe. Rhys rubbed cold hands together and glanced at Jebediah wistfully.

"All right, I'm not going to tell you any more about this than you already know," he said softly. "I've worked with you only a little more than I had with Gregory, so we should be starting from about the same place. Just relax now, as if I were about to work a normal Healing function. Are you ready?"

"Ready as ever," Jebediah replied, leaning his head against the back of the chair and closing his eyes.

With a glance at Camber, Rhys raised his hands to either side of Jebediah's head and slid his fingers into the dark, greying hair, letting his thumbs rest against the temples. Jebediah did not flinch at the contact, though a flutter of his eyelids did betray his tension. Without giving him time to worry about it further, Rhys sent his mind questing outward, slipping past Jebediah's well-disciplined shields along the familiar healing pathways and halting unerringly before the triggerpoint.

For just an instant he paused, confirming what a deep-rooted part of him already knew, then extended just a hair's breadth and felt the function snap into place. Jebediah's shields and abilities all vanished in a heartbeat, there one second and gone in the same. He twitched at the awareness of what had happened, and opened his eyes as Rhys, with a muffled little cry, glanced at Camber.

"Sweet *Jesu*, it worked!" he whispered, drawing away from Jebediah far enough to peer anxiously at his face. "I was sure it would, but a part of me still doubted. Are you all right, Jeb?"

Jebediah, his eyes as wide as they would go, raised one hesitant hand to a temple and then let it slip down his cheek and fall weakly to his lap.

"God damn, that's the oddest thing I've ever felt!"

"Shall I make it right?" Rhys asked. "Are you sure you're all right?"

Jebediah nodded tentatively. "No, don't put it back right away. If you're going to study this, somebody's got to put up with it for a while." He shook his head. "It's as if I'm trapped inside my own mind." He glanced at the door and shook his head again. "I can't project as far as the door. I can't even sense the four of you, except by what I see with my eyes. Mother of God, is this what it is to be human?"

"I—suppose it is," Rhys said uneasily. "Do the rest of

133

you want to read him? The effect feels the same as Gregory to me, but I could be mistaken."

In succession, they read Jebediah, who endured their touches and their probes in typically stoic fashion. Other than his awareness that he once had had power, there was nothing to indicate what he was or had been. And when Rhys went softly back into his mind and blocked his memory, even that was gone. Camber, reading as deeply as he could, could detect no telltale sign. Had he not known Jebediah, he would not have believed that such a thing was possible.

Rhys restored Jebediah's awareness of what had been done, for they needed his on-going assessment of what was happening, at least from a non-Deryni viewpoint; but he did not restore the triggerpoint yet. There was no doubt in his mind that he could do that. Instead, he opened his medical kit and began assembling a succession of small cups of wine, dumping in powders from various packets and stirring them carefully.

Merasha was the substance which gave them the most concern, for it was *merasha* which was best known to humans as a drug specific to Deryni in its action. A high enough dosage could act as a sedative in a human, but even a minute amount was sufficient to disrupt Deryni function for hours, incapacitating a Deryni's physical coordination as well as extending the insidious mind-muddling effect for which *merasha* was so famous. They had decided to try a moderate dose on Jebediah first, of about the strength any Deryni might expect if detained by nervous human warders.

Jebediah's expression, as Rhys put the cup into his hand, was one of resigned distaste. Like all formally trained Deryni, he had experienced various such drugs and was well aware of the effect of this one, had he been in his normal state. None of them knew how he would react in his present condition.

"Do you want me to drink the whole thing?" Jebediah asked, peering into the cup suspiciously. "It certainly looks like a lot."

"I used a lot of wine. It should diminish the aftertaste. Go ahead and drink it down."

"You're the Healer," Jebediah replied, tossing off the dose and automatically making a face, then raising one eyebrow in surprise. "Hey, that did reduce the aftertaste."

He gave the cup back to Rhys. "Are you sure there was *merasha* in it?"

Rhys raised an eyebrow at Jebediah, though his thought to Camber belied his next words.

"There's nothing wrong with your tongue, at least," he said, leaning out to take another cup from the table. "Try this one. The first was a blind, just in case you'd talked yourself into an expected reaction."

As Jebediah shrugged and took the second cup, Camber watched even more closely, knowing that this was the blind and not the first cup. Jebediah drained the second cup as efficiently as he had drained the first, again shaking his head as he handed it back to Rhys.

"No aftertaste to that one, either. And none of the classic drug-signs. My hands are steady, my vision is clear, no nausea. . . ." He grinned. "Looks like your talent is good for preventing a *merasha* reaction, all right —though the cure may be worse than the disease. I'm putting on a brave facade for you, but if you tell me you can't put things back aright, I'm likely to go to pieces on you."

"I can put things back," Rhys said confidently, raising an eyebrow in thoughtful deliberation. "Can you feel that, other than physically?" he asked, laying a hand on Jebediah's forehead and extending his mental touch to probe the areas usually affected by the drug. Even with perceptions stretched to their uttermost limits, he could detect no sign that *merasha* was in his subject's system.

After a few seconds, Jebediah shook his head.

"All I can feel is your hand."

"That's what I thought. Evaine? Anybody else?"

In turn, the others confirmed what Rhys had already tried. With a sigh, the Healer laid his hands on either side of Jebediah's head again and reached out toward the triggerpoint.

"Brace yourself, if you can. The drug has had enough time to enter your system completely. I think it's going to hit you like a catapult."

The Michaeline doubled up with pain as the return was triggered, and Rhys caught him to his chest and tried to ease some of the effect. As the other three entered rapport with him, Rhys confirmed full restoration— and *merasha* disruption—of all Jebediah's Deryni senses. Wordlessly he signalled for Evaine to hand him yet another cup from the table, holding it to the stricken

135

knight's pale lips and encouraging him to drink. The medication would not neutralize all the effects of the *merasha*—nothing could do that except time and sleep —but at least it would help the nausea and splitting headache.

Rhys triggered the block again, this time without asking Jebediah first, and that enabled the grand master to get the contents of the third cup swallowed and to lie back in the chair again, exhausted, color gradually beginning to return to his face as the new drug took effect. After a few minutes, Rhys restored him again, keeping a firm hold on his pain centers, and this time the backlash was bearable. Jebediah winced and closed his eyes, moaning a little as he brought both hands to his forehead and rubbed it gingerly, but at least he did not double up. After a few minutes more, he was able to open his eyes and look at them again.

"It was really bad, wasn't it?" Rhys asked softly.

Jebediah managed a weak smile. "It still is, my friend —but it's bearable. *Jesu,* do they really use that high a dosage in the prisons?" His speech was labored and required all his discipline.

"That's my information," Rhys replied. "When I blocked you that second time, did it help at all?"

Jebediah thought about it for a moment. "I think it did. It's hard to tell for certain, though. I was so woozy already, I can't be sure. God, I'd rather take a dozen battle wounds than go through that again!"

"Well, I hope neither will be necessary," Rhys said. "I want you to know that your ordeal is appreciated, though. Do you want to rest for a while?"

"I'm not good for anything else," Jebediah said wistfully, shaking his head, but gently. "Just put me to sleep and let me go away for a while. Maybe when I come back, it will all be like a bad dream."

"Your physician agrees with the diagnosis and the prescription," Rhys grinned, putting one hand under Jebediah's arm as the knight shifted forward to stand, and signalling Joram to support him on the other side. "Let's just get you over to Joram's bed and tuck you in for the night. You'll feel a lot better in the morning."

"Have to," Jebediah murmured thickly, as he staggered off between the two. "Felt any worse, and I'd be dead."

As the two helped Jebediah into the bed and got him

136

settled, Camber glanced across at Evaine. He was more shaken than he would have admitted to Rhys over what he had just seen and witnessed, and he knew with a certainty born of working many years with the Healer that his daughter would be the next to taste what Jebediah had experienced. She knew it, too—he could see it in her eyes—and he went to her and held her close in his arms for just a moment, surrendering her only when Rhys and Joram returned.

With a bright, feigned smile, Evaine arranged herself in the chair which Jebediah had lately vacated. Rhys picked up another cup from the table and glanced at it thoughtfully; then, almost as an afterthought, he handed it to Joram and sat on the chair arm beside his wife.

"Before I have you drink that, let's just make certain that the effect works in you the way it did with Jeb." He laid his hands gently on either side of her head. "If you can, give me a little resistance with your shields—a *lot* of resistance," he amended. "Sweet Jesu, the triggerpoint isn't protected by normal shields at all! I can't get past your shields to any other part of you, but the triggerpoint is there, totally exposed. Can you feel me next to it?"

She whispered, "No," and Rhys glanced at Camber and Joram.

"Do the two of you want to link with me and watch me do it, the way you did with Gregory? I don't think it's going to make a bloody bit of difference, but you're welcome to try."

Apprehensively, Camber laid his hand on Rhys's arm, slipping into familiar rapport and feeling Joram do the same. With Rhys's guidance, they could sense the area to which he was referring, intertwined among the partially-exposed Healing pathways, but Camber knew that he could never have located that point on his own. Joram knew it, too. That aspect was almost certainly a Healing function—the ability to sense levels that other Deryni not so gifted could not. He wondered whether the triggering of that point was also a Healing function, and not for the first time wished that the Healing talent had been among his gifts.

"All right, this is what it's going to feel like, if it works through the drugs and cancels out their effect," Rhys said softly, looking into Evaine's eyes.

Camber felt something shift, and it was done. Suddenly Evaine was psychically invisible. She blinked in

137

surprise, trying to run a rapid mental assessment, as she had always been taught—but there was nothing to assess beyond the usual senses of sight and hearing and touch. She was Blind!

She swallowed and returned her attention to Rhys, who had not moved his hands from her head.

"It—works on me, too," she whispered, staring into his eyes and seeing only eyes, instead of the psychic windows they had always seemed for the two of them.

Almost heartsick, he reached out and reset the trigger-point again, then leaned down and kissed her hard on the mouth as normal Deryni senses came flooding back. She clung to him for a moment, then drew back and took a deep, steadying breath. At her nod, he took the cup from Joram again and put it in her hand.

"Are you sure you want to do it?"

"No. I don't like *merasha,* but I like what just happened even less. The sooner we get on with it, the sooner it will be over."

She drank down the cup and made a face, screwing her eyes shut and shaking her head, then sat back in the chair and drew another deep breath.

"I've certainly got the bitter aftertaste," she murmured, after a few seconds. "My tongue's going numb. My vision is starting to tunnel and blur, too. Nothing wants to focus."

"Normal reaction," Rhys replied, professional detachment restored as he laid a monitoring hand on her near wrist. "You're getting a slower effect than Jebediah did, because you're getting it gradually."

She closed her eyes and grimaced, and he moved his free hand to her forehead.

"Easy, love. I know it's getting bad. Take another deep breath and flow with it. All right, read her with me," Rhys said to the others. "She's essentially got the full effect of the drug now. Her shields are in tatters—not that this apparently matters, where my little trick is concerned. Her Deryni functions are still there, but they're mostly inaccessible. If she tried to use them, she might get a reaction, but it would undoubtedly be the wrong one. Control is gone. This is a classic *merasha* disruption, such as we've all experienced in training. I'm moving in to the triggerpoint now, and—there!"

As he spoke the final word, Evaine's eyelids fluttered and then she looked up at them, pain gone from her eyes, but also all trace of her Deryni powers. As they probed her mind, she looked around in amazement, astonished at the disappearance of the *merasha* effect which had been so excruciatingly apparent only a moment before. When the others had read in all the depth they cared to do, Rhys held another cup to his wife's lips and bade her drink. After she had drained it, he led her into the next room and laid her down to sleep in Camber's bed, not removing his block until he was sure the second cup had done its work. He returned to find Camber and Joram waiting by the fire, and settled in the chair between them without a word. Almost as an afterthought, and without warning, he reached out his right hand to touch Joram's forehead. Before the priest could react, Rhys had triggered and reset the triggerpoint in him, leaving Joram with an astonished expression on his face and Rhys shaking his head.

"That's what I thought," he said, slumping in the chair and looking at the flames on the hearth as he rubbed at his eyes wearily. "I'm getting tired—this *does* seem to be akin to the kind of energy outlay used for Healing— but there doesn't seem to be any kind of advance preparation necessary. We needed to know that, too. Joram, do you feel any kind of after-reaction?"

"It was just a—a blankness, for the split second." Joram swallowed. "Jesus, you scare me, Rhys!"

"I know. I scare me, too." Rhys took a deep breath, then looked up at Camber. "I suppose that to round out our knowledge, we really should see what this will do to your shape-change. If anyone else can do what I do, it could be a danger to you."

Steeling himself, though he knew that would do no good, Camber returned the Healer's gaze.

"Only one way to find out, isn't there?" he said evenly. "Go ahead. I'm ready." And he watched dispassionately as Rhys's hand moved unerringly toward his head.

He felt the touch of Rhys's hand on his brow, and he closed his eyes as the contact was made, knowing at least part of what was almost certain to come. For an instant more he continued to take in information with all his Deryni senses.

Then it was as if a light had been extinguished and there was only darkness and the psychic sensation of being muffled in heavy, shrouding wool, close and claustrophobic. Immediately he opened his eyes to search for

Rhys and was startled, in spite of himself, to see Rhys still sitting where he had been a moment before. He knew where he was and what had happened, at least intellectually, but he could not remember how it had felt not to be Blind; only that something was lost.

At least his appearance seemed to be causing no alarm. He saw Rhys and Joram staring at him intently, and knew they must be reading him, but he could feel nothing. After a moment, Rhys smiled and nodded, brushing his temple with a fingertip, and full awareness came flooding back. With a quick sensation of vertigo, Camber shook his head and swallowed.

"I take it I stayed Alister," he whispered, after a slight pause.

"You did that," Rhys agreed. "Curiously enough, your dangerous alter-ego remained shuttered away, too, though if someone knew to look for it, he might be able to dig it out. That isn't likely, I don't think. At least we now know I can do it to anybody. And we know what *merasha* will do. Now we only have about half a dozen other common drugs to test, to see whether *they* affect blocked Deryni. I think we're going to have a busy week, not to mention that it's going to be hard on my volunteers."

Neither Camber nor Joram could quarrel with that.

They continued their experiments throughout the rest of the week, drawing on Gregory and Jesse one night, Davin and Ansel another, Jaffray and then Jebediah again on a third, to finish testing all the substances Rhys felt needful. By the Feast of Saint Teilo, the day of Cinhil's state funeral, all of them were ready for a break—even a Requiem.

Cinhil's funeral was rich with all the pomp and dignity which the regents could muster from Church and State. Gwynedd had not seen a royal funeral of a reigning monarch for more than thirty years. Cinhil had been neither a great king nor even a greatly loved king, but he had been human and Haldane, and he had ousted the hated Imre and prevented Imre's sister from taking back the throne. No one could deny that these were all good things; and for these, at least, the people had been grateful.

They were grateful, in their grudging ways, but they did not understand him. They did not comprehend the personal piety and commitment which had made Cinhil long for a return to his priestly life, for the setting aside of the Crown won at such high cost.

What they did know and understand was that Cinhil, while not a brilliant or particularly wise king, had seemed genuinely concerned for the welfare of the people entrusted to his governance—even if he had not always known how to govern well or choose suitable advisors—and that he had been infinitely better than a child on the throne of Gwynedd.

Now they faced that latter situation, and knew that the kingdom would be ruled for at least the next two years by regents. The regents were fairly popular among their human constituents, but they were still regents, and many folk were aware of how some of them had already taken advantage of their positions at Court to gain offices and lands and titles. No, regents would not be the same at all as an adult king on the throne.

Still, the charm of three young princes was undeniable. No one knew a great deal about the children, since their father had protected them fiercely from too much public exposure during his lifetime, but it was said that at least the heir and the youngest were intelligent and engaging boys, though the heir was a trifle sickly.

They did not talk much about the middle son, club-footed Prince Javan, who bore the mark of God's displeasure in every step he took. Some there were who felt sorry for the boy, but no one was sorry that it was Alroy and not Javan who was to be crowned in May, on the twins' twelfth birthday. It was not thought seemly that a cripple should sit upon the throne of Gwynedd—though law did not prohibit such a thing.

But, perhaps that, too, would change under the rule of the regents. It was said that the boy required a Healer at his side, day and night. Perhaps he would die, and save them all the further embarrassment. Had the regents been asked, and answered truthfully, they could not have argued with that rationale. Rhys Michael was a full year and a half younger than Alroy and Javan—with a correspondingly longer minority.

The princes' first public function after Cinhil's death, other than their brief appearances at the chapel royal beside the bier, was to walk behind their father's coffin in the funeral procession. From the castle, where Cinhil's body had lain in state for the past week, the procession wound its way out the courtyard and down the narrow, serpentine streets of the town, finally ending at the great Cathedral of All Saints, back near the castle.

Young Alroy, a royal prince's circlet of gold shining on his raven hair, walked directly behind the bier. Still a little pale, and very austere looking, he held his head high and looked neither right nor left; he had been well-coached by his tutors for the past week in royal deportment. He wore black, befitting the solemnity of the occasion, but the undifferenced shield of the Haldanes was blazoned bold on his chest and back to mark him as the heir. His brothers walked behind him, also in black, though without the shields, and wearing silver circlets.

Javan limped a little less than usual that day—a surprise to those who had never seen him, for many had thought him hideously deformed, to hear the common rumor. His manner was as cool and regal as his twin's; but those who watched would never know of the special ministrations given him by Tavis that morning, to block the pain of so long a march; nor would they know the price that walk cost him later that night, when the damage must be faced and Healed. For now, he was a royal prince and knew it.

And beside Javan, spritely and engaging, a sunny-dispositioned Prince Rhys Michael moved out confidently, in rapport with the crowd as only a natural-born leader could be, only barely able to refrain from smiling and waving to the people as he passed.

Next came the regents—all except Bishop Hubert, who would be assisting at the funeral and was already waiting at the cathedral with the other prelates. They walked four-abreast behind the princes, garbed in funereal black but by their bearing leaving little doubt of their own estimation of their importance in the future of Gwynedd.

Cinhil's Requiem Mass was celebrated by Archbishop Jaffray and Bishops Cullen and MacInnis—friends of Cinhil, all, though not universally of one another—a fitting farewell to a most pious king. It was attended by Deryni and humans alike.

When it was over, Cinhil was laid to rest in a crypt in the cathedral undercroft, near the tombs of the Festil kings who had once ruled Gwynedd. The regents had announced earlier in the week that Cinhil's body would be removed to Rhemuth later and reinterred with his

Haldane ancestors, as, indeed, the entire Court would relocate to the old Haldane capital as soon as rebuilding was sufficiently advanced. The regents had even made inquiries to locate the graves of Cinhil's father and grandfather: Alroy, known as Royston, and Aidan, known as Daniel Draper.

The pronouncement was an auspicious one for the new regime. Such a poignant outward sign of piety and respect for the past touched responsive chords in Deryni as well as humans, and put the regents in a very positive light from the start. The veneration of the Haldane line, the planned retreat to the old human capital, with its associations of more fortunate days, seemed positive auguries for a more enlightened and responsive reign ahead.

Hence, for the first few weeks after Cinhil's funeral, the regents were careful to do nothing which might diminish their carefully nurtured first impression. While the Court was still in mourning, the regents occupied themselves with making quiet preparations for Alroy's coronation in May, the while setting out their long-term strategy for the months and years ahead. The council having been purged of all its Deryni members save one, it now became the regents' quiet task to ease out Deryni members of the royal household, the while rearranging staffs and quarters and schedules to extend even more rigid control over the three princes.

To begin this reorganization, the boys were moved into separate apartments—in the same wing, but separated by intervening suites occupied by staff and some of the regents themselves. Their schooling went on, as it must, but now in a more concentrated format, with even more rigid schoolmasters; and Alroy was often absent from the formal sessions still held in the old common room of the nursery, the regents avowing that he could learn more by travelling around his kingdom and observing his government at work firsthand. In fact, what now began for Alroy was a carefully calculated program of isolation and growing dependence.

Tavis was permitted to stay at court, to avoid royal tantrums on Javan's part before the new king was safely crowned, but castle rumor had it that his days were numbered, and he walked a very narrow line of tolerance. He was one of a very few Deryni who did not taste the regents' cool rejection in those early days—and knew it.

143

For the Deryni dismissed from office, like Camber, those weeks of late February and early March were a time of making arrangements for other occupations, other livings; and many of those anticipating dismissal did likewise. Archbishop Jaffray had requested Camber's participation in Alroy's coronation, giving him an excuse to remain at the capital yet a little while longer, and perhaps mitigate some of what the regents planned; but eventual departure was inevitable, Camber knew. Fortunately, he still had Grecotha. At least at Grecotha, he would have a secure base from which to function—which was more than many could say.

Mostly, though, Camber spent his time in prayer and contemplation, considering their situation as a race and trying to cement strong ties of friendship and mutual aid with those who would remain at Court when he was gone. Also high on his list of priorities was to learn all he could about the men who now held Gwynedd's destiny in their avaricious hands.

As if that were not enough, he must also worry about Davin and Ansel, who were actively trying to break up the bands of young Deryni bravos who increasingly terrorized the roads now that spring was upon them. The identity of some of the ringleaders was now known, thanks to Joram's briefing, and Davin, as Earl of Culdi, had tried and hanged two in his county court for raping and killing a farmer's wife at Childermas. Vigilante bands of humans had begun to roam the roads of late, too, sometimes clashing violently with the Deryni. Some said that it was such a band which had burned a mostly-Deryni monastic school near Barwicke, a scant week after Cinhil's funeral.

Nor had Gregory and Jesse been idle in the Ebor area. Of the men who had attacked Camber and Joram, a full half-dozen had been known to Jesse or his father, and had been detained and questioned accordingly. A lynch mob had almost taken them the first night they were jailed, but Gregory's men had been able to prevent it—at the cost of four Deryni and two human lives. The prisoners had now been moved to safer quarters, but Gregory doubted he could hold them much longer. The young men's fathers were clamoring for their release, claiming that the Earl of Ebor could not keep them safe. Besides, boys would be boys. . . .

In the face of such frustrations, Camber's one positive

idea for utilizing Rhys' talent seemed almost brilliant—until he began examining its ramifications in depth. Synthesizing the basic concept took the better part of several weeks, and even when it came, he explored the concept for days with Rhys and Evaine and Joram before he even considered taking it to the Camberian Council. He and Jebediah spent an entire day and night going over the military and religious implications and arguing about all the things that could go wrong.

Finally, even Camber had to admit that it was a terrible idea, that it had only a ghost of a chance of working —but it was also the only idea they had, at that point. Only desperate circumstances could warrant its use, for it was a mere survival plan for certain of their race—and saving some of them would mean the loss of much of what they had gained.

Yet, it was better than no plan at all. And if there was even the most remote chance that such a drastic plan might one day have to be implemented, then preparations must be begun. They could always abort the plan, if it became no longer necessary.

"I know the outcome is risky," Camber said, after he and Rhys had just summarized the proposal to the Camberian Council, meeting informally around the great, ivory council table. "But at least it would give some of our people a chance, especially the ordinary Deryni of no particular training or rank, who haven't access to the hiding methods of many of us."

"I don't know," Jaffray said, shaking his head doubtfully. "To begin with, I don't like this idea of using a religious framework to present it. God knows, there are enough religious hoaxes that can't be helped, without deliberately inventing one."

"I agree," Camber said. *And if only you knew,* he continued to himself. "You must admit that it's a perfect foil, however."

"Yes, I suppose so." Jaffray sighed for at least the fourth time that evening. "That isn't my only reservation, though."

Camber smiled. "I had hardly dared hope it would be."

"I'm serious!" Jaffray protested. "In addition to the dubious theological aspects of what you propose, this whole plan hinges on whether other Healers can be trained to do what Rhys can do. What if they can't? If that comes to be the case, suppose something should happen to him? With no one else to reverse the block, we don't know whether people's powers would eventually return spontaneously or whether they'd be lost forever as Deryni. That could be the death of our race just as surely as if we all fell beneath human swords or died at the stake."

"Maybe Deryniness is transmitted to the children, even if the parents' powers are blocked," Evaine said quietly. "Maybe the children would still be Deryni."

"And maybe they would not!" Gregory said pointedly. "You have children, Evaine. Would you want to take that chance?"

As Evaine shook her head, Jebediah sighed and shrugged.

"We may have to take that chance, Gregory. We *might* succeed. There's even the chance, albeit slim, that the persecutions we fear might never come—or that they might be far less severe than expected."

"And snakes can fly!" Gregory said emphatically. "Come on, Jeb, you know better. You've seen the signs. How many of your officers have been 'transferred' to other assignments and replaced by the regents' human cronies, even before you were dismissed as earl marshal? How many of our friends and acquaintances have suddenly been eased out and their places filled by men we never heard of, but who have the regents' ears? And then, there are our own people who simply *invite* the regents to move against us, the ones that Jesse and I and your nephews, Evaine, have been trying to take out of circulation so they won't provoke even more vicious retaliation than we saw at Nyford."

"But the highway bands weren't responsible for Nyford," Evaine protested. "Besides, I thought they were being put down. You said they were."

Now thoroughly agitated, Gregory slapped both hands flat on the table and rolled his eyes toward the crystal sphere hanging above the center of the table.

"My dear child, how *can* you be so naive? A mere pittance! A tear in the ocean-sea! If there were no more bands—if the harassment stopped now, tonight—it would be too late for that! You say the persecutions may not come? I say that they're here already, growing in small, insidious ways. Given our fine, self-righteous, Deryni-hating regents, *and* given a two-year minority of our new king—or his next brother, if Alroy shouldn't last that long—or more than *three* years, if Rhys Michael should come to the throne before his majority—you can bet that it's only going to get worse! The only questions in my mind now are how bad and how soon?"

He sat back explosively. "I'm sorry. That's been building for a very long time. But that's how I feel."

The rest of them stared at him in shocked silence for several seconds until Camber finally cleared his throat and glanced around self-consciously. They had deserved that—all of them. Perhaps they had all been too far-removed, too blindly trusting that fate would intervene to save them. But it was not too late—was it?

"Your warnings are well taken," Camber said, unusually subdued for Alister. "Perhaps we've all been guilty of refusing to recognize how serious things are. Oh, we've realized what was happening in a day-to-day sense, in bits and pieces, but I think it's only really begun to sink home since Cinhil's death. We do *not* have Cinhil's tempering influence to protect us anymore, however tenuous that protection might have been. We *do* have a set of unscrupulous and avaricious regents whose next specific moves are unpredictable, but whose general attitude is quite clear: *they do not like Deryni!* I think we have—perhaps—until the coronation to decide what we're going to do to protect ourselves, as a race as well as individuals. And frankly, Rhys's talent presents the best hope I've seen so far."

There were nods of agreement at that, even Gregory giving grudging acquiescence. But when all attention had returned to Camber, he glanced casually at Rhys, across the table. The Healer was staring at his two hands lying palm-down on the table—slender, fine hands with supple fingers and short, well-kept nails. Rhys felt their scrutiny, but he did not lift his gaze from his careful study of his hands. His voice was almost fragile as he spoke.

"You wonder that I stare at my hands," he said softly, not looking up at them. "There is a reason for that. They are a Healer's hands, consecrated to the service of mankind—human as well as Deryni. I pledged that service in my Healer's oath, many years ago. I have often held life itself between these hands—sometimes *your* lives. Now it appears that I have been given not just the lives of individuals, but of our *race*—here, in the span of these two frail hands. Do you wonder that I feel the burden?

147

"Gregory, you've been our doomsayer tonight, our gadfly, our goad, our Nesta, who foretold the fall of Caeriesse—except that no one believed Nesta, and she was right. I hope that you aren't." He looked up finally, directly at Gregory.

"But even if you are, I'm not ready to concede this fight. And I don't think the others are, either, or we wouldn't be here together, looking for a miracle. We need you with us, Gregory. We need your strength and —yes, we even need you to warn us when we've gotten off our focus, as you did tonight. Especially, we need you for that."

"I'm with you," Gregory said gruffly, blinking an unaccustomed brightness from his pale blue eyes. "I never meant to imply that I wasn't, or that I doubted you. It's just that—damn it all, man! I'm a soldier. I don't understand your poet's ways. Speak to me in a language I can understand!"

"All right. Progress report," Rhys replied briskly. "If you want to be military, I can be that, too. Item: we have established that the Deryni-specific drugs most commonly accessible to humans do *not* affect blocked Deryni. This means that Deryni could be hidden right under the noses of the authorities and they'd never be detected, as long as no one knew they were Deryni to begin with. For the ones who are known, but choose this option, it means a massive relocation program, once we get the operation underway in earnest. That's a much later problem.

"Item: unfortunately—or fortunately, depending upon your point of view—my blocking talent seems to be exclusively a Healer's function. So the next question is, can other Healers learn to do it, or am I a fluke? And can *all* Healers do it, or can only a few learn how? Jaffray, a while back, you offered to get me access to other Healers. I assume you were referring to Gabrilites?"

"That's correct."

"Very well. Bearing in mind that we almost have to tell them the background on this, including at least some background about the Council, whom were you considering?"

"Well, Dom Emrys comes to mind first of all," Jaffray said promptly. "You'll not find a better Healer or teacher of Healers anywhere. And since he declined a seat on this Council years ago, I think we need not worry about his discretion. I would trust Emrys with my immortal soul—and have done so, on occasion."

Rhys returned Jaffray's wistful smile with a chuckle. "I know what you mean. I thought you might recommend him. I was going to, myself. I only trained under him a short while, but I admire and respect him greatly. I do have some reservations about his age, though. What is he, close to eighty?"

"Maybe more. He's in good health, though. And if anyone can learn to do what you do, he should be able to. Also, he'd be able to help train others."

"A telling point. Very well. Who else?"

"Queron Kinevan," Jaffray replied. "I haven't seen him in years, but he's one of the finest Healers I ever knew. Some of you will remember his demonstration at the synod which canonized Saint Camber. Sorry to bring up a sore point, Joram, but his performance *was* brilliant."

"I know," Joram whispered.

"So, do you know where he is, these days?" Jaffray continued. "Didn't you say you'd seen him at Dolban, a few weeks ago?"

Joram had lowered his eyes guardedly as Jaffray extoled Queron's abilities, and Camber knew that his son must be remembering their chilling personal encounter with the Healer at the synod Jaffray had mentioned. Then Joram had nearly been forced to bare his mind to Queron's ruthless scrutiny, threatening the betrayal of every detail of his father's change of rôle. Camber, as Alister Cullen, had managed to avert Queron's probe by himself seeming to conduct a Truth-Read of Joram regarding his supposedly-dead father, but the terror which both of them had felt while they worked to reach that goal had been too real, the threat of Queron's rumored ability to strip away all deception, all too powerful. Joram was not now in danger, if Queron were chosen to try to learn Rhys's new talent; but Rhys could be. Neither Camber nor any of his kin wished to have Queron delve any deeper into the inner workings of anyone who knew the truth of Camber.

Not daring to speak first, Camber gazed across the table at Joram and caught the quick thought, troubled and angry despite himself, yet resigned, which his son sent only for him. He watched as, with a slow intake of breath, Joram cautiously raised his eyes to Jaffray.

"I'm sorry, sir. I have—vivid memories of Queron, as you may well imagine. Time has eased my feelings somewhat, but—yes, we did see him at Dolban. We even visited the shrine."

"You did?" Gregory's surprised delight was written all across his narrow face, for he was a devoted adherent of Saint Camber, despite all Camber had been able to do to discourage him. "Joram, you have no idea how happy I am to hear that. I *knew* you'd come around eventually. Your sainted father—"

"His sainted father," Camber interrupted smoothly, shaking his head and trying to smile, "is still a delicate subject for Joram, and you know it, Gregory. Can we get back to the subject?" He faced Jaffray again. "Understand that I don't know Queron except from a few brief meetings—at the synod, mostly. As Deryni, he's—formidable. But I'm no Healer to judge in that area. Can you tell us more about him? You and he were Gabrilites together. You know his abilities better than any of us."

Thoughtfully, Jaffray sat back in his chair and scanned them all, clicking his ring of office against one large front tooth.

"He's good, Alister," the archbishop finally said. "One of the best I've ever met, as I said. We were very close at one time, before I became a bishop and left the Order. I can tell you this: in his prime, he made most Healers look like first-year apprentices by comparison. In those days, you couldn't find a man with better Healer's credentials—outside this room, of course," he ended, nodding deferentially to Rhys.

"And now?" Rhys asked. "No idle compliments, Jaffray. I have to know. By his own admission, he's not been an active Healer for years, except in his own community. That may or may not make a difference."

"That's one reason I suggested Emrys first," Jaffray replied, "though I don't think it will make a difference with Queron. I've seen him do things that made me doubt my own perceptions. But he was always inclined toward the dreamer, the wild-eyed idealist—witness his departure from the Gabrilites to set up the Servants of Saint Camber. You, on the other hand, have both feet firmly on the ground. That's important, but you're also unafraid to delve into the unknown. This new Healing quirk is a case in point. In all, though I haven't seen you work as much, I think you have the potential to be at

150

least as good as Queron." He paused. "Do you need any further comparison?"

"No further. Thank you," Rhys whispered.

"Very well, then. On that somewhat less than enthusiastic recommendation," Jaffray said with a slight, wry smile, "I propose that we go ahead with plans to get you together with Emrys and Queron as soon as possible. I think Alister should go, too, since he has observed your work rather more than anyone else excepting, perhaps, your lady wife. Evaine, I would have suggested you, except that I think another priest would do better than a woman in dealing with Queron—and someone who is not related to Saint Camber," he added, for Joram's sake.

Camber's secret amusement at Jaffray's last statement almost overshadowed his reluctance to face Queron again. At least as a non-Healer, he would not be expected to enter as deep a rapport with Queron as Rhys would. And since Queron had known Alister Cullen only after Camber's assumption of that identity, and Camber hardly at all, consistency should be no problem. Still, both he and Rhys would be at least somewhat vulnerable in the sort of rapport necessary for Rhys to show and teach his odd, newfound talent. They would have to be careful to put Queron off balance from the beginning in that regard, so he simply would not have the leisure to read them too deeply in any but pertinent areas.

"Good. That's settled, then," Evaine said, lacing her fingers together and placing her joined hands precisely on the table before her. "I think that now we need to talk more about the framework in which our Healers are going to work—assuming, of course, that the talent can be taught. We've been skirting the issue because of its theological implications—my brother has already voiced his objections, in private—but it has to be faced. Alister?"

Camber nodded slowly. "Very well. I'm no more comfortable with the idea that the rest of you, but it does seem the lesser of a number of evils at this point. And there *is* historical precedent for the kind of movement we talked about earlier. The concept of dying to the world and being reborn is a fairly universal one, going back even before Judaic traditions. John the Baptist was neither the first nor the last to preach it."

"That much I'll grant you," Jaffray said. "And the

idea of dying to one's 'evil' Deryni powers, to the extent that they really are gone and not just denied—well, that's a stroke of genius, Rhys."

Rhys shrugged. "I don't know about genius. It still makes me a little uncomfortable. But it may work."

"It *will* work," Evaine said. "However, to make it work, we're going to need an undeniably human front-person, whose background and motivations will be unquestionable, both to us and to those to whom he'll be ministering."

"And you have the perfect candidate," Jaffray guessed, an amused smile tugging at the corners of his mouth. "Ah, Evaine, my child, I can see that you've inherited a full measure of your father's legendary duplicity."

"I'll take that as the compliment I'm sure you intended," she retorted with a matching grin.

Jaffray nodded. "So be it. And who is this paragon of human competence and suitability who is to be our voice in the wilderness?"

"His name is Revan. Some of you have met him."

"Revan?" Gregory's eyebrows were raised in surprise. "Not the clark?"

"The same."

"Who is Revan?" asked Jaffray.

Evaine lowered her gaze, remembering with some reluctance. "When Imre was still king, one Lord Rannulf, a Deryni, was found murdered in the village below my father's keep. Though Willimite terrorists were blamed, Imre took fifty villagers to be executed, two each day. My brother Cathan tried to intercede—and was granted one life, which he must choose! He chose Revan, then a boy of about thirteen. After Cathan was killed, I took Revan as my confidential clark and saw that his education was continued. For the past five years, he has been tutor to our two younger children."

"And you think *him* suited to our purposes?" Jaffray asked. "With his Deryni connections?"

Jebediah raised an elegant eyebrow in speculation. "Has it occurred to you that it might be precisely those Deryni connections which would make his apparent defection all the more believable? Also, those who keep track of such things will remember his part, however small, in the Rannulf affair, and the alleged Willimite ties. It's said that the Willimites are active again, by the way. Some of my men reported an entire community of them living in the hills near Saint Liam's. If we send Revan in there, with the right background, he'll have a ready-made movement to assimilate. God knows, the Willimites hate Deryni—though they do have several renegades among them, who Truth-Read for them but use no other of their powers."

"Renegades, eh?" Jaffray mused. "His cover will have to be impeccable, then, if he's to stand being Truth-Read. One almost wonders whether the Willimites hate Deryni too much, though. Suppose Revan can't convince them of his mission?"

Joram crossed his arms across his chest and scowled. "Oh, he'll convince them, all right. He has all the marks of a messiah, don't you know? He was a carpenter's apprentice when Cathan found him, and he walks with a limp, just like Prince Javan!"

"Joram, that's enough!" Evaine snapped. "I know you don't approve of this plan, and I know why. But since you have no better suggestion, I'll thank you to keep your trepidations and pious quibbles to yourself!"

With an expression of angry amazement, Jebediah brought the flat of his hand down hard on the ivory tabletop.

"Now, stop it! Both of you! This bickering is—"

"It's none of your concern, Jeb!" Joram retorted. "Stay out of it! Evaine, I'm getting a little tired of your—"

"Children!" Abruptly Camber stood, the thought behind his word carrying his paternal shock even as the verbal exclamation underlined the consternation of the part of him that was Alister. Joram and Evaine both froze in amazement as they realized what they had done.

"I'm sorry, Father Alister, Joram, Jeb," Evaine murmured, not looking at her brother or her father.

Joram, too, bowed his head.

"Sorry, Jeb, Evaine. But you know how I feel about such things. Alister, I'm sorry that you had to step in that way."

"It's understood, son," Camber murmured, once more taking his seat, and thankful that the outburst had been covered so well, though he still was concerned at Joram's obvious hostility. "We'll talk about it later. For now, though, don't you all think we should get back to the subject? Gregory, Jaffray, the rest of us know Revan to varying degrees, and are reasonably satisfied with his

153

suitability for the job at hand. Even Joram has no objections to the man. It's the job that gives him problems. How do you feel?"

Gregory glanced at Jaffray, and the archbishop nodded slowly.

"It seems to me that you're asking a great deal of one so young," Jaffray said. "How old is Revan, did you say?"

"Twenty-six or twenty-seven, by now," Evaine replied.

"Gregory, what do you think?" Jaffray asked. "I'm reserving my opinion, for the moment."

Gregory shrugged. "He does seem a little young for what Alister has in mind—but Our Lord was little older when He started His mission. Besides, who would expect Revan to be involved in such a thing, even if they should come to suspect a subterfuge?"

"Exactly the point," Rhys agreed. "The very fact that he is so well known to be devoted to Evaine and me will work in our favor, to convince people that his conversion is genuine, when he starts preaching our message."

"Provided he has someone to work with," Jaffray said quietly.

"What do you mean?"

"I mean," said Jaffray, "that right now, you're the only one who can do what you can do, as a Healer. Suppose it can't be taught? What then?"

"Then I'll simply have to make the sacrifice and do it myself, won't I?" Rhys said lightly. "We'll have to figure out a rationale for *me* to appear to defect and renounce my powers, and go on from there. I'm hoping that won't be necessary, though. I don't really think I'm cut out to be a messianic figure."

"Neither was Camber," Joram muttered under his breath, "and look what happened to him."

"What was that?" Rhys asked.

"Never mind. I think you'll make a fine latter-day John the Baptist, Rhys—running around in the desert, eating nuts and berries and—damn it, this whole thing is too risky!"

"So it's risky," Jaffray countered. "So is being wiped out by humans, because we're Deryni. So unless you have another solution, I think we'll all thank you to keep your objections to yourself. Evaine, Rhys, I think you should talk to Revan as soon as possible. If he's willing to do it, he's going to need all the time we can give him to build his cover with the Willimites. Have you considered what happens if he *won't* do it, by the way?"

Evaine sighed. "He'll do it. He has no more choice than we do. We'll try to go to Sheele by the end of the week."

"Good. And in the meantime, I'll see about setting up Rhys's and Alister's meeting with Emrys and Queron."

CHAPTER ELEVEN

Whom shall he teach knowledge? And whom shall he make to understand doctrine?

—Isaiah 28:9

A few days later, on a morning bright with sunlight for the end of winter, Evaine and Rhys rode to their manor at Sheele, ostensibly to visit their children. Once there, Evaine pleaded a slight indisposition, leaving Rhys an ideal excuse to take the children riding while she rested at the manor with Revan for company.

Revan's limp was far less pronounced than usual as they went into the winter-dead garden. Pleasure and contentment lit his eyes as he sat at Evaine's invitation. Together they watched the seven-year-old Rhysel demonstrate her newly forming riding skills to her father, astride the gentle bay pony her parents had given her at Twelfth Night. Tieg, half her age, had to be content to sit in front of his father, wedged securely between him and the high, tooled-leather pommel. The boy crowed with delight as Rhys's big chestnut pranced and cavorted. The picture wanted only Aidan, the eldest of the three children, to make Evaine's pride complete; but Aidan was at Trurill, near Cor Culdi, fostered to his cousin Adrian MacLean, a grandson of Camber's sister Aislinn, and father of another Camber, called Camlin, who was a year Aidan's senior. Evaine saw her firstborn mostly at holidays.

With a wistful sigh, she brought herself back to Revan sitting at her side. His fine hands, stained with ink around the nails, cradled a scroll of creamy new parchment—no ancient scrolls for Revan. Though Evaine could not bring herself to ask, she suspected that it was some new verse or song which Revan himself had written. The lame carpenter's apprentice had become a learned scholar and bard in the years since his rescue by Cathan. A twinge of guilt assailed Evaine as she considered how what she must ask would end so much of that. And yet, there was nothing else to be done.

"How go the children's studies, Revan?" she asked, trying to delay the inevitable for yet a while longer.

Revan smiled, brushing a strand of light brown hair back from his face. Like many men of the younger generation, he wore his hair long, brushing his shoulders.

"Lord Tieg is too young for much formal training yet, my lady," he said easily, "though he knows most of his letters and shows great promise. Lady Rhysel is the one who gives me the most delight. She will be another scholar like you, if she continues."

Pleased, Evaine plucked a dead twig from the hem of her gown and twirled it absently between her fingers.

"A family trait," she said with a smile. "She favors her grandfather, too." She studied her twig as if she had never seen one before, searching for the words. This was not going to be easy.

"Revan, you have served my family for many years now. Do you enjoy your work?"

He smiled, a quick, sunny grin which was typical of his nature, then dropped his gaze a little shyly.

"My lady, you know I do. You and Lord Rhys have been very kind to me. The children are almost like the brothers and sisters I never got to know. In fact, I— sometimes like to think I am more than just a tutor to your children—that I am a part of the family, if only a poor cousin." He dared to glance up at her. "You're not angry, are you?"

"Angry? Of course not! You *are* a part of this family. With you here, Rhys and I have never had to worry that we must spend so much time away from the children. We have always known that they were in good hands."

He did not reply to that, though he looked pleased, and Evaine knew that she could no longer delay the inevitable.

"Revan—Rhys and I did not come here today only to see the children. Nor am I at all unwell. I wanted to discuss the nature of your service with us and to ask whether—you might be willing to consider a different kind of service, much more difficult than anything which you have done hitherto. If we did not consider you as family, I would not dare to ask you what I must."

"What *different* service, my lady?" Revan murmured. Suddenly his face had become more serious, the lights of laughter fading from his eyes. Laying aside his scroll, he turned his full attention on Evaine, waiting, fearing.

"We—Rhys and I—have a problem." She broke off a piece of the twig she still was holding and let it fall to the ground. "No, there is nothing wrong between the two of us," she added, catching the look of concern which flashed across Revan's face. "Rhys and I are mated in our souls, as well as hearts and bodies. We could not ask for closer union in this life."

Questing out with her mind, she caught Revan's relief at her assurance, knew as she had never realized before just now much the young man idolized Rhys, worshipped her. Firmly she forced herself to withdraw.

"No, this has to do with Rhys as a Healer," she continued, worrying at a strip of bark on her twig with one snagged thumbnail. "In the past few weeks, Rhys has discovered an important new facet of his Healing powers, and we feel that it could benefit all of our Deryni people. But it's an odd sort of talent. It enables the Healer to block out the powers of a Deryni, to make those powers disappear so completely that they cannot be used, detected, or even remembered. So far as we know, no one has ever been able to do that before."

As she glanced at him, sidelong, Revan shook his head slowly, confusion showing in his pale brown eyes.

"But, why would you want to take away a Deryni's powers, my lady? Give them, maybe, but take them away? I don't see the point."

"Neither did we, at first. But—" Sighing, she rose and began pacing back and forth in front of the bench, gestured for Revan to remain seated when he would have stood, too.

"Revan, you're surely aware of the way people feel about Deryni, especially since the death of the king."

"Well, some people, my lady," he admitted, with a

disparaging shrug of his shoulders. "I don't, and the others of the staff here at Sheele don't."

"But many do," Evaine replied. "And what is more important, at least four of the five regents do. With the young king guided by such men as Murdoch and Rhun and that despicable Bishop Hubert for the next two years, who is to say what the official policy on Deryni will be in the future? Remember, when Imre was toppled, it was a Deryni regime which fell with him. Deryni have been tolerated in the new government only because Cinhil personally felt an attachment to such particular Deryni as gave him comfort and support. The regents have no such attachments, and long memories for what Deryni did to their kin during the Interregnum."

"Archbishop Jaffray still sits on the regency council, my lady, and he is Deryni," Revan said.

"Aye, but it is not by choice of the regents. Jaffray is tolerated, for the present, because he must be. It is the undeniable right of the Archbishop of Valoret and Primate of Gwynedd to sit on the council of Gwynedd, whether it be a regular council or a regency. But Jaffray could very easily meet with a convenient accident, and be replaced, too. And other Deryni, such as Bishop Cullen and Earl Jebediah and Rhys himself, have already lost their appointments at Court. By coronation, we must all be gone from Valoret. We fear that this may be just the beginning, that lost appointments may be only the prelude to lost lives. What if there is another Nyford?"

Revan frowned, nodding slowly. "I see what you're saying." He paused. "But, what does all of this have to do with taking away Deryni powers? It seems to me that a Deryni would want even more power, to protect himself, if you truly fear that the regents will move against all Deryni."

"So one would think," Evaine admitted, both pleased and heartsick that Revan should understand so well. "But we Deryni have limitations, too, you know. And when it comes to a contest between Deryni powers and a dozen swords, or arrows, or spears—well, magic takes time, and force breeds force. It isn't always a very good defense."

"Is *lack* of magic a good defense, then?" Revan asked, almost to himself.

"Well, no—not if it's known and can be proved that the person is a Deryni. However, I ask you to consider this: if even another Deryni could not discover whether a person is or is not Deryni and if a Deryni himself cannot remember that he once was Deryni, then perhaps lack of magic *would* be a good defense."

While Revan pondered that, Evaine sat down again and willed her racing heart to slow. After a few moments, Revan raised his head and stared out across the meadow. Close by the oak grove which lay at the other side, they could see Rhys and his daughter leading their mounts, young Tieg now sitting proudly alone in his father's deep saddle. Quickly Revan looked away, but not before Evaine realized that he suspected, in some as yet inarticulated way, that she was about to ask him to give up the children.

"My lady, you haven't yet said how this affects me or the children."

She sighed. "Aidan should be safe enough with his cousins for the present. Rhysel and Tieg would stay here, for the time being—we'd have to engage another tutor—but arrangements are being made for them to go to a Michaeline establishment with my brother, if that becomes necessary."

"I see."

"For yourself, we have an idea how you might aid us in using Rhys's discovery to protect at least some of our people. You would become a prophet, in the style of John the Baptist, and a follower of Saint Willim. We would make it appear that you were removing the powers of Deryni, neutralizing their magic to save them from the evil against which the Willimites preach—though, in fact, you would be working with a Healer, who would be blocking those powers. You would do this to as many nonessential Deryni as possible, especially women and children, who are not likely to be well known in their own rights. Such folk could relocate in places of safety and make new lives, disassociated from the stigma of being Deryni, until times were safer and they could be restored."

Revan was shaking his head by the time she finished.

"It's incredible! It could never work! I've been in the service of Deryni all my life. Who would believe it? Who would believe *me?*"

"We've thought of a way. Would you like me to tell you?"

By the time she had outlined further details of their

159

plan, Revan's disbelief had been transformed to awed discipleship.

"I think it *could* work, my lady," he said, hardly daring to speak aloud. "And—you really think that I could do it?"

"I do."

Revan swallowed noisily, his throat working with emotion, then awkwardly slipped to his knees at her feet, took her hand, and pressed it to his lips in homage.

"Then, I am your man, my lady, as I have always been," he whispered.

"Thank you, Revan," she breathed, touching her free hand lightly to his head and reaching with her mind. "Now, come and sit beside me again, and we shall talk further. We have many preparations to make."

His eyes took on a glassy look as he rose and moved back onto the bench, still clasping her hand.

"That's right," she murmured. "Relax and let me hold your mind, as we have done before. And for your own safety, remember nothing consciously of what we shall discuss unless you are with Rhys or me."

Later that evening, Evaine and Rhys returned to Valoret, well pleased with what had been started at Sheele that afternoon with Revan, instrument of their plan, though their hearts ached for Revan the man. Their progress was duly reported to the Camberian Council, and further plans were set in motion as the days wheeled on.

And at Sheele, young Revan almost overnight found himself violently enamored of a young woman of the village named Finella, who mysteriously sickened within weeks of when Revan first met her, and whose health steadily declined, even under the ministrations of Rhys, who came at Revan's urgent call.

Rhys tended the young woman diligently, aided by his wife and overseen anxiously by Revan, who had stated his intention to marry the girl at Pentecost; but despite all that Rhys could do, his efforts wrought little change in Finella. And on the day when poor Finella's coffin was lowered into the ground—filled with rocks, the girl having been spirited away the night before with new memories and enough money to make a start in another village—something seemed to snap in Revan's mind.

"You could have saved her!" Revan screamed, in front of several dozen guests who had gathered at Sheele with Rhys and Evaine to celebrate the Feast of Easter. "You let her die, you Deryni monster! You could have saved her, but you let her die! You killed her!"

Ripping off the badge of his service to the household of Rhys Thuryn, he trampled it on the floor at his master's feet and ran weeping from the hall. Evaine tried lamely to explain to her dinner guests of mixed humans and Deryni that it had not been at all as Revan claimed; that he had become increasingly deranged as Finella's illness progressed, despite Rhys's efforts to effect a cure of either the girl or Revan himself—but the mood was ruined, and so was dinner. What had started out as a festive celebration ended very early, almost as the last course was removed from the table.

By the following week, news of the incident had spread through all the Court—for Evaine had made certain to include among her Easter guests certain minor personages of the Court who could be counted upon to repeat what they had seen and heard. By Lady Day, the story had been embellished to the point that Rhys was now being rumored to have deliberately let Revan's young lady die, perhaps for motives of jealousy. Rhys had feared that Revan would leave his service, if he married Finella and started a family of his own. No, Rhys had himself wanted Finella, but had been spurned by the girl in favor of Revan—and *that* was why Rhys had let her die. After all, was Rhys not Deryni, for all that he was a Healer? Had not Bishop Hubert preached in a sermon of only a few weeks ago that Deryni were treacherous, that eventually, even the truest-seeming of them would revert to type, like Imre?

As the coronation approached, word began to trickle in of Revan. By mid-May, it was learned that he had surfaced with a band of neo-Willimite brethren in the hills east of Valoret. Rumor had it that he was being viewed by his new colleagues as something of a madman; that he spent a great deal of time alone on a mountaintop conversing with a large bluestone boulder; that he ate but sparingly and spoke hardly at all, save in his meditations. No one seemed to have any doubt that Revan's defection was anything other than the action of a man driven to dementia by the persecution of his Deryni masters.

Bishop Hubert, on hearing the news, preached a sermon in the chapel royal on the conversion of Saul on the road to Damascus, and hinted very strongly that humans who still served Deryni should pray for a conversion such as Paul's.

And while Revan was establishing his cover with the Willimites, readying himself to become a new voice in the wilderness, his temporarily disremembered allies were continuing to develop the Deryni facets of this jewel of race salvation. To that end, Jaffray pursued the contacts for arranging the required meeting of Rhys with Emrys and Queron.

For the site of their meeting, he chose Saint Neot's, the Gabrilite monastery and school where Dom Emrys ruled as Abbot, famed for uncounted generations as a center for Deryni learning and Healer training. Since Saint Neot's was part of the old ecclesiastical Portal network established by the Deryni clergy centuries before, it was easily accessible not only to Rhys and Camber, who would be coming from Grecotha, but to Jaffray, who must make the initial arrangements with Emrys and, through Emrys, with Queron. Most of the cathedrals and major religious houses with present or former Deryni connections had at least one Transfer Portal on the premises, even if their current communities did not always know of their existence or whereabouts.

Jaffray took advantage of that network, winking across the Portal link from his own chapel at Valoret to the semi-public Portal which any Deryni clergyman might use, in the sacristy of Saint Neot's abbey church, at an hour when he had a fair expectation of finding Emrys alone at meditations. The Gabrilites kept perpetual vigil before their famous shrine of Saint Gabriel and the Lady, in a rear chapel of the abbey church which was accessible to outside visitors as well as the brethren and students. Emrys had kept the midnight vigil as the week turned to the Sabbath for as long as Jaffray had known him, and he had not changed his routine in the intervening years, as Jaffray discovered.

Their meeting was warm, if brief. Finding Emrys before the Lady's shrine as he had hoped, Jaffray gave his old colleague fair greeting and then took several minutes to renew their friendship in mindlink before turning to the reason for his visit. The information passed was sparse, but Jaffray did reveal that it was important council business which Rhys felt need to bring to Emrys and Queron.

He left it to Emrys to infer that the meeting might involve Healer's business as well as that of the council.

Emrys was given the responsibility for ensuring Queron's participation in the meeting, for Jaffray feared that the visit of a Deryni Primate of Gwynedd to the principal shrine of a Deryni saint might raise unwelcome questions; Jaffray was already walking a precarious enough balance as the only Deryni member of the regency council, without giving the regents more cause for suspicion. Besides, Jaffray preferred not to reveal his Camberian Council connections to Queron yet.

Several weeks were therefore required to arrange the actual meeting at Saint Neot's, since there was no Portal at Dolban and ordinary messengers must be sent back and forth with Emrys's written words. Queron was not particularly cooperative in the beginning, either, requiring several exchanges before he could be induced to come only on the strength of what Emrys had leave to tell him. Though he eventually agreed and arrived on the appointed day, he was suspicious and a little nervous that Alister Cullen, who was not a Healer, would also be there. Nor could Emrys reassure him on that point, for even Emrys did not know why Rhys wished to bring a non-Healer to the meeting; and he could not tell Queron of Alister's Camberian Council connection. The abbot could speculate, but he knew little for certain. Jaffray had not disclosed the reason for Alister's inclusion, and Emrys had not asked.

The appointed day dawned brisk but clear in Grecotha, a brilliant mid-April morning marked by fresh-scoured skies and the heady perfume of a dozen different flowers in Camber's episcopal gardens. After Mass and a light breakfast, he and Rhys climbed the one hundred twenty-seven steps of Queen Sinead's Watch in silence. Rhys was as apprehensive as Camber had ever seen him at the prospect of presuming to instruct Emrys, his former master at Saint Neot's, and the almost legendary Queron Kinevan.

Both men squinted against the brightness as they emerged in the sunlight of the open rampart walk, pausing to let their eyes adjust again when they had ducked under the timbered roof of the tower chamber. Rhys fidgeted uneasily in the doorway, framed green-mantled against the April sky, as Camber knelt to trace out the perimeter of one of the floor tiles in the northeast corner.

"I wish I knew how you keep track of that," Rhys said, making nervous small talk as Camber stood and adjusted the white sash binding the waist of his bishop's cassock. "Oh, I know the theory, but I can't help being suspicious of a Portal that moves—and that I can't feel."

Chuckling a little to put Rhys at his ease, Camber stepped onto the square he had traced and held out a hand for Rhys to join him.

"Well, *I* can feel it—and that's what matters this morning, isn't it? I know what your problem is, though. You just don't like the idea of having to relinquish control to use it." He smiled as he laid his hands on the younger man's shoulders and drew him onto the square in front of him. "You Healers are all alike. You always want to run things."

"Now, that's a perverse thing to say!" Rhys replied, with a hearty indignation which gave lie to the pulse racing wildly in his throat. "On the other hand," he added with a deep breath, "it's occasionally good to let someone else take over." He turned to look at Camber squarely, took another deep breath and let it out with a sigh.

"Listen, this is going to be very difficult, and not just for me," he said softly. "You're not a Healer, and they're the best. Are you sure you want to risk—"

Camber shook his head. "No, I'm not sure at all. But I won't send you into that one alone, Rhys. I'll take the risk. It won't be the first time."

"No, it won't."

"Then, stop worrying. They're not your teachers anymore. You know something that they don't know how to do, no matter how good they are at anything else. Remember that."

"I'll try."

With a smile, Camber laid his arm around the Healer's shoulder once more and took a deep, relaxing breath, let it out, gathering the energies close about the two of them as he felt Rhys slipping into familiar rapport to be carried through. Visualizing their destination, he made the proper mental shift and warped the energies just—so.

Instantly they were standing almost in darkness before a small but incredibly detailed vesting altar of ivory, the shadows relieved only by the flicker of a lone vigil light on the wall above. As they turned, Emrys and then Queron stepped from the shadows.

"Ah, Dom Emrys, Dom Queron," Camber murmured,

164

taking his cue from Emrys's calm expression and inclining his head slightly in greeting.

"Welcome to Saint Neot's, Your Grace," Emrys said softly, cool hand taking Camber's to kiss the bishop's amethyst. "And, Lord Rhys, I am pleased to see you again, after so many years. I hear that you have done well in the world."

The old Healer appeared fragile and almost ghostlike in the dim light, skinny Gabrilite braid all but invisible against the bright white of his robes. The eyes, too, were almost colorless, glinting like shards of sunset frost in the thin, ascetic face. Only the Healer's badge on the left side of his chest interrupted the stark play of white on white.

Queron, as the last time Camber had seen him, wore the grey habit of the Servants of Saint Camber, though he had donned a Healer's mantle for the occasion, of a more subdued green than the one Rhys wore. As Rhys exchanged nervous bows with the two men, Camber suddenly realized that Queron looked almost as tense as Rhys; this was going to be far from easy for any of them. He was glad for the calming refuge of Emrys's mental presence as the old man smiled gently and beckoned them toward the sacristy door.

"Come, my lords. I've provided a warded and secure room for our discussion," he said, unlatching the door and pushing it back with an almost transparent hand. "And since I believe Bishop Cullen has not been to Saint Neot's before, I thought we might guide him through a short tour of the abbey before settling down to work. Is something wrong, Rhys?" he finished, turning to cock his head at the obviously dismayed Rhys.

"Well, it's just that we have important business to dis—"

"And you think that you are in a suitable frame of mind to do so?" Emrys returned, brushing one of Rhys's hands with a gentle feathertouch. "You're tied in knots, son. Where is the discipline I taught you? Granted, it has been many years, but you cannot have forgotten everything you learned. By your reputation alone, I know better than that."

Suitably chastened, and more than a little embarrassed to have been corrected in front of Queron, Rhys managed to murmur an appropriate apology. Camber, sympathetic but not *too* sympathetic, merely allowed himself a small, gruff Alister smile as he turned his attention on the abbot. He had noted, during Rhys's outburst, that Queron had used the time to make a concerted effort to reduce his own uneasiness. Queron, too, was feeling the pressure of the unknown. Perhaps he was not as formidable an opponent as they had feared.

"Thank you for saying that, Dom Emrys," Camber said with a dry chuckle. "I've been trying to get him to relax since he came to me last night—though with little more success than you seem to have had with Dom Queron."

He ignored the sharp look which the other Healer gave him and went blithely on, as if he had noticed nothing.

"As you are aware, I have little knowledge of Healer's training, though I have heard much about it from Rhys. I should be quite interested in seeing a little of it while I am here. In fact, should your brethren think that the true reason for my visit, so much the better."

"My thought, precisely," Emrys agreed, with a glance at Queron and a slight inclination of his head. "If Your Grace will accompany me, then, I will be pleased to show you some of the more important aspects of our community here. Queron, Rhys." His tone was that of master to wayward students. "I shall expect both of you to be in better control by the time we are ready for serious discussion."

With no more comment than that, he was guiding Camber out of the sacristy with one pale hand at the bishop's elbow, already pointing out the detailing of a particularly fine mosaic of the Archangel Gabriel on the wall just outside.

Rhys and Queron, after an exchange of wary glances, retreated into their respective modes of calming and followed mutely behind.

CHAPTER TWELVE

Show new signs, and make other strange wonders.
                                    —Ecclesiasticus 36:6

To the left Emrys led them from the sacristy, following a narrow ambulatory aisle *jesh*-wise around the apse to avoid crossing the sanctuary—for whisper-soft chanting within told of devotions being conducted in the choir. They paused briefly at the eastern end of the apse, directly behind the high altar, and there Emrys bade Camber peer through a watch hole pierced in the carving of the reredos.

His first, overwhelming impression was of white. White marble and alabaster paved and faced the entire expanse of choir, nave, and what he could see of the transept arms extending north and south. Even the wood of the choir stalls and the benches in the nave beyond was bleached to an almost colorless finish. No rood screen separated choir from nave in this monastic church, so his view was unobstructed all the way to the great western doors and the graceful rose window above, done in rich azures and golds. There, just to the right of a doorway which must lead to Saint Neot's famous belltower, a play of blue-filtered sunlight told of the Lady Chapel where the Order kept their perpetual vigil before the Sacrament. Even now, he could discern a white-cowled figure moving slowly down the center aisle from that chapel.

The figure approached between the rows of backless benches with their brightly tapestried kneeling cushions tucked precisely beneath, quietly joining the dozen or so brethren already bowed in prayer in the choir. Each of the men wore the single braid of Gabrilite priesthood falling along the hood cast back on his shoulders, and each also bore the badge of an ecclesiastical Healer on the left

167

shoulder of his habit, like Emrys: a green, open-palmed hand pierced by a white star of eight equal points—the reverse of the white hand pierced with green which Rhys wore on his Healer's mantle.

As though the arrival of the last man had been a signal, the entire company stood and began to sing, alternating the verses back and forth between the two halves of the choir.

"Adsum, Domine. . . ."

Here am I, Lord. . . .

Thou hast granted me the grace to Heal men's bodies.

Here am I, Lord. . . .

Thou hast blessed me with the Sight to See men's souls.

"Here am I, Lord. . . .

Thou hast given me the might to bend the will of others.

O Lord, grant strength and wisdom to wield all these gifts.

Only as Thy will wouldst have me serve. . . .

The hymn was the ancient and haunting *Adsum Domine,* heartstone of the ethical precepts which had governed the conduct of lay and ecclesiastical Healers for nearly as long as there had been Healers among the Deryni. Only once before had Camber heard it sung, though he had read the words a dozen times or more, and knew them all by heart. Rhys's rich baritone had managed to convey only a little of what could be in the singing.

Now the voices of the Healer-priests wove spine-tingling harmonics which touched at deeper chords within his being, seeking but never quite finding in Camber those differences which made some men Healers and some not.

The singers had reached the Versicle, the pivot-point of all the Healer's conscience and mystical experience, and for just a moment, Camber let himself slip back to Rhys's singing—saw in his mind's eye a sacred circle in a tower room at Sheele, on the night Evaine had given birth to her second son. Even before his coming into the world, they had known that the child Tieg would be a Healer like his father.

That night, an awed Camber had watched with Evaine and Joram and Jebediah as Rhys held the newborn Tieg in his arms and sang the song the monks now sang, dedicating his son to the service of his Healing patrimony and to the Ancient Powers whom they had all called to witness by their joint invocation.

The voice in Camber's memory blended with those of Emrys's monks as the *Dominus lucis* floated in the stillness.

"Dominus lucis me dixit, Ecce. . . ."
The Lord of Light said unto me, Behold:
Thou art My chosen child, My gift to man.
Before the daystar, long before thou wast in mother-womb,
thy soul was sealed to Me for all time out of mind.
Thou art My Healing hand upon this world,
Mine instrument of life and Healing might.
To thee I give the breath of Healing power,
the awesome, darkling secrets of the wood and vale and earth.
I give thee all these gifts that thou mayst know My love:
Use all in service of the ease of man and beast.
Be cleansing fire to purify corruption,
a pool of sleep to bring surcease from pain.
Keep close within thy heart all secrets given,
as safe as said in shriving, and as sacred.
Nor shall thy Sight be used for revelation,
unless the other's mind be freely offered.
With consecrated hands, make whole the broken.
With consecrated soul, reach out and give My peace. . . .

Camber felt Rhys's presence close at his shoulder as the singers shifted into the final Antiphon, and knew that his son-in-law had remembered that other time and was feeling Camber's wonder at the mysteries hinted in the song. A wave of longing swept through him then, a tightening of chest and throat which nearly brought tears to his eyes. But before he could be completely caught up, Emrys was touching his arm in understanding and beginning to move him gently but firmly on along the ambulatory aisle.

Suddenly he knew, with an indescribable certainty, that the abbot had read and understood that bereft sense of not belonging which had welled up all unbidden in Camber at the magic of the hymn—and it was not through any Deryni Sight, for Emrys would not have dreamed of intruding, and Camber was closely shielded to all but Rhys.

Gratefully, Camber fell in behind the abbot and fixed his attention on the swaying white braid, stilling his sense of loss and taking in the calm which now radiated both from Emrys and, surprisingly, from Rhys and Queron, who followed. Peace became an almost tangible presence surrounding all of them.

The hymn's final verse floated with eerie majesty on the incense-leavened air as they went out through a side door.

Here am I, Lord. . . .
All my talents at Thy feet I lay.
Here am I, Lord. . . .
Thou art the One Creator of all things.
Thou art the Omnipartite One Who ruleth Light and Shade,
Giver of Life and Gift of Life Thyself.
Here am I, Lord. . . .
All my being bound unto Thy will.
Here am I, Lord. . . .
Sealed unto Thy service, girt with strength to save or slay.
Guide and guard Thy servant, Lord, from all temptation,
That honor may be spotless and my Gift unstained. . . .

They exited into a narrow slype which led between the transept and a round building which Camber surmised must be the chapter house. Joram had once likened Saint Neot's chapter house to the ruined temple they had discovered under Grecotha, so Camber casually expressed an interest in the building to Emrys, as the four of them emerged in the eastern cloister walk. The abbot obliged his visitors by leading them into the center of the cloister garth, presenting an overview of the general groundplan before they went inside.

Aside from the church itself, which the Gabrilites referred to as their chapel, though it was larger than any chapel Camber had ever seen, the chapter house clearly dominated the rest of the monastic complex. Its graceful dome of sky-blue faience gleamed clean and pristine in the morning sun, matching those of the chapel itself—for, indeed, Saint Neot's was famous for its multiple domes. The overall effect was of an extension of the southern transept to include the chapter house. On the chapel, Camber could count six—no, seven—domes, and knew that there were at least four more that he could not see

—and the chapter house made twelve, a sacred number.

Other details also became apparent from this close proximity, among them the imprint of a golden Gabrilite cross on each faience tile of the domes, equal arms touching a solar ring at the four quarters, the arms flaring slightly at the ends. That motif and others which seemed somewhat familiar were repeated in the carving of the heavy bronze doors framing the entry portico of the chapter house—subtle, but there for those who knew what to look for. The overall impression rather confirmed his suspicion that the origins of the Gabrilites, like the Deryni themselves, stretched back much farther in history than most folk assumed. While it was not much discussed, especially among the more orthodox clergy, those who studied such things were well aware that many faiths besides Christianity had contributed to the body of knowledge which was the legacy of Deryni magic.

But he would ask Rhys more about the symbols, once they were alone. He had sensed Rhys' eager interest, but also his warning, as the Healer became aware of the sweep of Camber's scrutiny. No, this was not a safe subject for Alister to explore.

And so he stood wide-eyed and only Alister-interested while Emrys pointed out the more mundane features of the monastic complex, nodding knowledgeably as he was shown the location of the reception rooms and refectory and kitchen ranges along the southern side of the cloister.

The brothers' sleeping quarters lay along the western perimeter, both at ground level and above; but unlike many cloistered orders, the Gabrilites provided separate sleeping cells for their brethren rather than dormitories, privacy being thought essential to the kind of mental and spiritual discipline expected of their company. The students, Emrys explained, were lodged around a second cloister beyond the refectory range and chapter house. There lay the formal classrooms and training chambers, and also their own destination.

First, though, Emrys knew that Bishop Cullen would wish to see the inside of the chapter house, though he feared that the usual impact of the chamber would suffer a little, as it was undergoing its twice-weekly cleaning just now.

As they approached the heavy bronze doors, Camber was able to take a closer, if brief, look at the symbols and scenes carved there and to file them away in his memory for future contemplation. Feigning ignorance of what he saw, he made no comment other than to admire the workmanship, but he could feel Rhys's fascination meshing with his own as they followed Emrys through the open doorway.

If the outside of Saint Neot's held revelations, entering the chapter house conveyed more the sense of a psychic shock, albeit a pleasant one—like being suddenly transported into a cave-chilled jar carved of aquamarine and gold: in honor of the Archangel Gabriel, whose color was blue and whose element was water, Emrys informed his visitors. Cool blue light filtered through the tinted clerestory windows like an airy counterpart of the water which Gabriel ruled, engulfing all in a shifting whirlpool of sky-hue. A brighter shaft of light lanced through a clear-glassed skylight in the center of the dome—which was the same pale blue faience as the outside, though strewn with tiny, eight-pointed stars instead of solar crosses—and its slant-beamed radiance transformed the white marble tiles of the floor to creamy gold where it touched.

A waist-high cube of pale, polished bluestone, devoid of any decoration, occupied the exact center of the chamber, surrounded by white-robed brethren scrubbing the floor on hands and knees, habits kilted up between their legs. Along the perimeter, other brothers moved among the three tiers of wooden benches with polishing cloths, wiping fragrant cedar oil into the deep carving and buffing the wood to a warm, mellow finish.

The scent of the oil conjured poignant memories for the Alister part of Camber, momentarily whisking him back to another place and time, when his being and his faith had been newer and less complicated—but then reality quickly tugged him back to Saint Neot's with a snap. Something odd about the bluestone cube. . . .

Whatever it was, he quickly realized that Rhys had sensed it, too—a somehow familiar perception, but one which the Healer had not known how to recognize when last he had been at Saint Neot's as a student. With a mental nudge of reassurance for Rhys's sake, Camber reached toward the cube with his mind, outwardly only watching the monks and listening to Emrys's low-voiced commentary.

He soon realized that his uneasiness had been born of no sinister connection, but only of the perception of power unexpected, clashing softly against his shields to set men-

172

tal warnings resounding. The chunk of bluestone was a power focus, likely used by the Gabrilites at Chapter meditations much as the Michaelines were trained to focus on a flame or the Sword of Saint Michael for their special workings. Residual power, neither good nor evil, radiated from the cube; but it was only undirected power. There was nothing to beware in that, especially in the hands of Gabrilites. It reminded him of the black and white cube altar in the ruins beneath Grecotha—and that, he knew, was a power nexus. He wondered whether there was a connection.

Breathing a little sigh both of relief and continued curiosity, he blinked and made complete his return to time and place, the scent of cedar oil still strong in his nostrils.

"Is anything wrong, Your Grace?" the old Healer was asking softly.

He found Emrys staring at him curiously, the pale face otherwise unreadable. Some of the brothers had slowed their cleaning and were glancing at him surreptitiously, recognizing the rank betokened by his purple cloak and white sash, even if they did not know his particular identity.

With a shake of his head, Camber seized on the pungent cedar smell as an excuse for his psychic wanderings.

"Nay, Father, I had a flash of my own youth, that's all. We used cedar oil for the wood at Cheltham. I was reminded of my novitiate."

"Ah." Emrys nodded wisely. " 'Tis strange, is it not, how one returns to such memories more and more, as age advances? My earliest training was in another tradition than either Gabrilite or Michaeline, and it was sandalwood oil which used to take me back. Cedar is better, though, I think. We find that the scent deters moths. But, come. We should not distract these good brothers in their work. Some of the younger ones are still learning the discipline of manual labor. All share equally here—ordained priest and Healer, as well as novice, apprentice, and student. Is it so among your Michaelines?"

It was, though not as fully as among the Gabrilites, Camber allowed, as they continued on past the chapter house and through a range of domestic buildings to the south and east. But though he and Emrys then launched into a lively discussion of the philosophical differences between the two orders, Camber did not pursue the seemingly offhand reference Emrys had made to training in a different tradition, especially in front of Queron. The more he learned about the Gabrilites, the clearer it became that there was much he did not know about them and, especially, their reverend abbot. He resolved to ask Evaine about it. Perhaps she had come upon information which could elucidate the matter further.

They moved along the students' cloister walk until they came upon a group of young boys sitting under a tree in the cloister garth, their plain white tunics identifying them as students. A youngish looking man in the habit and braid of a Gabrilite priest was lecturing them softly, though his voice did not carry to where Camber and Emrys paused to watch. Camber wondered whether it was by design.

"These are some of our ten and eleven year olds in general training," Emrys murmured. "They have been here only about four months. Dom Tivar is a weapons master, among other specialties, but so far he has not allowed any of them even to touch a weapon. First they must learn to sense an opponent's moves through their Sight—even a Deryni opponent. But of course you Michaelines have much the same kind of schooling in this regard."

"Yes, we do."

Even as he replied, the boys were scrambling to their feet at some unknown signal and pairing off to practice, closing their eyes and beginning to move slowly through the routine of a fighting exercise, swaying and dipping and blocking each other's blows with hands and forearms which seemed almost to sense the movements by themselves. Camber had done similar exercises as a young man, and his dual awareness as Camber-Alister could appreciate the training even more than he alone.

"Ah, yes, I remember that one—though we did it a little differently at Cheltham," he added. "Do you remember the bruises, once the exercises were brought up to speed? Or, do Healers receive the same martial training?"

"I did not, but many do." Emrys smiled. "Come and I'll show you some more direct Healer's training, if you'd like. This will be very familiar to Rhys, I'm sure."

They strolled on around an angle of the cloister walk and paused again just outside a latticework door opening off the corridor. Inside, a boy of twelve or fourteen lay motionless on a cot with his head toward the door. A Gabrilite Healer sat on a stool at the boy's head with his back to them. His fine, unlined hands were held just a little way apart from the boy's temples as he spoke in a soft, lulling monotone.

"That's good, Simonn. Relax every muscle. You know how. Very good. Now, center in and let yourself slowly become aware of the blood whispering through your veins. Feel the pulsebeat. Now be aware of your heart pumping that blood. It's beating a little faster than it needs to, but you can slow it, if you really want to. Give it a try . . .

"No, you're trying too hard, son. Relax. Don't *make* it happen; *let* it happen. Now, take a deep breath and let it all the way out. Again. Now you're getting it. That's right. This is the way every Healer has to start—learning to control his own body before he can control others'. Good. Now, let's slip a little deeper and go on to other awarenesses. Deeper . . . deeper . . ."

And as the man spoke, Camber was aware of Rhys's appreciation for what they were seeing, sensed the Healer's own flash of memory to a time when another boy had lain on a similar cot and learned to rule his body in precisely the same manner as this boy was learning.

A little while longer they watched. Then, after only a short walk down another corridor, Emrys paused before a door and pushed it ajar. Beyond a short passageway lay a dim chamber lit only by a brace of candles on a small cabinet with many drawers. Camber scanned quickly as the others came into the room behind him.

The walls were hung with heavy drapes of a rich, midnight-blue, almost black, the ceiling likewise swathed in thick fabric which drank the sound. A narrow couch occupied the approximate center of the room, with two well-padded chairs facing it on one side. Camber guessed that the room was ordinarily intended either for solitary meditations or else for paired workings. He sensed a cold fireplace behind the hangings on the left, and a small window directly opposite, for ventilation, though the window was now shuttered.

Underfoot was a carpet of Kheldish weave, but no design had been worked into this piece to distract attention. Its dark, midnight hue swallowed up visual sensation as it swallowed up most sound. Camber did not even hear the second door close behind Emrys as he joined them.

"Being abbot has certain undeniable advantages, Your Grace," the old man murmured, white face and robe stark against the darkness of the room. "This is my personal meditation and Healing chamber. Rhys, I assume that you will wish us warded for our discussion?"

"Please."

With a slight inclination of his head, Emrys drew breath and raised his hands to either side of his head at shoulder-level, his eyes shuttering for just an instant as he turned the palms slightly inward. As the old man exhaled, Camber felt the tingle of energy rising around them, the unmistakable prickling of a ward circle strongly in evidence just at the edges of the room.

Surprised at the ease with which Emrys had done that, Camber drew in his own shields until they no longer collided with the shields of the warding circle, moving to one of the chairs as Emrys casually lowered his hands and took a place on the couch with Queron. Rhys sat uneasily in the chair beside Camber's.

"My lords, we are now warded against both sound and psychic intrusion. Rhys, I am told that it was you who requested this meeting?"

"Just a moment." Queron glanced at all of them with only partially veiled hostility. "Emrys, you didn't mention that. Who is Rhys to request a meeting of the four of us? And if this is Healer's business, why is Bishop Cullen present?" He glanced at Camber. "I mean no disrespect to your office, but there are certain confidences of our vocation which we usually do not share with non-Healers, even other Deryni."

Rhys sighed and moistened his lips with the tip of his tongue. Camber could sense his underlying anxiety as he faced the older Healer, though he knew that even Queron could not penetrate Rhys's precise control at this level.

"Your last statement is certainly correct, Dom Queron." Rhys drew a deep breath. "However, I have requested this meeting not only as Healer to other Healers, but under the seal of the confessional, to which Father Alister, as my confessor, is already sworn. I must charge you and Dom Emrys likewise to seal it so, on your office as priests, or I may not tell you more. Have I your pledge?"

Queron froze for an instant, only the intense brown eyes widening just a little in the otherwise well-schooled face. Then he glanced at Emrys, who nodded minutely, returned his attention to Rhys and gave a curt nod of assent.

"Thank you," Rhys breathed. Camber knew he was steeling himself for the first revelation.

"Tell me, Dom Queron, what do you know of the Camberian Council?"

Queron's jaw dropped and a tiny intake of breath marred his previous composure before he could regain control.

"Then, it *does* exist!" Queron breathed. "All these years, I've *dreamed*—but. . . ."

He glanced at all of them as he recovered himself, much taken aback as he realized that even Emrys had not reacted to Rhys's question.

"Emrys, you knew of this?"

"Of the Council's existence, yes."

"Are you a member, then?"

"Let us name me *amicus concilium,*" the old man replied with a faint smile.

"But, you *knew* of it, then! And you did not tell me!"

"You did not ask me," Emrys replied. "Allow me also to reassure you that Rhys's by-now obvious connection with the Council is the extent of my knowledge of this present affair. I was asked by someone else, whose identity I may not reveal, to bring you here for a meeting with Rhys and Bishop Cullen. I have done so."

"I see." Queron turned that over in his mind, then looked squarely at Camber.

"And what of you, Your Grace? Are you also of the Council? It is understandable that Rhys should be a part of it, for he is husband to the Blessed Camber's daughter. But you—you did not even support his canonization. Are you now a member of the consortium named in his honor? Or was it in hypocrisy that you and Joram came to the shrine in February?"

"Bishop Cullen is here at the behest of the Council, the same as yourself," Rhys replied, before Camber could frame a suitably misleading response. "For now, I put it to you that he is present as an unbiased but interested fourth party, and because he has knowledge of what I am about to reveal to you."

"Which is?"

"I have discovered a new Healing function."

"Ah," Emrys breathed, nodding slowly.

Queron, his brows furrowed in question, glanced from Rhys to Camber to Emrys and then back to Rhys.

"A new Healing function? Of what sort? And why such

177

secrecy? Emrys, are you sure you know nothing of this?"

Emrys shook his head. "No more than you do, son. But I gather that Rhys is prepared to tell us of it, or he would not have asked us here. Rhys?"

"I would prefer to show you, rather than tell you, sir," Rhys said carefully. "As you may recall, Dom Queron once made that same request of a court convened to canonize my late father-in-law. As I hope to teach other Healers this working, I should like you to observe while I demonstrate on Dom Queron—provided, of course, that he is willing."

Queron had started at Rhys's words. Now he shifted in his seat, glancing at Emrys uneasily. "Emrys, would you allow this?"

"You need not be injured in order for me to demonstrate," Rhys responded immediately, Queron's apprehension on that count blatantly obvious. "The function is akin to what you worked with Guaire at the court, in that respect. I ask only that you give me the full cooperation which Guaire gave you, that you open completely and let me do what is necessary to demonstrate the effect. Father Alister will bear witness that what I propose will cause no permanent damage. I swear this by my powers of Sight and Healing. Nor is it painful—a little frightening, at worst. I will also give you what I would not ordinarily give with the practical use of this working, and that is the awareness and memory of what I have done, after it is accomplished. You may also follow the undoing."

"Well, you've succeeded in making it sound ominous," Queron replied, almost snappishly. He glanced again at Emrys, but got no support one way or the other, so he turned his attention on Camber.

"Your Grace, I would not ordinarily believe someone of your station party to anything untoward, but I am not entirely certain you understand our Healer's ethic. Is it your recommendation that I accede to this request?"

"I would not be here, if I did not," Camber replied truthfully.

"Emrys?"

The old man shrugged. "The decision must be yours, Queron. Rhys is clearly wary of your strength, yet he has chosen you as the most suitable subject for demonstration. You know his training and his reputation. You know, also, that I shall be monitoring. His request is unusual, but you yourself set the precedent. I *will* say that I trust both of these men implicitly."

"I see." Queron weighed all that had been said, then gave a short, explosive sigh.

"Well, it seems that I shall learn nothing more unless I agree. What must I do, Rhys? I warn you, after working only with my mostly human Camberians for so long, I am ill-accustomed to relinquishing complete control to another, especially when I do not know the expected result."

In spite of his own apprehension, Rhys could not resist a slight chuckle as he got to his feet. Camber suspected he was enjoying Queron's uneasiness just a little.

"I'm sorry, and I do commiserate, but I want to be certain that your foreknowledge doesn't affect the outcome. Also, I want it to work the first time. Now, would you prefer to remain sitting, or would you be most comfortable lying down?"

"I'll sit, thank you," Queron murmured, watching warily as Rhys came around behind the couch.

"As you wish. The important thing is that you relax as much as you can," he said easily. "The first time I did this, I had an unconscious patient who was also sedated, and the few other times, my subjects were consciously cooperative. Also, they were not Healers. I don't know whether that will make a difference, but at least I'd like to be assured that you won't panic and snap your shields shut on me."

"Come, now!" Queron began indignantly. "I have better control than that!"

"I'm sure you do," Rhys agreed. "So let's show me. Center in and relax."

He laid his hands lightly on Queron's shoulders and drew him back to lean against his chest, but the muscles beneath his fingers were rigid. He said nothing, but as Queron took a deep breath and let it out, he could feel the tension draining away, too. Deeper relaxation followed as Emrys laid one weightless hand on Queron's left wrist.

"That's better already," Rhys murmured, as he sensed a slow rapport building. "Why don't we all take a few deep breaths and center in now? Alister, come around to my other side and go with us, if you will. You've watched me do this before, so if we should have any problems, you'll have a unique vantage point as a trained non-Healer. Do you agree, Queron, Emrys?"

His dropping of the others' titles indicated that Rhys was fast regaining his equilibrium, now that he was actually working. Camber was already slipping into familiar rapport with Rhys as he laid his hand on the Healer's forearm.

Welcome, Rhys sent, as Camber settled into linkage.

"All right, let's all go deeper. Queron, whatever you may feel, don't resist. That's right. Take another deep breath and let yourself go down another level."

As Queron's eyelids fluttered and then closed, the rapport extended until his mind was like a still, clear pool awaiting the ripple of another's touch, the other poised quiet but expectant on the bank. Gently Rhys reached out with his mind, searching for the triggerpoint. When he touched it, the result was so abrupt that even Camber almost missed the transition.

One moment, Queron's considerable talents and potentials were spread there for all three of them to see, dormant and controlled by Rhys's touch, but there. The next moment, they were gone, and Queron was no more than human.

Startled in spite of himself, Camber drew back mind and hand simultaneously and watched Queron blink and tense for just an instant in sheer, naked panic. The Healer quickly regained just enough presence of mind to twist around and stare at Rhys in undisguised horror. Emrys looked equally stunned, the only time Camber had ever seen the elderly abbot's composure shaken.

"Sweet Jesu, what have you done to me!" Queron cried, beginning to tremble as he realized just what Rhys *had* done.

He clapped both hands to his temples and shook his head several times, unable to assimilate what he was feeling—or *not* feeling—then subsided weakly, to suck in deep, shuddering gasps, as if he had not the physical strength to cope with his helplessness. Instinctively, Emrys gathered him in the circle of his arms and held him close for comfort, glancing across at Rhys in shocked disbelief.

"You took away his powers!" Emrys whispered, his tone both accusatory and awed. "One of the most powerful Healers I have ever trained, and you made him human—Blind! You *can* undo it?"

"Of course."

"Then, do so. At once!"

Emrys's voice was soft, but it crackled with command, nonetheless, and Camber felt Rhys's surprise and consternation at the abbot's reaction. Without hesitation, Rhys drew Queron back against his chest, and slipped his hands to Queron's temples, accutely aware of Emrys's rapier mind right behind Rhys's, watching, guarding.

"Go deep, Queron," Rhys murmured, pausing for just an instant as Camber dropped into the linkage once again with him and Emrys. "And now, know what it is not to recognize what has happened to you."

With a deft mental touch, he nudged the memory of past power into temporary forgetfulness and allowed a moment for the knowledge to register on the most conscious levels, frighteningly aware of Emrys poised behind him, almost menacing in his protectiveness.

"And now I'll bring you back to your normal state, with all intact, remembering both the not-knowing and what it felt like to have your powers blocked. Relax, now, and feel it all return."

Camber watched in fascination as Rhys reached out once more and reset the triggerpoint, relinquishing control and backing out hastily as the other two also withdrew. Queron's shields rebounded into place with an almost audible snap, nearly brushing them all with the force of the return.

Queron blinked and sat up abruptly, took a few deep breaths, then looked slowly at Rhys coming around to take his seat again. In those first instants of recovery, Queron was taking inventory, as all Deryni adepts learned at a very early age, re-establishing balance as he would have done after any dangerous magical operation and assessing for hidden triggers or controls which might have been left behind.

After a few seconds during which no one dared breathe a word or move, Queron gave a little sigh and shook his head just a trifle wistfully.

"Whew, I'll no more have my reputation, if that gets out." He rubbed a still trembling hand over his ashen face.

"Are you all right?" Emrys demanded.

"Yes, I'm fine."

"Are you sure?"

"As sure as I can be, after *that*."

He gave another little shudder, then turned to look at Camber, still sitting attentively to his right.

"And you, Alister—you *will* forgive the familiarity, I hope?"

"Of course."

"Thank you. I—have to say that despite all the other surprises of the past little while, I was pleasantly surprised at the strength of your—presence. You have a sureness of touch that one seldom finds in one not Healer-trained. I'm amazed that your reputation has you as a man reluctant to use his powers—or, is it convenient cover for the fact that you *are* of the Camberian Council, and now accustomed to working with the likes of Rhys, here?"

Camber managed to keep his Alister smile from becoming an uncharacteristic grin at the implied compliment —and real truth—though he chose his words carefully.

"Let us say that I have learned a great deal through my association with Rhys and his lovely wife and my secretary Joram," he replied easily. "As for the Council, yes, I am a member. And as you undoubtedly have guessed by now, the Council is very interested in you and Dom Emrys, especially if you can learn to do what Rhys has just done."

Queron's brow furowed. "You—the Council, that is —you see a practical application, then, for neutralizing a person's Deryni powers?"

"We believe it's a blocking rather than a neutralization," Rhys replied. "Granted, this would be a desperation possibility, but consider how selected individuals might be blocked and hidden away, safe from discovery as Deryni, once the persecutions start. And if it *is* a blocking, rather than a taking away of powers, then the Deryni potential should be passed on to the children, even if it should happen that the parents cannot be restored to knowledge, for some reason. Of course, preventing the persecutions in the first place is the better solution, but we can't count on that, given the present political situation."

Queron nodded, his equilibrium obviously returning.

"I fear you may be right. But—do you really think that Emrys and I can learn to do what you just did, on command and without preparation or detection? I've never heard of anyone doing that before."

"Neither have I, so I suppose we'll be breaking new ground."

Emrys, who had kept silent, once reassured of Queron's

182

return to full function, shook his head incredulously and folded his arms across his chest.

"I'm not certain I like the idea, Rhys. Is the Council truly behind this plan of yours?"

"They think it bears further study, at any rate," Rhys replied. He shifted his attention back to Queron. "How about it? Shall we do it again, so that Emrys can watch from my perspective instead of yours this time?"

Queron opened his mouth to speak, then swallowed with a visible gulp, though the sound was muffled in the heavily draped room.

"You *are* good at destroying a man's self-confidence, aren't you?" he murmured, controlling a shiver of apprehension. "Do you really know what you're asking? No, don't answer that. You're right, it should be me, so that Emrys can observe. No sense in *both* of us being set off balance."

Rhys grinned and glanced at Camber. "Healer's pride. You can bet that this is the last thing in the world that he wants to do right now, but he's going to do it anyway. Thank you, Queron."

"He need not do it on my account," Emrys said, laying a restraining hand on Queron's shoulder. "Why not give him a day or two to settle? Only God knows how hard that must have been on him."

"Not as hard as if we wait and I get to think more about it, without knowing how it's done," Queron interjected, shaking his head vigorously. "Let's do it now, Rhys, before I lose my nerve. Do you want me here?"

"Let's try the couch," Rhys said, getting up as Camber rose to make room for Queron to recline. "Lie down and really make yourself comfortable this time. I'll try to go more slowly, so Emrys can have a chance for deeper reading."

"Just don't go too slowly, or the suspense will have me gibbering," Queron said with a nervous grin, stretching his wiry frame on the couch and arranging his body for maximum relaxation as Rhys came around to sit on his left.

"And Alister," Queron added, "why don't you pull up a chair on my right and keep me from edging into hysteria while Emrys studies me like a prize beetle?" His voice held more than a hint of tension, and Camber realized he was deliberately using speech as a means to channel off some of it. "Emrys, you link with Rhys and try to figure out what he does."

Emrys looked dubious, but he came around and stood in the angle between Rhys and the head of the couch, resting one weightless hand on Rhys's shoulder. Camber laid his right hand over Queron's right, then watched as Rhys took the first of his centering breaths to begin easing into Healing mode. Matching his rate of descent with Rhys's, he extended to sense Queron's shields, felt them already beginning to collapse as Rhys began to work.

"Excellent," Rhys murmured, slipping his hands lightly along either side of Queron's head. His thumbs came to rest firmly on the temples, the long fingers threaded in the wiry, reddish-brown hair.

"Good. Now let's show Emrys what we did before, all right? Take another deep breath and let it out, and let the shields go with it. You know it's safe here, even though you know what's coming this time. Don't tense up. That's right, let go. I'm going to allow you to keep your awareness of what's happening, so you can describe it to Emrys, once it's done. That's right," he continued, as Queron closed his eyes.

"Now, Emrys, follow where I go, and watch what I do —watch carefully, or you'll miss it. It's—now."

And again, seeming even more quickly than he had done it the first time Camber witnessed the feat, Rhys reached out and gave that little wrench—and Queron was once more bereft of Sight. The eyelids trembled, but they did not open. Rhys glanced up quickly at Emrys.

The Master Healer's pale, unlined face had taken on a look of concentration such as Camber had never seen before. As Rhys withdrew his hands, making way for Emrys's more direct probe, Queron opened his eyes and hesitantly met Emrys's gaze, very uneasy, but with his panic in control this time. Rhys pulled back discreetly from all rapport, until finally Emrys sank to his knees beside the couch and turned to stare him full in the face, slowly shaking his head.

"I'm afraid I missed it again," Emrys murmured. "It's truly incredible. I saw it before, but I still can't believe it. He even let me read his memory, his sensations, of what you did before. None of it prepared me for this."

"It must be a frightening experience," Rhys agreed.

"You just—reached out and—twisted something," Emrys said, searching Rhys's golden eyes with his pale, colorless ones. "Don't you have any idea how you do it?"

"A little," Rhys admitted. "I've had my wife read me,

and Alister, and several others, but never another Healer. They could only give me hints. I was hoping that you would be able to see what I did." He sighed. "Emrys, if you or Queron can't learn this, I'm not sure it can be learned. Maybe this is to Healers what Healing is to other Deryni."

"Well, let's not jump to conclusions, son. No one said anything about not being able to learn it," Emrys retorted, sounding almost a bit annoyed, though Camber could not be sure. "I simply wasn't watching closely enough; and Queron was in no position to watch." He glanced at Queron, who was studying them all tensely from his frozen position on the couch. "Remove the block again, and let's take another crack at it. Alister, you watch this, too. A Michaeline point of view could be very useful. I may be missing something entirely obvious."

Bringing his hands to Queron's head again, Rhys took another deep breath and let the linkage settle in with Emrys and Camber, deftly guiding both of them to the location where he thought the function was occurring. With a reassuring smile at Queron, projecting what he hoped was his best bedside manner, he reached out mentally and took Queron down as easily as if he were dealing with a human child of no training whatsoever. All trace of the formerly magnificent Healer was undetectable.

Then, as he had done before, he shifted that ineffable something—and Queron was restored. Emrys, like Camber, could only shake his head.

"Damn, I missed it," Emrys whispered, almost to himself. "Do it again?"

And Rhys did.

He did it to Queron. He did it, after several more repeats, to Emrys. He did it as slowly as he could to each of them, while the other watched and tried to learn. He did it to each of them while in an almost normal state, and even while resisting. His only limitation seemed to be the necessity for physical contact between Rhys and his subject—but then, that was a limitation under which Healers had always had to work. The laying on of hands was an established requisite for the Healer's vocation.

He did it to two different student Healers, leaving their memories blocked after it was over. He even, as Emrys's suggestion and Queron's exasperated agreement, did it with Queron sedated to the eyeballs, as Gregory had been the first time. He did not do it to Camber, but he explained that by saying that at least one of them should remain neutral and untouched by the phenomena, and that Alister was not a Healer. They accepted that.

But nothing seemed to work, so far as learning was concerned.

"I can only conclude," Emrys finally had to admit, while they sipped at wine, "that this may, indeed, be a talent which is unique to you, Rhys. We've certainly tried to learn it, but in this, I'm afraid you've far outstripped your teachers. I honestly don't know what to tell you."

Exhausted, Rhys stretched and craned his neck from side to side to ease cramped muscles. It was late afternoon, and other than the present wine and a slab of hard yellow cheese which Camber was slicing, all of them had been working without proper respite for far too many hours.

"Well, maybe our baptizer cult wasn't such a good idea, after all," he said, gnawing at the rind-end of a piece of cheese which Camber handed him. "If I'm the only one who can do this, we're going to have to rethink the whole concept. I said, somewhat facetiously, that I'd play the role of religious fanatic if there were no other way—and the stage is set for it to work, regardless of who takes that role—but I'd sure like to find an alternative."

"I'm sure we all would," Camber replied, passing cheese to Queron and then to Emrys. "We'll have to see what can be done."

Chapter Thirteen

Strangers conspired together against him, and maligned him in the wilderness.

—Ecclesiasticus 45:18

Unfortunately, the Council had no ready answer to Rhys's dilemma. A philosophical setting was being established by Revan's presence among the Willimites, ready for a Healer of Rhys's gifts to step in and activate it; and

Joram and Evaine, in turn, kept secretly feeding Revan more and more information to build his cover more tightly; but only time would tell whether Rhys's talent could be taught or whether he himself would be forced to assume the role of associate messiah. The slim chance also remained that the plan might never have to be set in motion.

But if Deryni were not yet setting drastic plans in motion, during the nearly four months between Cinhil's death and Alroy's coronation, others certainly were. Though the actions of the new regime were no more outwardly spectacular than those of the Camberian Council, they were no less precise and efficient, bespeaking serious long-term implications for those not in the regents' favor. No violence broke out during those early months of spring, much to the relief of Camber and his colleagues, but change was definitely in the air, and not to the advantage of Deryni.

One of the first and most insidious changes had to do with the army of Gwynedd. The regents well understood the importance of the army as a power base, and knew that here, among Jebediah's Michaeline-trained officers, human as well as Deryni, lay the most likely seeds for a successful Deryni revolt. It was therefore necessary that the army be cleansed of all taint of Deryni and Deryni sympathy.

Accordingly, the army underwent a massive reorganization at all levels of rank, with younger, less experienced officers and commanders—humans, all—gradually being phased in to replace Jebediah's seasoned troops. Helpless to prevent it, Jebediah watched his army change into a conscienceless tool which might eventually be used against him and his people. All he could do was to despair and try to find positions for his displaced men.

His task was not an easy one. Such a political climate as the regents were engendering did not bode well for men born and bred to live by the sword. Most Deryni nobles already had a surfeit of retainers, Deryni and human, and were disinclined to take on any more, especially in light of the apparently declining opportunities at Court for those of their race. Some were even letting men go, no longer anticipating the wherewithal to pay large numbers of private troops.

As for the human nobility, they were becoming increasingly reluctant to employ fighting men dismissed by the regents. Where once Michaeline military training had been prized for producing outstanding soldiers, tacticians and strategists, human and Deryni, now it became more and more a stigma connected with the old days of Deryni domination, a liability instead of an asset.

Fortunately for Gwynedd, Michaeline training also instilled discipline and responsibility, so the land was not plagued by bands of masterless Michaelines riding aimlessly through the countryside as their noble counterparts still did. Most actual members of the Michaeline Order, Deryni and human, simply retreated to the commanderie at Argoed, or one of the provincial houses in Gwynedd or without, there to hold themselves in readiness or, in some cases, to return to duties related to the teaching which had long been the other Michaeline specialty besides fighting. A few of them began organizing small, clandestine groups to preserve Deryni and Michaeline training and tradition, ready to become islands of refuge, if the worst came to pass.

It was only a matter of time, Jebediah guessed, before the Order would be suppressed as brutally as it had been in the last year of Imre's reign. The plans for the entire Order going underground again must be brought up to date and readied. At least until Alroy came of age and the regents were out of power, Michaelines would have to tread almost as carefully as Deryni, and Deryni Michaelines must be doubly careful.

Among those only Michaeline-trained, however, without the formal guidance and protection of the Order, there were far fewer options available, especially to men with families to support. As a consequence, many of these of Jebediah's officers simply disappeared, taking their families with them into Torenth, Forcinn, Llannedd, Howicce, and further lands where others unlike the Festils had left gentler memories of Deryni living among them, and where no one knew of their former Deryni connections. Human and Deryni alike, they went, taking some of the finest military minds of their generation out of Gwynedd forever. Jebediah regretted their going, but he could not, in conscience, bid them stay. At least in foreign lands, they might have a chance to survive unmolested.

Domestically, too, there were changes in Gwynedd, beginning slowly in the weeks right after Cinhil's death. Deryni household retainers and officers at Court, never really numerous even under Cinhil, were gradually given leave to return to their homes, as new human replacements were rotated in. Rhys and Evaine, most prominent of the Deryni formerly in Cinhil's personal service, were among the first to be dismissed, with the excuse that they deserved lives of their own after so many years of faithful service; but it was clear that if Deryni were no longer desired at Court, then the daughter and son-in-law of a Deryni saint were doubly unwelcome.

So Rhys and Evaine moved out of the quarters in the castle which they had occupied intermittently for the past twelve years and took up temporary residence at Rhys's townhouse in Valoret, the house he had bought as a young Healer and had maintained through the years as a hostelry for Healer's apprentices. Periodically, they travelled back to Sheele to see the two younger children and check on the new tutor they had hired. There, during one idyllic week in mid-May, they conceived their fourth child —a daughter, to be born early the following year. But they would not return to Sheele permanently so long as Camber still lodged in the archbishop's palace by the cathedral—and Camber could not leave until after the new king's coronation late in May.

Rhys's departure from Court left the post of royal physician vacant, but the regents chose to fill it with two human physicians. Humans, they said, could tend the young king's colds and other ailments just as well as Deryni, for in treatment of illnesses, magic had little edge over medical knowledge. It was in the Healing of physical injury that the Healers were clearly superior—and in that eventuality, the regents still had Tavis O'Neill.

Not that they wanted him. He was Deryni, after all. But given Prince Javan's proclivity for throwing tantrums which made him ill, whenever the possibility of Tavis' leaving was even mentioned, the regents decided it best to wait at least until after the coronation to resolve the issue. Javan must appear to be the picture of princely decorum on his brother's coronation day.

Besides, Tavis was among the most inoffensive of Deryni, never having shown evidence of any but Healing abilities for as long as anyone could remember. He might almost be human, were it not for the Healing gift. And as Bishop Hubert grudgingly pointed out, though the state of Tavis's soul might definitely be in question because of his Deryni birth, at least he was only using his magic for good, for Healing. And so Tavis stayed, if rather closely watched.

Archbishop Jaffray also stayed, even more closely watched—tolerated because he must be, at least for the present. However, the archibishop's aides, human and Deryni, and even minor members of the human Court were already warning him to guard himself—that the regents desired nothing less than his terminal illness or fatal accident, so that death might oust him from the regency council, since they could not.

But Jaffray flourished, despite their ill wishes, and continued to report regularly to the Camberian Council on the regents' latest plans, at least so far as these were discussed with the full council and not just among the regents themselves.

One topic which came to be discussed with alarming regularity, though nothing serious had yet come of it, was the regents' increasing awareness of the roving bands of young Deryni such as Camber and Joram had encountered on the road near Dolban. The regents did not know of that particular incident; but they knew of the one involving Hubert's brother. Fortunately, even Manfred had not been able to allege more than rowdiness and lewd conduct, but God knew what the summer might bring, after the excitement of the coronation was past and life settled down to a new and more restricted routine. The regents were already talking of harsher measures.

The problem was not unique to the Deryni, though it was most apparent among their numbers. The position of younger sons had never been a strong one, and traditionally these men had ended up as clerics or soldiers or, if they were fortunate enough to gain some kind of inheritance, rakes and men-about-town. Some few managed to win titles on their own merit, but opportunities for this kind of advancement were rare, especially in times of peace.

Under the guise of rotating appointments and positions at Court, the regents had shifted the human-Deryni ballance of the Court from a nearly half-and-half arrangement to more than three-quarters human, in scarcely three months. Deryni who had patiently waited their turns to serve the Crown under Cinhil, and who depended upon royal stipends for part of their income, now found themselves without employment and without preferment —yet they were still expected to fulfill their feudal obligations of military service, tithe and tax, and peacekeeping in their areas. This Michaelmas, at the end of the summer would see not only the traditional tithes come due, but also a set of new taxes. The regents had already informed the peerage, human and Deryni, to be prepared for that.

Such developments did not set well with many Deryni. And chief among those who were less discreet than they should have been about their dissatisfaction were the bands of Deryni younger sons who now began to roam the countryside, short of funds as well as bored and unfulfilled.

In fact, there were probably no more than one hundred or so of these impetuous young men, comprising perhaps half a dozen bands; but they were conspicuous for being Deryni, and most still had sufficient connections of family, name, and title to ensure that disciplinary action was never carried out. Who were local sheriffs and constables to argue with the sons of earls and barons? These officers complained, but they had not yet been given the authority to deal with the problem.

Increasingly, during the months before Alroy's coronation, Jaffray brought his fears to the Camberian Council, and increasingly, Davin and Ansel and Jesse reported that they were doing the best they could; but three young men and Gregory, their mentor, simply could not be everywhere at once, even by delegating some of their patrol duties to their sworn men. Little more could be done on the Council's behalf without risking exposure of their existence—and that, no human must ever know.

Alroy Bearand Brion Haldane was crowned on his twelfth birthday, in a festival to celebrate both the installation of the new king and the coming of spring after the long and dismal winter. His father had run an austere and conservative court, but the regents had decreed that this was not to be the case for young King Alroy. Amazing things had been planned for the amusement of the king and his brothers, once the solemnities of the coronation were over, not the least of which were a tournament and a great fair. By comparison with these latter events, a coronation seemed tame. The boys could hardly wait until Alroy's crowning was past and they could get on with more exciting things.

The boys' day began early. Alroy and his brothers were roused for morning prayers and baths—but not breakfast —and then separated so that Alroy might be drilled a final time for his part in the ceremony. While the royal dressers clad him in his coronation robes of white and gold, the boy was made to rehearse his lines to the exacting satisfaction of Bishop Hubert, who had been tutoring all three children exhaustively for the past month.

Alroy was pensive but letter-perfect as he repeated the words he had been taught. Too pensive, as Hubert later complained to his fellow regents. The boy had actually asked the bishop whether he thought that Alroy would make a good and wise king. Hubert, of course, had assured him that he would, especially if he heeded the advice of his counselors, but the bishop was not pleased; it would not do for the boy to get the idea that he really was king, so long as the regents ruled.

The coronation procession left the castleyard precisely at Terce, led by a troop of household guards in the livery of Gwynedd and then by every peer of the realm who had managed to get to Valoret for the occasion—nearly fifty in all, human and Deryni, though of the latter there were far fewer than Camber had hoped. Davin, Earl of Culdi, rode among them, with Ansel at his side; a tense Earl Gregory rode with his sons; and Baron Torcuill de la Marche, who had just returned from his eastern estates and looked as if he wished he were back there.

But most of the rest were human, Camber noticed, as the procession neared the cathedral steps where he and Jaffray and Bishop Hubert waited. Many of the most powerful and influential Deryni of the kingdom simply had not come!

With a sinking feeling in his heart, Camber shifted the heavy fabric of the cope on his shoulders—the vestments Cinhil had given him so many years before—and watched the first of the procession begin to dismount and file into the cathedral. Some of the absences he could have predicted; and some of those not in the procession were already inside, like Rhys and Evaine. But this poor a showing had been quite unforeseen—almost a slap in the face to the regents by those of his race. He prayed fervently that the regents would be too occupied to notice the slight, but he knew the prayer to be but wishful thinking. The regents would notice. Even if Murdoch did not, Tammaron or Rhun would. Or Hubert.

He glanced sidelong at the corpulent Hubert standing opposite Jaffray and saw that the bishop-regent had already noticed. The tiny rosebud lips were set in a petulant pout of disapproval, and occasionally the cherubic face would turn slightly to dictate a few terse words to a clark lurking by his right elbow. The page on which the man wrote was dark down nearly half its length.

Joram, what is that man writing? Camber sent mentally to his son, who was standing just behind him and Jaffray, and in a much better position to see.

Names, Joram's mind whispered in Camber's. *He's making a list of those in the procession. What do you want to bet that there's someone inside, too, taking notes on those already seated?*

No bet, Camber responded. *Are Evaine and Rhys in their places?*

Yes.

Thank God for that, Camber thought to himself. *Go inside and see. If the regents are making lists, then we'd better do the same, so we can warn those who didn't show up. I can understand their distaste, but in this case, I can't help wishing they'd been a little less principled.*

Dom Emrys is inside with the Gabrilites, Joram returned. *Shall I ask him to make note? He won't have to write it down, and I can reach him without arousing suspicion.*

Camber nodded, recalling that the Abbot of the Gabrilites had a perfect memory. Then he gestured for Joram to bend closer.

"Joram, would you please bring me some water?" he asked, for the benefit of any listening ears. "An old man like me shouldn't be expected to last through a long ceremony like this, without refreshment."

"Right away, Your Grace," Joram replied with a bow, his face solemnly belying his momentary amusement.

As he backed off, to merge with the peers filing inside, the first of the royal party entered the cathedral close, to the accompaniment of a trumpet fanfare and a roll of drums. First came the king's brothers on matched chestnuts, led by Earls Hrorik and Sighere, crimson-clad and wearing silver princes' circlets on their heads. Behind them, Ewan bore the great sword of Gwynedd, which had been Cinhil's, and Murdoch the royal banner.

Finally came the king, bareheaded and looking very young and vulnerable as he sat his tall, albino stallion.

Earl Tammaron, the new chancellor, led the boy's mount, curbing the animal's proud prancing with a white leather lead that shone in the sunlight. Rhun of Horthness walked on the other side of the king's horse with one hand on the bridle, hardly able to keep the sneer of triumph off his angular face.

The sunlight glittered almost as brightly from the jewelled surcoats and coronets of the regents as it did from the king's own royal robes, and flashed from chains of gold, silver spurs, and raiment stiff with embroidery such as no mere subject had worn in decades—only kings and clergy.

As the king's robes were adjusted a final time and his long white mantle arranged to trail gracefully behind him, four earls' sons stepped into place with the canopy of cloth-of-gold, shading the boy from the bright spring sun. As the cathedral doors were thrown open a final time to admit the royal party, the choir of the *Ordo Verbi Dei* broke into the traditional strains of the coronation hymn:

"I was glad when they said unto me, let us go into the house of the Lord!"

The coronation party began to move down the nave: first the choir monks in their burgundy habits, singing as they processed; then a full dozen altar boys in hooded white robes, scarlet-sashed, each bearing a taper in a bright-reflecting silver holder.

A lone thurifer came next in the procession, his censer spewing a cloud of sweet incense smoke which hung in the air where he passed and through which the ornate processional cross of the Primate of Gynedd seemed to float almost unsupported by the young deacon who bore it. Archbishop Jaffray followed the cross, accompanied by his chaplain and a second deacon, and behind him walked Archbishop Oriss of Rhemuth and his attendants. Both archbishops wore heavy copes of white and gold, stiff with embroidery and appliqué; and the jewel-encrusted miters of their offices, rich as any crowns, carried the carved and gilded croziers which proclaimed them shepherds of their flocks.

The king's portion of the procession came next, with Camber and Hubert walking to the left and right of Alroy, just under the canopy of cloth-of-gold which the four earl's sons carried. The rubric had called for Alroy to rest his hands on the inside hands of his escorting bishops, but at the last minute the boy had refused to go along with that part of the ceremony, complaining that their hands were too high, and his arms would get too tired. Camber suspected that the true reason was that Alroy simply had not known whom he might trust, so had decided to trust none of them.

Now the boy walked quietly between them—but not touching them or allowing himself to be touched, head held high and chin set firmly in a pose which Camber had seen many times on the boy's father and had learned not to argue with. Perhaps Alroy had a mind of his own, after all.

More bishops followed the king and his canopy, and then Father Alfred, the boys' confessor. After him came the four lay regents bearing the regalia: Ewan with the sheathed great sword; Murdoch now bearing the scepter instead of the banner he had carried in the procession to the cathedral; Rhun with the Ring of Fire on a small silver salver; and Tammaron carrying the scaled-down replica of the Gwynedd State Crown which had been made for Alroy, with its leaves and crosses intertwined. Earls Hrorik and Sighere were last in the procession, escorting the Princes Javan and Rhys Michael.

Into the choir the royal party went, each rank pausing at the foot of the sanctuary steps to bow before moving to assigned positions on either side. While Alroy knelt at a faldstool to the right of the altar, beside the low throne which he would later occupy, Camber and Hubert stood with the other bishops on either side of the archbishops' thrones which had been set up at the left of the choir.

The two archbishops prayed uncovered at the altar steps until the processional hymn had ended, then had their miters replaced by their respective chaplains and went to raise up Alroy. The young king trembled as they led him before the altar for the Presentation, looking very small and frail in his heavy robes and mantle.

As at Cinhil's coronation thirteen years before, Camber was aware that Jaffray, like his predecessor Anscom, followed Deryni as well as human custom in this part of the ceremony. Common tradition taught that the Presentation at the beginning of the coronation was to the four corners of the kingdom—perhaps to the four winds—that word of the new king might be proclaimed to the farthest reaches of the land. To this end, the presiding archbishop always announced the new king's name and claim to the four cardinal points of the sanctuary for the people's acclamation. So it had been for as long as anyone could remember.

But trained Deryni understood a more esoteric meaning in the action: the bringing of the sacred king to the notice of the Elemental Lords, as personified by the four great Archangels, whose guardianship and protection were invoked for any serious working of Deryni magic. This invocation, plus the ritual censing of the sanctuary later in the ceremony, would ensure that the actual sacring of the king took place within a consecrated circle, guarded from potentially hostile forces. And if the hallowing of a king were not magical, then what was? How odd that most people did not see their religion as magic.

Jaffray knew this, even if the human Oriss did not. Taking the boy's right hand in his, and with Oriss holding the left, Jaffray guided Alroy to the eastern end of the sanctuary, to the foot of the altar steps, where all such ritual began. There, all three of them raised their arms in salutation as Jaffray intoned the traditional words.

"All hail Alroy Bearand Brion, our undoubted king! Be ye willing to do homage and service in his behalf?"

"God save King Alroy!" the people shouted, only Deryni—and not even all of those—aware that they were participating in the very magic which the young king's regents would later swear to suppress.

To the south the archbishop led the young king, raising his arms as before and repeating the recognition.

"God save King Alroy!" the people repeated.

To the west and then to the north they went, each time repeating the ancient formula and hearing the answering affirmation of the people. When the last echoes had died away from the northern recognition, the archbishops led the king back to the east, up the steps of the altar itself. There lay the open book of the Gospel, an elaborately calligraphed and illuminated document beside it. With a bow, Jaffray released the young king's hand, half-facing the people once again as he said:

"My Lord King Alroy, are you now prepared to take the hallowing oath?"

"I am willing," the boy replied, though in a voice so soft that even Camber, standing within a few feet of the boy, could barely hear him.

Gently Jaffray took the boy's hand and placed it on the open Gospel, picked up the scroll and began to read.

"Alroy Bearand Brion Haldane, here before God and

196

men declared and affirmed to be the lawful heir of our late liege lord, King Cinhil, do you solemnly promise and swear to keep the peace in Gwynedd, and to govern its peoples according to our ancient laws and customs?"

"I so swear," Alroy murmured.

"Will you, to the utmost of your power, cause Law and Justice, in Mercy, to be executed in all your judgments?"

"I so swear," Alroy repeated.

"And do you solemnly pledge that Evil and Wrong-Doing shall be suppressed, and the Laws of God maintained?"

"All this do I swear," Alroy repeated, yet a third time.

"Let the Lords Regent come forward," Jaffray said, turning toward them and bowing slightly as they approached.

Oriss drew back to stand with folded hands beside Camber as the five regents made their obeisances and ascended the steps on either side of Alroy.

"Murdoch of Carthane, Tammaron Fitz-Arthur, Rhun of Horthness, Ewan of Rhendall, acting for his father, Sighere of Eastmarch, and Hubert MacInnis: having been charged by our late Sovereign Lord Cinhil with the duty to govern our young king until he shall come of age, do you solemnly swear to uphold the selfsame oath which His Highness has just sworn, to serve as loyal stewards and faithful regents of the Crown of Gwynedd, so help you God?"

"We so swear," the regents replied, in perfect unison.

The archbishop placed a quill in Alroy's hand and watched him neatly trace his *Alroi Rex* at the bottom of the page in his careful, childish hand. When the regents had added their signatures and seals to the document, and Jaffray and Oriss and Camber had witnessed it, Alroy gravely laid his small hand on the Gospel and, without further prompting, turned slightly to face the people.

"That which I have here promised, I will perform and keep, so help me God," he said, in a much louder voice than he had hitherto managed.

Then he stood a little on his tiptoes to kiss the Book, waiting until his regents had done the same before descending the altar steps to kneel and be divested of his mantle and outer robes. As he prostrated himself before the altar, now clad in only a simple, alblike garment such as the priests themselves wore, the bishops and priests knelt all around him and the choristers began to sing the

197

Veni Creator, words written by a centuries-dead king of Bremagne and long reserved for the hallowing of kings, priests, and bishops:

"Veni, Creator Spiritus, mentes tuorum visita, imple superna gratia, quae tu creasti pectora. . . ."

A sacring prayer was recited while Jaffray and his assistants censed the altar and the prostrate Alroy, and then the choir monks intoned the ancient coronation formula: *Zadok the priest and Nathan the prophet have anointed him king in Gihon, and they are come up from thence rejoicing. . . .*

As the song ended, Alroy was raised to his knees by Camber and Hubert and the canopy brought into place. Under this protection, Archbishops Jaffray and Oriss began the anointing which would make Alroy a sacred king.

"Be thy head anointed with this holy oil, as kings, priests, and prophets were anointed," Jaffray said, pouring oil on the bowed raven head in the form of a cross.

"Be thy breast anointed with holy oil," the archbishop continued, tracing the sign on the boy's chest through the open neck of his alb.

"Be thy hands anointed with holy oil," the archbishop concluded, tracing the symbol on each upturned and trembling palm. "As Solomon was anointed king by Zadok the priest and Nathan the prophet, so mayst thou be anointed, blessed, and consecrated to the service of these, thy people, whom the Lord our God has given thee to govern in His Name. *In nomine Patris, et Filii, et Spiritus Sancti. Amen."*

They raised him up then, and garbed him in robes befitting a king: a tunic of cloth-of-gold, a jewelled white girdle, and a mantle of fur-lined crimson, thickly encrusted with gems and gold bullion.

On his heels they placed the golden spurs; in his hands, momentarily, they placed the kingly sword which had been his father's, before giving it into the keeping of Ewan, the new marshal, to be laid on the altar. On his finger they placed the Ring of Fire, sized down now to fit his boy's finger—though the jewelled band had already done its most important work. The scepter, a slender wand of gold-encrusted ivory, was placed in his hands long enough for him to feel the weight of it, then set aside on the royal throne.

Finally, solemnly, the boy knelt at the archbishop's feet, before the altar, as Jaffray took up the crown and raised it high above the boy's head, his eyes riveted on the tracery of gold and silver leaves and crosses intertwined.

"Bless, we beseech Thee, O Lord, this crown. And so sanctify Thy servant, Alroy, upon whose head Thou dost place it today as a sign of royal majesty. Grant that he may, by Thy grace, be filled with all princely virtues. Through the King Eternal, Our Lord, Who lives and reigns with Thee in the unity of the Holy Spirit, God forever and ever. Amen."

So Alroy was crowned King of Gwynedd, as a silvery fanfare underscored the completion of the moment and the people shouted, "God save the king!"

After that, the bishops and lesser clergy and then the nobles, led by Alroy's brothers, came forward to render homage and fealty and to receive the royal recognition, the regents standing triumphantly to either side of the throne as the others came forward. Mass followed the fealty, with the king himself bringing forward the offerings of bread and wine, and then the procession from the cathedral—the procession of a very tired young king.

Nor could the king's day end with his return to the castle, for there was yet the obligatory coronation feast to be endured. Though the Vesper bells were ringing as the procession passed into the castleyard, and though Alroy's head ached abominably from the weight of the crown and the heat and the lack of food since late the night before, little respite would be allowed.

An hour they had—long enough for Alroy to discard his heavy robes and crown for a little while and lie down, there to succumb to exhausted sleep, which Tavis made more than just a brief nap. On both the other boys, Tavis likewise worked his Healing of forced sleep, and delayed waking them until the regents would be put off no longer. He did manage to insist that they eat something substantial and nourishing first, but beyond that there was nothing else he could do except watch from the sidelines and be prepared to make a rescue, if necessary. If the king fell asleep at table before the evening's festivities were through—well, older kings than Alroy had been known to nod over their cups or doze into their plates.

So the king and his brothers were escorted into the hall for the feast, to a trumpet flourish and the cheers of the assembled nobles. Alroy sat on the dais at the center of the high table as official host, dwarfed by the royal throne which had been his father's and flanked by his regents and their wives, all in furs and jewels and the badges of their offices. Javan and Rhys Michael were isolated at either end of the high table and likewise surrounded by adult courtiers who were far more interested in the prestige their seating gave them than in easing the public discomfort of children forced too soon into adult roles. Other than the pages and squires who helped serve the feast, the royal brothers were the only children in the hall. The evening was to be the first lesson, but not the last, on the loneliness of the Crown.

Lonely or not, the evening was not without its pleasures, even for the boys, though they might have enjoyed it more, had they been better rested. The food, if over-rich and exotic for young palates, was wonderfully presented, to madrigal and instrumental accompaniment, and usually paraded about the hall for the amazement of all, before being served: roast venison and stuffed capons; sturgeons arrayed in aspic, so that they appeared still to be swimming; cygnets and doves stuffed inside pheasants; great tarts and meat pies; eels seethed in wine; and a peacock roasted to perfection, still bearing all its jewel-glowing, iridescent feathers as it was brought to table. There was even a subtlety of the Haldane Lion done in gilded marzipan and spun sugar, with glazed cherries for eyes, of which Alroy got the tuft at the end of the tail and one ear for his portion.

Some of the entertainment also held appeal for children as well as adults—acrobats and harpers and a few of the less bawdy of the troubadours. Alroy was particularly taken with a short mummer's play depicting his father's defeat of the hated Deryni Imre—though he would never know how the story had been altered by the regents to show Imre falling on his own sword, rather than willing himself to die by his powers, to avoid being taken captive by the Deryni-supported Cinhil and his Deryni allies. Other than Imre and Ariella, Deryni did not even appear.

By then, it mattered little anyway, so far as the princes were concerned. Despite Tavis's earlier ministrations, it was not long before the day's accumulation of fatigue began to tell on all three boys. Indulged by their adult companions with as much wine as they wished, first Rhys Michael and then Alroy nodded off, before the third course had even been completed.

A squire nudged Alroy unobtrusively to present a

finger-bowl for his use, and Alroy thanked him sheepishly but by then, Javan, too, was yawning mightily and Rhys Michael had slipped groggily from his chair to curl up in the rushes beneath his end of the table and go to sleep. None of his dinner companions even seemed to notice.

Tavis noticed. From his vantage point in the gallery above the hall, he had been watching all three boys throughout the feast, and waited for a time when he might finally take action. During a particularly rowdy dance interlude at the far end of the hall, he and two squires slipped quietly onto the dais and woke the now-drowsing Javan, the squires accompanying Javan and Alroy while Tavis collected the sleeping Rhys Michael from under the table and took him out.

Tammaron saw them go and waved his approval to Tavis, for he had young sons of his own at home in bed. Other than Tammaron, no one else even missed them. By the time the dance had ended, Murdoch and Rhun could be seen lolling on the arms of the throne and hoisting cups in toast while they led the assembled nobles in a rousing rendition of one of the bawdier tavern ballads currently making the rounds in Valoret town. Ewan and his brothers, Hrorik and Sighere, started a wagering game in one corner of the hall with four other men. Bishop Hubert was rapidly drinking himself into red-faced and exuberant inebriation, much to the distress of his fellow regents' wives or any serving maid who chanced too close to His Grace's chair.

Jaffray, one of the very few Deryni present in the hall that night, and one of the handful of either race who remained relatively sober, could only shake his head to himself and wonder how they would manage to survive the next few years, if these were the men who were to govern Gwynedd.

Fortunately for the princes, the next day boded better. For one thing, it started later. By the appointed hour of noon, the regents were only beginning to revive from the previous night's festivities, and they were nearly an hour late collecting the boys for that day's events.

The first afternoon's offering was but prelude to a week-long series of entertainments devised to please young boys of ten and twelve and keep their young minds from the serious business of ruling. For further diversion, the regents brought their own children and kin of about the princes' ages, and Hubert brought his brother's children; no sense in all the expense being used for just three boys.

Prime among the performances was a troupe of puppeteers and Morris dancers, who mimed several tales of Gwynedd folklore to the accompaniment of a gaily clad troubadour; and jugglers and a young harper, hardly older than the twins, who sang and played so sweetly that the boys were held in thrall by the tale she wove in song, and seriously discussed how they might keep her there at the castle—though none of them was old enough or experienced enough in the world to know what they might do with her other than have her sing. After the harper had finished, the Morris dancers did a fierce sword-clashing drill to the accompaniment of pipes and drums, which nearly frightened the ten-year-old Rhys Michael at first, whirling and interweaving their swords in patterns, first slow and then fast, which were nearly as ancient as the history of the land.

An added attraction was the presentation of a menagerie which was to be displayed at the fair opening in the town the following day. The boys had never seen such animals: a dancing bear, which roared and growled most ferociously when prodded to perform; several strange, dust-colored animals with humps on their backs; a pair of real lions, like the one on the Haldane arms, brought from beyond the borders of Bremagne and kept in a stout cage; and, the gift of the small, quick man who owned the menagerie, three exquisite R'Kassan yearling colts, jet-black now, but promising to turn to purest white by the time their young owners should be old enough to ride them as warhorses.

The boys' excitement knew hardly any bounds, and that night they slept the gentle sleep of normal, boyish fatigue. Tavis began to relax a little.

The second day saw a resumption of more vigorous activities. First among the royal duties—and a fascinating task it was, which the boys minded not in the least—was a state visit to open the town fair which had been proclaimed in honor of the new-crowned king. Alroy and his brothers personally witnessed the official opening, standing by eagerly while a herald read the official decree and commanded all, in the name of King Alroy, to keep the king's peace within the boundaries of the fair.

The royal party progressed through the fairgrounds to

drum and trumpet after that, while a liveried attendant bore before them the gilded gauntlet on a pole, which was symbolic of the king's protection and patronage. To the populace, the king and his brothers dispensed copper coins struck with Alroy's likeness for the occasion of the coronation, in return sampling the wares of several of the stalls and being given numerous small trinkets and gifts which the regents even allowed them to keep.

But there was no time to linger, for the king must attend a tournament being held that afternoon in his honor; and so they had to leave the fair long before boyish curiosity had been satisfied. Cinhil had not believed in such frivolity, and so the boys had never been permitted even to see a fair or marketplace. For that matter, they had never attended a tournament other than as spectators, though they had been taught the skills of horsemanship requisite for participation in such an activity. Tournaments had only been introduced during the latter days of King Blaine, Imre's father, to keep the skills of war honed even in times of peace. All manner of martial accomplishment might now be tried in the name of sport.

Therefore, a tournament designed, at least in part, for the participation of children held a special allure for the princes. After the initial ceremonies, and the first skirmishes between adult horsemen, a squires' list was held, and then one for Alroy and Javan's age-group.

The king had a slight cold, and so was not permitted to ride—though he was promised that he might on the morrow, if his health was improved—but Javan tilted at rings and ran at the quintain most stylishly, to the great surprise of most folk watching, for on horseback, he was as secure as any other rider, and the long surcoat he wore obscured the special boot on his right foot. He even won a second place in pole-bending: a chaplet of wildflowers which the Countess Carthane, Murdoch's lady, bestowed.

The ten-year-old Rhys Michael also acquitted himself quite nobly against the young pages of his age group, managing to snag several more than his share of rings in the ring-tilting competition. The crowd cheered for him in particular, for his sunny disposition was fast making him the popular favorite. All three boys again slept the sleep of the righteously exhausted when they went to bed that night.

Commitments were far less rigid on the third day. Though the king's presence was expected at the continuing tournament, and he had, indeed, been given permission to compete this time, the two younger boys were not required to attend. A little judicious pestering of Earl Tammaron, who was known to be indulgent with his own boys, produced the exhilarating permission to go to the fair with Tavis instead of to the tournament, taking only a small guard escort with them.

The boys were ecstatic, and their enthusiasm was so infectious that Tavis was even prevailed upon to let them dress as pages rather than princes, so that they might pass for ordinary boys on holiday at the fair. Tavis's own tunic, with its badges of Healing and royal service bold on the sleeve, he covered with a short cape of grey, for the day was warm and the event informal. Even the guards were cajoled into the spirit of the day's adventure, somewhat disguising themselves by wearing plain harness and throwing worn, nondescript cloaks over their badges of household and personal rank.

It mattered not to the boys. They had the semblance of freedom, if only feigned, and the guards were sympathetic, several of them with small children of their own. Almost, the boys could imagine that they were, indeed, the simple pages that they appeared to be. It was a delicious taste of what they had always imagined it might be like to lead an ordinary life, and they revelled in it.

All day long they ran through the aisles of the fair, inspecting stalls and booths, watching with awe as a man breathed fire here, produced fresh flowers from a woman's hair there. They saw women weaving baskets out of sleek, sweet-smelling reeds, gaped in astonishment as a bowl grew under the supple fingers of a master potter.

A baker's stall provided fresh-baked pastries and tough, chewy brown rolls at midday, far different from the fine white manchet bread to which they were accustomed at home; and from a cheesemaker's booth they procured fragrant, frothy milk kept cool in a crock which had been buried in the ground the day before.

And there were comfits to be munched greedily—rare treats which Tavis only occasionally permitted—and small bundles of fragrant herbs to be tucked into belts against the less pleasant smells of such a large gathering, such as those of the butcher's stalls, which both boys avoided when they realized what happened there. Violent death, even of animals, had not yet become a part of their reality.

In a cutler's booth, Rhys Michael found a dagger scaled just right to fit his boyish hand, and Tavis was finally persuaded to let him buy it.

Javan's purchase was more poignant, still, for while ferreting about in a saddler's stall for a suitable sheath for Rhys Michael's blade, the elder prince came upon a length of supple white calf's leather about a handspan wide and nearly as long as he was tall. He made no particular reaction when he first found it—merely looped it twice over his arm and continued helping his brother's search—and soon they located a sheath of Haldane-red leather tooled in an interlace design.

But while Rhys Michael and one of the guards, Sir Piedur, haggled with the saddler over the sheath's price, Javan fingered his length of white leather thoughtfully and then drew aside another of the guards, Sir Jason. The two spoke confidentially for several minutes, Tavis unable to ascertain what was passing between them; but when Rhys Michael paid the agreed-upon price for his sheath, Javan bought the strip of white leather without even arguing the price, an expression of grim determination on his face as he tucked his rolled-up prize in his belt pouch. It was not until half an hour later that Jason was able to come casually to Tavis, while Javan and his brother watched a glassblower at work, to tell him how Javan planned the white leather to become the belt of a knight. Jason, who was known for his skill at leather-working as well as his knightly virtues, had not had the heart to tell the boy the futility of his dream—that his club foot would almost certainly bar him from that rank unless, somehow, he should become king.

Tavis said nothing further of the matter, though he thanked Jason for telling him. But his heart ached for Javan—this prince who would be all things to all men, whom fate had flawed in a way which had nothing to do with his noble spirit but which would forever mark him, nonetheless. Not for the first time, he wished that his Healer's powers could somehow make of Javan the whole prince which he was in everything excepting body.

Other treasures the boys also found on that afternoon, though they were not permitted to buy everything that they saw. For their royal brother, they picked out a fine leather riding crop, its handle tooled with mysterious designs from far Torenth. Rhys Michael insisted that the carved leather would match beautifully the white headstall on the R'Kassan colt Alroy had received two days before.

For old Dame Lirel, who had been the boys' chief nurse up until the previous year and still kept their quarters tidy, they bought a length of sky-blue ribbon the color of the Lady's mantle; for Botolph, who kept the horses, a fine cambric shirt embroidered at neck and wrists with the odd, geometric cross-stitching of his Forcinn homeland.

The four guards received handsome leather pouches worked with each man's badge or device in bright dyes and threads while they waited. And for Tavis, the boys picked out a leather hunt cap in Healer's green. The pleased Tavis wore it proudly for the rest of the day.

But for the most part, all of them simply looked and marvelled at what the fair had to offer. The day passed quickly, as the boys enjoyed their unprecedented adventure and freedom, and they remarked several times that they wished Alroy could have been there to share it with them.

One brief incident threatened to mar their outing, though nothing came of it at the time. Toward midafternoon, when the boys' boisterous running around had been temporarily abated by a pause for cheese and fruit, Tavis had stopped to relace Javan's special boot, the boy perched genially on a vintner's empty barrel while he munched on an apple. As Tavis crouched there, gently massaging the boy's foot and unobtrusively delivering a little Healing energy, he was jostled by a passing group of richly-dressed young men whom he instantly recognized as Deryni in his heightened state of awareness.

He lost his balance momentarily, as one of the men's feet grazed his heel in passing, and his cloak slipped far back on his sholders as his arms flailed out to keep him from sitting hard on the ground. The movement exposed the Healer's badge and royal device on his sleeve, and he caught a quick psychic gasp from one of the men, a mental grimace of distaste, quickly damped and shielded, before he could recover his balance and twitch his cloak into place and try to locate the precise source of the reaction.

He managed only a glimpse of the men's backs before they melted into the throngs. He tried to reach out with his Deryni senses and touch them again, to learn why the one had recoiled at his badge, but he could detect nothing. The men must be shielding heavily. As swiftly as their bodies, the men's auras had disappeared in the crowded area.

Thoughtfully he finished lacing Javan's boot, aware and thankful that the boy had scarcely noticed the incident. There was probably nothing to it. The fair had been crowded all day, and this was not the first time one of them had been jostled. Sir Robear made a good-natured comment about some people's rudeness, but his attention was soon engaged by an exotic-looking dancing girl performing in front of a stall farther down the aisle.

Tavis, with a mental shrug of resignation, dismissed the incident as a fluke and took Javan's hand as they and their guard moved on. He had long been aware that there were Deryni who did not approve of Deryni service to humans, just as there were humans who did not approve, like the regents. It really mattered little to Tavis, since his service was to Javan and not to humans in general. Let them presume to think what they liked. So long as Javan needed him, he would stay.

He thought no more about the incident for the rest of the day. The boys were full of energy and had to be watched constantly, lest they wander off unescorted to investigate some new temptation which beckoned from booth or stall or brightly-clad entertainer; and Tavis himself found many things to catch his eye.

By dusk, as they were heading back through the narrow streets and alleys toward the castle, Tavis was concerned only with getting two tiring and sleepy princes to bed for the night. Javan, his foot finally having given out on him a little while before, was gleefully but sleepily riding the shoulders of Piedur, the largest of the guards, while Rhys Michael, still somewhat energetic, continued to foray off with Jason, Robear, and Corund, to peer into side streets and shopfronts.

The streets were crowded with jostling, merry people, some of them in masks, for tonight was carnival and celebration. One group passing by sang a three- or four-part marching song, and Piedur joined in. Tavis did not notice that he was in the midst of a rather different kind of merrymakers until suddenly he was seized by either arm and jostled into the mouth of an alley.

"Deryni should not aid the enemy!" a voice whispered in his ear, just as a blow struck the back of his head and he momentarily lost track of what was happening.

CHAPTER FOURTEEN

And I will cut off witchcrafts out of thine hand.
—Micah 5:12

He staggered, stunned, but he could not even fall while gripped so tightly. His reeling senses told him only vaguely that he was being half-propelled, half-carried, further into the alley—and that the men around him were masked, and his escort still in the main street with the princes, only now becoming aware that something was amiss.

"What should we do with Deryni who aid the enemy?" another voice rasped, as Tavis began to struggle weakly and tried to reach out with his mind.

He felt an answering surge of shields locking into place around him—his captors were Deryni! He shook his head and tried to scream for help, but to no avail. A gloved hand was clamped over his mouth, his head immobilized against a velvet-clad chest.

He continued to squirm, all the while being dragged further into the darker reaches of the alley, and again he sought to reach out with his mind, somehow to break the bonds of those other minds surrounding him, as well as the physical restraints; but another blow to the side of his head jolted him so that it was all he could do just to stay conscious.

"This is one Deryni who will aid the enemy no more!" the first voice said.

And Tavis heard a sword whisper from its scabbard, steel against well-oiled steel.

There were shouts coming from the street now, as his escort began trying to make their way to his aid, yet still protect their royal charges—but suddenly he knew that they would be too late.

208

He struggled even more frantically, though already almost resigned to the fact that he was not going to be able to escape them. They were too many and too strong, and he was not trained as a fighting man.

But then, in an even more horrifying realization, he felt his left arm being jerked out to his side, the hand and forearm being pinned against the wall beside him. Through the swell of an even greater terror than the threat of mere death, he saw the sword gleaming in ruddy torchlight as it drew back and then descended, flashing inexorably toward the join of hand and wrist.

God, no! Not his hand!

He convulsed with dread and tried to scream again, strained and wrenched with even more frenzied strength in that instant. But those who held him pinned were stronger, and the hands which gripped his body and his arm were like tempered steel; he could do no more than force an anguished gurgle of horror.

If thy hand offend thee, cut it off! The words rang in his mind.

He felt the steel strike his wrist with hot, numbing force, felt his stomach knot as he saw the flesh and bone part beneath the blade—but not all the way through—not with that first stroke, for the wall had deflected the blade a little. As he retched and felt his world lurching askew, he knew that the blade struck two more times, saw the black shower of his blood spurting from his severed wrist with each terrified beat of his pounding heart, heard the guards fighting through to him in earnest now—though he knew, as his senses faded, that it was too late.

They released his head then, and he screamed with all his strength, his shriek escalating to one of sheerest agony as he saw that they were not yet done with him. A torch approached, in the hands of a man whose face he would remember until the day he died, despite the fact that the man wore a mask across his eyes.

The last thing he remembered, before he mercifully passed out, was the sickening, pungent-sweet stench of his own seared flesh, and the excruciating anguish of a hand which was no longer there.

By the time the guards won through the crowd at the entrance to the alley, the attackers were nearly out of sight at the other end. Two of the guards started to pursue, but their fellows called them back. They dared not leave their royal charges, and Tavis must have help immediately.

Grimly, then, for an initial glance as they passed had told them there was nothing they could do to save Tavis's hand, they returned to find Prince Javan crouched beside the unconscious Healer and surrounded by a growing press of spectators. The boy had clamped one hand over the end of the severed wrist, trying to staunch the blood which spurted between his too-small fingers, and with his other hand he was searching for the pressure point under Tavis's upper arm. From his actions, it was clear that the boy remembered the theory, but he did not have the sheer physical strength to hold the pressure firm.

The guards did not pause for further reflection. While one of them ran to commandeer a cart and a pair of mounted town constables, another began to clear away the crowd, so that his remaining two colleagues could see to Tavis. Working quickly, they knotted a tourniquet around Tavis's upper arm, where Javan had tried to find the pressure point, then eased the prince's hand from the wound and bound up the bloody stump as tightly as they could. Rhys Michael, who had been huddling by the bloodstained wall in stunned shock until now, chose that moment to begin weeping hysterically, his mental state not improved by stumbling over Tavis's severed hand when one of the guards tried to turn him away from the bloody scene.

Javan watched all in stony silence, trying to stay out of the way until the cart arrived. While the guards loaded Tavis into the cart, he quietly retrieved the severed hand, wrapping it carefully in the sleeve which he tore from his own shirt. He cradled it against his chest all the way back to the castle, hoping that by warming it against his own body, it might be kept sufficiently alive for another Healer to reattach it. Sir Jason tried half-heartedly to take it from him, but the boy gave him such a look that he immediately backed off. Nor would he wipe Tavis's blood from his hands.

But locating another Healer proved difficult. Rhys had moved from the castle weeks before, but was reported to be living at the opposite end of town, so they sent a constable to inquire. When they paused at the archbishop's palace to ask whether Jaffray knew of a Healer nearby, the archbishop's secretary recommended several, then remembered that Rhys Thuryn had gone riding with

Bishop Cullen, though they were expected back momentarily. Should Rhys be sent to the castle when he returned?

He should. Further, there in the shadow of the castle walls, the guards judged that at last it was safe to divide their number, so Robear and Corund borrowed horses from the archbishop's stables and went out to look for Rhys, while the other constable returned to town to search for one of the other Healers named. Jason and Piedur carried Tavis into the castle and laid him in a room near the princes' quarters, at Javan's grim insistence.

The royal physicians were summoned then, and did what they could while they waited for a Healer to arrive, but they were only human. To keep Tavis from hemorrhaging to death, they were obliged to cauterize the wound further with red-hot steel, searing flesh and bone beyond even a Healer's ability to reconstruct.

Nor was Tavis their only patient. Rhys Michael remained so hysterical that he had to be put to bed with a sleeping potion; and they would have done the same to Javan, but the elder prince would not allow it. With a show of royal hauteur which would have made even the regents take notice, he insisted upon being allowed to wait for word of his friend's condition—though even threats would not persuade them to let him wait inside the room.

Alroy and the regents returned from the tournament shortly after that, and were told briefly what had happened. The regents mouthed suitable regrets over Tavis's injury, but Murdoch got it in his head almost immediately that the attack had really been aimed at the princes, as part of a Deryni plot. Bishop Hubert was even heard to remark that it was typical of the soulless Deryni that they should attack and maim their own kind, and good riddance.

Word arrived that a Healer had been located and was on his way, and Alroy asked to wait with his twin for news, but the regents would not hear of it. The king had already had a tiring day, and must guard against the return of the cold he had so lately shaken.

So Alroy, too, was put to bed with a sedative; and when Murdoch would have insisted that Javan do likewise, he was met with such cold resistance that even the normally merciless Rhun softened, suggesting that in the case of this prince, perhaps it might be better if he were permitted to keep vigil until the Healer's condition was stable.

So Murdoch relented, though, not until he had seen Tavis's blood washed from the boy's hands. Javan was permitted to curl up in a chair outside Tavis's door, wrapped in a warm blanket, after which he was promptly ignored. Hubert stayed with the physicians inside, but the other regents went down to supper. To Javan, the minutes seemed to crawl.

The Healer finally arrived from town, one Lord Oriel by name, a young, almost beardless man only recently matriculated from his final training at Saint Neot's. But though he was reasonably skilled, there was little he could do for his brother Healer at this late date other than to plunge him into even more profound sleep and try to ease the trauma done to tissue by cautery of flame and iron. Even if Tavis's wrist had not been so brutally seared—though the searing had saved his life—the hand which Javan had guarded so carefully had been severed too long for even a Healer to reattach. Butcher's leavings, Bishop Hubert observed, just before leaving, as Oriel sadly bade a squire dispose of the sleeve-wrapped hand.

So Oriel and the physicians administered a sedative to the unconscious Tavis, to ensure against his waking while they worked, and set to cleaning and dressing the raw first-aid already given, before Oriel could attempt a further Healing. A dusty Rhys arrived shortly, with Evaine, Joram, and Bishop Cullen in tow, to see Oriel preparing to work a final Healing of the stump, to seal a better closure and set in play long-term Healing so that Tavis might eventually be fitted with a hook.

The royal physicians were only too happy to defer to Rhys. Surgery was not their favorite occupation, especially something this gory, and they had been nervous enough about working with an unknown Healer. Rhys's arrival was ample excuse to bow out and leave their patient to his fellow Healers' care—and bow out, they did, though they did look in on the sleeping Alroy and Rhys Michael before retiring, and tried once more to persuade Javan to go to bed.

But Javan was having none of it, and almost succeeded in bullying his way into the room while Rhys and Oriel conferred. Only the arrival of Father Alfred, the boys' childhood confessor, kept Javan from making another scene. Camber, waiting with Joram near the door, where he would be out of the way, could only note Father Alfred's actions with approval and vow to put in a good word for him with Jaffray. The last thing Rhys needed was a hysterical prince disrupting things just as he and the other Healer settled down to work.

Rhys, meanwhile, began attuning himself to the grim business awaiting him. When he had scrubbed the grime from his hands and made a brief examination of Tavis's condition, he went into Healer's rapport with Oriel and reviewed the younger man's plans. He found Oriel inexperienced but imaginative—a combination he could work with easily enough. After only a brief exchange of information and techniques, they settled down beside their patient.

While Evaine monitored Tavis's life functions and kept him in deep sleep, beyond even the sedative already in his system—a task which seemed to surprise Oriel, since Evaine was not a Healer—Rhys controlled the area where Oriel worked, stopping bleeding, anchoring severed muscles and tendons and ligaments, sealing major nerve-endings, holding all in suspension as Oriel removed a bit more bone and smoothed the jagged ends and drew new flesh and a flap of skin over what once had been a Healer's hand.

When they were finished, they bandaged what was left and propped his left arm upright at his side, resting on the elbow, the forearm tied loosely to a chair drawn near the bed—though they covered arm and chair with a light blanket to disguise its lines. They would not have him see too much of it too soon.

Since they were approximating what a healed amputation should look like, rather than using the body's natural tendency to be whole while still in one piece, they knew that the Healing could not be completed that night. The body must be free to reroute blood vessels in its own way; and until that happened, there was danger of blood pooling in the stump and pressure building, making further surgery necessary on an even weaker patient. Besides, there would be less pain when Tavis woke, with the injured member elevated.

Oriel stayed with them a little while longer, observing their patient's condition and picking up fine points of technique from the Master Healer. After some discussion, it was agreed that Rhys should take over the case, reckoning it likely that Tavis might respond better to a Healer with whom he was acquainted, once he regained consciousness and must begin his terrible adjustment as a Healer with only one hand.

Oriel left around midnight, and an anxious Javan slipped into the room through the opened door. The boy was exhausted, wound up as tight as a catapult skein, dark smudges undershadowing the grey Haldane eyes. His face was streaked with tear-tracks through the day's accumulation of grime. His limp was more pronounced than Rhys had ever seen it as he made his way to the foot of the bed.

"Is he—alive?" Javan whispered, as though afraid to speak the words.

"Of course he's alive." Rhys smiled. "You didn't think we'd let him die, did you? It takes more than that to kill a Healer."

"I suppose." The boy stared hard at his toes. "Did—did you put his hand back?" he asked plaintively. "I wrapped it up as well as I could, and I tried to keep it warm. . . ."

Slowly Rhys crouched down before the boy, taking his slender arms and trying to get him to look him in the eye.

"I'm afraid that wasn't possible, Javan. It had been too long. We can Heal a lot of things, but even we have our limits. Can you tell me how it happened? A guard said you were attacked."

Angrily Javan jerked his arms away and moved to the right side of the bed, touched tentative fingertips briefly to Tavis's remaining hand, knuckled away grief-stricken tears from his bleary eyes.

"I was riding on Piedur's shoulders," he said shakily. "There were lots of people around us, singing and laughing. Some of them were wearing masks, because it was carnival time."

He sniffed and drew himself more erect. "All of a sudden, Tavis wasn't with us anymore. I looked around and saw him being rushed into the alley by a couple of men who had hold of his arms. They were wearing dark cloaks and masks. And there were others around him, too, and they were part of it, even though they didn't all have hold of him.

"I—saw one of them hit him in the head," he continued, his voice quavering a little, "and I yelled and pointed, and Piedur saw what was happening and put me down." His voice strengthened. "The other guards came running, but I couldn't see what happened next. There were people running everywhere and screaming. I managed to squirm through the crowd, but it was too late. T—Tavis was lying on the ground, and there was blood everywhere, and the guards were starting to chase the other men.

"I tr-tried to stop the bleeding, but I w-wasn't strong enough to hold the pressure point. Piedur came back then and helped me, and I—found his hand and wrapped it up in my sleeve." He shuddered, his tired shoulders slumping in dejection. "But, it didn't do any good, did it?"

Camber, standing across from the sleeping Tavis, could hardly control his amazement and horror at the tale the boy told.

"Oh, my poor boy, you're wrong about that," he murmured, starting to reach out to him. "If you hadn't tried to staunch his wound, he might have bled to death before Piedur could even get to him. You probably saved his life."

The boy did not look up, but he drew away slightly and swallowed hard. A fresh tear rolled off the lad's dirt-streaked cheek to splash on Tavis' hand. The unconscious man did not react, but Evaine did, moving in to lay her arms around the boy's rigid shoulders.

"I won't go to bed," Javan murmured, stiffening and shaking his head. "Not yet."

Evaine only smiled gently and pulled a straight-backed chair closer, on Tavis's right, near the head of the bed, and urged him to a seat on it.

"You don't have to go to bed yet, Javan. You're not a child anymore. You've proven that today. Sit here, where you can keep watch with us. Your good thoughts and prayers can help him Heal faster, you know. In that respect, everybody has a little bit of Healer in him."

"Really?" Javan whispered, heartened both by her statement and her acknowledgment of his maturing.

"Of course," Evaine replied. And she brought a blanket and tucked it around him in his chair, gently smoothing his hair and reaching out for control as she glanced at her father and her husband.

But her expression soon showed she was not making contact. She could not touch Javan, other than to read his presence as a hazy area of shielded consciousness as he gazed down at his friend.

She sent her surprise to the others, relaying to them what she was feeling—or not feeling—but she could not get through to Javan, and dared not try harder for fear of being detected.

Cinhil must have given him shields, Camber surmised, as he read his daughter's frustration. *Probably the others, as well. I wonder if he realized what he was doing?*

Rhys moved in to check his patient again, meanwhile sending: *Well, at least we know about it now, instead of finding out during an emergency. It's going to make things more difficult in the future, though. A logical protection, but I wish Cinhil hadn't done it.*

What about Javan now? Evaine queried. *He's exhausted, but he won't let himself go to sleep.*

Just ignore him for a while, then, Joram returned. *As you've pointed out, he's exhausted. By the time Tavis comes around, Javan may have fallen asleep on his own. It isn't worth a fight, at this point, and that would only antagonize him.*

Joram is right, Camber interjected. *But force isn't the only way to put a prince to sleep. Watch this.*

He yawned and pulled up another chair, making a show of settling in with every appearance of falling asleep himself.

"Evaine is right," he said aloud, giving a deep sigh as he let his eyelids droop. "I think we should all try to rest for a while. When Tavis wakes, he'll need us. And we'll be much more help if we're rested."

And as the others took his lead and began settling in to keep drowsy vigil, Camber covered a smile with yet another yawn as he saw Javan already yawning widely in response, the weary eyelids drooping lower and lower.

Soon Javan was asleep, and Evaine and Joram dozing in chairs around the bed while Camber and Rhys kept dreamy watch. Several hours passed before Tavis finally stirred, moving his head to one side with a low moan. Camber was instantly alert.

"Rhys?" he called softly.

The Healer had been grinding a posset of herbs blended with another sleeping potion, but he returned immediately to Tavis's side and laid his fingertips along the man's good wrist.

"He's coming out of it. That's a good sign. I was beginning to fear he might have lost too much blood."

Gently Camber touched the unconscious Healer's forehead, almost recoiling at the churning awarenesses beginning to surface.

"I fear that blood may be the least of what this man has lost," he said softly. "Rhys, are you certain he's ready to face what has happened? Maybe we should just force him back down for a while yet. Despite what you and Oriel have done, there's Healing that only his body and mind can do, and that only with time."

Tavis moaned again, and Rhys laid his Healer's hands lightly on either side of Tavis's face, beginning to extend his awareness around the reviving mind. Evaine woke and moved back to her position at Tavis's head.

"He's going to have to face what has happened, Alister," Rhys said, his face reflecting his concentration. "And for a Healer, the sooner the better. Tavis, can you hear me? Tavis, it's Rhys. Open your eyes, Tavis. You're all right. You're going to live. Open your eyes and let me know you understand."

Slowly Tavis obeyed, pain washing outward in increasing waves even through Rhys's rigid control and the drugs in his system. His glance flicked to the Healer's face first, to Joram, beyond, and Evaine, near the head of the bed, then to the bishop standing at his other side. Then he swallowed and tried to move his left arm. Gently Camber restrained him, taking a firm grip on the injured arm just below the elbow, through the folds of shrouding blanket. Rhys turned the pain-wracked face back toward him, away from the maimed arm.

"Don't look. Not yet," he commanded.

"How—" Tavis swallowed hard and had to start again. "How long have you been here, Rhys?"

Rhys dropped his grip to Tavis's shoulders and shook his head sadly. "Not long enough, I fear, my friend. I was out riding with Bishop Cullen. The royal physicians saw you first, and then a young Healer named Oriel. But it took them a while even to find him. By the time I got here—"

He sighed and bowed his head. "Tavis, there was nothing any Healer could have done, that late. It wasn't Oriel's fault. It wasn't even the physicians' fault. They did the best they could. At least they saved your life."

"They saved my life," Tavis repeated dully, turning his face to the left, to stare blankly at the shroud over his arm, "but not my hand. Why did they bother? What good is a Healer with only one hand?"

"Why, the same as one with two hands," Rhys began puzzledly.

"No!" Tavis croaked. "The balance won't work, don't you see? I'm flawed, defec—"

"Tavis!"

"No! Listen to me! Even the scriptures—"

"Tavis!"

"The scriptures agree: 'They will lay *hands* on the sick, who will recover.' *Hands,* not *hand!* And the *Adsum* confirms it. *Cum manibus consecratus*—with consecrated hands, make whole the broken. . . ."

"The *Adsum* also says, *Tu es manus sanatio mea*—thou art my healing *hand* upon this world," Rhys interrupted, thinking fast. "And all your arguments and self-pity to the contrary, there's nothing in scripture to suggest that *two* hands are necessary to heal. Jesus put forth His *hand* to heal the leper—"

"No. . . ." Tavis wailed, near hysteria.

"Tavis, stop it!" Rhys snapped. "Stop dwelling on what you *don't* have, and think about what you *do* have. You're still a Healer! It wasn't your mind that was affected by what happened to you today—only your hand!"

"Only my hand!"

Tavis laughed, a clipped, broken sob, then seemed to crumple inward as the pain took him once more. Rhys clamped one hand to Tavis's forehead and tried to curb the pain again, then shook his head and raised the other hand as well, shifting to Tavis's temples for finer control.

A difference of balance? Perhaps. But nothing said that a new balance could not be learned—though this was not the time to give Tavis an object lesson. Now Rhys must use his own familiar balances to calm his patient's hysteria and keep it from nudging him into shock again. As the pain eased off, and the injured Healer cautiously opened his eyes—still a bit disoriented-looking for Rhys's tastes, but not raving at least—Rhys took a deep breath and sighed, casting his glance grimly over the others.

"Tavis, we need to know who did this to you," he said.

"I don't know."

"Do you know why, then?" Joram asked. "It doesn't sound as if they were after the princes."

"They weren't," Tavis whispered, swallowing another sob. "They were after me."

"You?"

"But, why?" Evaine gasped.

"If thy hand offend thee, cut it off, one said. And, *Deryni should not aid the enemy."*

Joram frowned. "Now, what the hell is that supposed to mean?—*Deryni should not aid the enemy.* Tavis, they weren't Deryni, were they?"

As Tavis nodded, the flood of repeated memory triggered the real agony all over again, and it came surging through to conscious levels. Tavis screamed.

Rhys moved in at once and set about damping the pain, but still it reverberated among the four of them so acutely that Evaine paled and looked as if she might faint. Joram hurried around the bed to steady her with arms and mind, but even his strong shields could not completely insulate her from Tavis. Backlash from his tortured memory surged around the room in waves as he vacillated in and out of consciousness, until finally Evaine turned and stumbled from the room, Joram going with her.

Rhys glanced after her for a moment, probing beyond the door, then returned the greater part of his attention to his patient.

"I should have had her leave before this," he whispered distractedly, stroking Tavis's forehead as he tried to soothe his pain. "This next daughter will be a Healer, like her father."

"A Healer!" Camber breathed. "But female Healers—"

"Are extremely rare. I know. I can name four alive today. Evaine was affected because the child already senses extremes of pain in others and yearns to control it, though she has no strength to do so yet, of course." A quick grin lit his face. "On the other hand, what would you expect of my child by the daughter of Camber of Culdi?"

"But Tieg didn't—"

"Tieg is a boy. Apparently the male line carries the gift more easily than the female, though Evaine had a few twinges when she was expecting him, too. This child. . . ."

He gazed toward the door again, his expression touched with awe, but then Tavis moaned, edging from unconsciousness into delirium, and Rhys turned his full attention back on his patient.

"It's all right, Tavis," he murmured, letting his entire consciousness submerge in his questing task, now that his wife was safely out of range. "Let go and let it flow.

219

I'll help you channel off the pain. Let it detach. I'll bear it for you, and so will Father Alister."

As Tavis calmed beneath his hands, Rhys let himself begin to sink even deeper, beckoning with another part of his mind for Camber to link into rapport and follow where he led, gradually suppressing physical discomfort and forcing the tortured mind downward into deep, Healing sleep. As Rhys emerged from Healing trance, he saw Camber leaning heavily on the side of the bed, rigid and white-faced with shared fatigue. Rhys, after a few deep breaths to steady himself, reached out to Camber with hand and mind.

"Are you all right?"

"I will be." Camber took a deep breath and shook his head. "God, the *bitterness!* That our own people should do this to him!"

"Aye. And if he doesn't master it, that bitterness can kill him—just as surely as if he'd bled to death in that alley."

"Is there anything we can do?"

Rhys shrugged and shook his head. "I don't know. He's not likely to listen to much of anything I have to say, after what I did to him the night Cinhil died. Oh, I blocked the specific memory, but I wasn't able to block all the emotion that went with our little scene. There's resentment there, even if he doesn't remember precisely why. You're no better choice—too much of an authority figure. Besides, you're not a Healer."

"What, then?"

"A second opinion, I think. Not Oriel. Oh, he's a competent enough Healer, with a lot of potential, but he doesn't have the experience, or the grand overview, the way we do—though it's times like this that I almost wish *we* didn't, either."

"Amen to that!"

"I think—Queron," Rhys said, after a thoughtful pause. "Or maybe Dom Emrys would be even better. Tavis must have studied with Emrys at some time. Most Healers do. Maybe Emrys can get through. If we get a message off tonight, they should be here by tomorrow noon. I don't think we should wait any longer than that, though. He could go critical on us at any time, and I don't mean physically."

"I agree," Camber said. He started to turn toward the door, then paused.

"Is it all right to leave him alone for now, do you think?"

Rhys touched a hand to Tavis's forehead and probed lightly, then nodded and turned toward the sleeping Javan.

"I think he should sleep until morning. Javan, too." He held his hand a little way from Javan's forehead, then shrugged. "I'll be damned if I can figure out those shields of his, though. Cinhil must have understood a great deal more than we gave him credit for."

He peered closely at Javan, then tucked the blanket more securely around him.

"Poor little fellow. He's really had a hard day. We'll let him sleep where he is, for now. Come on. I want to get those messages off to Emrys and Queron."

But when they had gone out of the room, and the door had closed, a young raven head was raised cautiously from its rest against the high-backed chair.

Chapter Fifteen

I will not be ashamed to defend a friend; neither will I hide myself from him.
—Ecclesiasticus 22:25

Blinking sleepily in the candlelight, Javan peered around the room, comfirming that he was now alone with Tavis. Other than that, he did not move for several minutes. He wanted to make certain they would not come back.

He wondered what they had been talking about, while they had thought him asleep. He *had* been asleep for a little while, but he had awakened while they worked with Tavis. He remembered hearing Evaine and Joram leave the room, and then something about a child, Evaine's child, who was going to be a Healer.

He sat up at that and tried to remember more, recalling

a long period of silence and then a strange conversation between the two men, Healer and bishop.

Our people, Bishop Alister had said. *Our people did this to him!* And then they had worried about whether Tavis would be able to master the bitterness.

Our people. . . . Did they mean Deryni? Javan wondered. Had Deryni done this to Tavis?

O monstrous thought! If Deryni had done this to his friend, maybe the lords regent were right. The Deryni *were* evil! And those who had done this to Tavis must be punished!

He sat there brooding for several minutes, imagining in his mind all the possible tortures suitable for Deryni who attacked people in alleys and cut off their hands, then glanced back at his friend.

Rhys had said something about Tavis not listening to him, because Rhys had done something to Tavis the night his father died. What was it now? Rhys had *blocked the specific memory,* but he had not been able to block all the emotion. And Rhys had mentioned a scene, and the fact that Tavis resented him. *What had happened that night?*

Brow furrowing in concentration, Javan sat up straighter and tried to think back to that night. So much had happened since then that things were a little hazy, but he remembered that Rhys had come to see them after supper and had *given them all a physick against colds!*—even the squires.

By all the saints, could that have been more than a physick? He remembered that he had gotten very sleepy very quickly, and his brothers, too. And yet, Rhys had said that his father had ordered it. Why would his father have wanted them to sleep so well?

Or, had his father even known? Maybe Rhys had lied!

He shuddered at that thought and tried to find a motive, but he could not. He had not been harmed, had he? If Rhys had intended to poison them, it had not worked.

He scratched his head and rubbed his eyes and tried to go over it again. He was getting confused. Somehow, Rhys was apparently involved in some strange goings-on, but he didn't seem to have hurt anyone. Yet Tavis didn't trust him anymore, and Rhys knew it, and Rhys had alluded to something he had done to Tavis, the night his father had died. And Javan's memory of that night wasn't very clear, either.

Then there was that final comment, just before Rhys

and Bishop Alister had left the room—what was it, about shields? And he had said something about Javan's father understanding more than they thought.

What were shields? And what had his father known that Rhys and Alister hadn't expected?

He shook his head at that, then glanced at Tavis and slid off the chair to his feet. The Healer seemed to be resting peacefully enough, pale but relaxed, but Javan wondered whether it was safe to let him sleep on, with Rhys saying those kinds of things. Maybe Tavis should be told. If Rhys was trying to hurt Tavis, was it right to let him continue doing whatever it was he was doing, especially with Tavis injured and helpless?

He moved closer to the bed and stared at Tavis's face, finally reaching out cautiously to touch the Healer's hand. When Tavis did not move, Javan pulled his chair closer, then settled down in it and took Tavis's hand again. For a long time he stared at the sleeping man, holding the hand and trying, the way he had seen Tavis do so often for him, to will strength into his friend. After a while, he started to doze, and finally came back with a start to realize that Tavis was looking at him.

"Tavis?" he whispered.

The hand squeezed his weakly, and the swollen lips parted in a dazed smile.

"My prince," Tavis breathed. "How did you get here?"

"They think I'm asleep," Javan replied confidentially, scooting forward in his chair and leaning closer to the Healer's head. "They said you'd sleep 'til morning, too. Why didn't you?"

For a moment, Tavis's eyes unfocused as he apparently searched for an answer to that question, but then he glanced at their two joined hands, back at the boy's face.

"Didn't you call me, my prince? I—remember, I was far, far away—" His glance flicked away from Javan's momentarily. "—And I thought you were lost, but then I thought I heard you call my name, and I knew I must come back."

Awed, Javan returned the Healer's gaze, hardly daring to believe what he seemed to be suggesting.

"You—heard me call?"

"Aye."

"But I—I only called you with my mind," he whispered. "I tried to give you strength, the way you do for me. It was a childish dream—I thought. . . ."

"A—childish dream," Tavis repeated haltingly.

Without thinking, he started to reach out to Javan with his left hand, only to be reminded by the tug of binding cloths that the arm was caught in place—and why. In numb fascination, his eyes were drawn to the blanket shrouding his arm and the chairback which supported it. Almost without will of his own, he started to pull his hand free of Javan's to draw the blanket away.

"No," Javan whispered, holding his hand even tighter. "Don't look. I have to ask you something. It's important."

"More important than what has happened?"

"I don't know." Javan's gaze flicked down to their joined hands, then back to the Healer's pain-taut face. "Tavis, what did Lord Rhys do to you the night my father died?"

Dazedly, Tavis stared at the boy. Slowly his lips parted, his hand tightening convulsively on Javan's.

"What—makes you think Rhys did anything to me, Javan?"

"He said he did," Javan whispered. "He thought I was asleep, but I was only pretending. He said he—'blocked the specific memory,' but he wasn't able to block something else—the emotion, I think it was. He says that you resent him because of it, but you don't remember why."

Tavis's brow furrowed as he tried to fathom that. "He blocked my memory? I don't understand. I remember that he came to your quarters that night and that he gave all three of you a physick—your brother had been sick all week."

"That's right," Javan agreed. "And my brothers and I fell asleep almost immediately. The next thing I knew, Lord Jebediah was waking us up, and the regents were there to tell us that Father was dead. You were still asleep, and you didn't want to wake up."

"Aye, I do remember that. I don't recall much of that night, quite frankly, but I'd never given it much thought." He looked carefully at Javan. "You think that Rhys was responsible?"

Javan shrugged. "He said he did something. He thought I was asleep. He thought only Bishop Alister was listening. Why would he say that to Bishop Alister, if it weren't true?"

"I don't know," Tavis said, shaking his head in pained frustration. "I can't imagine what he's talking about— God, I'm too drugged to think clearly!"

"What's the matter? Can't you keep your shields in place?"

Startled, Tavis stared at Javan again, surprise momentarily driving much of the pain from his expression. "What do you know about shields?"

"Well, I—Rhys said that I have them, and he can't figure out why." The boy swallowed, taken aback by his friend's reaction. "He said—he said that my father must have understood a good deal more than they gave him credit for—whoever *they* are. What did he mean? What did my father understand, and what are these shields that Rhys says I have?"

"I wonder," Tavis murmured. Slowly he disentangled his hand from Javan's and reached up toward the boy's face. Javan was puzzled, but he leaned closer so that Tavis could reach him.

"Sweet *Jesu*, my head hurts!" Tavis whispered haltingly. "Try to let yourself relax, as if I were going to work a Healing on you. This isn't that difficult a function. I should be able to do it—and the fact that I'm talking about it means I'm terrified I won't be able to. But let's try."

Obediently Javan closed his eyes and let himself think of nothing, feeling almost immediately the soothing sensation he had come to associate with Tavis's touch. He nodded, relaxing even further, then came back with a start as the Healer removed his hand. Tavis looked relieved as he flexed and relaxed the fingers of his right hand.

"Well, at least I'm not going to be totally useless to you," he said softly. "That was excellent, considering my present state. Now let's try something else. I want you to pretend that I'm not Tavis, that I'm someone else—say, Rhys—and I'm going to—try to make you go to sleep. Use your imagination, now, and try to stop me."

"All right."

Again, Tavis reached toward the boy's forehead, meeting a stony gaze where, before, there had been warmth. Javan steeled himself, almost fancying he could see Rhys's face superimposed over Tavis's in his concentration.

But this time, there was no soothing intrusion of peaceful relaxation—only the hard, returned stare of grey eyes against pale blue ones. Tavis could not keep up the effort for very long, but it was long enough to tell him what he wanted to know. With a deep sigh, he withdrew his hand and let it fall slack on his chest.

"Congratulations, you have shields," Tavis whispered, "though I couldn't begin to tell you how you got them. I never saw a human with shields before. Did you feel anything, when I was trying to read you?"

Javan shook his head. "No. You told me to try to keep you away."

"And you didn't feel anything?"

"Nothing. Should I have?"

"Damned if I know," Tavis whispered. "You shouldn't have shields to begin with. Since you do, I haven't the slightest idea whether you should be able to feel pressure against them. If you were Deryni, I could give you some answers. But you're not. Damned if I know what you are."

Taken aback, Javan swallowed heavily and then covered Tavis's hand in his again.

"Is—is there something wrong with me?" he asked in a very small voice.

Tavis, in the midst of shifting his position in the bed, turned his attention back to Javan with a start.

"Wrong? Goodness, no, I don't think so. In fact, if Rhys *did* do something to me, maybe you can help me find out what it was. Not now, of course. In any case, I don't think he'll be able to make you do anything you don't want to do."

"Or you either!" Javan whispered fiercely. "Oh, Tavis, he's afraid you're going to have a hard time a-adjusting to what's happened to you, so he's bringing in some other Healers to help him."

"Other Healers?" Tavis whispered, chilled.

Javan nodded. "Aye. Two Doms—Dom Emrys and Dom Qu-Queron, I think he said."

Tavis whistled softly under his breath. "Emrys and Queron, eh? High-powered Healers, for the likes of me. Emrys was my teacher for a little while, and I've heard of Queron."

He stared at the ceiling for several seconds, until Javan could stand the suspense no longer and jostled the hand he still held.

"Tavis, what if they *do* help him? Not just to—to help you adjust, but to—do more of whatever it was Rhys did to you that other time."

226

After a short silence, Tavis turned his gaze back on Javan.

"Well, we're just going to have to be progressed to the point that I don't need any more Healers, then, aren't we?" he said. "Would you like to help me?"

"Can I really, even though I have shields?"

"Especially because you have shields, my prince," Tavis breathed. "I warn you, it's going to make you very tired—but what I need to do is draw energy from you. I won't harm you. I would never do that."

"I trust you, Tavis," the boy whispered. "I don't care that you're Deryni. You're—different."

"Oh, I do hope so, my prince," he murmured. "I do hope so."

Lifting his head, he glanced around the room, then lay back and released the boy's hand.

"Bring your chair closer, so you can be comfortable."

The boy obeyed, moving his chair right up against the side of the bed. He brought another blanket and laid it in the chair, padding the edges, then pulled the other blanket around himself against the chill of the room.

"That's right," Tavis murmured, guiding the boy to curl up with his head resting on the edge of the bed. "Scoot down just a little farther, so I can touch your head. Now give me your hand and make yourself comfortable. Make sure you won't be cramped."

Squirming a little, Javan did as he was bidden, shifting a fold of blanket under his shoulders where chair met edge of bed, then gazing up trustingly at what he could see of Tavis's head. He took the Healer's hand and cradled it against his cheek, finding a comfortable position at last, curled up on his side.

"That's fine," Tavis whispered, his voice now hardly a whisper. "Now open to me as if we were Healing again. I'm going to try to draw energy from you the same way you usually do from me. You may feel a faint sensation of pressure inside your head, as if something were being pulled slowly through your body and out through your head, but it's nothing to be afraid of, and I won't even start until you're nearly asleep. That's right. Let go and let me guide us both. Sleep now. You're safe."

And as Tavis's voice died away, Javan felt the familiar lethargy of the Healer's touch steal across his limbs; he sensed himself slipping into that twilight state he had felt so many times before, and he dreamed. He felt the warm, satisfying shift of energy stirring within him, prickling at the base of his skull, not at all unpleasant.

And as he drifted, other sensations sifted along the edges of his consciousness—of standing in a darkly shadowed room, surrounded by people who should have been familiar but somehow were not. His father was there, and held a strangely glowing cup to his lips. And then, there was a kaleidoscopic display of lights and sounds and spinning sensations—not frightening, but merely strange.

Then he was sinking deeper into sleep.

He felt Tavis's hand, reassuring against his cheek, and held onto it as if it were an anchor. But then he was aware of nothing, nothing at all, and would remember nothing when he woke.

Rhys and Camber found them that way half an hour later, but by then neither man could read any pattern other than normal sleep. Curious, but not at all alarmed, Camber gathered up the sleeping prince and carried him into his own room next door, while Rhys saw to their patient.

But Tavis was resting peacefully, the deep sleep of Healing, and so Rhys did not disturb him further, but contented himself with settling into the chair Javan had just vacated. Camber looked in on him briefly, after he had put Javan to bed, but Rhys told him there was nothing more they could do for several hours, and to get some sleep, himself. Camber obliged, taking Joram and Evaine back to his quarters in the archbishop's palace, where temporary housing was found for Joram's sister in the section reserved for the nuns on the lower level. All of them slept the sleep of physical and emotional exhaustion until dawn.

Tavis woke at first light, his slight stirring rousing Rhys with a start. Rhys was heartened to see that his patient's color was much improved with a night's sleep—in fact, Tavis looked considerably better than Rhys felt—but as he laid cool fingertips gently along his patient's wrist, he felt rigid shields surge into place across the other's mind. At Rhys's murmured, "Good morning," Tavis allowed his body to be read—but that was all. His attitude was almost hostile. Rhys wondered at the response, but he was careful not to react outwardly. The last thing Tavis needed was to have his grief and depression fed.

"Well, sleep did its usual wonders," Rhys said, when he

had finished his initial evaluation. "You're past the danger of shock. How do you feel?"

Slowly Tavis turned his head to gaze at Rhys, his pinched face unreadable. "How should I feel? I am a Healer who has lost a hand."

His voice was neutral, flat, and Rhys was a little concerned at the apparent lack of emotion as he went around to the other side of the bed.

"You *should* feel a loss," Rhys observed. "You still have your life, however, and you are still Deryni, and a Healer. There will doubtless be many things you still can do."

"Will there? Perhaps you're right."

Rhys had no answer for that. Silently he removed the blanket which shrouded Tavis's wounded limb and began untying the strips which bound it to the chairback. Tavis went white at the sight of the bandaged stump—obviously too small to contain even part of a hand—and turned his face away, trembling.

Moving quickly, Rhys unwrapped the wrist, intending only to change the dressing and, perhaps, work a bit more Healing, but he froze as the last layers of bandage came away. Hardly any blood stained the linen strips, and what there was, was dried. The stump, which still should have been raw and barely beginning to Heal from the inside, was smooth and healthy looking, faint scars visible where the skin had been joined to cover bone and tissue, but essentially Healed.

Containing his surprise, and working quickly to confirm what appeared to be, he bathed the stump gently with warm water which a servant brought, sluicing away the last of the dried blood and scabbing in amazement. The skin was fine and smooth, like the inside of the forearm. He could hardly believe that the injury had occurred only the day before, even with the miracle of Healer's aid. Thoughtfully, he wrapped a clean bandage lightly around it.

"Tavis, do you know anything about this?" he asked softly.

Tavis did not move his head.

"Anything about what?"

"About your arm," Rhys returned, gripping the forearm a little more tightly as he tried to catch the younger man's attention. "It's Healed, Tavis. I would have expected it to take days or even weeks, even with a Healer's full attention, to get to this stage. You could be fitted for a hook today."

Tavis turned his face even farther away.

"I will wear no hook," he breathed.

"No?" Rhys shrugged. "Well, suit yourself. You don't have to make any decisions about that yet. I want to know what happened, though. Did another Healer come in here last night, perhaps? Or—" A quick mental image of Tavis and Javan came and went. "God help you, Tavis, you didn't try anything with Javan, did you?"

Slowly Tavis turned his face back to Rhys, though he pointedly avoided looking at the arm Rhys held.

"What do you mean, did I try anything with Javan? What could I have tried? Javan is human. Besides, you know I would never do anything to harm him."

"I—don't know," Rhys said thoughtfully. "But I—we —found him asleep beside your bed early this morning, and you had your hand cradled against his cheek. Did he —say anything to you?"

"I was unconscious," Tavis whispered, staring at the ceiling now. "He must have thought to comfort me."

"I see." Rhys thought about that for a moment, some-how bothered by Tavis, but not in any way he could put his finger on, then slipped the Healer's arm into a loose restraining loop to keep it elevated.

"Well, he seems to have been good for you, whatever he did. How about something to eat?"

When Tavis did not reply, Rhys shrugged and headed for the door.

"Well, you have to eat. I'll be back in a little while. In the meantime, I suppose you could use a little time to yourself. That's going to take some getting used to."

And how would you know? Tavis retorted bitterly, but only in his mind, as the door closed behind the other Healer.

He lay there glaring at the door for several minutes be-fore giving it up as too tiring. In frustration, he rolled his head from side to side on the pillow, then stopped as his eye caught what he had been trying to avoid ever since he woke. There at his left, his arm was propped against the back of the chair, only a very light bandage covering the place where once a hand had been. A single loop of cloth held his upraised forearm against the chair back.

Slowly he reached his right hand across his body and touched his forearm where the cloth loop crossed, made

230

his eyes slip up to the bandage so close above. He swallowed to keep from choking, forcing himself to continue looking at it.

Alone now, with no false pride to make him brave and no pain to goad him into constructive action, the true extent of his loss was starting to come through as he had not permitted the night before. In his then state of shock, he had been able to tell himself that it was all a bad dream, that when he woke, the hand would be whole.

Except that this dream would go on. There would be no waking in the future as a whole man again. The hand was gone, and he was not. He was going to have to live a long time with that realization.

A moment more he procrastinated, biting back angry tears. Then his hand was fumbling at the cloth which supported his forearm, releasing the knot, easing his truncated arm down across his chest.

He rested there awhile, cradling his arm, his eyes closed, calming his mind against the horror which he must eventually face. Slowly he explored the sensations of his injury, hesitantly testing, probing. A muscle twitched in his arm, and he thought he felt a finger move—but he knew that could not be. Only phantom fingers would ever serve that hand again.

At that thought, his muscles twitched again and it was as if his phantom hand had made a fist. The feeling was so real that he opened his eyes, his gaze drawn irresistibly to the bandaged stump.

That brought him up short. He stared at the bandage in horrible fascination for several seconds, forcing himself to study every fold of the clean linen. Then he slid his hand up to the bandage and, in one quick motion, swept it away. A chill, awful nausea assailed him, but he forced himself to face what he now was, forced himself clinically to inspect every detail.

It did not take long. After a long moment of control, he abandoned all pretense of the cool, professionally-detached Healer and let himself weep, curling over onto his right side and cradling his phantom hand against his chest and sobbing for all that he had lost.

When Rhys returned with his breakfast a little later, he found Tavis asleep in that position and surmised what had happened; mercifully, he left the food within reach on the right side of the bed and went out again. He would let Tavis rest until Emrys and Queron arrived later on.

For now, sleep was surely the best possible medicine for Tavis O'Neill.

Sleep did seem to work its expected wonders, for when Rhys next looked in on Tavis, just before midday, he found that the Healer had eaten most of what was on his tray and was talking casually with the servant who had come to take away the remains. When he came back again, a little later, with Camber and the two Gabrilite Healers, they found him sitting up in bed. Other than the fact that Tavis kept his left arm under the blanket when they entered, he appeared to be rested and hale. Even his color was good, which Rhys found extremely unusual, considering the amount of blood he estimated Tavis must have lost.

"You're right, he does look well," Emrys said, as Rhys followed Camber and the two Healers into the room. "How are you, Tavis, my son? I was so sorry to hear of your unfortunate loss. This is Dom Queron Kincvan. I don't believe you've met."

Tavis eyed the white-robed Emrys evenly, but with little warmth, and gave Queron a neutral nod.

"Good afternoon, Dom Emrys, Your Grace. Dom Queron, I've heard much about you. Rhys, I'm surprised that you would bother these eminent lords with my small plight."

"Small plight?" Emrys said. "That isn't the way I heard it." He and Queron moved in on either side of the bed. "May we see your injury? We're told that you have effected a somewhat miraculous cure."

Tavis stiffened, his arm jerking slightly under the bedclothes, but he did not bring it out; merely laid his good hand protectively over the outline of his forearm beneath the blanket.

"I'm not certain it was a miraculous cure," he said guardedly. "Two Healers worked on me last night, as you know; and I am still a Healer myself, regardless of my— loss. A Healer's body, properly trained, should be able to Heal itself much faster than a Healer can Heal another's body. Dom Emrys, you yourself taught me that at Saint Neot's. Do you now question me, because I have been a good pupil?"

Dom Emrys, frail and almost transparent in his white robes, pale albino eyes ghostlike in his ageless face, laid a hand gently on Tavis's right shoulder, ignoring the quick flinch, tightly controlled.

"Nay, son, you have always been a good pupil. But sometimes the pupil surpasses the master, and that is what we would like to know. Even if there is nothing further we may do for you, you may, perhaps, help us by letting us see how we have taught you so successfully."

"We understand your defensiveness," Queron interjected quickly, from the other side of the bed, "but your loss must be faced, eventually. Is it not better to begin facing it among those who will understand what it has cost you? And you *can* learn to compensate, you know."

Angrily, though he tried to control it, Tavis lay back on his pillows and stared at the ceiling, tight-lipped and tense. The others waited. After a few minutes, Tavis sighed and slowly withdrew his left arm from underneath the blanket. A pale silk cloth was wrapped loosely around the stump, but he did not protest as Emrys reached gently across and withdrew it. The skin under the silk was smooth and white, like a baby's skin, with hardly a scar to show where the repairs had been made. The wrist now terminated in a smooth knob of flesh.

"Amazing!" Queron breathed. "If I had not seen it, I would not believe it."

With a nod, Emrys poised his hand above the wrist.

"May I read it, Tavis? I will be gentle."

"If you wish," Tavis replied tersely. "And there's no particular need to be gentle. I don't feel anything—except that, sometimes, I think my hand is still there, and that I can almost touch things with it."

Queron nodded. "A fairly standard response to an amputation. Battle Healers often run into that sort of reaction. There's sometimes phantom pain, too, as if the missing limb or part were still there and injured."

Emrys, slipping deep into his Healer's mode, laid his hand more firmly on Tavis's arm, signaling for Rhys to come to his side and share the probe. As Rhys obeyed, Queron, too, touched his fingertips to Tavis's arm and eased into the linkage. After a moment, all three men opened their eyes and broke the contact.

"This is quite amazing," Emrys said. "I've not seen that kind of thing except in people born that way. The ends of the bones have fused, and the musculature has redistributed as if it were meant to be that way. You have also managed somehow—and don't ask me how—to bring your blood level back almost to normal." He glanced at Rhys. "Are you certain he lost as much blood as you thought he did?"

Rhys shrugged. "Not certain, no, since I wasn't there when it happened, or even for the first hour or two thereafter. But his condition last night seemed to indicate a greater blood loss than he shows now. I can't explain it."

Puzzled, Emrys turned back to Tavis again.

"Can *you* explain it?" the old man asked. Tavis shook his head. "Then, will you allow me to read you more deeply? For some reason, your shields are very rigid, Tavis. There's no need for that with me, your old teacher. I had hoped you would realize that."

"I—cannot, sir," Tavis whispered, turning his head away and swallowing heavily. "Please, don't try to make me do it, either."

"But, I don't underst—"

"Then, understand this: *they* tried to batter down my shields!" he gasped, clutching his arm to his chest once more and plunging both arms beneath the blanket again. "They tried to—to force my mind! *Men of our own kind* held me fast while they chopped off my hand! They said I was aiding the enemy! Does Javan look like the enemy?"

There was little they could say to that. After making perfunctory apologies, Emrys and Queron were ushered from the room by a pensive and silent Rhys, Camber following wordlessly. The four men said nothing as they returned to Camber's quarters in the archbishop's palace, but they discussed the plight of Tavis O'Neill in hushed tones for several hours that evening, joined by Joram and Evaine.

"It's as if he's just shut down psychically," Rhys said. "And there's a core of bitterness there that's really making me uneasy. I don't know what to make of it."

"I hope that *I* don't know what to make of it," Queron said, after a long pause. "I once saw a case like this when I was still teaching at Saint Neot's. Do you remember, Emrys? We had a marvelously gifted young Healer's novice—Ulric was his name."

Emrys nodded and sighed, then shook his head sadly as Queron continued.

"Well, one day he simply—went berserk. He challenged the novice master to a duel arcane. He'd had almost no formal training in such things, but he defeated and killed the novice master! And the novice master was a high-level adept, a Healer himself and a very powerful practitioner!

"Anyway, the point of similarity is that young Ulric showed the same kind of adamant shielding for some time before he went mad, and there was no way to reach him, psychically. He called us devils and blasphemers and tried to bring down the entire abbey. Emrys put an arrow through his heart, right there in the cloister garth, or Ulric would have destroyed us all. He had turned on his own kind."

"You think Tavis might do that?" Evaine asked, after a stunned pause. "He's always seemed so gentle."

Queron shook his head slowly. "I don't know, my dear. I'm not certain I want to find out, either. Rhys, I don't suppose you might feel justified in trying out your little Healing quirk on Tavis, would you? To block his abilities until we're sure he's stable enough to handle them?"

"A touchy point of ethics," Rhys replied. "Besides, it may already be too late for that. We've established that cooperation isn't necessary—and you *know* he'd never cooperate for something like that—but the odd way his shields are fluctuating, I'm not sure I'd want to try it and risk the possible backlash. Something very strange is going on in that man's head."

"Do we just give up, then?" Camber asked. "Rhys, he's in a potentially very dangerous position, not only for himself, being the only Deryni in the regents' household right now, but for us. If he should become sufficiently disillusioned with us, that he'd side with the regents—why, with Tavis working for them, the regents could sniff out Deryni no matter where they went."

"Not if I can teach someone how to block Deryni powers," Rhys replied.

"But who are you going to teach? That's just the point. Emrys, Queron, God knows, you've tried—but suppose it can't be learned? Rhys, can you really go out and work with Revan? Are you prepared to make the necessary sacrifices? And even if you are, there's no way of ensuring that our manufactured cult will catch on. Besides, we're only talking about a few Deryni to be protected that way. They can't even be the best of us, because the best and best trained must stay aware to transmit our heritage to our children!"

With a surprised gasp, Queron sat back in his chair and

stared at Camber. Emrys, ever-calm, shook his head in disbelief and laid his hand on Camber's arm.

"Alister, Alister, don't *you* despair on us!—you, who are usually the rock of calm and courage. Do you truly think that no one else can learn to do it?"

Camber leaned his forehead on the heels of his hands and wearily shook his head. "I don't know. Forgive me, Emrys. It's just that all of us have been fighting for so long, in our own ways, and the situation seems to get worse instead of better, with each passing day. And I think I *have* raised a valid question: if we block the best to save the best, who will teach the children? Oh, we were as mad as your Ulric to even think it might work!"

Chilled, Rhys reached across to touch Camber's shoulder, at the same time reaching out with his mind.

Courage! You must not do this in front of Emrys and Queron! Or, is it your intention to tell them everything?

With a mental start, Camber jerked himself back into psychic focus, forced himself to look up slowly at Rhys. God knew, it was *not* his intention to tell the others everything. They thought Camber long dead, and a saint; better they remain thinking so. But Rhys was right. If he didn't get hold of himself, he was going to end up revealing everything in spite of himself.

"I'm sorry," he whispered, bowing his head again. "Lord, help Thou my unbelief. Perhaps it will work. Maybe some other Healer? Maybe Oriel? Rhys, could he have been responsible for Tavis's recovery?"

They discussed the possibility, though Rhys, who had worked with Oriel, had detected nothing in the young Healer which should have made him special from any other Healer. Nor could Oriel have returned without being seen.

They did not discuss the suspicion that Prince Javan might have had a hand in things. And especially, they did not discuss what had happened that other night, when Javan might, indeed, have gained the power to do what they were beginning to suspect.

Javan, too, wondered increasingly about that night, and about the strange link he seemed to have formed with Tavis, but he did not mention either one directly, when he spoke with his brothers that evening. He had taken supper with Tavis earlier, but by tacit agreement, neither had mentioned the events of the night before.

But when Javan joined Alroy and Rhys Michael just before evening prayers, to report on Tavis's progress, he did turn the conversation to what they remembered about the night their father died. Alroy's recollection was no better than Javan's own, however, and Rhys Michael could not be induced to take any of their discussion seriously, being preoccupied with the setting up of his toy knights. Alroy was interested in Tavis's progress, and was glad to learn that he was doing better, but he preferred not to talk about the attack.

"But, we've *got* to talk about it," Javan whispered, drawing his brother into an alcove near the fireplace. "He was attacked by Deryni! Deryni cut off his hand—a *Healer's* hand, Alroy! *My* Healer! What if he'd been one of *your* friends? Then you'd do something!"

"Well, what could I do?"

"You're the king! You could order their arrest!"

"But, Javan, I don't even know who they are! Besides, I'm only the king in name. If the regents don't agree, I can't do anything."

"Then, get them to agree!" Javan argued fiercely. "Listen, you told me yourself that there had been reports in the council about bands of young Deryni bloods running around and molesting people. These men who attacked us could have been from one of those bands. They were nobly dressed. But this time, they maimed a member of the royal household. And Rhys Michael and I might have been killed or maimed, too! Can't you do something?"

Alroy sighed and looked at his twin sourly. "Javan, you're not making it any easier for me. You're only a boy, just like me. We can't change the world."

"You're not a boy, you're a king!" Javan snapped. "And if you allow this kind of thing to continue, next time it may be *you* they're attacking! At least ask the regents to do something. They hate Deryni. They should be more than willing to round up some so that Tavis can check them out. He's certain he'd recognize them again, you know."

Alroy drew himself up straighter and looked at his brother. "He would?"

"Of course."

"Ah, but would he tell us?" Alroy asked. "He's Deryni, too, after all. Would he betray his own kind?"

Javan's jaw took on a tight set. "He'd betray those who mutilated him," he said softly. "Believe that!"

Alroy seemed to think about that for a long time. Then he slowly nodded.

"Very well. I'll ask them. But don't expect any miracles. They're not all that fond of Tavis anyway. They've only let him stay because you made such a scene about it."

"They'll see another scene or two, if they don't do this," Javan muttered under his breath. "I *want* the men who did this to him, brother! And I want them to suffer the same fate as they cast on Tavis—before I have them killed. They must learn that *no one* trifles with the servants of the royal House of Haldane!"

CHAPTER SIXTEEN

For the elements were changed in themselves by a kind of harmony.

—Wisdom of Solomon 19:18

The Camberian Council met several nights later, with Emrys and Queron in attendance, as well as Davin and Ansel and Jesse. The only topic was Tavis.

"Well, I still think you're overestimating the seriousness of the situation," Gregory said. "Tavis O'Neill is a conscientious Healer and a good friend of Prince Javan. He protects the boy from the regents. Even if he isn't one of us, he's a Deryni in the heart of the castle. If we needed him, I feel certain we could call on him."

"You *feel*. Ah, but do you know for sure?" Camber asked. "That's the real question. Right now, it's been nearly a week since the attack, and in all that time, Tavis has not let himself be read, other than on a purely physical level. His shields are so strong that I don't think anything or anyone could get through except by force— and that could destroy him."

"Drugs are a possibility," Rhys volunteered. "If everyone is as worried about what he's planning as it appears,

I suppose I could find some excuse to slip him a doctored cup and force the rapport."

"It's certainly tempting," Camber replied. "I question whether you could 'slip' it to him, the way he seems so suspicious of us lately, but the longer we wait, the stronger he seems to get and the less likely you probably are of succeeding. What does everybody else think?"

"I think it's a damned-fool notion!" Gregory replied. "Tavis is not a traitor, he's a victim. Unless you know something about this case that you're not telling us, I don't see why all of you are so concerned."

Evaine, sensing the direction the conversation could go if not headed off immediately, sighed and shook her head.

"We know he's a victim, Gregory. But he's still close to the princes, especially Javan. And today we learned that one of them—and we have to assume that it's Alroy, though Javan probably put him up to it—one of them persuaded the regency council to start hunting down those bands of Deryni bravos. Jaffray, why don't you tell him what happened in council today?"

Jaffray nodded.

"Evaine is right. The king was not present today, but Tammaron presented the idea. The story now is that the attackers were really after the two princes, but settled for Tavis, since they couldn't get at the children. Naturally, it's said that Tavis will help to identify the attackers—which, no doubt, he will. If I'd gone through what young Tavis did, I shouldn't doubt I'd want my revenge, too."

Jebediah, who had been out at the Michaeline commanderie at Argoed for the past week, traced one of the golden inlays of the table with a scarred forefinger.

"It sounds to me like we need someone to keep an eye on Tavis better. It's too bad all my men have been cashiered from the guards. The royal household is going to be moving to Rhemuth this summer, unless I miss my bet, and a well-placed guard could really keep us posted."

"A human?" Evaine asked. "That's the only one who would be acceptable, for Tavis would be able to detect another Deryni. But a human sworn to our service would also be detectable, if Tavis became the least bit suspicious."

Jebediah nodded thoughtfully. "That's true. And if we used a human, and gave him sufficient protection to escape detection, he'd be little use for reporting back." He sighed and thought a moment, then raised his head again. "Rhys, how about your little trick? What if we were to send in a Deryni with his powers blocked?"

Joram raised one cynical eyebrow. "Same problem. If his powers are blocked, how would he be any better than a human? We could set up a link and monitor him from here, I suppose, and that could be useful if he could remember what he was supposed to be watching for—but if he could remember that, then it could also be read by Tavis."

Davin raised his hand tentatively. "Maybe we just need to take a bit of a chance, then. Surely Tavis O'Neill has better things to do with his time than to read every paltry guard who comes into the royal service. For that matter, you could send your man in with his powers blocked initially, then remove the block after he's established as a trustworthy member of the household."

Camber nodded. "Now, that I like. Good thinking, Davin." He glanced at the others. "Of course, the next question is, where do we find someone suitable? He's almost got to be someone unknown, but he also has to be someone who can be trusted with the knowledge of this Council. That narrows our choices considerably."

"Aye, it does, that," Jaffray agreed. "Queron, Emrys, any ideas from your connections? Queron, is there someone within the Servants of Saint Camber who might do?"

Queron shook his head. "There are few Deryni within our ranks, Your Grace. And the few who are have not the martial training to carry off such a deception. The idea of recruiting such a man from cloistered ranks is a good one, though." He turned toward Emrys. "Perhaps one of your Gabrilite novices, Emrys? Or you, Jebediah? Even better. How about some young Michaeline trainee?"

It was Jebediah's turn to shake his head. "Those of sufficient training were in public positions too recently. No, what we need is a highly trained Deryni from outside those ranks."

"How about me?"

It was Davin who had spoken, and all eyes turned toward him in astonishment. Evaine started to shake her head, a horrified look on her face, but Davin held up a hand and swept them all with his gaze.

"No, listen. It's perfectly logical. I have the martial training, I'm associated with this Council, and I—"

"And you're instantly recognizable wherever you go,

Earl of Culdi," Camber interrupted, shaking his head vehemently. "No, I won't hear of it."

"Pardon me, Bishop Alister," Davin said softly, "but it isn't entirely up to you. Uncle Joram, didn't you once tell me how, after my father was killed, my grandfather placed your shape and Rhys's on two of the servants, so that you could escape to rescue Prince Cinhil?"

There was a low whistle of amazement from Gregory, and several sighs around the table, as Joram slowly nodded. Camber, controlling his apprehension only with great effort, could see the pulse beating wildly in his son's temple.

"Didn't you tell me that, Uncle?" Davin repeated softly.

Slowly Joram forced himself back into control, willing his hands to relax from their white-knuckled grip on the edge of the table, swallowing once, taking a deep, calming breath.

"Yes, I told you that."

"And you, Uncle Rhys," Davin continued. "You were there. You experienced it, too. And I'm sure that Aunt Evaine must know how to do it." He glanced from one to the other of them, trying to read their reactions.

"Don't you see? It's the perfect solution. One of you puts a shape-change on me, and Rhys temporarily blocks my powers. You give me a false identity as a human soldier, newly recruited to the guards. No, even better, you actually snatch a guard who's just been assigned to the royal household, and I take his place. Then, after I've established myself, Rhys removes the block and I report regularly through a prearranged contact—Jaffray, perhaps. Or maybe a psychic link. It's the perfect solution, I tell you."

As the young man eagerly searched all their faces, Gregory glanced at Joram.

"Well, can you do it?"

"No."

"Joram!" Evaine chided. "Of course you can."

"But I won't. It's too dangerous," Joram replied stubbornly. "I know it was necessary then." *And other times, too,* his further thought echoed in her mind. "But it's too dangerous now. What if he's found out? He's your nephew, too, Evaine."

"I know that."

Quietly Evaine glanced across the table at her husband.

In the back of her mind, she could feel the shocked rapport of her father, helpless, once again, to do anything to prevent what now seemed to be inevitable.

"Rhys, what do you think? Could Davin carry it off, given your block and a shape-change? I can handle the latter, if you don't feel competent."

Rhys sighed, knowing the reluctance both Evaine and her father were feeling, yet unable to find a good reason to object.

"I can block him. I'd feel safer if someone else also knew how to undo it, in case anything should happen to me, but I'm afraid I must agree that Davin seems to be the only man for the job—if, indeed, this is a job we need to have done. Unfortunately, I've been racking my brain ever since he mentioned it, and I can't think of any other way to keep tabs on Tavis and our wayward princes and their even more wayward regents. I say we let him try it, if he's willing."

"And if he fails, will you take his blood on your hands, too?" Joram asked harshly. "Can we afford to risk one of our own number on something this chancy?"

"There is blood already on our hands," Evaine murmured, remembering the many, many who had already died. "But if there is to be more, then better there be the chance of our best blood succeeding rather than the greater chance of failure by those less qualified."

"Amen to that," Jaffray breathed.

"Then, are we agreed?" Evaine asked. "I say aye, and Rhys, and Jaffray, and Davin, of course. And Joram says nay. Gregory, how say you?"

"Aye."

"And Father Alister?"

He felt her sorrow and her resignation across the bond of her love, and knew that she was right. Slowly he nodded, not daring to meet his son's eyes. He felt his daughter's swell of support, deep and bolstering, as she turned her attention to Jebediah.

"And you?"

"He is right. There is no one else. I say aye."

"Then so be it," she murmured. "I'm sorry, Brother," she added, as Joram hung his head and gnawed his lip.

After a long silence, it was Davin who dared to speak. "Well, then, it's all settled. When can I start?"

"It will be a week or so," Jebediah quickly replied. "We must find guard officers who know our replacement guard, but not too well, and then you must review the guard protocols, so you'll know what you're doing. It's a little different from being an earl. I'd say at least a week. Evaine, Rhys, do you agree?"

Both nodded simultaneously.

"I'll need to work with him on the blockage and memories we must instill," Rhys said. "Then there must be a compulsion for him to appear, after things are safe, where I can join him to remove the blockage and restore his real memories. Somewhere the guards can go when off duty. And I'm sure that Evaine will want to work on the physical shape-changing more than once."

Two weeks later, they were ready. A week it took to drill Davin in his military manners, for he would be playing a far lower rank than ever he would have held in his own right as earl; and another week he worked with Rhys and Evaine, practicing the total relaxation which would be necessary for optimum effect. The while, Jebediah sought out the officers who would be able to vouch for Davin in his new role. The soldier he was to replace was also found: one Eidiard of Clure, a slender young highland man of Davin's approximate coloring and build who had only lately been assigned but had not yet reported to court. On the appointed evening, the full Council, less Jebediah, gathered in the *keeill*, below the Council chamber.

Keeill: the term meant chapel or sanctuary, and this one had been ancient when the first Haldanes pacified what later became Gwynedd, nearly three centuries before. It, and most of the Council chamber above, lay hidden beneath a high, rock-girt plateau of the rugged Rhendall mountains, almost within sight of the sea. An ancient Deryni brotherhood known only as the Airsid claimed credit for the *keeill* itself, and apparently had at least started work on the chamber which now housed the Council, but they had disappeared before it could be finished—no one knew why.

Neither *keeill* nor Council chamber were now accessible except by Transfer Portal, and no one could even guess how the first one might have been placed there. Even the existence of the complex had been discovered only by accident, from a chance reference in one of the ancient manuscripts which still occupied most of Evaine's leisure time. After that, many more months had passed before they were confident enough of their visualizations of the described Portal there to risk an actual Transfer.

Eventually they had done it, though; and discovery of the then only partially completed Council chamber and *keeill* had given them both a secure meeting place and a sanctuary for ritual workings. They had felt at home immediately.

The *keeill* was heavy and massive, the walls curved instead of faceted-in-eight. Roughly-dressed ashlar pillars, twelve of them, stood flush against the perimeter, with enough space between for a person to stand. The single bronze door in the northern quarter opened between two of them. Four bronze cressets held torches which gave smoky, wavering life to the four quarters, thrusting vague, dancing shadow-shapes in and among the recesses of the pillars. The ceiling was somewhat more finely finished, having geometric vaulting of a blue-grey stone that glittered slightly in the torchlight.

A dais of grey-black slate occupied most of the center of the room, the first of its seven shallow steps starting only an armspan from the heavy mass of the pillars. Precisely in the center of the dais was a square of stark white marble, an armspan on each edge and a hand's-breadth thick. Around that slab knelt Rhys, Evaine, and a taut-looking Davin, the three of them putting the final touches to a Ward Major construct which wanted only final activation, once its components were placed at the edge of the dais.

The others waited among the pillars, Jaffray and Gregory standing at the eastern and southern quarters and Camber and Joram by the door in the north—though Joram still was not resigned to what was about to take place. As those in the center began moving the ward components into position, the door opened to admit Jebediah and a sleepwalking young man who wore the harness of the Gwynedd Royal Guards. The grand master closed the door behind them, then turned slightly toward Camber and Joram, his gloved hand resting lightly on his companion's arm.

"It's necessary, Joram. You know that," he said.

"So you tell me."

"But you don't believe it, do you?"

Joram shrugged. "It simply seems that we're getting into more deception, all over again."

"You reconciled yourself to the others," Camber murmured.

"Those were different."

"How, different?"

"They just—happened. There was no premeditation. This is—cold. And your victim, there, has nothing to say about it. Before, all the participants were willing ones."

Camber nodded thoughtfully. "That's true. Crinan and Wulpher agreed to help us. Evaine chose to do what she did. And for Alister, it didn't matter." He glanced at the silent Eidiard, at the blank, unseeing eyes, the slack expression, then back at Joram.

"But this young man has not been asked. And that bothers you?"

"It does."

"He will not be harmed by what we do. He merely will be held incommunicado. It will be a very honorable confinement."

"But his life is ruined, especially if this fails," Joram pointed out. "Even if we change our minds and pull Davin out before anything happens to him, this man's military career is finished. You could never fill in the gaps so that he could step back into his place as it exists today."

"No," Jebediah agreed. "But we can make him another place. And even if we can't—well, sometimes soldiers in a war serve in many different ways. This will be his."

"But he wasn't allowed to choose, it," Joram said.

"No, he wasn't, son. But that's the way it has to be."

Joram made no answer to that, merely folded his arms across his chest and watched sourly as Jebediah took the compliant Eidiard up the seven shallow steps of the dais and transferred control to Evaine. Then, as Jebediah came back down to rejoin Camber and Joram, Rhys raised his arms and focused on the cubes, speaking the words which brought the Wards to life.

"Primus, Secundus, Tertius, et Quartus, fiat lux!"

Light flared in the perimeter of the dais, flickering blue-white starshine in a circle defined by the four ward components. Evaine touched her fingertips lightly to Eidiard's temples and deepened his trance. After a few seconds he swayed on his feet and would have overbalanced, had not Rhys moved in to support him. At that, Evaine drew her hands away and glanced at Davin, who had watched all in tense silence.

"He will know nothing of what we do. Come and change clothes with him now."

Beneath the steel-gray robe he now removed, Davin already wore the simple linen undertunic and breeks of a guardsman. Wordlessly he and Rhys began removing Eidiard's battle harness, only the muffled clank of leather-cased plate and the jingle of buckles intruding on the hollow silence of the wards. When the guardsman had been stripped down to the same garb as Davin, Davin began putting on the other's clothing.

Close-fitting leather britches of a deep, rich brown; then the gambeson, heavy linen quilted over sheep's wool in a lozenge design. Next, a leather brigandine of the new design, sewn with hand-sized metal plates between the two layers, covering all the torso and shoulders and reaching to midthigh. Over that, the crimson surcoat of Haldane service, with a lion's head blazoned on the shoulder.

He pulled on heavy, knee-high boots after that and buckled on plain steel spurs, a sword-belt of brown leather carrying a plain sword, and a dagger which appeared to have seen much use. Eidiard's gloves were slipped under the belt. His mantle and helmet had been left outside the circle.

"Let's see you now," Evaine said, as Rhys helped their nephew tug the last strap-end into place. "Stand here beside him. Yes, the resemblance is uncommonly good, even without the shape-change. That makes it easier."

Davin shifted the weight of the armor on his shoulders and tried to scratch between his shoulderblades. "I'm glad you approve," he murmured with a grimace. "I could have wished for a little less realism, though. I think there are bugs in this gambeson!"

"Welcome to the life of the common soldier," Rhys grinned. He glanced at Evaine, the amusement going out of his eyes. "Are we ready?"

"As ready as we're going to be."

Gently she took Eidiard's hand and led him into the center of the circle, guiding his step up onto the square white slab which marked it. When she had placed him to her satisfaction, she turned to Davin and gestured for him to step up beside the man he was about to become. Davin, with a deep breath, obeyed.

"Now, you understand how important it is that you open completely for this?"

"I understand."

"Good," Evaine replied, exchanging glances with Rhys as he came to stand behind Davin. "Because the deeper you can go, the wider you can open to me, the better image I'll be able to put on you. That's important, since you won't be able to do anything to help stabilize your shape for the first few weeks, while your abilities are blocked." She laid her hands lightly on his shoulders. "Now, take a deep breath and let's get started. Good. Now, another."

Davin obeyed, letting himself begin to sink into familiar trancing. The first stages were not difficult, but as he sank deeper and deeper under Evaine's subtle guidance, he could feel himself reaching new depths which were not easy to keep open in the smooth, passive widening which Evaine demanded, even though they had done it many times in the past week.

He drew another deep breath, pushing himself down another level as he let it out, and then was dimly aware of Rhys's gentle hands slipping along either side of his head from behind, the Healer beginning to draw him even deeper, so that he lost track of his surroundings.

His eyes were closed now. He could not see with his vision, but his mental Sight was increasing with every breath—and those were becoming farther and farther apart, as his body settled into the relaxed, receptive state which Evaine guided and encouraged.

He was no longer master of his breathing now—though that did not matter, since Rhys guarded that function with his Healer's touch. Nor was he certain that his heart would have continued to pump, were it not for Rhys's Healing hands. His whole being was now contained between those other hands resting on his shoulders, now slipping up to touch his forehead. Something seemed to settle into place at that new touch—something which gave over, for all his present existence, the control of his destiny. Now, even if he had wanted to break the rapport, he was not certain that he could—and did not care.

Evaine's hands left him briefly then, and vaguely he sensed that Eidiard was being similarly prepared, that his pattern was being brought into the linkage. He teetered there on the brink of knowing and unknowing, precariously balanced between Rhys's two hands, until Evaine's touch once more glittered just behind his closed eyes.

Hold steady now, her mind whispered into his, as she poised between him and Eidiard on the balance point.

Then the energy began to flow, and he abandoned himself to its filling. He could sense the power tingling in his limbs, an eerie sensation like hundreds of tiny insects crawling all over his body—yet, oddly, not an unpleasant feeling—a vibrancy which permeated every part of him. He felt it as his own, and yet there was a part of it which was not his.

Suddenly it was over. His body was his own again, all strange sensation gone. As Evaine drew hand and mind apart from him, he felt himself surfacing from the place where he had been—swayed a little with the sheer giddiness of so rapid a return to normal consciousness. Rhys's hands steadied him, the Healer's mind withdrawing more slowly as functions were returned to Davin's control. When Davin opened his eyes, Evaine was gazing at him with a pleased smile on her face, one hand resting on the shoulder of the still-entranced Eidiard.

Rhys came around to face the northern boundary of the Ward Major and open a gateway toward which Jebediah was ascending. Evaine laid Davin's discarded robe around Eidiard's shoulders, then turned him over to Jebediah, who took him out. When Jebediah had returned, and Rhys had secured the wards again, she turned back to Davin.

He could see in her eyes that he had changed. From the movement outside the circle, seen only dimly through the haze of the warding, he could tell that the others were similarly impressed. Fleetingly he wished that he had a mirror, then dismissed the notion as frivolous, almost as soon as it had come.

He needed no mirror to tell him what he looked like now. In the week just past, he had looked like every one of them, with Evaine's help. Besides, the most difficult part was yet to come—and the most frightening part, though he knew that he would not remember that. They had worked with the block numerous times during the past week, though in their training sessions, Rhys had always let him retain his awareness of what was happening. This time, Davin knew that he was to remember nothing of his true identity. Even to Deryni scrutiny, he must appear to be only what his exterior proclaimed: a soldier, human, of no particular consequence other than being assigned to the princes' guard.

Then Rhys was standing before him and flashing that peculiarly reassuring smile that Healers were wont to display when about to attempt some particularly difficult or unusual Healing—except that this was not a Healing; and for the next few weeks, Davin would be completely at the mercy of whatever they chose to leave him with. Was he sure that he wanted to go through with this?

But they had gone over all of this before. Though he had volunteered on impulse, his capabilities and motives had been carefully scrutinized and studied all through the past two weeks. Father Alister and Joram had been particularly against his taking on this mission; but it had been clear, in the end, that there was no one better suited to do the job, and that the job needed to be done.

With a deep breath to banish his conflicting emotions, he returned Rhys's lopsided little smile and held out his hands to the Healer. Rhys took them. Without a word they settled into the rapport they had practiced so often in the past two weeks.

Evaine's hands were on his shoulders as he slipped deep into trance once more, and Davin knew that she was monitoring in the same way that Rhys had done, during the first part of the working. He achieved a good depth of trance immediately at Rhys's urging, then slipped even deeper, gave up control wholly to Rhys as the Healer's mind insinuated itself in ways far different from Evaine's touch.

This was the control of a Healer now, light yet firm, pushing down all his conscious reflexes and protections, gentle yet insistent, irresistible. Davin's last conscious thought, as the Healer's mind took hold and began the odd, sense-wrenching operation which would block his powers, was that he might die from this—but that somehow, it did not matter. Here, safe between Rhys and Evaine, he could sleep forever. His life was in their hands.

And Rhys, as he took control and tilted the energies, touching the triggerpoint and shifting it as he had before, felt the familiar jolt in his own mind as the block was set in place and he slowly began to withdraw.

Evaine pulled out completely then, only lending her physical support as the changed Davin slowly crumpled under Rhys's continuing touch and sank to the marble slab. As Davin dreamed on, human now, Rhys continued his patterning, securing the controls he had planted, weaving the background in what would become the conscious mind of a soldier named Eidiard, while Evaine went about the business of releasing the wards.

When Rhys finally looked up, Davin-Eidiard slept still and sound beneath his hands. Rhys let out a deep sigh as he withdrew his final contact, glancing around at all of them.

"That's about the best I can do," he murmured, "but I think it will stand the scrutiny. Go ahead and test, if you wish. You won't disturb him."

One by one, they did, each withdrawing after a time to nod agreement or shake a head in disbelief at what they read. Camber and Joram alone did not accept his invitation, Camber because he did not need to and Joram because he did not wish it. When they were finished Jebediah stood and dusted the knees of his blue riding leathers with a gloved hand.

"Well, that's done, then. I'll take Davin back to the horse Eidiard had waiting and see him off to his new assignment. Several of my Michaelines are waiting there, and will take the real Eidiard back to Argoed with them. They're Deryni, so there won't be any problem."

"That sounds fine," Rhys agreed. "And beginning tonight, I think one of us should always try to be in the chamber above and monitoring for him, ready to pull out quickly and notify Jaffray immediately, if anything should go wrong. Jaffray, you'll be the only one within physical reach, in such a case."

Jaffray nodded. "Understood."

"I'll take the first watch, if you like, then," Camber said. "I'm apt to be missed in the daytime. Father Willowen runs Grecotha as if it were his, and gets almost indignant when he can't find me."

"Sign of a good dean," Jaffray said with a tight little smile. "He'll keep things running, whether you're there or not. I'll take tomorrow night, though, since I, too, am likely to be missed in the daytime. Besides, I can't let those regents run amok in the council."

An hour later, they were all gone except Camber, who sat silently at the great table in the Council chamber and thought about what they had done this night.

More deception, Joram would have said—*had* said, though not in so many words. And Camber had to agree that it was so. They had worked no such deception in all the long years since Camber had assumed Alister's form.

And now it began again, with Camber's grandson also in a position of jeopardy and not even knowing the fullness of why it must be done.

Oh, there were immediate reasons, of course, and they were all good or at least reasonable ones. But the fact remained that all they did today was predicated on what had happened so many years before, was bound up with the deception of Camber taking the form and shape of Alister, to try to retain some influence over the royal family which they themselves had placed in power.

And if things had been shaky during the reign of Cinhil at times—and only a fool could claim that they had not— what were they now, with a child on the throne and avaricious regents controlling that child and his even younger brothers?

Not that *all* the children were totally under the influence of the regents. Javan had shown surprising spunk in the past few weeks. His support of Tavis O'Neill, while not unexpected from a purely human standpoint, had become far more than that on a psychic plane.

No one had been able to get close to Javan to see precisely what had happened. But even in the short contact which Camber and Rhys had had with Javan that night of the attack, it was clear that something about Javan had changed—whether from what they had done to him that night of Cinhil's death, or from working with Tavis, or what, Camber didn't know. But if it had come of what they did to him, then they were to blame for whatever happened. And a human who could shield like Javan could be dangerous, indeed.

In the meantime, there was Davin to be watched and guarded, and a host of other things to be tended now that Camber was back at Grecotha permanently.

And where was Davin now? Ah, yes: mounting his horse, where Jebediah had just left him. The entity was Davin, but the part which was Davin himself was so deeply submerged that Camber must constantly remind himself just whom he was tracking. He certainly could not read a distinctive spark.

Only soldier thoughts were on the surface of Davin's mind as he guided his horse onto the main road and began cantering easily toward Valoret. He was concerned with his new commission, eager to enter the king's service, pleased that his commanders had esteemed him sufficiently competent to procure him the new assignment.

Few other thoughts crossed his mind as he rode along, but he was not aware of the shallowness of his existence in this shell of the real Eidiard, so he did not think it amiss that his mind seemed occupied only with soldier thoughts.

And Camber, as he watched idly with one part of his mind, let himself drift off to contemplation of other things as the dawn approached.

CHAPTER SEVENTEEN

A faithful friend is a strong defense: and he that hath found such an one hath found a treasure.
—Ecclesiasticus 6:14

The days passed, and the weeks, and the summer solstice came and went. For the first month after the coronation, Valoret remained in a state of unease bordering on shock, the attack on Tavis now being openly regarded as an actual attempt on the lives of the two younger princes, perpetrated by Deryni.

To make matters worse, an unusually hot summer brought with it a mild but debilitating plague to which humans, for some reason, seemed far more susceptible than Deryni. Few folk of either race died, other than the very young or the very old, but human victims were apt to be bedridden for a month or more with alternating bouts of vomiting and loose stools, and might be badly scarred thereafter as a result of the shiny white pustules which sometimes accompanied the disease. Deryni either did not catch it, or else recovered within a fortnight, usually with no permanent ill effects.

Rumor began to run that perhaps the Deryni had had a hand in the coming of the plague, for certainly there seemed no other reason that Deryni should suffer less than humans. In some areas, rumor even had it that certain

Deryni Healers were spreading it rather than curing it—and that magic was being used to try to undermine the new regime. Hubert preached a fiery sermon on the dangers of black magic, and the regular prayer for the king's health was modified to include a plea for deliverance from magic.

The summer wore on. Alroy and Javan finished their formal schooling at the beginning of July, though they would be continuing their practical education for many, many years, and immediately the entire Court packed up to move to Rhemuth at last. Restoration of the ancient capital, begun in earnest during the latter years of Cinhil's reign, had been stepped up almost immediately on his death, as soon as the weather allowed. By midmonth, when king and Court actually arrived in the city, the royal architects and master masons could report that at least the keep and the gatehouse of the old castle were now habitable. They hoped to have all the old castle fully secure before the first snow. The regents felt very strongly that a relocation to the old Haldane stronghold, with its positive associations for the old regime, would greatly strengthen the claim of the new one. Progress thus far, on both counts, had been impressive.

The massive octagonal keep, the heart of the castle complex, had been made weathertight and secure even before the Court arrived from Valoret, with new lead sheathing laid down on the conical roof and good grisaille glass inserted in all the windows of the top two floors. The keep was still somewhat more drafty than the old apartments at Valoret, for little could be done to keep the damp from rising through the garde-robe shafts and unused chimney flues; but garde-robes could be curtained or partitioned off, relegating the worst of their unpleasantness to times of actual use; and fires were kept burning most of the time in the fireplaces that had been restored thus far. The insulation of thick tapestries and carpets brought from Valoret also helped to make the rooms more hospitable.

Earls Tammaron and Murdoch and their wives shared the top floor of the keep, with separate sleeping quarters and the restored solar occupied in common. The solar gave access to a roof walk circling the top of the keep, and connected, via wall walks, to the castellan's quarters in the gatehouse at the south, and to the yet uninhabitable residential tower in the west. Rebuilding of the gatehouse, captured and then slighted during the Festillic takeover, had been the first project the masons tackled, when Cinhil gave the order to begin repairs. The gatehouse and keep now constituted a nearly impregnable defense, even without the added protection of the curtain walls and secondary defenses.

The king and his brothers were quartered on the floor beneath the regents, still with separate sleeping quarters, but once more sharing a common dayroom. Tavis, the royal squires, and Father Alfred, the boys' confessor, were also housed on that level in a series of tiny intramural chambers adjoining those of the appropriate prince, though these were suitable for little other than sleeping and storage of a few personal belongings. Below the princes lay the two-storied former great hall of the keep, now relegated to auxiliary kitchen facilities and quarters for the royal bodyguards; and the lowest floor was occupied by the many clarks and scribes who carried out the written business of the new regime. The keep's all-important well, storerooms, and cellars took up the three underground levels, these gradually being stocked with grain, flour, wine, and other provisions necessary to see the household through the winter.

A number of wooden outbuildings had also arisen in the castleyard to augment the facilities of gatehouse and keep. Chief among these was a large, hammer-beamed hall with a good slate roof, set against the north curtain and connected to the keep by a covered walkway, doubling as audience chamber, court, and feasting place. A stable with barracks above and a smaller servants' hall adjoining the kitchen tower had also been built, with bedchambers above and a buttery and pantry. A free-standing chapel and a temporary building containing an armory and smithy were also nearly completed, and a practice yard for horse and foot combat had been laid out between the two. Nothing was as spacious as Valoret, but it was adequate, and becoming more so with each passing day.

Perhaps the most comfortable accommodations in Rhemuth were enjoyed by its archbishop, the same Robert Oriss who once had been King Cinhil's superior in the *Ordo Verbi Dei*. In the thirteen years since the archbishopric had been reactivated, a new cathedral and episcopal residence had been completed, started and finished even before Cinhil had begun the restoration of Rhemuth as

254

the royal capital. The Cathedral of Saint George, built on the foundations of an older church of the same name, and whose undercroft still sheltered the remains of almost all Gwynedd's Haldane kings, became the first of many edifices planned to enrich and glorify the former Haldane capital. The archbishop's residence was a fitting companion to such an architectural jewel.

Upon realizing the cramped and somewhat ordinary conditions at Castle Rhemuth, Hubert wasted no time in approaching his archbishop for a favor, one bishop to another; and soon Hubert was lodged in relative luxury and comfort with his brother bishop, who was flattered and somewhat awed that one of the royal regents should deign to grace his house with his august presence.

Earl Ewan became Duke Ewan that summer, his father, Duke Sighere, having been among the first of the old and already infirm to succumb to the plague; and shortly after the Court went to Rhemuth, he and Rhun returned to Valoret to supervise the army there, Ewan assuming his new duties as earl marshal in name, as well as in fact, and Rhun assisting him.

While this move divided the regents geographically, and diminished their immediate influence as a group over the king and his brothers, it also put Ewan and Rhun into daily close contact with the officers and men of Gwynedd's army—which reflected sound military reasoning, even if it did nothing to reassure the Camberian Council. By mid-August, the Council learned that Ewan had called up a large part of the Gwynedd levies and divided the by-now largely human army into two parts, the lesser one moving nearer Rhemuth under the direct command of Murdoch and Tammaron, with Hubert's brother Manfred executing their orders, while the rest encamped and held military exercises on the plain just west of Valoret.

No one knew why they had assembled, or against the threat of what enemy they conducted their maneuvers and practiced their battle skills, but some Deryni had their suspicions. Ewan was shaping to be a man without conscience, totally dedicated to carrying out the policies being determined by the regency of which he was a part; and Rhun the Ruthless could only serve as a further dehumanizing force.

But most Deryni ignored the warning signs, and said that nothing could happen.

Alroy and his brothers were little aware of what went on outside Rhemuth, other than to note that Ewan and Rhun were no longer so often about. Alroy's physical health had never been better, there in the milder climate of the plains country, and even Javan had far less pain in his foot than was his usual wont. Several times a week, royal duties permitting, the three boys would ride out on the rolling plain of Candor Rhea to hunt or fish or simply race like the wind on fine, blooded horses, sometimes taking their hawks, but more often accompanied by the great, red-eared coursing hounds which Earl Murdoch had given them. All three boys grew inches in that summer of 917, to the despair of the royal tailor, who must keep them in decent-length tunics; and the twins, especially, began to take on the leaner lines of young manhood as they wore into their thirteenth summer. In many respects, it was the happiest time the boys had ever known.

Yet, if the boys waxed strong in body that summer, mental stimulation was quite another matter. At the heart of all their waking activities were Murdoch and Tammaron and Hubert, who made a point of subtly stifling any royal interest in affairs of state. The king and his brothers were trotted out on feast days and for other ceremonial occasions, and the regents regularly brought Alroy piles of documents requiring the royal signature; but they discouraged him from participation in most of the actual decision-making unless he had been carefully coached in advance. True, Alroy was a king, but he was also a boy of twelve, they reminded him, and most matters of state were far too complicated for him to understand. There would be plenty of time to worry himself about such things when he was grown.

Given sufficient repetition of such indoctrination, Alroy began to accept it. He had never been particularly strong-willed; and the spark of defiance which had surfaced briefly at his coronation was soon replaced by boredom. Subtle medication prescribed by an obedient royal physician and given him on a regular basis as a tonic further helped to erode resistance. By summer's end, Alroy was essentially the placid, compliant prince who was all the regents' dream. Rhys Michael, too, appeared to be a model child, biddable and diffident to his elders while still retaining that merry, carefree outlook which had always been his trademark. Only Javan, of the three, was beginning to see through the regents' benign facade; and from the beginning, he was careful to conceal his true feelings.

Javan's first concern after the post-coronation turmoil, of course, had been Tavis's recovery. Though Tavis seemed to have effected a miraculous physical recovery, he had sunk into a profound depression once his life was no longer in danger, withdrawing for much of the time into his own private prison of grief and agonized loss. Many were the days when he hardly left his bed, staring at the walls and ceiling of his tiny sleeping cubicle while an increasingly concerned Javan sat and talked or read to him for hours, eliciting only minimal response. Only gradually did Tavis emerge, Javan's monologues at last evolving to long discussions and walks along the castle ramparts.

Tavis would not speak of Healing, however; and it was only when necessity compelled, in the form of an injury to Javan, that the maimed Healer could be induced to try to Heal again. Javan had twisted his crooked foot painfully while wrestling with one of Murdoch's sons in the castleyard, and could obtain no relief from the cold compresses which the royal physicians prescribed for the swelling. Tearfully Javan begged his friend at least to try to ease the pain. And when love for his young charge had finally overcome his self-loathing for his own fate, Tavis had agreed, laying hand and stump on Javan's foot—to Heal.

The Healing was a milestone in Tavis's recovery, for he soon found that the contact thus established was just as sensitive as it had been through the missing hand. The balance of energies was different, as he had maintained to Rhys all along, and any physical manipulations must be done with his right hand—but he could compensate for those. The discovery placed his future in an entirely different light, and restored him to his previous partnership with Javan.

That accomplished, the only other adjustment he had to make was to the reactions of others. He had tried to hide his maimed arm in the early days, wearing it in a sling held close to his body. After resuming Healing, he abandoned the sling entirely, and contented himself with merely having an empty cuff to his sleeve, though he was still a little self-conscious about it.

But his occasional patients other than Javan were often

initially squeamish at the sight and touch of his handless appendage, and Bishop Hubert complained rather peevishly that the empty sleeve was unaesthetic. In an effort not to annoy Hubert unduly, Tavis did experiment briefly with wearing the hook he had sworn he would never use, but he found that it interfered with his function as a Healer. After that, he quietly returned to his empty sleeve, adopting a series of postures which would minimize the notice of others. Javan gave him a great deal of support in those early days, insisting that the Healer resume his regular duties as soon as possible, and encouraging him to share his talents with such others of the royal household as had need of a Healer's services. His dogged devotion to Tavis also helped to keep him out of the regents' sight.

By the time Tavis had recovered, of course, the royal household included Davin. Davin-Eidiard had been assigned directly to the command of Sir Piedur, who now headed the younger princes' personal bodyguard. After an initial apprenticeship and testing under the older man's tutelage, he was permitted to assume regular duties which kept him near the royal children a great deal of the time. He immediately proved excellent both with horses and with weapons, and a good teacher, as well, so he soon became a favorite companion of all three boys, but especially of Rhys Michael.

Unfortunately, this proximity to the princes also kept him near Tavis—which, while it was a major part of the reason he had been sent, also presented the greatest danger of discovery. To guard against this, and as part of Eidiard's personality, Rhys had given Eidiard a nervous distrust of other Healers, hoping that this might keep him from coming under Tavis's close scrutiny for as long as possible. Unfortunately, the need for that scrutiny did come; fortunately, it came only a few weeks into Davin's royal service, while he was still deeply blocked of all Deryniness and Tavis was still new enough in his restoration to Healer's function that he was not likely to notice any discrepancy.

Davin had been ground-driving one of Javan's new R'Kassan stud colts in the breaking pen, dogging the animal a little too closely, and the beast had shied and skittered backwards, kicking him hard in the knee. The pain was excruciating. Javan and Tavis had been watching, and both of them had gone to Davin immediately for Tavis to assess the damage.

But when the prince's Healer probed the great, already purpling bruise, he read nothing in his patient either Deryni or suspicious—only the surface apprehension which so many humans displayed when constrained to deal with a Deryni in these current times. Pronouncing the bone intact, Tavis sent cleansing warmth into the injury and cleared it in the space of only a few minutes, apparently thinking nothing further of it. Jaffray, when he learned of the incident while reading Davin later that evening, could only breathe a sigh of relief. At least the first hurdle had been crossed.

Unfortunately for Tavis, not all of his healing encounters were so benign.

As had been decided at Tammaron's recommendation, and to fuel the theory that the Deryni who had attacked Tavis had really been after the princes, despite what Tavis claimed, the regency council set up regular patrols to scour the countryside and begin rounding up the marauding bands of both races. Humans were dealt with through the regular assize courts, tried where they were arrested and receiving ordinary punishments befitting vandalism, occasional assault, and general disorderly behavior—usually no more than a figurative slap on the hand for those of noble blood. The Deryni, however, Hubert caused to be brought to Rhemuth for trial, since it had been Deryni who had attacked Prince Javan's Healer. There, as Jaffray had warned that he would, Hubert offered Tavis the opportunity to search among the prisoners for his attackers.

Especially in the beginning, Tavis needed little encouragement, for his desire for vengeance was strong when his injury was most recent. He had no desire to betray Deryni in general but he *was* desirious of finding out which, if any, of the prisoners had had a part in his mutilation. To get past balky shields, he was willing to resort to reason, threats, the many subtleties of his Healer's craft, and even Deryni-specific drugs and force, if need be.

But once he had read them deeply enough to determine that they had not been involved in his attack, he had no interest in them. He would not delve deeper just to please Hubert, who was looking for any excuse to execute or at least incarcerate Deryni. As the weeks went by,

Tavis's lust for vengeance diminished and Hubert's frustration grew.

Tavis actually did find one of the men just before the man clamped down immensely powerful shields. His name was Dafydd Leslie, a nephew of the same Jowerth Leslie, who had been a council lord under Imre and Cinhil until his death a few years before. He was also a friend of a number of high-ranking Deryni, among them Davin and Ansel MacRorie.

But Dafydd was not the one who had cut off Tavis's hand, or even one of those who had held him for the butcher. Nor could Tavis pull forth any more information, for Dafydd panicked at having his shields assaulted so doggedly, went into convulsions, and died rather than betray his friends.

Hubert tried in vain to persuade Tavis to attempt a death-reading—a procedure he had heard of, and which he was sure a Healer of Tavis's talent ought to be able to perform. But Tavis had no stomach for it, even had he known the procedure. What Hubert asked was from the arcane side of Deryni knowledge, and Tavis had always dealt primarily with the Healing arts. Besides that, Dafydd had known what he was doing, and had deliberately blurred out all portions of his consciousness before he died. Even a Deryni skilled in the working which Hubert mentioned could not have gained usable results.

This only spoke to Hubert of plots, and plots within plots, for he found it difficult to conceive that a Deryni nobleman, especially a petty noble like Dafydd Leslie, would take his own life in defense of another man's crime. Dafydd himself had done nothing except witness other men's offenses. For that, he might have gone free, had he been willing to name his companions. That he had not been willing only confirmed Hubert's belief that Dafydd must have been involved in some kind of conspiracy.

Tavis could say little, once Hubert had made up his mind, other than to point out that nothing could be proved, now that Dafydd was dead; but his enthusiasm for Hubert's prisoners waned even further, after that. In addition, the encounter with Dafydd had triggered Tavis's own nightmares of the incident. In trying to suppress them, he kept returning to that terrible day and night, and Javan's incredible role in helping him cope with what had happened. And that raised the further mystery of Javan's shields, and what might have happened the night Cinhil died. As though by tacit agreement, the two of them had not discussed the matter further, Javan perhaps sensing that Tavis needed the time to heal, emotionally as well as physically, and Tavis choosing not to think about it.

After Dafydd's death, Tavis mulled the situation for several days, wondering how best to broach the subject with his young lord, but it was Javan himself who finally took the first step.

It had rained that afternoon, curtailing their plans for a quiet ride to the hills across the river, so they had repaired to Javan's chamber, where the Healer had thought to show the prince a copy he had secured of the current royal budget—an item which they had discussed several times with great interest, and which Tavis knew his young master was keen to see.

Javan glanced dutifully over the first few columns of tight, crabbed script, then pushed the scroll aside and glanced up at Tavis. In the common room outside, they could hear Javan's brothers arguing over a game of cups and triangles, Father Alfred's voice raised in reprimand. A rushlight burned on the table between them, intended to dispel the gloom of the rainy afternoon, but it only highlighted the boy's angular cheekbones and made of his eyes two enormous pools of polished serpentine.

"Tavis, we need to talk," he said in a low voice.

"Are we not doing that?" Tavis replied, raising one dark red eyebrow.

"That's not what I mean, and you know it," Javan whispered. "What happened the night my father died? I only refrained from asking before because I thought you needed time to heal. Well, now you're healed. And I want to know what you did to me that night of your injury, too. And I want to know about my shields."

Tavis sighed, a low, weary exhalation, and rubbed his hand across his eyes. "You ask much, my prince."

"Did you not ask much of me, when you lay near to death in Valoret?"

"Yes."

Another sigh. Then Tavis rose and motioned the boy to come with him, leading him to a seat in the window embrasure. There they settled, Tavis next to the rain-streaked grey mullion panes and Javan to his left. Tavis flexed his fingers and massaged his stump with the palm of his right hand.

"First, I suppose, there's the matter of what happened to you that night of my injury," he said quietly. "I took far greater liberties than I normally would have with a human, but you seemed willing, and there was that which I could tap into, though I didn't stop to think about the reason at the time. You mentioned shields that night, and you were right. You had them, and you do have them, and you seem to be able to raise and lower them at will. I've never heard of someone not Deryni who could do that before."

Javan frowned. "These shields—do you think they are somehow connected with the night my father died?" he asked, after a thoughtful pause.

"I don't know. You could have had shields for a long time, and I just wasn't aware. I remember that you were a little slow to open up to me when I first came to Court—but even then, you'd dealt with other Healers before. Once you came to trust me, there was never any resistance beyond what one might expect of a boy who occasionally wants to do what he thinks is best, rather than what his elders think he should."

A quick grin crossed Javan's face. "Was I a trial to you, Tavis?"

"Only occasionally, my prince. And that night of my injury, you were anything but a trial." His eyes and his voice dropped. "If it hadn't been for you, I don't know what I would have done. Certainly, I would not have healed so quickly—in mind or in body."

"What—did I do?" Javan asked.

"You gave your very soul into my keeping, if only for an hour," Tavis said softly. "I asked you to let me draw on your very life-force, praying that I would be able to prevent myself from drawing out too much, and you gave yourself completely into my hands—or, rather, my hand. I might have killed you that night, Javan. You must have sensed that. But you never hesitated. You gave me the energy of Healing and of life."

Javan's eyes had grown round as Tavis spoke, and now he reached across and took the Healer's hand.

"Have you not done the same for me, countless times?" the boy asked quietly. "I was awed and honored to be able to do it for you. And yet—"

"And yet?"

"And yet, I did not think humans could do such things for Deryni, Tavis. How is it that I can?"

"I don't know," Tavis whispered. "I really don't know. And yet, I think this thing is not something which has always been. As close a time ago as just before your father's death, I would *swear* there was only the ordinary rapport of patient and Healer between us."

"Then, what happened to change things?" Javan asked. "What happened the night my father died? Rhys himself claimed to have done something to you. And we know that he gave me and my brothers a so-called physick that night. Perhaps he did something else to me, as well as to you. Do you think we can find out?"

"I don't know," Tavis replied thoughtfully. "God knows, I've searched my memories as best I can alone, but perhaps—" He glanced at Javan tentatively and gave his hand a squeeze.

"Will you help me, Javan? With your rapport, perhaps we can both go back to that night. The more I consider the timing, the more I begin to suspect that the key lies there."

"What must I do?" the boy replied. "You know I want to help. Tell me what I must do."

"All right."

Quickly Tavis slued around on the cushion until he faced Javan, his left leg curled up on the seat in front of him. Javan did the same, tucking up his right leg. Gently Tavis took the boy's left hand in his right, laid his other forearm along Javan's right. He felt the boy's right hand cradle his left elbow to steady the link, since he had no hand of his own to seal that bond. He took a deep breath and let it out, watching Javan follow his example.

"All right," Tavis said softly. "I want you to relax and let yourself go, the way we did that night you helped me before. You'll feel the same kind of slight pulling sensation, but this time, I want you to stay conscious. You may feel drowsy, but don't go to sleep. Try to center in on that night when Rhys came into your room and gave you the wine. See yourself with your brothers now, back at Valoret."

As Tavis concentrated on his breathing, he felt the boy slipping into a trance state as easily as if he had been doing it all his life. In half a dozen breaths, his eyes were closed and he was as deep as he had been the night of Tavis's injury, relaxed and yet alert, even as Tavis had instructed him.

Gently, lightly, Tavis initiated mind contact, letting

Javan experience it at first as only an intensification of the physical touch they shared. Deftly he guided his thoughts back to that night, feeling Javan moving back with him through time. He closed his eyes and let the scene take shape, integrating his awareness with Javan's point of view as the boy, too, began to relive the night in question.

The three princes and their squires had gathered around Rhys after supper, where Rhys had produced a packet from his pouch and emptied it into the flask of sweet Fianna wine which one of the squires had fetched. As Tavis watched curiously from a seat in the window, cups were poured for princes and squires and emptied by all. Prayers had followed, and then sleepy climbings into beds.

Now they both rode Tavis's memories as the Healer glided down to the table and picked up the empty flask, wondering what Rhys had given them.

"What was this?" Tavis asked, as Rhys rejoined him by the table.

"I told you, a physick against colds. The king ordered it. Taste it, if you like."

Tavis had shaken his head and put down the empty flask, and had watched Rhys head toward the chamber door. With a yawn, Tavis had picked up his scroll and wandered over to the pile of furs beside the fireplace, had read for a little while, had drifted off to sl—*no!*

In his agitation at finally seeing the crack in the memory, Tavis stirred a little from his trance, some of his indignation spilling over undiluted to Javan, who gasped under the emotion of it.

Swiftly Tavis reschooled his thoughts to calm, reassured Javan, and went back to the beginning.

Back to the point where you fell asleep, he ordered Javan. *Rhys returned to the common room, but the flask wasn't empty!*

It was not until he had said it that he realized he had spoken in his mind, and that Javan had responded.

He picked up the flask and sniffed the contents, and this time he could feel the shock which had first surfaced in his mind that night.

"You lied!" he had whispered.

"I did?"

"That was no physick against colds. You drugged them. You gave them enough to put them to sleep until tomorrow. What are you up to?"

264

He watched as Rhys returned his gaze, the picture of righteous amazement, and it was only in this remembering that he realized how deftly the older Healer had inserted himself between Tavis and the door.

"Up to? Why, I'm simply following His Grace's instructions, seeing that the children get a good night's rest."

Feeling his suspicion anew, Tavis relived the instant he had touched a finger to the dregs in one of the cups, brought it to his nose.

"Rest in peace, more likely. You won't mind if I check with His Grace, will—what's this?" He could hardly believe what his senses were telling him. "Wolfbane and mer—Rhys, you didn't!"

His shields went up, all in a rush. He felt the swift, tentative probe of Rhys's mind, and shuttered his own all the more tightly, the while trying to decide what he was going to do.

Without warning, the elder Healer's fist slammed into Tavis's solar plexus! As Tavis collapsed, gasping for breath, Rhys seized the wine flagon and pressed it to his lips, forcing him to drink.

Pain!—of chest, laboring to breathe—of throat, forced to swallow once, again, again. . . . Indignation. And now, genuine fear, though physical function had started to return—for mental function had begun to haze as Rhys's potion took effect.

"I'm sorry I had to hit you, Tavis," Rhys had said. "But it was necessary for you to drink, since you had the ill-fortune to be here tonight, and I doubted you would do so of your own accord."

Tavis's mind whirled with growing disorientation, and it had been all he could do to get out the words.

"But why? My God, Rhys! You've given them m-m-merasha! And—anhalon. Merasha and anhalon, and they're not even Deryni!"

"It has been done at His Grace's command, and with his full knowledge," Rhys had murmured. "Beyond that, I may tell you nothing more. And even if I might, you wouldn't remember . . . would you?"

But Tavis did remember, now, and lived again the altered vision, the increasingly sloppy shields as the drugs invaded his controls and opened them to Rhys's probe.

Now, as he forced himself down, taking Javan with him, he knew the places where Rhys had touched him; knew how to restore what Rhys had changed.

But there was little more to change, beyond that point, for the unconsciousness brought about by Rhys could not be reversed. There was no way to restore memory of what had not been witnessed. There was nothing to do but return to waking consciousness and try to determine what it all meant. Javan's eyes went wide and amazed as he came out of his trance and stared at Tavis.

"Why would he do that?" Javan murmured. "For some reason, he drugged us all that night, and then he made you forget about it." He paused for a moment, then stared at Tavis in horrible suspicion. "Tavis, you don't suppose he knew that my father was to die?"

Tavis gazed back at the prince neutrally, not daring to follow that suggestion to its logical conclusion.

"How could he have known that, Javan?"

With a shudder, Javan turned partially away and drew his knees up under his chin, hugging them tight against his chest, not looking at Tavis. "No, that's impossible. He's a Healer. Healers don't kill people."

"Not by choice, anyway," Tavis murmured. "And if Rhys knew ahead of time that Cinhil was to die, then there must have been a choice involved." He slammed his fist into the cushion beside him in frustration. "It doesn't make sense. He said he'd drugged you and your brothers at your father's orders. If he *were* part of some ghastly plot to kill the king, why would he have wanted you and your brothers only to sleep through it? The drugs he gave you were potent, but certainly not deadly."

Javan thought about that for several seconds, then glanced uneasily at Tavis again. "Tavis, could magic have been somehow involved?"

"Magic?" Tavis cocked his head at the boy quizzically. "What gave you that idea?"

"Well, he gave us Deryni drugs—which, I gather, aren't supposed to work on humans."

"A mixture, actually. Some of them were not specific. They would have worked on anyone."

"Nonetheless. And then, there's the matter of my shields. I *must* have gotten them that night. Is it possible that—well, that he and my father—did something to us that night?"

"Did something? Such as—what?"

"Oh, I don't know," the boy pouted, swinging his clubbed foot across to rest on the cushion on the opposite side of the window seat. "You're the Deryni. You tell me. Maybe they were going to—I don't know—put shields on all of us, and they didn't want you to know."

"Why would they do that? And who are *they?* I thought we were talking about Rhys."

"Well, he can't have done it alone, can he? Maybe Evaine helped him. She's his wife. Or Bishop Alister!" The boy sat bolt upright. "That's who he was talking to, the night I heard him say he'd done something to you! So Alister must know! Maybe he was a part of it, too!"

Slowly Tavis nodded. "And that would also make Joram a part of it, and probably Earl Jebediah. They were all in the chamber when the regents brought you in to see his body, except Evaine—Rhys, Alister, Joram, and Jebediah. And all of them except Jebediah were there the night of my injury! There's *got* to be a connection."

"But, what?"

"I don't know. They're not likely to tell us, either."

Javan thought on that a moment. "Is there a chance *I* could tell us?"

"What do you mean?"

"Well," Javan continued thoughtfully, "whatever happened to me, I must have been there. Can't you make me remember?"

Tavis frowned, gazing unseeing back into the dim bedchamber.

"You were drugged. I don't know whether I could get past that or not."

"*You* were drugged, too, but you got past it."

"I'm Deryni," Tavis answered absently.

Javan scowled. "Don't you *dare* use that excuse on me," he muttered. "Can't you at least try to make me remember?"

"I don't know." Tavis cocked his head. "Unless you regained consciousness between the time you fell asleep from the physick and when Jebediah and the regents woke you, I doubt there's anything to remember."

"But, there must be—something. . . ." Javan's voice trailed off and he squinched up his face in concentration. "There was a . . . dark room, I think, and my father . . . damn!"

"Don't swear," Tavis said automatically.

"Well, I can't help it!" the boy fumed. "There *is* something—maybe I just dreamed it, I don't know. For just a second there, I had a flash, though. Can't you try to follow that?"

"Right now?"

"Of course, right now. You won't hurt me."

"I know I won't hurt you, Javan," Tavis sighed. "I don't want to tire you, though. You're not used to this."

"You're damned right I'm not used to this!"

"And if you're going to get yourself all overwrought—"

"I am *not* overwrought! I'm—" Abruptly he broke off and dropped his gaze, a reluctant grin playing at his mouth. "You're right. I *was* overwrought. But—can't you at least try?"

Echoing Javan's grin, Tavis glanced around the seating alcove, then fetched a cushion from the opposite bench and put it on the seat between himself and Javan.

"If it's that important," he said, patting the cushion. "Lie down and make yourself comfortable. Let yourself go into trance exactly the way you did before."

The boy lay back with a triumphant little smile.

"Don't think you're getting away with anything," Tavis added good-naturedly, resting his hand lightly on Javan's forehead. "I just happen to agree with your argument. Now, close your eyes and center in. Let yourself slip back to your last waking memory of that night."

Javan did as he was bidden. Gradually he gained the impression of being warm and safe in his old bed, winged back to Valoret and February by agile memory, and then of Tavis's active presence receding. As the reality of it all intensified, he shifted onto his side and snuggled his face against the cushion, only a minute part of him still vaguely aware of the Healer's hand maintaining contact with his brow. Then he felt himself being gently nudged forward from bed and into dreamless sleep.

At least, he thought it was sleep, in the beginning. There were the usual flitting images of things he'd done at play or at his lessons that frigid winter season. But there was also an elusive flickering of something else, after a while: faces, familiar, yet strange; a cloudly haze around lights gold and red and green, the feeling that one was somehow missing; a footed cup whose whiteness blocked out all his view of anything else—and colors, feelings, sounds, spinning and tumbling together—and nothing, nothing. . . .

He clawed his way up from the odd, white darkness to find Tavis staring down at him, a puzzled expression on his face. He sat up and shook his head to clear it, then looked at the Healer again, almost afraid to ask.

"What did you see?"

"It was odd," Tavis replied. "I can't tell whether it was a dream or something that really happened but was distorted by the drugs they gave you."

"Well, what did it look like?"

Tavis shook his head. "I honestly don't know, my prince. Damned if I do!"

"Don't swear," Javan retorted without thinking, bringing an amused smile to Tavis's lips. "Tavis," the prince went on, "we've got to find out what it was."

"I know."

"Well, then, *do* something."

Tavis considered, then looked at Javan again.

"All right. I do have one idea, but you have to promise not to nag me while I work out the details."

"What is it?"

"Well, you were drugged when—*whatever* happened. So I think it's worth our time to try duplicating the drugs Rhys gave you, then dose you and let me try to break through the memories that way. I'll have to do some research, though. I know most of what was in there, but I'll have to work out the proportions and dosage."

Javan wrinkled his nose. "Another 'physick'?"

"Aye, as close to the original as I can manage. I don't really relish the idea, but I haven't got any better ones just now. Are you willing, before I go to all that trouble?"

With a perplexed sigh, Javan nodded. "I suppose so."

"Just what I love to hear—enthusiasm," Tavis said, slapping the boy's shoulder affectionately and getting to his feet. "I don't suppose you'd like to give the whole thing up?"

"And just forget about my shields?" Javan replied archly.

"There is that," Tavis agreed. "But, we've given ourselves enough to think about for one afternoon. Let's go bother Cook. I'm starving."

CHAPTER EIGHTEEN

The voice of him that crieth in the wilderness, Prepare ye the way of the Lord, make straight in the desert a highway for our God.

—Isaiah 40:3

Tavis and Javan were not the only ones given much to think on, as the summer wore on and temperatures and tensions rose. Though a certain normality had begun to emerge from the reign's rather tumultous beginning, it was far different from what anyone had known before. The uncertainty of a regency and a child king on the throne did nothing to lessen the growing sense of foreboding, especially among Deryni who had an inkling what was taking place.

This sense of foreboding certainly permeated the actions of the Camberian Council. Gregory and Jesse continued to patrol their lands and keep the peace there but, after the attack on Tavis, Gregory grew withdrawn and grimly thoughtful. The idea that Deryni would attack Deryni deliberately had affected him more than he was willing to admit. He came and worked his turn at monitoring Davin, and attended the meetings of the Camberian Council, but he had become a dour and troubled man. Camber learned that he had purchased a small, isolated estate in the Connait, and was preparing to move his family there. Camber could not say he blamed him.

Jaffray, too, began to show the strain. He continued to report the actions of all the Court from his vantage point inside the regency council, and kept a more normal contact with Davin, now that Rhys had been able to remove the blockage and restore his true memory. The young man was functioning with full powers restored. But the move to Rhemuth had forced Jaffray to spread himself entirely too thin. He had duties in Valoret, as archbishop, which could not be entirely delegated; and he knew that the regents were aware of this, and even counted on it to keep him away from meetings of the council as much as possible. Still, such eyewitness reports as Jaffray was able to provide were infinitely more valuable than the slanted view they got from monitoring Davin, in his relatively sheltered position guarding the princes. So long as they had Jaffray more or less securely in the council, at least they might have some advance warning of any drastic measures the regents might be contemplating.

Jebediah also kept a feverish pace, circulating among the various Michaeline houses and directing preparations for going underground again. Even Crevan Allyn, his human vicar general, understood and feared the signs which were becoming all too clear—though with his Order so scattered throughout Gwynedd, he dared not begin an open abandonment of Michaeline facilities too quickly, lest their retreat seem to give credence to suspicions about Deryni elements in the Order. When the army of Gwynedd had been purged of Michaelines earlier in the year, both Crevan and Jebediah had hoped that anti-Michaeline sentiment would diminish; but by Lammas, it was clear that this was not to be. Several Michaeline knights and men-at-arms, human and Deryni, had been arrested and imprisoned by the regents for various vague reasons. To protect these men, nothing must be done by other members of the Order which might further antagonize the regents.

Given these factors, Michaeline withdrawal from Gwynedd had to be accomplished more subtly than the overnight operation of Imre's time. The commanderie at Argoed, in particular, could hardly be closed down without arousing suspicion; but its complement was cut drastically, all its remaining brethren and knights having definite assignments in the event of a general suppression. Cùilteine, second only to Argoed in Gwynedd proper, kept a token force of brothers and knights within its precincts and endeavored to make them look like twice their number.

Many of the remaining knights Jebediah sent to the three Michaeline houses outside Gwynedd, a few at a time: Brustarkia, in Arjenol; Saint Elderon, across the border into Torenth; and desert Djellarda, the orginal mother house of the Order, which overlooked the Anvil of the Lord.

Even the teaching brethen of the Order were slowly recalled from their posts and sent to safety. As the summer wore on, those few schools still staffed, at least in part, by Michaeline teachers found those men being replaced, seemingly at random, by brothers and priests of other, human orders. Reassignments were quietly arranged by Jaffray and Bishops Cullen, Trey, and Descantor, who also managed to "lose" the records of several small but strategically placed houses which might later become places of refuge.

Camber himself stayed in Grecotha through the summer, Joram running interference with Father Willowen and the rest of the cathedral chapter while Camber continued to work with Rhys, Emrys, and Queron on discovering how Rhys's talent might be passed on to other Healers. But try as they might, they could not isolate the function well enough to teach it. Though Emrys and Queron were probably the most skillful Healers of Rhys's acquaintance, neither could offer him a solution.

Meanwhile, there was Revan to consider. Revan's uncertain position kept matters in a perspective of ongoing urgency, which was complicated by the fact that no one of the Camberian Council had seen or spoken to him since his flight from Sheele at Eastertide—though they knew approximately where he was. Everyone assumed that his cover was still intact—else they would have heard of it—but no one knew for sure.

In addition, it became increasingly likely that for Rhys's plan to work, he was going to have to carry it out himself. They might never find another Healer who could learn; and against that eventuality, Rhys must begin easing himself into a working relationship with the exiled Revan.

Accordingly, on one hot afternoon toward the end of August, Rhys and Evaine made their way to the Willimite encampment in the hills above Valoret, dull as mice in the greyed russet firze of common folk, with bright hair darkened to nondescript dust-tones by the art of Deryni illusion. They were careful to be diffident and wide-eyed as they approached the Willimite perimeter, a properly meek peasant couple who had come to seek out a holy hermit. Their going among the Willimites was a somewhat risky venture, for the martyred Saint Willim had been a victim of Deryni ill use, and his adherents believed Deryni to be the Devil's own spawn, deserving a suitably terrible fate unless they recanted their detestable heritage; and there were known to be several "reformed" Deryni who lived lives of penitence among them and might Truth-Read suspicious strangers in defense of the brotherhood. Rhys and Evaine must be careful not to arouse the wrong kind of attention.

"Your pardon, good sir," Rhys murmured, with a tug at his cap as he approached the first man he saw. "I wonder if you could tell me where I might find the holy hermit who is said to live in these hills."

The Willimite, a weathered and emaciated-looking man, looked over the colorless couple with an appraising eye, noting their shabby clothing and the woman's obvious pregnancy, then relaxed a little and favored them with a thin smile and a slight bow over piously-folded hands.

"A holy hermit, y'say? Well." His voice held the clipped lilt of the Mooryn highlands. "Can ye perhaps be more specific? We have several holy men among us—and all are sworn to resist the evil of the godless Deryni, curst be their souls!"

"Oh, aye," Rhys murmured, nodding earnestly and making a gesture of agreement wth one hand. "The man we seek is a youngish man, they say. He walks with a limp, like the young heir. They say he used to be the servant of a Deryni house, and that he ran away. They say, that he has—visions—and that the Lord favors him greatly, and that—his touch brings luck to them as he esteems."

The Willimite nodded self-importantly. "Ah, that would be Brother Revan. 'Tis said his former master killed his sweetheart—and the master a Healer, and all!—and after that, young Revan went a little strange." His voice took on a tinge of genuine awe.

"But he's touched by God, he is! Everyone says it. He has speech with a great stone on the mountain top, and it tells him what to preach. He says a great doom is coming upon the Deryni—that many will be slain—and the only ones that might be saved are those who repent of their evil ways. He says the Lord will reveal how some Deryni might be spared, if they approach the throne of heaven with humble and contrite hearts!"

Evaine, who had pretended to be listening raptly to

every word the man said—which she was, though she was also casting out all around them for danger—plucked at the man's sleeve with awed urgency.

"Then, praised be the Lord, for what we have heard is true! They say he can even remove the taint from those who have been forced to serve the Deryni—that his touch can make one clean!"

"Och, aye, he's a very holy man," the man returned, a little taken aback at her apparent fervor. "As ye say, he does give blessing to them as ask."

"Will you take us to him?" Evaine begged. "Oh, please, good sir. You do not know the weight which has been upon us these many years, forced to live in the village of a Deryni lord. Now we mean to—to run away! But for the sake of my unborn child, I would have us cleansed before we go. I know this holy man's blessing can wash away the taint!"

Rhys cleared his throat self-consciously. "My wife—she is overwrought in her condition," he said faintly, extricating Evaine's fingers from the man's sleeve and bobbing his head apologetically. "But we would seek Brother Revan's blessing, if you would be so kind. Please, for my wife's sake. . . ."

They had manged to gather the attention of several other men and women of the Willimite community as they spoke, one of them a woman with shorn hair and a pinched, lined face who was almost certainly Deryni, though she made no attempt to reach out and probe them. Just to be safe, however, Rhys reached into Evaine's mind and sprang the triggerpoint, blocking everything else which was not appropriate for the peasant woman she appeared to be. With his hand still on her arm, he caught her slight stumble as she made the transition, then withdrew deep into himself where a casual probe from the woman would not touch his shields. As the first man began leading them on through the camp, the others fell in behind in a little parade, including the Deryni woman.

They crossed the Willimite encampment, with its motley collection of tents and rudely-constructed lean-tos, then began a steep climb up the side of the mountain. The gorse and felderbloom were parched and sere from the summer's heat, but a breeze stirred increasingly as they climbed. By the time they had reached a small plateau halfway up the mountainside, the wind was blowing steadily from the east, cooling steamy faces and dispelling the odor of bodies too seldom washed and clothing too long worn. Across the plateau, just in front of the mouth of a narrow cave, stood an almost unrecognizable Revan, with nearly a dozen men and women crouched in a semicircle around him.

He was clad in an ankle-length robe of some greyish homespun stuff, threadbare and much patched, though cleaner than the garb of most of those around him, and he cradled a twisted staff of what looked to be olivewood in the crook of his left arm. His hair had grown several inches since they last had seen him, and he had a full beard which looked almost blond in the strong sunlight. He was preaching as they first saw him. Gradually his words became discernable as they came closer.

"The day is coming when those who have walked in darkness must be tried in the forge of the ages, and all imperfections burned away. Even as our Lord foretold, the wheat shall be separated from the chaff, and the good seed from the bad.

"But I say unto you that even for those who have walked in the uttermost darkness, the Light may yet be seen and known. To him who doth earnestly repent of his evil and renounce the darkness forever, the Lord shall give a sign of His grace. The evil ones shall be changed, the dross refined from the true gold, and the Kingdom shall thrive in the fullness of the Lord's love."

A murmur passed among them at that, dying away as one woman spoke up.

"But, Master, how can this be? Are you saying that even the accursed Deryni can be saved?"

"So I am given to understand," Revan answered, so low that Rhys and Evaine, still approaching from the path, could barely hear. Rhys checked the assembled group for more Deryni, but there were none; only the one woman in the little band behind them, who still had made no move to use her powers.

". . . been told how this will come to pass," Revan was saying, "but I have faith that it will be made known to me in God's time. The Lord of Hosts will do all these things, even as it has been foretold."

"Blessed be the name of the Lord!" one of the men murmured, scrambling to his knees and clasping his hands rapturously.

"Amen!" another cried, following suit.

A third dropped from his perch on a rock beside Revan to kneel at his feet, face upturned in shining hope.

"Will you give us your blessing, Master?"

"Not my blessing, but the blessing of the Lord," Revan murmured, laying his right hand on the man's head.

"The Lord bless you and keep you," he said, moving on to touch each person's head, in turn. "The Lord give you peace and rest, and the certainty that you will be with Him, at the day of reckoning. May He forgive you your sins, and bless you, and be gracious to you, and cleanse you of that which troubles you. In the name of the Father, and of the Son, and of the Holy Spirit. Amen."

He concluded by making the Sign of the Cross over them and upon himself, then bowed his head and closed his eyes, one hand on his staff and the other held lightly to his breast. Those who had received his blessing slowly gathered themselves and their belongings and began filing back toward the path, past Rhys and Evaine and their escort. Rhys began leading Evaine forward, but Revan did not seem to see them as he turned and ducked his head to retreat into his cave.

"Brother Revan, these people have come to see you," the Willimite called, bowing respectfully as Revan turned to gaze at him. "They are fleeing from a Deryni master, and they seek your blessing before they go."

With a weary but patient blink, Revan turned the pale brown eyes on them, no flicker of recognition registering even to Rhys's watchful study. He peered at them mildly and blinked again, then nodded and beckoned for them to follow as he disappeared into the inky darkness of the cave mouth. The Willimite, with a startled glance at both of them, scrambled after Revan and motioned for the two to follow. The rest turned and went back with the folk who had just left, and Rhys at last dared to release Evaine's block, giving her his view of all that had transpired between camp and plateau as they followed their guide into the cooler darkness of the cave.

Inside, as their eyes adjusted to the dimness, they could see that Revan had lit a shallow clay tallow lamp from a piece of kindling on a rude hearth, and was gesturing by its light for the three of them to be seated. Several dingy grey sheepskins lay on the sandy floor around a slab of smooth stone which evidently served as table, and Revan settled on the nearest one as he moved the tallow lamp from hearth to stone.

"Sit between our brother and sister and pray with me for them, Brother Joachim," Revan said to the Willimite in a gentle voice. "I sense our Lord's mission in their presence, though even they may not be aware of His purpose yet. We will pray together."

They still could not tell by Revan's behavior whether he had recognized them or not, but Rhys noticed how Revan's body now blocked the hearthlight from Joachim's line of vision, and how Evaine cast a shadow from the brighter light of the cave entrance, so that it, too, never reached Joachim. The tallow lamp, on the stone in front of them, was the brightest light that Joachim could see.

As Revan held out his hands to them, Rhys on his left and Evaine on his right, both of them knew in that first instant of contact that he had set it up that way specifically for them, so they might ease Joachim under their Deryni controls. He had learned his early lessons well in dealing with Deryni. The pair of them relaxed as Joachim joined hands with them and the linkage was complete.

"Let us pray to the Lord," Revan murmured, throwing back his head and closing his eyes. "Let us allow the Holy Spirit to descend upon us and guide us. Wait and watch in silence for the Spirit to come upon us."

There was silence, then, except for the sound of gentle breathing, as the four settled into waiting. Through slitted eyelids, Rhys watched the silent Joachim beside him. He reached out with his mind to Evaine and moved with her simultaneously to insinuate controls on the unsuspecting Joachim so that the transition from contemplation to forgetful, oblivious trance would be so smooth as to be undetectable. When it was done, and Joachim's head had nodded forward on his chest, Evaine gave a great sigh and took Revan's hand in both of hers, looking at him and shaking her head with a smile.

"Revan, it's been too long."

"I trust I did right by Joachim," he said shyly, glancing back and forth between the two of them. "I never dreamed you'd come to me here, out in the open. And when he came with you, it seemed there must be some way to use his presence to advantage." He glanced doubtfully at the sleeping Willimite. "He can't hear us, can he?"

Rhys shook his head. "No, and we can give him some perfectly harmless memories to cover the time we're here. I don't know how long we'll have before someone else comes, though—and there's at least one Deryni who knows we're here, though she doesn't know what we are —so we'll need to make this quick."

"Of course. How can I help you?"

"We primarily wanted to let you know what progress we'd made, and to see what you'd done," Evaine replied. "We heard you preaching. It sounds as if you're on the right track in that regard. Any problems?"

Revan gave a sour grin. "None that two Deryni can help me with, I fear—unless you're wanting to become the first two object lessons in our little scheme." He glanced at Rhys. "Is it to be you, then, or have you managed to teach anyone else?"

"So far, no," Rhys replied. "We still have hope, however. How soon do you think you'll have to start producing results? I'll make the sacrifice if there's no other way, but if you can hold off, I still hope to find you another Healer."

With a low chuckle, Revan shook his head. "I think I can stall a bit longer. The Lord's ways are historically slow. Besides, I haven't yet told them what to expect, so I can really do just about anything. My notoriety is only now beginning to spread beyond the immediate area. And once the winter comes, things will slack off. It's going to be grim up here, once the snows start."

"We'll try to stay in touch," Rhys agreed. "You think you can hold off until spring, then?"

"I think so. What about you? Do you think you'll find somebody?"

Evaine sighed. "That is anybody's guess right now. But, we're losing precious time. Rhys, did you want to do a quick probe, just to make certain everything is still as it should be? We shouldn't keep our friend Joachim under for much longer."

"Right. Will you watch him, please, and keep a probe out for strangers?"

As Evaine shifted her attention to the still slumbering Joachim, Rhys laid his hand on Revan's shoulder and gave a nod. For reply, Revan simply closed his eyes and drew a deep breath, instantly locking into a deep rapport with the Healer. The exchange took only seconds, as

Rhys plunged deep and read detailed memories of the background Revan had thus far forged as prophet and sage, testing also the limits of the safeguards which he and Evaine had given Revan against casual probing by other Deryni. The camouflage held, undetectable unless one knew precisely where to look.

With another deep breath, Rhys emerged from trance, steadying Revan with his hand as the younger man followed a heartbeat behind. Evaine grinned at both of them, then held out her hand to reestablish the link.

"Someone is coming up the path—not our Deryni lady, though. Let's slip back into character, Brother Revan."

With a nod, Revan bowed his head once more and half-closed his eyes, feeling the support of Rhys's and Evaine's hands to either side.

"The Lord of Hosts be praised, for He has given you the courage to leave the ways of darkness and seek a new life," Revan murmured, glancing at the two of them, once more the slightly wild-eyed evangelist. "Joachim, you have done well to bring me these two lost children." Joachim lifted his head with a slight start at the sound of his name. "The Holy Spirit has spoken in my heart and doth vouchsafe to give you peace, my children."

"Then, we may be free of the Deryni taint, Master?" Evaine whispered, staring at him almost glassy-eyed. "We may receive your blessing?"

"Not my blessing, but the blessing of the Lord of Hosts," Revan said, releasing their hands and lifting his to rest on both their heads. "Bow your heads and pray for His blessing and protection, in the name of the Father, and of the Son, and of the Holy Spirit."

"Amen," came their whispered response, all humble peasant folk now, as Joachim looked on with awe.

"Go now, in peace, to love and serve the Lord," Revan said gently, dropping his hands to pick up the tallow lamp before it should be overturned in their passage.

As he stared into the flame, not moving from where he sat, the two of them got up, followed by Joachim, and stumbled out of the cave. Others were waiting outside, but Joachim bade them sit and wait, explaining that the master was tired now, but would come to them shortly. As he moved among them, himself seemingly transformed by the apparent sanctity of the man he had just left, Rhys and Evaine made their quiet way down the path and out of the Willimite encampment. They met no more Deryni.

CHAPTER NINETEEN

There is no healing of thy bruise; thy wound is grievous.

—Nahum 3:19

Rhys's and Evaine's visit to Revan was not entirely reassuring, despite its apparent success. True, Revan had met the challenge of surviving alone in the dangerous and even deadly company of the Deryni-hating Willimites, but they could not put aside a vague sense of disquiet at how easily Revan seemed to be assimilating his developing role as savior and seer. Revan had not yet realized the full potential of the power he might someday direct but, when he did, would he be able to resist the seductive lure which such power presented? For that matter, would any of them be able to control what they were creating? Though it seemed advisable for a religious movement to arise from their efforts, if Deryni were to be spared as a result, suppose it got out of hand, as "Saint" Camber had?

Rhys and Evaine reported both their reassurance and their uneasiness to the Council. Jaffray and Davin continued to relay their observations from among the regents and royals at Rhemuth, and the summer dragged on with little expectation of any marked change for the better.

Developments on the Michaeline front did little to ease the sense of impending doom which increasingly permeated their thinking. By mid-September, Jebediah could no longer delay telling his fellow Council members the long-unwanted news: Crevan Allyn was dispersing the Order. Already, most of the brethen had been secretly relocated to places of greater safety. The coming Michaelmas would likely be the last ever at Argoed, their commanderie of the past thirteen years.

The decision had been made a few weeks earlier. With the August redeployment of the Gwynedd army to Rhemuth and Valoret, and scattered regiments constantly on the move elsewhere, it had become clear to the most naive lay brother that the regents were gearing their military strength toward the capability to command all of Gwynedd on very short notice. Castles and garrisons were being invested all over the kingdom, and new keeps thrown up almost overnight. There could be no benign reason for such a state of readiness, when no enemy hounded at Gwynedd's borders, and the regents had made their feelings about the Deryni-dominated Knights of Saint Michael quite clear when they had purged them from the army the previous spring.

And so, at the beginning of September, Crevan Allyn had begun his final departure from Gwynedd. Most of the nonfighting brethren had already been shifted out of the kingdom, but now the rest of his knights went, too, the majority of them retreating to Djellarda, at the southern tip of the Forcinn. One of the petty Forcinn princes feared Moorish invasion, for which there was ample historical precedent, and had promised refuge, additional land, and employment if the Knights of Saint Michael would relocate on his border. In a way, it was a homecoming, for the Michaeline Order had had its beginnings there on the edge of the great desert called the Anvil of the Lord. After the Michaelines had been welcomed into Gwynedd, the little commanderie at Djellarda had been relegated to a minor outland holding of the Order, as the headquarters were moved to Cheltham at the invitation of King Bearand and his successors. Soon Djellarda would be restored to its former status.

Now only a handful of Michaelines remained in Gwynedd, no more than a score besides the three of the Council, spread mostly between Argoed and Cùilteine to suggest at least that the Order still functioned under the Haldane regency. Haut Eirial and Mollingford, never restored to their full strength and size after Imre's suppression, had been given over to their local bishops in late summer; and the bishops, never ones to disdain gifts of land and buildings, had promptly installed new communities of monks on the abandoned premises. The regents' officials did not notice that the habits of the occupants had changed, only that bodies still came and went. As Michaelmas approached, the Michaelines were little missed.

The Michaelines were not the only group about whom the regents had made their feelings quite clear, as the summer wore on into fall. Especially in the towns, Deryni continued to bear the brunt of regency harassment in increasingly blatant ways. Deryni nobles were not deprived of their holdings or titles—yet—but new offices and preferments invariably went to non-Deryni. When a Deryni official died in office, or his term expired, he was replaced by a non-Deryni. Deryni artisans and merchants, formerly under royal patronage, found their services no longer required. By early September, there were virtually no Deryni in positions of responsibility in Rhemuth except Archbishop Jaffray and Tavis O'Neill.

The phenomenon of Tavis gave the regents pause to consider. Tavis himself could be pushed only so far, but other Deryni might be more pliable, and more useful, if there were adequate controls to keep them in line. Healers, in particular, could be very valuable, so long as one had ample guarantee of good behavior.

Not all of the regents were in favor of pursing this line of reasoning initially. Rhun and Ewan, in particular, simply fed one another's anxieties, where the subject of Deryni conspiracies was concerned. But when they considered further, all of them had to admit that if one wished eventually to be rid of Deryni once and for all, it would behoove one to be able to tell for certain whether a given captive were Deryni or not. Of course, there were drugs which would detect such things, but those would only incapacitate or kill a Deryni, not render him vulnerable to use himself. It took a Deryni to discover a Deryni, to force a Deryni—unless, of course, the methods of force used were not against the Deryni's particular strength at all, but against more universal considerations.

Accordingly, toward the beginning of September, it was decided to begin a trial program of limited Deryni "recruitment." Rhun was given the assignment, for it was felt that he would test it most efficiently, being generally suspicious. And so, on a single night in mid-September, he and his captains surreptitiously swept through a score of different hamlets and towns and took to hostage several dozen known Deryni and their families, the women and children to be held against the good conduct of their menfolk. The swoops were repeated for several nights running, until more than fifty new "agents" had been taken. All of the captives were held incommunicado for several days, the men separated from their families and all of them dosed heavily with Deryni-specific drugs so that none might use their powers to attempt escape. They were then offered the terms of the regents' service.

Within a week, nearly every regiment or other military group of any size had a "Deryni sniffer" attached to its command staff, with orders for immediate execution of the Deryni and all his family, no questions asked, if any harm befell the commander. After several recalcitrants, suitably bound and drugged to helplessness, were forced to witness the execution of their families, including children and small infants, before themselves being tortured and killed, the word spread quickly among the remaining captives, and Deryni began to collaborate. The promise of reward, and a kind of tolerance, even induced some Deryni to offer their services on their own initiative, as Hubert had suspected they would.

The very existence of the collaborators was not widely known, especially outside the towns and villages, but it was well enough known to begin driving zealous men to desperate deeds. Perhaps it accounted, in part, for what finally happened on the eve of Michaelmas, near Rhemuth, touching once more on the royal family itself.

The day was sunny and fair, though the nip of fall had been in the air early that morning. All three princes had planned a day of riding and hawking, but that morning a court had been scheduled in Rhemuth town which required Alroy's personal attendance, so he was not permitted to go.

Hence, they were nine as they rode out that morning: Javan and Rhys Michael; a squire apiece, to see to their lunch and carry the game the party hoped to snare; four guards, including Davin; and a pleased Tavis O'Neill, bearing a gentle merlin on his leather-clad forearm, delighted to find that this was one sport which was not denied him by his loss. Javan, though entitled by his rank to a much more flashy bird, had chosen a favorite kestrel for the day, because she had been his first really well-trained falcon. Rhys Michael did not like birds—they made him sneeze—so he had merely come along for the ride and the opportunity to be out. He and "Eidiard" had struck up quite a good friendship, and the prince, whose passion was horses, had been pestering Eidiard for the past month to begin teaching him some of the advanced horsemanship which Eidiard made look so easy.

They rode throughout the morning, Rhys Michael amusing himself with periodic races with the guards and squires while Javan and Tavis flew their hawks with fair success. By midday, all of them had worked up appetites befitting the enormous amount of food the squires had brought along; so, after some discussion, a suitable site by a stream was selected and the squires set about laying a noon repast. While the guards unsaddled the horses and set them to graze and water a little downstream, Corund jessing their birds to a convenient tree limb, Javan excused himself and disappeared into the trees and brush up the hill. When he returned, a few minutes later, his young face wore a thoughtful expression. Quicky he found Tavis and drew him aside, watching only distractedly as Tavis unlaced the leather hawking vambrace from his left arm.

"Tavis, would you come with me, please?"

His voice was low, pitched so that the others could not overhear, and something in his tone made Tavis take notice even more than he usually would have.

"What is it, my prince?"

"Come with me. You'll see," the boy insisted, catching Tavis's sleeve and drawing him up the hill, the way he had come.

They climbed only a short way, picking a path through underbrush and several levels of shrouding trees until they came out into a wide, grassy clearing.

"Look you. There's a fire ring, and a little cairn of stones, over there. Do you suppose the little folk use this place?"

Tavis's jaw dropped, and he had all he could do to keep from laughing.

"The *little folk?*"

"Don't laugh at me, and don't look at me as if I'm mad!" Javan returned with tight-lipped solemnity. "I've heard the soldiers' talk. Do they or do they not dance at the turnings of the seasons and kindle the bonfires on the hilltops? Look out there." He gestured toward the other side of the clearing, where the hillside dropped away sheer and spilled onto the plain. "It could have been seen for miles. Is it true, Tavis? Do the little folk come out and dance around the bonfires?"

To cover his amazement and confusion, Tavis moved closer to the fire ring and prodded the long-dead embers with a booted toe, crouched down to hold his hand above the cold ashes.

He was aware that strange customs were still practiced among the country folk. Bonfires were lit at the major turnings of the seasons, as was well known. With the equinox but a week past, it was quite possible that Javan had, indeed, stumbled on the remnants of one of those bonfires.

Furthermore, there *had* been power raised here, benevolent, but real. Tavis could sense the residuals of it in the ashes, faint but unmistakable. Anyone with Sight could hardly help noticing, but Javan did not have Sight. How could he have noticed? And, *little folk?*

"What makes you think this is anything more than a shepherd's fire, Javan?" the Healer finally asked, raising his face squarely to the boy's.

Javan shook his head. "It's no shepherd's fire. The autumn equinox was last week. The common people build fires then, and they—they dance around the fire. I read about it. Why do they do that, Tavis?"

"Well, it's tied in with very old beliefs," Tavis began uneasily, wondering where the boy had found such reading material in Valoret's or Rhemuth's austere libraries. "It's supposed to ensure the health of the people and their animals. It's said that sometimes they leap through the flames, and that they drive their cows and sheep through, too."

"It's said—it's supposed—do they or don't they?" Javan wanted to know.

"Well, I really don't know about the animals," Tavis replied, scratching his head sheepishly. "Those are old, superstitious customs. Only the peasants practice them anymore, so far as I know. I do recall something about the theory behind the dancing, though—something about generating a—why do you want to know, Javan? Why is it so important?"

Javan gave a perplexed shrug. "I don't know. It's just that this place felt—strange, somehow. Magical, maybe."

"Magical?" Grinning, Tavis stood and knuckled the boy playfully under the chin. "And how would you know about that, my little human prince? Who's been filling your head with tales of magic?"

"It isn't funny, Tavis," the boy muttered. "I *felt* something. I still do. I would have thought, after the times I've helped you, that you'd realize that!"

Angrily the boy turned on his heel and limped back down the hillside, slapping his gauntlets against a leather-clad thigh in annoyance. Tavis watched for a moment in shock, hardly knowing what to think, then scrambled down the hill after him. They reached the campsite together, and Javan put on a pleasant expression for the benefit of the guards and the squires, but Tavis could sense the turmoil still churning behind the polite facade. He thought about their conversation while they ate their lunch.

Everyone settled down for a rest when they had finished eating and cleaned up. The guards took themselves off near the horses, and Rhys Michael flopped down, bored, under a tree to nap when the squires wandered over to relax near the stream.

Javan plunked himself on a rock near but out of earshot of his brother and began flicking pebbles into the shallow water. Tavis, after a casual glance to locate the others, made his way slowly to Javan's side, where he crouched on his heels and studied the ripples the boy was making with his rocks.

"I'm sorry if I made light of your questions, my prince," he said in a low voice. "I wasn't thinking. You know I would give my life for you."

"Your life, yes. But you no longer give me your confidence."

"I—*what?*"

"Did I or did I not help you the night of your injury?" Javan demanded, his voice not rising in volume, but all the more intense for that. "Did I or did I not help you remember what happened to you the night my father died? Did you or did you not promise to help me remember?"

"Javan, you know I've been tr—"

"Don't give me your adult excuses! For weeks now, I've held my peace. I've kept my part of the bargain and I haven't nagged you. What good has it done me? Tavis, I have to know. What happened to me the night my father died?"

Forcing down a shudder, Tavis glanced around surreptitiously. Robear, who was musically inclined, had unstrapped his lute from one of the sumpter horses and was tuning it softly while Corund napped. Jason and Eidiard were playing at dice. The squires, Dorn and Tomais, had disappeared upstream; he could hear their voices occasionally, floating on the breeze. But Rhys Michael was lying just across the clearing, apparently watching clouds build up against the horizon. If they did not keep their voices down, the boy would hear.

"I'm sorry, Javan," Tavis whispered. "You know I'm working on it. I think of little else. I thought you understood that. I'm not convinced I've identified all the ingredients Rhys used, though. I don't want to risk your safety more than once."

"Well, what's it going to take to be convinced?" Javan asked haughtily. "I can't wait forever, you know."

"I know," Tavis breathed, bowing his head. "I was going to talk to you about it later. I—suppose I need to take you back to the early part of that night one more time and re-read your impression of the taste and smell. I need to be sure it tallies with mine. Perhaps we can do it tonight."

"Why wait until tonight? Let's do it now."

"Now?"

"Yes, now. The others are asleep or occupied. Reach into my mind and see. We've done this kind of thing often enough by now. It needn't make a sound."

"But, your brother—"

"Bother my brother!" Javan snapped, though his voice was still low. "Put him to sleep, if his nearness bothers you. You can go get me some wine, and then stop to talk to him on the way back. The others won't think it amiss, and *he* won't know."

"But, Javan—"

"Are you my friend, or aren't you? Now, *do it?"*

With a smile which he hoped did not appear too forced, Tavis nodded and got to his feet, moving back toward the sumpter horses. Rhys Michael glanced up at him as he started past.

"Are you and Tavis fighting?"

Immediately Tavis stopped and dropped to a crouch beside the boy.

"Fighting? Certainly not. His foot is hurting him. I thought I'd bring him some wine to drink while I work on it. Why don't you take a nap?" Tavis suggested, clasping the boy's arm reassuringly and sending a strong compulsion to sleep as he did so. "You've had a busy morning. The afternoon will be a lot more fun if you're rested."

"I suppose you're right." Rhys Michael yawned, settling back against his tree. "Will Javan's foot be all right?"

"Of course." Tavis smiled, brushing the boy's forehead with his fingertips and getting up. "The stirrup just needs a bit more padding, that's all."

And across the clearing, a young soldier with curly blond hair watched out of the corner of his eye as the Healer picked up a wineskin and took it back toward the elder prince. With a part of his mind, Davin followed the dice his partner tossed. But he wondered what Tavis and the prince were talking about, as the Healer gave the wine to the boy and knelt at his feet, beginning to strip off the prince's special boot. He wished he dared extend his powers, but he knew better than that. Tavis might detect it, especially if he were preparing to go into a Healing mode.

The boot came off, and Javan gave a sigh of relief, smiling as he unstoppered the wineskin and took a perfunctory swallow. As Tavis pelled off his stocking, Javan put the skin down and shifted onto his left side, leaning his head against one hand propped on elbow.

"You're taking a big risk," the Healer murmured, as he dipped a towel into the water and began bathing the misshapen foot. "Furthermore, you're making *me* take a big risk."

"What are you doing that they haven't seen a dozen times?" Javan countered. "They're humans, Tavis. What do they know?"

"And you're not human?"

"Not like them. I have shields. You know I do."

"That's true," Tavis replied, drying the foot and beginning to massage it briskly. "And if you didn't have them. I would be sorely tempted at this moment to give you a psychic jolt you would not soon forget. You're acting like a spoiled child."

"How dare you!" the boy whispered. "I ask for your help, and you—will you or will you not help me, Tavis? I need to know what happened the night my father died. Don't you understand that? *I need to know!*"

Tavis lowered his eyes. "Will you stop that?" he whispered, controlling the urge to glance around surreptitiously again. "You're echoing psychically all around the campsite! God help us both if there's anyone with latent talents around here. You—"

"You mean, I was sending my thoughts to you?" the boy interrupted, sitting up and grasping Tavis's hand, an amazed look on his face.

"I'm sorry, my prince," Tavis said in a loud voice, bending over the foot and massaging it more attentively. "I didn't mean to hurt you." And then, under his breath, "Do you want to have the whole camp over here? Lie back, and I'll see what I can do."

Meekly, and much chastened, Javan lay back as he was ordered.

Tavis, with a glance at the guards, began to insinuate his consciousness around that of the boy. As he felt the oddly familiar meshing start to slip into place, he was relieved that the guards did not seem to have noticed anything out of the ordinary.

But Davin had noticed. Further, he had caught the force of Javan's psychic echo, if not its sense or its precise source. As he continued dicing with Jason, he tried to open for a further reading—though he did not want to encounter Tavis's sensitive shields. Some humans had natural resistance to probing and Davin had worked carefully to cultivate that kind of facade. But he must not draw close attention to himself. The Healer was the one person who could betray him now, if he should become suspicious and try to read the soldier known as Eidiard.

Yet, something was happening between Healer and prince—something which seemed to be outside the usual interaction of Healer and patient. He had an impression now that the psychic echo he had caught had come from Javan, not Tavis.

Someone else besides himself definitely should know about that. It was the very sort of thing he had been sent to watch for. He quested outward with his mind to see who was on monitor duty in the Council chamber, but when he realized it was Bishop Alister, he hesitated. The potential link was there if he needed it, passive but reassuring for its mere presence, but the bishop's active attention was off on some other item of importance— some mouldy scroll he was trying to make sense of—and Davin did not want to disturb him. Davin had grown very fond of the bishop. The old man reminded him of the few very early memories he had of his grandfather.

So Davin passed over that link and scanned about the camp again. Jason was engrossed in winning the last of his partner's meager stake of copper coins—they rarely played for greater amounts than that—and over near the horses, Robear was now strumming a soft shepherd's song while Corund continued trying to doze against a tree.

Rhys Michael was asleep, with a sense about him which suggested that the nap had not been all his idea, and the squires were splashing in the water a little ways upstream. Just as Davin took the dice from Jason, one of the horses whuffled—an inquisitive wicker halfway between surprise and fright.

Davin froze with the dice poised on his open palm.

"Did you hear that?" he whispered to his companion.

"Hear what?"

Urgently, Davin quested outward with his mind, the while staring into the trees across the clearing and listening with all his regular faculties. His mind encountered the faint snap of shields reacting to his probe and being raised!

Deryni!

And the snap had not come from Tavis!

Even as he bent to unsheathe his sword, the first arrow slammed into the tree just behind him and the second drove feathered death into the dozing Corund. With a stifled oath, Jason dove for his own weapon, scattering dice and copper coins but avoiding yet a third arrow which narrowly missed his head.

"To the princes!" Robear shouted, scrambling to his feet as half a dozen well-armed men burst from the trees and began running toward them. Arrows continued to thud home all around.

Tavis was already yanking Javan to cover behind a nearby tree, but Rhys Michael sat bolt upright and then froze, transfixed with horror, as a swordsman seemed to materialize from the brush not four paces away. Davin sprinted toward them and engaged before the man's sword could sheathe itself in royal flesh, sparks clashing from their weapons as they exchanged a first flurry of blows. He took a superficial cut to his left forearm before he remembered, just in time, that he had no shield.

Fortunately, his opponent was not quite good enough to take full advantage of Davin's momentary lapse; and with the second engagement, when one of Davin's two-handed blows finally connected, he collapsed with his skull caved in. The man's place was immediately taken by another attacker who pressed Davin hard. But Davin would not be moved from his defensive stance astride the cowering Rhys Michael, whose face was set in a silent cry of terror.

All around, battle was closing now. Arrows continued to fly, though the bowmen's aim was poorer, now that they must distinguish between friend and foe, all moving. Robear had blocked one such arrow with his beloved lute in those first seconds of confusion and then had been forced to parry a swordblow with it, to the instrument's total ruination. Now, leaping over the splinters of the delicate instrument, with Jason fighting desperately to shield them both so that they could make their way to Robear's bow, he lashed out and savaged a man's hand with his dagger, as partial repayment for the lute's destruction, the while staying close to Jason's back.

They won through to the saddles and equipment, but then it was a second struggle to keep from being cut down or shot while Robear tried to get his bow out of its casing and strung. An arrow whizzed under his arm as he shook out the bowstring, evoking a blasphemous oath from him and a brisk and furious retaliation on Jason's part against another swordsman who had harried them all the way there. The squires had come running at the first sound of battle, and were now doing a valiant job of fending off attackers with daggers and hastily grabbed hunting spears, since they possessed no swords of their own. Dorn, the younger of the two, was holding his own against a swordsman nearly twice his weight, with the aid of a handily seized sapling.

Even Tavis was engaged in a dangerous running skirmish with an attacker, though it consisted mostly of the untrained Tavis running and his attacker pursuing, with occasional clashes when Tavis would whirl to pit his dagger against the man's sword. But at least he was leading the man away from Javan. The white-faced elder prince, his bare, clubbed foot held up gingerly, was clutching his own dagger and trying to keep a tree between himself and the fighting, hopping on his good booted foot and wincing involuntarily whenever an arrow would occasionally thud home around him. On a horse, Javan could have acquitted himself well against any of them, but on foot and without his supportive boot, he was clumsy and knew it.

Davin saw the prince's dilemma, and he gritted his teeth as he tried to beat back an attacker half again his size. He had to get to Javan! But as he flat-bladed the man and one of the squires finished him, he heard Rhys Michael scream behind him and whirled to see a man with an axe grab the prince by one thin arm, axe poised to strike.

Almost without thinking, Davin launched himself across the intervening distance and swung his sword two-handed, half cutting the man in two at the waist before the axe could descend on the screaming prince with deadly force. Rhys Michael took a shallow cut across the top of his thigh and collapsed shrieking beside the dead man, hysterical as more arrows started to rain down. One took the squire Dorn in the stomach.

Davin engaged another enemy. Robear had finally begun retaliation with his own bow, and was now firing blind into the underbrush as fast as he could, hoping to hit or at least frighten off the enemy bowmen. His initial barrage seemed to have little effect, however, for the enemy arrows kept flying. Several slithered off Davin's mail as he fought, and one even skewered the calf of the man who had been pursuing Tavis.

With an oath, the wounded attacker sank to his knees and tried to snap off the arrow in his leg, but he had not reckoned on Javan, lurking behind his tree. The elder prince leaped onto the man's back with a blood-curdling yell and held on like a limpet, one arm locked around the mailed head, drawing it back as he jerked his dagger across the upturned throat with a deftness which would have made the most exacting weapons master proud. As the two of them went down in a shower of blood, Davin glanced aside and then threw himself across Rhys Michael, just in time to intercept an arrow meant for the prince. The shaft buried itself in his lower back, the jagged hunting barb searing pain through his body.

Gasping, legs no longer able to function, he clasped Rhys Michael to his breast even as he lashed out with his sword to hamstring an attacker who was harrying Jason. Someone screamed from the brush into which Robear had been continuing to shoot, and the enemy arrows stopped. A frantic rustling of leaves told of another bowman beating a judicious retreat. As Robear swung on the last two attackers still on their feet, one of whom had been trying to keep the squire Tomais from impaling him on a hunting spear, the men threw down their weapons and surrendered.

"All right! It's over!" Jason rasped, prodding the hamstrung man with his sword until the latter also surrendered.

As Davin slowly raised up on one elbow, he could hear a horse galloping away—the retreating bowman making good his escape, no doubt. Corund lay dead where he had slept, the young squire Dorn did not move from where he had fallen, and four attackers likewise moved no more. As Robear and the remaining squire lashed the hands of their two captives behind them at wrist and elbow, Jason trussed up his own crippled captive, then went charging into the brush to look for the second bowman. Rhys Michael, hauling himself from under Davin's protection, took one look at the wound across his thigh and began to wail.

"My brother! He's hurt!" Javin cried, scrambling so quickly to his brother's side that his limp was scarcely noticeable. "Tavis, help him! He's bleeding!"

Davin had rolled onto his side as Javan approached, so the blood-stained prince did not notice the arrow protruding from his lower back. But as the Healer came to kneel beside the younger prince, Jason emerged from the brush dragging a gravely wounded bowman and turned him over to Robear. Jason blanched as he came up behind Davin and saw the arrow.

"Eidiard! My God, man!"

"It can wait," Davin whispered, with a fierce shake of his head, though he did accept Jason's support and help in easing further onto his left side.

He was sore hurt—that much he knew. Too hurt, he expected, for even a Healer like Rhys to do much for him. He had no feeling below the burning shaft protruding from his back, and he had to reach back and brush its feathers with his fingertips to know that it had passed just beside the spine, leaving his lower body numb and lifeless. His heart sank with that realization, for he had never heard of a Healer being able to mend such a wound.

He could sense Bishop Alister's frantic inquiry, now that the fighting was done; and as he leaned against Jason's knee, he closed his eyes and let the older man read his injuries through his own faculties, praying that his pain and fear had exaggerated the seriousness of his situation.

But Alister's assessment came back stark and stunned, with the soul-chilling addition that the barbed arrowhead, besides grazing the spine, had lodged hard against one of the great blood vessels which fed from the heart—had, in fact, already cut partway through the vessel's wall. Any chance movement could complete the job. A really competent Healer, working very fast, might be able to Heal that damage before the pressure blew it wider and he bled to death internally, but it would require two good hands as well as skill, and Tavis O'Neill had only the latter.

Nor dared he let Tavis even try. For Healer's ease, a Deryni must lower almost all his shields, so that the Healer might draw from the resources of the patient's body, as well as his own strength—and Davin could not go shieldless before Tavis. It was inevitable that the Healer would learn that he was Deryni, but Tavis must learn nothing more. The Council and their work must not be jeopardized because a chance arrow had rendered one of their number a dying cripple.

Davin stifled a gasp as Jason jostled the arrow in trying to get a better look at his wound, knowing that the barbed head had moved him that much nearer to eternity, but he knew what he must do, and gave his decision to Bishop Alister. There was grief in the old man's response, but he understood all the logic which Davin had pursued, and that there was no other choice.

In a breath, though there was no outward sign, Davin opened all his soul to the bishop, sensing the answering absolution and blessing like a whisper of a caress flowing across the link which bound them. Almost he could feel the touch of the anointing oil as the last sacrament was projected through the link as real as if the bishop had knelt by his side and physically touched him with the holy balm.

He was at peace as Tavis finished healing Rhys Michael's leg, at peace as the Healer shifted on his knees to move to Davin's side.

"He's got an arrow in his back, m'lord," Jason said urgently, before Tavis could even touch him.

Davin's eyes fluttered open in time to see Javan's white-faced horror as he scrambled nearer.

"My God, Jason, why didn't you say something?" the prince gasped, staring at the reddened hand which the knight displayed for Tavis's inspection. "Rhys Michael could have waited. Tavis, do something!"

But as Tavis reached out, Davin grabbed the handless wrist with his good right hand.

"No! Lord Tavis, if you try to remove the barb, I will die immediately. There's nothing you can do. My legs are gone already."

Steadily Tavis reached out and released his stump from Davin's grip.

"Suppose you let me make the medical judgments around here, Eidiard. You're neither Healer nor D—you *are* Deryni!"

His hand jumped back from Davin's like one stung, his psychic shock reverberating. Javan's face was pinched and drawn so tight that Davin could not help wondering whether he had felt it too. Jason had simply frozen behind him in shock, and Davin extended just the slightest amount of control to make certain the knight did not leave him prematurely.

"Yes, I am Deryni," he whispered. "But I swear, it was not to do any of you harm that I came here—and I was *not* of those pigs who tried to kill us all just now. You must believe that."

"Who are you? How can you be Deryni?" Tavis managed to whisper. "I *probed* you! Right after you came, when that horse kicked you, I Healed you! I would have sworn you were not Deryni!"

"I was sent to guard the princes, and to keep watch over you," Davin murmured, sensing Tavis's growing intent to try to read him further and knowing he could not permit that. With a part of his mind, he reached out to Jason again and urged one of the man's supporting hands to move closer to the arrow in his back. "Believe me, Tavis, I am neither of these pigs nor of the butchers who took your hand. I am a friend."

"You deceived us—"

"It was necessary," Davin responded, playing for time as he set triggers in his mind to ensure that there would be nothing there to read, when his shields failed. "Had I not been here, you would have had that much less warning of the attack today. And this shaft which now sends me to my grave would have taken Rhys Michael instead."

"You're lying," Tavis whispered. "You must be lying. Who sent you? Why did you really come?"

His probe lashed out, clashing against Davin's shields even as the Healer's hand and stump pressed against his temples. The shields held, but Davin knew he could not hold them for long.

Into Thy Hands, Lord, he sent his final prayer, at the same time nudging Jason's mind just enough to move the man's hand awkwardly against the arrow shaft.

The barb shifted within him, but there was no pain. He felt only a warmth flood through his gut as blood began pumping where blood was never meant to go.

He gave a little gasp as his vision began to dim, and he knew from the look on Tavis's face that the Healer realized he was hemorrhaging internally, but the Healing energy which Tavis tried to divert to him was too late now. As he closed his eyes and sagged more heavily against Jason's supporting knee, he reached out a final time to the one who anguished in the Council chamber and tried to force his own strength across the fading link.

He had time only to sense that last futile caress, and to wonder again at how Bishop Alister reminded him of his grandfather Camber; and then, for just an instant, the old Camber presence that he remembered from childhood flooded through him and enveloped him in love.

His last image, as the final darkness descended, was of the face of his grandfather, weeping, and of the strong hands reaching out to buoy him up—and then a nothingness which was pervaded by a blinding, incredibly beautiful light of all the colors of time.

And Tavis, pressing relentlessly at those last vestiges of consciousness as he realized his subject was dying, gasped and pulled back in awe and momentary panic. Of all the things he had expected to encounter, the presence of Saint Camber had been the last! Almost immediately, he re-engaged; but it was too late by then. Davin was dead, and all his memories fled away, the erasing triggers having done their work.

Suppressing unbidden tears whose source he could not trace, Tavis withdrew, slamming his fist against the ground in sheer frustration—then catching his breath in awe as the still, handsome face seemed to shimmer.

Slowly the curly blond hair went straight and fairer, the chin became more pronounced, the face changed shape just enough so that it was no longer Eidiard's. The eyes, when Tavis peered hesitantly under one slack lid, had gone from brown to palest grey.

"Jesus Christ!" Jason murmured, letting the body slip to the ground and edging back a little on his knees as he wiped his palms against his thighs. "That isn't Eidiard!"

"I know him!" Tavis whispered, hugging his arms across his chest to keep them from shaking. "I've seen him before, but I can't remember—"

"Good Lord, it's the Earl of Culdi!" said Robear, joining them from his task of binding the prisoners. "But—that's Eidiard's harness, and—"

Javan, kneeling dazed on the other side of his sleeping brother, could only shake his head in stunned disbelief and whisper, "Why, Tavis? Why?"

Chapter Twenty

Let us see if his words be true: and let us prove what shall happen in the end of him.
—Wisdom of Solomon 2:17

"I'll tell you why!" Bishop Hubert raged, when the party with its prisoners had returned to Rhemuth Castle. "He was one of them!" He gestured toward the four kneeling prisoners with an angry chop of his hand. "Are they not all Deryni?"

Court had been convened in the great hall as soon as the king and regents could be summoned. The princes had been allowed time to wash and change their blood-stained tunics, but now they sat tensely on stools to either side of their brother, who nominally presided from the formal throne. A tense-looking Tavis crouched beside Javan's stool to the far right.

The three regents resident in Rhemuth were ranged in

rigid fury around the throne: Bishop Hubert, coped and mitered between Alroy and Javan, crozier clutched like a talisman against the prisoners; Earls Murdoch and Tammaron on Alroy's other side, wearing their coronets and long court mantles of rich, dark stuff lined with fur.

Archbishops Jaffray and Oriss were also present, and Earl Udaut, the constable, and several other lesser lords, but they had been relegated to places at the right of and perpendicular to the throne, with several clarks who were scribbling notes intently. Jaffray, the sole functioning Deryni in the hall besides Tavis—for the prisoners had been drugged before they ever left the campsite to prevent Deryni tricks—only wished he could be even farther from the center of attention. Deryniness would be a key issue this afternoon, as well it had to be.

He wished he knew more precisely what had happened. From what snatches of information he had been able to pick up from those around him, it appeared that there had been an attack on the royal hunting party by, among others, those now kneeling before the court, and that Davin had been among those killed, his true form returning at his death. The logical inference seemed to be that Davin had been a key part of a Deryni assassination plot—for why else would a Deryni of Davin's high rank join the royal household disguised as a common guard?

That Davin was dead, there was certainly no doubt, even if his psychic absence were not poignant enough reminder. His lifeless body lay on a litter before all the court, alongside those of the other four attackers who had been killed, plus the dead guard and squire. Beside them knelt the four bound and drugged prisoners who had been taken alive, each with a guard standing behind. They *were* Deryni—Jaffray had sent out a swift probe as they were brought in, though the shields he had encountered were hazy and confused from the drugs—but he did not recognize any of them except Davin.

"I therefore think it clear," Murdoch was saying, "that these—*Deryni*," he spoke the 'name with purest contempt, "did conspire to murder Your Highness's royal brothers—and would have threatened Your Highness's life, as well, had you not been called to your royal duties at the last moment and stayed in Rhemuth this morning. Nor is this the first instance of Deryni plots against the House of Haldane, as Your Highness will recall. Now, one of the loyal guards has been most foully slain, and another guard, who was trusted with the very safety of the Crown, has betrayed you."

He moved down a step and gestured angrily toward the body of Davin.

"There lies the Earl of Culdi, who, by some magic surely profane in the eyes of God, took the form of another and did deceive Your Grace and your royal brothers—and was revealed as the deceiver he is only when death forced him from his evil ways."

"He saved Rhys Michael's life," Javan protested. "He took an arrow meant for my brother."

Murdoch threw up his hands in disgust. "Oh, Your Highness, how can you be so deceived? It was merest chance that the arrow struck—*that!*" Again he gestured roughly toward the body. "His confederates miscalculated—that is all! There is another who was so wounded. It is not always possible to choose one's targets with great precision in the heat of battle, especially when the bowman shoots from a cowardly shelter in brush."

He stabbed a beringed forefinger at the body of the man Javan had finished, with the arrow still projecting from its leg.

"These Deryni are all in league," he concluded. "It is quite clear what dark Master of destruction and damnation they serve!"

It was all Jaffray could do to keep his seat, but he knew he dared not rise to Murdoch's bait and draw the regents' scrutiny on himself. Tavis had likewise blanched at Murdoch's statement, but with tight-lipped forbearance he merely dropped his hot gaze to the floor by Javan's feet.

Alroy, who had grown progressively paler as Murdoch spoke, gripped the gold-mounted ivory of his scepter as if it were his only link to sanity as he stared at the four battered captives.

"Have you anything to say to us?" he said, in a thin but steady voice.

The captives stared back sullenly, eyes a little glazed from the drugs they had been given, but none of them showed any inclination to speak.

"We do not wish it said that our justice is arbitrary," Alroy continued, almost a little pleading. "Your crime is irrefutable. We have done nothing to provoke such an attack upon us. Yet, if you had some quarrel—"

Bishop Hubert rapped twice with his crozier on the wooden floor of the dais, the sound an echo of doom for those who knelt before him.

"*No* quarrel may justify raising hand against one's lawfully anointed king, Your Grace!" he thundered in red-faced outrage. "And to strike against the king's heirs is to strike against the king! These *Deryni* were engaged in sacrilegious murder and treason. They must be made an example, that none may ever again raise hand against your royal house!"

Alroy, who had shrunk down in his throne a little as Hubert made his pronouncement, gripped his scepter even tighter, and Javan looked as if he might faint. Only Rhys Michael continued to stare evenly at the prisoners, his face a chiseled mask of ice. After a few tense heartbeats, Alroy turned his face slightly toward Tavis, crouching at Javan's side.

"Lord Tavis, perhaps a Deryni can shed some light on the motives of other Deryni."

Tavis, with an uncertain glance at the king, then at the prisoners, rose stiffly and crossed his arms so that his missing hand was shielded behind his other elbow.

"I would gather from Your Highness's request that my own loyalty is not in question, even though I am Deryni," he said softly. "If this is so, do I also assume that Your Highness is asking me to Truth-Read the prisoners?"

"If you can."

"With all due respect, Your Highness, I would rather not."

"Your own attackers could be among them," Murdoch offered smoothly. "Will you not serve yourself and your king in this small way, Tavis?"

Tavis returned Murdoch's gaze implacably, then drew careful breath, clearly about to refuse.

"Do not force me to command you, Tavis," Murdoch whispered.

For a moment, Jaffray thought the Healer might continue to defy Murdoch. Tight-jawed, he glanced at Javan, at Alroy, then gave a brisk nod, not quite a bow, before moving down the dais steps. The prisoners, even in their drugged lethargy, shrank against the guards who stood at their backs, but they could not escape his touch as he passed along their line, pausing before each man to lay his hand briefly on forehead and probe as well as he might. When he had read each one, he returned up the steps and made Alroy another almost-bow.

"I believe no useful purpose would be served by deeper probing, Your Highness. They appear to be only disgruntled younger nobility—the same breed of bully boys whose bands have plagued us for some time now. They are more young and foolish than conspiratorial, and seem as astonished as we that Earl Davin was among us."

Javan raised his head attentively, some of the color returning to his cheeks.

"Then, Davin was *not* lying. He *was* sent by someone else, to protect us."

"Aye, sent by someone else," Hubert replied archly, "but not to protect you, Your Highness. He deceived you. He deceived all of us. He took another man's form and identity. And where is the real Eidiard of Clure? No doubt, most foully murdered, so young MacRorie could come here in his place and plot his treason!"

Javan had no answer for that. Nor did Tavis. After a moment, Alroy looked at the Healer again.

"You believe there was no plot, then?"

"Among themselves, because they were personally outraged, yes, of course there was a plot, Your Highness. But it did not extend beyond their band, and it was not a *Deryni* plot. This was not a Deryni question, despite the fact that Earl Murdoch would have it so. I cannot speak for Earl Davin's motives, but these men appear to have acted out of purely human motivations."

"They 'appear' to have acted," Murdoch repeated, tight-lipped. "Then, you admit the possibility that there may have been other considerations which prompted their action, which you could not read?"

Tavis shrugged, a not-quite insolent statement of subtle defiance.

"I cannot read their souls, my lord, but so far as I may determine, on an admittedly superficial but drug-assisted reading, they acted to retaliate against those who symbolized the lessening of their prospects."

"And if more than a superficial reading were attempted?" Tammaron asked.

"They would die."

"What!"

"They had a pact among themselves, to resist any deep probing by triggering their own deaths. Bishop

MacInnis will remember a similar case early in the summer, when a prisoner willed his own death rather than permit the baring of his mind to my probe. I have the names of the living and the dead, including the one who escaped. There is nothing further to be gained."

Hubert nodded, the pink lips pursing in the cherub face.

"He's right. I remember."

"I see." Murdoch hooked both thumbs in the leather of his earl's belt and rocked back and forth on his heels. "And I assume that if anyone else of your kind were to attempt to read them, he would likewise encounter this?"

"Undoubtedly, my lord."

"Even Archbishop Jaffray," Murdoch pursued it, "who is forbidden by his vows to kill?"

As Jaffray caught his breath, praying he would be spared the necessity to find out, Tavis gave a curt nod.

"You are welcome to have it tried, my lord. Archbishop Jaffray was one of my teachers, though he is not a Healer. It may well be that he has skills which I do not; but I do not think even he can elude a death-trigger."

Murdoch turned his attention to Jaffray slyly. "Well, Archbishop, can you serve your king in this?"

Chilled, Jaffray stood.

"Your Highness," he murmured, with a slight bow to the wide-eyed Alroy before returning his attention to Murdoch. "Lord Tavis was, indeed, my student at one time, and if he says that no one could avoid such a trigger, then I am certain that it is so."

"I would question that, Archbishop," Murdoch replied. "However, I will not demean your office by putting you personally to the test. Sir Piedur."

The guard captain, standing by the side door nearest Jaffray and Oriss, snapped to attention.

"Excellency."

"Ask Lord Oriel to attend the King's Grace. Do not tell him anything of what has just been discussed."

"At once, Excellency."

"And you, Tavis, do you go to the clarks and give them the names that you have learned, while we wait for Oriel to join us," Murdoch added.

As Piedur left and Tavis came down from the dais, Jaffray sank wearily back into his chair and folded his hands, realizing some of the worst of his fears as he watched the young Healer come and stand before a clark. He had heard vague rumor for the past month that the regents were recruiting Deryni agents by inducement and threat, and now he knew that it was true. The collaboration was beginning, Deryni against Deryni!

Tavis had nearly finished dictating to the clark, arms clasped sullenly across his chest, not bothering to look at what the man wrote down; but Jaffray could see the names over the clark's shoulder, and knew with a sick feeling in the pit of his stomach that the men had come from some of the oldest families in Gwynedd. When Tavis had finished, he returned to the dais and crouched once more by Javan's side. Murdoch, displaying a typically prim, careful smile, leaned one arm casually on the back of Alroy's throne, surveying Tavis and Jaffray by turns.

"We thank you, Lord Tavis," he said silkily. "And I believe you will remember Lord Oriel from the night of your injury?"

Tavis gave a curt nod.

"Good. And you, Archbishop—do you know him? He is in our employ now, as you will have gathered. It seems he has a wife and tiny daughter of whom he is inordinately fond. But, I didn't hear your answer, Archbishop. Do you know Lord Oriel?"

"Only by reputation," Jaffray murmured dully. He looked up and saw Murdoch's peculiar, twisted smile— and just for an instant, he wanted to smash Murdoch's prim, disdainful face.

"Well, you shall meet him shortly," Murdoch was saying. "But just to keep both you and Tavis honest, I should warn you that if either of you should attempt either to influence what Oriel does or to interfere with his reading of the chosen prisoner, he will tell me—and I shall know where your true loyalties lie." The sour smile was replaced by a grim, tight-lipped scowl. "Do I make myself clear?"

Resignedly, Jaffray nodded assent, glancing aside as Piedur re-entered the hall, escorting a young, blondish man with a wisp of reddish beard who looked far too young to wear the Healer's green, even though he fit the description Rhys had given them in the Council. Tavis, crouching still by Javan's stool, followed the younger Healer with narrowed eyes. Jaffray suspected that Tavis had little use for the Healer who had failed to save his hand—though it had not been Oriel's fault, God knew. Murdoch smiled his bitter smile again and folded his hands piously, though he did not remove his elbow from the back of Alroy's throne.

"Lord Oriel, we have here a situation which is at once a serious matter of state and a test—of whom, I shall not say." He gestured toward the four kneeling men with a thrust of his chin. "These prisoners were taken following their ambush of the Princes Javan and Rhys Michael whilst hunting. They killed the guard and the squire you see yonder, and the other dead are of their band. At least one man escaped. We know them to be Deryni. What I want to know first is, what are the names of all the conspirators?"

Oriel glanced coolly at the prisoners, then returned his attention to Murdoch.

"May I ask the Lord Tavis a question?"

"Ask, and I will tell you whether he may answer," Murdoch replied.

"As you wish. Lord Tavis, I note without actually probing that the prisoners have been drugged in some manner. Am I to assume the usual combination of substances?"

Tavis glanced up at Murdoch, who nodded, then turned his attention briefly to Oriel.

"The usual combination," he admitted reluctantly. "The minimum dosage consistent with safety for those around them, while still ensuring breakdown of defenses."

"Very well. Earl Murdoch, have you any preference as to which prisoner I should interrogate, or did you wish all of them read?"

"The bowman, there on the left," Murdoch said, folding his arms across his chest and fondling his close-trimmed beard with one hand.

He made no move to say anything further, and Jaffray realized that he did not mean to tell Oriel of the death-triggers. He was going to see whether Oriel detected them on his own. Where Oriel went from there was anyone's guess, though Jaffray did not think Oriel would kill on orders from the regents. He was, after all, a Healer sworn.

Oriel turned and looked at the prisoners, then walked slowly to the bowman, on the far left of the line. The broken shaft of an arrow still protruded from his right shoulder, but he was no longer bleeding much. The pain showed in his eyes as he looked up at the Healer, though, for neither drugs nor his now-crippled Deryni-ness could ease the ache of arms still lashed tight at wrist and elbow, the throb of arrow still impaling, the cold dread of certain knowledge that psychic invasion was now imminent. As Oriel slowly raised his hands toward the man's temples, he winced and screwed his eyes shut and tried to shrink back from the Healer's touch; but the guard supporting him merely tightened his grip on the prisoner's shoulders, at considerable additional pain, and held him fast for the contact.

Jaffray did not dare to extend and find out precisely what Oriel was doing in those first seconds of contact, but very shortly the prisoner started trembling, his eye-lids fluttering involuntarily, as Oriel intensified his probe. Almost immediately, Oriel opened his eyes, apparently having withdrawn slightly, since his subject had stopped shaking, and half-turned his face toward Murdoch, though he did not take his eyes from the bowman's.

"I have their names and families," Oriel said softly, "including the man who escaped."

"Speak them," Murdoch ordered. "Clark, check these against your list."

"This one is Denzil Carmichael. The other three are Fulbert de Morrisey, Ranald Gilstrachan, and Ivo Lovat, the Baron Frizell's youngest son." The two clarks collaborated over their list, nodding as each name was found and checked off. "The dead are Dylan ap Thomas, Shaw Farquharson, and Amyot and Trefor of Morland. Those last two are cousins. The one who escaped is Sholto MacDhugal."

At the senior clark's final nod that the lists tallied, Murdoch breathed, "Excellent."

"And what of the Earl of Culdi?" Hubert asked.

The Healer's eyes went a little unfocused as he apparently read again, but then he shook his head, a puzzled expression on his face.

"Carmichael has never seen him before, Your Grace. In fact, he thought the man was a guard until he—shape-changed?"

With that, he looked up, not breaking the forced rapport he maintained, but seeking Murdoch's face for confirmation of what he had just read. Murdoch went red, and Jaffray did not even need to use his Sight to read the anger in all three regents.

"He's lying," Murdoch whispered. "He has to be. We

know that MacRorie was part of a massive Deryni plot to overthrow the Crown. Read deeper!"

Troubled by their reaction, Oriel returned his gaze to the face between his hands, closed his eyes for a moment, then shivered visibly as he turned his face slightly toward Murdoch again.

"My lord, I dare not go deeper. This man has a suicide block of some kind. If I force his shields further, it will kill him."

"Then kill him!" snapped Murdoch. "I want to know about the conspiracy, and I *will* know!"

"But, there is no conspiracy, at least not with anyone named MacRorie," Oriel whispered. "These men sought vengeance for the death of a friend, but this Earl of Culdi whom you mention was no part of their design."

"Read deeper, Oriel!" Murdoch commanded, taking a step toward the Healer. "If you value your life and your family, obey me!"

For a moment, Jaffray thought the Healer would refuse the order. Oriel squeezed his eyes shut as if to block out the sight of all around him; but then his shoulders sagged in defeat and his face relaxed to stony indifference.

It was over in an instant, as Tavis had promised and as Jaffray had known it would be. As the man collapsed against the guard, Oriel gave a shudder and let his hands fall away, having to steady himself on the guard's shoulder to keep from falling himself.

Murdoch was scowling as Oriel turned toward the throne, and Hubert and Tammaron showed similar signs of displeasure. Tavis stared across at his fellow Healer with a look of raw fury which Jaffray had never seen in the pale blue eyes before. Oriel caught the look and blanched, hardly daring to lift his eyes to Murdoch.

"He is dead, Excellency, as His Highness's Healer apparently knew would happen before I came. Why did you not tell me?"

"I told you, it was a testing. Besides, it is not for you to question us," Murdoch said evenly. "What more did you read?"

Oriel sighed. "A few small, petty sins; terror that what he himself had set in motion could not now be recalled. But I read no conspiracy beyond the pact the nine of them shared. The one called Trefor of Morland was apparently their leader, if you could call it that; they were

306

hardly that well organized. He was a foster brother to a —Dafydd Leslie, who was executed this summer?"

Hubert snorted, a priggish, perplexed sigh, then motioned the man away with a plump hand. "Never you mind, Oriel. We know the name. You may go now."

Speechless, Oriel sketched a helpless, sorrow-laden bow to Alroy, then turned and followed Sir Piedur out of the hall. Jaffray could not help noticing the contempt in Tavis's eyes as his gaze followed the younger Healer out. His own reaction he could not resolve just yet.

"Very well, Your Highness," Murdoch said, when Piedur had returned to the hall alone. "I think it clear that pursuing this course of action will only cheat the executioners. I therefore ask Your Highness, what is your pleasure toward these men who would attempt to slay your royal brothers, and who have killed two of your good men?"

Alroy swallowed and turned slightly toward his chancellor, standing at his left hand.

"Earl Tammaron," he said softly, "name a fitting punishment for men who would seek to murder my brothers."

With no outward sign of emotion, Tammaron turned his gaze on the three remaining prisoners.

"Such men should be executed at once, Your Highness. Furthermore, their lands and titles, if any, should be attainted, and their heirs declared outlaw and put to the horn. In the case of younger sons, I would recommend that their fathers receive the same punishment, for having exercised so little control over their kinsmen."

"Execution for these and attainder and outlawry for their families?" Alroy asked.

"Precisely."

"And the method of execution?" Alroy murmured hesitantly.

"To be hanged, drawn, and quartered, befitting traitors," Tammaron replied promptly. "The parts should be sent to every major town in Gwynedd and displayed for all to see and learn the fate of traitors and assassins."

Alroy's face had gone ever whiter at Tammaron's pronouncement. Javan had closed his eyes. Rhys Michael did not change expression at all, even when Alroy stood shakily to pronounce judgment.

"We concur with the recommendation of our chancellor," he said in a surprisingly strong voice. "The sentence will be carried out at once."

The three kneeling Deryni blanched, even through their drugged state. Murdoch watched their reaction, then leaned close to the king to whisper something in his ear. Alroy's knuckles whitened even further on the scepter he held, but he nodded curtly.

"We further command that the bodies of these others suffer the same sentence," Alroy added, gesturing toward the bodies with his chin, "including the Earl of Culdi. The Earldom of Culdi is hereby confiscate to our Crown."

"No! He saved Rhys Michael's life!" Javan protested, half-rising from his stool.

"This is the king's command!" Murdoch said in a loud voice. "So let it be done. Sir Piedur, you will assemble the castle garrison to assist in the executions and to witness the king's justice."

As Javan subsided on his stool, the king turned and went out of the hall through a side door, attended by the regents and followed by Rhys Michael and several guards and squires. Oriss and Udaut and the clerks followed them, for note would be taken of any statements the prisoners made at the time of death, but Jaffray paused to kneel briefly by the body of the dead Denzil Carmichael. As he rose, the guards took the body and began dragging and herding the live prisoners out to the courtyard at the far end of the hall. With a sigh, Jaffray moved on through the side door with the others.

When the prisoners, living and dead, had been taken from the hall, and all that remained within were a pair of guards by the doors at the far end, Javan finally roused himself from his dazed introspection and turned his gaze on Tavis, still crouching at his feet.

Was there a conspiracy, Tavis?"

"I don't know, my prince. I honestly don't think so—and I say that not as Deryni, but as your loyal servant and friend. Even Oriel, who is now the regents' tool, could find no evidence of a larger plot, it seems." He chuckled bitterly. "In truth, I suspect they were after me, for killing Dafydd Leslie and for serving you—though it would have been a masterstroke to kill both the king's brothers, too."

"And Davin MacRorie—was he a traitor?" the boy asked softly.

Tavis could only shake his head in bewilderment.

"Not a traitor—though what he *was,* I cannot begin to guess." He paused for just an instant, then looked up tentatively. "Javan," he whispered, "I did not tell the Court, and there was no time to tell you earlier, but when Davin died, I thought I sensed another presence with him."

"Another presence? What do you mean?"

"A—" He sighed and shook his head, finding it difficult to express himself in words. "Forgive me, my prince. You know of Saint Camber, who was young MacRorie's grandfather?"

"Of course."

"Well, it was *his* presence I thought I sensed. Davin acknowledged him as Camber. Camber was *with* him— I would almost swear it on my Sight! There was such a peacefulness about Davin as he died—not as if he willed it, precisely, but he—accepted it. And Camber upheld him."

Javan's eyes had grown round with wonder as Tavis spoke, and now he grasped Tavis's good arm so tightly it almost hurt.

"You think that Saint Camber came to him at the moment of death?"

Tavis swallowed. "So it—seemed."

"Oh." Then: "Do saints do that often?"

Tavis gave a semblance of a nervous chuckle and shrugged helplessly. "Damned if I know. I don't think so, though," he concluded on a more sober note.

Javan mulled that for a moment, then cleared his throat uneasily.

"Maybe they only appear to their families."

"I suppose it's as possible as any other speculation. But—why do you ask that?"

"Well, Davin had a younger brother, didn't he? Maybe we could ask him."

"About Saint Camber? Ansel?" Tavis shook his head. "He will be long in hiding by now."

"In hiding? Why? How could he know?"

"The two were brothers, and Deryni, Javan," Tavis whispered impatiently. "He will have known of Davin's death the instant it occurred, and he will have known what that would mean, for he cannot have been unaware of the secret game his brother played."

"What about Father Joram, then?" Javan insisted.

"He was Davin's uncle, and he's a priest. If anyone should know about Saint Camber, he should. Or, what about Lady Evaine, or Rhys?"

"Rhys, my prince? After what he did to us the night your father died? And the others are no less involved, I feel more and more certain."

"But, how can we find out? Tavis, we must know the truth! We *must!*"

But they were allowed no further time for discussion just then, for the royal party was filing along an open passageway running just beneath the rafters of the hall toward the gallery at the far end. That gallery overlooked the hall in one direction and, in the other, the pitched stone courtyard which lay between the hall and the great octagonal keep. There it was that the executions were about to take place.

Sir Jason appeared in the side doorway with a cloak for Javan, for the afternoon was growing chill as evening approached, and Javan glanced plaintively at Tavis in appeal; but the Healer shook his head and helped the prince up with a hand under his elbow. Grisly though the executions would be, Javan must witness them; and Tavis would not leave the boy to face that alone. Already, the mutilation of the bodies would have started, the better to terrify the three living prisoners awaiting execution. They could delay no longer.

Sir Jason laid the cloak around Javan's rigid shoulders, then withdrew discreetly; and Tavis, with a grim expression, began walking the boy firmly up the hall, where another narrow stair led to the gallery where the others were already assembled.

"Courage, my prince," he murmured. "We shall find a way to get more information out of my fellow Deryni, I promise you. Let me think on it for a day or two. It may be that Rhys can be our key, after all. He and I are Healers, two of a kind. I may be able to use some of his own craft against him."

CHAPTER TWENTY-ONE

*An enemy speaketh sweetly with his lips, but in his
heart he imagineth how to throw thee into a pit: he
will weep with his eyes, but if he find opportunity,
he will not be satisfied with blood.*
                                    —Ecclesiasticus 12:16

In a dim underground passageway deep beneath Caerrorie, Rhys had his hands full trying to comfort the devas-
tated brother of Davin MacRorie. From Camber to Joram
the word of Davin's death had gone, shattering Joram's
composure all the way in Argoed, where he and Jebediah
had waited for Camber to join them for Michaelmas. The
two Michaelines had returned to Camber, via Portals, as
quickly as they could decently make their excuses to
their vicar general. The details of the tragedy they read
from a still-stunned Camber before deploying to gather
the others, Joram to bring Rhys and Evaine from Sheele
and Jebediah to try to find Gregory. To Rhys it befell to
bring back the next MacRorie heir.

Ansel had known, of course. Rhys found the seventeen-
year-old Ansel huddled miserably in the passageway outside the Portal chamber, arms clasped around his knees,
tear-bright eyes lifted in dread expectation as the panel
slid aside to disclose Rhys. He scrambled to his feet as
the Healer emerged, stumbling blindly into the older
man's arms and weeping bitterly as Rhys's hand stroked
the silver-gilt hair in futile comfort. Several minutes
passed before Ansel regained sufficient composure to
speak, but Rhys did not try to hurry him. The bond Ansel
had shared with his older brother had been far stronger
and of longer duration than even Camber's tie.

"Oh, God, I felt him go, Rhys!" Ansel finally managed
to choke out. He sniffled and swallowed with difficulty, a
loud, painful gulp. "I couldn't tell exactly *how* it happened, but I knew! The master of horse must have
thought I was having a seizure or something."

311

"I know," Rhys murmured, keeping an arm around Ansel's shoulders as the young man smeared an already damp sleeve across his eyes.

"What—what did happen?" Ansel asked, after a few more deep breaths to regain better control.

"There was a hawking expedition," Rhys said quietly. "The princes' party was ambushed by Deryni, at least six or so. We don't yet know who they were or why they did it, but Davin took an arrow apparently meant for Rhys Michael. It—entered in the lower back, damaging his spine in passing, and lodged against one of the major blood vessels, Alister says."

Ansel winced and bit at his lip to keep from groaning, but he did not interrupt as Rhys took a deep breath and continued.

"The injury was—very severe, and Davin knew it. He assessed the damage, and his chances of surviving, while still keeping his shield integrity from Tavis, and decided not to allow Tavis to try to Heal him. After the initial wound, there would have been very little pain. He was even able to receive the last rites through Alister before inducing an unwitting guard to ease him on his way."

"You mean, he—let himself die?" Ansel whispered incredulously.

Rhys sighed. "Ansel, try to understand. He knew that trying to remove the arrow would almost certainly kill him. He also knew that Tavis would discover that he was Deryni, the instant the Healer tried to work on him, and that he would try to force his shields. There was also the probability of drugs being used to force his cooperation."

"Oh, God!" Ansel moaned.

"So he set mental triggers to prevent Tavis from being able to work a death-reading," Rhys continued softly, "and then he reached into the mind of the guard who was supporting him from behind and—had him jar the arrow, just slightly. Do I—have to go into the medical details of what happened next?"

Ansel shook his head quickly and swallowed.

"Was it—quick?"

"He would have lost consciousness within seconds."

Ansel rubbed a shaking hand across eyes bleary from weeping, then shook his head when Rhys would have touched his temple to read his mental state with greater accuracy.

"It's all right. I'll be all right." He sniffed and swal-

312

lowed, finally managing to raise a more composed face to Rhys.

"So, what now? Will we at least be able to get his body back for burial beside Father?"

Rhys sighed and shook his head, remembering Cathan's grave in the little village churchyard only a few hundred yards from here.

"I doubt it, Ansel. His own shape will have come back upon him when he died. Those who were there will have seen it. By now, the regents surely know. Unless I miss my guess, they'll hold Davin just as much to blame as the others."

"But, he didn't—"

"You know that, and I know that," Rhys agreed, "and the regents may even know that—but do you really think they're going to pass up an opportunity like this to accuse a high-ranking Deryni of treason?"

Ansel heaved a heavy sigh, his shoulders slumping in dejection. "No. You're right. For that matter, they'll probably be after me, next, as the brother and heir of a traitor."

"I fear they will." Rhys glanced at his feet, then looked up at Ansel again. "The Council is gathering to make plans. We'd like to include you. It will help to take your mind off what's happened."

Drawing a deep breath, Ansel squared his shoulders and then raised his head.

"I'll come."

In the *keeill*, the others were gathering as the word spread. Evaine and Joram sat cross-legged to Camber's right beside the white slab in the center of the dais. A single sphere of silvery handfire rested at the center of the slab, the only illumination in the vast chamber except for torches burning in the four bronze cressets.

In the hour since Evaine's and Joram's arrival, the three of them had been sharing Camber's experience of Davin's death and remembering his short but valiant life, trying to find some meaning in those last minutes for which he had died. Davin's final suspicion about the unpredictable Prince Javan had provided only bittersweet soothing to their sickness of heart. Evaine had wept, and Camber, too, but now the tears were past. Joram had not cried at all, but perhaps he would have been better off if he had, for every line of his body, huddled inside the heavy Michaeline greatcloak, spoke of grief and anger only barely contained. His face, lit mainly from below by the glow of Camber's handfire, was a mask as cold as the white marble before them.

After a while, Jebediah and Gregory joined them, with Gregory's son Jesse, all three haggard and drawn-looking in the crimson light which Jebediah brought. The Michaeline took his place quietly at Joram's right and extinguished his handfire, knowing the extra measure of grief which was Camber's at losing a grandson as well as a young and promising colleague.

But Gregory did not know, and did not fathom the depth of mourning of the three others already assembled there. Outrage was his overweening emotion.

"Has Rhys gone for Ansel?" he asked.

Evaine gave a brief nod.

"And Jaffray?" Gregory pursued.

"Still at Court," Joram said, his words clipped with his own emotion.

A little subdued by the sparseness of their responses, Gregory sat down in his accustomed place between Joram and Evaine, hands propped belligerently on his thighs. Jesse settled quietly and to his father's right.

"I'm sorry," Gregory said gruffly. "I know how much Davin's death must have shocked you. I didn't mean to seem callous, but I'd like to know the circumstances. Alister, you were monitoring when it happened?"

Camber nodded and held out his hand.

"Go ahead and read it," he whispered, opening the Alister part of his mind to the other man. "We lost another of our people to our own kind."

Gregory, who had started to take Camber's hand, jerked back his own as though he had encountered red-hot iron.

"Not *our* kind! Those were none of ours!" he said, with an emphatic shake of his head. "Deryni, yes, but— Jebediah told me some of what happened. They sound like the same breed of misfits that stopped you and Joram on the road last winter."

"No!" said Camber. "*Those* were bored, mischievous children, by comparison. These were assassins, set on killing the princes—vicious cutthroats, of the same ilk as those who maimed Tavis O'Neill!"

"And I say you're both wrong!" Evaine interjected angrily. "Those were *sadistic* children, and since no one

314

was able to stop them, they have become assassins, murdering in their frustration, trying to destroy what they think keeps them from the lives they used to lead. What they fail to realize is that the House of Haldane and those who serve them are not the enemy."

Joram snorted and pulled his ankles in closer. "As I recall, the esteemed regents supposedly serve the Haldanes. If our bored young compatriots are so eager to seek redress, why don't they go to the source of their grievances?"

"Joram, Joram, there's nothing to be gained by bitterness," Camber sighed, extending his hand again for Gregory. "Go ahead and read it, Gregory. Then see if you are still inclined toward charity for the men who caused Davin's death."

With an indulgent sigh, Gregory made the contact and closed his eyes, slipping into rapport with the Alister portion of Camber and reading all that Davin had sent save his shriving and the final exchange. When Gregory emerged from trance, his narrow face was drawn. The reality of what he had witnessed through Alister's experience pulled stark and poignantly at all the father instincts of Ebor's earl.

For a moment, Gregory bowed his head, high forehead cradled in the long fingers. He was saved from the need to speak by the arrival of Rhys and Ansel, the latter stumbling a little as he and the Healer mounted the dais steps. As all of them rose to meet him, Camber saw the dead Davin's echo in his younger brother, stripling-man almost still boy. The two stopped on the top level at Camber's left.

"This is—not the Michaelmas I would have wished," Ansel said haltingly. "I—" He had to stop and swallow hard to keep from crying again, finally regaining enough semblance of control to lift his eyes to Camber with some degree of steadiness.

"Bishop Alister—" His eyes wavered for just an instant before he went on. "I—Uncle Rhys tells me that you were—that you—"

"Read my memory, son," Camber murmured, holding out both his hands and moving within reach of his grandson. "Go ahead," he urged, when Ansel glanced uncertainly at the others. "The others know, and so should you. He was your brother."

As Ansel made the contact, Camber gently let slip his

Alister shields, at the same time drawing in Ansel's tentative probe and solidifying the necessary rapport. He did not spare the boy the full feeling of the memory, for he knew that neither Ansel nor Davin would have wanted that. Instead, he spread the entire encounter there for the other to read, saving only the confession and the Camber interaction.

Tears were rolling down Ansel's beardless cheeks when he came up from his trance. Camber gently gathered him in the circle of his arms as Rhys had done, seeing this time that all the grief came out, so that when Ansel finally drew away, there were no tears left—only the rich memory of the man who had been his brother and who had given his life for a cause in which they all believed.

They settled down around the marble slab to wait for Jaffray then, and shortly he joined them, disbelieving anger and despair laced through every step as he sank to his knees among them. He placed a black leather case on the slab beside Camber's handfire. The top of the case was stamped with tiny gold crosses.

"I came as soon as I could," he said, in a voice edged with bleak fatigue and grief. "When they got him back to Rhemuth, they—weren't finished with him." He sighed heavily. "Alister, I have to talk this out, or I'm going to lose whatever hold I've managed to keep on my anger and fear. Would you please take care of this while I talk? We'll need a place to work."

As he pushed the black case closer, Camber shook himself free of the immobility which had held them all, then reached a blind hand for the Ward Cubes he carried in his cincture. He drew out the familiar black velvet bag and untied the scarlet cords, upending it in his other hand as he had done at least a hundred times before.

Deliberately distracted from what Jaffray was saying, he recalled another time and place, before the *keeill*'s finding—indeed, before they knew for certain that any of the more complex cube possibilities were safe to work. Now there were several such which he counted as most routine, though they still had never worked the cube configuration which mimicked the altar at Grecotha.

He tucked the empty pouch into his cincture for safekeeping, then began methodically picking the four white cubes from the pile in his left hand and setting them into position on the slab, their sleek chill against his fingers somehow soothing in the tangle of emotions eddying around Jaffray and the others as he slowly drew himself apart.

"What happened, Jaffray?" Jebediah was saying.

Jaffray breathed in deeply, as if trying to pull in strength and resolution from the very air. "There were four prisoners taken alive initially, all of them Deryni. You would recognize most of the names, if I told you. One of them died in the hall, when Lord Oriel set off a death-response which he knew was there."

"Oriel?" Rhys gasped. "He's helping the regents?"

Jaffray nodded. "Joram, you and Alister and Jebediah have been warning us for years that Deryni would turn against Deryni, and now it's happening. I didn't want to believe the rumors I'd been hearing, the little hints around Court, but now I've seen it with my own eyes. The regents have been soliciting collaborators. In Oriel's case, they have his wife and infant daughter to hostage. I have no reason to hope that this is an isolated case."

"Sweet *Jesu*," Joram whispered under his breath. "And Oriel just set it off, knowing it was there? He deliberately killed the man?"

"Not exactly. Tavis had found it initially and warned the regents what would happen. He did a superficial reading and gave the regents the names of those involved— they were all dead or captured anyway, except for one who got away—and then they brought in Oriel to check on Tavis. In all fairness to Oriel, he did it reluctantly."

As Jaffray continued recounting the incident in detail, Camber took a deep breath and made his conscious mind block out what the archbishop was saying, laying a finger on the white cube in the upper left of the square before him and projecting its *nomen*.

Prime!

He had not spoken the word aloud, but immediately the cube lit from within, glowing with a cool white light.

Seconde!

The upper right cube gleamed like its companion.

Tierce!

So followed the cube below the first.

Quarte!

The last cube's activation made of the four of them a single, softly glowing square of cool white light, whiter than the slab on which they lay. A moment Camber paused to shift his perspective to the other side of Balance, from white to black, then touched the black cube next to Prime. Jaffray's voice was a meaningless buzz as Camber formed the first black's name:

Quinte!

The touched cube sparkled to life, a dark, blue-black glitter of darkest opal fire, as he moved on to the next.

Sixte!

The fire seemed to leap instantaneously from the first black cube to Camber's finger to the one so-named, and to follow as he touched the remaining black cubes in rapid succession.

Septime! Octave!

As the fires stabilized in the heart of the last cube, Camber drew a deep breath and let his conscious resume its attention to Jaffray's words, wincing a little as what he had blocked now came through in full force, filling in the gap of his brief psychic absence.

"When Oriel first found the death-trigger, he withdrew a little," Jaffray was saying. "He told them what would probably happen if he pushed too hard, but they made him go on by threatening the safety of his family. Perhaps he thought he could get past it—I don't know. He couldn't, though. The man's name was Denzil Carmichael. I think I may have known his grandfather. At least his death was easy, compared to the others."

"What happened to the others?" Evaine asked, horrified yet fascinated.

"The three remaining prisoners were executed in the castleyard, as befits traitors and assassins."

"Drawn and quartered?" Gregory murmured, with a great lord's knowledgeable raise of an eyebrow.

"Aye, and hanged first, though not to death," Jaffray whispered. "The regents wouldn't even let them see a priest before it started. Poor Alroy and Javan. . . ."

With a shake of his head, Camber flung up his shields again and blocked out Jaffray, taking but an instant to balance between black and white as he placed his first two fingers on Prime and Quinte and shaped the *phrasa*.

Prime et Quinte inversus! He switched the two cubes' positions and felt the energies warp slightly.

Quarte et Octave inversus! Again, the change of place, an intensification of the weaving, the stranding, of the power being harnessed. He laid his fingertips on Septime and the transposed Prime.

Prime et Septime inversus!

And *Sixe et Quarte inversus!* The final *phrasa,* suiting action to words.

The cubes lay in a saltire configuration now, one diagonal glowing a deep blue-black and the other gleaming white on white against the marble slab, their arrangement and the working he had done steadily drawing in more energy and laying in new strands to be commanded. He came back to the others, their words of the past few seconds flooding into his consciousness and making him wince with the intensity of accompanying emotion.

". . . terrible thing for children to have to witness," Evaine was saying, one protective hand cradling her own swelling abdomen. "Sweet Mary and Joseph, is it to be this kind of bloody reign forever?"

"So long as the regents hold sway, I fear it will get worse before it gets better," Jaffray replied. "Their vengeance reaches far. Already, they have issued writs of attainder and outlawry against all males of the families of the assassins. And Ansel, I saw your death warrant signed myself."

"Then, they counted my brother as one of the assassins!" Ansel said bitterly.

"They did—though both Tavis and Oriel insisted there was no evidence. Of course, they are both Deryni, and therefore suspect."

"What—what about Davin's body?" Ansel asked, almost dragging the words from his lips.

Jaffray bowed his head. "The regents determined to make an example of the assassins. Parts of—parts of their bodies were ordered sent to all the major towns of Gwynedd. The heads hang even now at the gates of Rhemuth as warning. They—did the same to the bodies of those already dead," he finished lamely.

"To Davin?" Ansel gasped.

Jaffray could only nod.

A groan escaped Evaine's lips, and several of the others shook their heads, Jesse blinking back tears. Rhys embraced his wife and would not meet anyone's gaze. Joram's jaw tightened even more than it had been throughout, the grey eyes hard and cold.

Camber tried to resist the raw emotion, for reason told him that it made no difference what happened to Davin's body. Blinking back tears which nonetheless threatened, he tilted back his head and made himself focus on the vaulting high above their heads. He could only let the horror run its course and be thankful that at least Davin had not suffered the torture that the others had—and pray for the repose of all Deryni dead.

At last, under control once more, he glanced at the waiting cube configuration, then at Jaffray, sending a silent query. Jaffray made no response, caught up in his own working out of the day's tragedy, so Camber resignedly took charge, drawing a deliberately audible breath as he extended his right hand over the cubes. Gradually he gained everyone's dazed attention.

"This will be a new working for some of you," he said, voice steadying as discipline displaced the flux of mere emotion. "Ansel, Jesse, you're about to see one of the few second level configurations we've had the nerve to try— and one of even fewer that we've gotten to work. It seems to have limited application, so far, but we're still learning. We have Evaine's research to thank for it."

As Evaine smiled weakly, Camber carefully picked up the cube named Septime and placed it on Quinte, black on black.

Quintus! he spoke in his mind, feeling the energy lick up around his fingers for just an instant before he moved on to Quarte, stacking it on Seconde, white on white.

Sixtus!

"More energy, twining with the first," he murmured, gesturing for them to sense it for themselves.

He felt their support and Ansel's and Jesse's increasing curiosity as he set Prime atop Tierce, Sexte on Octave.

Septimus!

Octavius!

He did not know whether the words themselves were important—he suspected not—but the mental energies behind them were, and he could feel them woven among his fingers as he held his hand above the cube he had formed. *The pillars of the temple,* Joram had called the configuration, the first time he saw it. It reminded them all of the shattered altar beneath Grecotha.

Carefully, Camber got his feet under him, ready to stand, then let his right hand rest squarely on top of the cube. With his left he motioned the others to move back slightly. Then he actively engaged the energies.

He could feel them tingling in his hand and all up his arm, even tickling at the edges of his mind, as if hand and cubes had fused in one vibrant unit. As he wrapped his mind around the strands of energy and wove the grid, he could feel the potential building, so that by the time he began slowly to lift his hand, the cube rose, too—and also the marble slab, soundless save for the faint whisper of polished stone in passing.

The slab continued to rise, as effortlessly as if it were feather instead of marble, supported by four large cubes, black and white alternating. Camber stood as the rest of them rose, his upper body still bent over the smaller cube whose power he had harnessed. A second course of black and white cubes began to appear, these set in opposition to the first course, finally revealing a black base of the same size as the *mensa* on top. Pillars the size of a man's arm stood at the four corners of the cube thus revealed, alternating black and white like the broken ones under Grecotha.

When the black slab had risen to the same thickness as the top one, the entire mass stopped. Camber, with a slight sigh, withdrew his hand out to the side of the small cube and flexed his fingers experimentally, then glanced at his intrigued audience as he scooped up the wards and returned them to their pouch.

"Its own weight will take it back into place when we're done," he said matter-of-factly. "One only needs the cubes to raise the thing." He looked at the archbishop. "Jaffray?"

"Aye. Ansel, I wish I could have brought back your brother's body, but since I could not, I thought to bring you our Lord's. I thought the Blessed Sacrament might offer us all some measure of comfort."

Ansel inclined his head, unable to reply with words, but then Jaffray's hands began shaking so badly that he could not even unfasten the straps which closed the leather case. Camber stepped in at that, moving the box away from Jaffray and himself unbuckling the latches to raise the leather lid. Inside were all the accoutrements needed to celebrate Mass.

"It was a fine and thoughtful idea, Jaffray," he murmured, touching the small gold chalice and paten reverently. "I should have thought of it myself. It will help all of us to center in and clear our heads so we can make cogent plans."

Jaffray shook his head doubtfully. "I don't know now, Alister. Maybe it wasn't such a good idea. I didn't even bring any proper vestments, I was so anxious to get away from the stench of blood. Do you think He will mind?"

"Surely not," Camber said gently, as Joram roused himself from his stunned lethargy to shake out the linen cloth which his father handed him.

"But—we don't really know what kind of altar this was before," Jaffray continued. "We don't even know whether the Airsid celebrated the Mass as we know it."

At his distress, Evaine moved around and laid her hands on his shoulders, leaning her cheek against his back.

"Oh, Jaffray, I'm sure they must have," she said, as Rhys picked up the box and nudged Camber's handfire higher, so Joram could spread his linen. "And even if they didn't, I think it's high time a Mass was said within these walls. It would be a beautiful and fitting memorial for Davin."

Even Jaffray, in his distraught state, had no quarrel with that, and watched numbly as Joram laid a small crucifix in place, set out the two half-burned candles in their simple wooden holders, passed his hands over them, and brought them to life, at the same time quenching the handfire.

Camber took out the chalice and paten and set them in place, then extracted four large unconsecrated Hosts from a flat metal box he found in the case and laid them carefully on the thin gold plate; Joram removed the water and wine, in their leather-covered glass flasks, and set them to one side. The narrow purple stole, much folded and creased, Camber shook out and laid across Jaffray's trembling fingers with a slight bow. Jaffray stared at the stole for a moment, then shook his head.

"I can't, Alister," he whispered. "God help me, for the first time since I was ordained a priest, I can't. I *saw*, Alister! I had to watch while they hacked his poor, murdered body to pieces! There's no charity in my heart for what they did. God, I had come to love that boy like a son!"

"So had I," Camber whispered under his breath.

But he took the stole from Jaffray's stiff fingers and touched it to his own lips, put it on, moved to the west side of the altar as one walking in his sleep, and waited for the others to range themselves around him. Jaffray he motioned to his left, with Rhys between him and Ansel. On his right stood Joram and Evaine, ready to serve him. Jebediah, stoic and silent outwardly, but churning inside, stood opposite with the shaken Gregory and Jesse.

"In nomine Patris, et Filii, et Spiritus Sancti. Amen," he whispered, as his hand moved in the sign of their faith, the familiar words beginning to give him an anchor to sanity. *"Introibo ad altare Dei."*

"Ad Deum qui laetificat juventutem meam," the others responded, Joram leading them coolly in the response.

I will go up to the altar of God, to God Who gives joy to my youth. . . .

"Judica me, Deus . . ." Camber continued. *Judge me, O God, and distinguish my cause from the nation that is not holy: deliver me from the unjust and deceitful man.*

"Quia tu es, Deus. . . ." For Thou, O God, art my strength; why hast Thou cast me off?* the others replied. *And why do I go sorrowing whilst the enemy afflicteth me?*

They offered up the Mass for Davin and his memory. They willed the meaning of every word to penetrate beyond their grief, lifting them into a renewal of their purpose. They had no book of scripture for their use that night, so each of them contributed from memory a verse which meant something to him or her in this troubled time—something to give comfort, or hope, or courage to go on.

Camber celebrated the Mass in the Michaeline manner, giving both Host and Cup to all who shared the rite. Now he moved among these loved ones of his, laying a piece of consecrated Host in each reverently outstretched palm, while Joram followed with the Cup. When he had finished, he had gained a measure of peace which almost transcended the tragedy of Davin's death. Somehow, he resolved, Davin's death would not have been in vain.

Ansel returned to Grecotha with Camber and Joram that night, for there was virtually no place in Gwynedd where the last Earl of Culdi might show his face and live, once the regents' writ was circulated. But another monk would not be noticed, especially in the household of a bishop; and so, with his bright locks shorn in a clerical tonsure and dyed a light brown, Ansel was introduced to the Grecotha community as Brother Lorcan, a Michaeline lay scribe sent to augment Bishop Alister's clerical staff. The difference of garb and hair, surrounding a face which had not been that well known anyway, was sufficient to hide Ansel without benefit of magic.

Father Willowen and the rest of the Grecotha congregation welcomed the new brother warmly, and thought nothing amiss the next day when, after the commemorative Mass which the bishop celebrated for the chapter, the newcomer was invited to share the bishop's private Michaelmas observances with his secretary. Everyone knew that Michaelines stayed together, especially for this important feast day. Camber and Joram used the time to good advantage to instruct Ansel further regarding ecclesiastical deportment and the Order to which he pretended. Within a few days, he was sufficiently informed to be able to move among the priests and monks of Grecotha without suspicion.

The others, too, returned to their various abodes, though all of them strove to keep as low a profile as possible in the days and weeks ahead. With no further need to monitor poor Davin, Gregory retired to Ebor and began making quiet arrangements for his family to leave Gwynedd, though he himself would return as often as the Council needed him. Jebediah went back to Argoed and bade farewell to his Michaeline brethren. Rhys and Evaine kept the feast of Michaelmas at Sheele with their children, but their celebration was much subdued by having to tell the children that their cousin Davin was dead. Little Tieg was too young to understand fully, but the eight-year-old Rhysel cried and cried.

Jaffray returned to Rhemuth to conduct the appropriate religious observances at Saint George Cathedral the next morning with Archbishop Oriss; but that night he slipped out of his apartments in Oriss's episcopal residence and made his way to a little-known Portal in the cathedral's sacristy, whence he whisked off to Saint Neot's and his old Order.

He spent that night and most of the next day closeted with Dom Emrys and the Elders of the Order, telling them of all that had happened in King Alroy's hall the day before and seeking counsel. His visit sparked a flurry of speculations and consultations among his brethren at Chapter; and when Jaffray met with the Camberian Council the following week, he told them of the Gabrilites' growing concern. If the Michaelmas Plot, as it had come to be called, pushed human reaction to the breaking point, the Gabrilites felt that the Deryni religious houses would be among the first to feel the regents' wrath. Nowhere else could one find so high a concentration of Deryni in close proximity. And the Gabrilites, as teachers of the most sophisticated Deryni practitioners in the known world, would be prime targets.

There were other Deryni establishments—the Varnarite School, and Llenteith, near the Connait, and the newly established *schola* near Nyford—which had already been burned out once and partially rebuilt—and the Council saw to it that all of these were warned, Camber and Jaffray making especial use of their episcopal rank to help the religious houses formulate escape plans. They could only hope that there would be time to use those plans, if the worst came to pass.

For nearly a month, their luck held. But then, in late October, during a last wave of near-summer weather, the balance swung once more against the Deryni and their cause.

The unseasonable heat, then in its second week, had brought a resurgence of the so-called Deryni plague which had swept through Gwynedd in high summer; in Valoret, a mob of irate townsfolk and farmers had whipped themselves up to stone a merchant family which had been spared the plague and was, therefore, suspected of being Deryni. A riot ensued when the town guards tried to rescue the intended victims, and they had been forced to summon a troop of the archbishop's household guards to assist them.

The archbishop himself led the sortie, since he was then in Valoret on one of his now-rare pastoral visits, a snow-white surcoat over his hauberk and a closed-face helm covering his head. A burnished bronze crucifix laid along the nasal and overshadowing the eyes proclaimed his identity, but he carried no weapon himself, save his crozier of office, for his Gabrilite Order was sworn to nonviolence. Jebediah, visiting Jaffray on his way back to Grecotha from a trip to Argoed, rode at the archbishop's side in full Michaeline array.

They had ridden out well-armed and twenty-strong in the noonday sun, alert, but not as vigilant as they might have been—for who would have thought that scarcely-armed townsmen and farmers could seriously threaten mounted knights on the city streets? The knights pressed their destriers into the fray, the weight of the great horses seemingly insurmountable by men on foot, laying about them with weighted riding crops and the flats of swords.

Only Jebediah at once recognized the danger from hoes, bills, and pitchforks, or the stones which whizzed past their ears and occasionally rang against steel helm or thudded hollowly against a shield. Too late he tried to call them in to regroup and guard one another more closely—too late, as one of Jaffray's men was suddenly yanked from his horse and buried under shouting, poking, pounding men. All at once, the milling, muttering gathering of disgruntled but basically law-abiding subjects had become a ravening animal, intent on destroying any who stood in its way.

Even Jebediah's swift blade was not fast enough to block the chance thrust of a bill-hook before it buried itself to the haft in the eye-slit of Jaffray's helmet. The archbishop was dead before his body even hit the cobblestone pavement.

The act took an instant only to register. Stunned by the sacrilegious murder of their archbishop and primate, both sides shrank from the still, white-garbed form as if expecting lightning to arc down from the heavens and slay them all where they stood.

But lightning did not strike them; and when the immensity of what had happened reached other levels, it was Jaffray's Deryniness which did strike them—and the fact that a Deryni had fallen at their hands—that so high a Deryni as the Primate of All Gwynedd could be killed like any other man!

Even the swords and horses of the soldiers could not stop them then! Not only did the original family of suspected Deryni perish in the violence which followed, but many townsfolk, as well, and fully a third of the archbishop's household guard. Jebediah's Michaeline garb made him a ready target—fortunately only rarely reached, and then by no blow which did him any real harm. It was sheerest luck which brought him through unscathed, for his Deryni faculties were so shocked by the proximity of Jaffray's violent and unexpected death that he could not think for a time—could only let his soldier's reflexes take over as he tried to stay alive. He was later to speculate that the only thing which saved him was his fortunate presence with the tiny group of knights who took Jaffray's body to safety; even in their fury, the mob fell away from the white burden which one of the knights carried over his saddlebow, as if it were some awful apparition.

Jebediah saw them safely to the gates of the episcopal palace, his wits returning as they gradually won through to open streets, but there he took his leave of them and made his way out of the city, not wishing to endanger them any further by the presence of a Deryni among them. With Jaffray's death, the last highly-placed Deryni was gone from Valoret. And the mob's reaction to Jaffray's murder and to Jebediah had proven that Valoret was no longer a safe place for a Deryni to be, even as Torcuill de la Marche had predicted a full nine months before. As he made his way past the troops coming in to aid the failing episcopal guards, Jebediah wondered how long any place would be safe.

CHAPTER TWENTY-TWO

For the chief-priest has his proper services, and to the priests their proper place is appointed.
—I Clement 18:18

The shock waves set into motion by the sacrilegious murder of Archbishop Jaffray reverberated through Valoret well into the night, and would eventually have repercussions throughout Gwynedd. Once Duke Ewan's men had rescued the embattled episcopal guards, many of them apparently became convinced that Deryni were to blame for the disturbance. Jebediah's presence at Jaffray's side had now been magnified to the point that many believed that *he* was Jaffray's murderer. And while, for the most part, the troops did not *help* the townsfolk to hunt down more Deryni, neither did they go out of their way to prevent it. In all, over fifty people were killed that day— not all of them, by any means, Deryni, though many were so accused; and several Deryni in "protective custody" in the town bailey were taken out and hanged, before Ewan could intervene and stop the murders.

The only fortunate aspect of the entire day was that Baron Rhun had taken his hot temper and nearly half the Valoret garrison out on field maneuvers earlier in the week, to occupy the energies of the more restless and more anti-Deryni among them, or even Ewan might not have been able to control the reaction of his men. By rigid enforcement of curfew, he was able to restore order soon after dark, but several more days were to pass before affairs settled to a somewhat more steady truce.

Word spread quickly. Camber and the others of the Council, of course, had known the mind-wrenching shock of Jaffray's death at the instant it occurred, and had learned the details as soon as Jebediah could reach Rhys's and Evaine's Sheele Portal and come with them to the *keeill*. Numbly they pondered what to do next, how to proceed. Two of those closest to them had now fallen victim to blind violence not aimed at any individual—and if the situation had been a slow simmer before, it was now approaching a full boil.

Word reached Rhemuth almost as quickly, for Duke Ewan, even in his moderation, was not above ordering one of his Deryni collaborators to take a messenger to Rhemuth through a Portal. The Court at Rhemuth received the news just at the end of supper, the messenger delivering his account in a brisk but stunned voice while regents, king, and princes listened avidly, but for different reasons. The boys were genuinely horrified and grieved, for all of them had grown somewhat fond of Archbishop Jaffray, Javan especially so. The regents pretended sorrow at the loss of a member of the regency council, Hubert even leading them in a prayer for the repose of Jaffray's Deryni soul, but their pious mouthings were soon replaced by a lively and oath-punctuated discussion of who should succeed to Jaffray's office.

Javan and Rhys Michael were all but forgotten in the ensuing hour, as the regents began naming off and assessing all the bishops of Gwynedd; and Alroy, too, would have been ignored, had they not been mindful that his support must go behind whomever the regency council eventually recommended to the bishops' synod which would now have to meet in Valoret to elect a new primate. When they had narrowed the field until Hubert seemed the only possible choice, only then did they turn their attention once more on the young king. With the weight of their positions and the boy's fatigue on their side, they were very quickly able to persuade Alroy that Hubert's election would be in the best interests of the kingdom and to elicit from him a promise to sign formal recomendation to that effect, as soon as the document should be drafted.

It was further decided that the Court should return to Valoret as soon as possible, so that the regents might better oversee the elections. The accommodations at Valoret were far more satisfactory, Rhemuth not yet being finished to the degree of luxury which the regents preferred. Under the circumstances, Valoret would be a far more suitable location to winter and hold Christmas Court.

As they called in stewards and chamberlains to begin making travel arrangements, their air was almost festive. Javan's quiet leavetaking with Tavis, ostensibly to go up to bed, went almost unnoticed. Rhys Michael was already asleep in his chair, so Tavis gathered up the slumbering prince and carried him after Javan as they made their way out of the hall. For Alroy, he could do nothing; the bleary-eyed king would not be allowed to sleep until his signature had been affixed to all the necessary documents.

But Javan was only feigning fatigue, Tavis discovered, as he followed the limping prince up the winding turnpike stair in the wall of the keep and emerged on the top level but one, where the boys' apartments lay. After putting Rhys Michael to bed, he went into Javan's quarters to find the boy huddled over a single lighted candle set on the sill in the window seat, as far from the door as he could get.

Javan did not protest as Tavis draped a fur-lined cloak around his shoulders against the cold which penetrated through the glass of the mullioned windows. The boy warmed chilled fingers a little over the candle flame, but he did not speak. His distress was almost palpable. Tavis drew another robe over his own shoulders, then eased down on the cushion opposite the prince. He started to touch the boy's forehead, to try to ease the agitation which was radiating from him, but Javan would have none of it, shaking his head and withdrawing even further into himself.

"Don't, please," he murmured, huddling deeper into his cloak. "It hurts, and I want it to, so I won't be tempted to avoid telling you what I must."

"What are you talking about?"

Javan swallowed audibly. "Tavis, I do not want Bishop Hubert to be elected archbishop."

"I certainly agree with that," Tavis said amiably. "But, why do *you* not want him to be elected?"

"Because he—*lies*," Javan whispered, half-turning his face toward the candlelight reflected in the windowpanes. "And it isn't just polite lies. You heard their discussion of the other archbishop candidates. I don't even know most of them, but somehow I *knew* that Hubert was telling lies about them, to promote his own candidacy. A man of God should never do that, Tavis!"

Tavis stared at the prince's profile for a long moment, then lowered his eyes uneasily, almost afraid to voice his suspicion.

"Javan, I have the impression that you're not really as disturbed about Hubert's lying as you are about the fact that you know." Javan nodded. "And you're trying to find a way to tell me that you—don't know how you know."

Javan nodded miserably. "I've been noticing it a little for several weeks. It's as if I can hear another voice, just like his real one, and it's contradicting what he says out loud. It's happened with a few others, too."

"Truth-Reading," Tavis murmured under his breath.

"What?"

Tavis sighed and laid his hand on the boy's shoulder. "It sounds like Truth-Reading, my prince. It's—another Deryni talent."

"Oh, God!" Javan buried his face in his hands for a few seconds, then raised his head again. "Is it like shields?"

"A little—only a kind of reverse effect. And more advanced. Much more advanced."

"But, it doesn't always work!" Javan protested weakly.

"No, but I'll bet it gets more reliable every time you become aware of it."

Javan nodded reluctantly, and Tavis sighed and slapped his palm against the top of his thigh in renewed frustration.

"God, what I'd give to know what happened the night your father died!" he whispered. "There *has* to be a connection!" He sighed again, then laid his hand on one of Javan's.

"They did something to you, Javan. I'm more and more convinced of that, even though we haven't been able to get any deeper. It was something very strange, and secret and mystical, and—" He squeezed the boy's hand and released it. "And I haven't the faintest notion what it was. You keep growing psychically, and you shouldn't. It's almost as if you were Deryni."

Javan gave a little shiver, then clasped his hands and brushed his thumbs together, studying them carefully before looking up at Tavis again in the candlelight.

"Do you remember how we talked about Rhys, after Davin was killed, and you said that you and he were two of a kind, and that maybe you could use some of his own tricks on him to get him to talk?"

"I remember."

"Well, I was just wondering whether he might not come to Valoret in the next few months, since Bishop Alister will be there for the synod. He and Lady Evaine live at Sheele, you know. It isn't far. And Bishop Alister is getting on in years. He might need a Healer. And if Rhys were to be visiting in Valoret, maybe we could invite him to come and see us."

Tavis raised an eyebrow. "Just to *see* us, my prince?"

"Not—exactly." Javan stared into the candlelight. "It's only courtesy to offer a man refreshment when he comes visiting, especially if it's cold outside and the man has ridden a long way. If there were something in the refreshment—"

"If there were, he'd likely detect it," Tavis said guardedly. "We've been sufficiently hostile to him in the past that I think he'd be somewhat suspicious even to be invited there."

"Not if he were needed as a Healer," Javan offered. "Suppose that you were to send word that I was ill, that you needed his help. Don't you think he'd come then?"

"Probably."

"And if you were to give me some—wine, for instance, and then offered him some, quite casually?"

"Something you had already drunk?"

Javan nodded.

"It would affect you, too. You know that," Tavis said tentatively.

"But, you could read him," Javan whispered. "It would be worth it, if you could find out what he did to me that night. In any case, I can't go on like this; having shields, knowing people's lies—not without knowing where it comes from, and why!"

Tavis closed his eyes for a moment and thought, then looked at Javan again.

"The most difficult part will be getting the right dosage

in him—enough to break his resistance, yet not enough to destroy him as a Healer. He doesn't deserve that. I can counteract most of the effects in you as soon as I've gotten the drugs into him, but you'll have to wait for the other effects to wear off, and you'll probably have a beastly headache afterward."

"I don't mind that, if it will get us some answers. Can you really make it so he won't be able to detect anything?"

Tavis nodded. "I think so. What I have in mind is tasteless and odorless. It has a bit of color, but in a dark wine, that won't be noticeable." He glanced at Javan. "I'll have to come up with something to simulate symptoms of illness in you—serious enough that he'll believe I couldn't handle it by myself, but not serious enough to put you in any real danger—but I have an idea for that, too. That part isn't going to be pleasant for you, either, by the way. You really will be sick, for a time."

"I told you, that doesn't matter, so long as we find out the truth. Do we try it?" he whispered, clutching Tavis' good wrist and staring into his eyes.

"Aye, my prince. We try it."

Several weeks passed while word of Jaffray's death went out and the summons was conveyed to all the bishops of Gwynedd to gather at Valoret and elect a successor. On the Feast of All Saints, beneath the floor of a cathedral named for that feast and in which he had presided as archbishop for a little more than twelve years, Jaffray was laid to rest beside his friend and predecessor, Anscom. Camber, as Alister, presided, and Jebediah and Rhys attended, though the latter two left immediately afterward. Evaine stayed at Sheele with the children, because of her advancing pregnancy. Queron had also come to Sheele to work with Rhys. Gregory and his family had gone to the Connait.

Alroy's Court returned to Valoret as planned, but somehow the regents contrived to have them arrive the day after Jaffray's funeral, much to Javan's disappointment. The regents, of course, professed profuse regret. Hubert immediately set to greeting the other bishops who had already arrived, conducting what could only be construed as campaigning.

Ailin MacGregor, who had become Jaffray's auxiliary bishop in Valoret only the year before, played host to his brother bishops, assigning accommodations to them and their immediate staffs in the archbishop's residence as best he could, though the overflow of retinues and household guards had to be quartered in the town below. Still, there were no complaints from the bishops, for many of them hoped the archbishop's residence would be his before year's end. Only Hubert, who had retained apartments in the castle as regent, resided in any real comfort —and Archbishop Oriss, for whom Hubert also found quarters in the castle, reciprocating the archbishop's hospitality in Rhemuth.

By the middle of the second week in November, but a few days before Cambermas, all the prelates were assembled: five titled bishops, two auxiliaries, and five itinerant bishops with no fixed sees. Only three of the twelve were Deryni—none of them a likely candidate for archbishop, under the circumstances. Niallan Trey, who had only reluctantly come out of his retreat in the holy sanctuary city of Dhassa, was relatively safe even from the regents, so long as he lived and so long as he stayed quietly in Dhassa and remained neutral.

The long-suffering Kai Descantor, so shabbily treated by the regents after Cinhil's death, left semi-retirement only at Camber's express urging. He had summered in Kheldour, where the regents' writ ran only sluggishly, and then only at the behest of Earls Hrorik and Sighere, Ewan's brothers, who paid little mind to the doings in Valoret and Rhemuth unless it suited them. Kheldour had been an independent earldom, almost a petty principality, for far too long for dead Sighere's sons to bow easily beneath the yoke of vassalage, even if their elder brother was a regent. In any case, since a titled see had not yet been created in Kheldour, Kai had been kept amply busy.

And of course, Alister Cullen's candidacy was least likely of all, if the regents had anything to say about it, he having already been crowded out of the regency once for his politics and his race. Camber had reached Valoret a few days before Jaffray's funeral, accompanied by Joram, a small guard escort, and Ansel. Now lightly bearded, as well as tonsured, hair still dulled to nondescript brown, "Brother Lorcan" looked nothing like the renegade Earl Ansel of Culdi, whom the regents still sought for outlawry. And where better to hide him than under the regents' very noses? Ansel would be far safer at Valoret, under the watchful eyes of Camber and Joram, than cloistered at Grecotha amid relative strangers, however benign, who would not know whether or when he needed protection. Besides, as Brother Lorcan, Ansel could stay secluded most of the time in his master's quarters, caring for his bishop's domestic needs.

Robert Oriss, the Archbishop of Rhemuth, presided over the convocation. He was joined, in seniority, by the Bishops of Nyford and Cashien, Ulliam ap Lugh and Dermot O'Beirne, both veterans of the synod which had elected Jaffray archbishop and made Camber a saint twelve years before, and both considered possible candidates for archbishop this time, though Dermot was still very young.

Three of the five itinerant bishops were also veterans of that synod: Davet Nevan, the jocular Eustace of Fairleigh, and, of course Kai Descantor. Turlough, though unable to make the last election synod, had been among the first to arrive for this one. Zephram of Lorda, former vicar general of the *Ordo Verbi Dei,* had not been a bishop at the time of the last synod, but he had been present at the inquiry leading to Camber's canonization, and it was he who had been elected to fill Jaffray's former post after Jaffray's election. Camber did not know where either Zephram or Turlough stood, but Eustace had told him that he thought Zephram might be leaning toward support of Hubert.

Hubert MacInnis, of course, had not been at that famous synod. In those days, he had been a poor and obscure parish priest attached to the household of the then-Baron Murdoch of Carthane; and his rise had come with Murdoch's own rise to favor. Murdoch's restoration to his family's ancient lands and earl's title had brought Hubert election as an itinerant bishop; and he had become Auxiliary Bishop of Rhemuth a scant year before Cinhil's death, when Robert Oriss had declined to be named as a potential regent, on the grounds of age, and recommended Hubert in his stead.

Now the Regent-Bishop Hubert MacInnis sat in Valoret cathedral's chapter house in the first of the six ecclesiastical thrones to the right of Archbishop Oriss. Niallan Trey sat to Hubert's right—a matter of seniority, rather than affinity, for there was no love lost between Hubert and the Deryni Niallan—and to Niallan's right were ranged Dermot O'Beirne and three of the itinerant bishops, Kai among them. Across the chamber, in a similar arc of five, sat Ailin next to the empty primatial chair, followed by Ulliam, Eustace, Camber, and Turlough, each with his secretary-attendant seated on a stool to his left.

The first day of the convocation was devoted to procedural business: the setting of operating rules, the reading of precedents, and the enlargement of the Council of Bishops by the creation of three new itinerant bishops. Two of the appointments Camber had anticipated, but the third was something of a surprise, and definitely had Hubert's hand in it.

Alfred of Woodbourne, long the confessor of Cinhil and his family, was an obvious choice, and one which Camber could hardly fault. The only real reservation Camber had was that Alfred might be too closely in the regents' scrutiny and debt to remain his own man, and might let himself be manipulated, out of a false notion of what was best for his young charges.

The other expected appointment was one Archer of Arrand, another of Oriss's and Zephram's *Ordo Verbi Dei* priests who had distinguished himself as a theologian— though of late, he had been speculating on the relative godliness of the Deryni as a race, and that made Camber nervous. Camber had heard him preach several times, and he was not certain he liked the conclusions Archer was drawing. If the man truly believed what he had been preaching for the past six months, then he could easily become a pawn for the regents' use. Hubert had been making overtures in Archer's direction, too.

But even Archer could be endured, were it not for the third and unexpected candidate. Paulin of Ramos had come very highly recommended—by the regents—and that alone would have been sufficient to make Camber take a second look at him. About five years before, Paulin had founded a small but steadily growing religious order called the Little Brothers of Saint Ercon, based beside the river near his native Ramos, a little south and west of Valoret. Saint Ercon had been a scholar and historian of some repute, brother, local legend had it, to the well-known Saint Willim, child martyr to Deryni ill use, whose cults had sparked the overthrow of Imre more than thirteen years before. The Erconites were not vocally anti-Deryni like their Willimite brethren, apparently devoting themselves to teaching; but they did not denounce the Willimites, either. Speculation persisted that

335

there was more connection between the two groups than mere brotherhood of their two patrons, but nothing presented itself which could be grasped or examined. Camber only wished he had more to go on than a vague mistrust of someone the regents wanted.

But Camber's mental reservations did not stop the ratification of the three men, and the next day saw them consecrated bishops with the full panoply of the Church. When the bishops were finally seated to begin the real business of the synod, they were fifteen, not twelve, and still only three of them Deryni. A vote of ten would be necessary to elect a new primate.

They met each day except Sundays, their first task to explore the state of the kingdom and determine the way it should be led in the future, theologically speaking. They assessed the leadership which Jaffray had given them, Camber and his Deryni colleagues holding their tempers only with difficulty when Hubert made his first bid for power by denouncing Jaffray as a self-seeking Deryni who had manipulated his office for his own ends, and against the best interests of the kingdom. Only Bishop Ulliam dared to call him on it, and then only in general terms before suggesting that they return to discussion of other matters. Each of the titled bishops reported on the state of the parishes in his care, and then the itinerant bishops told of the course of their ministries since the synod had last met. The Deryni issue had been defused for at least a little while longer.

But avoidance could not last indefinitely. Hubert willingly would have broached the subject again, but Bishop Alfred inadvertantly beat him to it—though not precisely as Hubert might have hoped. Alfred had been present at the questioning of the assassins, as well as their executions, and he wondered at the propriety both of forcing Deryni to work against their own kind and of refusing the condemned men the final rites of the Church.

This, of course, set Hubert off again. After soundly berating Alfred, *a very junior bishop,* for even suggesting that there was anything wrong with that, Hubert launched his attack on the Deryni in earnest. It was fact, Hubert pointed out, that Deryni had tried to kill the Princes Javan and Rhys Michael, not once but twice. Bands of Deryni continued to roam the countryside and harass honest subjects, and to harry Crown officers in the performance of their duties. Deryni obviously were members of a subversive element; and to uncover their plots, any means were justified.

This led to guarded discussion of magic in the context of the Church—a topic which the three Deryni prelates would have preferred not to discuss and which the others did not know enough about to discuss. It did no good to try to point out that much of what Deryni could do was not really magic at all, but only a heightened form of awareness which enabled them, at times, to harness energies not normally accessible to other men.

Bishop Niallan broke his self-imposed discipline of silence and spent an entire afternoon trying to make his brother bishops understand the added dimension of spirituality accessible to a Deryni who used his powers to enhance his meditation and prayer life—which was fascinating to a few of them, but threatening to far more, who began to find themselves roused to jealousy by the idea that some people, especially laymen, might have a more effective link with Deity than they did. Unfortunately, Niallan did not realize this, and likely did more harm than good by his discourse.

Of course, none of them brought up the other aspects of their talents, and the fact that some of the things they could do really *did* appear to be magic. Events such as Camber had experienced the night of Cinhil's death could not be explained by anything in Camber's experience except magic; and there were other examples, too numerous to recount.

But, was it magic, or was it religion? Or were the two the same?

The mere time of year at which the convocation met brought problems, too, for Cambermas fell during the first full week—an event of some embarrassment to Camber himself and one which opened a whole new line of questioning on the part of many others. The matter of Camber's sainthood was not reopened—then—but it was noted even by the usually flexible Eustace that for the common people, Saint Camber's veneration seemed to have lost a little of its luster over the years. Paulin of Ramos was quick to agree, pointing out that the Deryni saint's failure to intervene in the matter of the plague had not gone unnoticed by the people.

Camber, as Alister Cullen, said nothing one way or the other on the matter, and so neither of the other two Deryni made an issue of it, either. As a result, the synod made no judgment on Camber's sainthood, contenting themselves with the declaration that perhaps Camber would be more appropriately deemed an optional saint, whose feast might be celebrated or not, according to the dictates of one's conscience. Hubert had agitated for more stringent measures, but he could gain no real support— too many of his colleagues had seen and heard the testimony which led to Camber's canonization in the first place.

By the first week of Advent, the bishops had finally come to the major reason for their convocation: the election of a new primate. By then, the regents had already made their preference known in ways none too subtle but, to cement the issue, they had the king address the assembled bishops in the castle's great hall on the Tuesday of that week, there delivering a speech on which he obviously had been heavily coached.

"For the sake of future harmony in this our realm," Alroy concluded, "we commend to your affection our well-beloved servant, Hubert MacInnis, and entreat you, out of the love and obedience you bear us as King, to confirm him as Archbishop and Primate in this, our kingdom."

Hubert pretended some degree of modesty, and little was said until the bishops had returned to the chapter house that afternoon; but there Dermot O'Beirne, who fancied the office for himself, had the temerity to suggest that Hubert's seniority was not sufficient for the job, even if his bold-faced campaigning were seemly for one seeking so exalted a position—and that brought on the expected tirade from Hubert and an ensuing free-for-all argument among all of them which did not end until they recessed for the night.

Camber had several late-night callers from among his brother bishops who were concerned at the active role the regents seemed to be taking in the election. If tempers had gotten this heated before the balloting even began, what chance was there for things to proceed rationally, once the voting did start?

The next morning, tempers seemed to have cooled somewhat, however, and the other candidates got the chance to have their own virtues presented and discussed. Niallan started them off on a light note by dismissing his own candidacy on the grounds that the Bishop of Dhassa must remain neutral, and that this was a safe and responsible place for a Deryni, especially in view of the regents' preferences. He had made it amply clear from the beginning that he would not consider accepting such a position even if it were offered. That somewhat mitigated Hubert's animosity over the remark about the regents.

Balloting began the following morning, with a preliminary vote giving no candidate more than three votes. Hubert was visibly annoyed, for he had fully expected to do better than that, but his angry reaction did nothing to endear him further to his brethren. On the second vote, no candidate still had anywhere near the requisite two-thirds vote necessary to elect. Hubert had five, Dermot O'Beirne had four, Ulliam two, and Oriss, Ailin MacGregor, Eustace, and Kai one each.

Ballots were taken again and the numbers did not change; again, and those supporting Ailin, Eustace, and Kai threw their support to Oriss, who did not want it but could do nothing about it. Camber merely shook his head as the next ballot was taken, for the results of that balloting left them with five for Hubert, four each for Dermot and Oriss, and two for Ulliam. The vote stayed that way for the next three ballotings.

It was obvious that something was going to have to be done. Each day began with a Mass of the Holy Spirit, to implore Divine guidance, and each balloting, with its speech-making and prayer session before it, took close to half a day—which meant that only two votes might be taken each day, and the convocation did not meet on Sundays. As Advent wore on, and the bishops appeared no closer to a choice than they had been at the beginning of December, the regents grew more anxious and Hubert's disposition became more sour. It became increasingly obvious that he was not going to become primate the easy way.

Sometime during the third week of Advent, someone got to Ulliam and frightened him into withdrawing his name from further consideration, but one of his supporters went to Dermot and one to Oriss. The balloting remained anchored at five each for Hubert, Dermot, and Oriss through six long days of deliberation and twelve deadlocked ballots.

It was the night before the Vigil of Christmas, and Camber and Joram were at prayer in the little oratory of the apartment Camber had used when he had been chancellor under Jaffray and Cinhil. Ansel had already gone to bed in the adjoining room. Camber and Joram had joined in deep rapport, father and son, at the conclusion of the night's prayers. A gentle rapping on their outer door jarred them from their meditations, and they glanced aside at one another in surprise.

"Are we expecting anyone?" Camber murmured, glancing toward the door.

Joram shook his head as he rose and went to answer it. "Not this late. It's long past Compline."

Though Camber remained in the oratory, easing his knees on the cushioned kneeler, he followed his son in mind as the priest slipped the latch and probed beyond the door, reading Joram's faint surprise to encounter firm but supportive shields surrounding two of the four men. As he, too, turned to look, and the door swung back, he knew through Joram's recognition as well as his own that they were his brother bishops outside—Niallan, Kai, Dermot, and Oriss. At Joram's startled glance in his direction, he nodded for his son to admit them, then turned back to the little altar for just a moment and breathed a quick prayer for guidance before signing himself and getting to his feet. As the four men filed into the sitting-room portion of his chamber and grouped themselves tensely before his fireplace, he thought he knew why they had come. He hoped that he was wrong.

"Good evening, my lords," he said softly, coming to face them squarely in the firelight. "Joram, please bring some stools for our visitors. Gentlemen, I fear that the accommodations are hardly adequate for entertaining on a large scale, but you are welcome to what hospitality we can offer. Please be seated."

As the four took seats in the two chairs and on stools which Joram brought, Camber tried to read them better. Niallan and Kai he could not read at all, other than the faint, underlying uneasiness which had been Kai's ever since he had been removed from the royal council. But Oriss was a frightened man, though he kept admirably tight rein on his fear, for a human. Dermot, on the other hand, appeared wistfully resigned to something. Camber could not quite read what it was, and dared not probe more deeply with Niallan and Kai watching.

"Thank you, Joram," Camber said, settling on a chest which Joram had brought for him to sit on, all other seating now being occupied. "Well, then. What can I do for you, my lords? Shall I ask Joram to leave? This is hardly the hour for a social call, so I can only assume that you have come to speak to me on business."

Oriss, who by seniority and rank should have been their spokesman, twined his fingers together and appeared to be trying to screw his courage together, but then gave a little sigh and glanced at Niallan in appeal.

"You do it, Niallan. I—can't."

With a sigh, the Deryni bishop raised an eyebrow and glanced back at Oriss, pursed his lips, then turned his attention to Camber.

"I don't think it's necessary for Father Joram to leave," he said, nodding reassuringly to Joram, who stood like a silent blue shadow behind his bishop. "Tell me, Alister, can you ward this room without going to a great deal of trouble and without scaring our human colleagues to death?"

Camber's heart sank. Now he was certain what they wanted.

Without a change of expression to betray him, Camber breathed in deeply and closed his eyes, casting out with his mind to touch the triggers which he, Joram, and Ansel had set in this room the first day they came. With the regents now using Deryni, it had been a necessary precaution they had hoped they would never have to use. Now the wards flared up cool and supportive around them, not obtrusive from the outside, for he had not wanted to attract attention when he used them, but sufficiently balanced that any attempt at intrusion would be immediately sensed. When he opened his eyes, he saw Niallan nodding approvingly, Kai wetting his lips, aware. The other two merely stared at him with varying degrees of curiosity and apprehension, gradually evening out to relief as they realized that he had already done whatever he was going to do, magically speaking.

"Will that do?" Camber asked softly.

Niallan nodded. "Well done, indeed. Kai was afraid you would not have made advance preparations. You are not reputed to use your abilities overmuch."

"I came to believe, long ago, that it does not pay to be too blatant," Camber countered. "Such has never been my way. There is a time and a place for the gifts we have been given." He flicked his cool, pale Alister glance to Kai, to Oriss and Dermot.

"But, I think you did not come here at this hour to discuss my abilities—not my Deryni ones, at any rate."

"No, we did not."

Niallan, sitting in one of the two chairs, folded his hands and tapped steepled forefingers against his lips briefly, steel-grey eyes framed by steel-grey hair, beard, and mustache.

"Alister, in exchange for certain minimal assurances, Dermot and Robert are prepared to withdraw their candidacies and to throw their support to you in the next balloting tomorrow."

CHAPTER TWENTY-THREE

And they shall scoff at the kings, and the princes shall be a scorn unto them: they shall deride every stronghold.

—Habakkuk 1:16

Even having anticipated what Niallan would say, Camber could not help a pang of momentary queasiness, once the words were said. He felt Joram's mental shock reverberate almost like a physical blow as the sense registered of what Niallan was offering, but he did not allow his own stunned reaction to show.

"Domine, non sum dignus," he managed to murmur, lowering his eyes.

"Nonsense!" Dermot retorted. "You're certainly as worthy as either of us." He gestured toward himself and Oriss with a vague wave of an amethysted hand. "And far more worthy than that pig of a Hubert MacInnis that the regents are trying to foist off upon us!"

"He's right," Niallan agreed, as Oriss and Kai nodded in unison.

Shaking his head, Camber half-turned toward the fire and kneaded the lower part of his face with one hand, trying to block out Joram's mental turmoil and thankful, at least, that his son was not radiating to the other Deryni in the room.

He did not want this—any more than he had wanted

342

to become Alister, or to become a saint. Oh, the position was certainly an influential one, in theory. Sitting on the regency council again, by unassailable right, would enable him to observe and guide the young king and his brothers—and God knew, they needed guidance, with the likes of the regents continually insinuating their poison into the three young minds. It would more than compensate for the functions they had lost with the untimely deaths of Davin and Jaffray.

But realities proclaimed that the regents would never accept him as archbishop and primate, which negated whatever worth the office might otherwise hold in that regard. The regents knew his politics, just as they knew his race and lineage—or that of Alister Cullen. If he were to be elected archbishop over Hubert, the regents would take it as a deliberate challenge by Deryni—never mind that only three of the ten votes cast for Alister Cullen would have been Deryni votes.

"I'm not sure you know what you're asking," he finally said, after a deep sigh. "The regents want Hubert. And Kai, you, of all people, should know how they feel about me. They've already ousted me from the regency council once."

"Because they *could,*" Kai replied, with a grimace of distaste. "This time, they wouldn't be able to. The Archbishop of Valoret sits on either a regency council or a royal council by right which no one can contravene. The Valoret archbishops have held that prerogative since the time of King Augarin. And in the matter of the election of that archbishop, the king—or the regents, in this case—can only recommend to the Council of Bishops. We're not obliged to follow that recommendation. Besides, it would do my soul good to see them have to swallow their pride and accept another Deryni Primate of Gwynedd."

As the others nodded emphatic agreement, Camber half-controlled a smile and shook his head again.

"Retribution, Kai? It is unworthy of you. Besides, I think you underestimate Hubert. He would never give obedience to a Deryni primate—especially *this* Deryni."

Dermot chuckled, a low, dangerous rumble. "Then, you would be within your rights to suspend him, and have done with the lout. I, for one, have had enough of that priggish hypocrite."

"And I," Oriss agreed. "Besides," he added, on a more

practical note, "you're the only candidate on whom all of us can agree. Some of my supporters won't support Dermot, and some of his won't support me. But since Hubert has five firm votes, it's obvious that some of *us* are going to have to change our minds—and whoever is going to beat Hubert has to have the unanimous assent of all the rest of us."

"So, now the truth comes out." Camber smiled again. "I am your compromise candidate. Tell me, what makes you think that I will be acceptable to all, when neither of you is? I *am* Deryni, and therefore in questionable spiritual status, according to Hubert's reasoning."

"You are Alister Cullen, who *happens* to be Deryni," Dermot replied. "We know your record, Alister. We know that you would never abuse your powers. We know that we can trust you to keep intact the honor of the Church and her people. The fact that you are Deryni has nothing to do with our selection of you."

"Well, it will have a great deal to do with the regents' reaction," Camber murmured. "We know Hubert's feelings about anyone other than himself, and a Deryni would be unthinkable. Duke Ewan is a civilized and even an honorable man, by most people's standards, so I don't think he'd do anything outrageous on his own, but Murdoch would be livid. Tammaron would go into an apoplectic fit. And Rhun—God, I don't even want to think about what Rhun might do."

"There's nothing they could do," Kai returned. "And if they refused to acknowledge you, you could excommunicate them!"

"Excommunicate them? For a difference of political philosophy? Come, now!" Camber retorted. "Dermot has just said that you would trust me never to abuse my powers. I suspect that he was talking about Deryni ones at the time, but that applies equally to those of an archbishop."

Kai shrugged. "Well, all right, you wouldn't have to excommunicate them. But they still wouldn't have any choice over whether or not to accept you. No more than they had with Jaffray."

"And suppose he meets the same fate as Jaffray?" Joram asked, daring to interrupt for the first time. "I beg your pardon, my lords, but has it occurred to you that Archbishop Jaffray's death could have been set up by the regents?"

"Enough, Joram," Camber soothed, trying to shush his son with a movement of his hand. "He is right, though, gentlemen," he said to the rest of them. "All of us have known, from the night King Cinhil died, that Jaffray was in danger as long as he remained at Court. Unless you want to go through this election process again quickly, perhaps another candidate would be better suited. How about Ulliam? He had a steady support there for a time."

"Of two votes," Niallan said. "Alister, you're not going to be able to wiggle out of this one. You tried the same thing when we elected you a bishop in the first place. I fear you're going to have to accept the inevitable, now as then. What do you say?"

Camber could not answer just then. Bowing his head over his clasped hands, he turned over in his mind the arguments they had given him and tried to find the errors in their logic; but Niallan and Kai's shields were too close, pushing at his own, and Joram's jangled perceptions and fear for him were not aiding his concentration.

Abruptly he rose and turned back to the oratory, where he sank to his knees and lowered his head on the heels of his hands to try to think. He raised his eyes to the little carved Christus on the wall and used it as a focus, letting serenity and calm wash around him.

To be Archbishop of Valoret and Primate of All Gwynedd—God, he had never wanted that! Of course, he had never wanted to be a saint, either—or Alister Cullen.

He could not fault their logic, so far as it went, but they did not have all the facts, and he dared not tell them. It was doubtless true, at this point, that he was the only one of them who could gain the necessary ten of fifteen votes to be elected. But being elected archbishop and staying archbishop were not necessarily one and the same thing. Joram had raised a very valid point. What if the regents *did* have a hand in Jaffray's death?

He clasped his hands against his forehead again and tried to think past it. Jaffray's death might or might not have had any connection with the regents' actions but it definitely had been convenient. Jaffray had been a thorn in their sides for the better part of a year.

Now, to replace him with another Deryni, and one who had been chancellor before—

In law, they could not stop it, if that was the way the bishops voted; but who was to say that the regents were necessarily bound by law? Laws had been bent before.

He gave a heavy sigh and shook his head. Niallan and the others were waiting for his answer; and he realized, as he examined both mind and conscience, that there was no good reason he could give them which would not also compromise his very existence. The fact remained that there was no one else who could win the election. For better or for worse, Camber must be their candidate. Alister Cullen must sit on the throne of the Primate of Gwynedd, and Camber must allow himself to be swept along by destiny once more.

Rising, he crossed himself with a heavy hand, then turned and went back to them. They stood as he approached; and at his slight nod of acquiescence, the four of them dropped to their knees and kissed his hand.

When they had gone, after a few more minutes of discussion, only then did he dare to look squarely at Joram. His son's eyes were dark with emotion, the grey deepened to burnt-out coals in the pale, handsome face.

"I know. You don't approve," Camber said.

"Why should tonight be different from any other time?" Joram returned. "You've made your decision. You obviously had your good reasons—even if they *will* be your death."

Camber sighed. "Aye, perhaps you're right. But what else could I do? It goes on, doesn't it, Joram? First one lie, then another, until we are so bound up that we cannot escape our fates." He shrugged. "Well, tomorrow will tell many things. Perhaps someone will decide that they don't want a Deryni archbishop after all. That would be a relief, wouldn't it?"

Despite himself, Joram could not restrain a flicker of a proud smile. "For you, perhaps—but not for Gwynedd. From a purely objective point of view—"

"And you are certainly objective," Camber interjected with a smile.

"From a purely objective view," Joram repeated, his smile matching Camber's, "you *are* the best candidate. I only hope you get the chance to do the job."

"That *would* be desirable, now that we've come this far." He lowered his eyes thoughtfully, then looked up at Joram more soberly. "I think I should like to have Rhys here, under the circumstances. I hate to ask him to leave Evaine just at Christmastime, and with the new baby due so soon, but I'm not as young as I used to be. Even if everything goes perfectly at this end—and well we know how often it does not—the next few days are going to be gruelling. I'd feel much better having Rhys here to call upon."

Joram nodded. "I think both he and Evaine would agree to that. Queron would still be there, in case she did need help. Shall I go and fetch Rhys?"

"No, wake Ansel and send him with the message. By the same reasoning that I want Rhys here, I think Ansel would be better off there. He can help Queron keep an eye on Evaine. Take him to the Portal in the cathedral sacristy. That way, if you're seen, you can always say you've simply gone there to pray."

Joram took up his Michaeline greatcloak and threw it around his shoulders. "How soon do you want Rhys here?"

"Have Ansel tell him to ride," Camber replied. "We don't want to flaunt our Deryniness by obvious use of Portals. He should be able to get here by midmorning, even if he snatches a few more hours of sleep. And I doubt that anyone will miss Ansel. They'll be too busy watching me."

"I daresay you're right," Joram said, laying his hand on the door to Ansel's anteroom.

Camber threw a grateful look in Joram's direction, and then his son was gone. Camber stood there, staring after him, for several seconds, then sank into one of the chairs still drawn up before the fireplace. He watched the flames for a long time, and had found some measure of resignation by the time Joram returned.

The bishops reconvened at Terce the next morning, the "third hour" of the ancient world, when the Holy Spirit had come down upon the apostles at Pentecost. After Mass and the by-now familiar prayers for concord, the vote was taken as it had been each day for nearly a month, only the fifteen bishops present in the circular chamber. The December sun shone weakly through the colored glass above their heads, but the tile floor was cold beneath Camber's feet, and the chill in his heart was colder still.

In silence, each prelate came forward and dropped his folded ballot into a large silver chalice set on a portable altar in the center of the chamber, after which Zephram of Lorda and Niallan, whose turn it was to count, began drawing the ballots from the silver vessel. Hubert's reaction, the first time Alister Cullen's name was read, was everything Camber and Joram had envisioned the night before.

"One vote for Hubert MacInnis," Zephram read, fully prepared to be bored again.

Niallan plucked the next ballot out of the chalice and read it in a neutral voice.

"One vote for Hubert MacInnis."

"A vote for—Alister Cullen!" Zephram gasped, nearly letting his second ballot slip from his fingers as he glanced at Hubert in shock.

Hubert had half come to his feet at the name, and watched with mouth agape as Niallan fished the next ballot out of the chalice and unfolded it with steady hands.

"Another vote for Alister Cullen," Niallan said with a nod, his face absolutely unreadable.

"That's impossible," Hubert muttered under his breath, still frozen between standing and sitting as yet a third time Zephram read, "Alister Cullen."

Niallan's glance flicked to the ballot in Zephram's hand as he pulled another slip of parchment from the chalice and unfolded it, looked down at the name in his hand.

"Hubert MacInnis."

As he laid the ballot on the first stack they had started, Hubert nodded slightly and settled back on the edge of his seat.

"Hubert MacInnis," Zephram read.

"Hubert MacInnis," repeated Niallan.

But then: "Alister Cullen . . . Alister Cullen . . . Alister Cullen . . ." until the chalice was empty. All the ballots lay in two piles only, and Hubert's pile was obviously far smaller.

"For Hubert MacInnis, five," Niallan said softly, spreading the ballots and confirming the number. "For Alister Cullen. . . ." He counted the ballots, then counted them again as everyone in the room also counted the slap of each parchment piece being placed on the altar.

"Ten for Alister Cullen, Bishop of Grecotha," Niallan said finally, raising his eyes to scan them all in confirmation. "The Holy Spirit has granted us accord. Praise be to God, we have a new Primate of Gwynedd!"

"That's impossible!"

But Hubert's gasp was all but drowned out by eight other voices affirming Niallan's proclamation. As Archbishop Oriss rose and stepped down from the dais, to be the first to kneel at Camber's feet and kiss his hand in homage, the others who had elected him also rose in a scrape of chairs and made their way to join him and similarly pledge their loyalty.

When they had finished and stood ranged to either side of their new archbishop, nine strong, Hubert still had not moved from his place. Zephram and the three new bishops had joined him, and were now clumped nervously to the left of him, wearing varied expressions of uncertainty and shock.

Slowly and deliberately, Camber rested his hands on the arms of what had now become his primatial throne, ice-colored Alister eyes gazing evenly across the chamber at the man who had just been defeated.

"Bishop MacInnis, please believe that I did not seek this office," he said softly. "We had been laboring with a deadlocked vote for many weeks now. Last night, four of our brethren, including your two former opponents, sought me out in my chambers. They said that I was the only compromise candidate who could consolidate our august brotherhood, and begged me to accept their combined support, for the sake of the kingdom and the health of our holy Mother Church. I feared to agree, knowing how you feel about me on many levels and aware of the stated wishes of His Highness, but the deadlock seemed otherwise insurmountable. Finally, I told them that they might nominate me only if God could give them no better choice. Apparently, He has not seen fit to do so, and so here am I, your duly elected archbishop and primate. If you cannot see it in your heart to give recognition to my person, will you not at least acknowledge my office?"

"Never!" Hubert blurted, lurching to his feet and glaring across the chamber at Camber and those who stood around him. "You have defied the king! The king and his regents chose *me* to be Jaffray's successor, and you knew that. It was your *duty*, the duty of *all* of you to support the king's wishes in this matter! *We* have done our duty, we five. We go now to report *your* failure to *him!*"

With that, Hubert pushed past his supporters angrily and stalked out of the chapter house, the other four following uncertainly.

Niallan turned to Camber with a deferential bow. "Well, my Lord Archbishop," the Dhassa bishop said, addressing Camber by his new, formal title for the first time, "I think it wise if, under the circumstances, you do not delay your enthronement. Do you agree, my brothers?"

The others nodded and muttered agreement, though many of them were clearly nervous in the wake of Hubert's outburst and threats. At their assent, Niallan returned his attention to Camber and raised an eyebrow in question.

"Alister?"

"Very well."

"Good, then," Niallan said. "Today is the Vigil of Christmas. I would recommend that the ceremony take place tomorrow morning, before as many witnesses as we can manage. Give the regents as little time to think about it as possible. The cathedral will be packed for all the Christmas Masses, especially when the people hear that Alister Cullen is to be their new archbishop."

Camber allowed a wry smile to touch his lips, matching Niallan's own. "I thank you for your confidence in my popularity. However, it should be pointed out that opening the cathedral will also open the possibility of retaliatory action on the part of the regents, who *are* going to have the time to think about it, and who are *not* going to be pleased when they learn of my election. It will also not be easy to maintain control in that large a crowd."

"Or to move against you without being quite blatant," Dermot countered. "Even the regents are going to have to think twice before they try to stop your enthronement in front of so many people."

Murmurs of agreement and vigorous noddings of heads punctuated Dermot's observation as he continued.

"To that end, I believe we *must* take precautions. Were I in your place, I think I would want Earl Jebediah of Alcara in charge of my household guard. I suggest that you call him back to Valoret as soon as possible—assuming, of course, that you know where he is. I can think of no man better qualified to ensure our safety."

"I quite agree," Camber replied. He glanced over the others, then settled on Kai Descantor. "Kai, I do not usually ask a bishop to be my messenger, but would you please go and tell my secretary what has happened and ask him to contact Jebediah? He knows how."

He had not intended an open reference to Deryni methods of contact, but all of them knew that Alister Cullen's secretary was the son of Camber of Culdi; and he had further asked a Deryni bishop to convey his message to a Deryni priest. His words elicited first a grin and then a low, appreciative chuckle from Niallan. Camber surveyed them all, the pale Alister-eyes gone uncharacteristically mild, then glanced innocently at Niallan.

"Dear me, I don't suppose I should have said that, should I? Well, I dare say, you all knew that you were getting a Deryni when you elected me, gentlemen."

"Aye, we did that, Your Grace," Dermot said with a smile of genuine warmth. "I'll go and tell Joram if you wish—though he may already have anticipated you."

"Thank you." Camber drew a deep breath and let it out with an emphatic sigh. "Now, Robert, as the only one here who has ever been enthroned as an archbishop, suppose you review for us what's going to be involved. If we're to do this thing tomorrow, we all had better get our parts straight. The regents will be enough to worry about."

Robert Oriss gave a slight bow and moved closer, taking a seat at Camber's gesture as the rest pulled chairs and stools closer and settled around him.

The news of Alister Cullen's election was even less well received by the rest of the regents that it had been by Hubert himself. Rhun, whose reaction Camber had most feared, was still out on maneuvers in the Lendour highlands, so the effects of his wrath would not be known immediately; but Murdoch and Tammaron more than made up for Rhun's absence. Only Ewan handled the news with anything approaching dignity and restraint, though he, too, was clearly displeased.

Just before Hubert arrived, his three fellow regents and the young king had been hearing morning petitions in the great hall. Alroy's presence, of course, was more formality than necessity, since it was the regents, and usually Tammaron, who would judge the merits of a case and then recommend a disposition, to which Alroy had only to give formal assent. But the king's presence was a useful fiction in establishing a suitable royal image. He was a Haldane, descendant of great Haldane kings. He was in his Court, listening to the problems of his people. Surely the kingdom was in good hands.

The true holders of the reins of government were equally in evidence. Murdoch and Ewan sat impressively behind an ornately carved table to Alroy's right, quietly ostentatious in their coronets and fur-lined court robes, respectively officious and merely official. Tammaron, the chancellor's collar of H's rich against his robe, stood directly left of the throne. Farther to Alroy's left and down off the dais, a second table served as desk for a pair of tonsured clarks huddled myopically over several stacks of scrolls and parchment documents. Three liveried heralds maintained order among the score or more petitioners still waiting to be heard.

The current suit was a domestic one, typical of the sort which it was traditional to bring for the king's judgment at Christmastide, like half a dozen others which the Court had already heard that morning. The presiding herald, who must read the petition, sounded as bored as king and regents looked as he recited the background of a complaint brought by one Master Gilbert, silversmith, against his neighbor, Dickon Thompson the baker, whose son had presumed to court the silversmith's daughter, against the orders of both sets of parents. The girl's condition was obvious, enhanced by the fact that she clasped her hands protectively over her swollen abdomen. The matter was routine. The court would order that the two should wed.

And far at the rear of the hall, in a deep window recess that overlooked the snow-covered courtyard at the side and gave view of the old keep beyond, Prince Javan and his Healer sat unobtrusively and listened to the proceedings—though that occupation would not have been apparent from outward appearances. Tavis had propped his booted feet on the opposite seat cushion and leaned his head against the white-washed wall at his back as if he were dozing, while Javan stitched diligently on a red leather headstall he was making, apparently quite absorbed in his work.

But both he and Tavis were using their apparent activities to mask their true intent, for the regents generally were not in favor of either Javan or Rhys Michael attending Courts or council meetings unless there was a particular need for them to do so. Ignorance, they felt, would help to keep superfluous princes in line until and unless needed.

It had not taken long for Javan and Tavis to figure out this rationale, and even less time to decide upon a course of action to counteract the ill effects. They had not been blatant in their protests, or pressed the matter publicly, once they realized the game the regents were playing. They simply had begun to find valid and seemingly innocent reasons for being in and around the great hall when business was being conducted, coupling with that a few careful indications that perhaps Prince Javan was just a little simple, a deficiency quite in keeping with the expectations of those for whom Javan's club foot was already an issue. The charade was distasteful to Javan, but he and Tavis had finally decided that it was the most feasible ploy if he wished to stay clear of the regents' attention and continue to learn.

And so he and Tavis had begun to make a practice of spending their mornings and often their afternoons in the little window recess at the rear of the hall, whether or not anything was happening there, taking the meager sunshine which managed to slant in and warm them as they sat and whiled away the time. The acoustics in the window recess were excellent, and made it quite unnecessary for a would-be listener to reveal himself to the front of the hall as long as he was content only to listen and not to see.

Now Javan and Tavis sat in that recess, as had become their usual wont, seemingly relaxed and totally oblivious to the fact that Court was in session at the other end of the hall. Tavis was still motionless, and Javan had just finished attaching the last of a series of thin silver discs to the browband of the headstall he was making, when the doors at the end of the hall opened and Bishop Hubert came through, followed by Bishop Alfred and three other prelates whose faces were familiar to Javan but whose names he did not know. Javan nudged Tavis to get his attention as the quintet strode down the hall, looking neither left nor right.

"Look, it's some of the bishops," Javan whispered, edging closer to Tavis so that he could watch them a little longer before they disappeared from sight. "Do you suppose they've finally elected an archbishop?"

"If they have, I don't think it's Hubert," Tavis murmured in response, automatically casting out just a little with his Deryni senses to try to read more of the bishop's mood. "Good God, he's angry. I don't dare try to read any deeper, for fear that one of the regents' trained spies is watching, but I wouldn't care to have that kind of hatred directed at me."

As Hubert and his party disappeared behind the edge of the recess, Javan slipped onto the cushioned bench nearer the front of the hall and eased closer to the opening, peering cautiously around the corner. At least for a few minutes, the attention of those at the other end of the hall would be occupied by the men who had just arrived. If he were careful, he probably would not be spotted.

"Your Highness." Hubert came to a halt and sketched a quick bow to Alroy as his companions did likewise. "I beg pardon for this intrusion, but I must speak with my fellow regents."

And then, as the others straightened and stood where they had stopped, Hubert beckoned Tammaron and strode over to Murdoch's and Ewan's table. Despite the acoustics, neither Javan nor Tavis could hear what Hubert said, though Javan could see his head wagging emphatically, but Tammaron's face went red and Murdoch's voice was a near-bellow.

"They *what?*"

There followed some incoherent sputtering, and then Tammaron crossed back to the king and bent to whisper something in his ear. Alroy's jaw dropped at Tammaron's words, but then he was nodding and renewing his grip on his scepter, raising his chin to address the petitioners, who had been waiting and watching curiously the while.

"Good gentles, we must beg your indulgence for this interruption, but a matter has come up which requires our consultation with our regents. If you will leave your names with a herald as you leave, we shall make every effort to hear your petitions in the same order we would have heard them today, but on the day after Christmas."

With that, he stood, and the heralds began ushering people back out of the hall. Quickly Javan jerked his head back out of sight, staring at Tavis wide-eyed as people began to pass them en route to the doors at the end of the hall.

"Do you know what's—"

"Sssssssh," Tavis breathed, holding a finger before his lips and closing his eyes briefly. "And, yes, that's what I thought I'd heard, but I wanted to make sure." He opened his eyes and looked at Javan. "The other bishops have elected Alister Cullen Archbishop of Valoret."

Javan pursed his lips as if to make a low whistle. Almost all the petitioners were gone now, and they could hear the scrape of chairs as Murdoch and Ewan moved from behind their table, Murdoch's whiny voice muttering something about not standing for this.

"Then, let's do something about it," Hubert answered. "Let's call Oriel, and have him sent to Rhun—"

"Let's not talk about it here," came Tammaron's voice, cold and precise in the growing quiet of the empty hall. "Guard, have Lord Oriel join us in the withdrawing room. Your Highness, I think you'd best go to your apartments. This is adults' work."

They heard Alroy's thin, reedy assent, reluctant, by the sound, and then the echo of light footsteps. After that, even the voices of the regents died away as they, too, left the hall. When Javan chanced another peek around the corner of the alcove, only the clarks and two of the heralds remained, clearing away the clutter of the interrupted court.

Mystified, Javan turned back to Tavis, almost afraid to speak.

"What do you think they're going to do?"

"I don't know," Tavis whispered, "but I'm almost certain I'm not going to like it." He considered for a moment, then cocked his head at Javan. "Do you want me to try to find out?"

"Could you?"

"Perhaps. If they're going to have Oriel contact Rhun, I might be able to pick up something more of their plans from him, without his knowing. It would be good practice for dealing with Rhys, too. He's come back to Valoret, you know. He arrived early this morning."

"He did? Why didn't you tell me?"

"It slipped my mind. I didn't see the connection, earlier. Now, I suspect that Alister must have found out last night that he was going to be elected, and sent for Rhys to come."

"I see," Javan said thoughtfully. "But—let's get back to Rhys in a moment. What about Oriel? Do you really think you can read him without his knowing?"

"Not 'read' him, precisely, but—never mind. Someday I'll try to explain it." He stood and peered around the corner, then smoothed his tunic with his hand and drew his mantle closely around him as he glanced back at Javan.

"Go back to your chamber and stay there, my prince. Plead indisposition. I'll join you as soon as I can. If I've not returned by dark, start discreetly trying to find out why. It may mean that I've been discovered, in which case you're the only possible one who might be able to save me."

"I understand," Javan whispered. "Be careful, though."

"Sound advice." Tavis grinned. "You follow it, as well."

With that, he made a casual bow and headed quite unhurriedly toward the far end of the hall, nodding to the clarks as he passed. Javan gathered up his cloak and leatherwork and limped slowly in the opposite direction, out the main doors of the hall and along the covered walk which led to his quarters.

He reached the common room which he and Rhys Michael shared, but there he encountered his younger brother and two of the squires playing at strategy with some of Rhys Michael's toy knights. That necessitated that he stop and talk with them for a few minutes, pretending not to understand the tactical situation they had set up and showing them the headstall with its little silver roundels. But then he let a little of his real nervousness show as a headache and went on into his own room, ostensibly for a nap.

There he stood and shook, his back hard against the carved oak door which separated him from the eyes of his brother and the squires, until he realized that his shaking was as much from the cold as from after-reaction to what was taking place. With that, he roused himself from his apprehensions and built up the fire, curling up before the hearth in a pile of sleeping furs and, in truth, dozing. Finally, just at dark, a quick rap at the door heralded Tavis' return. Javan scrambled to his knees as the Healer entered and closed the door behind him. Tavis's face was still and solemn with tension and fatigue, the pale, water-blue eyes like stone.

"What did you find out?" Javan asked.

"That the regents do not much care for Deryni archbishops."

As Javan stared up at him quizzically, Tavis crossed to the sleeping furs and collapsed to sit cross-legged beside Javan.

"I waited out of sight near the withdrawing room until Oriel came out," he said wearily. "He looked ashen, bereft of hope or solace. They'd made him work in front of them, directly reaching out to Rhun's Deryni; they usually let him work through a relay, to conserve his strength."

"How do you know? Did he tell you that?"

"Not in so many words. But I saw his face as he left the withdrawing room. When I then 'chanced' to meet him a little while later in another corridor, there was still a great deal of spillover from his shields. As Healer to fellow Healer in distress, it was no unexpected matter for me to probe a little. Of course, his shields immediately strengthened, but there was enough of a delay that he couldn't hide everything from me." He averted his eyes. "I almost wish I hadn't read him at all."

"Why? What did you learn?" Javan breathed. Then, with growing suspicion, as Tavis at first did not respond: "Tavis, what did they have him tell Rhun?"

"They had him send a death sentence," Tavis replied evenly.

"A death sentence? Of Bishop Alister?"

"Not directly, though they may have talked about that, too. Tell me, though, to what Order does Bishop Alister belong?"

"Saint Michael," Javan replied promptly. "But, you know that!"

"Aye." Tavis nodded wearily. "And to what Order did Archbishop Jaffray belong?"

"Saint Gabriel," Javan responded again. "Tavis, what are you trying to tell me?"

"Just one more question," Tavis said, massaging his forehead with his hand as if he hoped to knead out the memory. "Think about the major religious houses of both those Orders, and their locations, and then tell me where Baron Rhun and his troops are."

"In the Lendour highl—" Javan's voice broke off and a horrified look came across his face. "Tavis, they're not going to have Rhun destroy Saint Neot's and Haut Eirial!"

Tavis closed his eyes and let his chin sink down to his chest with a slight nod. "I think so. I have reason to believe that Rhun and his men are within a few hours' ride of either house—both, if they split up—and that this has been planned for some time. I suspect that this is why Rhun is still in the field so late in the season—because the regents were awaiting the election results, and perhaps even hoped for just such an excuse as this to vent their hatred on the Deryni houses. Jaffray was Gabrilite. Besides, the Gabrilites train other Deryni. As for the Michaelines, they were already in bad odor, especially once the regents ousted Alister as chancellor. That's connection enough, so far as they're concerned."

"But, we can't let them do it!" Javan whispered. "It isn't right. Deryni didn't elect Alister. It takes ten votes, so seven of those *couldn't* have been Deryni. And to blame the Deryni Orders is—is—outrageous!"

"I quite agree. However, they are likely enough targets, if you hate like the regents. Consider: Jaffray is dead, so they can't do anything to *him*, but they *can* do something to his Order. That's vengeance, of a sort. And Alister . . ."

"*Bother* Alister! The regents are going to condone the destruction of both the Orders," Javan whispered. "We can't just stand by and allow innocent holy men to be murdered. We have to warn them!"

Tavis huddled down in the furs and thought for a moment, rubbing the soft skin at the end of his stump against his lips, then looked at Javan.

"All right. I have an idea that might work, and it could solve another problem at the same time. How are you feeling?"

"What? All right, I guess."

"No," said Tavis, reaching aside for pen and parchment, "you feel terrible." He touched the end of his stump fleetingly to the boy's forehead, then exclaimed aloud and shook his head. "Ach, you have a roaring fever —or will have, by the time this reaches its destination," he added with a tight little smile. He dipped the pen into the inkwell and began writing.

"In fact, I'm worried for your very life, Javan, though I would never tell your beloved regents that, for fear they might blame me. But if I send our friend Rhys the information about the religious houses—which I managed to gather this afternoon, only to return and find you taken gravely ill—do you think Rhys will be able to resist coming to your aid?"

With an expression of sudden dawning, Javan slowly nodded.

When, an hour later, a royal squire came to deliver Tavis's message, he found Rhys ensconced with the new archbishop. Joram, Jebediah, and Bishops Niallan and Kai were also there. It was just past Vespers, and the six Deryni had taken a light supper together before settling down to discuss the ramifications of Camber's new office and the precautions which needed to be taken.

By now, the regents' displeasure at the outcome of the election was certain. Word of the initial reaction in the great hall had come from one of Bishop Ailin's contacts in the castle, late in the afternoon, and they could imagine the tone, at least, of later discussions. The next twenty-four hours appeared to be the critical ones. If they could see Alister safely enthroned and reinstated on the regency council, as was now his due, there was a good chance that further reaction against their kind might yet be avoided or at least delayed.

So deeply were they immersed in their discussion, safe from either human or Deryni eavesdropping behind the defense of Camber's wards, that they did not note any physical approach outside until a tentative knock at the door jarred them hollowly from their intense concentration.

"Good God, who can that be?" Camber murmured, as much in annoyance as in apprehension. Simultaneously, he raised his shields to full protection, checked to be certain his colleagues had done the same, and dispelled the wards with a wave of his hand and a mental command.

He did not stand or turn in his chair as Joram went to answer the door, but he did cast out with his mind to identify the caller. An unknown human mind waited on the other side of the door, vaguely familiar yet not attached to any name that Camber knew. Joram eased the door open and then stood aside to glance at Rhys.

"Rhys, he wants to speak with you."

Rising, Rhys went to the door where one of the royal squires waited, Camber lightly linking in and observing through the Healer's eyes.

"Bertrand, isn't it?" Rhys asked.

Bertrand gave a nervous bow.

"Aye, my lord. A priest downstairs said I might find you here. I—hope I'm not disturbing you. I'm sorry, Your Graces," he added, as he spied the three bishops now turning to peer at him.

Rhys favored the boy with a reassuring smile. "It's all right, Bertrand." He noticed that the boy held a folded and sealed square of parchment. "Do you have a message for me?"

"Aye, my lord. I've come from Lord Tavis, on behalf of my master, Prince Javan." He glanced beyond Rhys at the others, then lowered his eyes uncomfortably. "His Highness is very ill, sir," he continued in a lower voice. "He's burning up with fever. Lord Tavis heard that you had arrived in Valoret this morning, and hoped you might come to His Highness. He bade me give you this." He held out the parchment packet. "He begs you to attend him."

"He *begs* me?" Rhys said, taking the boy by the shoulders in alarm and making a quick, subtle probe.

Instantly, Camber shared Rhys's perception of Tavis's taut face giving instructions and the message to the squire . . . the boy's view of the prince tossing feverishly on his bed, kicking off the blankets in his delirium. . . . Tavis and the frightened squire sponging down the pale, hot body with water only just melted from snow fetched from outside. . . . Javan thrashing and moaning under Tavis' efforts to comfort him.

Good God, what was wrong with Javan?

The perception took only an instant, and was surely interpreted by the squire as only a searching glance of disbelief that one Healer should so entreat another. Then Rhys was shaking his head and taking the message the boy still held in one hesitant hand and running a sensitive fingertip across the seal to confirm that the message did, indeed, come from Tavis.

Camber glanced at the others and brought them into the link to share the contents of the message—first Joram and Jebediah, and then, after the slightest of hesitations, Niallan and Kai. Through Rhys's eyes they watched the parchment unfold, scanning the shakily penned lines with growing consternation.

I have learned, by reliable means, that the regents plan to move against the Gabrilite and Michaeline establishments in the Lendour highlands. Baron Rhun and a sizable force are there now, and have been given orders to take retaliatory action for the election of Alister Cullen, though I do not have specific details. His Highness was so distraught by the possibility of the murder of these good holy men that he has taken some kind of fever that I do not know how to deal with. Please warn Archbishop Cullen to guard his Order and that of his esteemed predecessor, and then come and aid me. Prince Javan's life may depend upon your aid.

The message was signed and sealed: *Tavis O'Neill.*

Chapter Twenty-Four

They plundered the sanctuary of God, as though there was no avenger.

—Psalms of Solomon 8:10

"Oh, my God!" Rhys murmured, lowering the parchment and glancing at Camber with a stricken expression.

His mind turned over the implications of the dreadful message he had just read, but already his hand was on the boy Bertrand's shoulder, guiding him back through the open door.

"Wait outside, please, son," he said. "I'll be with you in just a moment." He closed the door and rested his forehead against the smooth wood for just an instant, then turned and came back toward the fire.

"I think we'd better have the wards back, Alister," he whispered, kneeling by the fireplace and holding the parchment to the light to scan it a second time. "If the regents should find out that we know about this, and how, Tavis O'Neill's life won't be worth a damn."

"Unless they sent him," Joram said.

Camber shook his head. "No, I don't think so. That wouldn't jibe with what Jaffray told us about Tavis's behavior before the Court after Davin's death. Read the message again and see if you don't agree."

With that, he closed his eyes and performed the mental processes which would re-establish the wards. When he looked up, once more aware of the faint tingle of protection surrounding the room, Joram and Jebediah were crouched tensely to either side of Rhys to read Tavis's warning with their own eyes. Niallan and Kai had not moved from their chairs, waiting for him to take the initiative. As Camber stood, they stood, too. Rhys pivoted on his heels at the sound and glanced up at the three of them, though he addressed only Camber.

"You don't think it's possible that it *is* a ruse?"

Camber shook his head slowly, clasping his arms across his chest in a gesture that had nothing to do with cold.

"That he would gamble with the lives of so many of our people? No," Camber said softly. "I fear that the regents do, indeed, plan what he says they do. It's my fault, too. I should never have let myself be talked into accepting election as archbishop." He sighed explosively and glanced at Joram. "And Joram is thinking that all the *mea culpa*'s in the world cannot now undo it, and he is absolutely right. However, the damage now being done, we must do what we can to minimize the effects. Niallan, will you and Kai help us?"

The senior of the two other bishops gave a quick nod. "What do you want us to do?"

"For now, simply cover for me, if necessary," Camber said. "Joram and I will have to go to Saint Neot's and warn Dom Emrys, if it isn't already too late. Jebediah, you must go to Haut Eirial and make certain that all of our people are out of there."

Jebediah nodded. "They are, but I'll go anyway. Other brothers took over the abbey when we moved out. Rhun's troops may not be able to distinguish between Michaelines and another Order, if they're in blood lust. I'll go on to Mollingford, after Haut Eirial. That's also within range."

As Jebediah spoke, Joram's hand had crept toward the hilt of the sword he was not wearing, there in the relative safety of a bishop's chambers. Now he chewed at his lower lip distractedly, the pale grey eyes like cold iron.

"My lords, I beg your pardon, but—something still isn't quite right about this. It's too—convenient, somehow."

"You suspect a trick?" Kai asked.

Niallan nodded simultaneously. "I think I understand Joram's uneasiness, Kai. It *is* a little handy—luring Alister into making a move directly against the regents—"

Camber glanced from the two bishops to his son, a bushy Alister eyebrow raised in query. "Is that what's bothering you, Joram?"

"Something like that, Your Grace."

Rhys shook his head and cast the parchment on the fire, watching it curl and burn as he stood. "Well, I don't know about plots within the regency, but I do know that Prince Javan is very ill. Bertrand isn't capable of deceiving me on that, whatever motives Tavis himself might have for sending us his information. And as shocked as I am about what the regents apparently have planned, you people are going to have to decide what's to be done about that. Right now, I think my place must be with Javan."

"I think it must be, too," Camber agreed, picking up Rhys's Healer's mantel and holding it for him. "Give the boy our best wishes, when he's out of danger, Rhys. And we shall all pray that it's only a simple childhood fever."

"I hope you're right," Rhys replied, picking up his Healer's satchel and heading for the door. "It isn't like a Healer of Tavis's ability to panic about something that common, though. Maybe he's just rattled because of what he found out. Or maybe he's finally remembered he's Deryni, too. Wards?"

As he paused beside the door, Camber smiled and let the wards dispel.

"Good luck, son. Our prayers go with you."

"I think you'll need them more than I," Rhys returned with a smile. "I may not be back before morning. Don't wait up."

As he opened the door and slipped through, Camber could see the boy Bertrand look up anxiously, his expression changing to one of relief as Rhys spoke to him in a low voice, and then the door shut them both off from view. Joram and Jebediah began buckling on their swords while Camber riffled through a garment press. Niallan watched impassively, Kai a trifle less so, as their superior pulled out a heavy, copelike mantle of gold-embroidered burgundy and slung it around his shoulders.

"What, specifically, do you want us to do while you're gone, Alister?" Niallan asked.

"You may have to celebrate the Midnight Mass for me, if I don't get back in time," Camber said, worrying at the clasp beneath his chin. "It's nearing Compline now. But if you do have to cover for me, say that I'm indisposed and resting for tomorrow. I'm told that Archbishop Anscom once used that excuse, when he went to marry Cinhil and his queen, on another Christmas Eve."

He caught Joram's hidden smile as the Michaeline donned his greatcloak, Joram remembering that Camber himself had heard Anscom say it.

Niallan nodded agreement. "I understand. We'll do the best we can. I assume you're going by Portal?"

"Aye, there's a private one in Jaffray's chambers that very few people know about," Camber replied, heading toward the door. "Fortunately, Ailin didn't think to quarter anyone there—presumptuous, you know, until the new archbishop was chosen, despite the shortage of housing—so it should be just a matter of manipulating the lock and getting in without being seen. If we should be intercepted, I'll explain our presence by saying that I wanted to pray in Jaffray's oratory before being elevated to his office. With luck, such subterfuge won't be necessary."

"I certainly hope you're right," Niallan murmured, as Joram eased the door open and he and Jebediah slipped outside. "Do be careful, Alister."

"My plan, precisely," Camber said with a wry Alister smile. "Let it be your plan, as well. Godspeed, my friends."

He started to clasp both men on the shoulder, but Niallan deftly caught his hand and knelt, pressing his lips to the bishop's ring in homage. Kai, too, knelt to repeat the process. There was nothing Camber could say to that —only lay a hand on each man's bowed head and bless him.

Then Joram was peering back inside and beckoning him to come, and he was slipping outside. They strode briskly but softly down the corridor. They saw no one. When they came to Jaffray's old apartments, Camber bent quickly to the lock while the other two Michaelines kept watch. No one interrupted. Within a few more seconds, they were safe inside the episcopal apartments, Joram conjuring handfire to light their way in the cold and darkened chamber. Camber, too, produced a sphere of handfire, and gestured for the two others to follow him.

The oratory was set in a deep alcove opening off the main sleeping chamber, its interior hidden from casual view behind a rich damask curtain. No light burned on the altar when Camber pushed back the curtain on its wooden rings, for the altar had been stripped and the Sacrament removed to the cathedral after Jaffray's death. A thin layer of dust covered the floor, the *prie-dieu,* and the bare altar itself, but a faint hint of incense still clung to the curtain and kept watch. The Inhabitant of the tiny, open tabernacle had not abandoned His house—only left it for a time, and would return.

The feeling of the place sparked vivid memories for Camber, even though he did not come here often. Once, long before he had become Alister Cullen, he had come here to plead the aid of Anscom of Trevas, Jaffray's predecessor, now these twelve years deceased. Anscom had hidden him within this very chamber while he arranged for another priest to cover his own Christmas Eve duties so he could come with Camber to solemnize the marriage of Cinhil and Megan, parents of the present king and his two brothers.

With a blink, Camber made the mental transit back along the passage of the years and sighed. Jebediah was standing on the Portal square set in the floor between the *prie-dieu* and the altar, the fine eyes dark and troubled in the rugged, handsome face.

"Are you all right?" he murmured.

"I'm fine," Camber replied, clasping Jebediah's arm and nodding assurance. "Just remembering another time. Shall we say that whoever gets back first will wait for the other?"

"Very well. You *will* be careful, though, won't you? Both of you!"

"See that you follow your own advice, as well," Camber said with a smile. "Godspeed, Jeb."

"And you. God, I hope that Tavis isn't playing us false."

With a nod of agreement, Camber stepped back and watched Jebediah lay his hand on his sword hilt and close his eyes. When Camber blinked, Jebediah was gone. With a sigh, Camber turned to Joram.

"Well, Rhys and I made this trip once before, though from a different Portal. We'll come out in the sacristy at Saint Neot's." He spied Jaffray's crozier standing in an ornate base beside the altar and hefted it experimentally. "I wonder whether Jaffray would mind."

"Why should he? It's yours now," Joram replied, picking up an embroidered miter and bringing it to Camber. "Besides, it will make a good weapon, just in case one's needed. Here, bend down and let me put this on you. You'll make a more identifiable silhouette when we come bursting in on Dom Emrys and his brethren unannounced."

"What makes you think it won't make me a more identifiable target for Rhun's men?" Camber retorted, stepping onto the Portal square with his son, who extinguished the handfire which had lit their way eerily while they made their preparations.

Both of them let the long-familiar link spring up between them, Camber assuming control. Then they were standing in a different kind of darkness, slightly lit by the familiar glow of a red glass Presence Lamp.

The silence was reassuring as they glanced about, surrounding them all at once with the sense of security which the familiar sights and scents and sounds bespoke. No clash of fighting or attack assailed their ears; nor was the silence that of carnage already done, of slaughter already completed. Rather, it was the profound and reverent stillness of a church at prayer, the tranquil murmur of voices raised to God, accompanied by the warm psychic glow of scores of highly-trained Deryni united in adoration of the All-Holy.

With a little thrill of relief, Camber moved toward the open sacristy door, Joram watchful at his heels. He ducked a little so that his miter would not hit the doorjamb as he passed into the corridor guarded by the mosaicked Saint Gabriel on the wall, pausing just inside the entrance to the sanctuary. Save for the Presence Lamp hanging to the side of the tabernacle and the obligatory altar candles, the chancel was nearly dark. But as he turned toward the choir and nave, he could see the back of Dom Emrys standing at the foot of the sanctuary steps, a pure silver light streaming from behind him to illuminate the filled rows of choir stalls to either side and beyond him.

The Office in progress was Compline, which closed the canonical hours for the day, and in two orderly lines the Gabrilite brethren, priests, Healers, and a few older students were filing out of their stalls and up the center aisle to make a reverence before their abbot and then conjure handfire symbolically from the light in his hands. As Camber and Joram watched, each man took his light back to his place in the choir and knelt, the silver glows gradually taking on individual tints of color as each man merged his own meditations with the spark which the abbot had given. It was a uniquely Deryni devotion, but under the circumstances its beauty was a little lost on Camber as he took another impatient step into the sanctuary. Could it be that they were not aware of his arrival, these most highly trained and aware of all Deryni?

The physical movement did finally produce results. Camber saw one of the priests take note of his presence and then bend to murmur something in Dom Emrys's ear. The old Deryni nodded, but he did not turn—merely kept passing handfire to his spiritual sons as if it were the most natural thing in the world for the Bishop of Grecotha, now Archbishop of Valoret, to appear suddenly in his chapel at Compline on Christmas Eve.

Camber waited, wondering whether he could have been wrong about the danger, if Tavis could have lied, or been mistaken. He could hear no untoward sounds outside the chapel, could detect no psychic sign of impending doom, though something vaguely menacing seemed to crawl at the very edge of his consciousness—possibly of his own creation, he acknowledged.

He waited until the last of the assembled Gabrilites had received the symbolic light from their superior, then sighed with relief as Emrys turned to bow deeply to Camber, his brethren doing the same. Curbing his impatience, Camber made a hurried genuflection toward the Presence on the altar, then strode quickly down the steps to Emrys's side and let the old man kiss his ring.

"You are all in great danger," he said, motioning them to move closer and congregate on the sanctuary steps before him. "Baron Rhun and his men are on their way to destroy Saint Neot's and all who remain within its precincts. We believe that Haut Eirial and Mollingford are also threatened, and there may be more. You must leave immediately."

Emrys nodded, his lined face betraying no sign of anxiety or tension. "I feared you might have such news, Your Grace. Indeed, we have seen soldiers in the vicinity for several weeks now, and wondered why the king's men stayed in the field so late in the season. Now it is clear."

"Then, Tavis was *not* lying," Camber murmured. "Dom Emrys, have you made preparations to defend yourselves?"

"To defend? No. Regardless of our resistance, Baron Rhun could not allow a Deryni training center to survive, no matter what the cost to him, if he has finally taken it in his mind to destroy us." He turned briefly to his brethren. "We will go now, my sons. You have your instructions. Let us file into the sacristy in an orderly fashion and be away. Those of you who are to gain us time know your assignments."

As he finished speaking, the men began lining up by twos, teachers and students, each still cupping a sphere of handfire in his palm. Three of the priests moved briskly to the altar, where they drew aside the veil of samite from

367

the tabernacle and began removing the altar vessels containing the precious consecrated Hosts.

A student with his robe kilted up between his legs came bursting through the doors at the west end of the church and ran breathlessly down the center aisle, followed by a handful of other students and lay servants.

"Father Abbot, we're under attack! There must be fifty knights, and twice that many men-at-arms! They've breached the outer walls beyond the fields and they're moving on the abbey itself! Brother Gillis and Lord Dov are slain!"

"God help them, we are too late!" Camber whispered, his knuckles whitening on the staff of his crozier.

Emrys, with a shake of his snowy head, moved into action, though his pale face had gone even paler against the white of his habit.

"Not too late for some of what must be done. Stephen," he addressed the student, apparently regaining his customary composure, "have the students bar the gates as best they can, and then all of you come into the chapel. We will take as many through the Portal to safety as we can."

As the young man turned to obey, Emrys came between Camber and Joram and laid his hands urgently on each one's elbow, pushing them toward the sacristy doorway. Camber, aghast at what he had just heard, drew back and stared at Emrys.

"Do you not mean to resist?"

"What good would it accomplish, other than to show that Deryni do, indeed, use their powers to kill?" Emrys replied. "We are a teaching Order, a Healing Order, Your Grace. You know that. We are sworn to do no harm, even in our own defense."

Dozens of younger students and lay brothers were pouring into the chapel now and barring the doors, strangely serene and calm for unarmed men and boys about to be set upon by steel. Emrys's pressure on Camber's arm became more insistent.

"Come, Your Grace. We are prepared to do what must be done, and you should not be seen among us by our attackers. Your office will protect you yet a little longer, and in that time there is much that you may be able to accomplish—but only if you are alive and free."

"But, they will be cut down like lambs!" Camber protested.

"Aye, some of them will. But perhaps only martyrdom of a few of us will keep the impeccable reputation of the Gabrilites intact for history. None of our Order has ever harmed a human with his powers. We must make it clear that this is yet the case, even when we ourselves are threatened unjustly. Now, *please* go! Your presence delays those who would make good their escape, for they will not interfere with your use of the Portal."

More of the youngest students surged past Camber in an orderly wave, forming a triple line with the priests, Healers, and other students, but several dozen students and lay brethren and a handful of priests remained at the doors, barricading them against the stout blows which were now battering at the carved oak from the other side. Beyond the rose of the western facade, the sky glowed redly, though sunset was long past, and Camber knew that the marauders were already putting beautiful Saint Neot's to the torch.

Choking off a sob, he let himself be propelled past the queued Gabrilites and into the sacristy, where Joram was already waiting beside the Portal, one hand toying anxiously with the hilt of his sword—for though Gabrilites would not kill, Michaelines had no such compunctions about defending themselves. Camber watched the Gabrilites part as he approached, making room for Joram to step onto the Portal square and beckon Camber urgently.

Camber's eyes filled with tears as he took his place beside his son and lifted his hand and crozier in final blessing of those whom he would likely never see again. Then he closed his eyes, bowed his head and let Joram take them back across the stomach-wrenching leap of the Portal. The beginning cries of slaughter as the intruders broke through into the chapel at Saint Neot's were cut off abruptly as the two of them jumped back across the safety of the miles to the Portal in Jaffray's apartments.

And back in the chapel at Saint Neot's, an aged and frail Deryni abbot prepared to make his last stand against the intruders who were slaying his brethren and students even then. Joining hands and mind with an experienced Healer named Kenric, Emrys let their combined shields extend between them and the battered doors, creating a shimmer of illusion to hamper those who were now hacking their way down the nave. He could feel his brothers surging past him to disappear on the Portal, two and three at a time, and knew that he would never see them again —that for him, there was no escape.

The explosive crash and tinkle of broken glass assailed his ears, and he could hear missiles striking the floor inside with tremendous force as the great rose and the clerestory windows were attacked and shattered. He flinched at the splintering sound of delicate wooden screens and railings being smashed by the fury of the attackers, and knew the flare of fire being set at the rear of the church, the red glow visible even through closed eyelids. Still, he and Kenric held the illusion which hampered the soldiers' progress, making the men believe they fought through cobwebs and mire which weighted their feet and slowed their advance.

The sounds of carnage were getting closer, and as Emrys opened his eyes and let the illusion go, he could see that the intruders were halfway down the nave, their path now blocked only by the unarmed resistance of a last band of students and teachers who were throwing themselves in the soldiers' paths. Quickly Emrys glanced around, seeing the last of the men by the Portal disappear, then drew his Healer companion toward safety as fast as they could manage.

."Go to the Portal at Dhassa, Kenric. Dom Juris will hold it open yet a little longer, until you are safely through. Then it must be set as a trap and manned constantly. I have a final task to perform."

"Aye, Father Abbot. God keep you," the Healer murmured, tears streaming down his face as he kissed the old man's hand.

"And you, my son. Now, go!"

Even as the Healer stepped onto the Portal and was gone, Emrys was kneeling beside it and slipping his hands beneath the carpet square to touch the stone, questing forth with his mind to rip the Portal's existence from the universe. He could hear heavy footsteps pounding in the hallway outside, the shouts of the men overrunning the sanctuary, the clatter of weapons clashing against the doorway where no weapon had ever before been drawn in anger, but he did not lift his head as he poured all his remaining strength into the destruction of the Portal. He was dead and his task completed an instant before a soldier's axe shattered the back of his skull.

And from the sanctuary doorway, a blood-spattered Rhun of Horthness saw the old priest die even as he tried to stay his man's weapon—for he had guessed what the abbot was doing. He had hoped to be able to use the Portal to track down at least a few of the fleeing Deryni, as well as to ease communication with his fellow regents in Valoret.

But it was too late, even if the soldier's axe had been stopped. The old priest lay as lifeless as a broken doll across the Portal square, only a little blood staining the carpet which covered the floor and marked the Portal's location. Later, when his men had slain the last of the inhabitants they could find and set about the methodical destruction of the abbey, Rhun confirmed the destruction of the Portal by bringing in one of the two captive Deryni who travelled with them in chains. The man was inured to his condition by now, for his wife and sons were held hostage for his service, but he wept when he laid his hands on the blood-stained carpet beside the dead abbot and knew the Portal's destruction.

Another hour the marauders stayed, smashing, looting, and desecrating. They could not overturn the main altar because of its size and weight, though they tried; but they smashed the delicate carving on the sides, cracked the *mensa* slab in two, and threw the gory body of one of the dead monks across it so that the snowy marble was stained with his blood.

Nor did they spare the Lady Chapel, with its cool, jewel-like panels of blue glass let into the walls, and its rich hangings; or especially the chapel to Saint Camber, set in the northeast angle of the nave. The statue of the Deryni saint was pulled from its base and beheaded, the arms hacked off to free the jewelled crown which the effigy had held aloft in commemoration of Camber's appellation as "King-Maker." Even the mosaicked hemisphere on which the statue had stood was attacked with club and mace. The gilded carving on the edge of the altar shelf likewise earned their special wrath, for the name of the Deryni Saint Camber must be obliterated from sight, if not from memory. Battle-axes and maces pounded repeatedly against the incised lettering until only imagination might supply the message once carved there: *Jubilate Deo* + + + *Sanctus Camberus.* A torch was set to the once-exquisite wooden screen which had taken years to carve, and the fire cracked and blackened what the soldiers had spared and which would not burn.

When the marauders had looted and desecrated all

they could, and set the final fires to destroy what remained, they mounted up and rode away. It was yet a little while before midnight, but the glow of the fires of Saint Neot's would stain the sky long after the moon had sunk behind the western horizon.

Only one Deryni gained even some small measure of satisfaction at Saint Neot's that night, and he was one of only two of his race to ride out of the burning abbey with Rhun and his men. For Rhun's captive Deryni never told his hated master of the message left in the blasted Portal by the dying abbot, of the warning sealed with the death of a Deryni Healer-mage, which would endure as long as this patch of earth:

Beware, Deryni! Here lies danger! Of a full one hundred brothers only I remain, to try, with my failing strength, to destroy this Portal before it can be desecrated. Kinsmen, take heed. Protect yourself, Deryni. The humans kill what they do not understand. Holy Saint Camber, defend us from fearful evil!

CHAPTER TWENTY-FIVE

In the day of our king the princes have made him sick with bottles of wine.

—Hosea 7:5

Though Camber himself would later count it as small victory, in a way Saint Camber did defend the inhabitants of Saint Neot's from fearful evil; for without Alister Cullen's timely warning, few if any of the Gabrilites would have escaped that night's grim work. When, after a few hours, Camber at last dared to reach back to the Saint Neot's Portal, he could only sense the lingering message of Saint Neot's last abbot and know its warning to be true: *the humans kill what they do not understand.*

Human understanding counted for even less at Haut Eirial and Mollingford, as Jebediah discovered. Apparently Rhun had moved first against Alister Cullen's Michaelines, splitting his forces to strike both houses simultaneously in late afternoon before reforming to march against Saint Neot's. For both locations, Tavis's information had come far too late.

True, the Michaelines had long since abandoned both sites to other Orders, but Rhun's soldiers had not known that, or perhaps had not cared. The poor monks who had counted it their fortune to be given the former Michaeline lands and houses found it no fortune at all when they were overrun on the afternoon of Christmas Eve and slain where they worked or prayed. By the time Jebediah reached them, he found only smouldering ruins, ashes and charnel heaps whose decent burial he did not even dare to undertake for fear of being discovered by any laggard soldiers still prowling in the area.

He found only Camber awaiting him when he returned to Valoret, a little past midnight. Joram was at Sheele, sent to warn Evaine and Ansel of the night's developments while they still had easy access to a Portal. And while Camber and Jebediah waited for Joram's return, Camber outlined the situation as succinctly as he could.

The birth of Evaine's daughter was expected toward the end of January. Hence, though she had longed to come with Rhys when word arrived of Camber's election, she had remained at Sheele with Ansel and Queron, the two younger children, and half a dozen loyal household retainers in what both she and Rhys had felt would be relative safety.

Now Camber was not so certain of that safety, and even less certain of the safety of Evaine's and Rhys's firstborn, Aidan, who was fostered with the grandson of Camber's sister at Trurill. If tonight's madness spread, any Deryni, and especially any of Saint Camber's kin, would be likely game for the regents' forces.

"And unfortunately, there's no way to get word to Adrian MacLean except by conventional means," Camber explained, as he paced the narrow confines of the oratory. "My sister Aislinn did not marry Deryni, so a Portal was never established at Trurill."

"Was her husband hostile to the idea?" Jebediah asked.

"No, there simply wasn't any real need. When we all were younger, she would use the old Portal at Cor Culdi when she wanted to visit us at Caerrorie—not that she came that often. She had her own life to lead, with three

373

growing sons and her duties as Iain MacLean's countess. In any case, the Portal at Cor Culdi is no longer accessible. You knew that the MacRorie lands had been given over to Hubert MacInnis's brother, didn't you?"

Jebediah's jaw dropped and then he shook his head. "I didn't know about Cor Culdi. I hadn't even thought about it. It was bad enough, when they took away Caerrorie." He paused thoughtfully, then went on. "This sister of yours—is she still alive?"

"Oh, quite. She was the youngest of the five of us— five years younger than I. I have another sister who's nearly eighty. She's abbess at Saint Hilda's, down in Carthmoor. I'm sorry, I thought you knew."

Again Jebediah shook his head, a bemused smile curving his lips. "You forget, I didn't really know Camber MacRorie very well before he became Alister Cullen," he said gently. "This Aislinn, though—she can't be the wife of the present Earl of Kierney."

"No, that's her eldest son, also named Iain. Her husband's other two brothers are dead, though they do have descendants."

"Then, she lives with her son and his family?"

"No, her grandson, Adrian, and his family. And Adrian's son, who's a year older than my grandson, is another Camber. They call him Camlin, for Camber Allin."

"I see." Jebediah ruminated on that for a moment, then glanced at Camber again. "Are you just going to have Evaine take Aidan to safety, then, or will the whole family go?"

"I hope that all of them will go," Camber said. "I certainly can't guarantee that it will be safe indefinitely at Trurill, especially that close to Cor Culdi."

"And where *will* it be safe?" Jebediah whispered.

Wearily, Camber sat down on the kneeler of the *priedieu* and rubbed his eyes.

"There's a monastery deep in the mountains beyond the Culdi highlands. It's called Saint Mary's in the Hills. Retainers of our family, not Deryni, established it more than a century ago. I've told Joram to send them there. It's in the diocese of Grecotha, so I was able to expunge the official records. When a new bishop takes over, he'll know nothing about it. Outside the local area, few people even know it exists."

"I see." Jebediah stroked his chin thoughtfully. "And

you—aren't you worried for Evaine, travelling the Gwynedd plain in winter, in her condition?"

"Of course I'm worried, Jeb," he sighed. "But better she should be there and free than a waiting target for the regents' retaliation. Besides, she'll have Ansel and the servants to protect her and the children, and Queron to handle any medical problems, and the roads on the plain are reasonably good. There was no other choice. Adrian and Mairi would never release Aidan to anyone other than a member of the family."

"That's both reassuring and inconvenient," Jebediah said with another shake of his head. "What about Joram and Rhys? Won't they also be targets, if it comes to that?"

"Aren't we all, if it comes to that?" Camber countered. "No, the rest of us will just have to take our chances. And speaking of Rhys, I think we probably ought to go back to my quarters, just in case he's come back. I'm a little anxious about Prince Javan. Besides, I suspect that Niallan and Kai will have finished Mass by now, and they'll be eager to learn what's happened. I only wish we could bring them better news."

"What about Joram?"

"I'm sure he's just stayed to see Evaine and the others safely on their way. He'll join us as soon as he can. Right now, I'm more concerned about Rhys. I certainly hope he's had better luck than we have."

After leaving Camber's quarters, Rhys followed the page Bertrand out a side gate of the archbishop's residence and along the castle walls until they came to a narrow postern door in the great southern gate, to which the boy had a key. From there, they had slipped around the perimeter of the snow-covered castleyard, until they could enter the apartment range which connected the west end of the great hall to the King's Tower. After that, it was a simple matter to make their way along the narrow passageways and up the stair to Javan's quarters. As the page opened the door to Javan's room, Tavis's white face was turned toward his across the tossing, feverish body of Javan.

"When did this start?" he asked, throwing off his mantle and laying his satchel aside as he came and laid his hands on Javan's fevered brow.

"About three hours ago. He's burning up. Vomiting, convulsions—I think I almost lost him a couple of times there. If I didn't know better, I'd almost say he'd been poisoned."

Rhys, scanning as best he could with the boy thrashing under his hands, shook his head. "No, there's some kind of imbalance, but it doesn't read like poison. What's he been eating?"

Tavis squeezed out a cloth in cold water which the squire held and began wiping down the slender body again.

"Absolutely nothing that he doesn't eat all the time. He had some cold symptoms last night, but he seemed all right this morning, and even when I left him in the hall this afternoon."

"Well, he certainly isn't all right now," Rhys said, running his hands down the boy's limbs and shaking his head. "Bertrand, bring my satchel, please."

As the boy obeyed, Rhys peeled back one of Javan's closed eyelids to note the pupil reaction, then rummaged in the satchel.

"All right, the first thing we have to do is knock down this fever. Have you got some wine to put this in?"

"Bertrand, pour some wine—about half a cup," Tavis ordered, gesturing toward a flask and cups on a small table nearer the fireplace. "This is a sweet wine, but it's the only kind he'll usually drink. I can get something else, if you'd rather."

"No, it won't make any difference. This is just some *talicil*. I'm surprised you haven't given him some already."

"I have," Tavis said, watching Rhys break open a parchment packet and dump the contents into the cup which Bertrand held. "Obviously not enough, though. He's sensitive to some drugs. I didn't want to overdo it."

Shaking his head, Rhys swirled the cup of wine and stirred it with his finger, made a face as he sucked the finger clean, and motioned for Tavis to raise Javan's head.

"God, that's bitter. Anyway, let's try some more. It's hard to overdose with *talicil*. That's the boy," he said, as Javan swallowed automatically, draining the small cup. "Good lad. Now let's cover him up and see if we can break that fever. He's going to have to sweat it out, I think."

For the next little while, they busied themselves covering Javan with extra blankets. Both Healers monitored their patient closely for nearly an hour, each pouring Healing energy into the thin body to help burn out whatever it was that was threatening it. Finally, a few tiny beads of perspiration appeared on Javan's upper lip and brow, heralding a full sweat, and then he seemed to lapse into normal sleep. When Rhys and Tavis had changed the boy's damp bedclothes and swathed him in a robe more suitable for the temperature of the room, Tavis dismissed the squire with a weary wave of his hand and an admonition to go get some sleep, then sank into a chair close beside the bed.

"I don't know how to thank you, Rhys," he said, shaking his head and rubbing his hand across his eyes. "I don't mind admitting that I was frightened. I don't think I've ever seen him so sick before."

With a slight smile, Rhys flopped into another chair not far from Tavis's and craned his neck muscles, sighing with relief.

"You just haven't gotten the feel of dealing with childhood ailments. My older boy used to get these odd little fevers all the time. He outgrew them, though. He's just a little younger than Javan."

Tavis snorted skeptically. "Alroy has never gotten them, sickly as he is." He stretched and yawned, then reached over to the decanter of wine and pulled out the stopper.

"God, I feel like *I'm* the one who's been fighting off a fever! Want some wine? Ordinarily, I wouldn't be able to stand something this sweet, but I'm too exhausted to call for anything else."

"Sweet wine is fine," Rhys said, nodding for Tavis to pour and thinking back to another time with Tavis. Then it had been the princes, the squires, and Tavis who had done the drinking—and Tavis not entirely of his own will.

The wine had been a sweet Fianna wine, much like this one, he remembered, as he watched Tavis set his cup aside and rise to check on Javan. He had chosen it partially to appeal to the children's taste, but also to mask the slight flavor and color of the drugs he had given them all that night. This was possibly an even better vintage, he decided, as he took a deep swallow and then another mouthful.

He had just swallowed what was in his mouth and was starting to take another sip when he realized that Tavis had sat down again, but that he had not picked up his cup. In fact, the other Healer had never even tasted his. And now he was sitting back in his chair and gazing across at Rhys with a look of incredible satisfaction.

Rhys lowered his cup and swallowed, suddenly dry-mouthed, testing for and finally detecting the slightly flat, metallic ghost taste on the back of his tongue that the strong, sweet wine had masked. Abruptly he knew why Tavis looked so smug.

"Tavis, what have you given me?" he whispered, setting the cup precisely on the chair arm and trying frantically to quell the subtle buzz that was beginning to sound in the back of his head.

Tavis raised an eyebrow, then rose and moved to the mantel, where he took down a small glass vial and brought it back to Javan. "It won't do you any more harm than what you once gave me," he said, raising the sleeping Javan's head and pouring the contents of the vial between his lips.

"What I gave you?" Rhys murmured, knowing that Tavis must be referring to the night of Cinhil's death, but aghast that he should have discovered anything was done. "What do you mean?" he denied. "And what are you giving Javan?"

"It's a partial antidote to what you just drank," Tavis replied. "Unfortunately for you, that was all there was—just enough to bring Javan around for what we—*you* inadvertently gave him." He sat casually on the edge of Javan's bed, within reach of Rhys. "I remember what happened that night the king died, Rhys. I didn't remember before, but I remember it now; and this young man helped me."

He gestured toward Javan, whose eyelids were fluttering as he started to regain consciousness. "The only thing is, now he wants to know what happened to *him* that night. And I'm going to help him find out."

"You must be mad!" Rhys whispered, trying to hoist himself out of his chair only to upset the cup of wine and find that his legs would not support him.

As the cup shattered on the floor, he crumpled to his hands and knees and his vision began to swim. The top was so evident now, he was astonished that he had not seen it before. All Javan's illness had been a sham, manufactured by Tavis to lure him here and take him unawares. Already, he could hardly think coherently, and

378

his body refused to obey him. His healing centers, especially, were almost totally inaccessible.

He could feel his shields slipping askew without Tavis even having to test them, and knew that almost all of his being would soon be open to Tavis's most minute inspection. He could not even shunt the most incriminating parts into deeper levels, for the shunting mechanism was one of the first things to go, under the drugs which Tavis had given him.

The night of Cinhil's death was buried deeply, but not deep enough to keep Tavis from it when he *knew* what he was looking for. The identities of the members of the Camberian Council were *perhaps* shrouded, but the existence of the Council was not. And the information about his new Healing talent was not hidden at all. Of all his most intimate secrets, only that of Camber's true identity was *perhaps* buried deeply enough that Tavis would not find it.

As he panted with the effort of staying on his hands and knees and tried to keep watching Tavis, he saw the other Healer bending over Javan, who moaned and blinked, then struggled to a sitting position with Tavis's help, pulling himself up by a handful of Tavis' tunic. As the prince's cold but clearing Haldane eyes met his, Rhys knew that he was doomed. He would find no mercy there. He felt his arms and legs collapsing under him and could not keep himself from lapsing into semi-consciousness.

"Tavis, you did it!" Javan whispered, struggling to a more upright position and staring at Rhys sprawled on his side against the chair. "Is he—asleep, or what?"

Tavis laid a fur-lined robe around the boy's shoulders, then went to Rhys and began hauling him back into the low-backed chair.

"He's not exactly asleep—more like a sort of twilight state. He can hear us, but he can't react much. His shields are all but gone."

Intrigued, Javan shrugged his arms into the sleeves of the robe and scooted to the end of the bed. Tavis eyed him dubiously as he swung his legs over the edge and stood down, but he seemed steady enough on his feet. Javan padded over to the chair, then reached out tentatively and touched Rhys's still left hand where it lay flaccid on the arm of the chair.

"He's awfully cold, Tavis," the boy whispered. "Is he all right? I don't want him hurt."

"Without what I gave you first to induce fever, the drugs lower the body temperature a little," Tavis said, pulling a blanket from the bed and draping it over and around Rhys's slumped form. "And I'll be as gentle as I can. but I may *have* to hurt him a little, if I'm to find out what you want to know. Here, why don't you sit on the other chair, opposite him? Are you sure you're all right? Of course the drugs don't affect humans as seriously, but—"

"I'll be fine. Just a little wobbly." Javan climbed into the chair and curled up, watching as Tavis peered under his subject's eyelid and then nodded to himself. "Are you going to read him now?"

"Yes, I think he's just about ready."

Slowly Tavis moved around to the back of the chair, his hand supporting Rhys's head on its slack neck. He slipped his hand onto Rhys's forehead and tipped the head back against him, at the same time laying his stump along the left side of Rhys's neck.

The pulse was steady and slow from the drugs. He reached out with his fine Healer's control, sending relaxation all through the taut body without resistance. Then, taking a deep breath and exhaling slowly to center, he sent forth his mind in search of that one incident, the night the king had died. Once-unbreachable shields parted before him like merest wisps of fog as he let himself descend deeper, deeper . . . and took Rhys with him.

He found the night first by his own presence, reliving the saga of that other wine as he had relived it half a dozen times in his own mind, with Javan's help. The details tallied, and he learned the precise proportion of the drugs Rhys had administered—cursed himself as a fool for having omitted a subtle but critical ingredient.

But all of that was from Rhys's view, not Tavis's own, or the even briefer memory of Javan. Here was new perspective. For when Rhys had left Tavis sleeping by the fire, and checked on the princes, he had gone to the closet and opened it wide—and there, behind a false panel in the back, had been Joram MacRorie!

One with Rhys in memory, then, and seeing through his recollection, he watched Joram pick up Javan, while Rhys swept Alroy into his arms and followed the priest into a narrow, rough-finished passageway lit only by green-ish handfire which floated just before them. They emerged in Cinhil's private chapel, where Rhys laid the sleeping

Alroy supine on a thick Kheldish carpet in the center of the room, next to a small table. He knew that Joram had put Javan down at the edge of the room and disappeared into the secret passageway again, but he did not see that happen because Rhys was kneeling with his eyes closed and his hands on Alroy's forehead, reaching deep for control points which were not at all familiar to Tavis. When he opened his eyes, Evaine was handing him a moistened swab whose scent was pungent and familiar, and Rhys was wiping the boy's right earlobe, piercing it with the needle which Evaine gave him, inserting a familiar looking ruby earring handed to him by—Cinhil!

Now Rhys was kneeling by Javan's side and repeating the operation, inserting an earring of twisted gold wire which Javan still wore. Strange, how Tavis had never noticed just when Javan had begun to wear it. . . .

Then Joram was laying the sleeping Rhys Michael at their feet, and the process must be repeated yet a third time. When that was done, Rhys laid his hand on Alroy's forehead once more and then relinquished all control to Joram.

Bishop Alister was also in the center of the room, quite near now as he exchanged a few words with the king; but Rhys had slipped into a meditative, neutral state, and was not paying attention to what they were saying. After a moment, Alroy opened his eyes, dreamy and slightly glazed, and Rhys and Joram helped him sit up and then stand.

Then Rhys was striding quickly to where Evaine waited with a candle in her hand to kiss him and let him pass to where the other two boys slept. As Rhys settled between them, taking up monitoring functions, Tavis was aware that his view of what went on in the center of the room was now obscured by a faint haze, and that Joram was walking a circle of magic around those within!

Stunned, Tavis almost withdrew, for of all the things he had imagined, he had never even considered magic; it had never occurred to him that another Healer might have decidedly different views than himself on the propriety of ritual magic.

And yet, as he followed what happened next, he realized that this was not only ritual magic, but high Deryni magic—that these four Deryni, plus Cinhil and his sons, had gathered that night for that very purpose, though the boys had been made to forget very thoroughly what had happened. No wonder he and Javan had not been able to retrieve the memory!

Three times, once for each of the boys, some strange working was done within the warded circle, followed by a quiet time when Cinhil would lay his hands on each boy's head as though in blessing and do—something. After that, each boy would collapse unconscious, to be brought out of the magical circle to Rhys and be replaced by the next one.

Javan was the second to undergo whatever happened there, but Tavis could read no more detail of his rite than he could of those for Alroy and Rhys Michael. With each working, Cinhil got weaker; and after each, Rhys must push strength into his failing body, even though both men knew that this was but hastening the end. After the third time Cinhil collapsed, even Rhys could do no more. The king was dying, and wanted only Alister and Joram to attend him.

When all had left the circle save the two priests and the dying Cinhil, the bishop and Joram gave Cinhil the Last Rites. Alister and Cinhil seemed to talk for a little while, until Alister finally told Joram to open a gateway in the circle with his sword—and then the circle disappeared and he knew that Cinhil was dead.

But that last part was strange and hazy, and Tavis had the feeling that there was something very special that he had missed. He withdrew from Rhys's mind with a shake of his head, oddly disturbed and yet awed by what he had read. All that magic—and yet. . . .

As he blinked and came back to reality, he was aware of Javan staring at him, and remembered that the boy had seen none of what he had seen. Nor could he even begin to tell him, he realized, though at least he knew now where to look in the boy's memory and how he might guide a fuller remembering on Javan's part.

"What was it, Tavis?" the prince whispered.

Tavis had to swallow before he could breathe the single word.

"Magic."

"Magic?" Javan gasped. "What do you mean?"

"I mean," said Tavis, drawing a deep, careful breath, "that the ones we suspected—Rhys, Evaine, Joram, and Bishop Alister—worked a ritual of magic with your father on the night he died." He took another deep breath. "You, Alroy, and Rhys Michael were all involved. That's why you were drugged—to make you receptive, and so you wouldn't remember until it was—time."

Javan swallowed noisily and stared at Tavis with an even more apprehensive expression.

"Time for what?"

With an explosive sigh, Tavis shrugged. "That, I couldn't begin to tell you. Even *his* memory is hazy on the whys of what I read. He was outside the magic circle, keeping watch over you and your brothers, while the others did—whatever it was they did." He glanced down at the still, calm face of Rhys, whose consciousness was now sunk fast in drug-induced sleep, then shook his head again. "Unfortunately, I don't think we're going to get too much more detail on that from him."

"Why not? Can't you probe deeper?"

"Not without great risk to both of us. Reading memories is one thing; probing for concepts, for explanations, ideas, is something else again. You did say you didn't want him permanently harmed."

"I don't. But how will we ever find out what happened to me, if he can't or won't tell us?" Javan asked plaintively.

Tavis rubbed his chin thoughtfully with his stump. "Maybe it isn't Rhys's memory of this particular incident that's important anymore," he said. "Don't you see? I've read what *he* remembers, but *you're* the one it happened to. He was outside the circle, and preoccupied with other things. He didn't really see the details, so of course he's not able to give them to us."

"But, Tavis, *I* can't remember—"

"Not now, you can't," Tavis replied. "But I may know how to help you reach your own memory now. Who knows better than yourself what really happened to you."

Javan stared at the Healer in awe, then scrambled out of his chair to grasp Tavis' arm.

"When, Tavis? When can we do it? Now?"

"No, later. In a few days, when you've had a chance for the drugs to get out of your system."

"But the drugs *help* you with Rhys," Javan murmured, sinking back on the edge of his seat and beginning to pout. "I don't understand."

"It's going to take some conscious effort and control on your part," Tavis said. "There are things that I can use to help you—and I will, when the time is right—but they're different from what I gave Rhys. Be still for a moment now. I want to check a few more things before his shields start coming back."

And this time, as he submerged himself in Rhys's mind, he sought out memories of Davin MacRorie, who had been Rhys's nephew by marriage—found that Rhys had known of Davin's imposture and had even helped in setting it up, though Tavis could not penetrate to other identities involved, no matter how hard he pressed for answers.

But the setting up—by God, it was *Rhys* who had made Davin seem not to have been Deryni! Rhys had discovered a way to block Deryni abilities in anyone!

He gasped at the revelation, reading hints of tries to teach the skill to others, the repeated failures, and then —the key itself!

Gingerly he reached out and probed the key, weighed the strength needed, found the cognate in his own mind and *knew,* without having to try it out, that he could do what Rhys could do!

But more important than that was the reason Rhys had sought to teach the skill in the first place. He read of Revan, who waited with the detested Willimites in the hills above Valoret for a Healer to come to him—a Healer who would be able to fulfill the plan which Rhys and—others—had laid out just after Cinhil's death: to help hide away at least some of the Deryni race from the ravening extinction of the regents who even tonight had begun their destruction of the Deryni religious orders. Tavis himself had given Rhys that information, and saw that it was to be acted upon by Bishop Alister and Joram and Jebediah, though whether in time or not, neither Rhys nor Tavis knew.

There was more, so much more . . .

Finally Tavis withdrew completely from Rhys's mind, leaving him to unviolated sleep. He opened his eyes to find Javan standing barefooted at his side, slender hands resting on his forearm as the wide grey eyes gazed at him in alarm.

Slowly, too stunned to speak, Tavis let his hand slip down the side of Rhys's head to his shoulder, let his stump fall away with Javan's hands still gripping it. When Javan would have questioned him, he could not answer, only reassuring the prince that all was well and bidding him go to bed now, that he would explain in the morning.

He sat in the other chair, watching Rhys for many hours after Javan slept.

Chapter Twenty-Six

So they set a fair mitre upon his head, and clothed him with garments. And the angel of the Lord stood by.

—Zechariah 3:5

Christmas of 917 dawned grey and cold, with a light snow drifting down over much of the Gwynedd plain. Camber watched the dawning from the window of his quarters in the cathedral complex at Valoret and wondered about his daughter, now making her way through that same snow toward Saint Mary's in the Hills and safety.

He drew some comfort from the knowledge that Ansel and Queron travelled with her for protection and medical assistance, but he did not envy her this trip in winter, heavy in her pregnancy and with the worst of the winter storms still to come. If only she could have been safely delivered of the child before necessity forced her to flee. If only the flight could have been delayed until the spring.

If only, if only. . . . He found himself playing the same old game over and over again. If only Cinhil had lived longer; if only the king had chosen less avaricious and close-minded men to govern his minor sons; if only the regents had proved to be endowed with better understanding and tolerance.

But he had not, and they had not, and now Camber and those who aided him must play out the movements of this mad, macabre dance, knowing that a head-to-head confrontation was as inevitable as breathing, as was the regents' eventual triumph, dealing from their position of legal strength, moving toward a massive reaction against all Deryni. Had it not already begun with the tragic retaliation at Saint Neot's and the two former Michaeline houses? And God and the regents alone knew whether there had been others as well. Suppose he were wrong in trusting that Saint Mary's was forgotten, and it had suffered the same destruction as Saint Neot's? Was Camber sending his daughter and the children to their deaths?

Brooding on that, he glanced through the rippled glass at the more immediate situation building here in Valoret. Though it was early yet, he could see a growing trickle of the faithful making their way through the outer gates of the cathedral complex and into the church itself, their footsteps gradually darkening the snow and turning it to mud. Cathedral guards, now under the supervision of Jebediah, stood unobtrusively along the way and at the main gates, not interfering but watchful. The Michaeline grand master himself was out there somewhere. He had left to see to the defense of the cathedral complex almost as soon as Joram returned from Sheele, in the early morning hours.

Rhys, however, had not yet returned, though Camber and Joram had waited up past Matins, the great Office of the Night. Finally, Camber had forced himself to nap for the last few hours before dawn, reinforced by deep Deryni trancing to restore what there was no time for normal sleep to do; but even then, his rest had not been easy. He had expected Rhys at least to send word, even though he had said that they should not wait up for him. Could Javan be as sick as all of that, and further word not have come? Javan was the heir-presumptive, after all.

Shaking his head, Camber turned away from the window, beginning to admit real misgivings about Rhys's safety. He had no official obligations until the noon Mass —Robert Oriss and Dermot O'Beirne had offered to take the two earlier services, as Niallan had taken the one at midnight—but he dared not initiate personal action to find out what had happened to Rhys. The quarters of the heir-presumptive would be off-limits to the Deryni bishop who had taken away Hubert's coveted office.

He heard a stirring in the next room, and shortly Joram joined him with a sheaf of documents which required his signature for issuance after his enthronement; after that, he and Joram must both attend to their morning toilette, in the absence of any servants to assist them—for Ansel

386

was gone, and they did not wish to call attention to that fact.

Camber was kept busy; but as the morning wore on, and he still received no word from Rhys, he became more and more uneasy. It was not like Rhys to be so thoughtless. He *must* know that Camber and Joram would be worrying. Why did he not at least send word?

And at about the same time that Camber was watching in the dawn, Rhys slowly began to regain consciousness—though it was of a hazy, two-dimensional sort that was not at all familiar or reassuring. He became aware that his neck was stiff, his head lolling heavily against his chest and slightly to the right; but when he started to ease it, simultaneously trying to raise his hands, he could not. His wrists were restrained against the arms of the chair in which he sat, and something bound him upright at mid-chest level. Memory of the night before surged back into his mind so quickly that he almost moaned aloud with the terror, but he managed to choke it back and make no sound.

Forcing himself to breathe slowly in the patterns of sleep, he willed his body to relax against its restraints again and tried to evaluate his present condition. He knew at once that he was not recovered from the effects of the drugs Tavis had given him; his head was pounding behind his closed eyes and at the base of his skull, and his stomach was only just short of rebellion; but neither was he totally under their influence anymore. Unless Tavis worked very hard at it, Rhys did not think his shields could be breached again—though that did not necessarily mean that Rhys could do anything active to defend himself. And of course, if Tavis should dose him anew—

Fighting down a momentary wave of mindless panic, he ordered his mind as best he could and tried to evaluate how much Tavis might have done to him. His Healing functions had been among the first of his faculties to go, and would remain blocked the longest, being most delicately balanced; and he knew that he had lost motor function and shielding ability for a time, though rudimentary levels were now restored. But he could not remember what memories Tavis might have touched, and that frightened him. Since the other Healer had probed him with the specific purpose of reading his memory of the night of Cinhil's death, Rhys had to assume that the foray had been successful, and that Tavis now knew the full story of the other drugged wine—God, how could Rhys have been so blind as to fall into so similar a trap!—and that he had followed it, as well as he could, to its logical conclusion: the rituals in Cinhil's chapel.

In that lay at least a measure of comfort, however; for of all of them who had participated that night, Rhys's actual knowledge of what had gone on inside the circle was the least complete. Oh, intellectually he knew approximately what had occurred; but he had not seen it clearly, and he had heard very little, from the outside looking in. He gained further comfort from the guess that Tavis probably had not understood a great deal of what he had seen through Rhys's memory—though Javan's part in it would surely provide a key for eventually digging it out with Javan himself. By the jangled state of his mind, he was forced to surmise that he was still all but at the mercy of whatever Tavis decided to do with him.

Without warning, something touched his temple. Somehow, even in his drug-befogged state, he knew it was Tavis's hand. He tried to block his reaction, to play at being still unconscious, but he knew, even as he tried it, that he could not fool the other Healer. He heard Tavis's snort of amusement at his sluggish response and knew it would do no good to keep feigning sleep. He opened his eyes and raised his head, focusing on Tavis with rather more difficulty than he had hoped for.

"Well, I'm glad that you decided not to play games with me," Tavis said. "How do you feel?"

Tentatively moistening his lips with a tongue which felt at least three sizes too large for his mouth, Rhys peered at Tavis through what appeared to be a tunnel and tried to swallow. It was the wrong thing to do.

"Damn you and your drugged wine!" he managed to gasp, his sudden paleness apparently giving Tavis ample warning to get one of last night's water basins under his chin before he began retching.

Memory blurred for a few moments then, and the next thing he was aware of was Tavis wiping his mouth with a cloth. He sat with his eyes closed for a few seconds when Tavis had finished, fighting down the still rampant nausea and abhoring the awful, metallic taste in his mouth, until he felt Tavis's steadying touch on the side of his neck again, something cool held to his lips.

"What is that?" he managed to croak, opening his eyes to draw away from the cup Tavis was holding.

The other Healer's eyes were pale, washed-out aquamarines in the weary-looking face, the firm mouth set in a line of almost bemused tolerance.

"It's something for the nausea, nothing more. I promise."

"Of course it is," Rhys whispered. "And last night's little refreshment was only wine."

"I never promised you anything about last night's wine," Tavis said patiently. "I do promise you about this. And if you won't drink it willingly, I know several good techniques for making you drink it, that I learned from you. I won't even have to hit you in the stomach first. Now, which is it to be? I'm in no mood to clean up after you again."

It was obvious that Tavis meant what he said; and Rhys had no doubts that the other Healer had, indeed, learned from his own experience. Another queasy roll of Rhys's stomach convinced him that acquiescence was the better part of wisdom in this case, so he gave a slight nod, leaned forward slightly, and made himself swallow the contents of the cup in four determined gulps. The slightly minty taste was familiar—a decoction of herbs which was a mainstay of any Healer's pharmacopoeia.

He closed his eyes and concentrated on making his stomach accept what he had just put into it, even relaxing a little as the cramping eased. When he opened his eyes again, vaguely sensing that he might have dozed, Tavis was standing in the window alcove across the room with Javan. The prince apparently had just awakened, for his hair was tousled and his eyes were a little sleepy-looking above the thick, fur-lined robe he clutched around himself. Tavis was telling him something in very emphatic terms, though his voice was too low for Rhys to catch the words in his still-drugged state. The boy kept glancing over at Rhys appraisingly.

After a few minutes, Javan and then Tavis came back over to him. The prince stared down at him quite dispassionately for one so young, almost as if revelation of the previous night's work had given him an extra measure of maturity which had not been there before. The expression sent a little chill of apprehension through Rhys's aching body.

"So, it was magic which you and the others worked on me that night," Javan said.

Rhys did not need to ask which night. He could only hope to convince the boy that no harm had been intended, that the reasons for the action would be seen as acceptable in due time.

"Is that so wrong?" he answered back. "We meant no harm. Your father would never have countenanced that."

"Just what *did* he countenance?" Javan asked softly. "Tavis said you were outside the circle, that he could read no details of what was done, and why. I am—*changed,* Rhys. I believe your Joram and Evaine and Alister did that to me."

"And your father," Rhys reminded him, not daring to take his eyes from the boy's face for fear of losing what little grip he had regained of control.

A flicker of uncertainty passed across the boy's face and then was gone. "My father. Yes, he was there, I understand. But was what he did at your behest or at his own? I wonder."

Rhys heard nothing, but suddenly Tavis motioned Javan toward the door. The prince went without question, standing in a listening attitude and nodding as footsteps approached.

"I think it's Rhys Michael and some of the squires," he whispered.

Instantly, Tavis took Rhys's face between his hand and stump, catching and holding Rhys's gaze with his own.

"I'm sorry to have to do this to you, Rhys, but you leave me no choice. If Rhys Michael wants to come in here, I can't refuse him, and I can't permit you to raise any kind of alarm. You taught me this, too, though I don't think you ever dreamed someone would use it on you."

Even as Tavis spoke, Rhys realized what must be coming, a part of his mind cringing in stark terror while another, more analytical portion noted, quite logically, that at last he had apparently found someone else who could learn it.

All at once, what little of his senses he had regained was dampened once more and he was confined to normal, human sensory input. He felt numb, as if his mind were wrapped in cotton wool which muffled and obscured his usual heightened senses. And even in this state, he was aware of Tavis's further touch, making his whole body relax as if in sleep, though the Healer left his hearing.

He felt the bonds being slipped from his wrists and chest and could not stop his body from slumping even deeper into the chair. He wondered why Tavis had left him his hearing, why he had chosen a semblance of normal sleep to show Javan's would-be visitor, instead of simply rendering him unconscious. If only he could raise some kind of outcry, could move, could see, could *See*— but he could not.

"Javan, are you feeling better?" the young voice rang out. "Good morning, Lord Tavis."

It was Rhys Michael's voice, and Rhys heard the older prince's *Shhhh,* and then muffled footsteps as his brother was apparently admitted.

"Yes, I'm fine. Lord Rhys came to help Tavis last night, and they took good care of me. He's asleep now, though, so try not to wake him. Tavis says he sat up with me almost all night."

"Oh. Well, we thought you were still sick, so we went to an early Mass without you and then had breakfast. Do you know what they're doing outside?"

"What who are doing?" Tavis asked.

"Bishop Hubert and the other regents. They wouldn't talk much about it in front of me, but Alroy told me after breakfast that they're going to surround the cathedral as soon as the noon Mass starts. If the other bishops enthrone Bishop Alister, Alroy and the regents are going to take them all prisoner and make them hold the election over again. They won't let me go, though. Alroy says I'm too little. They'd probably be mad if they even knew he'd told me." He sighed. "They never let me do anything."

Rhys Michael chattered on for several more minutes about inconsequentials, but Rhys hardly heard him. He was trying to figure out how he was going to get away and go warn Camber. When the door had finally closed behind Rhys Michael, with Javan having established that he really did not feel quite as well as he had first indicated and that he thought he would stay in bed for the day, Rhys still had not come up with a plan. His mind did not seem to want to function well with wool stuffed inside.

"Well, Rhys, did you hear that?" Tavis muttered, touching his forehead and allowing him to open his eyes and regain limited motor function, though he did not restore Rhys's Deryni abilities.

Cautiously, Rhys shifted in the chair and looked up at the other Healer. Javan, too, was watching as if unsure of

Tavis's plans. Suddenly Rhys found himself wondering whether he had missed something he shouldn't have.

"Tavis, please don't toy with me at a time like this," he murmured. He tried to make his voice as firm as possible, under the circumstances. "Did I hear correctly, that the regents are going to attack the cathedral if the bishops enthrone Alister?"

"That's what it sounded like to me," Tavis said.

"And you're going to *let* them?" Rhys gasped. "Don't you understand what that means?"

Javan frowned, glancing from Rhys to Tavis and then back.

"What should it mean, other than the fact that the bishops must obey the king's commands? My brother had stated his choice for archbishop. The bishops should not have gone against that choice."

Rhys shook his head and immediately regretted it, forcing himself to fight down the vertigo the movement had cost him.

"Good God, they've trained you well," he protested. "Javan, the regents have lied to you if they told you that. The king may recommend, and very often the bishops abide by the Crown's recommendation, but they are *not* bound to do so by either Crown or canon law. Do you really think that Hubert MacInnis should be the next Primate of Gwynedd?"

"No! I hate him," Javan whispered. "But the Crown's prerogatives—"

"That is *not* a prerogative of the Crown!" Rhys interrupted desperately. "The regents would have you believe it so, but it is to serve their own purposes, not the good of the realm. Look to the *law*, Javan!"

Javan lowered his gaze, shifted it uncertainly to Tavis. "Is he telling the truth? Is that the law?"

Tavis looked at Rhys. Rhys knew the other Healer must be reaching out with the light probe of Truth-Read, but he could feel nothing. So this was what it was to be Blind. Thank God he was telling the truth.

"He believes it is the truth," Tavis said guardedly. "That is what he has been told. And the question regarding Bishop Hubert is a telling one. You yourself said, weeks ago, that you did not want him to be archbishop."

"But, the king's word—"

"Has been shaped by the man who would be elected," Rhys interrupted, a hint of hope tingeing his thoughts for the first time since he had regained consciousness. "Hubert MacInnis is not a temperate man. You know that. I have no idea whose idea it was to give the orders against the Deryni religious houses yesterday, but I would be very surprised to learn that Hubert had no hand in it. If you allow the regents to go through with their plans today, in defiance of law, then you condone what happened yesterday, as well. If the king, who has all power in temporal matters, cannot be balanced by the clergy in spiritual matters, then soon our faith becomes but a hollow shell—a facade for despots to hide behind!"

"My brother is no despot!" Javan began hotly.

"No, but his regents are, and for another year and more, they will hold the real reins of government. If Alroy is very lucky, there will still be a kingdom for him to rule, when he finally does reach his majority."

Javan had gone rigid at Rhys's words.

"Tavis, is this true?"

Tavis, too, had gone very still as Rhys spoke. Slowly he reached out and touched Rhys's forehead, closing his eyes briefly. Again, Rhys guessed that he was being Truth-Read, even more deeply this time. He did not move under the other Healer's hand, only praying that Tavis would see and understand that he spoke the truth, for all their sakes. After a moment, Tavis withdrew and opened his eyes again, clasped his arms across his waist and shuddered violently.

"God, I wish he did lie," Tavis muttered. "But he's right, Javan. If the regents aren't stopped now, there will be no stopping them later on. Rhys believes they mean to destroy every last Deryni they can find. Last night was not even the beginning. There have been more subtle moves long before this."

"Well, can we stop them?" Javan asked.

Tavis shook his head. "I don't know how."

"I do!" Rhys said. "At least I know how to try."

"How?" Javan blurted, clipping off Rhys's last words in his urgency.

"Let me go and warn Alister," Rhys pleaded, leaning forward in his chair. "The enthronement cannot be stopped, for that would accomplish the same thing the regents want. But it can be done in such a manner that the people will know the truth and the regents will not dare to oppose Alister openly. The bishops chose the noon Mass because it would be well attended. If they have advance warning, the situation can be turned to our advantage."

Javan's lips had compressed in a thin, tight line as Rhys spoke.

"You ask a great deal, Rhys Thuryn. In effect, you ask me to betray my brother."

"This would be no betrayal," Rhys protested. "Alroy is not to blame. He has had poor counsel. If Alister is safely enthroned as Archbishop of Valoret and Primate of Gwynedd, he will be entitled to a seat on the regency council, and the other regents will be able to do nothing to stop it. Your father *wanted* him to be a regent—don't you remember how the others ousted him? Alister was your father's loyal chancellor. Do you think he will serve your brother any less well?"

"As he served them with magic?" Tavis interjected. "Rhys, I still want to know what really went on the night King Cinhil died."

"You saw—" Rhys began.

Tavis shook his head vehemently. "No! I saw your memory of that night. I still know nothing of what it was I was watching, or why those things were done. If you can tell us that—"

"Well, why not just rip it from my mind?" Rhys lashed out, anger at their procrastination taking the better part of prudence. "Fill me full of some more of the drugs you swore to use only for Healing, and then wade right in! You'll probably find out what you want to know!"

He knew he had probably ruined whatever chance he might have had for mercy from the man who had already stripped him of his powers—but it was done now. Javan was staring at him as if he'd just witnessed some strange transmutation, and Tavis—Tavis's face was contorted in some unfathomable expression.

He consoled himself with the thought that at least if Tavis took him at his word and ripped his mind, he would probably never know what hit him—he had probably goaded the other Healer beyond all possibility of reasoned response—but Tavis surprised him. He could only guess that Tavis had been reading him all the while, and knew it was truth behind the words he spoke. Smoothly, as if nothing had happened, Tavis composed his face and turned to Javan, his manner taking on a certain brittle formality.

"My prince, before today I have misled you. Rhys

speaks the truth. With your permission, I propose that we release him and permit him to go and warn the bishops."

"Just like that?" Javan whispered.

"Precisely like that."

At Javan's tight little nod, Tavis turned back to Rhys and reached out with his hand and stump. Warily Rhys sat back in the chair and allowed the other to touch him, forced himself to take a deep breath and let it out.

"I certainly hope you know how to put things back," he murmured as he closed his eyes, doing the best he could, without the feedback of his Sight, to slip into relaxation.

Tavis's voice seemed to come from a long way away, just as a slightly heady sensation of falling threatened to overcome him.

"We're about to see, aren't we?"

Then, abruptly, his Sight was restored, at least to the level it had been before the blocking, still muddled by the drugs in his system. With an incredulous smile which grew to a grin, he opened his eyes to see Tavis drawing back, a little awed. Javan was watching with an expression which Rhys could only describe as amazed.

"Are you—all right?" the prince asked.

Nodding, Rhys sat forward and started to stand, then thought better of it and sank back into the chair. "I *have* felt better. We still haven't counteracted what I drank last night. Tavis, I don't suppose you were lying when you said all the antidote was gone, were you?"

"No, but I can make up some more. It won't counteract all the effects, though."

"It will make things better than they are now. Do the best you can. How late is it getting, by the way?"

"Well past Terce," Javan said, watching in fascination as Tavis began rummaging in his Healer's chest for appropriate vials. "Perhaps as late as eleven. I think Rhys Michael had been back from Mass and breakfasted some time before he came here."

"But it isn't noon yet?"

Javan shook his head. "I'm sure it isn't."

A period of silence descended, punctuated only by the clink of Tavis working with his drugs and potions. When he had finished, he handed the result to Rhys in a small cup. Rhys probed it as best he could, with his limited abilities, but realized he was just going to have to trust Tavis. After raising the cup to both of them in salute, he downed the contents in one enormous gulp, making a face as he held the cup out to Tavis again.

"God, that tastes awful. Couldn't you do any better than that?"

"Sorry, it's in water. Without sending out for more, the only wine we could have used wasn't really suitable. You sampled it last night, and told me so yourself."

Rhys could feel the drugs already working their miracle of clearing his head, counteracting the fogginess in his mind, and the exhilaration of returning to near normal was sufficient to let him appreciate the wry humor of Tavis's remark.

"Pour me some water to chase this with, will you?" Rhys said, holding out the cup again.

Javan picked up a ewer and poured, filling it to the brim, then filled it again when Rhys drained the first one and held out the cup for more. Tavis merely sat down on the edge of the bed and watched the two of them, gradually pulling in his shields as Rhys's reached equilibrium and steadied. When Javan had put aside the ewer, he came closer to the chair where Rhys still sat massaging his forehead and trying to get himself together. As Rhys looked up, he had the distinct impression that the prince wanted to ask him something.

"Question, my prince?"

"Rhys, I—I'm sorry for what we put you through. But —damn it, you still haven't told us what happened that night!"

"I can't, Javan. I gave my word."

"To whom?" Javan persisted. "To my father? If I'm never to know, what good did it all do? Will I never find out?"

Sympathetically, Rhys reached out and brushed his fingertips across the boy's forehead, was heartened to see that Javan did not flinch.

"Someday, perhaps. And if you do, I think it will all have been to the good—even last night and this morning."

"But you can't tell me now?"

"No."

With that, Rhys made another attempt to get out of the chair, this time with better success. The walls undulated a little until he got his equilibrium established, but the effect was definitely better than he had felt since he first was drugged the night before.

"All right, I'm at least ambulatory again, though I definitely have felt better. I'm going to need some help getting out of the castle, though. Tavis, can you come with me?"

"I can!" Javan volunteered.

Tavis shook his head. "No, I'll go. You're too recognizable. Besides, if there's fighting, I don't want you anywhere near it."

"I agree," Rhys nodded, bending carefully to pick up his Healer's mantle. But he was stopped by Tavis before he could put it on.

"I don't think I'd wear that, if I were you. Deryni in the cathedral this morning are going to be about as welcome as wolves among the sheep."

Tavis opened a chest at the foot of Javan's bed and pulled out two heavy woolen cloaks, one black and one a deep royal blue. The blue one he tossed to Rhys before donning the black one himself. The cloaks only reached the knees of either man and were snug across the shoulders, but at least they were less conspicuous than Healer's green.

"Let's go, then," Tavis said, moving toward the door. "Javan, you wait here. Or, if you must get closer, stay on the higher levels of the keep where it overlooks the cathedral close and stay well out of sight. If the regents ever get wind that you're involved in this, we all might as well give it up."

Christmas at noon was hardly brighter than it had dawned. The snow fell more heavily, if anything, but that did not deter the faithful who came to observe the Feast of the Newborn King and to see their new archbishop enthroned. Word had spread quickly the previous day, and the hostility which had marked the aftermath of Jaffray's death a few months before seemed to have evolved to embarrassed acceptance, as if the election of another Deryni archbishop somehow was expiation for the murder of the one before. Besides, Alister Cullen had the reputation of being one of the most unassuming of his race, and had served fairly and faithfully as chancellor. And if King Cinhil had deemed it meet to have the Deryni bishop at his side all those years, then his counsel could hardly have been bad.

Inside the Cathedral of All Saints, the gloom of the weather outside was even more pronounced, for the church was old, and the windows high and few, most of them filled with glass of a darker, more opaque sort than was favored in more recent constructions. The contrast between this ancient church and the newer one at Rhemuth was evident. Even the candle sconces and candelabra, blazing with their scores of lights, could hardly dispel the shadows which huddled almost like living things in the aisles and far corners. The cathedral was packed with presences seen and perhaps unseen. The mystique of enthroning an archbishop had never been more evident.

The sanctuary, beyond the choir, was the sole oasis of real light in the building. There, before the high altar, on the wide dais which had seen the enthroning of kings as well as bishops, the man whom the world knew as Alister Cullen had been seated as Archbishop of Valoret and Primate of All Gwynedd but half an hour before. There, in the seat which had been Jaffray's and Anscom's, Camber had received the ring and miter from Archbishop Robert Oriss's consecrated hands, taken up the great primatial cross which was now emblematic of his rank, given it into the keeping of the ever-faithful Joram as the prayers continued.

There, seated on the throne, he had received the homage and allegiance of the nine other bishops who had supported him, still hoping, even to that moment, that at least a few of the others would have broken free of Hubert's domination and joined their brethren in obedience. But none had.

The rest of Christmas Mass had followed then, with Camber as principal celebrant and Oriss and Ailin to assist him. Through it all, a part of Camber had remained detached, worried, for Rhys still had not returned or sent word. Just before leaving his quarters for the cathedral, he had even tried to link with Joram and reach out to the Healer with his mind, to force a contact, if he could—but he had encountered nothing save a vague reassurance that Rhys was not dead. Could it be that Rhys had deliberately damped down his distinctive mental echo for some reason, perhaps so as not to interfere with whatever bond might exist between Tavis and Prince Javan?

But there was also the possibility that something was wrong—not as wrong as dead, but wrong, nonetheless. Under ordinary circumstances, Camber was sure Tavis was no match for Rhys, but who was to say that these were ordinary times?

Now Camber sat on the primatial throne once more

while several assistant priests purified the Mass vessels and put them away and the monks of the chapter here at Valoret chanted the day's antiphon. Once the priests had finished at the altar, only his first primatial blessing and address to the faithful would remain. Gazing down the choir and into the nave, he could see the kneeling masses, upturned faces staring back with rapt attention, waiting for his words. All were poised, not even the usual shuffle of feet and coughs and whispers marring the stillness which underlined the monks' chant.

Joram brought the jewel-encrusted miter which had been removed for Mass, and Camber bent his head slightly so Joram could set it into place. The crozier of the archdiocese was already in his left hand—a marvelous piece of workmanship inlaid with gold and ivory and odd grey baroque pearls surrounding plaques of ivory painted with scenes from the lives of saints. The primatial cross on its heavy, gold-leafed staff Joram held, standing now by the right arm of the throne. Out of deference to shaky public tolerance for Deryni, Joram had donned a knee-length white surplice over a plain black cassock this morning, instead of his familiar Michaeline blue. A Michaeline archbishop was quite enough for one day.

Camber could see Jebediah quietly making his way up a side aisle, also anonymous in a cloak of deep grey rather than the possibly inflammatory Michaeline blue, a look of grim alarm on his handsome face. Camber glanced at Joram and saw that his son had seen Jebediah, too. But it would take Jeb several minutes to make his way to them without being obvious. What was wrong? Had the grand master received some news of Rhys? Camber longed to reach out with his mind, but he knew he dared not, across that distance. He would simply have to wait until Jebediah could get to him.

And in the sacristy, Rhys and Tavis winked into existence via Portal. For the first time in twenty-four hours, Rhys's luck held; the sacristy was deserted. He stumbled and staggered a little on the deep Kheldish carpet, grabbing onto Tavis's arm for support as he glanced around wildly to assess their safety.

"We must be mad!" Tavis muttered under his breath. "What if there had been someone here?"

"Well, there wasn't," Rhys returned, drawing a deep, steadying breath as he moved toward the doorway. "And there was no other way to get here in time."

The little corridor outside the sacristy was likewise deserted, but, as Rhys slipped along it and moved toward the door which let into the sanctuary, he could see and hear that he had arrived only just in time. The Mass was over, the altar nearly restored to its usual configuration. The cathedral monks were singing the last Gospel. As soon as they finished, the recessional procession would form up and, after a blessing and short exhortation from the new archbishop, all of them would file back up the packed nave—straight into the waiting clutches of the regents and their soldiers.

Several priests and deacons were standing in front of the doorway, and Rhys had to crane his neck to see whether Camber was sitting on the primatial throne. He spotted him, apparently absorbed in staring down the left side of the nave. Rhys stepped farther into the doorway, still not visible from the nave, but apparent to Camber, if he would only look this way, but the archbishop did not. In desperation, Rhys raised an arm and began slowly waving it back and forth behind the priests, hoping that the movement would somehow catch Camber's attention, or Joram's. Finally, Joram glanced his way.

Breathing a sigh of relief, Rhys watched Joram bend slightly to whisper in Camber's ear, saw Camber's slow, controlled turn of head to look where Joram indicated.

A look of relief mixed with alarm flashed across the craggy Alister-face almost too quickly for any but an intimate to assess. Camber glanced down the nave once more, then returned a sidelong glance to Rhys.

Rhys, what's happened? Are you all right? came the sharply focused thought, so intense it almost seared in Rhys's still groggy mind.

In reflex, Rhys shook his head and shut his eyes, unable either to modulate the intensity of Camber's question or to return an answer. When he looked up again, he saw Camber's face taut, the tall body tensed as if he were considering rising and coming to Rhys directly.

But he must not do that! Desperately, Rhys shook his head, trying to think of a way he could go to Camber without making a major spectacle. At least in this, though, Tavis had anticipated him and was pulling the short cloak from Rhys's shoulders.

"What are you doing?" Rhys whispered, at the same time seeing the white fabric bunched over Tavis's left arm.

"Here, put on this alb," Tavis replied, dropping the

cloak on the floor and lifting the other garment over Rhys's head. "In the confusion, you can pass as a priest. Hurry."

Without argument, Rhys slipped his arms into the sleeves and tugged the robe into place, glancing at Camber as he took the cincture which Tavis proffered and knotted it around his waist. Now, if he could only manage to make his way across the sanctuary without arousing special attention . . .

But first, he must be certain that Tavis got away safely.

"Listen, you mustn't stay here," he whispered. "You mustn't be seen and recognized, if you're to be of any use to Javan in the future."

"But, I can't just leave you here, unprotected," Tavis murmured. "You're not nearly back to your full strength. How will you get away?"

"Once I get out there, I'll be with Alister and Joram," Rhys replied. "If we fail, at least we fail together. Now, promise me you'll go back to safety. You now know where the Portal is in Jaffray's apartments. Go back there and then make your way to Javan as quickly as you can."

"All right," Tavis agreed sullenly.

"Promise me!" Rhys insisted.

Defiantly, Tavis took Rhys's hand from his shoulder with his good hand and pressed him toward the door. "All right, I promise. Now get out there and warn them, before it's too late."

With a quick prayer, Rhys gave a nod and turned back toward the door, took a deep breath and folded his hands before him. The priests and deacons moved aside to let him pass, but already the recessional line-up was forming in the choir. Rhys paused to bow before the high altar; then he had reached Camber's throne and knelt, taking Camber's right hand in both of his and kissing it fervently to cover his unscheduled appearance.

"The regents are waiting outside to take you all prisoner," he whispered. "I got here as soon as I could."

Camber, now with physical contact to work with, could not control a gasp of shock and consternation as he reached out with his mind and encountered Rhys's still-addled state.

My God, Rhys, what's happened to you? he sent, glancing at the doorway from which Rhys had appeared and seeing Tavis still waiting there, though in shadow. *Did Tavis do this to you?*

Yes, but there isn't time to explain now, Rhys managed to reply, without verbalizing this time. *How are we going to get out of this?*

The procession was forming in earnest now, and Archbishop Oriss and Bishops Dermot and Niallan were approaching to escort Camber to his place. In desperation, Camber reached out into Rhys's mind with force, probing deeply as the Healer let fall all his shields to give as much information as possible in the shortest time.

Under the circumstances, Camber's touch could hardly be gentle. As he withdrew, his own mind reeling with the implications of what he had just read, Rhys teetered dangerously on his knees. Quickly Camber slipped his right hand under the Healer's elbow and raised him as he himself stood. He was so appalled at Rhys's mental condition that he could hardly think; and Joram, who had been catching the overflow from his exchange with Rhys, had no ideas either.

He must somehow defuse the situation. If the regents dared to enter the cathedral to try to take him, the people must know what was happening. As yet, he could detect no sign of intrusion at the far end of the cathedral.

The people were standing shoulder to shoulder, waiting for his blessing when his procession should move out of the cathedral. But as he eased into place behind Joram and his processional cross, flanked by the unsteady Rhys on one side and Archbishop Oriss on the other, he saw Jebediah finally making his way up the steps from the nave to the choir and heading toward him. The procession began moving, to the low chant of a psalm whose words eluded Camber in the confusion of trying to assess what was happening, and he met Jebediah just in the center of the choir. The head of the procession was already down the steps which Jebediah had just ascended, and beginning to move slowly up the center aisle. Jebediah looked surprised to see Rhys dressed as a priest.

"Alister, the outer courtyard is filled with armed men," he reported, loud enough that the other bishops near Camber could also hear. "Murdoch, Tammaron, and Ewan are there on horseback, with several of their captains, and I think I saw Hubert and the king. We couldn't stop that many. I'm sorry."

"Then, it *is* a confrontation," Camber said in a low

voice, taking a closer grip on the crozier in his left hand. "Rhys says they plan to take all the bishops prisoner and force a new election."

"More likely kill you all," Jebediah breathed. "At least it wouldn't surprise me if those men had orders not to be too careful with some of the bishops. Bishop Niallan, Dermot, I would think you're prime targets, along with Alister."

As those within earshot reacted, Camber nodded grimly.

"I fear you're right, Jeb. Well, I suppose this calls for drastic action. My Lord Bishops," he called, raising his voice and his crozier, "stop the procession and attend me. Quickly."

At his words, those nearest him gasped, jostling those ahead of them and passing the word until the entire procession had halted and the choir monks had ceased their singing. A murmur of surprise and curiosity rippled through the congregation, quickly subsiding as the procession melted back to either side of the choir screen to frame the new archbishop coming forward to stand there on the steps. Quickly the other bishops clustered to either side of him, those who had not been close enough to hear Jebediah's warning staring in amazement at their new leader, gaping as those who had heard spread the essence of the news until their archbishop raised his hand for silence. At his right, Joram moved into place with the jewelled processional cross of the primatial office, underlining Camber's authority as he began to speak.

"Good people of Valoret, I pray your attention for yet a little while longer."

His words brought an almost immediate cessation of sound in the rest of the cathedral.

"This day you have seen me enthroned as your archbishop and primate. As you are doubtless aware, choosing a worthy successor to Jaffray of Carbury was not an easy task. After many weeks of deadlocked voting in which I was not even a candidate, two of the men who *were* candidates came to me and begged me to be their leader. They said that both, with their supporters, could endorse me; and combining both factions would give us the majority vote we needed to elect a new archbishop.

"I was reluctant to accept their proposal, for I knew that there were certain other of our brethren who would never support my candidacy; but finally I told them that, if the next day's vote proved their earnest, I would accept the yoke which they and the Holy Spirit chose to lay upon me."

Outside in the yard, he could hear voices shouting, and the sound of steel-shod hooves echoing against the paving stones, and he realized he had not much time.

"I do not shrink from that duty or that yoke, for I believe that I have something to offer the people of Gwynedd. But now I have learned, even as I was preparing to leave this cathedral and give you my blessing, that there are those who would dispute the right of your bishops to elect their primate from among themselves."

A murmur of consternation began to grow in the congregation, but Camber held up his hand and raised his voice to keep above them.

"Not only would they dispute that right, but they would force the bishops of Gwynedd to elect an archbishop of *their* choosing, whether or not the bishops agree."

"Who would do that?"—"Who?"—"Who?"—"Give us their names!" the shouts began to ring out.

At that moment, the doors at the rear of the cathedral were thrown back and a mass of horsemen appeared, silhouetted against the snow. The lead riders wore the livery of the House of Haldane, but as those parted, Camber could just make out the device of Murdoch of Carthane.

"Alister Cullen, come out into the yard!" Murdoch cried, spurring his horse right into the doorway, to fidget and slip on the inlaid tiles of the floor.

"There is your answer, good people!" Camber cried, gesturing toward Murdoch.

Furious, Murdoch wheeled his horse around in a tight little circle.

"Bishops of Gwynedd, I command you, in the name of the king, to cease this folly. Your king will be lenient, but only if you abide by his will!"

"Since when is the synod of bishops bound by the will of the king in such a thing as this?" Dermot shouted back. "Or rather, by the will of the regents! Alister Cullen is our legally elected, properly enthroned archbishop. The regents have no right—"

"The regents have *every* right to protect the kingdom for its king!" Murdoch retorted. "Alister Cullen is an agitator, with his Deryni powers and his Deryni insinuations into the affairs of this kingdom. He is not acceptable to the Crown!"

Eustace, usually so jovial and light-hearted, took a step forward. "Has the king said that? I think not!"

"Then, he *shall* say it!" Murdoch retorted, before Eustace could continue. He sidled his horse closer to the doorway again. "Make way for the King's Grace! Stand aside, you! Make way!"

And as Camber and the others watched incredulously, the soldiers parted behind Murdoch and King Alroy came riding through on a white horse bedecked in scarlet bardings. He wore his scaled-down crown of crosses and leaves, a scarlet surcoat worked with the Lion of Gwynedd on his chest, and mail gleaming at neck and wrists and knees. The sheathed state sword of Gwynedd hung from his saddle, and a mounted knight followed at his stirrup, bearing the banner of the kingdom.

An awed murmur sighed through the cathedral, and Camber knew that they had lost. He had not expected Alroy to be with the regents on such a mission. The king's presence lent a legitimacy to which the people were already responding—the old Haldane mystique. The fine distinction between Crown and advisors was already blurring. Camber could feel it in the air.

"People of Gwynedd," Alroy said, in a clear, loud voice, "our regent has spoken truly. It is against our wish that Alister Cullen has been elected to this highest of ecclesiastical offices. We do therefore declare his election to be null and void. We command our bishops to meet again and reconsider our wishes. And if anyone defies us at this time, we order our regents and military forces to take them into custody to await our further pleasure."

A stunned silence met the end of Alroy's speech, but only for a few seconds. Then Dermot O'Beirne was stepping out from the others, his dark eyes flashing with anger.

"Sire, this is not meet!" he cried, pounding the iron-shod foot of his crozier once against the marble step in emphasis. "Further, it is against law and custom. Archbishop Cullen was elected by due process. Not even the king may—"

"The king," Murdoch interrupted in an imperious tone, "may do what he wills! Your resistance is very dangerous, Bishop O'Beirne!"

"And if you have advised the king in this matter, then

405

your counsel is dangerous, Earl Murdoch!" Dermot retorted. "The people will never stand—"

"The people will never stand for these insults to their king!" Murdoch snapped. "And those who continue to oppose his royal will could be construed as traitors!"

The word was a strong one. Murdoch had intended the shock value. As a murmur of outrage rippled through the assembled people, a few of the bishops exchanged uneasy glances, though Camber kept his head high and his eyes fixed unwaveringly on Murdoch—for it was Murdoch at whose word violence could erupt at any second. Behind the regent were mounted knights and men-at-arms for as far as he could see, almost blotting out the dingy, hoof-churned snow. These men, he knew, would have no qualms about riding into the cathedral itself, at the order of their leaders. And yet, for the sake of the Church which he now headed in Gwynedd, he could not accede to their wishes, even if it cost the lives of half the people in this place, as well as his own.

"My Lord Earl," Camber responded, raising his hand and trying to temper his words with just the right balance of strength and acquiescence, "there are no traitors beneath this holy roof, and certainly none among my brother bishops. Every one of us swore at His Highness's coronation to uphold his lawful commands and to support his throne. None of us has forsworn his oath."

"Then, obey this command!" Tammaron retorted.

"I cannot, for it is not lawful. Our oath pertained to temporal obedience. His Highness, in turn—and you, as his regents—swore to defend the spiritual well-being of his kingdom—which he does not do, if he tries to go against the lawful governance of the synod of bishops and their right freely to elect their primate."

He had hit the crux of the matter, and Murdoch knew it. For a moment, the regent's jaw worked in silent rage, his face going almost purple in his anger. Nor were Tammaron and Hubert able to conceal their indignation, though Ewan, good soldier that he was, betrayed no sign of emotion.

For a moment, Camber thought he might have won the point—that the regents would back down, at least for the nonce.

But then Murdoch turned slightly in the saddle toward Alroy and mouthed something incomprehensible from where Camber stood. Alroy seemed to pale a little, but then he gave a tight little nod and raised his chin a trifle higher, his young face stiff and strained under the crosses and leaves he wore.

"Take them!" he said, in a voice which carried the full length of the cathedral.

Chapter Twenty-Seven

As for the illusions of art magick, they were put down, and their vaunting in wisdom was reproved with disgrace.

—Wisdom of Solomon 17:7.

An instant of shock immobilized everyone within reach of his words, but only until Murdoch and Alroy eased their steeds to either side and the knights and mounted men-at-arms began pressing their big warhorses down the center aisle. Carpet had been laid for the ceremony, and it gave the chargers footing. The riders and following foot soldiers had penetrated perhaps a quarter of the way down the nave before the fact of their actions truly began to register. Then people began to scream and scatter before the hooves of the great horses and their riders.

"Sweet *Jesu*, I didn't think they'd dare to do it!" Dermot gasped to Camber, as all of the bishops began surging back into the choir. "Alister, you must get away. Don't let them take you!"

"Niallan?" Camber called. "Can you give us sanctuary?"

Niallan, pushing his way toward the sacristy door, gave a curt nod. "Aye, just let me go ahead. Dhassa's set as a Trap Portal just now, you know."

"Let me come, too," Dermot said. "Whatever happens, they've heard what I said today, and they count me as yours. They'll have Cashien away from me, in any case. Better that I'm free, if in exile."

"Come, then," Niallan nodded, pushing closer to the sacristy doorway.

407

The soldiers were more than halfway down the nave now, and the screams of the frightened and the inevitably injured echoed among the columns and arches of the great cathedral. In the sacristy, an appalled Tavis O'Neill cowered behind a garment press and watched as Bishops Niallan and Dermot scurried into the sacristy and stopped on the Portal square. Dermot spotted him as Niallan slipped into place behind him, and the human bishop turned his head to murmur something to the Deryni; but Niallan only shot Tavis a stern, forbidding look and then pulled Dermot closer. Then both men disappeared.

With a shudder, Tavis came out of his hiding place and scurried toward the Portal square himself. He had already stayed too long. He had to get out before someone else saw him.

He glanced out the sacristy door and almost collided with Jebediah. The Michaeline knight had his sword drawn and a murderous expression on his face, and he grabbed Tavis by the upper arm and shook him like a terrier.

"What the hell are you doing here? Get back to Javan!"

"I'm going now," Tavis managed to mutter. "I—wanted to be able to report what had happened to Javan. Besides, you might need a Healer."

"We have Rhys!" Jebediah retorted. "Now, will you go? If you should be taken, or even seen by one of the regents' men, Javan will have no one!"

"But Rhys can't Heal right now!" Tavis protested. "And it's my fault!"

"And it will be your fault if you leave Javan stranded. Now go, or I'll knock you senseless and take you out of here myself!"

Against that kind of determination, Tavis dared not protest further. With a little sob of fear, he gave a quick nod and drew himself up on the Portal square. Jebediah released him and stepped back, his attention already turning to the sanctuary, where foot soldiers and a few mounted men had now penetrated and were taking clerics into custody. A number of priests and three of the more timid bishops—Turlough and Davet and Ulliam—had surrendered, but those remaining were putting up a resistance.

Tavis craned his neck. He saw Joram lay about him with the heavy processional cross, and the new archbishop thrust his crozier under the nose of a startled war-horse, which immediately reared and slipped, falling and dislodging its rider.

But then he saw another mounted man urge his horse around behind Rhys, shouldering him aside with the heavy destrier and sending the Healer sprawling. Rhys slipped in blood and fell without being able to break his fall, the back of his head hitting the edge of one of the altar steps with a sickening, hollow crack.

Tavis cried out and started to go to him, but Jebediah's face had gone white at the sound, and he now brandished his weapon as if he would enjoy using it on Tavis. With a sob, Tavis hugged his arms tightly around himself and closed his eyes, forcing himself to make the jump back to the safe Portal in the archbishop's apartments.

And out in the sanctuary, close by the sacristy door, Camber saw and heard Rhys fall. Using his crozier like a pole weapon, he fought his way past the horseman who had been responsible and even managed to unhorse him before ducking under Joram's guard to kneel by the fallen Healer. Joram continued to fend off would-be assailants with the processional cross, and Camber could see Jebediah fighting his way to them. Gently he touched the Healer's forehead, trying to force himself not to acknowledge what he had felt as Rhys fell.

Throwing aside his crozier, he stripped off the rich cope of white and gold and wrapped it around the fallen Healer, gathered Rhys tenderly into his arms and staggered to his feet, to begin pushing his way to the sacristy, now guarded on both sides by Joram and the grim-faced Jebediah. His face was terrible in his grief as he eased his way through the doorway into the tiny corridor, then into the sacristy itself.

Half a dozen priests and deacons were already gathered there for safety, though all of them knew it was only a matter of time before the soldiers won through. They parted before him like water, none daring to ask his intention as he stumbled to a halt on the Portal square.

"All of you, out!" he managed to croak, Joram and Jebediah reinforcing his words as he swayed under the weight he carried. He lowered Rhys's feet to the floor, then held the limp, cope-wrapped form hard against himself as the room cleared, reaching out with his mind across the miles to Dhassa.

Eager, caring hands were waiting at the other end,

there in the little side chapel at Dhassa, but Camber shook his head and carried his burden a few steps outside the mosaic boundaries of the Portal, finally to drop to his knees before the altar and lay his burden on the soft carpet. Almost immediately he was aware of Joram and Jebediah dropping to their knees on either side of him, Jebediah already stripping off his grey mantle to make a pillow for Rhys's head.

"It wasn't even a weapon that did it," Camber whispered plaintively, taking the slack head between his hands and probing with fingers and mind. "He fell and hit his head on the step."

"He's still breathing, but not very well," Joram murmured, running his fingers through the thick red hair and closing his eyes for better concentration. "Damn! He's got a depressed fracture here big enough to put an egg into!"

With an increasing sense of despair, Camber moved his hands to where Joram indicated and felt the awful indentation. The skin had not even been broken—there was no blood at all—but he could feel the irregular edges of bone beneath the scalp. All the life signs were depressed, along with the section of skull; and as he reached into the brilliant Healer's mind, he found the Healing channels hopelessly obscured and drug-muddled. Now he knew just what the encounter with Tavis O'Neill had cost Rhys, besides the information he had been made to reveal. There was no way that even Camber could try to link into Rhys's Healing resources. Another Healer was Rhys's only hope, and soon.

"Niallan!" he called over his shoulder, the word almost a sob. "You haven't got a Healer nearby, have you?"

The other Deryni bishop knelt beside him with a shake of his head. "I've already checked. My household Healer is out on a call. I've sent for him, but I don't know whether it's going to be in time, Alister."

Beneath Camber's hands, Rhys's breathing was becoming shallower and more irregular, the pulse thinner and more thready. In desperation, Camber tried to reach out with his mind to ease the pressure on the brain, to lift the shattered portion of the skull. He could feel the depression lessening slightly under his fingertips, but he could also sense the fluid beneath the broken skull, building yet more pressure to quench the vital functions. Rhys's breathing became more erratic still, and Joram began to blow his own breath into the failing man's lungs as he once had done for Camber, while Jebediah laid his hands over the laboring heart and tried to regularize its pace.

Despite all their efforts, Camber finally had to admit that Rhys was dying. After a few minutes, he became aware that Niallan had left them and then returned to kneel beside him again; his brother bishop was unstoppering a vial of holy oil and preparing to perform the Last Rites, still in his full vestments, less miter. Camber could not bring himself to participate. He could only watch and listen numbly, still doing all he could to keep this man who was more than a son to him from slipping away.

While Niallan prayed, Camber himself assaulted the heavens with his petition, not for the first time resenting the fortune which had given some the Healing gift, but not himself, or even the man whose identity he wore. The thought of Alister brought him the image of another time, however—of Alister in death; and of Alister's killer, the beautiful but treacherous Ariella, impaled on the sword flung by Alister with his dying strength, her fingers cupped in the attitude of a spell which might have saved her—a spell thought by most Deryni to be but legend.

For a moment, hope flared. He knew why Ariella had failed, at least in theory. As surely as he now despaired for Rhys's life, he *knew*. Had Rhys been even remotely conscious, he could have fed the Healer the procedure and helped him work it, he was sure. The spell did not even depend on Healing function. He could have worried later about how to bring Rhys back from the spell's stasis. Again, he knew the theory. With another Healer close at hand, he felt certain he could have muddled through it somehow.

But Rhys was not conscious and might not have agreed to try so desperate a measure, even if he had been. The Healer was not as conservative as Joram, but there was an ethical question, nonetheless. Did Camber have the right to answer that for even one so close as Rhys? Dared he be another's conscience?

Almost, he decided to try it anyway. It was really little more than the stasis that could be put on bodies to prevent decay—well, perhaps a *little* more, to keep a soul bound to a suspended body. . . .

But while he argued with himself, and agonized, and even made a tentative probe to see whether he could work the spell on an unconscious subject, he realized

411

that it was too late. Rhys was dead. As Niallan's voice wrapped around him in the traditional prayers, joined by the responses of Dermot and a handful of priests in the white of the Gabrilite Order, Camber felt the bleak emptiness and knew that Rhys was gone.

He waited until Niallan had finished, his hands still resting on the thick red hair which hid the damage done to the skull beneath, then signalled minutely that Joram and Jebediah should cease their ministrations. As they sank back on their heels, drained and exhausted, he gently gathered Rhys into his arms again, cradling the red head close against his cheek.

"Dear God, *why?*" he whispered, his voice breaking as the tears began to come. "Forty years to make this man, and now—this! A fall! Death should be more difficult!"

The regents wasted no time in extending their vengeance, especially once they learned that their principal quarry had managed to elude them. In all, only five of the ten renegade bishops remained in custody by the end of the day, three having escaped by Portal and two by death. Davet Nevan was kicked in the chest by a warhorse and died before help could be obtained, and they found Kai Descantor sprawled in the center of the sacristy floor without a mark upon him. Oriel told them later that a Portal had previously been sited there beneath the carpet, and judged that Kai had died destroying it, after the escape of his colleagues.

But five of the ten bishops would be enough for the regents' intentions. After chaining the captives in a dungeon overnight to let them contemplate the folly of their disobedience, the regents set in motion the mechanism for rounding up those who had escaped. Writs of attainder and outlawry were issued for Alister Cullen, sometime Bishop of Grecotha (suspended), Niallan Trey, sometime Bishop of Dhassa (also suspended), Father Joram MacRorie, Earl Jebediah of Alcara, Lord Rhys Thuryn, and also Bishop Dermot O'Beirne, suspended Bishop of Cashien, who was not Deryni but who had fled with them, and who had supported the illegal election of Alister Cullen as archbishop.

As an afterthought, the regents also ordered the apprehension of Rhys's wife and children and any other of their kin who could be found, for the regents were beginning to suspect that the entire clan related to the so-called Saint Camber were probably involved in plots against the Crown and regents.

In keeping with the writs, the regents also sent new orders to Rhun of Horthness, who henceforth was to be Earl of Sheele for his brilliant work of Christmas Eve. Dhassa, which the regents immediately guessed as being the renegade archbishop's place of refuge, was to be besieged by Rhun's forces. The siege of Dhassa, however, would be a long and weary business, for the worst of the winter was just beginning. Unless the Dhassa Portal was still operational, and at least one other open to supply it, no one would be going in or out of Dhassa until the spring.

Meanwhile, the regents continued to cement their ecclesiastical power in Valoret. On the day after Christmas, a little way outside Valoret in a town called Ramos, the remaining bishops, five of them in chains, convened to reconsider their actions of two days previously. It soon became clear, however, that most of the five captured bishops were going to remain obdurate—one, Turlough, was won over with the promise of a new see to be created at Marbury—so Hubert and his faction took the opportunity to nominate six new itinerant bishops to the council, one of them Edward, the twenty-year-old bachelor son of Hubert's brother Manfred, who had already received the rich earldom of Culdi. Since confirmation of the nominations required only a simple majority, the six nominees were approved without difficulty.

Consequently, when the first ballot for archbishop was taken that afternoon, after Ulliam also went over to Hubert, thirteen of the sixteen possible votes went to Hubert. The three abstentions, not surprisingly, were Robert Oriss, Archbishop of Rhemuth, Ailin MacGregor, Auxiliary Bishop of Valoret, and the only remaining itinerant bishop who had not just been elected at the synod itself, Eustace of Fairleigh.

Hubert was enthroned the day after he was elected, but in a much more private ceremony than Alister Cullen's had been, for Hubert had work to do. That very afternoon, the Council of Ramos convened and began taking measures to stop the further incursions of Deryni into the control of Gwynedd. Hubert, with this much power in his hands, could not be restrained.

They began by suspending and laicizing all Deryni priests and other clergy, that the Church might be purged of their magical influence and evil taint. No Deryni might ever again enter holy orders of any kind, even as a layman. There was even some talk regarding whether Deryni might continue to receive the other six sacraments, but fortunately more prudent heads prevailed. Barring Deryni from normally sanctioned religious functions might lead to even more monstrous practices than those of which they were already suspected. Better to keep the average Deryni in the fold of the Church as a wayward child than to cast him out altogether, where one would never know what he was up to.

Alister and Niallan, of course, were included in the general suspension and laicization, and stripped of their offices. Joram, son of the infamous "Saint" Camber, was also declared to be a priest no longer. Dermot O'Beirne they likewise suspended and stripped of office, as a Deryni sympathizer, but they did not strip him of his priesthood altogether, since he was not Deryni. His see of Cashien they gave to Zephram of Lorda. Alister's old see of Grecotha went to the new Bishop Edward MacInnis, and Niallan's to Archer of Arrand—though Bishop Archer would have a difficult time taking possession of his new diocese until the siege of Dhassa was over.

Joram's specific naming in the suspensions and laicizations brought up the subject of Camber's sainthood again, and this time it did not survive. The canonization of twelve years before was repudiated. Camber's name was forbidden even to be spoken, on pain of flogging for a first offense and having one's tongue cut out the next time. The order was issued to destroy all written records of his name and family. Anyone tempted to write anew of the *quondam* saint risked the loss of the hand which wrote it.

Nor was that sufficient for the regents' retribution. Declaring all magic anathema, with Deryni sorcery the chiefest among the heresies, they proclaimed Camber a heretic besides. Had they been able to find his body, they would have burned it at the stake, but unfortunately it had been established at his canonization that the body had been miraculously assumed into heaven. Now Bishop Zephram was led to suggest that perhaps the body had, indeed, been spirited away by Camber's son; but he and the others doubted whether anyone would have any luck finding it now. In any case, since punishment for heresy could not be meted out to Camber in person at this late date, the bishops decided that it would be a fitting penalty to exact on his adherents instead. On Childermas, the

Feast of the Holy Innocents, they made an example at Dolban, the mother house of the Servants of Saint Camber, burning more than three-score men and women to death at stakes set row on row in the abbey yard. Only a few of them were even Deryni.

One reluctant exception the bishops made to the general condemnation of Deryni magic, and that was to permit Healers to continue to function, though under far more rigid regulation than they had known hitherto. Philosophers and theologians had long agreed that Healing came of God—but the Healers were also Deryni, and therefore at least suspect of having other, darker allies than the Lord of Hosts. Eventually, it was hoped that even Healers could be phased out of practice, but none of the bishops was really ready to think out all the implications yet. In any event, Healers were few, and their services had always been somewhat limited to the aristocracy of both races; so as long as the bishops and regents could call upon Healers when they needed them, they decided not to worry too much about the common people. It was also judged appropriate to continue the use of Deryni collaborators to hunt down other Deryni, for nearly anything may be justified in time of war.

The impropriety of Deryni magic finally defined, the bishops next considered nonreligious sanctions against Deryni in general. While even Hubert would not go so far as to advocate the wholesale annihilation of all Deryni at this time, he was very much in favor of rigid controls. All high-born Deryni were to be stripped of their titles and ranks. Henceforth, no Deryni would be permitted to own land, except under the strictest of supervision. Deryni could not hold offices of any kind, or marry or inherit without the express leave of their liege lord. And any Deryni discovered to be teaching his evil abilities to another would be summarily executed.

The Council of Ramos met each day of Christmas week, the bishops returning to their quarters at the cathedral complex only to sleep, except for Archbishop Hubert, who still occupied his suite in the keep, and who dined each evening with his fellow regents and briefed them on the day's accomplishments. The young king was permitted to join them for the meal and the first part of the briefing, to make him feel he was a part of the policy-making process, but liberal amounts of strong wine served with the meal always set him to nodding by the time more serious discussions began, and he was bundled off to bed by a few squires. Javan and Rhys Michael were not included at all.

This exclusion, as the days wore on, bothered Javan and Tavis more and more, for rumor was spreading of the general tone the bishops were taking in their daily meetings, and Javan was beginning to fear for Tavis's safety. Tavis found himself being watched very closely whenever he went out of Javan's quarters, for he and Oriel and a few other collaborators were now the only Deryni at large in the keep. He took to staying in Javan's rooms in the daytime, but often he would disappear at night and even Javan did not know where he had gone, though he always covered for him. The Healer made a thorough exploration of the walls and passageways deep in the bowels of the keep. By Saturday night after Christmas, he had made several interesting discoveries and several difficult decisions. His heart was heavy as he talked with Javan late that night.

"I just don't see what we can do to stop them, Javan," he concluded, after he had reviewed all he had managed to glean of the bishops' rulings of the past week. "Hubert has gone mad with power, and he'll use it as a scourge against every Deryni he can track down. It's a miracle that I'm still allowed to be with you. I can only surmise that it's an oversight, because of the bishops still being in conclave, since the only other Deryni in the castle are under heavy guard almost all the time, even Oriel. Either that, or they're simply not ready to contend with you."

Javan stood and began to pace back and forth, in and out of the window embrasure where they both had been sitting. Under the long, fur-lined dressing gown he wore, his limp was hardly noticeable. He had grown several more inches since the fall, and was now taller than his twin.

"I won't let them take you from me, you know that," he said solemnly.

Tavis shook his head. "I know that you don't want to let them take me, but you may not have much choice, my prince. What we have to decide, I think, is what to do if they do try it. Do I let them take me, or do I escape? In either case, I leave you to their less than gentle ministrations—and that's the last thing I want."

"Or I. Find another option. You know I can't—wait

416

a minute! You said escape—you mean, from Valoret? How?"

"Through a Portal."

It took an instant for the import of Tavis's words to sink in. Then, all at once, Javan was scurrying back to crouch at Tavis's knee, grabbing the Healer's one good hand in his two and staring up in excitement.

"A Portal? Then, we could *both* escape! Oh, Tavis, do you think we really could?"

"We?" Tavis looked at the boy with a stricken expression. "My prince, you can't go. You're the heir-presumptive. If I left, and you went with me, it would be taken by the regents as a renunciation of your claim to the throne—and that's exactly what they want. They could manage Rhys Michael; they can't manage you. Oh, I know it doesn't seem that important now, but think about it. Who else can hope to undo what the regents and bishops are doing now, except you? Do you think Rhys Michael can, or would?"

As Javan's shoulders slumped, he shook his head, and Tavis continued, laying his handless forearm along the boy's right shoulder in comfort.

"All right, then. We're agreed on that point, in any case. Your place is here, regardless of whether or not I can stay with you. Once you're king—or even once you're of age—you can have me brought back to Court. For that matter, if and when I do have to leave, I'll try to come back for brief visits as long as the Portal isn't discovered."

"But, you *will* go, rather than be taken?" Javan whispered. "I couldn't bear to see you killed by them."

"Yes, I'll go. But not before it's necessary."

"And I can't come along?"

"No."

With a sigh, Javan bowed his head over their joined hands for a moment, touching them to his forehead, then got up and moved to the window without looking at the Healer. He stood there with both hands resting on the stone tracery for several seconds, staring out at the darkness, then dropped one hand and turned slightly toward Tavis, though he still did not look at him.

"Have you any idea how difficult it is to be a prince?" he asked in a low voice.

"Very little," Tavis whispered, shaking his head

slightly. "I wish it were something that you did not have to learn, and so young."

The prince glanced at the floor, at his clubbed foot in its special boot, protruding from beneath the hem of the fur-lined robe, then looked back at Tavis. The young Haldane face was now composed, every inch the prince that he must be.

"This Portal that you mentioned—I take it that you don't mean the one in the archbishop's apartments, since that's impossible to reach with Hubert there now; and you said Bishop Kai destroyed the one in the cathedral. Where—"

"Beneath the King's Tower," Tavis replied. "There are probably several more, in other portions of the castle which were built during the Interregnum, but this is the only one I've manged to locate. Stories say that on the night Imre was taken in his tower room, his pregnant sister darted through a secret opening in the king's chamber and made good her escape. I was hardly older than you at the time, but I remember thinking that she must somehow have gotten to a Portal. So I've been searching all the likely hiding places all week. I don't know whether what I found is the one Ariella used, but it *is* a Portal. I wasn't going to tell you."

"Why not?"

"Because it's dangerous to use one, these days. I know the location of several Portals, but I don't know their status. They may not be working, or they may be set as traps. I'm afraid to try the few that still seem to be operational, for fear I can't get back."

"What do you mean, 'traps' and 'can't get back?'" Javan asked in amazement.

Tavis sighed. "Well, you can Transfer into them, but then you can't leave, even to go back where you came from, unless someone at that end releases you. I've also heard stories of other things that can be done to Portals so that you—never come back anywhere. No one knows where those unlucky souls go."

"Would they do that at Dhassa, or would they just have destroyed it?" Javan asked, after a thoughtful pause.

"At Dhassa? Why do you ask?"

"Just answer my question," Javan said evasively. "Would they do that at Dhassa?"

"Well, no. Not that last, at any rate. No reputable Deryni would. It isn't destroyed, either. I'm almost certain they'll have set it as a trap, though. That's probably where Rhys and the others went, when they escaped from the cathedral. Dhassa's under siege now, you know."

Javan was silent for several minutes then, but Tavis could not penetrate beyond the boy's rigid shields to find out what he was thinking—not without forcing and revealing his intrusion. After a little while longer, Javan looked up. The grey Haldane eyes were quicksilver cool and compelling.

"Tavis, I want to go to Dhassa," the prince murmured. "Will you take me?"

For just an instant, Tavis almost said yes. Then, with a blink and a shake of his head to loose the boy's spell, he stared at Javan in amazement.

"How did you do that?"

"Do what?"

"What you just—never mind." He took a deep breath and remarshalled his thoughts. "Why do you want to go to Dhassa? Haven't I just told you how dangerous it is? Do you even understand what you're asking?"

"I understand exactly what I'm asking."

"But—Javan, you're far more than an ordinary human, God knows, but you're not Deryni! For God's sake, you've never even been through a normal Portal. If that *is* a Trap Portal at Dhassa, we could wait a long time, and it might be very unpleasant in the waiting."

"It won't be long," Javan said confidently. "Under the circumstances they'll have it manned at all times. Tell me about the unpleasant part."

He could not counter the boy's logic about the waiting. Grimly he racked his brain for a description that would mean something to Javan's limited experience.

"Do you remember how you felt the night I made you sick? The mental part of it, not the physical illness, though it could also have physical manifestations."

Javan shuddered a little. "Yes."

"Well, it could be worse than that, depending upon what they've done. Besides, why do you want to go to Dhassa?"

Javan clasped his hands and glanced down at them. "First of all, I want to apologize to Archbishop Alister," he said in a low voice. "I think we were wrong about him. I want him to know that we see now what he and Rhys and Joram and the others were trying to do all along.

And I want to make certain that Rhys is all right. I've had an uneasy feeling about him, ever since you told me about seeing him fall."

"I see." Tavis rubbed the end of his stump in an unconscious gesture of uneasiness. "Javan, I understand your feelings, and I'd like to be reassured, too, but it *is* dangerous. We could get caught at any of a number of points right here in the castle, we don't know what the Portal situation is like, and once we get there, *if* we get there —well, after what we did to Rhys, we may not be terribly welcome."

"I know that, but it's too late to undo it. That's another reason I think it's important that we go."

"Suppose I go," Tavis offered. "I probably exaggerated about the danger of the Trap aspect of the Portal. They wouldn't dare make it too dangerous, for fear of catching one of their own people trying to make an escape. At worst, they'd keep me prisoner, which has to be better than being the regents' prisoner. You shouldn't have to—"

"No! I won't send you where I wouldn't go myself!" Javan interrupted. "Princes don't do that. I want to go, Tavis. And if the archbishop wants to be angry with us because of Rhys, then I guess we'll just have to bear his anger. But we have to let him know that we're on his side now, and that we'd never have done what we did to Rhys if we'd only understood that we're all fighting parts of the same battle, against a common enemy." He sighed resignedly. "And if they don't want me to know what happened to me the night my father died—well, I guess I'll just have to wait until it's time."

"It may not be that long a wait," Tavis said tentatively. "The two of us might be able to dig it out on our own, now that we're both recovered. You have a right to know."

Javan shook his head. "Maybe I don't. In any case, that's not the issue here. I want to go to Dhassa, Tavis. Now. Tonight. Will you take me there?"

CHAPTER TWENTY-EIGHT

It is the part of a brave combatant to be wounded, yet overcome.

—Polycarp 1:14

Half an hour later, having made provisions to cover their absence as best they could, Tavis and Javan eluded several guard patrols and then slipped along an intramural passageway and down a stair beneath the King's Tower. Around the curve of another passageway, they came to what at first appeared to be an ordinary garderobe—except that the floor was solid. Javan began trembling as Tavis paused before the opening, but he stepped in boldly when Tavis gestured for him to enter.

"Are you sure this is a Portal?" he whispered incredulously, as Tavis took the torch and urged him further into the dank closeness.

"Well, it's hardly in a class with the one in the cathedral, but yes, it's a Portal. I'm going to put the light out now. Don't move."

The end of the torch continued to glow for several seconds as Tavis straightened and slipped his right arm around Javan's neck from behind, the hand resting lightly at the base of the throat. His left forearm he slid along the other shoulder so that his wrist touched the side of the boy's neck. Javan tensed under his touch, for he knew that this was going to be different from the workings they usually did with Healing magic.

"Now, remember what I told you about the need to relax and let yourself go completely, so that I can carry you through," Tavis whispered, his lips directly beside Javan's left ear. "Take a few deep breaths and let them out slowly, as if we were going to work a Healing. Open and let things drift. Come on, you can do better than that."

Javan tried, but he was too nervous to relax the way Tavis had taught him. He reached out and brushed the damp wall with his fingertips for reassurance as he took another deep breath and let it out, repeated the process —even sensed the tentative touch of Tavis's mind reaching out to float against his shields. He could not seem to make himself let go.

"Tavis, I don't think I can do it," he whispered, beginning to shake his head. "Maybe you were right. You should go on without me. I'll wait here. I promise, I won't make a sound."

"No, that won't do," Tavis breathed, the tone still infinitely patient. "Let's try something else. Don't fight it, just let it happen. I'm stronger than you, and you couldn't get away even if you wanted to—which you really don't."

As he spoke, he shifted his hand upward on Javan's neck and began to exert pressure on either side, gentle but firm, and increasing as Javan became aware of what he was doing and started to tense up even more.

"Relax!" Tavis commanded. "This is just for a moment, to get you through the Portal. You won't lose consciousness for more than a few seconds. Believe me, it's easier this way."

Javan could breathe, but he could feel the blood pounding beneath Tavis's fingers, sensed his vision beginning to blur, even in the stark darkness of the alcove. Now he forced himelf to exhale deeply and let his arms fall heavily to his side, even leaning farther into Tavis's pressure to speed the process, though it was against all instinct. In only an instant, the darkness of the alcove was replaced by an even greater darkness which was but prelude to an odd, stomach-stirring sense of vertigo and falling. He felt Tavis's arms supporting him as he passed out.

In Dhassa, Camber hastily threw on a dressing gown which Joram held for him and then followed him and Niallan down a series of corridors to the chapel. There he found Jebediah and a handful of Niallan's Deryni elite guards surrounding a shimmer of purplish light which stood over the Portal in the side chapel. Inside the shimmer, Camber could just make out the forms of Tavis O'Neill and Prince Javan. Both Healer and prince looked tense and apprehensive, and more so when they saw Alister Cullen approaching, but there was no place they could go, trapped in the Portal as they were. For some reason, they were both wearing black tonight.

With a hand-signal, Camber bade Niallan release the Trap and dismiss the guards. Tavis gave an audible sigh of relief as the purplish light died around him, waiting until the guards had gone out and closed the door before making a short bow to Camber.

"Thank you, Your Grace. Before you chide me for bringing His Highness here, please let me explain that he insisted. We've been gathering information which we thought you should have, and this seemed to be the best way to get it to you. Where is Rhys?"

Camber stiffened at the name, feeling both Joram and Jebediah reverberate psychically with the shock, seeing Niallan's inadvertant expression of sorrow—quickly masked, but not quickly enough. Dhassa's bishop had grown closer to all of them in the past week, in many ways beginning to fill some of the void which Rhys's absence left.

The reaction of a previous stranger was not lost on prince or Healer's searching eyes. As Tavis took an involuntary step toward them in surprise, Javan caught his arm and followed.

"Something's wrong. I knew it!" the boy whispered. "What happened?"

"Rhys—died," Camber said simply, unable to think of any way to soften the news. "He died almost where you are standing, shortly after we left the cathedral."

O God! Javan mouthed silently.

Tavis shook his head incredulously.

"But, he *can't* be dead. He can't be. He just can't be!" the Healer repeated, over and over.

Javan whirled to face his faithful Healer, his eyes like deep pits of shadow, all pupil and horror, his mouth working jerkily several times before he could choke out the words.

"Oh, God, we killed him, Tavis! We should never have drugged him! He couldn't Heal himself because of us, and he *died!*"

Camber could not force down a surge of agreement, as the boy collapsed into hysterical weeping in Tavis's arms, for it was undoubtedly true that the fact of Rhys's diminished capabilities had not helped his condition. But it was also true that, given the nature of the head injury Rhys had received, he would not have been able to Heal himself even if he *had* started out at full capability. The fall had been no one's fault in this room—an awful, senseless, tragic accident!

He told the two so, reiterating his belief that the only thing which might have saved Rhys would have been the immediate presence of another Healer; but then Tavis merely began berating himself for leaving when he did, returning to Javan when he might have gone to Rhys to Heal him.

Jebediah pointed out that Tavis had not known the extent of Rhys's injury when he left, and that he had been obeying Rhys's own instructions and Jebediah's sword in going back to guard the prince. That finally seemed to begin satisfying Tavis's guilt.

Camber said little during this exchange, for he could not prevent a part of his pure emotion from clinging to the futile belief that Rhys might have lived, if only Tavis had not drugged and then abandoned him; but he forced himself to submerge those last flickers of resentment. Rhys had made his peace with Tavis and his prince. Camber had read it in that fleeting instant when Rhys had knelt at his feet in the cathedral and given him all the night's fear and reconciliation in one quick burst of intimate rapport—his last, as it turned out. In that, at least, Rhys's death had not been in vain; for in addition to the warning he had brought, he had given them two new and impressive allies: Tavis O'Neill, a Healer of increasing potential, it seemed, who had mastered Rhys's own Healing quirk in the last hours before the end; and a surprisingly talented son of Cinhil.

They spoke a little with Javan after that, finally making it clear that though Alroy was the king, it was Javan to whom they looked for aid and an eventual return to sanity, where relations between Deryni and humans were concerned. They knew he would not betray his brother, nor would they dream of asking him to, but he must be prepared to take his brother's place when the time came. No, they would not harm the sickly Alroy, but neither was Alroy fit to rule, held as he was under the thumb of the regents, even if he had been physically fit.

When they were sure he understood, they knelt before him there in front of the altar and gave him their pledge of support—not full homage, as must be reserved for a king, but a commitment to him, personally, nonetheless. Javan acknowledged it solemnly, and said little thereafter, but the atmosphere seemed to have eased a little for the exchange. Their major remaining concern now lay with Tavis.

"I'd like to know whether you've thought any more about what you learned from Rhys," Camber asked, without further circumambulation of the issue.

The Healer stiffened defensively. "What was that, Your Grace?"

"The new Healing function," Camber returned, avoiding the other, more magical topic which he knew both Tavis and Javan really wanted to talk about. "He told me you'd learned how. If it's true, you can be more help than you know."

Tavis's face, guarded already, became positively mask-like.

"It's true." He hesitated, then went on. "I don't know how that can help anything, though. Deryni aren't our enemies—except some of them," he concluded. He jogged his chin toward the empty wristband of his sleeve. "This wasn't done by friends."

"Also true," Camber agreed. "However, suppose you show me what you can do. Then I'll tell you why it's useful."

Tavis shrugged, relaxing a little. "All right." He glanced at the other three, then back at Camber. "Any preference of subject?"

"How about Niallan?" Camber replied softly, a little reluctant to ask for a demonstration of this particular talent when they were not yet sure of Tavis, but knowing that he had to find out. He didn't think that Tavis would use it as a weapon against them now—he'd only used it on Rhys to prevent an inadvertent betrayal—but if he would, best to find out now.

What Tavis did not know was that the Portal behind him was still set to prevent departure, and that the entire chapel was warded from without. And he could not overpower the Deryni guards outside and make them lower the wards to allow his escape. Only Niallan's mental order could do that—which meant that Niallan had to be restored.

But all of this was but an instant's thought. As the Healer glanced at the other bishop, Camber sensed that Tavis was trying to be open with him, that he did not want to have to play these sparring games, but was as wary as the rest of them. Niallan gave a lopsided smile and stepped out bravely from the other two, and Tavis glanced at Camber once again.

"No tricks?" he asked.

Camber shook his head. "I could ask the same of you, but there comes a point when we all have to trust one another. I've asked you to demonstrate on Niallan because he's never experienced it before. Would you rather someone else?"

Tavis flexed his fingers nervously, considering, glanced at Javan for reassurance, then shook his head and moved within reach of Niallan.

"I've only done this once before," he murmured, starting to raise both arms toward Niallan's head, then dropping the left one, as though suddenly embarrassed by his missing hand. "My last subject was drugged, too. I'll try not to hurt you."

"Go ahead," Niallan whispered, outwardly composed, but unable to suppress a flinch as Tavis's hand touched his forehead.

Nothing outward happened, but suddenly Niallan gasped and drew back a step, eyelids fluttering in shock, reeling a little dizzily as Joram and Jebediah quickly caught him under the elbows and gave him support.

"Christ, he did it!" was all Niallan could murmur, absolutely astonished as Tavis backed off and waited, uneasy, and Camber glanced at the others.

Gone? he sent to Joram and Jebediah.

Joram nodded minutely. *As clean as you could want.*

"Good," Camber said aloud. "Now, remove the block, please, Tavis."

"Very well."

Again Tavis moved in to touch Niallan's forehead, his expression far calmer at the second approach. In the space of Camber's blink, Niallan was restored. His wide, relieved grin was all the confirmation Camber needed.

That left only the question of whether Tavis could truly be trusted in matters they did not know about. They talked; and as Tavis related what he had observed of the regents and the bishops during the past week, he seemed sincere, but he also seemed anxious—far more anxious than he really had a right to be.

This alarmed Camber, for at first he feared that the nervousness might herald some hitherto unsuspected deception. As they continued to talk, he extended delicate and subtle probes to try to detect what it could be. Finally, he realized that something else underlay what was happening: Tavis had always been aloof, even before his injury, but now he seemed to be making clumsy attempts to open and reach out.

Amazed and relieved, Camber tried to maintain patience, to encourage, to let Tavis take it at his own speed, now that he suspected what the younger man was about. During an appropriate lull in the conversation, he had the other three Deryni take Javan aside, across the chapel, ostensibly for Jebediah to brief the prince on military theory but, in fact, to give Camber and Tavis some semblance of privacy. Tavis was still awkward and somewhat ill at ease, but he seemed grateful.

"You know that there's something else, don't you, Your Grace?" The Healer folded his arms uneasily across his chest so that his empty cuff was hidden. "I don't know how to ask—no, not to ask, but to offer—damn, I don't know what I mean to say!"

"For a beginning, why don't you try calling me Alister," Camber said gently. "I find titles can sometimes be a hindrance, when one wishes to address a friend."

"But, you're an archbishop—" Tavis began.

"No, you yourself have told me that there are no bishops in this chapel," Camber said with a smile. "The Council of Ramos has said so. However, there *are* priests here, regardless of the words of the new archbishop. If it helps, I can assure you that anything you wish to share with me will be held in the strictest of confidence—under the seal of the confessional, if you like."

Tavis plucked at a fold of his sleeve with thumb and forefinger. "It isn't that. I trust you, as far as that's concerned."

"But not where other things are concerned?" Camber said gently. "If you don't, I'll understand. These things take time."

"No, I think I do trust you in that." Tavis looked up at Camber squarely. "I was wrong about you—about all of you. So was Javan. Rhys never lied when he told me we were all fighting on the same side, but I wouldn't believe him until it was almost too late—and it *was* too late for Rhys." He paused to swallow and gather his courage again. "God knows, I've paid for my arrogance and petty suspicions, and made others pay, but I think I really can help now, instead of hinder. I *want* to help; I just don't know how—Alister. . . ."

Slowly, so as not to break the growing rapport, Camber stood away from the altar rail and took a careful step toward Tavis, another, until he was less than an armspan away. Tavis stood, fearful, expectant, yet not retreating. It appeared that the Healer sensed what should come next, but he could not seem to bring himself to initiate it.

With a slow, deliberate blink, Camber purposely stepped-down a little of the rapport—and the tension— allowing a ghost of a smile to curve his lips.

"I'm afraid I have you at a slight disadvantage, Tavis. We Michaelines are trained in the old rituals, the formulae for contacts, as are Gabrilites, and we sometimes assume, erroneously, that all others of high training are, too. But your Healer's training wasn't Gabrilite, was it? And it certainly wasn't Michaeline."

Tavis shook his head sheepishly.

"Varnarite?"

"Yes."

"Ah, that explains much. Their approach tends to be more pragmatic than philosophical—an acceptable variation on the art of Healing," he added, at the beginnings of a defensive expression on Tavis's face, "but it often ignores some of the more subtle nuances which would be useful in a situation like this. Let's see, you would have learned the standard Healer's approaches, but not the secondaries. Correct? You see, after many years of working with Rhys, I am somewhat familiar with the terminology."

Tavis allowed himself a slight nod, and Camber echoed it reassuringly.

"I thought as much. Give me just a moment, will you?"

Without waiting for Tavis's assent, he turned and went inside the altar rail, pausing to reverence the altar before removing one of the smaller candles from its holder. As he returned, he sent a quick command to Joram to keep the others back unless summoned. Then he was standing in front of Tavis once more, holding the unlighted candle in his left hand as he re-engaged Tavis's eyes.

"I'd like to show you an exercise that many Deryni children learn at a very early age," he said softly. "Joram and Jebediah learned it from their fathers, and I suspect that Niallan learned it from his. I, on the other hand, did not learn it until I was a Michaeline novice. The point is, I suppose, that it's never too late to learn something new. Now, this could come under the category of a spell, but it's time you learned that there's nothing to fear in a name." He held the candle a little closer to Tavis. "Put your hand over mine, so that we both hold the candle."

Tavis hesitated for just an instant, then obeyed. His fingers were icy cold, but Camber did not move—simply let Tavis settle for a few seconds, take a few deep breaths which finally began to have an effect.

"Good," Camber whispered, after a few more breaths. "Notice that *you* are the one who will be in control in this working. Your hand is over mine—I'm not holding you in any way. If at any time you begin to be afraid, or feel that you can't bear what we're sharing, feel free to withdraw as much as you need to. I won't be offended. I gather, from some of your reactions, that you've been hurt in the past, and God knows, I don't want to hurt you any more."

Tavis swallowed. "How did you know that?"

"A good guess?" Camber smiled. "You *have* been hurt, though, haven't you? Perhaps in your training?"

"Yes. I was—"

"No need to dwell on it now," Camber murmured, with a slight shake of his head, his voice lulling and soothing as he lifted his right hand to the same level as the other and turned it palm-out, toward Tavis. "We'll just see if we can't ease past that point. There's been more pain since then, too, hasn't there?" he continued, as Tavis's left arm began slowly rising in echo of his own—though he did not think the Healer was aware of that. "You've never resolved the loss, have you? Don't pull back!" he added sharply, but no louder, as Tavis became aware of his handless arm hovering beside Camber's and he drew it away in embarrassment.

"No, I can't—"

"Make the contact," Camber whispered, glancing deliberately at the now-trembling forearm Tavis held clenched against his chest.

Tavis was sweating now, even though it was cold in the chapel at this hour. The Healer's hand on Camber's below the unlit candle gripped like a vise.

"Go ahead, Tavis. Make the contact," Camber said again, gently. "Do you think I'll be disgusted? Do you think the beauty of your soul has been marred by the loss of a mere hand? Think what you still can do with what you have, Tavis. Why, you can do things with one hand and a stump that other men can't do with two good hands and all the armies in the land!"

He had felt Tavis cringe at the word "stump." He was sorry, but denying its existence would not bring back what was lost. Tavis had to accept that. Camber almost held his breath as he stared into Tavis's eyes, desperately willing the Healer to loosen up. He could not help unless Tavis wanted to be helped.

Finally Tavis began to respond. His teeth were still clenched tightly in his jaws, the eyes fixed and staring, but now the arm moved jerkily toward Camber's hand. In the periphery of his vision, Camber could see the tension in the muscles of the lower forearm, where the sleeve fell away from the handless wrist, but he did not allow his gaze to waver from Tavis's unblinking eyes.

The movement seemed to take forever, but finally Tavis made the contact, shoving the stump of his wrist firmly against Camber's palm with a sob and closing his eyes. After a few seconds, the Healer was able to stop most of his trembling and look up again. Camber continued to gaze across at the other man mildly, in all acceptance.

"I know," he whispered. "It was very difficult, wasn't it?"

He had let the fingers of his right hand cup lightly and naturally over the end of Tavis's wrist, supporting yet not confining, and he was encouraged by the perception that the Healer truly had stopped trembling. As Tavis gave a nod, breathing more easily now, and even beginning to relax a little, Camber allowed himself the ghost of an Alister smile.

"Are you feeling better?"

Tavis swallowed and nodded. "A little drained, but not nearly as frightened as before, God alone knows why. Apprehensive, but not really—frightened."

"Good," Camber nodded approvingly, "because there's really nothing to be frightened of. You'll find, I suspect, that it doesn't feel a great deal different from Healing rapport, except, perhaps, for the fact that it's an equal sharing, rather than one person being in control. It may also seem more intense but that depends on you." He raised a bushy Alister eyebrow. "So, do you think you're ready to learn a childhood spell now?"

"I think so."

"Good. Let's take a few deep breaths, then, and center down as if you're preparing to do a Healing. That's right. And when you're ready, *if* you're ever ready—some people never are—you can close your eyes for better concentration. The idea is to let the link form slowly, just a little at a time, so that each new meshing can be examined and digested at your own pace, with you controlling the depth of interaction, but passively—letting it happen, letting it flow."

As he spoke, he could see the Healer's eyelids beginning to flutter, the gaze becoming less intense, more dreamlike, and he knew that Tavis was shifting into his Healer's trance. The level of control was excellent.

"That's good," he continued. "Just let yourself float with me, as far as you want to go. And when you're ready, the spell will go something like this:

"Join hand and mind with mine, my friend. And let the light flare up between our hands when we are one. Let the light flare up between our hands when we are one.

"It's all a mental set, of course," he went on softly. "The words, of themselves, mean nothing. Their essence is what's important—that as our minds join, there will come a point when we are sufficiently in rapport to do useful work—and when that occurs, the light will flare between our hands, as an outward sign that that level has been reached. And it *will* happen. . . ."

Tavis was visibly nodding now, blinking very slowly, his breathing light and moderate. On one of the deep blinks, he did not open his eyes again. When Camber was certain that he was not going to, he closed his own eyes, beginning to reach out just a little across the bond of flesh to search for that other bond.

He brushed the other's shields almost immediately; but to his relief, they began to subside, slowly, tentatively, at first, then with greater confidence, as superficial levels of Tavis's consciousness encountered and accepted Camber's gentle questing out. Camber went carefully, gathering all of his Camber essence back beyond what he intended to share with Tavis and beginning to reveal the Alister aspects, intending to go slowly, gingerly, so as not to startle the Healer.

But then, to his surprise, Tavis lowered every vestige of shielding and subterfuge, in one dizzying surge of blind, submissive trust. On instinct, Camber swept in behind the disintegrating shields, ready to pull out quickly if Tavis started to panic, but then letting himself merge with Tavis's thoughts in a breathless mingling of memories and perceptions.

It was the most nearly perfect rapport Camber could have dreamed of, under the circumstances, approaching that long-ago first contact with Jebediah for sheer ecstasy of psychic communion outside the bonds of blood kin—excellent by the most exacting of standards. He was dazzled, by turns awed and appalled, but all of it was Tavis, and real; and some of the insights he gained into what was developing in Javan positively took his breath away.

The candle held between them had burst alight spontaneously in that first surge of raw awakening; but as the depth of rapport increased, and Tavis began to weave on his feet, the watching Joram came and took the candle away, to keep either of them from being burned—for the candle was the last thing on either man's mind by then.

It was as well as he did, for Tavis's knees buckled shortly after that, voluntary muscle control melting away with his resistance as he settled into even deeper psychic realms, though at least he did not faint away as some people had been known to do at the intensity of such a first encounter. Camber caught him and eased him to the floor, managing not to lose contact or rapport, then settled down beside Tavis and let himself resubmerge. Javan tried to go to them, alarmed at Tavis's apparent collapse, but Jebediah restrained him and tried to explain, guessing what Tavis must be experiencing and remembering his own first rapport with Camber. Tavis, of course, did not know that it was Camber, but the force of Alister Cullen alone was more than sufficient to give Tavis an experience he would never forget.

Camber shared all he could of Alister Cullen, and his relationship with all the others—Joram and Jebediah and Rhys and Evaine, and even Jaffray and Emrys and Queron—giving Tavis the background of their mission over the past twelve years and even projecting the details of the Camberian Council's function and existence—for he sensed instinctively that Tavis should eventually be among their number, and told him so.

He did not share his part in the events of the night of Cinhil's death, or his real identity as Camber, but other than that he opened his mind as fully as his priestly office would allow. Even the pain of Rhys's death was worked through, the guilt and remorse expiated, the grief laid to rest.

One subject it was essential that they explore further, now that Tavis seemed the sole inheritor of Rhys's Deryni-blocking talent, and that was the need of a Healer to work with Revan. Tavis did not exactly volunteer, for he was torn between his loyalty to Javan—the need to aid his prince as long as possible—and the recognition that the Revan movement also presented increasingly important potential to protect a large number of Deryni. However, he did agree to begin working wth Queron to round out his training as a Healer, to take on the search for other Healers who could also learn and, if another Healer had not been found by then, to consider joining Revan when his position with Javan became no longer tenable. It was a precarious balance of *if*s, but without consulting Javan, Tavis did not feel he had the right to make a more definite commitment. Camber had to agree.

Tavis, when he finally opened his eyes, found himself lying flat on his back with a benignly smiling archbishop sitting on one side of him and a worried-looking prince kneeling on the other. Joram crouched beyond Javan, holding a lighted candle and wearing a tight little smile. Jebediah and Niallan stood beyond them, Jebediah looking especially pleased.

"How—how did I get on the floor?" Tavis asked sheepishly.

"You unlocked your knees," Camber said easily. "It's quite common. Some people, like Joram, can go to just about any level while on their feet and even functioning. Others, like Jebediah, go completely limp when they go into trance. I don't know whether it has to do with training, or what. Perhaps there's a physiological difference—rather the way different patients will respond to a Healer's sleep commands. I noticed such variations when I used to work with Rhys."

Tavis seemed to consider that carefully, but without the pain which Rhys's name would have evoked before rapport with Camber. His shields were back in place, but not tightly so. Now there was casual seepage around the edges, so that Camber could constantly catch vague impressions of the direction of Tavis's thought, much as he could do with Joram or Jebediah when in close proximity. He caught Tavis's shift back to contemplation of what had just happened between the two of them and smiled as the Healer glanced up at him incredulously.

"Alister, did we really just do what I think we did?" he whispered.

Slowly Camber nodded, amazed and a little sad that Tavis apparently had never managed to experience that level of rapport before tonight, in all his twenty-five years. He realized now how much he had taken for granted all his life, that there must be many Deryni like Tavis, some of them even highly trained as he was, who had never achieved that awesome sharing which was their birthright.

"You did incredibly well, Tavis," he said with a smile. "I don't know how we managed to miss you all these years, but I think you're going to be an enormous asset to our cause."

"I'll certainly try to be," Tavis returned warmly. "I'm only sorry I fought you for so long."

"What about me?" Javan blurted, brash yet a little fearful as he edged closer on his knees. "I want to help, too! I can, you know."

"Javan!" Tavis chided, sitting up the rest of the way with Camber's help.

"No, it's all right," Camber said, wondering whether he really wanted to cope with Javan, too, after the emotional drain of Tavis. The exchange had been a heady one, and one which he would not have missed, but it had left his equilibrium a bit askew, as so profound an initial rapport often did. Still, if Javan was ready to trust them now, ready to open those impossible shields, this was an opportunity not to be passed up. A quick probe in the direction of Joram and Jebediah revealed that they shared his expectation and backed his reasoning.

"Javan, do you understand what just happened between Tavis and me?" he asked softly.

"I—think so."

"What did happen?"

"Well, you both—let down your shields and you—went into each other's minds?"

Camber nodded. "Essentially, yes. But that's only the most superficial of explanations. Tavis trusted me, and he offered me the knowledge of everything he is, in equal sharing. It's the most intimate gift that two people can share, Javan, for it's the gift of perfect, unquestioning trust and acceptance. One does not give that gift indiscriminately; but when it is given, it must be without reservation, save for details which would violate another's confidence. Can you comprehend that?"

Javan swallowed audibly, wide-eyed with awe, then gave a careful nod.

"*I* have shields, Father Alister," the boy whispered tentatively. "Did Tavis tell you?"

"He did. And that you have learned to raise and lower them at will, just as we can. Have you really?"

Javan stared at Camber uncertainly, glanced at Tavis, back at Camber. For a moment, Camber was sure he was going to back down from what he had begun; but then the boy lowered his eyes shyly and spoke in a whisper.

"Do you want to see? I've—never done it for anyone except Tavis, but I'll try, if you like."

As he looked up at Camber a little fearfully, wanting to trust yet still uncertain whether he dared, Camber still was not sure how or whether he wanted to attempt this tonight. Fortunately, Tavis took the matter out of his hands.

"I have a suggestion, Alister."

"Yes?"

"Well, this is very alien to Javan. If it overwhelmed me, with my training, you can see how it must be doubly frightening to him."

"Are you saying that you don't think he's ready for this?" Camber asked.

"Maybe not for your touch—yet—but he does know mine," the Healer replied. "Why don't we let him lower his shields through me, and then you can establish a light link indirectly."

"Fair enough."

Javan looked visibly relieved at that, and as he settled down cross-legged in front of the Healer, Camber beckoned for Joram to attend him. Joram blew out the candle he was still holding and gave it to Niallan, then took a place between Camber and Javan, resting his hand lightly on Camber's knee. Jebediah came and crouched behind the two of them, leaning an elbow casually on each man's shoulder.

Healer and prince settled quickly, the boy's eyes fluttering closed at a few low words from his mentor. After a few seconds, Tavis laid his hand lightly on Javan's forehead, himself nodding a little as he pushed himself down to working level and established the bond between himself and the boy, then signalled Camber to join the link. Rapport was tenuous this time, for Javan was not yet able to lower his shields very far, or with a great deal of consistency, especially with the link thus expanded, but the boy did have shields: bright, adamantine shields that would have done any Deryni proud.

For just a few seconds, Camber was able to hold the bonding, to see several levels into Javan's mind and perceive a bright, scintillating knot of *something* with tendrils extending outward from it—but then both Tavis's and Javan's control started to slip.

As Tavis withdrew, dissolving the link, he seemed puzzled about the brilliant knot, and looked at Camber in question.

"Do you know what that was?" he asked.

Camber nodded. "Yes, I do. Unfortunately, I can't tell you."

"You can't—does it have something to do with what happened the night his father died?" Tavis guessed, sitting forward avidly as Javan did the same.

Camber raised one unruly eyebrow, thoughtfully linking in with Joram and Jebediah as he considered the question. He could not tell Healer and prince all of what had occurred that night. On the other hand, by all that Tavis had told him of Javan—plus his own observation—the boy had not reacted precisely as they had planned, either. He should not have shields; he should not be spontaneously learning to Truth-Read; and that bright knot of incipient power was something which Camber had not thought to see until and unless Javan became king.

"I may not tell you precisely what happened," he said. "I gave my word to Cinhil, as did the others who were there. I can tell you, however, since you know some of the results already, that what was done has to do with the succession. Cinhil had planned for—certain effects to be manifested in Alroy first. In that, he partially succeeded. The potential is surely there. Unfortunately, the regents have your brother in too firm a hold. I doubt that he will ever use what he was given—and thank God for that, since he has become the regents' tool."

"That isn't his fault!" Javan began hotly.

Camber touched the prince's shoulder reassuringly. "I know it isn't his fault, son. But the fact remains that Alroy is not his own man, and may likely never be. He may not even live to be a man. Rhys was very concerned about his health."

"You mean he may die?" Javan gasped. "Tavis, is that true?"

Sighing, Tavis lowered his eyes. "He's always been sickly, Javan, you know that. I think the regents keep him sedated a good deal of the time, too. You've noticed how he sometimes nods off at Court. There was nothing either of us could do about it, so I didn't tell you. I didn't want you to worry any sooner than you have to."

Stunned, Javan looked from face to face, seeing confirmation even in the kindly Niallan's eyes.

"Is he—going to die because of them?" the boy finally asked. "Are the regents going to kill my brother?"

Camber shook his head. "No. In fact, it's much to the regents' advantage to keep Alroy alive as long as possible. They can control him, where they're not so sure about you. That's one of the many reasons they'd like to get rid of Tavis, too. He encourages you to think and he keeps them from turning you into the same kind of puppet they've made of Alroy. When Tavis is eventually forced to leave, you must be terribly careful. Don't think for a minute that they're fooled by your simple-minded act."

Javan stared at him in silence for a long moment, then looked down at his feet. "You said that what was done to me—had to do with the succession."

"Yes."

"Then, my shields, and the way I'm starting to know whether people are lying—"

"—are part of what should have come to you only if you became king," Camber replied. "You can see the reason for that, I think. If things had gone as your father planned, each of you three boys would have remained unchanged, so far as you were consciously aware, until and unless you came to the throne. Even then, awareness would have come only if there was need. I think your father was trying to set a precedent for the future: that only one Haldane heir should gain—what we gave you—at a time."

"Why has this happened to me, then?" Javan asked.

"Probably the same principle we spoke of earlier," Tavis interjected. "Different people respond differently to the same experiences." He glanced wistfully at Camber. "Alister, I don't suppose that we could just—oh, go ahead and let—whatever it was, run, since he's already discovering a part of it?"

"Do *you* think he's ready for that kind of responsibility?" Camber countered.

Tavis pursed his lips. "He's very young. Still, he's already learned a great deal."

"And will doubtless continue to do so, but better at his own speed. You're welcome to continue working with him and see what you can unbury," Camber said with a slight smile. "I'll be curious to learn how far Cinhil's intentions went awry. And it will be good practice for Javan, who has shields, and is learning to Truth-Read anyway," he concluded, tousling the boy's hair almost playfully.

They spoke for yet a little while longer, but Camber would reveal nothing further about Javan's magical destiny. They cemented plans and discussed alternatives of action for keeping both Javan and Tavis safe, and by the time Camber was ready to send them back through the Portal to Valoret, he was much heartened. Their immediate value was limited by Javan's youth, but it would increase in the months and years ahead, as each day brought Javan closer to legal age and, almost certainly, to the Crown. In the meantime, both of them would keep as innocuous a profile as possible, especially the Deryni Tavis, and try to avoid provoking the regents to drastic action. Tavis would begin exploring ways to work with Queron and, eventually, with Revan.

When the two had gone, and the Portal had been reset, Camber made further plans with Joram and Jebediah and Niallan.

"This news of the arrest warrants on all of us concerns me more than I indicated to Tavis," Camber said, pacing back and forth in Niallan's study. "I'm especially fearful for Evaine's safety now. It's bad enough that she must have sensed Rhys's death, and has no one really close to turn to in this time of need, but if she might be pursued, in addition. . . ."

"Alister, I don't think anyone from Valoret could catch up with her," Niallan said. "She's had five days' start. Besides, she has Ansel and Queron with her."

"I know. And you're probably right. But she doesn't know that she was definitely a fugitive now. It could make a difference."

Niallan shook his head. "What difference? Could it make her run the harder? She still has the children with her, Alister, and two to rescue, and another yet unborn. Don't you think she'll fight to keep them free? Joram, she's your sister. You probably know her best of all of us. Tell Alister that she knows what she's doing."

"She knows," Joram said, with a wan smile and a nod. None of them had been able to reach her since Rhys's death—though shock and distance could easily account for that. They were certain she was not dead. . . .

"She's probably all right," Jebediah agreed. "And while knowledge of the warrants *might* be useful, it might also just make her the more anxious. Besides, even if we wanted to intercept her, there are half a dozen routes that she could be taking between Valoret and Trurill— and from there, at least a handful more to Saint Mary's —which makes it difficult for us, but no easier for would-be pursuers. They might guess she'd go to Trurill for the boys, but Saint Mary's?" He shook his head. "You did a good job when you purged the diocesan files, Alister. I doubt that more than a dozen folk outside the immediate area even remember that there's an abbey called Saint Mary's in the Hills—much less remember where it is."

"You're probably right," Camber sighed. "And unfortunately, Dhassa is just too far to try to make concontact, even if she were expecting it. Maybe one of us should be at Saint Mary's to meet her when she arrives, though. If we could gain access to a Portal in the area, it could be done. Joram, you're the most familiar with Cor Culdi. I doubt that Hubert's brother could have tampered with the Portal there, if he even knew where to look for it. Provided that he hasn't, could a man get in and then get out alive?"

"*I* could," Joram replied, sharing Camber's uneasiness. "Is that what you want me to do?"

Slowly Camber nodded. "I think so. Much as I hate to send you off alone, someone needs to go. We also need a Portal at Saint Mary's, so we'll have another safe access to the *keeill*. You could begin setting up to construct it with Ansel and Queron, as soon as they arrive. I don't think you should count on Evaine's help until after the baby is born. The three of you can do it, can't you?"

"If we draw on Aidan and Camlin and a few of the

more discreet brethren to fill out the power component, yes. The boys are old enough."

"All right, then. I think there's time to get this started tonight. It's still a two-day ride from Cor Culdi to Saint Mary's, so you're going to have to move if you hope to get there before she does. Jeb, we'll need the plainest harness you can find for him—black, if we have a choice. Niallan, try to find him some good, lightweight provisions that he can carry without being weighted down. I don't want him having to stop at public inns. Joram, I want to work with you until they get back, so we can establish a long-range link for contact at set times. I wish we'd had time to do that with Evaine, but —no matter. Are you game?"

Joram smiled, knowing the flurry of activity was at least partially designed to take his father's mind off his anxiety.

"You still manage to think of everything, don't you?"

Chapter Twenty-Nine

But these two things shall come to thee in a moment in one day, the loss of children and widowhood: they shall come upon thee in their perfection for the multitude of thy sorceries, and for the great abundance of thine enchantments.

—Isaiah 47:9

The week had been interminable for Evaine, all but a few short hours at the beginning bleak and numb with loss. She had known Rhys was in danger when she left her beloved Sheele on Christmas Eve. She had feared for him as Joram told her of the destruction of Saint Neot's and helped them to pack. Rhys had gone to Javan's aid, but Evaine knew he had not trusted Tavis. The situation appeared to be fast approaching a crisis point. God alone knew whether they would all survive.

But she could not let herself be paralyzed by fear or indecision. Nor could she rely on husband, father, or brother to see her through this crisis. She counted it a miracle that Joram had even been able to come and warn her in person, especially after what he and their father had witnessed at Saint Neot's. They were doing their best to protect those entrusted to their care; she must see to the safety of those within her charge.

The servants at Sheele would not long be safe in Deryni employ, she decided. Accordingly, she paid and dismissed most of them, then left a favored few the gift of the manor, for she was fairly certain she would never be back. Four loyal young men-at-arms she kept in service—bachelors, all, for she would not risk others' families in what might lie ahead. The children were bundled in their warmest clothes, precious keepsakes hidden away beneath Sheele's Portal with a few of the scrolls she had been meaning to return to the *keeill,* and then the Portal was locked and sealed to all but those of blood relation. The few sumpter horses they allowed themselves must carry food for their journey, for they dared not stop at inns.

In addition, unbeknownst to Joram, she sent Queron into the hills to find and warn Revan of what was happening, for she could not bear to let that loyal friend of so many years merely pine away in solitude, waiting faithfully for orders which never came. She assured Queron that she would be safe; her child was not due for another month. Queron was uneasy about leaving her, but finally he obeyed. He did not know that she had not told Joram he was going.

Her apprehension about Rhys did not diminish during the night, but by midday she seemed to sense an easing. In the sunshine after lunch, she had been laughing with her daughter as they rode along, she on a favorite bay palfrey and Rhysel cantering happily on her matching pony beside one of the younger guards. The baby Tieg was perched in front of Ansel, who had shed his clerical attire in favor of mail, leather, and a sword; the child chortled with glee as he tried to count the sumpter horses following their train, though he could not get past three without giggling. Death was the last thing Evaine was prepared for on this sunny Christmas afternoon.

His end had not been sudden, she realized; only her realization that he was dying. The knowledge struck her like a physical blow, driving her breath from her lungs and almost making her lose her seat in that first instant of stark awareness. She pulled up sharply on the palfrey's reins and clung to the velvet covered pommel, her face ashen. Ansel immediately thrust the protesting Tieg into the arms of one of the guards and raced to her side.

"What's wrong? Is it the baby?"

"No—Rhys!" she managed to gasp.

Frantic, terrified that she had lost him already, she thrust herself down into trance and tried to search her senses for his plight—winced under the sharp, skull-crushing blow which had rendered him instantly unconscious, followed the gradual ebbing of all other sensation around him, a slipping into darkness where even she could not follow.

An odd, wrenching sensation twisted her orientation even as she tried to touch him. Then he was even farther away—Dhassa?—and slipping farther than mere physical distance, and she could only catch a faint echo of her father's anguish, her brother's, even of Jebediah's—but no longer any more of *his*.

She blinked and looked up, amazed that the sun still shone coin-bright in the winter sky, and saw by Ansel's stricken expression that he, too, had felt something of her shock. Then she buried her face in her hands and wept.

She remembered little, felt little, in the next few days. Later, she would recall riding endlessly, eating tasteless food when it was placed in her hands, and falling into deep, troubled sleep when they would bed down for the night.

Times there were, especially in the beginning, when all of them would race wildly down a snow-choked road, throwing up great gouts of ice and mud; and other times when they would sit their horses in some forest stillness, seemingly for hours, and Ansel would become very nervous if anyone coughed or a horse whinnied.

After a few days, the wild rides and forest waitings ceased, and they saw few travellers. Snow fell nearly every night, which slowed them, but kept others off the roads, for the most part. In those early days of her bereavement, she hardly spoke or made a move which Ansel did not direct. Ansel, fearing for her safety and the unborn child's, if she should fall in her condition, managed to obtain a covered, two-horse litter for her to ride in. It was not until dusk on Monday, the last day of the year, that she at last began to be aware of her surroundings again.

She apologized for her withdrawal over supper that night, playing a little with the children and, after they dozed, querying Ansel and the men-at-arms for news while they all huddled around a well-shielded campfire. But when she learned that they were but a few hours from Trurill and her son, she bade them press on. Taking the children into her litter, she lulled them to sleep with a song and the gentle, swaying motion of the conveyance as they journeyed on, later unbraiding her golden hair and brushing it loose down her back as her Aidan liked to see it. The guards had taken up brands to light their way, and their torchlight cast a glaring, ruddy glow on the new-fallen snow.

They were within an hour of dawn, with russet streaks beginning to finger upward from the eastern horizon behind them, when they made the turnoff toward Trurill. But now, as they approached the castle itself, it was as if another dawn stained the sky *before* them. As they topped the rise before descending into the rich, narrow valley which was the castle's demesne, Evaine held aside the curtains of the litter and peered aghast at the flames licking upward on the early morning breeze. Trurill Castle was burning!

With a gasp, she pulled herself to a sitting position and swung her feet to the ground. Ansel, sitting his horse uncomfortably at the side of the litter, squinted at the burning structure uncertainly, then leaned down in alarm to take Evaine's arm and steady her as she lurched to her feet beside the litter.

"Evaine, have a care!"

Shakily, she clung to his stirrup leather, her face terrible in the torchlight, her hair rising like a halo on the wind.

"Aidan is down there!" she cried, past tears already in the stillness of her horror. "Ansel, we must find him! They wouldn't hurt him, would they? He's just a little boy."

But she knew, as she said the words, that her son's youth would have made no difference to marauders. If prisoners had been their goal, then there was a chance that Aidan was still alive, even though she could not sense him with her mind. But if the raid had been a retaliatory one, then they would have spared no living thing—family, servants, animals—nothing!

For what seemed an eternity they stood there, she and Ansel both searching with their Sight for any remaining marauders. Thomas, who was hardly older than Ansel, left his torch with one of his fellows and rode quietly down into the valley. He was gone for some time. When he returned, his face was pale, his leggings and boot darkened along one side where, by the look and smell, he had been sick. He did not want to meet her eyes as he drew rein before her and the others crowded near.

"Well?" she whispered. "Are they all gone? Is it safe to go down?"

The man swallowed noisily and looked as if he might be sick again.

"My lady, don't go down there. It's no fit place. It's nothing you want to see."

Slowly Evaine went rigid, hardly daring to ask further yet unable not to.

"Did you find my son?" she asked. "Did you find Aidan?"

"Please, my lady, don't go. They were butchers who came to Trurill."

"And Aidan?" Evaine insisted, striding to his horse and laying her hand on the reins as she stared up at him.

The man bowed his head, a sob catching in his throat. "I couldn't tell, my lady. It was too dark to see faces. Mercifully, too dark."

With a little whimper of dread, she seized his near boot and pulled it out of the stirrup. "Get off. Give me your horse. And stay here with the children until we send it's safe."

As she spoke, the man was obeying, jumping off the animal on the other side and scurrying around to make a stirrup of his clasped hands. Ansel gaped at her, shocked, and urged his horse closer.

"Evaine, is this wise, in your condition? The child—"

"What of my other child, my firstborn?" she countered, struggling to raise her bulk into the saddle and settling there with a sigh of relief. "Aidan may be down there. And if he is, he may still be alive. I have to find out."

With a shake of his head, Ansel grabbed a torch from one of the guards and moved out in front of her. "All right. Thomas, you and Arik stay here with the litter and the sumpter horses. You can begin moving down into the valley as soon as it's a little more light, but don't bring the children inside until I tell you it's all right."

Thomas, who had no desire to see the castle again, nodded vigorously. "Aye, m'lord. You don't want these little ones to see what's down there."

The children, seven-year-old Rhysel and the baby Tieg, peered sleepily out of the litter, and Evaine blew each of them a kiss.

"Stay here with Thomas and Arik, darlings," she said tightly. "They'll bring you to Mummy as soon as they can."

Young Rhysel, golden-haired and wise for all her seven years, gazed up at her mother guilelessly. "Are you going to look for Aidan, Mummy? I don't think he's down there."

"We'll see, Rhysel," she managed to murmur, though her heart sank at the implication of her daughter's words.

Then, with a slight wave to the children, she was gathering the reins of Thomas's chestnut in her cold-numbed hands and kicking the animal into a painful trot down the slope to the valley below, Ansel scurrying to get in front of her in case her horse should slip. Behind them came the other two attendants, each bearing his torch, the four of them making a tight little knot of shadow and fading brightness as they picked their way down the hillside far faster than it was safe to go.

The first light of true dawn was just beginning to stain the snow around the castle as they approached the gatehouse, but already they could see some of the previous day's gruesome work. Outside the walls, six or eight mail-clad bodies lay in silent, snow-shrouded heaps where they had been thrown off the castle walls to die on the rocks below. Amid the splintered floes of ice in the moat, several more bodies floated just below the surface, and in one place a bloated face was lodged beneath a clear patch of ice, the eyes open and staring in death. Evaine controlled a shudder and pulled her cloak more closely around her as she urged her horse to take its first steps onto the lowered drawbridge.

The attackers had burned the castle, in addition to their other bloody work. Timbers of the guardroom above the gatehouse had collapsed in a still-smouldering tangle, nearly blocking one half of the gateway, but it was inside that the fire had done its major work. The roof of the tower keep and great hall were still smouldering, and the barracks, which had been built of timber against one curtain wall, was nothing but a charred heap of support beams, and still burning. The barracks door, barred from the outside, still stood in its jamb, mute evidence of the fate of those who had been inside. Bodies dotted the castleyard, each given a merciful shroud of new snow during the night, but the snow had not been able to cover the cloying stench of burned flesh hanging heavy in the air, or the scent of blood.

With grim determination, Ansel swung down from his horse and began checking the closest bodies, the hand on the hilt of his sword increasingly white-knuckled as he and the two guards found death after death, each more grisly than the last.

Several of the men had been stripped and dragged behind horses, so that there was scarcely an unbroken bone or a scrap of skin intact on the cold, bloody bodies. A venerable, silver-haired old priest had had his hands and feet cut off and his eyes gouged out, and had been left to die of blood loss in the snow—which was, perhaps, one of the more merciful forms of death.

In the kitchen yard, Ansel came upon the bodies of two servant girls who had been raped and then split open from crotch to breastbone with swords. One of them had been big with child, and the dead infant lay in a pool of congealed blood beside its mother, nearly cut in two by the same blow which had ended her life.

He was violently ill at that, retching repeatedly onto the snow until there was nothing more in his stomach to vomit up. As he regained control of his rebellious gut, wiping his face with a handful of clean snow to try to clear his head, he thought he had seen the worst. Then he spotted a thin young form standing more or less upright in the yard before the stable. Somehow he knew it was Aidan, even from that distance and in the dim light.

He whipped off his cloak and managed to wrap the small, naked body in its folds before Evaine saw him, to ease the pathetic little form from the stake which had impaled it and lay the boy out on a clean patch of snow. Only the face was unmarred, the pale golden hair riffling slightly in the cold morning breeze which began to rise even as Evaine fell heavily to her knees beside her son. Though the eyes were closed, at least sparing her that, the body was frozen in the configuration of its terrible death, the white skin of chest and limbs criss-crossed with the marks of the scourging he had suffered before his murderers went on to other sport. From this angle, Evaine could not see the damage done by the stake, but Ansel was not quick enough to place his body between her and the implement of her son's death, and he saw her blanch as she glanced at the bloody wooden upright and saw the slick of his blood frozen around the base.

He could not bear to look at her as she bent over the boy, her golden hair shifting like a pale, metallic curtain around them as she took the still-beautiful face between her hands and stared at the closed eyes. Still fighting down a terrible sickness of heart as well as of body, he looked away, another part of him wondering why Aidan had been done to death in this manner, and here, in the stableyard.

Then, in the shadows at the entry to what had been the stables, he saw why. Stunned, his jaw working convulsively in his effort to maintain control, he rose and crossed slowly to the stable doorway. Now he knew what had happened to Adrian MacLean.

If the captors of the castle had been brutal with Aidan and the castle's garrison, they had been savage with the castle's lord. They had beaten him, like Aidan, but that was the very least of the atrocities to which they had subjected poor Adrian. He had been stripped and flogged, branded with hot irons over a great deal of his torso, and even his eyelids deftly removed so that he must see every further act of wanton cruelty to the bitter end. They had tied ropes around his wrists and ankles and lashed him to the uprights of the stable entrance, hoisting him off his feet so that he hung spreadeagled a few feet off the ground. Whether they had castrated him before or after opening his belly to let his innards spill out, Ansel could not tell.

In a terrible flash of insight, he guessed at their intentions: degradation and torture for the lord of the castle, both in his own person and by being forced to watch the torture and slow death of the boy they had taken for his son—for Aidan and the still-missing Camber MacLean were similar enough in appearance to be brothers rather than cousins.

With a hoarse cry of outrage, he crossed the remaining steps to the stable entrance and drew his sword, to begin hacking at the ropes which bound Adrian's ankles and wrists. When the last rope was severed, and the frozen corpse fell to the bloody ground below, he turned and raced back to where Evaine still knelt with the body of her dead son cradled against her swollen abdomen and began hacking at the stake, his breath sobbing in his lungs, until the stake was chopped in two and lay in a pile of wood chips and blood-reddened snow. Then he sank to his knees and wept, his hands braced on the quillons of the sword and his head bowed in bitter grief.

When he looked up, Evaine was recovered sufficiently to begin looking around dazedly. Bartholomew, the oldest of their men-at-arms, had removed his cloak and spread it over Adrian's body. Damon, the other guard, was checking a pair of corpses lying near the ruined gatehouse, but then Ansel saw him look up at the raised portcullis and freeze for just an instant, then scramble to his feet and gaze upward into the shadows with a look of new horror on his face.

"Lord Ansel!" the man's cry came, almost strangled in its emotion.

Ansel lurched to his feet and ran to Damon's side, following his upturned gaze high among the smouldering beams of the collapsed guardroom floor. A pair of naked legs dangled, the toes flexing jerkily on one bruised and bloody foot. Up a little higher, he thought he could see a small white hand outstretched at an odd angle, the fingers cramped and clawlike and also twitching.

With a bellow for Bartholomew to attend them, Ansel began scrambling over the smouldering debris of the fallen timbers, accepting a leg up from Damon as he climbed. He reached a point where he could swing up on the portcullis, using its wooden crossbars as a ladder; but as he drew nearer to what he had seen from the ground, he almost faltered in his climb.

Vaguely he was aware of Damon and Bartholomew watching from below, of Evaine joining them, her face upturned in dumb amazement, but he dared pay them no more attention than that, for there *was* life above him, tenuously held, but there.

The marauders had crucified Camlin MacLean, Adrian's son. Ansel might not have recognized him, had he not known the boy so well from summers spent at the same family retreats. They had nailed him to the portcullis, hammering heavy spikes through the slim wrists and into the dense timber backing of the portcullis grid, before hoisting it aloft and setting the gatehouse afire.

And of course, before that, they had stripped and beaten him and perhaps committed other atrocities upon his young body that Ansel could not see, though he could guess at what might have been done.

There the marauders had left him to die, barely standing on tiptoe on one crossbar of the portcullis until fatigue should force his legs to give way and the full weight of his body hang suspended from his arms, gradually to collapse the chest and suffocate him.

But they had not reckoned on the action of the fire in the gatehouse above, sending the timbers crashing down around their victim, and they had not reckoned on young MacLean's massive will to live. For somehow the boy had managed to swing his left leg up and over one of the fallen beams, to support the bulk of his weight there instead of on his arms, and to brace the other knee against a second beam. The pain must have been excruciating, for he would have had to dangle with his full weight on his arms until he could work up enough swing to gain the support of the fallen beams, and every tiny movement would have been agony.

There would have been danger of burning, too, though the fire did not seem to have gotten terribly near. In fact, the warmth from the fire was probably what had thus far saved the boy from dying of exposure. What a miracle of coincidences seemed to have conspired to save at least this one young life amid the other carnage!

Ansel gained the boy's side and touched the bruised forehead, probed, felt the answering, groggy response of dim awareness. With a few orders snapped to the men waiting below, he sent Bartholomew to find tools for somehow removing the nails from the boy's wrists, while Damon came aloft to locate the portcullis mechanism and slowly begin lowering the grille to the ground. Working quickly, Ansel cleared away as much as he could of the debris that might interfere with the smooth descent of the portcullis, finally hooking one arm through the grillework and supporting the boy's body with the other.

The boy moaned and passed out fully as his weight was shifted, but Ansel knew that it was for the best. It took nearly a quarter hour to free him, once the portcullis reached ground level. By the time they had wrapped him in Damon's cloak and Bartholomew had carried him into the lee of a wall, out of the wind, he had begun to regain feverish consciousness. Evaine had torn strips from the edge of her under-shift while they worked to get him down, and had bandaged the mutilated wrists, but blood was soaking through. While Bartholomew stripped down to his tunic and held the cold little body close against his chest for warmth, Ansel and Damon began rubbing the boy's legs and upper arms in an attempt to restore circulation. Evaine knelt beside them and gently touched the boy's brow, but he tossed his head and nearly threw off her hands.

"Can you help him?" Ansel asked, laying another cloak over the boy's bruised and blood-streaked torso.

"I don't know," she replied. "He has a great will to live, but I'm not a Healer. Camlin, can you hear me? Camlin, listen to me," she insisted, as the swollen eyelids flickered open and then were closed almost immediately with the pain of returning consciousness.

Damon unstoppered a water flask and held it up, and she nodded.

"Just a little for now, Camlin," she whispered, bracing herself to reach out with her mind and take hold of the pain as the boy managed several tortured swallows.

Camlin gave a few pathetic whimpers, but slowly he began to relax under Evaine's touch and she knew that she was getting through, that there still remained a will to help, as well as a will to live. More forcefully, she reached out and intensified her hold on the edges of his mind, nodding a little in confirmation as his shields slipped a little further and he responded.

"Camlin, can you hear me?" she whispered. "Is the pain a little less?"

Slowly, painfully, the boy opened his eyes—eyes so like Aidan's—his breathing ragged and tentative from the strain of overtaxed chest muscles, but apparently with his discomfort at least a little controlled.

"Aunt Evaine," he managed to croak. "Can you make it stop hurting? Is Uncle Rhys here?"

With a pang of grief, Evaine shook her head slightly. "No, he can't be here right now, Camlin. I'll do what I can for you, though. Do you think you can go a little deeper into trance for me? We've got to clean your wounds, and it's going to hurt much more unless you can really let me take control. Will you let me do that?"

As the boy gave a little nod and closed his eyes, she pushed her link with him, feeling his shields yield and drop in obedience to her touch. Gently she eased him into deep, painless sleep, such as any skilled non-Healer might command with the patient's assent, then slowly began unwrapping the wounded wrist nearest her. Bartholomew, who still held the boy in his lap, turned his head away as blood began to flow again.

Ansel had gotten the little medical kit from his saddle and was opening a small flask of the pungent green fluid which Rhys used to clean wounds. He shook his head as he handed her a square of linen saturated with the fluid.

"Is it really any use?" he asked despairingly. "Can he possibly live, other than as a useless cripple? Look at the angle of his hand. Those nails just tore him up."

Biting her lip, and not wanting to accept that he was probably right, Evaine began swabbing out the wounded wrist, probing with cautious fingertips into the wounds themselves, where fresh blood pulsed from both openings faster than her cloths could blot it up. It was not until she had changed blood-soaked bandages several times, and had about decided that she could do little else than that to help his wrist, when she became aware of what was almost a ghost-brush of a presence. She glanced aside to see three-year-old Tieg peering owlishly at Camlin over her right shoulder.

"Tieg! Oh, for heaven's sake, you're supposed to be asleep!"

As she glanced at Damon, who was still chafing Camlin's cold feet and legs, she sighed and pressed her fingers firmly over the wounds on either side of Camlin's wrist, ignoring the blood which continued to stream down her own hands.

"Damon, take him back to the litter, please. He's too young for this."

"No! Not too young!" Tieg protested, clutching his mother's arm and clinging even more doggedly when Damon started trying to dislodge him. "No! Tieg help!"

Again, Evaine felt that odd prickling at the edge of her mind, a presence *like* Rhys's, but not his.

Tieg?

Startled, she shook her head for Damon to let go, then looked at little Tieg more intently. The boy stopped squirming and immediately slipped his chubby arms around his mother's neck, delivering a moist kiss to her cheek.

"Tieg help Mummy," he informed her gravely, hazel eyes meeting her blue ones in a forthright gaze. "We fix

Camlin, huh, Mummy? We fix, like Daddy does." The surge of accompanying Healer's energy, unfocused and untrained but nonetheless present, almost made her think they could.

Was it truly possible?

She realized she had been holding her breath, and she let it out slowly. It was worth a try.

"All right, darling. You can help Mummy. You hug Mummy's arm tight and watch Camlin and think about helping him. All right?"

"I do it," he said simply, shifting around to peer over her shoulder, chin settling dreamily against her upper arm.

Against all logic, she quested for the Healing paths and found them, drew her son into ever deepening rapport, felt out the same kind of link she had forged so often with Rhys in his Healing work. Against all logic, she felt the Healing energies stir in response to her touch!

The sensation was like what she had felt a thousand times, over the years, as she worked with Rhys. Only this was her direction and Tieg's power; she was a conduit of control and guidance through which the Healing energies were ready to flow. They *could* do it!

She knew that Ansel and the servants were staring at her, but she paid them no mind. She shifted Camlin's wrist in her hands and boldly pressed her fingertip into the bloody entry wound, while her son looked on in confident fascination. She felt the increased flow of blood around her fingertip, hot and vital with life; the hard reality of the bones of wrist and arm; the ligaments and tendons torn by the nail which had rent the flesh and forced the bones apart—and Tieg's amazed observation of all of this, clinical, but with all a child's naïveté and trust in the ability of his mother to make everything right. She shifted a portion of her mind and felt Tieg's energy flowing through her fingertip and into the wound —Healing energy, of the same kind which had been Rhys's and was now their son's.

She moved the wrist with her other hand and felt the bones shift back into place, sensed the flesh and sinews mending under her very touch as she slowly drew her fingertip out of the wound and it closed behind her retreat. She turned the wrist and drew her fingertip through the exit wound on the back of the forearm, and it, too, closed. Some faint scarring he would have to remind him of his ordeal, besides the scarring of mind which would take other Healing, for she had not the skill to Heal him as cleanly as Rhys could have done, but at least the bones were knit, the angry wounds closing.

Ansel had watched her and Tieg in amazement during the first part of the operation, but as he realized what they were doing, he unwrapped the other wrist and swabbed it as clean as he could for their next attention. Now she touched those wounds and Healed them, too; laid her bloody hands on the striped and stretched chest to ease the strain of muscles pulled almost to the point of collapse; erased the marks of the scourge.

The demand on her concentration was becoming very intense, and she was aware of the drain on Tieg's energy, as well; but when she bade Bartholomew shift the unconscious Camlin in his arms so that she might assess the damage to his other side, and would have let it Heal on its own, Tieg gave her a deeply reproachful look.

Smiling despite her fatigue, Evaine eased the weals on Camlin's back and buttocks, on the lean, well-muscled legs, then washed his blood from her hands and reached out with what little strength remained to touch his memory, blurring the details of what had happened until he should reach a time and place in which he might deal with them. When she had finished, her patient slept more easily, wrapped in the warmth of several cloaks. Tieg was curled up at her side, also asleep once the physical Healing was done, with a thumb in his pink mouth and a beatific expression on his freckled face. Gently she disengaged from her son's mind, gathering him in her arms to hold him in mindless gratitude before giving him over to Damon to return to the litter. As Bartholomew took the now peacefully slumbering Camlin, Evaine sat back on her heels with a sigh, easing the small of her back with both hands. As she relaxed her own controls, she felt a little shudder in her womb, and then a quick but strong cramp. She tensed, but the pain was almost too quickly gone.

"Are you all right?" Ansel asked, taking her arm in alarm as he saw the pain flash across her face.

Quickly she assessed her condition, then nodded tentatively.

"Seem to be. I think my other Healer-child was protesting the strain on her mother. She's done that before. When Tavis lost his hand, I was only a few months

pregnant, but I had to leave the room where Tavis was.
I guess she didn't like his disharmony."

Ansel signalled Thomas and Arik to come in with the
litter, then sent Damon and Bartholomew to search for
any other survivors in the keep while he scouted the rest
of the yard.

After a while, Bartholomew and Damon returned with
an armful of heavy cloaks and blankets and the body of
a thin, white-haired old woman, simply but richly clad.
There was no mark upon her; she might have died in her
sleep, so composed was the expression on her face. As
Damon laid her on one of the blankets which Bartholomew spread, Evaine came and stood beside her.

"Aunt Aislinn, my father's sister," she said in a low
voice. "Where did you find her, Damon?"

"In the solar at the top of the keep, my lady. The
room had been breached, but they never touched her. I
can only think she must have died from the smoke, before they broke in."

"Or else her heart just stopped," Evaine murmured.
"She could have chosen that way, knowing death was
near, and the form it might take."

She shook her head and drew a fold of blanket across
the old woman's face. "She was the Dowager Countess of
Kierney, Damon—grandmother to the castle's lord and a
very great lady. Are you sure you found no trace of any
other noble ladies? Lord Adrian's wife and sister should
have been here, since Aislinn and the children were."

"We've found nothing yet, my lady. Do you want me
to keep looking?"

She did, but before she could tell him so, she glanced
around the yard to see whether Ansel needed him. Ansel was checking on the litter, which had been drawn up
in an angle of the inner wall that would afford no view of
the carnage if the children woke and sneaked a look between the curtains. Arik, Bartholomew, and Thomas
were piling up unburned timbers and other combustibles
in the center of the yard. She stared at them for several
seconds before their intention registered.

"Ansel, what are they going to do?" she gasped, running to his side as fast as she could in her condition and
grabbing his arm.

"I told them to do it, Evaine. We can't take our dead
with us, we can't bury them in the frozen earth, and we

can't just leave them here for the wolves and the elements. It's cleanest this way, under the circumstances."

She knew he was right, but she could not keep the tears from starting again. Blindly she stumbled to where her firstborn's body lay still wrapped in Ansel's cloak, knelt and uncovered the still-beautiful face to stroke the fair hair off the smooth, untroubled brow. Like this, with his tortured body hidden from her sight and only the angelic face to meet her gaze, she could almost believe that he had died at peace like Aislinn.

She clasped her hands and tried to pray, longing for the presence of father or brother to add their prayers to hers to speed Aidan on his way, and wishing that there could be something more than a funeral pyre to mark the passage of all these victims of senseless brutality, but she knew that was not possible. This time, her blessing must suffice—and who better to give her son farewell than the one who had borne him, nursed him, taught him, loved him, and now must let him go? She could not even begrudge the fact that young Camlin lived, while her son had died—for anyone who had survived what Camlin had, deserved his life.

She prayed then, and bade him Godspeed, and by the time Ansel came to take the boy and lay him on the pyre, she could stand aside and watch dry-eyed as her nephew lifted the small, blanket-wrapped form, knowing that it was but a broken shell, that Aidan was not there.

They laid Adrian and Aislinn on either side of him—MacRorie kin all, although of different names—and then she joined her hand and mind with Ansel's to start the cleansing blaze.

She thought herself well in control until another cramp rippled up her abdomen and she felt the warm, familiar rush of her water breaking. The snow beneath her feet took on a pinkish hue.

She gasped with the surprise of it, though she knew well what it was; and now a frightened human urgency began to supplant the cool Deryni sorceress. The baby would be born within a few hours, almost a full month early, and there was nothing she could do to stop it. They were stranded in this ruin of death and torture now until she could deliver. And for this birth, she would have no gentle Rhys to ease her labor and Heal her pains, nor even a midwife to attend her. She wondered whether Ansel or any of the other men had ever even seen a baby born.

The men lost no time in finding her shelter. She would not go into what was left of the stable, with Adrian's blood still frozen on the snow outside, and they would not let her stay within sight of the funeral pyre still sending its greasy column of smoke upward on the morning breeze. They finally compromised on an alcove underneath the kitchen stair, which could be curtained off with blankets and made reasonably secure from the cold, for snow had begun to fall again.

A small fire was built, and the litter unhitched from the horses and brought inside, but Rhysel was awake and hungry, impatient to be allowed out. Evaine could not permit that, of course, but she did visit with her daughter while she ate breakfast, and had Ansel wake Camlin and Tieg long enough for them to eat a little, too, before sending all three children back to sleep inside the litter.

Evaine settled down to the business of labor then, losing track of the time as her pains grew closer together and the morning wore on. Ansel stayed with her most of the time, trying to absorb a little background on basic child delivery between her pains. The guards continued the grisly business of bringing the rest of the dead to the pyre. All through the morning Evaine could hear the crackle of the flames as they consumed each new offering.

It was near noon when the guards' voices took on a different note, and then Arik came bursting into the enclosure without even pausing to ask permission.

"My lady, my lady, look what we've found! They were hiding in the middens!"

She could have wept for joy to see the two dirty, bedraggled women who came into view behind Arik. They were her missing kinswomen. Fiona, small and dark and quick, gave a little cry and threw herself across the enclosure into Evaine's arms, shaking her head and laughing as if she could not believe what she saw. Mairi, wife to the slain Adrian, stood silently beside Bartholomew and let him support her arm, her gaze distant and unfocused, even when Fiona finally came and led her gently to a little stool beside Evaine. Evaine did not have to ask what Mairi had seen.

The men went out gratefully then, to continue with

their work and to keep watch, and Evaine and Fiona passed the time by talking. While Fiona washed herself and the compliant Mairi of the stench of the middens and changed both their clothes for dry ones which Ansel soon brought, she told Evaine of how she and Mairi had watched the horror of the day before from their solar window, then had managed to climb down a garde-robe shaft after the attackers torched the keep. The spunky old Countess Aislinn, too infirm to navigate the narrow space with them, had volunteered to stay and cover their absence, if the marauders gained the solar room before the fire did—for they had heard the screams of the men trapped in the barracks below, and knew that it was only a matter of time before the flames reached them, as well. The two of them had huddled in the middens all that terrible night, praying that they would not be discovered; and sometime during those awful hours, Mairi had withdrawn into her grief.

All afternoon Evaine's labor continued, as Ansel and the guards kept watch outside, and Fiona kept Evaine talking about Healing Camlin and her love for Rhys and anything else she could contrive to keep her mind from the pain. Always before, Evaine had had Rhys to speed her labor and ease its discomfort; this time she must let nature take its course. By the time the baby was born, just at dusk, both mother and newborn daughter were exhausted. Ansel let them rest until it was fully dark and made everyone eat a substantial meal; but then he had to insist that they move on.

With Evaine in the litter with Tieg and the baby, Rhysel on her pony, and Camlin and the two other women mounted before Ansel and two of the guards, they set out from Trurill at last. All through the night and into the day they rode, twice avoiding patrols of the new Earl of Culdi's men and stopping only to feed and water the horses and rotate riders. Toward dusk, however, Ansel realized that they had picked up an escort, far back on the road.

He did not tell Evaine of it, but she knew. She reached back with her mind and sensed their cold, brutal presence, somehow knowing them to be of the same ilk as the men who had tortured and killed her son. She hated them, and was impotent in her hate, drained as she was by the Healing of Camlin and the birth of her child. Ansel pushed on, but the road worsened as the light faded, and now he began to worry in earnest, for their pursuers were gaining, slowly but inexorably, and the litter was slowing them greatly. As they slowed even more for the litter-bearing horses to negotiate a particularly treacherous down-hill section of the road, slick with mud and ice, Ansel drew rein alongside the litter and put out a hand to steady it. Evaine's face, as she drew aside the curtains and peered up at him, was pale and gaunt-looking.

"They're gaining on us, aren't they?" she asked.

"I hoped you hadn't noticed," he said.

With a deep breath, she assessed her condition and decided that she just might be able to sit a horse now. It seemed their best chance to lose their pursuers, and this might be their only opportunity. With all of them on horseback, and pushing hard, there were several narrower tracks which they might take from here which would get them to the safety of the monastery by dawn or a little later. But they must lose their pursuers first, or risk leading them right to their only refuge.

"I'll ride, then," she said, pulling the baby from her breast and drawing her cloak around herself as she swung her feet down from the litter. "If we leave the litter here, we can make better time, especially in the dark."

Instantly Ansel was leaping down into the mud to support her as she tried to stand and staggered, instead.

"Don't be a fool! You're in no condition to ride," he muttered. "Do you want to kill yourself?"

She gestured for Damon to come and help her as she began unbuckling one of the traces on the lead litter horse.

"Of course not. But I don't want us to be taken, either, and I don't want to lead our pursuers to our only refuge. We've seen what they do to Deryni in this part of the country. Damon, you and Thomas unhook the litter and rig the horses so they can be ridden. The baby and I will ride with Fiona."

"Don't you think you at least ought to ride with me or one of the other men?" Ansel asked. "I don't know whether Fiona can catch you, if you start to fall."

Fiona, let down from the horse where she had been sitting with Arik, came running over to support Evaine under one arm and take the baby from her.

"She won't fall," Fiona said, "and I won't let her. The

horses can carry two women more easily than a man and a woman. It's the only logical way."

Ansel looked dubious, but he sensed that Evaine would not be budged, once her mind was made up—and they *could* make better time without the litter. After assessing the mounts they now had, he chose the largest and most smooth-paced of them for Evaine and Fiona, then had Arik switch his deeply padded travel saddle for the harness arrangement on the sumpter horse's back, knowing that Arik could ride bareback. The children were parcelled out among Arik, Damon and himself, and Mairi was put on the second sumpter horse, following alongside Thomas. Bartholomew brought up the rear with Rhysel's pony in tow.

They kept a slow pace at first; but when Evaine appeared to bear up reasonably well, they pressed on more quickly. Just at dark, a light snow began to fall, covering their tracks; and shortly after that, they passed through a succession of forks in the road which they hoped would further discourage pursuit.

Evaine felt herself begin to hemorrhage, a little after that, and held onto consciousness by only the barest of threads, her strength taxed more and more with each mile they completed. But she would not, dared not, tell Ansel and risk having him slow their pace and face possible capture. Better to die on the road than chance what those others had suffered at Trurill.

They did, indeed, lose their pursuers during that long night of flight through the new snow, as the date turned to the second of the new year and the cold increased. They rode through the darkness with but two brief stops for rest and meager rations, as much for the horses' sake as for their riders. Evaine continued to insist that she was doing well enough.

She would not get down from her horse the second time, though, for she had seen the blood staining the dark suede of the saddle seat the first time she got down —though Fiona and Ansel had not—and she knew that she must not let the others know. Instead, she sat nodding in the saddle and gave the baby suck from there, her voluminous cloak muffled closely around her and snowflakes resting unmelting in the rich golden hair which spilled from her hood and around the baby's face.

They rode on then, and Evaine slipped back into that twilight state which she had found to be the only way she could keep from passing out entirely from her growing weakness. She was hardly aware of the passage of the hours or the miles after that, but they reached Saint Mary's in the Hills just after dawn.

She managed to bring herself back to awareness briefly as they drew rein in the abbey yard, all her being rejoicing to see Joram running to meet them across the virgin snow. She stayed in the saddle just long enough to give the baby safely into the arms of a waiting monk, felt Joram's hands on her waist to lift her down, but then the world began to spin.

The next thing she knew, she was lying someplace warm and dry, snuggled under the reassuring weight of several soft blankets. She could feel the warmth of a friendly fire on the right side of her face. The aroma of something eminently edible wafted past her nostrils. She had been bathed and dressed in a clean garment while she lay unconscious—she suspected Fiona's hand in that —and as she flexed an ankle experimentally under the blankets, still not opening her eyes, she was reminded abruptly of the abuse to which she had been forced to subject her body in the past few days. A quick assessment reassured her that she had stopped bleeding, however, and that her general condition was far better than she had feared.

Returning alertness had brought the brush of other minds in the immediate vicinity, both strange and familiar, so she opened her eyes. She found herself lying on a narrow bed before a cheery hearth. The room's ceiling and walls were plastered and whitewashed, the exposed beams oiled to a dark, mellow finish. A black-robed monk sat on a stool to her right, stirring a cup of something which was the source of the enticing aroma. Another monk stood behind—she knew he was the abbot. On her other side, Joram knelt with his pale head bowed, in the black of the stranger-monks instead of his familiar Michaeline blue, and with a priest's stole around his neck. Behind him, she could see Fiona departing with a basin and armful of rough, grey towels.

Joram looked up then, aware by Sight that she was conscious. Before she could say anything, he was sliding an arm behind her neck and shoulders and raising her head so the monk could begin spooning broth into her mouth. When she would have protested, both men merely shook their heads stubbornly and the monk pressed the spoon to her lips. She gave in at that, obediently swallowing each spoonful of the warm, fragrant stuff which the monk presented. When she had finished the last drop, the monk rose and departed without a word, the abbot accompanying him. As Joram eased her back onto her pillows, she turned her head to gaze at him fondly.

"One might think someone were dying," she said with a faint smile. "That stole is not at all reassuring."

"I'll take it off, if you promise not to need it," he replied, taking her hand and kissing it gently.

She closed her eyes briefly and nodded, then smiled again. "I've never been able to tell for certain when you're joking, you do it so seldom," she said. "Will you take it off, though?"

"With your promise," he said doggedly.

"Given."

"That's more like it." He pulled off the offending stole with his free hand and touched it to his lips, then draped it over the blankets covering her, as if to include her in its protection. Then he took her hand in both of his and held it close against his chin.

"Sweet *Jesu*, Evaine, I was frightened for you! You were so pale when you rode in. Fiona said the birth was not particularly difficult, but you lost so much blood! You should never have ridden so soon or so far."

"It was necessary," she said.

"Well, at least you're going to be all right now. The shock might have killed you, though. And where is Queron?"

"I sent him to Revan, before we left Sheele."

"To Revan? In your condition, with the baby's birth so near?"

She gave a little shrug, wincing at the pull of sore muscles. "At the time, I didn't know it was that near. Is the baby all right?"

He nodded. "Everyone's sleeping. Ansel told me what happened, while Fiona and Brother Dominic cleaned you up."

"Brother Dominic?"

"The one who was feeding you soup. He's the infirmarian. They haven't any Healer, of course."

"No, I suppose not." She took a deep breath and let it out with a little sigh. "What about Alister?" she asked softly, using that name from habit, even though there was no one else in the room.

461

"Safe at Dhassa, for the nonce," Joram breathed. "I'll be in contact with him tonight and let him know you're safe. Your instincts about avoiding capture were sound, by the way—in more than a general way. The regents outlawed the whole family the day after Christmas. I suspect that's why Trurill was hit—that and the over-zealousness of the MacInnis clan. Anyway, Alister and Jebediah are waiting at Dhassa for news of the new synod at Ramos, before they come to join us. The new archbishop and his minions have already laicized all Deryni priests, suspended the bishops who wouldn't co-operate, and forbidden any future ordinations of Deryni to the priesthood."

She glanced at the stole lying across her blankets, then looked back at her brother. "I infer that you don't accept the laicization."

"What do *you* think?" he returned, the set to his jaw and the hard fire smouldering in the grey eyes telling her all she needed to know about that.

She smiled. "Understood. You mentioned a new arch-bishop—Hubert?"

"Who else? Niallan and Dermot got away with us to Dhassa, but Hubert must suspect that's where we went, because Rhun has put the city under siege. Kai and Davet Nevan were killed in the cathedral on Christmas Day, the same as—"

He bowed his head as his voice broke off, for he had not meant to speak of that, especially to her, but she pressed his hand in reassurance and brought her other hand across to pat his arm.

"I know, Joram. It's all right to talk about it."

"Evaine, I'm so sorry," he whispered. "God knows, we tried to save him, but with no Healer. . . . It was such an awful, senseless, tragic—"

"Hush, I know," she murmured. "It wasn't your fault. Do you think I didn't know that? Do you think I didn't feel it, when he died?"

She blinked back the beginnings of tears and stared up at the ceiling until she could go on.

"We won't be able to stay here indefinitely," she said more briskly. "We don't want to endanger the good monks who have so kindly sheltered us. Have you any plans beyond all of us meeting here?"

Joram nodded, also regaining his equilibrium. "Ansel and I are to begin setting up a Portal here as soon as we

462

can. We'll go to our old Michaeline sanctuary, where we took Cinhil. The Order has abandoned it now, but supplies were laid in months ago. With the Portal there set as a Trap, we should be safe enough, at least for a while."

"I can think of far worse places for exile. It will seem almost like home. You said you were going to set up another Portal here, though—you and Ansel can't do it alone. . . ."

"If you're thinking to offer to help, don't," he said gently. "We'd thought to have Queron, but we'll manage with some of the others instead. Fiona's fairly adept, as I recall, and we can use Camlin, too, if he's up to it."

She turned her face away slightly to stare at the ceiling again, biting her lip.

"Did they tell you about Aunt Aislinn and Adrian and —Aidan?" she whispered tremulously.

Joram nodded. "And how you healed Camlin. It was a miracle, Evaine!"

"No, it was Tieg," she amended, turning her eyes back to his. "He's a Healer, like his father. He—" She swallowed noisily, barely fighting back the tears. "Oh, Joram, his father would have been so proud of him!"

She could not hold back the tears after that, and sobbed in Joram's arms for a long time while he stroked her hair and murmured childhood endearments, gradually establishing the rapport to share all that had happened to both of them since their last meeting. When she finally regained control and opened her eyes, Joram was still there at her side—and the monk Dominic, with another cup of soup.

"I can't," she protested weakly. "There's too much to do."

But Joram was adamant. "The *only* thing you have to do for a few days is to get well," he said, with that firm set to his jaw which she knew so well. "Now, cooperate with Brother Dominic and eat. Ansel and I will take care of everything until you're strong enough to help."

CHAPTER THIRTY

For there is hope of a tree, if it be cut down, that it will sprout again, and that the tender branches thereof will not cease.

—Job 14:7

The new year began no more auspiciously for Camber than it had for his children, for it brought unwelcome news from Valoret, even before Joram's grim report. Camber and Bishop Dermot had been assisting Niallan at the noon Mass for the cathedral chapter, as had been their wont since their flight to Dhassa on Christmas Day, both of them waiting with folded hands to either side of Niallan while he read the last Gospel.

"In principio erat Verbum, et Verbum erat apud Deum, et Deus erat Verbum. Hoc erat in principio apud Deum. Omnia per ipsum facta sunt: et sine ipso factum est nihil, quod factum est. . . ."

In the beginning was the Word, and the Word was with God, and the Word was God. . . .

As Niallan read, the air above the Portal in the side chapel began to shimmer, then to solidify a slender, dark-cloaked shape in the purplish mist which proclaimed it still a Trap Portal. Niallan hardly looked up, for the passage and the Mass were almost finished, and Jebediah and Niallan's elite guards had already begun moving into position around the mosaicked pattern which marked the Portal, but Camber bowed unobtrusively and made his way across the chancel to join them. He doubted whether the black-muffled form was recognizable to most of the brethren in the chamber, but there was no doubt in his mind that it was Tavis, and without Javan.

With a nod to Jebediah and the guards to shift around and shield the newcomer from those kneeling for the final blessing, he stepped carefully into the purplish haze. The tingle of the Trap would render him half-Blind like its other occupant until Niallan reached them, but at least he could question Tavis verbally until that occurred.

"What's wrong? Where's Javan?" he whispered, taking Tavis's shoulders and staring into the pale acquamarine eyes.

Tavis sighed. "He's sitting in council with his brothers, hearing the regents ratify the Ramos conventions."

"The Ramos conventions? Today? All of them?"

"And more," Tavis mumbled.

In that instant, the haze of the Trap dissipated, and Niallan was moving in to lay a hand on Tavis's arm. Dermot was still at the altar, extinguishing the altar candles, and Jebediah and the guards moved out to shepherd the last of the morning's worshippers from the chapel. While the chamber cleared, Camber warned Niallan off with a flicker of thought, then turned his full attention on Tavis, offering rapport in place of words. The weight of information which came flooding back in that instant of communion was almost staggering.

Javan had learned the night before that the new laws were to be promulgated. The measures would spell the next thing to active extermination, for it would be nigh impossible to live as Deryni without infringing on at least part of what the regents were to decree. The regents had agreed to everything recommended by the bishops, and had added points of their own. Penalties for any deviation would be stringent.

The prince had told Tavis of this, and then had all but commanded the Healer to flee to safety in the morning. What followed had been their most profound mind-sharing to date, with Javan's response almost indistinguishable from that of a Deryni, albeit an untrained one. The two had spent the rest of the night and early morning talking and testing and sharing thoughts with growing facility, and had even arranged a system by which they could maintain occasional communication, once Tavis had gone.

But then, at midmorning, Javan had pulled himself together as a prince must, arrayed himself for court, and taken quiet leave. Tavis, torn by conflicting wants and needs, had made his way to their secret garde-robe Portal without incident—and the rest, Alister knew.

"Well, I suppose it could have been worse," Camber whispered, as he and Tavis withdrew all but a thread of contact and Camber quickly shared what he had learned with the other two Deryni. "At least you had time to make arrangements with Javan—and the manner of your leaving, on the day the laws are decreed, will lend credence to whatever you decide to do next. Do the laws take effect immediately?"

Tavis shook his head wearily. "Javan didn't know. It's likely, though. He saw the unsigned writs escheating all Deryni-owned lands to the Crown, and the attainder lists for the Deryni lords. There were some expressed exceptions, in the case of a few Deryni heiresses who will be married off to suitable human lords, but otherwise, I think every Deryni of any rank at all is on their lists. Listen, could we sit down somewhere? I didn't sleep last night, and I'm a little shaky from all of this."

"We can go to my solar," Niallan said promptly, ushering them toward the door. As they moved through the corridors, Camber continued to press the Healer with questions.

"What about the prohibition against teaching Deryni? Are they keeping the execution clauses?"

"Yes, in fact, there was serious talk of forbidding *any* education for Deryni, but Javan says they finally dropped that—too difficult to enforce. But Deryni won't be allowed to teach anything, for fear they might teach magic." He sighed. "At least our folk won't have to be illiterate."

They discussed the ramifications of Ramos in depth as they settled around a table in Niallan's solar, grudgingly concluding that the new laws could have been worse—though not much. Details of the arrangement for continued communication between Javan and Tavis were explored—for with Javan now isolated among the hostile regents, it was essential that he have an outlet, both for the exchange of information and for a timely escape, if his position became absolutely unbearable. Camber and his colleagues agreed that the garde-robe Portal should continue to be their rendezvous point, on a five-day cycle for exchange of messages, but suggested that Tavis warn the prince that any of the four of them who were Deryni might be his contact, and that if he needed to speak to someone in person instead of leaving a message, he should be on the Portal just after Compline on one of the scheduled days. His presence would indicate that it was safe for someone to come through and bring him back for a face-to-face meeting, though they must not do this too often, for fear he might be seen or missed.

"At least he's reasonably safe, so long as he keeps playing the cowed simpleton," Niallan commented, when they had fairly well concluded their assessment of Javan's situation. "But what about you, Tavis?"

As Tavis shrugged half-heartedly, Camber gave him a tight little Alister grin.

"That depends a lot on Javan, doesn't it, my friend? We hadn't thought to have you so soon, but since we do, we can certainly make use of the time. Are you willing to take on the role we discussed before, with Revan?"

"I'd have to stand with Rhys on that, Alister," the Healer replied. "I'll do it if no one else can be found. I'd be lying if I said I wanted to do it. And this is going to make me pretty recognizable," he concluded, holding up his stump. "Even a shape-change can't give me another hand."

"No, but your own appearance and apparent defection will seem all the more plausible, by the time we get through establishing your new cover," Camber said. "It's known that Deryni did that to you. You've already left Court under a cloud. And if Javan plays his part well— bitter and angry that you deserted him—you should be quite ready for the Willimites by spring. We'll have you look for other suitable Healers, of course, but we'll also have you turn up in a few major towns and cities all through the winter and lay some foundations. By the time you 'stumble' on Revan in March or so, you should be able to give quite a convincing performance."

With a grimmer look, Camber laid a hand on Tavis's upper arm. "I know it won't be easy, son. If it's any consolation, you won't be alone. Niallan, do you think you could take our young friend in tow for the next month or so? All of us will want to move on to the old Michaeline sanctuary as soon as possible, but Jebediah and I may have to go to Saint Mary's first, if they can't manage the new Portal there without help. We should be hearing from Joram on that in the next few days."

"I'll take care of him," the younger bishop agreed. "In fact, while I work with Tavis, this will be an ideal opportunity for Dermot to learn more about us." He glanced at his human colleague. "How about it, Dermot? Are you ready to be corrupted by heretical and God-curst Deryni?"

Dermot returned Niallan's grin without a trace of apprehension. "It seems I already am."

* * *

They spent that afternoon and most of the next day in planning. The evening of the third, Camber excused himself before the evening meal to prepare for communication with Joram. Jebediah went with him into his sleeping chamber, there to keep watch while Camber stretched out and pushed himself down into the profound state of relaxation which was the required precursor for such contact, especially over such a distance. The contact came on schedule, but it did not bring the news which Camber had expected.

He received Joram's account in numbed passivity, so shocked by the senseless brutality of Trurill that little else registered in those first stunned moments. Instinct prompted him to draw Jebediah into the link as a buffer against the horror, but even Jebediah could offer little but blind support and comfort in the wake of the dread news.

Camber could barely comprehend the extent of the butchery at Trurill. He had never been exceptionally close to his sister Aislinn or her children, and had met his cousin Adrian only a few times, but it was difficult to conceive of men who could subject any living beings to what had occurred at Trurill. The general slaughter and torture was bad enough, but emotions already torn raw by the tragedy of Rhys's loss could only throb and ache anew at the death of Rhys's eldest son, even softened in the telling by Joram at third-hand. This was the second grandson Camber had lost in the past half-year, and Aidan's death had been neither quick nor painless compared to Davin's. Even the miracles of those who had survived seemed pale, balanced against the atrocities of Trurill.

A little later, he and Jebediah related Joram's news to the others at a subdued supper gathering. After initial outrage on the part of all present, they determined that Alister and Jebediah should lose no time in reaching Joram and the others at Saint Mary's, so the Portal could be completed and all brought to safety. Accordingly, by midnight the two were stepping onto the rounded design of the Portal in Niallan's chapel, both dressed in worn black riding leathers and fur-lined cloaks. Plain swords were buckled at their hips, sturdy fur-lined caps pulled firmly over hair and ears. Mail shirts warmed but slowly under otherwise unremarkable tunics of leather and wool. Camber wore no insignia of his rank save his archbishop's ring, which he kept under glove, and a small gold pectoral cross, which he tucked into the front of his tunic.

Goodbyes had all been said before the two of them knelt for Niallan's blessing and Godspeed beside the chapel's altar. No further words were needed as they moved into the purple haze of the guarded Portal and felt it fall away at Niallan's unvoiced command. In silence Camber linked with Jebediah to warp the energies and they were gone. They reappeared in darkness in the ruins beneath Grecotha.

They had considered surfacing openly in Alister's tower Portal and taking horses from the episcopal stables. Such could have been construed as due the former Bishop of Grecotha, had these been ordinary times. But they did not know whether Edward MacInnis might already have taken possession of his new see. Besides, Hubert might have sent troops with his nephew, anticipating just such an event as the appearance of the Deryni Cullen at his former residence. Neither Camber nor Jebediah wished to risk a physical confrontation with great numbers of the enemy.

In caution, then, they used the Portal in the ruins, and spent most of the night working their way out, clearing a passage through the collapsed corridors by the light of handfire and the sweat of much toil until, near dawn, they reached the open air. A while they spent concealing the way they had come, and waiting for the city to wake. Then they must time the theft of two horses just to coincide with the opening of the city gates for the day, and cover their departure with a confusion at the marketplace, so that the city guards should be diverted until the two could make good their escape.

They were not pursued after the first few hours; and the jump to Grecotha had cut their total journey to only two or three days. They changed horses several times, and took a variety of lesser roads and tracks when they must eventually pass through the lands of Horthness and Carthane—though at least they knew that the lords of those holdings were not about in person; they were wreaking their mischief in Valoret and places farther east. Though they passed several mounted patrols each day, they aroused no special attention. In their plain black leathers and fur-lined cloaks, with unadorned swords at their sides and fur-lined caps drawn close around their heads and faces, they appeared little different from any pair of fighting men travelling on some winter errand—though a closer look would have revealed one of them to be rather older than one might expect still to be in military service, and the other was scarcely younger.

Still, in ordinary times, they would have aroused no special attention as they left the Purple March and began to penetrate the foothills which lay below Saint Mary's; and they had been careful to avoid both Cor Culdi and the ruins of Trurill. It was only the most unfortunate of ill luck that they paused at a tiny inn on the Culdi road to wait out a snowstorm and had to share the common room with, among others, a quartet of rough-looking knights wearing the livery and badge of the Earl of Culdi—the *new* Earl of Culdi, of course. And it was worse luck that Camber's pectoral cross slipped out of his tunic and flashed in the firelight as Camber shrugged his cloak back off his shoulders when he and Jebediah settled down to eat and drink in the room's further corner. Camber tucked it back inside with an automatic gesture as the barmaid plunked tankards on the table, and thought no more about it. The room was crowded, the jumble of thoughts chaotic, and no one was likely to attempt thievery of the cross here, in front of so many witnesses.

The cross alone might have elicited no more than passing interest on the part of the knights; for while the ornament was rather more valuable than most soldiers could afford, it was possible that its wearer simply had stolen it off some unlucky churchman—an abbot, perhaps, by the size of it. One of the knights had a ring he had stolen from a body only a few days before.

But when the two black-clad strangers did not remove their fur-lined caps while they ate, it prompted the knights to wonder. The men might simply have kept on their headgear against the cold—but on the other hand, such caps *could* conceal tonsures—and why would tonsured priests be travelling disguised as fighting men?

That question so intrigued the knights that they determined to get a closer look at their fellow travellers. Offhand, they could think of no logical reason for priests to be travelling incognito in this part of the country at this time of the year—unless the two were Deryni! Earl Manfred had told them only the previous week that all the bishops were supposedly at Ramos even now, drafting stringent new statutes against the accursed Deryni. He had expounded on the subject at length, before sending them out on that thoroughly satisfying raid of Trurill.

Trurill. Now, *there* had been sport! And condoned by

the Church, too! Earl Manfred's brother, now Archbishop and Primate of All Gwynedd, had sent his special apostolic blessing on everyone who took part; and young Bishop Edward, the earl's son, had also sent his promise of prayers for their intention.

They snickered over their tankards for a while, recalling choice details of the day's work, then returned to the more serious business of the two men across the room, since they had no better sport while they waited for the storm to pass. Soldiers or priests? Human or Deryni? Both of them were far older than the knights had at first estimated—perhaps as old as fifty. And why would they not take off their caps indoors? The taproom was not that cold!

So, in the next half hour, each of the knights contrived excuse to take a closer look, making his way to the tap to refill tankards with frothy brown ale, or to the privy to relieve a full bladder, or to the kitchen to commandeer more meat for their table—for knights in the service of the Earl of Culdi could exact some privileges. When they had all had a surreptitious look, they regrouped to compare notes.

Their combined impressions produced no other conclusion about the younger of the two men than the probability that he was, indeed, a soldier like themselves—perhaps gently born, but a fighting man, for sure. The dark eyes held a flintlike steadiness which was familiar to all of them, and the scarred and agile fingers were never far from the hilt of sword or dagger.

The older man, however, presented more interesting possibilities, though he, too, had that look in his light-colored eyes. His craggy features seemed vaguely familiar to one of the knights, who had spent some time at Court a few years back; and when he realized that what had appeared to be a plain gold band on the man's right hand was, in fact, a more elaborate ring with the stone turned inward, pieces began to sift into place.

Could the ring be a seal of office? A bishop's amethyst, perhaps, in keeping with the cross and the suspected tonsure? He had it! Could the man be Alister Cullen, former Chancellor of Gwynedd and Bishop of Grecotha? If that were true, he would also be Deryni, and a fugitive from the regents' justice. Cullen had been a Michaeline before his election to the See of Grecotha. He could easily play a soldier.

But why would the renegade Alister Cullen have fled to Kierney, of all places, travelling with but one companion? That companion would be Michaeline, too, they realized now, both by his bearing and the fact that Cullen was Michaeline, but who was he? Not Joram MacRorie, the heretic Camber's son and longtime secretary to Bishop Cullen. MacRorie was younger and fairer.

Who, then?

"What about Jebediah of Alcara?" one of the men guessed. Earl Manfred had said something about Alcara escaping with Cullen and MacRorie on Christmas Day. Could this be the infamous Earl Jebediah, grand master of the now-proscribed Michaelines?

The dual possibility sobered the four, for the thought of taking on two Deryni—and Michaelines, at that—was not reassuring. Of course, they could always enlist aid from others here at the inn; but princely rewards had been offered for the apprehension of both these men, especially if Cullen could be taken alive, and avarice demanded that the reward not be shared. Besides, as one of the knights recalled, those other Deryni at Trurill had not put up that much of a fight. They had died as easily as any other folk, their highly vaunted magic never making an appearance at all. If these Deryni were no different, what had they to fear on that account? And were not the blessings of Archbishop Hubert and Bishop Edward still upon them?

As for Michaelines, what were they? These Michaelines were old men, and only two of them. Against four elite knights, half their age, how good could they be?

Their courage thus bolstered by bravado and mellow ale, they settled down to plan their strategy. If these men *were* Cullen and Alcara, they still had not deduced why they were in Kierney—and that was doubtless something their lord would like very much to know. Perhaps it was all a part of some Deryni plot, such as Earl Manfred had been warned of by his brother only last week, when word of the renegade Cullen's suspension and condemnation had been received at Cor Culdi.

The possibility that the two were on their way to rendezvous with others of their kind whetted the knights' greed even more, for if they could lead their lord to a whole nest of Deryni, they would receive even greater reward than if they only brought in Cullen and Alcara. And if they could capture even these two alive, how much

472

greater pleasure might their lord derive—and how much greater reward give—if he could torture them before their execution? In the meantime, if they could but follow the two after the storm and discover their intention, they might find that they could handle the situation all by themselves. Then they would have to share their reward with no one.

And so the four did not confront the strangers that night, merely keeping watch, by turns, that the pair should not slip away before they knew it, as the storm waned.

And Camber and Jebediah, unaware of the scrutiny and the conspiracy they had inspired, now that they were so close to their destination, did not take it amiss that, as they rode out the next morning, close on the dawn, the four knights were also saddling up to ride.

They stopped near noon to rest the horses, pausing in the refuge of a small roadside shrine which also embraced an ice-choked stream and pool. While Jebediah led the horses to the pool, breaking the ice-crust near the edge with his heel, Camber crunched across the fine powder of the previous night's snow to the shrine itself to pay his respects, his boots leaving darker footprints in the virgin snow. They were only a few hours from Saint Mary's. Best to try to contact Joram and Evaine now, for there had been no opportunity in the closeness of the inn the night before.

The shrine was a miniature chapel set on a post, open toward the clearing, with a steeply-peaked roof to protect the wooden statue within. Little drifts had built up on the base and around the statue's feet, and Camber scooped them away with his gloved hands before bowing his head in a brief prayer for continuing guidance. The stillness was profound, broken only by the horses' soft slurping, occasional snorts, and the jingle of bits and curb chains.

He did not hear the approach of other riders until they were nearly upon them, for he was deep in trance, and the new snow muffled hoofbeats. Even Jebediah gave the four riders only cursory attention as they came around a close curve and walked their mounts toward the pool, for Camber's stallion chose that moment to raise its head and whinny menacingly at the other horses' approach, lacing back its ears and wheeling around to kick, so that Jebediah had to maneuver quickly to avoid being shouldered into the icy water. Camber turned, roused from his meditations by the commotion—he had *just* touched his daughter's mind in a first, fleeting brush of contact—but Jebediah's attention was occupied with getting the horses back under control, and he obviously could not see the four men reaching for their swords.

Too late Camber recognized their identity and their intention. They must somehow have spotted him and Jebediah, then followed and watched for a chance when the odds were in their favor—and the four could hardly have two Deryni at a better disadvantage!

Even as Camber shouted out a warning, jarring Jebediah with mind as well as voice and starting to dash across the clearing with drawn sword, the four were converging on the grand master, one of them nearly connecting a killing blow to his head but wounding a horse instead, as the Michaeline ducked.

The horse fell screaming, nearly knocking Jebediah down, but he managed to cling to the reins of the second horse and use it as a shield, ducking behind it long enough to draw his sword and reappear unexpectedly on the other side and slash an attacker deeply across the lower leg. The blood of the dying horse and the wounded man showered the snow, the man cursing as he yanked his horse back a few steps—but only far enough for one of his companions to move in for another try. While Jebediah dealt with that, a third assailant delivered a numbing blow to his left shoulder, the broadsword slicing through leather and mail and partway into flesh.

Jebediah cried out, releasing the reins of the horse he was still holding, and at the same time a great hoof thudded into his chest with almost enough force to shatter ribs. His mail saved him, though he had to gasp to breathe. He recoiled against the fourth horse and rider, half-stunned, but he retained enough presence of mind to use his position to twist around and fling the rider's leg up and over unexpectedly, dumping the man heavily onto the trampled snow before whirling once more to parry a sword thrust. Milling horses screamed and kicked, presenting almost as much danger as the attackers' swords.

Camber reached them then, snapping the edge of his cloak in the face of a startled warhorse even as his sword sought the rider of a second. The first horse shied and reared, throwing its rider into another and adding to the confusion, while Camber and the second man exchanged a flurry of blows. He did not see Jebediah take his next wound, though he heard him gasp and curse as he tried to retaliate, for Camber was busy avoiding his own assailant's blade. He only just succeeded in deflecting a potentially killing blow to a glancing one instead. The man's sword cut a bloody track down his leg from midthigh almost to knee, but he hardly felt it in the heat of battle as he continued to fight. He had to get to Jebediah and defend him!

Two men were unhorsed now, one of them not moving, but Camber realized that if he and Jebediah were to have any chance at all, they must better the odds by getting their other two attackers on the ground. Jebediah was trying to fend off one mounted attacker and one on foot, and his own mounted assailant was staying just beyond Camber's ability to harm him seriously, pivoting his horse to present trampling, steel-shod hooves whenever Camber would work his way too close. Seizing a desperate chance, Camber lunged under the horse's nose and grabbed for the reins, wrenching so savagely at the bit that the animal slipped and went down, first to its knees and then to its side.

Its rider was more skilled than Camber had hoped, though—perhaps too skilled for Camber in his present numbed condition. The knight managed to throw himself clear as his horse went down, landing on his feet and vaulting over his fallen comrade to engage Camber almost immediately. Camber felt the awful sluggishness of muscles growing fatigued, responding less quickly than they once had. He cried out as his opponent bloodied his arm and then traced another deep gash along his hip, just below the line of his mail, in a brilliant followthrough.

God, the man was fast!

He managed to stay on his feet, despite tripping over one fallen knight, but he did not know how long he could last. He could not prevent the numbing blow to his swordarm, though he did succeed in switching his sword to his other hand and warding off a follow-up attack. He even scored a minor wound, to the man's clear surprise. He supposed the knight had not expected him to be able to handle a weapon with his off hand.

His strength was ebbing, though, and he knew Jebediah's must be, too. He saw the grand master sink to a sitting position, clutching at his thigh with one hand while he continued to fight off the other dismounted knight with the other, but Jebediah looked bad, his face taut and desperate against the blood-stained black of his leathers and cloak. He did not seem to notice the lone remaining mounted knight working his horse around to take him from behind. Loose horses plunged and squealed, crazed by the smell of blood and the clash of steel, and Camber's opponent kept pressing him even harder, every time he tried to break closer to Jebediah's defense.

Desperation entered his own fighting now. Kicking his assailant's feet out from under him in a move he knew Alister had never learned in any chivalrous Michaeline school, he whirled toward the last mounted knight and called on one of his most poignant Alister-memories, hurling his sword left-handed with all his remaining strength and a prayer.

In that instant, the clearing seemed to erupt with light, a soundless and unexpected shock almost jolting him to his knees.

By sheer reflex, he launched himself across the intervening space and threw himself on the remaining knight who had been harrying Jebediah, cutting the man's throat with his own sword before the knight knew what had happened. As he released the collapsing form and drew back, ready still to fight, if he must—though he could not see, for the after-image of the flash—he realized that it had suddenly gotten very quiet. He could hear the horses crashing through the skeletal, winter-seared brush which surrounded the clearing, still snorting and whickering to one another in fright, but nothing moved nearby. After a few more seconds, his eyes began adjusting to the normal light level again.

He was spattered with blood, much of it his own. He was still too dazed to tell how badly he was hurt. Beyond his own dying victim, Jebediah was slowly curling into a ball, an oddly luminous sword sinking to the snow in his bloody fist. Behind, the man who had been the target of Camber's desperate spell lay in a charred and definitely dead heap atop his equally dead horse, the man's chest transfixed by Camber's sword. The hilt was blackened and twisted like another he had seen only once, in a clearing at Iomaire.

He drew breath sharply, wondering whether his spell could have caught Jebediah in its backlash, but another part of him argued that this could not be, for Jebediah was still alive. Then he realized that his own former attacker was also dead, though there seemed to be no serious wound upon him. The eyes were open and staring, the face frozen in an expression of surprise and terror. As Camber reached out a shaking and bloody hand to sense the cause, he felt a residue of darkling magic—suddenly *knew* its source. Stunned at that, he shook his head to clear it and scrambled toward the feebly moving Jebediah.

"What the hell did you do?" he murmured, catching the grand master's silvered head before it could sink back on the snow.

Blood was spuring from a thigh wound in bright, pulsating gouts, smoking in the cold winter air, and Camber clamped his hands over the wound in despair.

"Oh, God, Jebediah! Jeb, can you hear me?"

When Jebediah only moaned softly, Camber whipped the swordbelt from his waist with one hand and looped it twice around the thigh above the wound, his breath coming in ragged gasps from the exertion as he tried to tighten it down and stop the bleeding. The black of the supple leather brightened to scarlet almost immediately, but it did not seem to slow the flow appreciably.

"Jeb, answer me!" Camber pleaded, gathering the fainting man in his arms and pressing his hand to another gaping wound in the back, sick at heart. At Jebediah's side lay the fallen sword in a blade-shaped depression filled with melted snow. Somehow, Camber knew that if he touched it, the blade would still be warm.

"Good God, man, what did you do?" he whispered.

Jebediah breathed in sharply through his teeth and rallied enough to look up at Camber with a tight little smile.

"Don't tell me I've managed to come up with a magical application you don't know about," he murmured. "I'm afraid it was a little grey around the edges, but your friend might have gotten you, otherwise."

"A little grey? *What did you do?*"

"Just a little energy diversion. Never you mind. The important thing is that you're still alive. One of us had to —oh, sweet *Jesu,* it hurts to die!" he gasped, as a wave of pain took him.

"No! Don't say that!" Camber ordered, clasping the wounded man even closer. "You're not going to die! I won't let you!"

Jebediah closed his eyes and moistened his lips, controlling a cough before he could manage a faint, sardonic smile.

"You're not often wrong, my friend, but this time. . . ."

He sighed and sagged even more heavily against Camber's chest, though he was still conscious. Camber started to lay his hand on Jebediah's forehead—paused to wipe off the blood against his side—wiped it again on his cloak when he saw that it had only become the more reddened with his own blood. Then he stroked the pain-taut forehead and reached out with his mind for that familiar, tender rapport which had been uniquely theirs.

He could feel his own strength ebbing, as the surge of battle energy drained away, but somehow that did not seem nearly as important as the fact that Jebediah was slipping away in his arms. He was aware of Evaine's and Joram's touch, brushing insistently at the edges of his mind as he opened the link to Jebediah, but he shut them out for now. No time for that. Jebediah was dying, and there was only Camber to comfort him in his pain.

"Alister," Jebediah managed to whisper, after a few seconds. "Alister—no, Camber—hear my confession . . . please. . . ."

"Oh, God, Jeb, don't make me do that—"

"And die unshriven?" The grand master gave a little shudder, either of pain or dread, then looked up at Camber trustingly, crawling his hand up to grasp the little gold cross, bloodied now, which had again escaped from Camber's tunic in the battle. He brought it weakly to his lips and kissed it, then steeled himself to gaze up at Camber steadily.

"Bless me, Father, for I have sinned. Since my last confession, I have slain a man with magic, and with hatred in my heart—and I most heartily beg forgiveness."

Camber could no longer see, for the tears in his eyes and the lightheadedness he was himself feeling, but he did not need to see to exchange the ritual phrases with Jebediah and give him absolution, to trace the sign of their faith on the dying man's forehead. He closed his eyes and let their rapport intensify, reaching out to ease his old friend.

Again he felt the ethereal, detached sensation as the silver cord began to unravel and the ties of earth-binding were loosed. Even though they were not in a magic circle

478

this time, as he turned his Sight outward he could See the vague, insubstantial image of a younger Jebediah superimposing itself over the failing body in his arms, a Jebediah restored to vigorous, vibrant youth.

Jebediah was not looking at him, though—not any more. Instead, his face was turned toward the little shrine across the clearing, which blazed in Camber's Sight like a friendly beacon of cool, silver light. From it a familiar form in Michaeline blue seemed to grow out of a pinpoint of light, drifting slowly toward them, booted feet never quite touching the new snow. A wide smile was on his face—the same face which had looked back at Camber in his mirror for many years now, though younger—and he held out his arms in welcome to the man who was now rising out of the spent shell which once had housed Jebediah.

Forgetting to breathe, Camber watched as a new and young Jebediah rose from the ground at his knees and went to join the specter, the two men embracing like long-parted brothers in a joy which brimmed and overflowed even as far as Camber. They drew apart to turn and gaze at him then, first Jebediah and then the other stretching out their arms as though inviting him to join them. The lure was appealing, but even as Camber wavered on the verge of accepting, pain jarred the vision and shook his concentration. When he tried to look for them again, he could not See them.

He knew Jeb was dead in his arms then, and a mortal portion of him mourned the loss, though another part rejoiced to have been witness to that awesome and mystical reunion. Time seemed to stretch out infinitely, giving him all the span he needed to contemplate his own destiny. Though he sensed vaguely that he, too, was dying, as his blood pooled and congealed around him on the trampled snow, somehow that did not seem an issue of high priority. Something else was, but he could not quite identify it yet, so he retreated further into stillness.

He felt Jebediah slip out of his arms and let himself gradually slump to rest his head on the dead man's shoulder, as the sun passed its zenith and began to decline. He willed his own shape to return, feeling a little strange to be wearing his Camber face again, after so many years, yet somehow sensing that it was meet to do so, especially after having seen Jebediah's ghostly escort.

The return to his own form was a proper choice, he knew, and yet it seemed to open him once more to Evaine's and Joram's touch. He sensed them hovering frantically at the edge of his awareness, but he had no great desire to set the link and let them read in depth. Strangely removed from all their anxious questioning, their fears for his safety, he gave them a calm, dispassionate account of what had happened and certain indication as to how they might find the place where he now lay. Then, gently but firmly, and in an oddly-transmuted sense of love for them both which surpassed his previous appreciation of the beauty of their souls, he eased them from his mind.

Something remained for him to do—something important, something he had not yet discovered. His body, with a twinge, reminded him that it was failing, but he pushed that awareness into the background of his consciousness. He would be given time to do what must be done, he felt sure.

He drifted then, as physical shock and the cold began to take command of his body. The sun sank gradually lower, and a light snow began to powder the clearing.

He wavered between consciousness and dreaming, and his mind went back again to the man whose body lay so close against his own, chilling flesh against still-warm—and to the one who had come to greet the freed soul. That brought his contemplation once again to Alister, the real Alister, whom he had known so many years ago. Alister, too, had died a warrior's death, bleeding out his life with the wounds of battle in a clearing shared only with the dead, but in a cause well-served. Alister . . . Alister. . . .

His reasoning was sluggish now, he sensed, but he could not seem to help himself. As he drifted in an oddly disconnected lethargy, he found himself remembering Ariella next—beautiful, cruel, clever, incestuous Ariella—her fingers curved in death in the attitude of a spell which most men thought impossible. She had failed, but Camber knew why. He had almost tried the spell on Rhys, confident that he could make it work—but that would not have been proper, he knew now. No man had the right to make that choice for any other soul.

And yet, the matter of the spell would not be put aside. Time after time, his thinking made the same brief circuit

—Jebediah, Alister, Ariella, the spell—and he could not seem to break the cycle.

Did one who mastered it indeed elude death? Or did one but gain access to that other sphere which now he twice had glimpsed? Somehow, simple yielding up to death, at least for now, did not contain the answer, though Camber had never feared to die—had always thought he would be ready, in his time. And close upon these musings came another question: had he been given these glimpses of that other sphere for a reason. . . ?

With sudden, blindingly obvious insight, he knew that reason—knew why Ariella's working of the spell had failed, knew a greater part of the Master plan in which he was a keystone. He sensed, also, the reasons one might be granted such grace—not to die, for now, but instead to enter that other, twilight realm of spirit where one might serve both God and man in different ways—or were they different? And *he* had been given the knowledge whereby he might accept that challenge, might gird himself with the whole armor of God and labor on, in the service of the Light.

It was so simple. It was so beautiful. All he had to do was reach out with his mind, just—so. . . .

Toward dusk, one who had lain as dead stirred beneath his blanket of powdered snow and sneezed, clutching his head miserably and moaning as he struggled to sit up. His name was Rondel, knight in the service of Manfred, Earl of Culdi, and the last thing he remembered was his own fury as the Michaeline grand master grabbed his foot, twisted it, and sent him flying over his horse's shoulder. He did not remember hitting the ground.

Memory of the battle cleared his head tremendously, and he scrambled to a crouch and looked around wildly for signs of continuing danger, dagger in his fist. Nothing moved except the gentle snowfall, filtering down from a greying, darkening sky. Vague in the shadows at the edge of the clearing, several of the horses nibbled half-heartedly at the bare winter branches and sucked at the ice-choked pool. He counted five snow-shrouded forms around him in the growing dimness, and knew with a chill unconnected with the snow that he alone had survived.

Practicality began to assert itself at that. If his comrades were dead, then he alone was entitled to the reward

481

which the earl had promised for the apprehension of Cullen and Alcara—and there was no doubt in Rondel's mind, at this point, that those were the identities of the two black-clad bodies lying together a little way across the clearing. Now, if he could only catch a horse or two. . . .

The dusk was nearly full upon him by the time he succeeded in capturing one of the animals. Rondel stroked the neck of the horse he had caught for several minutes, gentling the animal with caresses and soothing words, then began leading it slowly toward the two black-clad bodies. His muscles ached from the cold and his fall, and his eyes did not want to focus, but he knew he dared not tarry over-long. He was several hours' ride from the inn where he and his comrades had stayed the night before, and there was no closer shelter along this road. He must pack up the bodies and be gone before more snow or the wolves which frequented these hills made him, too, a casualty of the day's work.

He was bending down to lift the nearer of the two bodies up across the saddle when he became aware of torchlight glittering through the dead trees in the direction opposite from that which he had come. He could not hear the sound of their horses across the several switchbacks, but there were close to a dozen men, by the number of torches, and they would reach him within a few minutes.

Torn between greed and fear, he crouched closer to look for some item of proof that he could take with him— the ring, perhaps, for he knew he dared not stay to see who the approaching riders were. The first body wore no ring, but clenched in the stiff fingers was the gold cross which he and his comrades had spotted back at the inn.

He had to pry it from the fingers of the dead man, and then break the chain which had held it around the neck of the other, but in his haste, and in the failing light, he did not notice the facial change which had come upon the older man since he had seen him in the noonday sun. He spotted the ring—and it was, indeed, a bishop's amethyst, engraved with crosses along the bezel—but he could not get it off, and he could hear the hoofbeats of the approaching riders now. They would soon be upon him.

He dared not delay. The cross would have to do as proof. There was no doubt in his mind that the dead man was, indeed, the renegade Bishop Cullen—and if the cross were not accepted as proof, well, at least the gold itself was worth something. And so, stuffing the cross into his tunic, he scrambled onto his waiting horse and sped away, gone in the twilight gloom.

Shortly, the others came, bearing light into the clearing, but sorrow out.

Epilogue

And they that shall be of thee shall build the old waste places; thou shalt raise up the foundations of many generations; and thou shalt be called, The repairer of the breach, The restorer of paths to dwell in.

—Isaiah 58:12

A dawn later, in the cold stillness just before first light, a numbed and sorrowing Evaine waited alone in the chapel of Saint Mary's in the high hills of Kierney. She sat on the kneeler of a *prie-dieu* near the altar rail, her back to the altar and her head leaned against the supports to the armrest. She was muffled in one of the ubiquitous black wool cloaks which everyone at Saint Mary's wore, a black monk's robe under that, her arms clasping the cloak around her up-drawn knees for warmth. Bright, burnished strands of hair escaped from beneath her hood, catching the light of Presence Lamp and altar candles as she turned her head slightly to the right.

The Portal, at least, would be completed as he had wanted it, she thought, letting her eyes roam over the carved wooden screen blocking off the northern transept. Behind that screen, Joram and Ansel and some of the monks had been tearing up the floor for days, so that now a circular space the breadth of a man's armspan exposed the living rock. Joram had chalked an octagon within that space but a few hours before, in preparation for the working planned for dawn, and was even now preparing the others who would help provide the energy to establish the Portal: Ansel, Fiona, Camlin, Rhysel and, at his emphatic insistence, little Tieg. After some argument, Joram had agreed that Evaine might also assist, but she was to conserve her strength until it was time. The ride the night before had already taxed her slowly-returning vitality, following so closely on the birth of Jerusha.

The ride . . . She sighed and turned her head slowly back toward the dark shape silhouetted at her left in the center aisle. Atop the more solid mass of the double bier, she could see the nearer of the two bodies without moving, the dim profile now restored to its familiar Alister-shape for the benefit of Ansel and the others. Jebediah lay on the other side, the two of them sharing a pall of black damask which covered them from neck to feet.

She had placed the illusion of Alister back on her father in those first few seconds when she and Joram had knelt in that blood-stained clearing, before they let the others approach. She held it now with a small corner of her mind—nagging, constant tension—until they could take the bodies through the Portal for burial with other Michaelines in that hidden chapel of so long ago. Rhys could have done the job with far less effort; but Rhys was dead now, too, and all Evaine's sorrow would not bring back him, or her father. Soon Camber would sleep at Rhys's side; and then, except for Joram and the children, she would be alone. An epoch had ended.

She and Joram—and perhaps a few others—would carry on the fight, because that was what Camber would have wanted; but it would not be the same. She felt as if her heart had been tugged out by the roots, and the empty place stuffed with straw. She would not die of it, but she feared it would be a long time before she again felt really alive.

She sighed heavily again, then eased herself to her feet and moved closer to the head of the double bier, aware that she had little time left for private goodbyes. The features of Alister Cullen, almost as familiar to her after so many years as the face this visage hid, were in repose, the candlelight flickering softly through the wiry grey hair with a wash of gold and spilling eerie highlights into the hollows of the closed eyes. Bowing her head, she laid her hand atop the mound of his hands underneath the pall and let his visage shift to the more familiar one, simply standing and gazing upon him in sorrow, for she had no tears remaining. Several minutes passed before she became consciously aware of the bulge of the hands and of a sense of strangeness.

She blinked at that, focusing her active attention on the shape beneath her hand. She glanced curiously at the smooth, low bulge of Jebediah's hands folded peacefully on his breast beneath the pall, then carefully folded back the black damask to see why Camber's were not the same. Strange . . . the arms were folded in approximately the same way, but the hands curved oddly on the still breast, as if cupped around something invisible and very precious. She touched one, but it resisted her tentative and then more determined attempt to ease it flatter, with something more than just the normal rigor of death or cold.

Puzzled, for an almost undetectable trace of memory had surfaced for just an instant, she closed her eyes and dipped into remembrance. The sought-for trace re-emerged almost immediately: a deep communing with her father many years ago, and his account of Alister Cullen's last battle . . . death in a glen at Iomaire, and a beautiful but deadly woman transfixed by a sacred sword, her hands curled in the same way, in the attitude of a spell which most Deryni thought only legend, with the most dubious chance of success; and Camber had said that *he knew why the spell had failed!*

She gasped as she returned to present time and place with a snap, mind reeling dizzily at the implication. In a wild flight of hope, she let her trembling fingertips gently trace the curve of her father's hand. Was it possible that Camber was not dead at all—that he was but bound in that most arcane of magicks, awaiting only the proper touch to bring him back?

Soft footfalls jarred her speculation. Instinctively she shifted the shape on the face before her, looking up almost guiltily. But it was only Joram who approached, weary and resigned, to lay an arm around her shoulders in distracted attempt to comfort.

She leaned her head against his chest for a moment, debating whether to tell him of her speculation. His shields loomed dull and lusterless, sealing him into his private grief, but after a few seconds she felt him relax a little, gradually admitting her to the light, superficial rapport which was their usual wont when in such close proximity. Seizing her resolution, she twisted around to glance at him sidewise.

"Joram, look at his hands," she whispered.

He looked, obviously seeing only that the pall was folded back so that the hands could be seen.

"Why? What's wrong with his hands?"

"Now remember Iomaire," she murmured. "You were there. Iomaire and Ariella. . . ."

She felt the rush of memory reverberate in his mind almost like a silent explosion. Staggering, he caught himself on the edge of the bier and stared at the body, balanced between horror at the audacity, the potential blasphemy of trying to deny death, and the wild hope that it just might be true. The image of Iomaire was strong in his thoughts.

After a moment, he jerked the pall back into place over the hands and crumpled to his knees. He was trembling as he leaned his forehead against the edge of the bier between his hands, eyes tightly closed. Evaine put her arms around his shoulders from behind and leaned close against his back to comfort him, caressing and cushioning his mind from the shock still echoing at all levels.

"It *is* possible, you know," she said in a low voice. "I can't be certain, but it's possible. He never spoke of it much, but I know he did some investigating in the old Grecotha records. They're scattered in various hiding places, but they can be reassembled."

He breathed in and out through his nose, an audible effort at control, then raised his head to stare up at the grey silhouette.

"Can you bring him back?" he asked softly.

"I don't even know for certain that he *did* work the spell, much less whether he succeeded. He was wounded badly, though. If he is under the spell, and we tried to bring him back, we would need to have a Healer at hand immediately. That might take some doing. In any case, we first have to determine whether the spell did work, then worry about how to reverse it, if it did." She sighed. "If it didn't work, then he is only dead, and there's nothing more that we can do."

Still uncertain, Joram shook his head forlornly, the final pretense of control dissolving as tears which he had not allowed before began to flow. As he sank back on his heels and wept, face buried in his hands, he let his sister hold him, clung to her and let her soothing presence fill him, merge with all levels in profound rapport, warring with heart, mind, and conscience in a tangle of emotion which only gradually began to sort into order. Evaine, in full communion with her brother as they had not been in a long time, held him close and let her own thoughts return to the man whose body lay on the bier above their heads.

She did not know for certain what had happened to her father, but she intended to find out. And if there were a way to bring him back, to Heal his wounds and make him live again, to release him from that twilight state which was not death, yet not life as they had known, then she and Joram would find it, if it took them the rest of their lives.

They would not be able to do it alone, she knew. But those whose aid they must seek need not know all. Besides herself and Joram, there was now no one else alive who knew the truth of Camber-Alister, and so it must remain. The myth of Saint Camber must be maintained. Once the Portal was finished, they would take their father's body to a secret hiding place, even as Joram had originally told the bishops he had done at the time of Camber's canonization, and at least that lie would be made truth. Alister Cullen could rest at last in his own right, with his beloved Jebediah at his side, and with the infant Prince Aidan—and Rhys. All of them would lie, at least for a time, in that secret and now warded Michaeline chapel where so much had started so many years ago.

And what had started would be continued. With Camber's body finally available, even though they hoped eventually to revive him, they had the focus for a new, small inner circle of Deryni adepts and human allies, quite apart from the foundered Camberian Council, which could assume the function filled until recently by Queron Kinevan's Servants of Saint Camber. Even Joram, with all his scruples and moral struggles, could support this cause; for in these awful past days of the regents' increasing madness, the extension of the long-feared reprisals and persecutions of their people, even he had come to acknowledge the importance of Camber's sainthood. Despite the literal truth or falsehood of their father's sanctity, Camber's example had been a source of strength and inspiration for countless people, human and Deryni, and one which neither of them would dream of destroying. While she and her brother searched for a way to bring Camber back in fact, the secret order which they would create could be the guardians of that example, carrying on the tradition that Saint Camber was not gone, despite the bishops' recent declaration to the contrary, and that his benevolent attention remained on Gwynedd, even beyond the death of his body.

Let the people keep their memory of Saint Camber to sustain them. There was much through which they must be sustained, in the months and years ahead, and only slim chance that Javan or Tavis or Revan or any of the rest of them could make a major difference. And if, in the meantime, she and Joram could restore a more active Camber to them—then that, too, would be all to the good.

She sighed and hugged her brother a little closer, a smile touching her lips as she sensed his gradual stilling, his return to the reasoned, ordered centeredness which was his usual wont, his acceptance of the future she offered. She let her mind blend with his in the comfort of their mutual resolution. For just an instant, it seemed that another presence brushed them fleetingly, like a familiar hand caressing her cheek, touching the top of his head, with a firmness which was as much a blessing as a sign of love, and far too real to be mere imagination.

It was gone, even as they became aware of it, both of them drawing apart to look at one another in wonder. Together they rose to stand with arms intertwined around each other's waists and gaze at the strange-familiar face of the body on the bier.

He was with them, they knew now—perhaps not only in the sense that all the dead remain with those they love, at least in memory, but in some more tangible way. Imagination or reality, memory or perception—it hardly mattered now. Together, Camber and his children had begun a task more than a decade ago. Together, they had seen it through the years and through the sacrifices, and together they would see it through the future, as long as they were able. Evaine and Joram were not the last; they were but early links in the great chain of Order which stretched backward and ahead in time to give support to all who would seize it, tossing on the seas of Chaos. Those of the next generation—Ansel, Rhysel, Tieg, and, yes, even young Camlin—those were the future, the next carriers of Camber's ideals. And those young ones—and others, and not even all of them Deryni—Healers and dreamers and keepers of the heritage of men like Camber —those would be the hope of all tomorrows.

As the others came into the chapel, and she and Joram turned to greet them, she could have sworn she saw her father smile.

In Appendices I and II, initials within brackets indicate that the person or place appeared in the volume indicated. Initials in parentheses indicate that the person or place was mentioned only in passing. References to the volumes are as follows:

CC=CAMBER OF CULDI (Book I)
SC=SAINT CAMBER (Book II)
CH=CAMBER THE HERETIC (Book III)

Appendix I

Legends of Saint Camber
INDEX OF CHARACTERS

ADRIAN MacLean, Lord—Master of Kierney; grandson of Camber's sister Aislinn and foster father to Camber's grandson Aidan Thuryn [CH].

AIDAN, Prince—only child of King Ifor Haldane to survive the Festillic coup of 822; royal name of Daniel Draper, grandfather of King Cinhil [CC, (CH)].

AIDAN Alroy Camber Haldane, Prince—infant son of Cinhil and Megan; killed by poisoned salt at his baptism, age one month [CC].

AIDAN Thuryn—eldest son of Rhys and Evaine, age 10; fostered to Lord Adrian MacLean at Trurill [CH].

AILIN MacGregor, Bishop—Auxiliary Bishop of Valoret [SC, CH].

AIRSID, The—an ancient Deryni fellowship, origin pre-500 AD (CH).

AISLINN MacRorie MacLean, Countess—Camber's younger sister; Dowager Countess of Kierney; mother of the

491

present earl and grandmother of Adrian MacLean, the heir [CH].

ALFRED of Woodbourne, Father—Cinhil's human confessor; later, Auxiliary Bishop of Rhemuth [SC, CH].

ALISTER Cullen, Bishop—Deryni; formerly Vicar General of the Order of Saint Michael; Bishop of Grecotha and Chancellor of Gwynedd under King Cinhil; briefly, Archbishop of Valoret and Primate of All Gwynedd; an original member of the Camberian Council [CC, SC, CH].

ALLYN, Crevan—human Vicar General of the Order of Saint Michael after Alister Cullen [SC, CH].

ALROY Bearand Brion Haldane, Prince—eldest living son of King Cinhil and twin to Javan, age 11; later, King of Gwynedd [SC, CH].

AMYOT of Morland, Lord—Deryni assassin killed in ambush of Princes Javan and Rhys Michael [CH].

ANDREW—farrier at Grecotha [SC].

ANDREW, son of James—the second "Benedict" at Saint Piran's Priory [CC].

ANSCOM of Trevas, Archbishop—Deryni Primate of All Gwynedd and Archbishop of Valoret [CC, SC, (CH)].

ANSEL Irial MacRorie, Lord—younger son of Cathan and grandson of Camber, age 17 [CC, SC, CH].

ARCHER of Arrand, Bishop—*Ordo Verbi Dei* theologian and preacher; later, Bishop of Dhassa [CH].

ARIELLA of Festil, Princess—elder sister of the former King Imre and mother of his son, Mark [CC, SC, (CH)].

ARIK—a guard of Rhys's and Evaine's household [CH].

ARMAGH, Master—an arms master to King Imre [CC].

AUGARIN, King—first Haldane King of Gwynedd; reigned 645-673 (CH).

BARTHOLOMEW—a guard of Rhys's and Evaine's household [CH].

BAYVEL de Cameron, Lord—uncle to Queen Megan [SC].

BEARAND, King and Saint—Haldane King of Gwynedd reigning 736–794; great-great-grandfather of King Cinhil (CC, SC, CH).

BENEDICT—King Cinhil's name in religion [CC].

BEREN, Sir—a Michaeline knight (SC).

BERTRAND—squire to Prince Javan [CH].

492

BLAINE, King—fourth Festillic King of Gwynedd, reigned 885–900; father of Imre (CC).

BORS—soldier under command of Coel Howell [CC].

BOTOLPH—horse-keeper at Valoret [CH].

CALEB—a guard of Bishop Cullen's household [CH].

CAMBER Allin MacLean—call Camlin, age 11; son of Adrian MacLean and foster-brother to Aidan Thuryn [CH].

CAMBER Kyriell MacRorie, Lord—Earl of Culdi; Chancellor under King Blaine; canonized as Saint Camber in 906; *Defensor Hominum* and patron of Deryni magic; sainthood rescinded by Council of Ramos in 917 [CC, SC, CH].

CAMERON—family name of Queen Megan [CC].

CARLE—one of Earl Maldred's men [CC].

CATHAN MacRorie, Lord—Camber's eldest son and heir; member of Imre's council; murdered by Imre in 903 for suspected treason [CC, (SC, CH)].

CHARLES, Brother—a Servant of Saint Camber at Dolban; formerly a baker in village at Caerrorie [SC].

CIERAN, Brother—lay brother at Saint Piran's Priory [CC].

CINHIL Donal Ifor Haldane, King—restored King of Gwynedd, reigning 904–917; formerly a priest of the *Ordo Verbi Dei* under the name of Benedict; kidnapped from his monastery by Joram and Rhys [CC, SC, CH].

COEL Howell, Lord—brother of Elinor, Cathan's wife; member of Imre's council; executed by King Cinhil in 905 [CC, (SC)].

CORUND—guard assigned to the service of Princes Javan and Rhys Michael; killed in hunting ambush [CH].

CREVAN Allyn—*see Allyn, Crevan.*

CRINAN—Cathan's squire; doubled for Rhys under a shape-changing spell [CC, (SC, CH)].

CULLEN, Bishop Alister—*see Alister Cullen.*

DAFYDD Leslie, Lord—nephew of Lord Jowerth Leslie; died during interrogation by Tavis O'Neill [CH].

DAMON—a guard of Rhys's and Evaine's household [CH].

DANIEL Draper—as Prince Aidan Haldane, only surviving son of King Ifor; grandfather of Cinhil [CC, (CH)].

DAVET Nevan, Bishop—one of Gwynedd's six itinerant bishops before the Council of Ramos [SC, CH].

DAVIN Elathan MacRorie, Lord—elder son of Cathan, age 19; Earl of Culdi [CC, SC, CH].

DENZIL Carmichael, Lord—Deryni bowman involved in assassination attempt on Princes Javan and Rhys Michael; died during interrogation [CH].

DERYNI (Der-ín-ee)—racial group gifted with paranormal/supernatural powers and abilities.

DERMOT O'Beirne, Bishop—human Bishop of Cashien [SC, CH].

DESCANTOR, Bishop Kai—see *Kai Descantor, Bishop.*

DOMINIC, Brother—infirmarian at Saint Mary's in the Hill, Kieney [CH].

DOMINIC, Father—priest at Saint Liam's Abbey; former teacher of Joram and Rhys [CC].

DORN—squire to Prince Javan; killed in hunting ambush [CH].

DOTHAN of Erne, Lord—former Festillic minister imprisoned for trial by Cinhil; son and daughter killed in assassination attempt on Cinhil (SC).

DOV, Lord—Healer slain at Saint Neot's (CH).

DRAPER—surname used by the Haldanes during the Interregnum: *see Daniel, Nicholas,* and *Royston Draper.*

DRUMMOND, James—*see James Drummond.*

DUALTA Jarriot, Lord—a Michaeline knight [SC].

DURIN, Master—a Healer at Iomaire [SC].

DYLAN ap Thomas, Lord—Deryni assassin killed in ambush of Princes Javan and Rhys Michael [CH].

EDMOND—a former Archbishop of Valoret (CH).

EDULF—ostler to Camber at Caerrorie; one of fifty peasants executed at Imre's command in retribution for death of Lord Rannulf [CC].

EDWARD, Father—priest who baptized Nicholas Draper (CC).

EDWARD MacInnis of Arnham, Bishop—twenty-year-old son of Earl Manfred, who is brother to Bishop Hubert; itinerant bishop and later Bishop of Grecotha [CH].

EGBERT, Brother—monk at Saint Jarlath's Monastery [CC].

EIDIARD of Clure—soldier replaced by Davin MacRorie; assigned to guard Princes Javan and Rhys Michael [CH].

ELINOR MacRorie, Lady—widow of Cathan; mother of Davin and Ansel; wife to James Drummond [CC, SC, (CH)].

EMRYS, Dom—Deryni adept and Healer; Abbot of the Order of Saint Gabriel [SC, CH].

ERCON, Saint—scholar and historian flourishing shortly after Saint Bearand Haldane; brother of Saint Willim (CH).

EUSTACE of Fairleigh, Bishop—one of Gwynedd's six itinerant bishops before the Council of Ramos [SC, CH].

EVAINE MacRorie Thuryn, Lady—daughter of Camber and wife to Rhys; an original member of the Camberian Council [CC, SC, CH].

EWAN of Rhendall, Lord—Earl of Rhendall and eldest son of Duke Sighere; a regent of Gwynedd; later, Duke of Claibourne and Earl Marshal of Gwynedd [SC, CH].

FARNHAM, Lord and Lady—parents of Megan de Cameron (CC).

FESTIL I, King—Deryni noble who engineered the Festillic Coup of 822 and founded the Festillic dynasty; reigned 822–839.

FESTIL II, King—second Festillic king; reigned 839–851.

FESTIL III, King—third Festillic king; grandfather of Imre; reigned 851–885.

FINELLA—Revan's "love" (CH).

FINTAN, Lord—human earl on Cinhil's council [SC].

FIONA MacLean, Lady—sister of Adrian and granddaughter of Camber's sister Aislinn [CH].

FULBERT de Morrisey, Lord—Deryni assassin involved in ambush of Princes Javan and Rhys Michael; later executed by regents [CH].

FULK—soldier under command of Coel Howell [CC].

GABRILITES—priests and Healers of the Order of Saint Gabriel, an all-Deryni esoteric brotherhood founded in 745 and based at Saint Neot's Abbey in the south Lendour mountains; especially noted for training Healers [CC, SC, CH].

GAVIN—Prince Alroy's squire [CH].

GELLIS de Cleary, Father—acting Percentor of the Michaelines [SC].

GIFFORD—manservant to Rhys [CC].

GILBERT, Master—a silversmith [CH].

GILLIS, Brother—Gabrilite brother slain at Saint Neot's [CH].

GREGORY of Arden, Father—Abbot of Saint Jarlath's Abbey [CC].

GREGORY of Ebor, Lord—Earl of Ebor and an original member of the Camberian Council [CH].

GUAIRE of Arliss, Lord—friend of Cathan; former aide to Alister Cullen; finally, a founding Servant of Saint Camber [SC].

GUTHRIE—sergeant of Bishop Cullen's household guard [CH].

HALDANE—surname of the royal House of Gwynedd.

HILDRED, Lord—human baron on Cinhil's council; expert on horses [SC, (CH)].

HOWELL, Coel—see Coel Howell.

HOWICCAN, Pargan—classic Deryni lyric poet (CC, SC, CH).

HRORIK of Eastmarch, Lord—middle son of Duke Sighere; Earl of Eastmarch [SC, CH].

HUBERT MacInnis, Bishop—a regent of Gwynedd and Auxiliary Bishop of Rhemuth; later, Archbishop of Valoret and Primate of All Gwynedd [CH].

HUMPHREY of Gallareaux, Father—Michaeline priest responsible for the death of Cinhil's firstborn son, Prince Aidan [CC].

IFOR, King—last pre-Interregnum King of Gwynedd; reigned 794–822; father of Prince Aidan (Daniel Draper) (CC).

ILLAN, Lord—a Michaeline knight [SC].

IMRE, King—fifth and last Festillic King of Gwynedd; reigned 900–904; died after defeat by Cinhil Haldane; father of Mark of Festil, by his sister Ariella [CC, (SC, CH)].

IVO Lovat, Lord—Deryni executed by regents following assassination attempt on Princes Javan and Rhys Michael; youngest son of Baron Frizell [CH].

JAFFRAY of Carbury, Archbishop—Deryni and former Gabrilite; successor to Anscom of Trevas as Archbishop of Valoret and Primate of All Gwynedd; an original member of the Camberian Council [SC, CH].

JAMES Drummond, Lord—grand-nephew of Camber and husband to the widowed Elinor [CC, SC, CH].

JARLATH, Saint—sixth century Bishop of Meara and abbot; founder of the Ordo Verbi Dei (CC, SC, CH).

JASON, Sir—knight assigned to guard the Princes Javan and Rhys Michael [CH].

JASON Brown—apprentice to Daniel Draper; inherited the business (CC).

JASPER Miller, Father—non-combatant Michaeline priest [CC, SC].

JAVAN Jashan Urien Haldane, Prince—twin brother of King Alroy; born with club foot [SC, CH].

JEBEDIAH of Alcara, Lord—Deryni Grand Master of the Order of Saint Michael, knight, and Earl Marshal of Gwynedd under Cinhil; an original member of the Camberian Council [CC, SC, CH].

JERUSHA Evaine Thuryn—infant daughter of Rhys and Evaine; a future Healer [CH].

JESSE, Lord—Master of Ebor; eldest son and heir of Earl Gregory [CH].

JOHANNES, Brother—lay Michaeline monk, servant of Alister Cullen [SC].

JOHN—factor who bought Dolban for the Servants of Saint Camber (SC).

JOHN, Brother—an alias of Evaine [SC].

JOHN, son of Daniel—the first "Benedict" at Saint Piran's Priory [CC].

JONAS, Father—old parish priest at Caerrorie (CC).

JORAM MacRorie, Father—youngest son of Camber; priest and knight of the Order of Saint Michael; confidential secretary to Bishop Alister Cullen; an original member of the Camberian Council [CC, SC, CH].

JOSEPH—one of Earl Maldred's men (CC).

JOWERTH Leslie, Lord—Deryni uncle of Dafydd Leslie; on Cinhil's staff until his death in 915 [SC, (CH)].

JUBAL, Brother—monk at Saint Foillan's Abbey [CC].

JURIS, Dom—Gabrilite priest [CH].

KAI Descantor, Bishop—Deryni itinerant bishop [SC, CH].

KENRIC, Dom—Healer at Saint Neot's [CH].

KINEVAN, Dom Queron—see Queron Kinevan, Dom.

KYRIELL—Camber's name in religion [SC].

LAUREN, Sir—a Michaeline knight [SC].

LESLIE, Dafydd and Jowerth—see Dafydd Leslie and Jowerth Leslie.

LIREL, Dame—former nurse to the princes (CH).

LLEW—a guard of Bishop Cullen's household [CH].

LORCAN, Brother—Ansel MacRorie's alias as a Michaeline lay brother [CH].

MACGREGOR, Bishop Ailin—see Ailin MacGregor, Bishop.

MACINNIS—see Hubert, Edward, and Manfred MacInnis.

MACRORIE—surname of Camber's family; see Ansel, Camber, Cathan, Davin, Evaine, Joram.

MAHAEL—ancient Deryni historian, author of History of Kheldour (CH).

497

MAIRI MacLean, Lady—wife to Adrian MacLean and mother of Camber Allin MacLean [CH].

MALDRED, Earl—one of Imre's warlords; assassinated by Coel Howell's hireling [CC].

MANFRED MacInnis, Lord—Baron of Marlor, and Earl of Culdi after Davin's attainder; brother of Bishop Hubert and father of Bishop Edward MacInnis of Arnham [CH].

MARIS—maidservant to Princess Ariella [CC].

MARK of Festil, Prince—son of Ariella and Imre and carrier of the Festillic line after his parents' death [SC].

MEGAN de Cameron, Queen—wife and queen to Cinhil; mother of Alroy, Javan, and Rhys Michael; formerly Camber's ward; lived 888–907 [CC, SC, (CH)].

MELISSA Howell, Lady—sister of Coel Howell; brought to court to tempt Imre (CC).

MICAH, Brother—a Servant of Saint Camber [CH].

MICHAELINES—priests, knights, and lay brothers of the Order of Saint Michael, a militant fighting and teaching Order, predominantly Deryni, formed during the reign of King Bearand Haldane to hold the Anvil of the Lord against Moorish incursions and defend the sea-lanes [CC, SC, CH].

MURDOCH of Carthane, Lord—human Earl of Carthane; one of King Alroy's regents [SC, CH].

NATHAN, Father—a Michaeline priest [CC, SC].

NESTA—Deryni seeress who foretold the doom of Caeriesse (CH).

NEVAN, Bishop Davet—see Davet Nevan, Bishop.

NIALLAN Trey, Bishop—Deryni Bishop of Dhassa [SC, CH].

NICHOLAS Draper—the third "Benedict"; grandson of Daniel; see Cinhil.

NIMUR, King—Deryni King of Torenth; connected to the Festils of Gwynedd through the female line (SC).

O'BEIRNE, Bishop Dermot—see Dermot O'Beirne, Bishop.

O'NEILL, Lord Tavis—see Tavis O'Neill, Lord.

ORIEL, Lord—a young Healer [CH].

ORIN—Deryni mystic and magician; author of the Protocols of Orin, a collection of scrolls containing extremely potent spells of Deryni magic (SC, CH).

ORISS, Archbishop Robert—Archbishop of Rhemuth; formerly Vicar General of the Ordo Verbi Dei [CC, SC, CH].

PARGAN HOWICCAN—*see Howiccan, Pargan.*

PATRICK, Brother—Prior of Saint Foillan's Abbey; later, Abbot [CC].

PAUL, Brother—monk at Saint Foillan's Abbey [CC].

PAULIN of Ramos, Bishop—stepson of Earl Tammaron; founder of the Little Brothers of Saint Ercon (912), a teaching order; itinerant bishop and later first bishop of new See of Stavenham [CH].

PHINEAS, Brother—gate-warder at Saint Foillan's Abbey [CC].

PIEDUR, Sir—knight assigned to guard the Princes Javan and Rhys Michael [CH].

PORRIC Lunal, Father—priest of the Order of Saint Michael and a candidate to succeed Alister Cullen as Vicar General (SC).

QUERON Kinevan, Dom—Deryni Healer-priest, formerly of Order of Saint Gabriel; a founder of the Servants of Saint Camber; later, a member of the Camber Council replacing Jaffray [SC, CH].

RANALD Gilstrachan, Lord—Deryni assassin executed by the regents [CH].

RANNULF, Lord—Deryni noble drawn and quartered by Willimite terrorists in 903 (CC, CH).

RAYMOND, Bishop—former Prince-Bishop of Dhassa and maternal uncle of Alister Cullen, whom he ordained to the priesthood (SC).

REVAN—lame former carpenter's apprentice saved by Cathan; clark and tutor to Rhys's and Evaine's children [CC, SC, CH].

REYNARD, Brother—infirmarian at Saint Foillan's Abbey [CC].

RHUN of Horthness, Baron—called The Ruthless, age 32; one of King Alroy's regents; later, Earl of Sheele [CH].

RHYS MICHAEL Alister Haldane, Prince—youngest surviving son of Cinhil, age 10 [CH].

RHYS Thuryn, Lord—Deryni physician and Healer; husband of Evaine and son-in-law to Camber; developer of the Thuryn technique of concentration; an original member of the Camberian Council [CC, SC, CH].

RHYSEL Jocelyn Thuryn—daughter of Rhys and Evaine, age 7 [CH].

ROBEAR, Sir—knight assigned to guard the Princes Javan and Rhys Michael [CH].

ROBERT Oriss, Archbishop—see *Oriss, Archbishop Robert.*

ROLAND, Bishop—Auxiliary Bishop of Valoret under Anscom; died 916 (CC).

RONDEL—knight in the service of Manfred, Earl of Culdi [CH].

ROYSTON John Draper—alias of Prince Alroy, who was father to Cinhil (CC, CH).

SAM'L—loyal retainer of Camber at Caerrorie [CC].

SANTARE, Lord—Earl of Grand-Tellie; one of Imre's warlords [CC].

SELKIRK, Master—an arms master to Imre [CC].

SELLAR, Wat and Tim—among the fifty peasants executed at Imre's command for the murder of Lord Rannulf [CC].

SHAW Farquharson, Lord—Deryni assassin killed in ambush on princes [CH].

SHOLTO MacDhugal, Lord—Deryni bowman who escaped from ambush/assassination attempt on Princes Javan and Rhys Michael [CH].

SIGHERE, Duke—former independent Earl of Eastmarch; first Duke of Claibourne; technically a regent of King Alroy, but failing health never permitted him to assume his duties [SC, (CH)].

SIGHERE of Marley, Lord—youngest son of Duke Sighere and later Earl of Marley [SC, CH].

SIMONN—Healer student at Saint Neot's [CH].

SORLE—Cinhil's squire; knighted by Cinhil at Twelfth Night, 917 [SC, CH].

STEPHEN—student at Saint Neot's [CH].

SULIEN of R'Kassi—ancient Deryni adept, author of *Annals* (CH).

TAMMARON Fitz-Arthur, Earl—one of King Alroy's regents; Chancellor of Gwynedd after Alister Cullen [SC, CH].

TAVIS O'Neill, Lord—Healer to Prince Javan [CH].

TERMOD of Rhorau, Lord—Deryni princeling, cousin of Imre, executed by Willimite terrorists in 903 (CC, SC).

THOMAS—a guard of Rhys's and Evaine's household [CH].

THOMAS—bailiff at Dolban, for the Servants of Saint Camber (SC).

THOMAS—a former Archbishop of Valoret (CH).

THOMPSON, Dickon—a baker [CH].

THURYN—surname of Rhys.

TIEG Joram Thuryn—younger son of Rhys and Evaine; a future Healer, age 3 [CH].

TIVAR, Dom—Gabrilite priest and weapons master at Saint Neot's [CH].

TOBAN—a hospice page [SC].

TOMAIS—squire to Prince Rhys Michael [CH].

TORCUILL de la Marche, Lord—Deryni baron; formerly a Festillic minister, now on Cinhil's staff; dismissed by the regents [SC, CH].

TORIN—a guard of Bishop Cullen's household [CH].

TREFOR of Morland, Lord—Deryni assassin killed in ambush on princes [CH].

TREY, Bishop Niallan—*see Niallan Trey, Bishop*.

TURLOUGH, Bishop—one of Gwynedd's itinerant bishops; later, first Bishop of Marbury [SC, CH].

TURSTANE, Dom—Gabrilite Healer; a stonecutter's apprentice before his Healer's training; an original member of the Camberian Council (CH).

UDAUT, Earl—Constable of Gwynedd [SC, CH].

ULLIAM ap Lugh, Bishop—Bishop of Nyford [SC, CH].

ULRIC—novice Healer at Saint Neot's who went berserk while Queron still taught there; killed by Dom Emrys (CH).

UMPHRED—Camber's bailiff at Caerrorie [CC, SC].

VALERIAN, Brother—Latin master to the princes [CH].

VARNARITES—Deryni adepts and scholars who founded a proto-university at Grecotha, late 7th–early 8th century; the Gabrilite Order broke off pre-745.

WAT—servant to Rhys [CC].

WEAVER, Mary, and brother Will, and cousin Tom—among the fifty peasants executed at Imre's command for the murder of Lord Rannulf [CC].

WILLIM, Saint—child martyr to Deryni ill-use; patron saint of the Willimite movement; younger brother of Saint Ercon (CC, SC, CH).

WILLIMITES—anti-Deryni terrorist group sworn to punish Deryni who escape justice through normal legal channels; mostly suppressed in 904 under Imre, but resurging during the latter reign of King Cinhil [CC, (SC), CH].

WILLOWEN, Father—Dean of Grecotha Cathedral and assistant to Bishop Cullen (SC, CH).

WULPHER, Master—Cathan's steward at Tal Traeth; doubled for Joram under a shape-changing spell [CC, (CH)].

ZEPHRAM of Lorda, Bishop—former Abbot of Saint Foillan's Abbey, a house of the *Ordo Verbi Dei;* briefly an itinerant bishop before the Council of Ramos; later, Bishop of Cashien [(CC), SC, CH].

Legends of Saint Camber

INDEX OF PLACES

ALL SAINTS' CATHEDRAL—seat of the Archbishop of Valoret, Primate of All Gwynedd [CC, SC, CH].

ARGOED—after 905, the Michaeline Commanderie (military headquarters) in Gwynedd, in the southern Lendour mountains [(SC), CH].

ARNHAM—birthplace of Manfred MacInnis's son Edward (CH).

BARWICKE—site of Saint Jarlath's Monastery, a few hours' ride north of Saint Liam's Abbey [CC, (CH)].

BRUSTARKIA—a Michaeline House-Minor in Arjenol [CH].

CAERRORIE—Camber's principal residence as Earl of Culdi, a few hours' ride northeast of Valoret [CC, SC, (CH)].

CARBURY—coastal town north of Valoret; an episcopal see as of December, 917 (CH).

CHELTHAM—site of the original Michaeline Commandderie in Gwynedd; destroyed by Imre's orders in 904 (CC, SC, CH).

CLAIBOURNE—principal city of Old Kheldour; later, name given to duchy created for Sighere of Eastmarch, after annexation of Kheldour by Sighere and Cinhil (SC, CH).

COLDOIRE—passage through the Rheljan Mountains, near the Arranal Canyon [SC].

COR CULDI—hereditary ancestral seat and fortress of the Culdi earls, near the city of Culdi, on the Gwynedd-Meara border [CC, SC, (CH)].

CÙILTEINE—a Michaeline House in western Gwynedd [(SC), CH].

CULDI—central city of the Earldom of Culdi, on the Gwynedd-Meara border [CC, (SC, CH)].

DHASSA—free holy city in the Lendour Mountains; seat of the Bishop of Dhassa, who is politically neutral, by tradition [(SC), CH].

DJELLARDA—original Mother House and Commanderie of the Order of Saint Michael, at the tip of the Forcinn Buffer States, overlooking the Anvil of the Lord; sometimes called "The Gate of the Anvil" [(SC), CH].

DOLBAN—ruined manor bought by Guaire of Arliss as a site for the first monastery of the Servants of Saint Camber. [SC, (CH)].

EASTMARCH—independent holding of Sighere, Earl of Eastmarch; later given to Hrorik, Sighere's middle son [SC, (CH)].

EBOR—earldom north of Valoret [CH].

FARNHAM—honor of the Camerons; a Crown holding after Cinhil's accession (CC).

FIANNA—coastal town across the Southern Sea from Carthmoor; famous for its sweet wines (CH).

GRECOTHA—university city, site of the Varnarite School; seat of the Bishop of Grecotha [SC, CH].

GWYNEDD—central of the Eleven Kingdoms and hub of Haldane power since 645, when the first Haldane High King began to unify the area; seat of the Festillic dynasty, 822–904; restored to the Haldane line in 904 with the accession of Cinhil Haldane.

HANFELL—site of a shrine to Saint Camber [CC, SC, CH].

HAUT EIRIAL—a Michaeline House in the southern Lendour Mountains, destroyed by Imre in 904 and again by the regents in 917 [(SC), CH].

HAUT VERMELIOR—site of a shrine to Saint Camber (CH).

HOWICCE—kingdom to the southwest of Gwynedd; loosely allied with Llannedd (CH).

IOMAIRE—site of battle with Ariella's forces on Gwynedd-Eastmarch border [SC, (CH)].

KHELDISH RIDING—viceregality broken off Kheldour after its annexation by Sighere and Cinhil in 906 [SC, (CH)].

KHELDOUR—small kingdom north of Gwynedd, famous for textiles and carpets; associated with Rhendall and the Festils through Termod of Rhorau (SC, CH).

KIERNEY—earldom north of Culdi, loosely linked to the Crown of Gwynedd [CH].

LLANNEDD—kingdom southwest of Gwynedd; loosely allied with Howicce (CH).

LLENTIETH—Deryni school near the Connait (CH).

MARLEY—small earldom carved out of Eastmarch and given to Sighere, youngest son of Duke Sighere, in 906 (SC, CH).

MARLOR—barony of Manfred MacInnis (CH).

MARYWELL—town in northern Gwynedd where a Festillic garrison ran amok (CC).

MEARA—kingdom/princedom northwest of Gwynedd; nominally a vassal state of Gwynedd (CC).

MOLLINGFORD—a Michaeline house in the central Gwynedd plain, destroyed by Imre in 904 and again by the regents in 917 (SC, CH).

MOORYN—petty kingdom at the southeast of Gwynedd; formerly a powerful ally under Imre's reign (SC).

NYFORD—river town in central Gwynedd near Saint Illtyd's Monastery, and seat of the Bishop of Nyford; site of Imre's abortive new capital (CC, SC, CH).

RAMOS—southwest of Valoret, the site of the Mother House of the Little Brothers of Saint Ercon; the Council of Ramos was held here in 917 [CH].

RENGARTH—a border town at the Gwynedd-Eastmarch-Torenth joining. [SC]

RHEMUTH—ancient capital of Gwynedd under the Haldanes; abandoned during the Festillic Interregnum; restored under Cinhil and Alroy [CC, SC, CH].

RHENDALL—lake region north of Gwynedd; formerly the Festillic holding of Termod of Rhorau; given to Ewan, eldest son of Duke Sighere, in 906, as the secondary title of the Duke of Claibourne and courtesy title of his heir (CC, SC, CH).

RHORAU—fortress seat of Lord Termod, cousin of King Imre, in the Rhendall lake region (CC).

SAINT ELDERON—a Michaeline House in Torenth, on the coast near the Eastmarch border (CH).

SAINT ERCON'S ABBEY—Mother House of the Little Brothers of Saint Ercon, in Ramos [CH].

SAINT FOILLAN'S ABBEY—an *Ordo Verbi Dei* House in the mountains southeast of Valoret, where Camber and Rhys found Prince Cinhil Haldane [CC].

SAINT ILLTYD'S MONASTERY—*Ordo Verbi Dei* House on the river near Nyford (CC).

SAINT JARLATH'S MONASTERY—Mother House of the *Ordo Verbi Dei,* two hours' ride north of Saint Liam's Abbey [CC].

SAINT JOHN'S CHURCH—parish church near Fullers' Alley

in Valoret, where the Draper family records were kept [CC].

SAINT LIAM'S ABBEY—a Michaeline-staffed abbey-school about four hours' ride northeast of Valoret; Joram taught there briefly [CC, (CH)].

SAINT MARY'S IN THE HILLS—isolated monastery in the highlands above Culdi [CH].

SAINT NEOT'S ABBEY—stronghold of the Order of Saint Gabriel, an all-Deryni, esoteric order specializing in Healer's training; in the Lendour highlands [CH].

SAINT PIRAN'S PRIORY—an *Ordo Verbi Dei* House about a day's ride north of Saint Jarlath's; Joram and Rhys interviewed the first two "Benedicts" there [CC, (CH)].

SAINT ULTAN'S PRIORY—an *Ordo Verbi Dei* House on the southwest coast of Mooryn [CC].

SHEELE—Rhys and Evaine's manor house north of Valoret; later, an earldom [CH].

TAL TRAETH—Cathan MacRorie's manor house in Valoret [CC].

TORENTH—kingdom to the east of Gwynedd; ruled by the Deryni King Nimur [SC, (CH)].

TRURILL—castle of Lord Adrian MacLean, Master of Kierney, near Cor Culdi [CH].

VALORET—Festillic capital of Gwynedd, 822–904 [CC, SC, CH].

WARRINGHAM—site of a shrine to Saint Camber (CH).

APPENDIX III

PARTIAL LINEAGE OF THE HALDANE KINGS

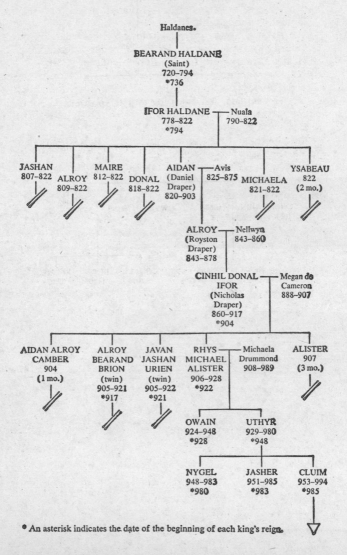

Haldanes

BEARAND HALDANE
(Saint)
720–794
*736

IFOR HALDANE ─── Nuala
778–822   790–822
*794

JASHAN   MAIRE   AIDAN ─── Avis   YSABEAU
807–822   812–822   (Daniel Draper)   822
    ALROY   DONAL   825–875 MICHAELA   (2 mo.)
    809–822   818–822   821–822

ALROY ─── Nellwyn
(Royston   843–860
Draper)
843–878

CINHIL DONAL ─── Megan de
IFOR   Cameron
(Nicholas   888–907
Draper)
860–917
*904

AIDAN ALROY   ALROY   JAVAN   RHYS ─── Michaela   ALISTER
CAMBER   BEARAND   JASHAN   MICHAEL   Drummond   907
904   BRION   URIEN   ALISTER   908–989   (3 mo.)
(1 mo.)   (twin)   (twin)   906–928
                905–921   905–922   *922
                *917   *921

OWAIN   UTHYR
924–948   929–980
*928   *948

NYGEL   JASHER   CLUIM
948–983   951–985   953–994
*980   *983   *985

• An asterisk indicates the date of the beginning of each king's reign.

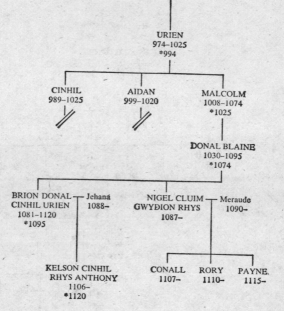

URIEN
974–1025
*994

CINHIL
989–1025

AIDAN
999–1020

MALCOLM
1008–1074
*1025

DONAL BLAINE
1030–1095
*1074

BRION DONAL
CINHIL URIEN
1081–1120
*1095

— Jehana
1088–

NIGEL CLUIM
GWYÐION RHYS
1087–

— Meraude
1090–

KELSON CINHIL
RHYS ANTHONY
1106–
*1120

CONALL
1107–

RORY
1110–

PAYNE.
1115–

THE FESTILLIC KINGS OF GWYNEDD AND THEIR DESCENDANTS

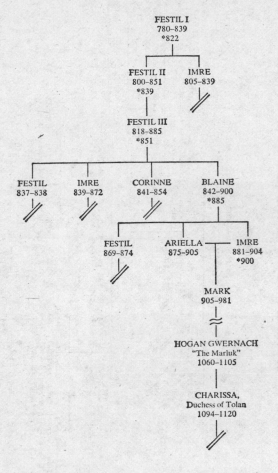

FESTIL I
780–839
*822

FESTIL II
800–851
*839

IMRE
805–839

FESTIL III
818–885
*851

FESTIL
837–838

IMRE
839–872

CORINNE
841–854

BLAINE
842–900
*885

FESTIL
869–874

ARIELLA
875–905

IMRE
881–904
*900

MARK
905–981

HOGAN GWERNACH
"The Marluk"
1060–1105

CHARISSA,
Duchess of Tolan
1094–1120

* An asterisk indicates the date of the beginning of each king's reign.

APPENDIX V
PARTIAL LINEAGE OF THE MacRORIES

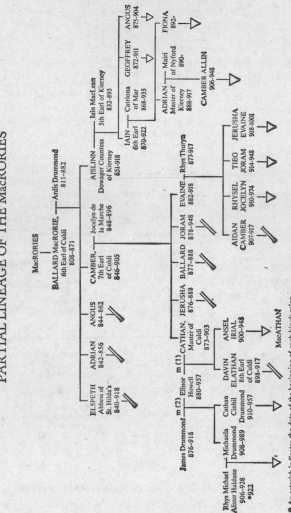

• An asterisk indicates the date of the beginning of each king's reign.

About the Author

Katherine Kurtz was born in Coral Gables, Florida, during a hurricane, and has led a somewhat whirlwind existence ever since. She was awarded a B.S. in chemistry from the University of Miami, attended medical school for a year before she decided she really wanted to write about medicine rather than practice it, and earned an M.A. in medieval English history from UCLA while writing her first two novels.

Miss Kurtz is interested in just about everything except baseball and business and has worked in such fields as marine science, anthropology, cancer research, cataloging of Chinese painting, educational and commercial television, and police science. She is also a professionally trained hypnotist, an avid horsewoman, and an avowed cat person, though she has nothing against dogs.

Miss Kurtz is active in the Society for Creative Anachronism, an organization which attempts to re-create the Middle Ages and Renaissance through tournaments, banquets, revels, and classes in medieval arts and sciences. As Bevin Fraser of Stirling in the SCA, she is an accomplished costumer, calligrapher and illuminator, herald, and expert on court protocol, as well as a student of medieval fighting forms (from the sidelines only; she bruises easily).

Q.

What is the most enchanting fantasy trilogy in years?

A.

Patricia McKillip's
The Quest of the Riddlemaster!

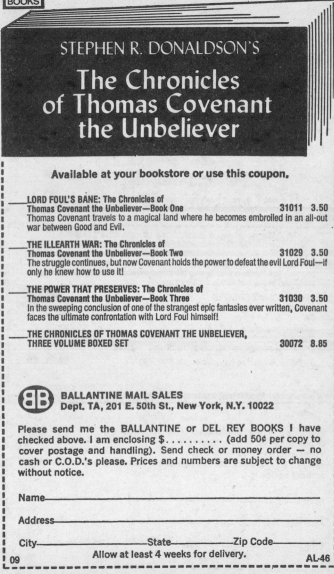